The
GIANT BOOK
of
SCOTTISH
SHORT
STORIES

The GIANT BOOK of SCOTTISH SHORT STORIES

Edited and Introduced by Carl MacDougall

PETER BEDRICK BOOKS
NEW YORK

First American edition published in 1989 by Peter Bedrick Books, 2112 Broadway, New York, N.Y. 10023. Published by agreement with Canongate Publishing Limited, Edinburgh, Scotland.

Library of Congress Cataloging-in-Publication Data
The Giant book of Scottish short stories / edited by Carl MacDougall.
—1st American ed.
p. cm.
Reprint, with new introd.
ISBN 0-87226-327-4. — ISBN 0-87226-217-0 (pbk.)
1. Short Stories, English—Scottish authors. 2. Short stories, Scottish. 3. Scotland—Fiction. I. MacDougall, Carl.
PR8676.G5 1989 89-33073
813'.01089411—dc20 CIP

Contents

1

Introduction

Scottish fiction has its roots in a tradition where stories were told to entertain. This imaginative pact between speaker and audience goes back to the oral traditions of the highlands and islands, or to the great border ballads, and is the stream from which Scottish fiction flows.

With the coming of books and the rise of a reading public throughout Europe, Scottish culture played an important role through the early influence of periodicals such as *The Edinburgh Review* and *Blackwood's Magazine*. Hogg, Scott and Galt are familiar enough names from this period, but it is sometimes forgotten that Hogg can be said to have anticipated Dostoevsky in the study of psychological division, while Galt's interest in family and social history pointed the way to the novels of Balzac and Zola. And of course Sir Walter Scott was internationally famous, and widely acknowledged by many European and American authors as a major influence on their work. So imaginative prose was well established in Scotland when Balzac was writing in France, and Edgar Allan Poe and Washington Irving were laying the foundations of American prose literature.

The old tradition lives on, and it is difficult to read a collection of Scottish short stories without becoming aware of the spoken voice and the power of first person narration. This is the basis of the present collection and indeed many of these writers have chosen to address the reader directly. John Galt and Alasdair Gray use the convention of letters; James Kelman, Alexander Reid, William Boyd, Jessie Kesson, Tom Leonard and Brian McCabe rely on versions of internal monlogue, while George Mackay Brown, in the middle section of 'Celia', allows, his character to speak for herself. The authenticity of a folk tale can be found in Scott, Cunninghame Graham, Betsy Whyte and Duncan Williamson, and even in Buchan's reported account of 'The Herd of Standlan'. Nor is the living voice of the community far from the narrative style of Grassic Gibbon, Robert McLellan, Alexander Reid, Tom Leonard, Alan Spence, James Kelman, George Friel or Neil Munro.

With the oral tradition comes the device of adopting an intimate tone to the reader, almost as if they were being taken into the writer's confidence. Whilst reinforcing what becomes a shared experience, this also allows the writer to take his audience into strange and unfamiliar territory otherwise inaccessible to them. Edward Gaitens, Eona Macnicol and Conan Doyle all use this technique to good effect.

There were other constants in Scottish Literature, the best known being an archetypal twinning of opposites when the ordinary rubs shoulders with the fantastic, when the Devil meets the Giro. Between them 'The Small Herdsman' and 'The Sailing Ship' have a lot to say about this breadth in the Scottish sensibility. They introduce not only many of the stories that follow but also the wealth of national experience which is balanced between the rural and the urban, the natural and the supernatural, the personal and the social, the ancient and the modern contained in this book.

There are other themes. Iain Crichton Smith's 'Murdo' and Alasdair Gray's 'Five Letters from an Eastern Empire' play variations on the problems of creativity and identity. Both struggle with their surroundings in the attempt to make some order out of their inner lives. Both are blackly humorous, and the same dark, disaffected comedy can be found in the stories by Willa Muir, Tom Leonard, Muriel Spark, Hugh MacDiarmid, Saki and John Herdman.

Jessie Kesson, Brian McCabe, Alan Spence and Bernard MacLaverty remind us that childhood can be a dark time while Elspeth Davie, James Allan Ford and Ian Hamilton Finlay make the same point from different backgrounds. Stories such as Fred Urquhart's 'Robert/Hilda' evokes a world which can be just as disconcerting, a notion interestingly extended in Betsy Whyte's 'A Man in a Boat' where the protagonist changes sex when he changes location.

Scottish culture is often accused of male chauvinism, yet the woman's point of view, and the plight of women in our society, is at the heart of many of our stories. There is Dorothy Haynes' 'Thou Shalt Not Suffer a Witch' and George Mackay Brown's 'Celia', one of his most powerful and painful stories. Galt's comic 'The Gudewife' and Hogg's 'Seeking the Houdy' make their own contributions to the debate from an obviously male point of view, and yet Hogg's story is subtly subversive in its account of a man at odds with a world of intransigent female forces. Jessie Kesson's 'Until Such Times' returns us to a contemporary female perspective, as do Rosa Macpherson and A. L. Kennedy, speaking for a growing number of Scotswomen who have found a new and urgent voice in their fiction.

Our fascination with the supernatural is not as simple as it might seem and Scottish writers have seldom opted for straightforward ghost stories or tales of the unexpected. Of course Scott and Hogg owe a lot to the uncanny world of the old ballads, while Cunninghame Graham, Duncan Williamson, R. L. Stevenson and even Conan Doyle satisfy the perennial demand for a mysterious tale well told. Even so, the strange stories of Robert McLellan and Eric Linklater make powerful social comments, while the uncanny experiences described in Margaret Oliphant's 'The Library Window' go behind the supernatural to provide an outstandingly sensitive acccount of a young girl's awakening sexuality. In quite different ways George MacDonald and Neil Gunn are haunted by intimations of a realm beyond our own that is somehow more real than realism. In this respect the stories by Betsy Whyte, Fred Urquhart and James Hogg deal equally strikingly with a world of changing boundaries and sexual ambiguity. Joan Ure and Brian McCabe take us back to Macnair Reid who reminds us that the real world can be just as strange and disorienting as any supernatural realm.

Scottishness and the reality of Scotland has been a constant theme in our fiction, and perhaps it is our status as a small nation, or a culturally occupied territory, that has led us to be so very aware of what our country is, or what it might be. Muriel Spark, Edward Gaitens, Alan Spence, George Friel, A. L. Kennedy and Ronald Frame all lay bare the nuances and the crippling divisions of class and class values within our society. James Kelman, J. M. Barrie, S. R. Crockett, Lewis Grassic Gibbon, George MacDonald Fraser and Neil Munro seem to speak from utterly different communities, and yet they all describe a Scotland which is, in one aspect or another, more than recognisable to most of us. Allan Massie's 'In the Bare Lands' and Douglas Dunn's 'The Canoes' take a new look at equally familiar themes to shake our complacencies about what being Scottish might ultimately mean.

Since George Douglas discredited the cosy world of the Kailyard and the popularity of the historical novel faded as a vehicle for serious literature, the focus has returned to the short story as a forum where Scottish themes could be seriously discussed. This encounter with realism has expounded and developed throughout the 20th century.

The whole, as always, is greater than the sum of its parts. Yet I hope the parts make for a various and occasionally surprising account of the healthy state of short fiction in Scotland over the last two hundred years.

Carl MacDougall

Eona Macnicol

In its time, Scottish literature seems to have been more than usually able to accommodate intrusions from the supernatural. Spirits, small folk and other less clearly defined manifestations of the unknown have exerted a malign or beneficial influence on generations of Scottish readers and listeners, and they still have their place today.

We are used to stories where the inexplicable emerges in the midst of the everyday, either to herald a quaint diversion into the picturesque, or to act as a device allowing the reader to redefine reality from a new perspective. In 'The Small Herdsman' Eona Macnicol takes this accepted format and turns it on its head.

Eona, Kathleen, Macnicol was born in 1910, and her first novel *Colum of Derry* was published in 1955. Since then she has continued to work in prose, producing both novels and short stories. 'The Small Herdsman' offers us an idyllic rural Scotland, complete with lilting accents and a curious young herdsman who might almost be mistaken for one of the fairy folk. Then the cold facts of another experience beyond the hills come pouring in.

5

The Small Herdsman

I FOUND THE children rough in Clachanree, even the girls. I looked with awe rather than pleasure at their spare-time activities—pushing each other down through the yawning rafters of the byre roof to fall on to the bedding bracken below, or hiding behind the half-doors and throwing screeching hens into unwary faces. My desire would go after Wattie, smaller than any of the children, yet going quietly on ways of his own.

He could often be seen here and there about An Craggoch, the croft next to my paternal grandmother's. His dry wind-bitten face was as small as a fist; below his thin neck his braces crossed so high they accentuated the tinyness of his stature: he never seemed to grow. He wore longish shorts of a ragged appearance, and went everywhere indomitably on bare feet.

I thought at first he was too small to play. I had the impression from his size that he was very young. Doubt came when I went up to Clachanree once in term time when all the children were at school. There in broad daylight, all young life else between walls, was Wee Wattie, tossing up bracken to dry in the sun for the cows' beds. Shocked by surprise out of observance of etiquette, I called out to him, 'What for are you not at the school, Wattie?' But I made nothing of the sheepish grin which was his only reply.

Then, seeing him close that summer on a sunny day, I noticed there was a fine soft whitish down about his cheeks, such as is on an adolescent's. His voice too, when I came to think of it, was not that of a young child. I began to wonder if he was not so much too young for horseplay, as too old.

His manner gave credence to this theory. He had the manner of a grown-up man. When he met anyone he would say, 'Well, so and so!' in the cheerful indulgent tone used by the elderly in Clachanree.

But in this gentleness there was a reserve. He seemed to stop either the playful attacks of the boys or the advances of the girls by some kind of repellent force. I never saw anyone jostle, even touch, him.

As my acquaintance with him went on, this question as to his age teased me. And once I cornered him, building up a fallen bit of the Craggoch garden wall. I did not this time ask bluntly, in the way of the world beyond, 'Wattie, how old are you?' I went more roundabout, in the way of Clachanree: 'And, Wattie, how old might yourself be, now?'

He stopped a moment from fitting the loose stones in, looked over at me, and said simply, 'How would I know?'

This gave me a delicious thrill. It was the reply a fairy changeling might have made; and it further whetted my curiosity. I reflected that Wattie, though he had quite absorbed our mode of life and outlook, and spoke in the intonations of our speech, was nevertheless not of Clachanree stock; he had come from 'the south'. His very surname was a matter of doubt, a fascinating circumstance when you came to think about it. Some said it had in any case been changed from his original one, but none could guess at the reason. After all, his Christian name was all he needed among us; among all the Donalds and Jocks and Alastairs it was distinctive enough.

He might be, if not too small, too old to play. Most certainly he was too busy. He worked constantly from morning till night. He was in the barn, in the byre, at the peat stack, in the garden, down at the well, hoeing the turnips, washing clothes at the Craggoch burn. His intelligent industry seemed to hold the Craggoch croft together. The other crofters used to talk about him: 'My, he's a proper worker, yon wee *eeshan* [nipper] o' An Craggoch's!'

'An Craggoch's well served wi' yon Wee Wattie o' his!'

The labours of so small a body had an uncanniness about them. It almost seemed as if he could be in two places at once. And always he worked with such gusto and energy; he was as if possessed.

Occasionally he and An Craggoch would appear together, at times of state or ease such as the Sabbaths and Fast Days, when it was the custom in Clachanree after the three-mile walk to and from the church to Lochend to inspect, though not to work, one's fields. They presented an incongruous appearance, the tall burly crofter and his diminutive henchman side by side. It was Wattie, surprisingly, who was the spokesman of the pair. 'Well, so and so!' he would say while the other stood silent. 'We are just taking a swatch [close look] at An Craggoch's barley. It's thin the year.' Or, 'Aye, aye! Soon's the Sabbath's over, if we're spared, it's me will be having to straighten yon post in An Craggoch's fence.'

He was a silent man, An Craggoch, upright and God-fearing in a gloomy kind of way, keeping his own counsel. His sons were all away out in the great world, his wife had died. He did for himself, quite competently, though the interior of his house when I went into it reminded me of an unusually clean byre, all untidiness simply swept to one side. He must have known enough about the art of cooking for survival. Yet it seemed an austere place to rear a child, and my kind mother sometimes said it weighed on her. 'It's a cheerless place, An Craggoch's, for a young boyan. My heart is sore for yon Wee Wattie o' his.'

Her heart was very sore once when Wattie was not seen for several days. She asked An Craggoch, who was a kinsman of my father's, and was told Wattie was ill and keeping his bed. She made some dainty dish for him, a cream blancmange with lemon—she was a rare cook even on a peatfire—and a little strong chicken broth, delicately flavoured with parsley. These she carried over herself. Her offerings were politely but resolutely refused. Wattie, starting up from bed, declared he had no stomach for food, it would make him sick. I think what she really wanted was to go near him, to stroke the short straw-coloured hair, to touch the small dry face, to murmur over him the ancient half-articulate endearments she murmured in my ears when I was on the verge of sleep. But Wattie, so I gathered from my mother's hurt and puzzled look, drew back from her and plainly wished her gone.

I do not think he liked women very much; he was more distant with them than with anyone, though always courteous to a degree. The only living things he seemed to love with any warmth were An Craggoch's four cows, Daisy, Dollag, Peg and Seonaid. He kept them clean as any mother her child, and was scrupulously regular in taking them out and in. 'You could set your watch by Wattie,' my father would say as the four cows and their small herdsman would go past our windows. And for good measure, as he tended them, he would caress them with a gentle pat here, a rub there.

I had been reading, all one summer, a book of Celtic legends. I began to conceive the notion under its influence that Wattie was no child, no youth even, but an adult of some short-statured race with powers of industry beyond our own; that he was a cattleman by right of oath or conquest of An Craggoch's, his passionless devotion like that of Cuchulain for the overlord. I longed to know for sure.

So came one day when, alone and at a loose end, I saw An Craggoch's four cows come lumbering out of their byre. They climbed the rocky knoll that gave the croft its name, and stumbled clumsily down the other side with tails in the wind. Across my grandmother's greensward they went, then down the hollowed road that took the precipitous slope of the first shoulder of the hill. I remember Loch Ness far below them, at that moment deep blue in colour, with a flake of white breaking here and there over its surface. There was often an aura of expectancy about it: what might not break from that surface as the flakes of snow-white foam broke here and there?

Expectancy rose in me at any rate as I saw Wattie and his cows go down the hill. I knew the pasture he was taking them to. It was called the Lon Vorlich, a clearing among the hazel woods, not far at all from where the Eas, our waterfall river, made its way to the Loch in secret of its high over-arching trees. My mother did not like the Eas. It was forbidden me at that time ever to go there, not only because of its dangerous steep sides but because to her it had an evil atmosphere. My Gaelic was imperfect, and only in Gaelic did she ever tell ghost stories, but I think she believed there were water spirits like mermaids there. I had not often been even to the Lon Vorlich, so near the Eas's course that you could hear the sound of the water falling.

It seemed the time had come. Now, I thought, now I will go down after Wattie, and in that secluded and unearthly place I will charm the mystery of his past life from him.

I was sanguine about it because Wattie was more tolerant of me than of anyone. My very helplessness seemed to make him less liable to repel me. He would often let me watch, even accompany him in his work, always keeping a protective eye on me. 'See and keep out of the bogs, *m'eudail*,' he would bid me, 'and you in your good shoes!' Or, 'Watch yourself, Ellen. There's a loose stone in the dyke; see will the sharp edge of it fall on you.' Surely then I might prevail on him?

So I climbed over the gate, and picked my way high up on the bank above the hollowed road which was all churned and sullied by the cows, away past the covered well and across the bogs below it, and so through the low hazel and rowan trees into the Lon Vorlich. I heard the sound of the cows tearing the lush grass, the impatient whisk of their tails as they were assailed by the clegs that breed in the bracken of the surrounding slopes. And then I saw Wattie. He sat perched on a rock, unwinding a length of rope. I knew he was about to go off and cut some bracken while he was herding, so I went swiftly up to him, but quietly, scared of putting him off, and said, 'Well, Wattie!'

A smile flickered over his small face, and, 'Well, Ellen!' he said with a wealth of good-natured tolerance in his tone, coiling the rope neatly round and round his scarred forearm. His hand sickle was lying on the grass at his side. I sat down and secretly spread the skirt of my dress over it in the half-conscious hope of removing the power of his work over him.

'Wattie,' I said, 'tell me a story. Come on!'

'I donno any stories, Ellen,' he answered reasonably. 'I'm no a good scholar. I wisna that much at the school.'

'A true story, I mean.'

He shook his head, that rather sheepish smile on his lips, and was looking round for his sickle.

'Tell me about yourself then, something that happened to you.'

He paused, and gave me a wary look. 'What would be happening to me, Ellen? I was in the Home. I donno where I put—'

'Well, but before that?' I urged softly. 'What sort of place would it be you were born in?'

His eyes were on the bracken slopes and he was feeling vaguely among the grass. Still, he had not actually repulsed me. I would have to be very quiet and casual and not put him off. 'What was it like, now, where you were born? Wouldn't you be remembering anything? Anything?' I spoke as softly as I could and kept the sickle covered. His questing hand grew still.

'I mind the water—'

I had scarcely dared hope for it, but Wattie was beginning hesitantly to speak. The constant sound of the Eas seemed to be lulling him, and he had forgotten his sickle.

'I mind the water,' he said in a tone as soft as my own.

'What water would that be?' I prompted, scarcely breathing.

'It was aye flowin',' he answered as if out of a trance. 'Flowin'. A leak it would be. Whiles it would stop, and then it would go dreep-dreep.'

There was something peculiar about his speech, but at first I did not realise what it was. My eyes fixed on him, my skirt over his sickle, I willed him to go on.

'Frae the la-avie . . . across the la-anding . . . frae wir room. And I mind the sta-airs. . . .' Fascinating! He was falling into a strange tongue. Yet I understood the gist of what he said, and listened spellbound until the image in his mind became implanted in my own, until the background dissolved round us, pasture and bracken and trees, and the hyacinthine Loch glinting between them; and we were in a dark tenement with its landing and stone stairs and a tap dripping.

The tap dripping was company for him and his brother as they crouched in their holey. . . .

'Holey?'

A cupboard under the stairs, empty except for bottles and tins. They were there so much it was like a kind of home; they seemed to pass their life there. It was very cold and damp, for it was below the la-avie, and the window opposite was broken and the rain came in. But it kept them hidden, safe—except when the wee yin coughed, he was an awfie yin for coughin'!

He was going on faster, his voice stronger, his speech stranger. He answered the question I had not asked: staggering feet coming up the stairs, loud bawling voices filling the cavity of the building. Yet here they lay still, close, till they could tell by the fumbling at the lock of their room door that danger was past.

In a pause I tried to speak, swallowing and licking my lip. But he went on, the strange accent still intensifying so that it was as much by intuition as by understanding that I grasped his meaning. When they got too hungry the wee yin would cry. Wattie must venture out, his heart in his mouth, and watch until the door opened, then slip in and seize whatever he could to make a meal. He was terrified he would be shut in and the wee yin be left alone.

'Wattie,' the effort to speak was like the effort in a nightmare. He turned to me, but his eyes were sightless, and went on speaking, his voice rising now in pitch until it was like the voice of a young child. Once or twice neighbours must have taken them in. He minded one time because of an oddity: it was pouring and the rain was driving into the holey; the man from the flat below had said, 'Jeese! Them weans is drooken wet,' and taken them into his room. There was a fire, a brown teapot on the hob and sausages jumping in a frying-pan, a smell to take the mice from the walls. The woman set them down on stools and gave them plates of sausages which they gulped down, and then a kind of fruit out of a tin with a sweet 'clarty' juice, and cream on it. But at the third mouthful of this he began to feel sick, the wee yin was already boakin'.

'Wattie,' I broke through my nightmare, 'didn't you have anyone to look after you?'

A wee dog sometimes came and lay beside them in the holey. It smelt something awfie and it started them itching, but it was a rare wee dog.

'But who looked after you? Hadn't you a mother?'

Again he turned blindly towards me, and answered in the shrill voice, 'Deed aye had we! Who my faither wis I never kenned, but we had wir mother. She was a ba-ad yin!' I put my hands over my eyes, but it was my ears I should have covered, for it was the words in the high strange speech that conjured up the evil visions: drunken brawling and obscene caresses and violence. 'It wis after a hammering he got the wee yin sickened. They took him away in the ambulance. They said he wis deid.' I must have got a cry out, and tried to struggle to my feet, for he said with something of his old gentleness, 'Na, I wisna sorry. He wis aye greetin' and coughin'. He wis a chairge on me. I didna mind.'

Then suddenly the angle of his head altered, the thin neck was stretched out, his eyes started, his mouth twisted in a grimace that showed his teeth. He said in a loud screaming cry, 'It wis the dog I minded!' He moved his head from side to side, crying words I had never heard before nor ever have heard again. 'The dirty drunken brutes, they hanged my dog on me! They tied one end o' the belt round his neck and threw it o'er the pulleys. And when I went for them they had me on the floor, and they all got their hands on me pulling me this way and that, laughin' and roarin', and herself the worst o' the lot. And then—

'And then—' He had put his two hands round his thin neck. I was compelled to understand what he was saying. I was in his power now, not he in mine. I could not stop him, could not escape from going down with him into his remembered hell. Successful in hanging the dog, they started on Wattie himself. But neighbours must have intervened; for he woke, gasping in agony, having gone all the way to the end of life and back again.

When I came to myself I was gasping too, my sobs strangling my breath. I was in terror I would never get back into my own life again. Yet the fearful incantation was over, Wattie was gone from my side. And slowly round me was forming the familiar scene: the damp pasture, the high arches of the Eas trees, and down below through the hazels, far down, the creeping water of the Loch greyed with evening.

Still I could not move, not even to rub away the burning tears that ran over my face.

It was Wattie himself who released me. I found him standing beside me, his sickle in his hand. His head poked forward from the enormous load of bracken on his back, so that he was comically like a tortoise in shape. Cheerful and dignified as ever, he looked at me, and gently reproved me, 'What for are you sitting there all the time crying, Ellen? Rise now like a good lassie. It is time to be taking up An Craggoch's cows.'

Edward Gaitens

Edward Gaitens (1897–1966) was born in the Gorbals and by the time he began to write in his mid-thirties he had already tried several ways of earning a living as well as having spent two years in Wormwood Scrubs as a conscientious objector during World War One. His first work appeared in print in 1938 and quickly attracted the attention and praise of other writers, including James Bridie and H.G. Wells.

With the exception of *The Dance of the Apprentices* (1946), which was a novel based on half a dozen previous stories, Gaitens stuck to short fiction and his work has consequently suffered from critical neglect. Although he was by no means prolific his work was regarded in his day as a realistic and vital record of working class existence. A review in the *Glasgow Herald* of June 20, 1942, acknowledged that he captured the life of the Glasgow tenements, 'with an understanding and knowledge that has seldom been bettered'. Certainly Gaitens avoided the pitfalls of sentimentality and melodrama which beset the authors of *The Gorbals Story* and *No Mean City*. He is the first Glasgow writer to portray the city's working class life with any degree of honesty and dignity and in this respect he has been a major influence on subsequent writers.

'The Sailing Ship' originally appeared in the *Scots Magazine* of May, 1939, and was later collected in *Growing Up and Other Stories*. Some critics have accused Gaitens of a lack of clarity and telling social comment, but the gently applied pressure of uncompromising honesty sustains his stories. He neither cheats his readers, nor lets them off the hook. His prose is both conversational and lyrical and he is at his finest when he describes the confrontation of the human spirit with the ugliness of emotional or physical desolation.

The Sailing Ship

MRS REGAN yelled at her son: 'Get up, ye lazy pig! Rise up an' look for work an' don't shame me before the neebors!' She stopped sweeping the floor and approached the set-in bed, brandishing the brush over him with insane gestures. The veins bulged in her scrawny neck, her eyes were crazy, she was red from her brow to the top of her breast, like a person in the throes of suffocation. 'Get up, d'ye hear? Get out o' this house an' never come back, ye lazy coward! Ye'll not be lyin' there day-in day-out an' neebors whisperin'.' She came closer, sneering: 'D'ye ken whit they call ye? "Johnny Regan, the dirty Conshy, the wee gentleman that's too good for work!"'

He stared in silent misery at the wall, holding in his rage, conquering the inherited violence in his blood. How he hated her! He would always hate her. Always! When she was long dead and gone, her memory would be nauseous! His hands gripped the undersheet in the vehemence of restraint. She screamed down at him: 'A conshense objaictor! My, ye're a rare son! A conshense objaictor an' socialish! Ma braw Terence is lyin' deid in France, while you're lyin' here safe an' weel!'

Why must she taunt him so horribly; making him itch to inflict the brutality he had witnessed so often since childhood? He had gone to prison, driven by wild idealism, believing his action would end life like this! He turned on the pillow and said quietly: 'Ach, shut up, will ye? Don't make yourself uglier than you are!' He could have plucked out his tongue. He had not meant to say that. But her nagging would enrage a saint! She became speechless and struck him with the broom handle, hard, vicious blows. Any reference to her disfigurement always infuriated her.

One of her aimless blows hit his elbow and he felt sick with sudden pain. He must stop this! He leapt from bed, as he was, in pants and semmit, and seized the broom handle. 'Stop it now, Mother! Stop it, for God's sake! D'ye hear me!' he shouted, pleading, at her crazed face. 'Have you gone mad? You'll hurt yourself!' But he could not wrest the brush from her, and he regarded, with horrified interest, her thin, red arms, amazed at her strength. Then rage gusted through him like a furnace blast. One good blow would settle her! He trembled, blinded by emotion, and let go his hold. She began receding from him as though from a ghost, walking slowly backwards holding the broom straight in front of her, terrified by the burning fixity of his gaze. He followed, slowly, ominously, with clenched fists. As she got round the lop-sided table, she darted from the room, slamming the door after her.

For several minutes he stood trembling and staring as if she was still there; then, aware that his bare feet were wet with the sodden tea-leaves she always threw down to lay the summer dust, he exclaimed: 'Ach, hell!' and stepped uncomfortably to the shallow window-bay, where his socks and trousers lay heaped on a chair. He pulled them and his boots on and sat regarding the street. Inflamed by a base desire to rush into the kitchen after her, he clapped his hands to his eyes. 'No! For Christ's sake! Not that!' His own mother! He ought to pity her and all warped people. A sense of the waste of life deeply affected him. One set of people embarrassed or bored by possessing much more than they needed, while others were continually distressed and dismayed by the lack of common human needs. Five years after the appalling waste of beautiful human energy and lives in war, he saw it still around him in slums, unemployment, preventable ignorance and disease.

Waste!

No one could call him a coward. He would have shouldered a rifle in a revolution. Let them whisper 'Coward' behind his back: none of them had the courage to step up and say it. But returned soldiers had said: 'Ah wish Ah'd had the pluck tae be a Conshy, like you, Johnny. It was four years of hell.' And those same men were unemployed, their lives as aimless and empty as his own. How gladly he would man any gun used to batter these tenements to the ground!

Why did he linger on here anyway? Some queer loyalty was keeping him, some faint hope of a return of the humble prosperity and friendliness and cheer that once had brightened this sad house. If only that recurring sickness did not afflict him. He would have adventured from here long ago. That two years' imprisonment, with underfeeding on bad food, had left him with some mysterious weakness. For days it disabled him; and these nights, crushed with three others in that bed it was impossible to sleep for the heat and the bugs.

He stood up vigorously and hustled into his waistcoat and jacket, trying, by activity, to divert his thoughts from their dark channel. What was the matter with him? He was only twenty-six and Life, fascinating, beautiful, waited for him to turn his youth to account.

He thought of going into the kitchen for a wash, but he knew she would set her tongue on him, and once more his feelings darkened. He looked at his collar and tie on the back of the chair. Why worry? Why bother putting them on! Why worry about anything? He strode into the lobby and met her waiting there, sullenly contrite. 'D'ye want ony breakfast, son?' she asked. He opened the door and passed out. 'I'm not hungry!' he cast back at her.

Ay, sure she would give him breakfast! he reflected as he turned out of the dark close into the main road. With his father and two brothers out of work like himself, bread and margarine and stewed tea was all the poor soul had to offer him this morning. And she would have nagged him like one of the Furies while he ate it. His heart turned back to her; he should never forget that she wasn't responsible for those mad fits; her nerves were fretted raw by worry and care; he believed she loved him, but he was aware that affection is a delicate thing, driven deep into people and lost behind the tough exterior they develop to face a sordid life.

Ach, if only he had a Woodbine! He raked his pockets for a stub. Across the street he saw a man stoop and pick a fag-end from the gutter, wipe it on his sleeve and stuff it into his clay pipe. His ache for a smoke tempted him to do the same, but with no food in him the idea made him squeamish. Never mind! He might get a few hours' casual work. Then his pockets would jingle!

The sky was sprinkled with gay clouds that sailed and shone as if there were no unemployment and slums in the world. At least he could smile at the sky! Perhaps the sea was like that today, limitless, deep azure, with ships roving about it like those clouds. He saw a cloud shaped like a swimming man with arms stretched in the breast-stroke. It sailed to a good wind, and he watched it awhile, wondering how long it would keep its form, till the wind tore it and bundled it into another shape. He laughed, and his heart stood up in him cheerful and fearless, his shoulders squared and he walked with manlier step.

From every by-street the sounds of the hordes of tenement children, on holiday these times, came to him; laughing and calling, each day they marvellously discovered happiness, like some lovely jewel, in the gutters and back courts of the big city. His soul joined with them as they sported and ran, and he was lightened with belief that war and poverty would sometime vanish away like an evil dream and that wakened Man would stand amazed at his blundering and turn to find happiness as simply and innocently as those ragged children were finding it now.

So exalted, he realised he had walked, without tiring, the four miles from his home to the docks. He entered the wide gates and strolled through crowds of idle dockers, vigorously discussing football, religion or politics in the assertive Scottish manner. Small chance of his getting work here! And even if he did, he would have to quit if the union delegate demanded to see his membership badge and card. But he was not saddened. The dazzled waters of the harbour immediately foiled his disappointment, and he inhaled the breath of travel and the smell of merchandise from the abounding light and heat. Flashing pinions curved in the blaze; he sensed them like a wreath around his head and smiled at the pigeons crooning their passion and quarrelling on the warehouse roofs, or seeking spilled grain and indian corn among the very feet of the men.

He watched a big tramp steamship manoeuvring into the first great basin. It was the only vessel there, and he recalled the prosperous days of the port, when every basin was so crowded with masts and funnels that it was hardly possible to row a dinghy between the herded ships. He sauntered around and, lifting his head to watch a wheeling gull, saw the towering masts and cross-trees of a sailing ship peering over the stern of a steamship. It was ten years since he had beheld a sailing ship and one of such a size as the height of those masts hinted she must be, and he almost ran towards her in delighted excitement.

He stood close and contemplated her with amazement as though she was a phantom which had sailed out of the past of buccaneers and pirates and which might at any moment fade from sight. She was a long, slim three-master, newly painted a pale blue, with the name *France* glittering in solid brass letters on her prow that pointed proudly at the bluff stern of the steamship like an upheld spear. She looked all too slender for her great calling; her spars were crowded white with resting gulls, still as sculptured birds, and as Regan gazed past them at the sky he was taken by desire to get a job on her.

He walked smartly up the gangway. There was apparently no one aboard, and he was elated by his solitary experience as he looked along the clean, bare decks where every hatch was battened down and everything stowed away. If only he might get work on her! That would be a manly break with the mean life of the tenements. Once he had faced the seas with her, he could never return to that life again. There was hardly a part of the ship he could have named, but he placed his hand fondly on her hot rail as though he had sailed with her for many years and knew her intimately. He leant over the side and saw hundreds of monkey-nuts floating, bright in the narrow space between the quay and ship. He had not noticed them when he hurried forward, with all his eyes for her, but now he saw them plentifully scattered about the dock and on the travelling crane, under which they shone like nuggets of gold on the coal-dust lying where a vessel had been coaled.

Monkey-nuts! They must have fallen from the hoisted sacks; they must have been her cargo; she had come from the tropics! His fancy wandered into passionate depths of tropical forests, he heard the chattering scream of monkeys, saw small bodies swing and little eyes flash in the green gloom; and he felt convinced that the tropic heat, soaked deep in her planks, was mounting from her decks through the soles of his feet into his body.

He turned to see an immensely tall, broad man in sea-going uniform stepping from a cabin away forrard. His heart bounded. Here was his chance! He walked towards him, summoning all his spirit to ask for a job, without the vaguest idea what to say, regretting his ignorance and inexperience of sea-life. The sailor, tanned and handsome, with blond hair gleaming under his officer's cap, stopped and looked dumbly at Regan, who felt most painfully at that moment the complete absence of breakfast in his belly. Trembling, he removed his cap and said shakily: 'Good-morning, sir! Do you need any sailors?' while he felt his blood scald his cheeks and seemed to himself the utterest fool alive. The officer stared a moment, then took a long, twisted black cheroot from his mouth and waved it vaguely about, as if taking in the whole harbour. 'All my grew iss 'ere!' he said. It was a Scandinavian voice. 'I haf no yobs! You haf been a sailor? Ya? No?' He replaced his cigar and stared stonily, then removed it and burst out with an uproarious laugh, pointing it at the dizzy masts: 'You could yoomp up there, ya? No, I sink you are yoost too schmall!'

Regan wanted to run off the ship. What bloody fool he was! Fancy the likes of him expecting to get a berth, with hundreds of seasoned seamen unemployed! He felt mortified by the officer's scorn of his physique. He was the last and slightest of eight strong brothers, but he had never been regarded as a weakling.

'Hi!' The officer was calling him back, and hope flared up in him again. As he approached, the officer took a cheroot from his outside breast pocket and offered it silently, with a vast grin on his face. Regan accepted it and descended to the dock where he stuffed his pockets with monkey-nuts and sat on the big iron wheel of the crane eating them and flicking the shells over the quayside. He shrugged his shoulders. Ach, well! At least, he could admire the beauty of the ship if he couldn't sail with her! He loved the way her slim bows curved, like the flanks of a fawn. *France*: that was a light little name that suited her beautiful poise. He had heard it said that the Clyde would never see a windjammer again; that they had all been requisitioned, dismasted and turned into steamships for war service. And here was a lovely one whose decks he had walked!

When he was sick of monkey-nuts, he begged for a match from a passing docker and lit the black cheroot. It was pure tobacco leaf and he thought he had burned his throat out with the first inhalation, while his head swam and he coughed violently. He stubbed the cheroot out against the crane and put it in his pocket as a souvenir.

In this great basin, where there were only three ships, all the light of day appeared to be concentrated, and in the intense path of the sun floating seagulls vanished as if they were burned away, like the phoenix bird consumed by its own fire, and Regan blessed his luck for coming upon this ship in such glad weather.

The steamship was unloading a cargo of Canadian wheat, through an elevator projecting from her hold on to the warehouse roof. He went and leant against the sliding door of the shed and watched the wheat pour an aureate stream to the ground in a rising, golden hill. Then he saw a big, red-headed man descending the gangway of the wheat boat. It was 'Big' Willie McBride, the stevedore, who lived in his neighbourhood and picked up a living as a street bookmaker, when there was no work at the docks. 'Hi, young Regan, come 'ere!' he called. 'D'ye want a job?' he asked as Regan came over. 'It's light work, shovellin' wheat for a couple o' days, an' worth thirty bob tae ye?'

What luck! Regan smiled eagerly. 'You bet, Mac! Glad to get anything! I'm skinned!'

McBride took him aboard the steamship and sent him down the hold, where he was handed a light, flat-bedded wooden shovel and joined nine other men, five of whom fed the endless belt of the elevator with wheat while four others poured it into huge sacks which were tied, roped together in fours and hoisted above by a steam-winch on deck.

Regan set-to shovelling the grain into the cups on the revolving belt. It was stifling down here; very soon he breathed with great difficulty, and his head was throbbing painfully when the ganger shouted: 'Come on, boays! Up on deck for yer blow!' They climbed up and were replaced by ten others. They could only work in shifts of half an hour, with fifteen-minute spells on deck, as the wheat-dust clogged their throats and nostrils, turning to paste in the moisture of breath.

At every turn on deck, Regan leant on the stern-rail and gazed down on the *France*. One time, in the evening, the other men joined him, curious at his quietness; and Paddy, a six-foot, handsome young Irishman, in dirty flannels and a blue guernsey, said loudly: 'Take a good look at the old hooker, me buckos, for she'll mebbe never come up the Clyde again!' Someone said: 'Ay, it's three years sin' she was last here. D'ye ken her, Paddy?' Paddy replied: 'Dew Oi know her! Shure Oi sailed wid that same win'-jammer three years ago. Her skipper was a darlin' sailor an' a dirthy slave-driver. A big, yella-haired Dane, he was, wid a wallop on him like a steam-hammer. Shure Oi seen 'im knock a dago clean across the deck wid a little flick uv the back uv his han'! She was a hell-ship, I'm tellin' ye, an' her grub wasn't fit for pigs, so Oi left her at Ryo dee Janeeraw an' sailed home to Belfast in a cattle-boat!' Regan, listening to him, knew proudly that he would have sailed with her had he got the chance, no matter how hard might be the life she gave him.

After midnight, when they all sat up on deck again, gratefully breathing the sweet air, Regan blessed the *France* for his luck. Her holystoned decks and every detail of her shone clear in the glow of the moon, as he whispered down: 'Thanks, lovely ship, for getting me this day's work!' Behind him, Paddy, who was tipsy, produced a bottle of whisky and sat swigging and humming by himself. Someone said: 'Give us a song, Paddy!' The Irishman stood up proudly, swaying, and passed the bottle round. 'Shure, Oi'll give ye'se a song!' he shouted. 'Oi'll lift yer hearts to the mouths of ye! Sing up, ye sods! Sing up!' They all laughed and joined him, singing:

'Oh, whisky is the life of man,
Whisky, Johnny!

Oh, whisky murdered my old man,
So it's whisky for my Johnny!'

Regan turned and joined them. 'Shut up, everybody!' he cried. 'Let Paddy sing by himself! Give us a solo, Paddy,' he said. 'Do you know "Shenandoah"?' He realised that the Irishman had a fine voice, but he was spoiling it with the drink. He wanted to hear a song that would honour the sailing ship, a sad old song of the sea. Paddy stared at him in drunken amazement and cried thickly: 'Dew Oi know "Shenandjo"! Will ye'se listen to him? Dew Oi know "Shenandjo"! Shure Oi lisped it at me ole man's knee!' He began singing. The lovely old shanty gripped him, and he sang it seriously, with romantic sweetness:

'Oh Shenandoah, I long to see you,
Away, you rolling river!
Away! We're bound away,
Across the wide Missouri!'

Someone produced a mouth-organ and played it softly and well, and it sparkled in the moonlight.

''Tis ten long years since last I saw thee,
Away, you rolling river! . . .'

From the ship across the basin a cook cast a pail of slop-water over the side. It flashed an instant tongue of silver and vanished in the dappled iridescence below, and the cook let the bucket dangle while he listened to the song quavering tenderly about the harbour. Regan was deeply moved. Ay, this was the song for a sailing ship! 'Shenandoah'. It was a poem in a name, and it sang of simple men who had travelled far, who carried pictures of relatives or sweethearts and were always promising to write home and always failing, men who had died abroad and never saw their homes again—the forgotten legions of wanderers in the long history of the sea. Ach, he must escape from the prison of the slums!

'Oh, Shenandoah, I love your daughter,
Away, you rolling river! . . .'

The big form of McBride suddenly loomed before them, and his mighty roar burst amid them like a thunderclap: 'Heh! Whit's this? A bloody tea-party? Get doon below, ye shower o' bastards! Yer spell's up ten meenits ago! Jump to it, ye lousy bunch o' scrimshankers!' They all scuttled down the hold, except Regan and Paddy, who, gleefully swinging his bottle, lurched into the stevedore, and the two big men faced each other. Highlander and Irishman, they were of a size and breadth, and they measured each other's splendid build with admiring, mocking eyes. Paddy offered McBride the bottle and the stevedore thrust it away. 'Tae hell wi' yer whisky, man! Ah've goat tae get the wheat oot o' this ship. Ah'll hiv a dram wi' ye efter that's done, no before!'

In spite of his hatred of the violence in himself, Regan sat watching, thrilled, expecting a fight. Paddy suddenly vented a great laugh and stumbled down the hold, shouting: 'Ach, we're buddies, Mac!'

McBride shouted after him: 'Sure, we're buddies, but you buckle intae that wheat, sod ye!' Then he turned. 'Whit's the matter wi' you, Regan?' Regan jumped out of his trance. 'Okay, Mac! I thought there was going to be a scrap!' McBride laughed good-naturedly. 'Ach, Ah wouldnae scrap wi' Paddy. He's okay! Noo beat it doon below!'

All night the wheat hissed down the elevator chute and the steam-winch rattled, hoisting up the sacks. Then the flanges of the bulk-heads showed clear and the many tons of wheat sifted surely down till the floor of the hold was visible. Late in the next afternoon the elevator stopped, the last few hundredweights of wheat were hoisted up in sacks and run down the gangplank in trucks on to the dock, and the whole gang left the wheat-boat to be paid off in the warehouse. 'It's me for the boozer an' a bloody guid wet!' Regan heard some of them say as they went away with their money. For two days' and a night's work he had earned over thirty shillings. He thrust it into his pocket and went and sat on the wheel of the crane. He was very tired, his head ached, and he coughed up wheat-dust from his throat, while he gazed longingly at the sailing ship till dusk descended. He had decided what he would do. He would give his mother half of his earnings, buy himself a second-hand pair of strong boots and tramp to London with his few shillings. But not before he had watched the *France* sailing down the Clyde. When he had bade her farewell he would never return. She would speed to the ocean, he would take to the road, and with every mile that he walked his thoughts would follow her.

After supper he picked up the newspaper which his father had just laid down and his eye fell on the 'List of Sailings'. Only a dozen ships were listed, but with excitement he read that the *France* was sailing next day on the afternoon tide. He threw the paper aside and hunched by the fire, staring at the invisible, voyaging with a sailing ship, till his mother, fretted by his immobility, said: 'Whit are ye starin' at, Johnny? Ye look daft, glarin' like that! Ye should go oot tae the pictures or doon tae the chapel for an hoor. Ye hivnae been tae Mass since ye came hame fae London'—she was always ashamed to mention the word 'prison'. He rose and thrust past her. 'Ach, I'm tired!' he said and went into the parlour, undressed and lay down, wakeful a long while, thinking of the *France*.

At her hour of departure next day he was by her side, waiting while ropes were cast aboard her from the pilot-tug, watching every pause and turn she made in the great basin till her prow pointed away from the city. At last she set out, very slowly, in the wake of the tug, with that tall blond man prominent on her deck, shouting instructions, the man who had given him the cheroot. Regan took that out and looked at it, and the keepsake seemed to bind him to her more as he followed along the dockside till his way was barred. Then he hurried out to the road and jumped on a tram and rode till he came to another free part of the river, and stood on the shore waiting till she came up. This way, riding on trams and buses, he followed her slow progress, while his heart grew sadder with every mile that she sailed beyond Glasgow. The flood was opening wider for her, the shores receding; she was leaving the grand little river, with its long and plucky history of shipmaking, maybe for ever. He recalled the Irishman's words. He would never see her again!

At the end he took a bus out to Dumbarton and stood on the shore nearby the great Rock. He saw the tug leave her and turn towards home with a hoot of farewell from its siren, like the cry of a timid friend deserting a gay adventurer. Then, like a gallant gesture, she unfurled all her sails and made her beauty terrible for his eyes. She was lovelier far than he had seen her yet as she came slowly on like a floating bird unfolding its wings for flight. She had a dream-like loveliness, and as she came opposite where he stood alone, he impulsively tore off his cap and waved it, then threw it on the ground and stood with his head proudly up, ennobled by her grace.

Sunset met her like a song of praise and his heart went after her as she rippled past. Ach, if he could only have served her on her last few voyages, before she was dismasted and broken up! She dipped slowly into the dying sun and the waters fanned out from her bows like flowing blood. Then the sun went swiftly down and her beauty was buried in the darkness. 'Goodbye, lovely ship!' he called after her. 'Goodbye! Goodbye, *France*!'

So ecstatic was his concentration upon that vanishing ship that he felt her decks quiver under his feet, saw her high spars tremble, heard the flap of her sails, as he gazed with uplifted head. He was sailing on, away from unemployment and slums and wretchedness, far from the ignorance and misunderstanding of his parents, to the infinite nobility of the sea! His eyes were moist, his hands in his pockets painfully clenched, his limbs shook like a saint's in the ardour of prayer. And for a long time he stood there bareheaded, unaware that darkness, with small rain and a cold wind, had enveloped his transported body.

Elspeth Davie

Elspeth Davie's work constantly reminds us that, as she says, 'the strange, the desolating and the ludicrous is happening to us all the time.'

Born in Ayrshire in 1919, Elspeth Davie spent her early years in the south of England. She was educated in Edinburgh where she attended University and the College of Art. She taught painting for some years and lived in Ireland before returning to Edinburgh where she lives with her husband, the philosopher George Elder Davie. Her novels and short fiction have been highly praised and she received the Kathleen Mansfield Award for short stories in 1978.

Elspeth Davie has the knack of making the familiar strange with surprising juxtapositions and combinations of character and event. 'Sunday Class' takes something as inoffensive and stridently conventional as a Sunday school lesson and uses it as a vehicle for disturbing doubts, bringing a strange and appealing atavism into a world of rigid hierarchies. What happens next is described with meticulous realism and splendidly dead-pan humour.

Sunday Class

THIS SEMICIRCLE crouched around the teacher are dead on time with their answers. A well-drilled lot, they flick them back, one after the other, while the question is scarcely out of her mouth.

'Flowers.'

'Birds.'

'Good food.'

'Homes.'

'Friends.'

'And loved ones,' snaps the oldest girl jealously.

Now they all turn their heads to the boy at the end. They know there is nothing left for him except 'good books', 'good music' or perhaps 'sunshine' at a pinch. They wait for it. He stares stubbornly down towards the end of the room.

'Come on,' urges the woman, Miss MacRae, her eyes wavering from her lapel brooch to her wrist-watch. 'Some of the things God wants us to be grateful for?'

'Dinosaurs,' says the boy.

There is a pause while the woman shifts the fur about her neck. She looks warm. 'To be *grateful* for,' she warns.

'I know that. I said "dinosaurs".'

'I suppose you know what they are?'

'I know all about them. Always have.'

'And you know how to spell them?'

'It doesn't matter.'

'What did you say?'

'It doesn't matter.'

'Can you not think of anything else?'

'No. I'm thinking of them all the time.'

'*All* the time?' Her eyes narrow in suspicion.

'Well, someone had better think about them. They were around for millions of years. I'm grateful for them!'

There is reason to be grateful for the swinge and whack of the monstrous, scaly tails in this stifling hall. A quiver of relief runs through the others in the circle as they momentarily throw aside good books, homes and loved ones. They stare up towards the high sealed windows expectantly. In this East of Scotland town it is common enough to see things swirling in the air even at that height. On the stormiest days tufts of foam have sailed past and whole sodden newspapers flattened themselves out against the glass. Besides being a meeting-place for various classes during the week this hall is sometimes used for a dance, and on Sunday morning the sweaty dust of Saturday night still hangs in the air. On the platform stands a grand piano, swathed in green cloth. Along the wall behind it are various Bible pictures, maps and travel posters. There is also a chart showing a fair-haired young man balancing on the apex of a large isosceles triangle, and at graded levels beneath him a variety of animals stare wonderingly up, except for one or two leathery creatures near the bottom who continue to stare glumly at their own tails. The chap standing at the top looks glad to be where he is, but not surprised. He is not naked, as in some charts, but wears a casual sports shirt and flannel trousers. His pink, open palms are turned outwards to show that he has nothing to hide. His bare feet are also turned outwards.

Down both sides of the room, separated from one another by thin, wooden screens, are a dozen or so small circles seated around a man or a woman. From behind each screen comes a strange murmuring, discreet and low. It is like the murmuring of visitors in a hospital ward—sometimes placating, sometimes insistent or impatient, but always mesmerically soft. The boy who has dinosaurs on the brain keeps turning his head first to the stage and then to the door. Sometimes he tips his chair forward and cranes his neck as though to see around the neighbouring screens and to catch another murmur, perhaps to compare one murmur with another. Then he returns his attention to the woman in front of him, watching her mouth closely like a lip-reader or like somebody following a conversation in a foreign language. This irritates her more than anything else.

'I'm afraid that's not quite good enough,' she insists. 'I want something more.'

The rest of the class fix him with their eyes. They are afraid that now for the sake of peace he will hand her a good book or even a single perfect flower. But the boy broods. Now he is dredging through the deepest pits of the sea. Things not quite good enough for Miss MacRae spurt from fissures or prod the blackness with phosphorescent eye-stalks. Further up are creatures frilled, beaked and scalloped, some whip-thin, others round and smooth as bells. And far above in steaming tropical forests the ground crackles and glitters with ferocious insects. He has made his choice. He scratches his knee thoughtfully, then raises his hands and demonstrates something in the air.

'There's a sort of insect—' he ruminates. 'A giant fish-killing bug with claws that fold up under its head like a clasp-knife . . .'

'I am taking no notice of you,' Miss MacRae interrupts instantly, her eyes riveted on him. 'Everybody else can understand what I'm asking. Are you different from everyone else?' He is silent. They are all silent, studying Miss MacRae. In striking contrast to her lack of love for wildlife she is made up of scraps from various birds and beasts. She is sporting a tuft of bright-coloured feathers, a couple of paws, a tail and a head and a carved bone or two. Her gloves are suede and she has a small purse-bag made of real pigskin lined with coarse hair. There is nothing artificial about her except the butterfly brooch in her lapel and the deep-set button eyes in the furry head that peers over her shoulder.

At the top of the room a handbell is struck loudly—signal that it is time to reassemble in the larger adjoining hall. Although most of the group snatch up magazines and Bibles and stampede off as usual, a few—mostly the older girls—linger as though protectively about Miss MacRae. Today there are mixed feelings about her. Her dismissal of dinosaurs and her withdrawal from fish-killing bugs has shown her to be wildly outside and utterly alone. It seems there is no place to put her now. All the same some of them feel for her in their hearts, and the oldest girl strokes the face of the little fox consolingly.

But the boy remains uncompromisingly stern. He gives them all time to clear off to the next room and in the meantime he takes a closer look at the chart on the wall behind the platform. This look confirms something he has suspected for a long time. Now there is no doubt about it. Miss MacRae is the true, self-appointed mate of the chap standing on the sharp, topmost point of the isosceles triangle. Her place is up there beside him. But could the man bring himself to step aside one fraction of an inch to make room for her?

John MacNair Reid

John MacNair Reid (1895–1954), was born in Glasgow and worked most of his life as a journalist, firstly on the *Inverness Courier* and later on the *Glasgow Evening Times*. He left his mark on Scottish literature as an author of both poetry and prose and as a prolific reviewer. His last years, before he died in a motoring accident, were spent in Wester Ross.

'The Tune Kilmarnock', published in the 1940s, is a remarkable piece in which Reid combines the emotional intensity of a young man's experience with a strangely controlled style. He has approached the twin taboos for an author hoping to avoid self-indulgence—writing about writing, and writing about a deeply personal grief—and yet he has triumphed.

Reid forces his readers to question the validity of the written word as a means of communication. Style and niceties of expression, he tells us, are in danger of isolating author, reader and subject. Yet it is the theme of isolation, intensified by a desperate need for faith and emotional contact, which gives this piece its remarkable impact.

The Tune Kilmarnock

IS NOT style an admission that you have found yourself and that, therefore, you are lost? When I said to my heart 'I will take your treasure up into the daylight and explain it to men,' my heart immediately doubted if it had a treasure at all. But I grew reckless as I thought of the chance this was of impressing men by my methods—my choice of words, my deft allusions, my outer rim of nonsense that marks the bull's-eye of sense.

'Yes,' I say to myself, 'you smiled when you thought of people saying, "Now, isn't it strange, but I've often felt such a thing and never could express it!" feeling as you did so powerful, so completely able to express it.

'Then a shadow came on your thought and you frowned. Why did men not add, ". . . but HE surely managed it"? Men read your work and discuss themselves into it, whereas they should see you only in it as it is your property. This treasure in your heart, for instance.'

Style is the body that wears you down and destroys you. It is conduct, three-fourths of life. The other fourth is the material which never goes down and which cannot be destroyed. Great men have had great style. They have stamped the record of existence upon the material Being as a lead embosses paper. I feel on Ayrshire soil that Burns's ribs are sticking out of it. Those great men may not see anything without wishing to impress their personalities upon it. Thus they alter and falsify it. It passes on to the next person—as it must pass on—man-soiled.

I will tell of this thing without style, for I know not how to tell it. I will not ponder on it: I will not be showy.

When I was young my mother said I was always showing off. But that was because she saw me doing things she had never seen little girls do when she was a girl. She knew nothing of little boys.

This thought will restrain me if some night when passing their bedroom door, with the candle shaded by my hand, I hear her saying to my father as they lie in the darkness, 'It's just like him to say he hears something in a tune that no one else has ever heard.' I shall pass on to my own room. They will not know that a part of them both has passed by outside and now lies in another square of the same darkness thinking of them. Such a picture makes me see myself as a tombstone glimmering in the moonlight with their names upon my brow.

But my mother's love would last through all that which she calls showiness, and would through other vices more incriminating. I do not fear her eyes upon my story. With others it is different.

There is Mark Ireland in my mind. We became friends at the time when friends are easily made, and have become enemies now when friends are sorely needed. (I suppose we are enemies now that friendship is over? It must be so when you think of the way things ended.) All my aims and aspirations, my tastes and prejudices were as open country to him. The more he explored the more I wanted to show him. Then, when ultimately my heart was entirely his, and he one of the permanencies of my heart, there came a pause. He seemed to draw back a convenient space to strike. He struck hard and cruelly: my heart shut tight, but it was too late. Now it hides the bruise, and lack of sun and light prevents its healing.

There, then, was someone separate from me, though he used my symbols and had my habits of living; someone from the beginning cast in the mould of enmity against me. If he should read my story he would sneer his sneer which is a duty to himself. And something of my heart would be wounded again.

Mark Ireland has been to Collashaig with me several times. We have slept together in the room above the parlour with its window facing the loch. All the days were spent fishing and mooning around. But on Sundays we went over the moor to the tiny church. He's bound to remember that sometimes. I wonder what his thoughts are when the memory comes and how he puts it from him again. Probably it bores him.

Certain it is that when I go to Collashaig nowadays I am not troubled by memories of him. He has not impressed himself upon the place. I never see his 'slow smile' break where the sun lights up the woods, and Cruachan amid the scurrying clouds stands aloof, as I like to picture him, free from all questionings of vanity. Yet such ears as Mark's have listened to prayer and Psalm in that little church, and such a voice as he possessed once aided in the praise. He was a voice in the days of my Belief.

My mother had a singing voice. When she first went to that little church on the hill-side at Collashaig one bright Sunday morning, the congregation stopped its breath, far less its voice, to listen to that one throat singing:

> 'I'm not ashamed to own my Lord
> or to defend His cause.'

There was something in her voice that got me. It was a soft contralto, and it was like the crushing of deep purple velvet in my hands. She loved her voice. And when she got a Psalm to sing it was like blending two colours, so suited to the Scottish Psalms was her lovely voice.

My childhood, however she remembers it (and when she talks she recalls window breakings, police chases, school complaints and running after lorries in busy Glasgow streets), is to me a composite picture of still moments in large Glasgow churches, where the sunshine sobered or blinded the vulgar coloured windows, a bowed figure in an exalted pulpit, and a voice swimming in the singing of the choir; that voice which sounded like the yield of rich purple velvet, or had I known of it then, was like the look of the faint purplish flush of the bloom of a peach. Yes, and of Sunday mornings and evenings in the little church at Collashaig, when the leader of the altos of a great Glasgow church became one of the congregation and mingled her voice in the quivering and hesitant singing of the rustic people around her.

Well, then, that is my memory. And it seemed to me that I was my mother's voice stealing unrecognized into the little hill-side church last Sunday morning. I am now thirty years old, and the last time I was in that church I was twenty-five. The last time my mother sang there I was fifteen. It was about that time she ruined her voice. One foggy night in Glasgow she attended choir practice and strained her throat. Add to that that she caught a chill on the road home. The purplish flush of the bloom was gone. Now she sings no more.

The last time, when I was twenty-five, Mark Ireland was with me. I had told him many times about my mother's singing, but it was not a topic upon which he could impose a triumphing example from his own little sphere, and so I felt that though I had spoken of it my memory remained undisturbed. When I went to the church last Sunday I knew I was something older than Mark Ireland, something that had been beautiful in the world before he was born: I was my mother's voice. Jubilantly I said to myself, 'Now I'll hear the magic words, "to the tune, Kilmarnock".'

And sure enough after the first prayer there it was, the decent minister chap announcing to a passive handful of people the Paraphrase, number fifty-four . . . to the tune, Kilmarnock.

The sun was shining mildly on the clear glass windows. I could see the field below the farm, and beyond its tufted edge the dark slate-grey line of the loch. A few sheep were grazing in the field, a wind was bothering some low-laid clouds, a patch of burnt heather looked like a perpetual cloud shadow on the far hill-side. The lady with the red hat was over at the wheezy harmonium, playing the first few bars; a shuffle of feet and we all arose.

The recent craving of my Unbelief, which was to destroy religion, has passed from my mind like a mist that leaves no trace. I say to myself there was once such a craving but it is now unconvincing as remembered pain.

Rejected his father's faith. When did I reject my father's faith? Was there a decisive hour? He took me as a child to a sunlit beach, he got me stripped in a small boat and plunged me into the waters. He was by my side and his gleaming arms were iron rods. Blue and a circle of diamonds were round me and a taste of salt that was the bite of the sunshine, the green, sleek body of the sea slipping past underneath me. 'Jesus, my Lord! I know His name, His name is all my boast.'

Someone who was dead was listening through me to the tune Kilmarnock.

A few shrill soprano voices were leading us all, and the men offered a shy and uncertain harmony. The absence of that other voice which flowed through my consciousness like the blood through my veins made the tune, and in this place, the property of other people. Was it like Mark Ireland's face, which on a meeting now, would pass with a distant stare, the light that animated it for me and shone out recognition of me being withdrawn? The love of this thing was not my mother's love of it, however hard I tried to make it so. It was different from my father's love of it as he had his memories rooted still farther back. It was a love new to man. I touched at the invisible, unformed pain awaiting me in the years of my full heritage and my mind reeled in its immaturity in rank sorrow. Someone who was dead was listening through me to the tune Kilmarnock.

And I do not mean my dead self. That would make the phrase mere chicanery. I was there certainly, my dead self was there: but someone else, or a whole people, was listening to a tune once revered as sacred with a gravity beyond my comprehension.

For if these old people could not understand my Unbelief, I could not comprehend their faith. Kilmarnock sings through me to them, of them to me. They had a formula I apprehend, and never was hate so feared as I feared theirs when in a sickness of love for this glory that is Kilmarnock I claimed their tune to chant my Unbelief. And when they listened to the words, 'Nor will He put my soul to shame, nor let my hope be lost,' the whole thing paused.

The sun was mellow on the clear glass window and the field was green without. That patch of burnt heather darkened the hill-side beyond like a cloud shadow and clouds moved slowly in the sky shadowless. That was the unaltered scene of fifteen years ago. The world of thought had moved on and left this little place a derelict scene in the wastes of long ago.

We were lost, those dead and faithful people and I their son with this handful of worshippers; and with us was an imperishable tune. In illimitable Arctic snows the explorer travels until he drops. All the little, hard, material things he gathered together for his use and safety lie around his melting body in the shifting ice. Some day, years and years onward, his tiny compass may lie in the white palm of a man, highly curious, wise and tolerant. The history of its survival will be recorded. . . . 'What I've committed to His trust, till the decisive hour.'

At the edge of my consciousness where those faces were crowding. Mark Ireland's among them, there was a rim of darkness. Each face had something about it that made it familiar, a something borrowed from my father's face to give it credibility and power. But I knew that while they listened and rejoiced they were blind, and could not explore the calm reserves of sense wherein my existence was secure without even scepticism: an indifference terrible as frozen snowdrifts on winter moors.

Youth stands with beseeching hands yearning toward the past, believing that the very ground he treads has become arid at the touch of his foot. But the ground I tread now is of holy ground for me, for the present must some day complete a past for which I shall yearn and remain uncomforted. The sanction of my Unbelief will then be final and my heart as calm and bleak as moonlight haze on snow. I shall turn my face to the outer darkness and go out. . . . 'Then shall He own His servant's name before His Father's face, and in the new Jerusalem appoint my soul a place.'

O mother, sitting at your hearth, with your black dress gathered round your legs like a silken rug and your white woollen shawl lying idle on the chair's arm near the fire, you have sung as I shall never sing, and as I shall never hear sung again a song that, being intensely grave and holy, is to a mind today only the more intensely pagan. I am standing here, my darling, in the sunlight of the little church, and the green fields are round me and the sheep are grazing in the fields as of old and the loch is still in the distance. Your father and your father's father are listening, and as the voices sing your voice breaks through and grows and grows and grows: it overflows my consciousness: I am dissolving in it; I am become your voice that has visited its old triumphant haunt. Even so I have wandered into the past and am among the lost.

Tom Leonard

Born in Glasgow in 1944, Tom Leonard has done much to take the everyday language of his city out of the realms of graffiti and comic relief. Published widely in many magazines and anthologies, his work transcribes living Glaswegian speech to prove that language is defined by class as much as by country. He has also shown that a working class form of expression is as suitable for poetry and serious thought as any other. Openly, and also by implication, he gives a lie to the idea that literature and truth are reserved for those who are fluent in standard English.

Leonard is better known for his poetry, but 'Honest' finds him exploring the predicament of the writer in general. For readers who expect their authors to sound, or at least write, as if they had been properly brought up, Leonard can come as a surprise. In this piece he unleashes an anarchic, irreverent narrator on hallowed artistic ground, but there is always a serious point to his humour and a real sense of celebration in expression.

As Tom Leonard says, 'All livin language is sacred.'

Honest

A CANNY EVEN remembir thi furst thing a remembir. Whit a mean iz, a remembir aboot four hunner thingz, awit wance. Trouble iz tay, a remembir thim aw thi time.

A thinka must be gon aff ma nut. Av ey thoat that though—leasta always seemti be thinkin, either am jist aboot ti go aff ma nut, or else am already affit. But yi ey think, ach well, wance yir aff yir nut, yill no no yiraffit. But am no so sure. A wish a wuz.

Even jist sitn doonin writn. A ey useti think, whenever a felt like writn sumhm, that that wiz awright, aw yi hud to say wuz, ach well, a think ahl sit doonin write sumhm, nyi jiss sat doonin wrote it. But no noo, naw. A canny even day that for five minutes, but ahl sitnlookit thi thing, nthink, here, sumdayz wrote that afore. Then ahl go, hawlin aw thi books ootma cupboard, trynti find out hooit wuz. Nwither a find out or no, it takes me that long luknfurit, a canny be bothird writn any mair, wance av stoapt. An anyway, a tend ti think if it's wan a they thingz that might uv been writn before, there's no much point in writin it again, even if naibdy actually huz, is there?

It's annoyin—a feel av got this big story buldn up inside me, n ivri day ahl sit down, good, here it comes, only it dizny come at all. Nthi thing iz, it's Noah's if a even no what thi story's goany be about, coz a doant. So a thinkty ma cell, jist invent sumdy, write a story about a fisherman or sumhm. But thi longer a think, thi mair a realise a canny be bothird writn aboota fisherman. Whut wid a wahnti write about a fisherman fur? N am no gonny go downti thi library, nsay, huvyi enny booksn fishermen, jiss so's a can go nread up about thim, then go n write another wan. Hoo wahntsti read a story about fishermen anyway, apart fray people that wid read it, so's they could go n write another wan, or fishermen that read? A suppose right enough, thi trick might be, that yi cin write a story about a fisherman, so long as thi main thing iz, that thi bloke izny a fisherman, but a man that fishes. Or maybe that izny right at all, a widny no. But a do no, that as soon as a lookt up thi map ti see what might be a good name furra fishn village, nthen maybe went a walk ti think up a good name for a fishermans' boat, nthen a sat nworked out what age thi fisherman should be, nhow tall he wuz, nwhat colour his oilskins were, nthen gotim wokn iniz oilskins, doon frae thi village tay iz boat, ad tend ti think, whut duzzy wahnti day that fur? Kinni no day sumhm else wayiz time? Aniffa didny think that ti masell, if a jiss letm go, ach well, it's iz job, away out ti sea, ana big storm in chapter two, ahd tend ti think, either, here, sumdyz wrote that before, or, can a no day sumhm else wi ma time? An in fact, if a came across sumdy sitn readn it eftir a did write it, if a hud, ad tend ti thinkty ma cell, huv they got nuthn behtr ti day wi their time?

A don't no that am sayn whut a mean. But a suppose underneath everythin, thi only person a want ti write about, iz me. It's about time a wrote sumhm aboot masell! But whut? Ah thought even, ach well, jist write doon a lohta yir memories, then maybe they'll take some kinda shape, anyi kin use that ti write a story wi, or a play, or a poem, or a film-script, or God only knows whut, on thi fly. So that's whuta did. Didny mahtr thi order, jist day eftir day, writn doon ma memories. N ad be busy writn it, thinkin, whut an incredible life av hud, even upti noo. Then ad be thinkin, they'll no believe aw this hapnd ti me. Then a looktitit, najistaboot threw up. It wiz nuthin ti day wi me at all. Nthi other people ad be writin about, thi people ad met an that, it wuz nuthin ti day wi them either. It might eveniv been awright, if you coulda said it was about me nthem meetin, but you couldny even say that. It wiz jis a lohta flamin words.

But that's sumhm else. Yi write doon a wurd, nyi sayti yirsell, that's no thi way a say it. Nif yi tryti write it doon thi way yi say it, yi end up with thi page covered in letters stuck thigithir, nwee dots above hof thi letters, in fact, yi end up wi wanna they thingz yid needti huv took a course in phonetics ti be able ti read. But that's no thi way a think, as if ad took a course in phonetics. A doant mean that emdy that's done phonetics canny think right—it's no a questiona right or wrong. But ifyi write down 'doon' wan minute, nwrite doon 'down' thi nixt, people say yir beein inconsistent. But ifyi sayti sumdy, 'Whaira yi afti?' nthey say, 'Whut?' nyou say, 'Where are you off to?' they don't say, 'That's no whutyi said thi furst time.' They'll probably say sumhm like, 'Doon thi road!' anif you say, 'What?' they usually say, 'Down the road!' the second time—though no always. Course, they never really say, 'Doon thi road!' or 'Down the road!' at all. Least, they never say it the way it's spelt. Coz it izny spelt, when they say it, is it?

A fine point, perhaps. Or maybe it izny, a widny no. Or maybe a think it is, but a also a think that if a say, 'Maybe it izny' then you'll turn it over in your head without thinkin, 'Who does he think he is—a linguistic philosopher?' Or maybe a widny bothir ma rump whether it's a fine point or it izny: maybe a jist said it fur effect in thi furst place. Coz that's sumhm that's dawned on me, though it's maybe wanna they thingz that yir no supposed ti say. An thirz a helluv a lohta them, when yi think about it, int thir? But anyway, what's dawned on me, or maybe it's jist emergin fra ma subconscious, is, that maybe a write jist tay attract attention ti ma cell. An that's a pretty horrible thought ti emerge fray emdy's subconscious, coz thi nixt thing that emerges is, 'Whut um a—a social inadequate?' N as if that izny bad enough, thi nixt thing that yi find yirself thinkin, is, 'Am a compensatin for ma social inadequacy, "by proxy", as it were?' An thi nixt thing, thi fourth thing, that yi find yirself thinkin, is, 'If av committed maself, unwittingly, ti compensation "by proxy", does that mean that a sense a inadequacy, unwittingly, huz become a necessity?' An thi fifth, an thi sixth, an thi seventh thingz that yi find yirself thinkin, are, 'Whut if ma compensation "by proxy" is found socially inadequate?' and 'Ivdi's against me—a always knew it,' and 'Perhaps posterity will have better sense.'

'Thi apprentice has lifted ma balls an cock,' said the plumber. Sorry, that comes later. Am no sayin that these seven thoughts necessarily come in the order in which av presented thim. Ti some people, ahl menshin nay names, these thoughts never emerge fray thir subconscious, particularly thi fifth, which is, yi can imagine, thi most terrible thought, of thi lot. Often it turns out that thoughts six and seven are thi most popular, though thoughts one ti five are largely ignored. But thi more yi ignore thoughts one ti five, thi more thoughts six and seven will out. Coz although thought five, 'Whut if ma compensation "by proxy" is found socially inadequate?' never emerges fray yir subconscious, there comes a day when, in a casual discussion about Literature in general, sumdy says, 'Your stuff's a lohta rubbish.' It might not even be so blunt—in fact, what usually happens is, that in the foyer of a theatre or sumhm, an in thi middle of a casual conversation about Literature in general, then sumdy introduces you ti sumdy else, an thi other person says, 'Who?' An although 'Who?' might no *sound* like a literal translation of, 'Your stuff's a lohta rubbish,' nonetheless, in the thoughts of a social inadequate, it's as near as dammit. So havin secretly thunk thought six, 'Ivdi's against me—a always knew it,' yi hurry hame ti write sumhm, ti get yir ain back. These ur thi symptoms. Coz yir that fed up wi ivdi yi know, so yi think, that writin sumhm seems about thi only thing worth dayin. Then at least when yir finished yi feel a hell of a lot better, coz whoever it was that was gettin onyir wick before, yi can go upty an say, 'A don't gee a damn whut you think about me, coz av jist wrote a poem, an that's sumhm, you huvny done. An even if yi huv, albetyi it wuz rotten.' Course you don't actually say all that—you don't huvti say it, even if yi could be bothered. An if it's sumdy that did say ti you, 'Your stuff's a lohta rubbish,' thirz no much point in goin upti thim anyway, is there? But yi can ey jist look thim in thi eye, in yir mind's eye, an think, 'Perhaps posterity will have better sense.'

'Ahma writur, your only a wurkur', a said, to thi plumbir.

'Fux sake Joe stick wan on that kunt,' said the apprentice.

'Ball an cocks,' said the plumber, 'Ball an cocks. A firgot ma grammur.'

'Gerrihtuppyi,' a said, to thi apprentice.

'Lissn pal yoor tea'll be up na minit,' said the plumber.

'Couldny fuckin write a bookie's line ya basturdn illiturate,' a said, ti the plumber.

'Right. Ootside,' said the plumber. 'Mawn. Ootside.'

Sorry. That comes later.

Joan Ure

NEW JOURNEY FORTH

Elizabeth Carswell (1920–78) began her writing career when she signed herself out of a TB ward and adopted the *nom de plume* Joan Ure. She produced twenty four completed plays and a body of largely unpublished poems, short stories and sections of drama. At the age of 58 she lost a long battle against the weakness in her lungs.

She was born in Newcastle of Clydeside shipbuilding stock but it wasn't long before the family returned to Glasgow. The city in the Thirties was not an easy place and Elizabeth's love of literature and reading was far from encouraged. Her first short story was burned when she gave it to her mother and although she was a bright girl, the economics of the family situation made it impossible for her to continue with schooling. At fifteen she started work as a typist. Married within a few years, she was left alone with a young daughter when her husband was posted abroad for the duration of the war.

It was a realisation that her time was limited that finally spurred Joan Ure to write. Her taut, accessible dramas use elements of fantasy, irony and poetry to deal with harsh social and political realities, and although her work was never popular with critics it added a delicate dimension to Scottish drama which few of her successors have felt able to explore.

With 'New Journey Forth' she proves herself to be a prose writer who could retain an almost painful vulnerability, allowing life to surprise her with its beauty and cruelty.

New Journey Forth

IT WAS a bright day but even that was not enough. She had not believed in the catkins that had budded and puffed out at her bedside. The convalescent mistrusted even the blackbird coaxing her out, serpentlike, with the beauty of his song. A song is shaped by art and art is a deceit. The Spring might drift back like a dancer, suddenly gone, as it had come.

Without any faith in it, she had dressed and now she opened the door and the air touched her face and hands, like lukewarm water, unbelievably tender. She drew on her gloves from the habit of city living, and closed the door behind her. She closed it as softly as she could so that there should be no sharp line drawn to emphasise that by stepping into the open she had completely changed her situation. To step out of the invalidity of sickness into the strength of the street is more of a step than moving one foot after the other is. She might want to go back soon. But moving one foot then the other accomplishes more than it seems.

Yellow stars of jasmine shot out like carnival surprises from their barren looking stems. Turning her head as if it were heavy, she saw a mist of pale green like a veil sprinkling a hedge. She had dared a deep breath before she had chosen to breathe at all and the surprise of the air was so sweet and new that she had to take care not to smile. A tiny dog like a rat on stilts trotted past her, newly released from a lead. It seemed to test the paving with its tiny paws, then, feeling safe, grew excited and pranced, its head and sharp nose high, trotting like a pony but so small, so ridiculous. The convalescent, suddenly sympathetic, laughed aloud. She dared to believe that she knew how free the little dog felt released from its lead. A lead or a sickness, they are very much the same. The world is not yours. It belongs to others but not to you.

She turned the corner and began to go down the hill rather uneasily, her head carefully high. She had lived on the horizontal for so long, the slope was alarming. It seemed like a precipice but her memory told her that it wasn't. It was a very manageable slope. She kept her gaze on the second floor windows of the tenement buildings beyond the road, gradually drifting down to first floor level. Pointedly she ignored the slope that would terrify her. At the foot, her conscious deep breath this time brought with it the elation of achievement.

All the tram lines had gone! The road was wide like a pond and smooth and beautiful. A Keep Left sign on an island divided the adventure of the road into two acts and made the crossing between the procession of cars just possible. 'Does everyone in the world possess a car then?' The sight of a grocer's boy on a bicycle balancing a large cardboard box set her mind at rest. His knees bobbed up and down at right angles to the direction in which he moved along, angular and not efficient enough. She smiled her gratitude to the boy because he rode on a bicycle instead of in a car and then she realised that she had made a mistake. He was hurriedly searching behind his almost rolling eyes to find her face in his memory. She would like to have called out to him 'I'm not one of your customers, it's all right, don't feel guilty,' but he had solved his problem for himself. He gave her a puzzled and very precarious salute with his forefinger towards his capless forehead and a little shy smile to suppress the guilt of his impossible memory. The bike wobbled the half of a figure of eight. She drew in a breath but the bike righted itself and passed on, the boy's body swaying from right to left as if he wove his way along the road. 'If I *must* smile, I shall smile up into the sky where no-one could possibly misunderstand,' the convalescent thought.

Four taxis in a shining expectant line waited around the red of the telephone box and the larger green of the police box. Three of the taxis were empty and in the fourth, the first in the line beside their own telephone, which was looped like a letterbox to a lamp standard, the men were sitting in the back of the taxi bent over their hands of cards. She stood beside the bus stop and waited. The women walking past her to the shops that glittered in bright paint and vitrolite were dressed in the odd, hesitant way that emerges between seasons. They dressed as if they made the weather in their minds and were afraid to interpret the barometer. An elderly lady in a fur coat and boots stood in the queue behind the convalescent and another, a younger woman, followed her, wearing a Spring green suit and a flowered hat with a wide brim. 'Are the skirts still short then?' the convalescent wondered. 'Or is she, as I am, six months behind?'

The green and yellow bus picked up the few people but already downstairs was almost filled with mothers and schoolchildren and some elderly women. A retired gentleman or two sat as if out of their depth in such a company. It showed on their faces even that they were a little ashamed to be travelling at such a time, just a little, a very little too early for the offices to come out. 'Seats upstairs please, no standing inside,' the conductor said after a stop or two. The older women murmured sympathetically and turned round disapprovingly. The convalescent thought 'There must be a new rule.' How much else had changed? The fare perhaps? No, the fare was still the same. 'Well, that's something,' she thought. 'I fully expected . . .' The conductor was a coloured man, slim and with scar marks in parallel lines on his cheeks. His voice was like butter. All the t's were d's. His teeth were strong and beautiful. He seemed very relaxed and yet he was conducting a bus in a busy city thousands of miles from where he was born. 'Strong people live on a razor's edge and never expect to cut their feet,' the convalescent marvelled, admiring and envious.

As the bus moved nearer to the city, the traffic became complicated. The deft interweaving of streams of city-going traffic filled her with a sense of dangerous participation. Men carrying rolled umbrellas and girls with white—yes, already with white high heels—skilfully shared the movement along the pavements. The nearer the city centre the greater the intricacy and the more astonishing the skill. The driver's face through his mirror was attentive but unconcerned and the hurrying pedestrians, looking sharply to right and left, set bold feet on to the road whenever there was a space. No-one doubted that they could negotiate their journey.

As the bus panted at the red light and cars from the side street turned into the main stream with their indicating light winking coquettishly, a stout woman in a black hat with a bobbing red rose on it was winding and nipping in and out towards the stationary back of the bus. Her long-handled handbag dangled from her arm, her umbrella swung back and forth and on the outstretched index finger of one gloved hand three or four parcels jostled and bumped as she ran. The people seated on the side seats at the end of the bus were drawn towards the hurrying woman in terrified fascination. The engine of the bus began to roar, but, no, the lights were still . . . The woman almost leapt. The conductor shook his head at her. 'That is not good,' he said. 'A person gets hurt and it is not our fault, you know.' But he held her elbow kindly till she steadied herself. Her flushed face relaxed and she looked pleased with herself. For a moment it seemed as if the passengers on the side seats who had seen it all were going to give her a round of applause. But they contented themselves by smiling down into their laps or among their parcels or looking quickly into their evening papers. Only one or two older people with the lines of experience around their old and beautiful faces had been too involved in the danger and could not so quickly release themselves from their fear. They contented themselves by muttering angrily a word or two and turning very deliberately away from the triumphant, wrongheaded rebel. Finding a seat soon, the rebel breathed deeply a long while and the red rose on her hat seemed to quiver until she had returned to being what she usually was, a conventional city lady doing conventional things appropriate to where she lived.

In the very hub of the city the convalescent woman came down from the bus and precipitated herself, feeling like an explorer but looking, she hoped, not too unlike everybody else, into the swarming street. She entangled herself inevitably in the queue of people who filed to get on as she got off. Once safely on the pavement through an accidental gap, she stood for a second afraid to move . . . less afraid perhaps than puzzled how to move. It seemed as if all the movement now were towards her, as if she were at the foot of a waterfall trying to get up. The effort needed, it seemed to her would be the equivalent of that of the salmon leaping up to the source of the intrepidly determined flow of the river. The salmon could manage it only because of the impetus of its instinctive drive, but what instinctive drive is there to help the individual in a city full of people all going the other way. Gradually, the convalescent noticed that there were a few people, just one here and there as it seemed, who were going the way she wanted to go. This was enough. The second step was easier. At first all apologies and awkward, indecisions, she too began to wind her way, out and in and, as she did, it seemed that more people were taking her direction and fewer were going against her way.

She was free to look up then. All along the telephone wires as if they were clothes pegs to hang the city's linen in full sight of its daily thousands, the starlings twittered an evensong to the hurrying human beings whose city they took over at first floor level every twilight. The sharp-pointed wings made spearhead movements across the strengthening blue of the sky and drew the eyes upwards to the ridiculous and beautiful invasion of the precise business centre. Inside the offices, banks, post offices, city chambers, everywhere, efficiency regulated the whole day. The anarchy of the starlings bespattered the buildings while the offices slept. The flight of these wreckers above and around the sharp-edged outlines of the roofs was beautiful. Their chatter from a thousand tiny throats sang like laughter.

A tall man with a wide brimmed hat asked the convalescent in an American voice where to go to find the American Consulate. He held a half-opened map in his hand. She faced the map with him and traced his way along the familiar names on the unfamiliar map. Here on some inches of paper were all the names of her city. She presented the freedom of her city and a welcome to it with her tracing finger as she told him where to go to find his own friends. He thanked her in his easy casual voice, he too, like the bus conductor, thousands of miles from home yet not afraid.

She turned into the crowd confident, moving at last in the chaos like everyone else. She thought of her job waiting for her to go back, her desk, its typewriter, her office files and believed that she too could move, like everyone else, part of the city madness. She could move on a tightrope day after day and never doubt the existence of the omnipotent safety net.

At a crossing where the lights had broken down a white-coated policeman had taken over. Cars that would have been impatient at the lights and pedestrians who never could quite trust lights anyhow moved across in the shadow of his arm. Lifting her head high, her eyes sad, she knew that she would try to cross even with the simple, mechanical guidance of the lights, the lights that were man-made and might fail at any time.

Iain Crichton Smith

MURDO

Iain Crichton Smith (b.1928) is a prolific poet, novelist and playwright in both Gaelic and English. He has written over fifteen books of poetry, published six collections of stories and ten novels, including the acclaimed *Consider The Lilies* (1968). His work often explores his own background on the island of Lewis, much influenced by the divisions of being raised in two languages, not to mention the rigid attitudes and certainties of the Free Kirk. These tensions have made him particularly sensitive to forces which threaten the freedom of the individual imagination. He is also good in dealing with the extremes of age, and many of his best poems reflect a compassion for the weakness of old age, coupled with tenderness for the young, who are unaware of the hardships life will bring.

Crichton Smith's novels and stories often avoid a broad social analysis, concentrating rather on the inward states of his characters. He has a dry, pungent humour, a gift for comic invention and a welcome ability to laugh at himself and his background while making a serious point and taking us to conclusions which are anything but obvious. 'Murdo' is simply one of the funniest stories I have ever read. Its comic desperation is inseparable from a deep and terrifying reality.

Murdo

WITH HIS pen in his hand Murdo looked out at the tall white snow-covered mountain that he could see ahead of him through the window.

He was trying to write a story.

He looked down at the green pen in his hand. The day was cold and white, and now and again he could see a black bird flying across the intensely blue sky.

His wife was working in the kitchen. After she had finished cooking she would polish the table and chairs and the rest of the furniture. Now and again she would come to the door and say,

'Are you finished yet?'

And Murdo would say, 'I haven't even started,' and he would look out at the mountain again, he would resume his enchanted scrutiny of it. The white stainless mountain that was so cold and high.

Murdo had left his work as a bank clerk and was trying to write. When he had arrived home and told his wife that he would not be going back to the bank any more, she had begun to weep and scream but Murdo had simply walked past her to his room and had taken out a pen and a sheet of paper. He had left his work in the bank on an autumn day when the brown leaves were lying on the ground, and now it was winter.

He would sit at his desk at a little past nine o'clock every morning.

The white paper lay on the wood in front of him, as white as the mountain that he could see through the window which itself was entirely clean since his wife was always polishing it. He had not written a single page so far.

'Your tea's ready,' said his wife at eleven o'clock.

'Right,' said Murdo.

He went into the kitchen where she was. The room was as neat as a pin, as it always was. He couldn't understand how she could spend her time so remorselessly cleaning rooms, as if it had never occurred to her that a particular table or a particular set of chairs could be elsewhere rather than where they were: that they could be in another house, in another country, on another planet even.

From the time of the dinosaurs, Murdo said to himself, was it predestined that this table should be standing by this window, that these chairs should be settled in the centre of this room? This was the sort of question that perplexed him and made his head sore.

He didn't say any of this to his wife for he knew that she wouldn't understand it.

They sat at the table opposite each other, and between them the pot of tea. His wife, Janet, was as neat and tidy as the room.

'When are you going back to your work?' she asked him as she did so often.

'I don't know,' said Murdo, putting a spoonful of sugar in his tea. His wife didn't take sugar, but kept saccharins for occasions like these. The saccharins were kept in a tiny blue box.

'Oh?' said his wife. 'You know of course that people are talking about you.'

'I don't care,' said Murdo drinking his tea.

'But I care,' said his wife. 'They're always asking me if you're ill. You aren't ill, are you?'

'Apart from a touch of the Black Death there's nothing wrong with me,' said Murdo.

'And my mother and father are always asking me when you intend to go back to the office.'

'Are they?' said Murdo, thinking of the red cross on the door. There was green paint on the wall. Why had he in those early days of happiness put green paint on the wall? Why not blue paint or yellow? Ah, the soul of man cannot be plumbed, Murdo sighed to himself. A clock, colour of gold, was ticking between two clay horses that he had once won in a fair.

Her father was a large red angry man who would sometimes become bloated with rage. He had been on the fishing boats in his youth.

Janet had left school at fifteen. When she married Murdo she expected that her life would be as limpid as a stream, that there would be money coming into the house regularly, that Murdo would at weekends be working stolidly in the garden reclaiming it from the wilderness, that they would have a daughter and a son, and that she would sit knitting by the fire when she wasn't talking to the neighbours.

She was a very capable housewife, small and alert. A good woman.

Murdo was trying to write a story about a bank clerk who had one day left his work and had begun to try and write. But one morning he had been enchanted by the white tall mountain with the snow on it and he had written nothing.

'This tea is very good,' he told Janet.

'Huh,' said Janet.

She would now begin to cook the dinner, and that was her life, and that life perplexed and astonished Murdo.

Why were the two horses set exactly like that, one on each side of the silently ticking clock?

'I'm going out tonight,' said Janet.

'Where?' said Murdo.

'Out,' she said. 'You can carry on with your writing.' She spoke simply, without irony.

'Where are you going?'

'I'm going to call on Mother,' said Janet.

'Oh,' said Murdo. 'I thought you had called on her on Monday.'

'I did,' said Janet. 'But I'm going to call on her again tonight.'

Your eyes are blue and cunning, said Murdo to himself. She was still pretty with her blue eyes, her dark hair, her red healthy cheeks.

'That's all right,' he said.

He rose and went back to his room.

He sat at his desk and gazed at the white mountain.

I should really, he thought, leave the house this minute and climb the mountain. I should leave my prints in the snow.

It occurred to him that his wife might have been lying, that she wasn't going to see her mother at all. But he said nothing about his suspicion to her at lunch or at tea. She left the house at five o'clock and he went back to his room again.

The red sun was lying across the snow like blood.

What am I going to do? Murdo asked himself. Am I going to stay here staring at this mountain without writing anything?

The house felt empty after his wife had left it. He wandered about in it, looking at the made bed, the still ornaments, the mirrors, the dishes, the books.

The whole machinery of her world was impeccably in its place, his wife had built a clean orderly world around them.

But this world wasn't as clean as the mountain.

At half-past five he left the house and went to his mother-in-law's house and rang the bell at the side of the door. There were actually two bells but only one of them worked. His father-in-law came to the door and his face was as red as the sun that shone on the white mountain.

'Is Janet there?' Murdo asked timidly.

'No, she isn't,' said his father-in-law and didn't ask Murdo to come in. Murdo could see through the window that the TV was on.

'Oh,' he said. 'I only thought . . .'

'You thought wrong,' said his father-in-law. The houses around them were quiet and grey. Murdo saw a man going past with a large brown dog. 'Oh,' he said again, shivering in the cold since he wasn't wearing a coat. He turned away and walked down the street. Where was Janet? He felt his breast empty and he had a sudden terrible premonition that she had run away with another man, a man who never tried to write, but who was happy with the world as it was and his own position in it, and he felt shame and fear as if the event had happened in reality. He went into a bar but she wasn't there either. When he came out he looked round him in the raw cold but he couldn't see the white mountain from where he was since there were houses between him and it. He stood on the pavement and he didn't know where to go next. Why had she lied to him?

Well, he said to himself, I shall have to find her or I shall have to climb the mountain. What shall I do?

I'll see if she is in this bar.

He went in and there she was sitting in a dark corner and there were some people with her.

He recognised John, who was a teacher in the only large school on the island, and his wife, Margaret. And another teacher (he thought) with a red beard, but he didn't know his name. And his wife as well. And a man who worked as a reporter on the local paper, a small pale-faced fellow who smoked endless cigarettes and whose name was Robert.

'Do you want a pint?' asked John, half rising from his seat.

'No thanks,' said Murdo. There was a glass of vodka or water in front of his wife. Murdo sat down on the edge of the company.

The bar was warm and dark with reddish lights and black leather seats.

'Where have you been?' Janet asked him.

'Oh, just walking around,' said Murdo.

'He's trying to write,' said Janet to the others.

'Write?' said Robert, his eyes lighting up. 'What are you writing?'

'Nothing,' said Murdo. 'I'm only trying to write.'

'Oh,' said Robert, the light almost visibly leaving his eyes as the light at the tip of a cigarette might cease to glow.

John and the red-bearded man began to talk about the school and Murdo listened to them.

At last he asked John why he taught.

'Why?' said John. 'Why am I teaching?' as if he had never asked himself such a question before.

'For the money,' said his wife, laughing.

'That wasn't what I meant,' said Murdo and in a whisper to himself, 'What the hell am I doing here anyway?' He was grinding his teeth against each other to prevent himself from howling like a wolf.

'This is a philosopher we have here,' said Janet in a sharp bitter voice, her lips almost shut.

'You must answer his questions.'

'Oh,' said John, 'I'm teaching History. What can people do without History? They would be like animals.'

'Right,' said Murdo, 'Right. Right.' And then,

'Are you an animal?'

John looked at him for a moment with such ferocity that Murdo thought he was going to leap at him like a wildcat but at last he said quietly: 'Animals don't teach each other History.'

'Very good,' said the red-bearded man. 'And now do you want a pint?' he asked Murdo.

'No thanks,' said Murdo and then quite untruthfully, 'My doctor has told me not to drink.' (He used the phrase 'my doctor' with an air of elegant possession though he had hardly ever been to a doctor in his life. He would also sometimes talk about 'my lawyer' in the same aristocratic tone.)

'It would be very funny,' said Robert, 'if animals taught History to each other.'

'It would indeed,' said Murdo.

They were silent for a while till at last Murdo said: 'Once I was sitting opposite a man in a café and there were cakes on the table, some yellow and some white. I took a yellow cake and he took a white one. What's the reason for that?'

'My coat is yellow,' said Margaret. 'That's because I like yellow.'

Janet looked at her own coat which wasn't as rich-looking as Margaret's and a ray of envy passed momently across her face.

'That's a question,' said John to Murdo. 'That's really a difficult question.'

'What café did this happen in?' said Robert as if he was about to take the story down for his newspaper.

'I can't remember,' said Murdo.

'Didn't I tell you he's a philosopher,' said Janet, sipping some vodka or perhaps water or perhaps gin.

Murdo was gazing at the bearded man's wife, a beautiful girl with long blond hair who was very silent. Beauty, O beauty, he said to himself, Yeats said something about that. My head is so heavy.

Margaret said, 'I just went into the shop and I bought this yellow coat. I don't know why I bought it. I just liked it.'

'Exactly,' said Robert. 'What more can one say about it?'

'What are you writing?' he asked Murdo again.

'Nothing,' said Murdo.

'Uh huh,' said John.

Murdo knew that his wife was angry because he had come into the bar disturbing people with his strange questions, and he was glad in a way that she was angry.

At the same time he was afraid that she would get drunk.

John said, 'Well, it's time I was going.' And he and his wife rose from their seats.

'You're sure I can't buy you a pint before I go,' said John again to Murdo.

'I'm sure,' said Murdo.

The bearded man and his wife also rose.

They all went away muttering their goodbyes and Janet, Murdo and Robert were left sitting in their dark corner by a table which was wet with beer.

'What are you writing yourself?' Murdo asked Robert.

Robert looked at him with small bitter eyes. What did he write but pieces about whist drives, local football matches, things without importance?

He didn't answer.

'Did you ever see,' Murdo asked him, 'the white mountain?'

'White mountain,' said Robert. 'What's that?'

'Don't listen to him,' said Janet. 'He doesn't know what he's talking about.'

'Sometimes you're right,' said Murdo.

Robert had been working as a journalist on the local newspaper since leaving school and he had never been out of the island.

'I read in your paper yesterday,' said Murdo, 'that a car was hit by another one on Bruce Street. Do you think that was predestined since the beginning of the world?'

'I don't know,' said Robert curtly, thinking that he was being got at. Murdo felt his head sore again, as often happened to him nowadays.

'It doesn't matter,' he said.

And again,

'But it does matter. Once I was looking at a triangle which was drawn on a piece of paper and it looked so clean and beautiful. And I saw a fly walking across it, across the paper on which the triangle was drawn, and I didn't know where the fly was going. But the triangle was motionless in its own world, in its own space. That was on a summer's day when I was in school. But I forget the year,' he said to Robert.

'I have to go,' said Robert. 'I have something to do.'

'Have you?' said Murdo.

The only people left at the table now were himself and his wife.

'Well,' she said, 'it didn't take you long to send them away with all your questions. What are you trying to do?'

'Why did you lie to me?' said Murdo. 'Why didn't you tell me you were coming to this pub?'

'I don't know,' said Janet.

'You knew I would find out,' said Murdo. 'That's why you did it.'

'Maybe you're right,' said Janet.

We are like animals right enough, said Murdo to himself. We don't know why we do the things we do.

And he saw his wife like a fox walking across the white mountain.

'Come on home,' he said.

She rose and put on her coat.

'Where's your own coat?' she asked Murdo.

'I left it at home,' said Murdo.

They left the bar and walked home down the street and Murdo put his arm round her.

He felt the warmth of her body on that cold winter's night and his bones trembled.

Then he began to laugh.

'Whist drives,' he said looking up at the sky with its millions of stars. And he made little leaps shouting 'Whist drives' at intervals.

'Are you out of your mind?' said Janet.

He pulled her towards him.

'Do you see that mountain?' he asked her. 'That white mountain. Do you see it?' She was like a ghost glimmering out of the darkness.

'Ben Dorain,' he said laughing.

'I see it,' said Janet. 'What about it?'

'Nothing about it,' said Murdo, looking at the mountain, his warm head beside hers.

The white mountain was shining out of the darkness.

The tears came to his eyes and he felt them on his cheeks.

'You're crying,' she accused him.

'No I'm not,' he said.

She turned towards him and gazed into his eyes.

'Everything will be all right,' she said.

'Yes,' he said. 'I'm sure of it.' And he looked into her eyes. 'Yes,' he repeated.

She tightened her arm round him as if she was frightened that he was going to melt like the snow.

'Come on home,' she said to him in a frightened voice.

'I won't leave you,' he said, 'though your coat is green.'

They walked home quietly together except that now and again Murdo would make another of his leaps shouting 'Whist drives' at the moon that was so bare and bright in the sky above the white mountain.

One morning murdo put on a red rubber nose such as clowns wear or small children at Hallowe'en and went downtown to get the morning papers. Norman Macleod's wife met him at the door of the shop and he said to her:

'It's a fine morning.'

'Yes,' said she, looking at him slightly askance, since he was wearing a red rubber nose.

'But it is not as beautiful a morning as it was yesterday,' Murdo said seriously. 'Not at all as good as yesterday morning. No indeed.'

'You're right there,' said Norman Macleod's wife, looking at his nose. Murdo pretended that he didn't notice her amazed stare.

'You're right there indeed,' said Murdo. 'I myself am of the opinion that it is not so warm this morning as it was yesterday morning,' glancing at the snow which glittered back at him from the roadside.

'Without doubt, without doubt,' said the wife of Norman Macleod.

'For,' Murdo pursued relentlessly, 'the clouds were whiter yesterday than they are today,' drawing nearer to Mrs Macleod and putting his red rubber nose quite close to her face.

'For,' said Murdo, 'when I got up from my bed this morning I nearly went back into it again, a thing that I did not think of doing yesterday. But in spite of that I put one leg before the other as we all have to do in this life at some time or other, indeed at all times, and I decided that I would come for the newspapers, for what can we do without them? What indeed?'

'You're right,' said Mrs Macleod, shifting slightly away from him.

'Yes,' said Murdo, 'in these days especially one must put one leg in front of the other. When the light comes out of the darkness we go in search of the *Daily Record*, those sublime pages that tell us about the murders that have been committed in caravans in the south.'

'Yes,' said Mrs Macleod in a voice that was becoming more and more inaudible as she moved further and further away from the red rubber nose.

'I myself often think,' said Murdo, 'how uninteresting my life would be without the *Daily Record*. That occurs to me often. Often. And often I think what would we do without neighbours? Their warmth, their love . . . These thoughts often occur to me, I may tell you.'

'I suppose . . .' muttered Mrs Macleod, her grip tightening on the newspaper she had in her hand as if she was thinking of using it as a weapon.

'For,' said Murdo intently, 'do you yourself not think that the warmth of the morning is like the warmth we derive from our neighbours. The sun shines on everything and so does the warmth of neighbours. There is a lot wrong with each one of us, we are all flawed in some way but our neighbours forgive us for they say to themselves, "Not one of us is perfect, not one of us is without flaw, so how therefore can we say that others are flawed." These are the thoughts that often occur to me anyway,' said Murdo. 'And I don't think I'm wrong.'

'I'm sure you're . . .' said Mrs Macleod trying to back steadily away while Murdo fixed her closely with his red rubber nose as if he were a demented seagull standing among the snow.

'Give me,' said Murdo, 'one neighbour and I will move the world.' He considered this for a long time, turning his nose this way and that, the only bright colour that was to be seen on the street. Mrs Macleod wanted desperately to leave but she couldn't move her feet and she didn't know what to say.

Murdo went closer to her.

'I am of the opinion,' he said, 'to tell the truth and without concealing anything from any man or woman, white or black, whoever they are and whatever their colour of skin, I am of the opinion without regard to anyone's politics or religion, for no one can accuse me of being biased, that yesterday morning was as beautiful a morning as we have had for many years. I'm not saying that there don't exist people who would deny that, and who would come to me if they liked with armfuls of records going back to the seventeenth century and before, that would prove that I was wrong, and even naive in that statement, but in spite of that I still hold to my opinion as I am sure you would under the same circumstances, for I have never thought of you as a coward. Oh I know that there are people who will maintain that neither the summers nor the winters that we endure now are as beautiful and unspotted as the summers and winters of their various childhoods but I would say humbly to these people that they are wrong. THEY ARE WRONG,' he shouted, pushing his nose as close to Mrs Macleod's nose as it could go.

'THEY ARE WRONG,' he repeated in a loud vehement voice. 'As wrong as people can be. I know in my bones that they are wrong. Totally wrong. Totally.' He sighed heavily and then continued:

'As well as that I know that there are professors who would oppose me on this matter. But I know that they are wrong as well. Though I have nothing against professors. Not at all, not at all.

'But I'm keeping you back. I shouldn't have done that. I know that you're busy, that you work without cease, without cease. Lack of consideration, that's what I suffer from, I admit it freely. But I wished to tell you how much more beautiful than this morning yesterday morning was. And I'm glad that you agree with me in my opinion. I am so glad. So glad. It is not often that I feel such gladness. But I know that you wish to go home. I am so glad to have met you.'

Mrs Macleod half walked, half ran, away, looking behind her now and then as if trying to verify that he did indeed have a red rubber nose. Murdo raised his hand to her in royal salute and then went into the shop, having first removed his rubber nose, and bought a newspaper. On his way home he would kick a lump of ice now and again with his boot.

'Drama,' he said to himself. 'Nothing but drama and catharsis. One must look for it even when there is snow on the ground.'

He arrived at a wall and opened out the paper and began to read it, glancing now and again at the white mountain.

He read one page and then threw the paper away from him, but after a while he picked it up and laid it flat on a large piece of ice.

The headlines of the paper said in large black type:

I STILL LOVE HIM THOUGH HE KILLED FOR ME

Murdo found an old boot in the ditch and laid it on top of this headline so that passers-by could read it and then went on his way whistling.

ONE NIGHT MURDO was on his way home with a half-bottle of whisky in his hand. He looked up at the sky that was trembling with stars and he began to shout to a group of them that were brighter than the rest:

'Lewis,'

and then

'Skye'

and finally

'Betelgeuse.'

He looked down at his shoes that were yellow in the light of the moon and he said,

'I'm drunk. Murdo is drunk. There is whisky on his shoes. On his shoes there is whisky.'

He then sat down on the road and took off his shoes and raised them towards the moon:

'Here is Murdo. There are Murdo's shoes. They are yellow. Murdo's shoes are yellow.'

'O world,' he said, 'how yellow Murdo's shoes are. Ah, Lewis, ah, Skye, ah, Betelgeuse.'

He thought of small yellow men with small yellow shoes drinking on Betelgeuse and he had compassion for them as they sat on the road with a half-bottle of whisky in the hand of each one.

'Ah,' said he, 'do you see the white mountain even on Betelgeuse? Do you have in your hands yellow pencils and are you writing on yellow paper a story about a clerk who left his work in an office on Betelgeuse?'

And the tears came to his eyes.

'Is there a split,' he said, 'between the soul and the body even on Betelgeuse? Is there on that illustrious star a woman like Mrs Macleod, of that ilk?'

And he began to laugh in harmony with the trembling of the stars which also seemed to laugh.

He looked at the sky and he shouted,

'Conscience.'

'Soul.'

'MacBrayne's boats.'

He looked down at his shoes again.

'Leather,' he said.

'Nails,' he said.

'Shoemaker,' he said.

'A shoemaker was born just for me,' he said and he felt pity for the shoes and the shoemaker, a little yellow man with little yellow nails in his mouth.

'Why,' he shouted to Betelgeuse, 'did you put skin on my bones, a worm in my head?'

And he felt the yellow worm in his head like a thin stream of whisky the colour of the moon.

'Existentialism,' he shouted to the moon.

'A lavatory of diamonds.'

'Plato in a thatched house.'

'Mist.'

He stood up and began to sing under the millions of stars a verse of a song he had composed.

'The Isle of Mull
has no grief or sorrow,
It is so green,
and will be here tomorrow.'

And he thought of his father and mother and they were like a pair of people who moved in and out of a Dutch clock, yellow and fat with fat red cheeks.

'And,' he said, in a mimicking voice, 'is it from Betelgeuse that you are yourself? When did you come home and when are you going away again?'—the age-old Highland questions.

'I was reared,' he said, 'when I was young and soft. When I grew a little older I thought that I myself was creating the morning and the evening. And at that moment I grew old. The mountains were like fangs in my mind.'

The stars winked at him and he winked back at them and he thought that there was a yellow crown on his head, a sharp yellow crown.

'Without me,' he said, 'sick as I am from *angst* and diarrhoea, you would not be there at all. Are you listening to me? Without me there would be darkness among all the planets.'

He lifted the half-bottle of whisky and he began to drink.

'Your health,' he said. 'Your good health.'

He reached his own house and he saw a ray of yellow light coming out from under the door.

'Like an arrow,' he said.

'Like a knife,' he said.

'Like a pen,' he said.

and

'Like a spade,' he said.

and finally,

'16 Murchison Street,' he said, 'with the green walls.'

'We are all,' he said, 'of a mortal company. Of a proud company,' said he swaying from side to side, the key in his hand.

'Drunkards of the universe,' he said.

'Glory be to the yellow universe,' he said in the yellow light.

He tried to fit his key in the door but couldn't.

'It is not fated,' he said, 'it is not fated that I shall open the door of 16 Murchison Street. The universe is against it.'

He thought of the key as a soul that could not enter its proper body.

'Lewis,' he said to Betelgeuse.

'Skye,' he said.

And finally as if he had climbed a high mountain,

'Tiree.'

And he fell asleep, the key in his hand and the yellow closed door in front of him and a heavy snore coming from him in that cold calm yellow night.

Murdo's Letter to the Poet Dante

Dear Friend,

Can you please tell me when and how you began to write first, and what magazines you sent your first poems to? And what was the animal you saw in the middle of the wood?

For myself, I see this white mountain all the time, day and night. With snow on it.

And in the room next to me there is a table and chairs as like each other as pictures in a mirror. Anyway I hope you will answer my letter for I am trying to write a story about a clerk.

And I don't know how to start.

With much respect and a stamp so that you can answer my letter.

Yours sincerely,
MURDO MACRAE

PS. You did very well, my friend, with that poem the *Inferno*. But what would you have done without Virgil? I think we all need a friend.

MURDO WAS (as they say) good with children and this is one of the stories he told to his nephew Colin who was six years old at the time:

There was a lad once (said Murdo), and he was seventeen years old. Well, one day he thought that he would leave home where he lived with his father and mother. It was a beautiful autumn day and he saw many strange sights on his way. In the place where he was, there were many trees and the yellow leaves were falling to the ground and they were all so beautiful and sad. But the most wonderful thing of all was that wherever he went—and the day very calm and now and again a fox running through the wood and red berries still on some of the trees—he would see his father's face and his mother's face. Wasn't that strange? Just as if he was in a land of mirrors. In the leaves, in the ground, he would see these faces. This amazed and astonished him. And he didn't know what to do about it. Once in a leaf he saw his house with the door and the windows and his mother standing in the doorway in a blue gown. And once in another leaf he saw his father bending down with a spade, digging.

Well this went on for a long time but at last he didn't see the pictures of his father and mother at all. And then he came to a small village and every man in the village was hitting big stones with hammers, every one of them. When he asked them the name of the village no one would tell him. In fact they wouldn't speak to him at all. But they just kept hammering away at the stones with their hammers. This was the only sound that could be heard in the village. Think of it, this was all they did all day and every day. And they never spoke to anyone. And he didn't know why they were doing this. He asked them a lot of times why they were hammering the stones but they wouldn't answer him. This astonished him and he himself sat on a stone in his blue dusty suit but they pretended not to see him.

At last he grew tired of sitting down and he went over and looked at one of the men and what he was doing. And he saw that this man was cutting names of people in the stone on which he was working. Murdo didn't recognise any of the names and he was just going to go away when he looked very sharply indeed and he saw that the man was cutting his own name in the stone.

Well, this made Murdo very puzzled and frightened him too, and before he knew what he was doing he was running away from that place till he reached a wood which was very quiet. Not even the voice of a bird was to be heard, and it was very dark there. However, there were some nuts on the trees and he began to eat them. He wandered through this wood for a long time till at last he saw ahead of him a high mountain white with snow though it was still autumn. He stood and stared at this mountain for some time.

Well, just as he was standing there who should he see but a beautiful girl in a green dress just beside him. She had long yellow hair like gold and she said to Murdo in a quiet voice:

'If you will climb that mountain and if you bring me a blue flower that you will find on its slope I will reward you well. My house is quite near here, a small house made of diamonds, and when you get the flower you will come to it and knock on the door and I shall answer.'

Murdo looked around him and sure enough there, not very far away, was a small house made of diamonds.

Well, Murdo made his way towards the mountain and in a short while he found a blue flower and he ran back to the small house with it and knocked on the door, but no one came to answer his knock. He knocked a few times but still no one came and he didn't know what to do, for he wanted the reward. At last he thought that it might be a good idea to return to the mountain and find an even more beautiful flower and bring it back with him. And with that he left the small house made of diamonds and he went back to the mountain. And he climbed with difficulty further up the slope and found a larger even more beautiful blue flower but he was feeling slightly tired by this time, and he walked much more slowly to the house. Anyway he reached it at last, and he knocked on the door again. The house was shining in the light of the snow and the windows were sending out flashes of light. He knocked and knocked but still no one came to the door. And Murdo returned to the mountain for the third time and this time he decided that he would climb to the very top and he would find a flower so lovely that the beautiful girl would be forced to open the door for him. And he did this. He climbed and climbed and his breath grew shorter and shorter and his legs grew weaker and weaker and sometimes he felt dizzy because of the great height. For four hours he climbed and the air was getting thinner and thinner and Murdo was shivering with the cold and his teeth were chattering in his head, but he was determined that he would reach the top of the mountain.

At last, tired and cold, he reached the top and he saw in front of him the most beautiful flower he had ever seen in his life but this flower was not blue like the other ones. It was white. Anyway Murdo pulled the beautiful white flower out of the ground and he looked at it for a long time as it lay in his hand. But a strange thing happened then. As he looked, the beautiful white flower began to melt and soon there was nothing left of it but a little water. And all around him was the cold white mountain.

Slowly Murdo went down the mountainside, feeling very tired and cold, and he looked for the small house made of diamonds but he couldn't find it anywhere. There was only a small hut without windows or doors. And Murdo looked at it for a long time and said to himself, 'But it may be that I shall meet that beautiful girl again somewhere.' And he continued on his way through the wood. But I don't think he ever met that beautiful girl again, though he travelled through many countries, except perhaps for one moment when he was lying on the ground, very tired, and he was staring at an old boot and he saw a flash of what might have been her. But perhaps it was his imagination for the moon was shining on the old boot at the time.

Murdo looked down at Colin who had fallen asleep.

'Well,' he said to himself, 'maybe he didn't like the story after all.'

THIS IS AN advertisement which Murdo sent to the editor of the local paper but which was never printed:

> Wanted: a man of between a hundred and two hundred years of age who knows the works of Kant and the poetry of William Ross, and who can drive a tractor and a car, for work on the roads for three weeks in the year. Such a man will get—particularly if he's healthy—two pounds a year. It would be an advantage if he knew a little Greek.

THE READER MUST now be told something about Murdo. He was born in a small village where there were twenty houses and which stood beside the sea. When he was growing up he spent a lot of his time drawing drifters on scraps of paper: and the most wonderful day of his life was the day that he jumped across the river Caras.

When he was on his way to school he would think of himself as walking through the forests of Africa, but the schoolmistress told him that he must learn the alphabet.

One day she asked him to write an essay with the title, 'My Home.' Murdo wrote twenty pages about a place where there were large green forests, men with wings, aeroplanes made of diamond, and rainbow-coloured stairs.

She said to him, 'What does all this stuff mean? Are you laughing at me or what?' She gave him two strokes of the belt.

After that Murdo grew very good at counting, and he could compute in his head in seconds 1,005 × 19. This pleased the schoolmistress and when the inspector visited the school she showed him Murdo with great pride. 'This boy will make a perfect clerk,' said the inspector, and he gave him a hard white sweet.

Murdo went home and told his father and mother what the inspector had said. But he didn't tell them that in the loft he kept an effigy of the schoolmistress which was made of straw and that every evening he pierced it with the sharp point of his pencil.

Nor did he tell them that he painted the walls of the loft with pictures of strange animals that he could see in his dreams.

One day when Murdo was fifteen years old the headmaster sent for him.

'Sit down,' he said.

Murdo sat down.

'And what do you intend to do now that you are leaving school?' said the headmaster who had a small black moustache.

'27 × 67 = 1,809,' said Murdo.

The headmaster looked at him with astonishment and his spectacles nearly fell off his nose.

'Have you any idea at all what you're going to do?' he asked again.

'259 × 43 = 11,137,' said Murdo.

The headmaster then told him that he could leave, that he had much work to do. Murdo saw two girls going into his study with a tray on which there was a cup of tea and two biscuits.

When he came out the other boys asked him what the headmaster had wanted with him and Murdo said that he didn't know.

Anyway he left the school on a beautiful summer's day while the birds were singing in the sky. He was wearing a white shirt with short sleeves and it was also open at the neck.

When he was going out the gate he turned and said,

'45 × 25 = 1,125.'

And after that he walked home.

His mother was hanging clothes on the line when he arrived and taking the pegs out of her mouth she said:

'Your schooldays are now over. You will have to get work.'

Murdo admitted that this was true and then went into the house to make tea for himself.

He saw his father working in the field, bent like a shepherd's crook over a spade. Murdo sat at the table and wrote a little verse:

He he said the horse
ho ho said the goat
Ha ha, O alas,
said the brown cow in the byre.

He was greatly pleased with this and copied it into a little book. Then he drank his tea.

ONE DAY MURDO said to his wife, 'Shall we climb that white mountain?'

'No,' she said with astonishment. 'It's too cold.'

Murdo looked around him. The chairs were shining in the light like precious stones. The curtains were shimmering with light as if they were water. The table was standing on its four precious legs. His wife in her blue dress was also precious and precious also was the hum of the pan on the cooker. 'I remember,' he told his wife, 'when I was young I used to listen every Sunday to the sound of the pot boiling on the fire. We had herring all during the week.'

'We too,' said his wife, 'but we had meat on Sunday.' She was thinking that Murdo wasn't looking too well and this frightened her. But she didn't say anything to him.

'Herring,' said Murdo, 'what would we do without it? The salt herring, the roasted herring. The herring that swims through the sea among the more royal fish. So calm. So sure of itself.'

'One day my father killed a rabbit with his gun,' said his wife.

'I'm sure,' said Murdo.

'I'm telling the truth,' Janet insisted.

'I'm not denying it,' said Murdo as he watched the shimmering curtains. And the table shone in front of him, solid and precious and fixed, and the sun glittered all over the room.

O my happiness, he said to himself. O my happiness. How happy the world is without me. How the world doesn't need me. If only I could remember that. The table is so calm and fixed, without soul, single and without turmoil, the chairs compose a company of their own.

'Come on, let's dance,' he said to Janet.

'What now?' she said.

'Yes,' said Murdo, 'now.'

'Let's dance now.'

'All right then,' said Janet.

And they began to dance among the chairs, and the pan shone red in a corner of its own.

And Murdo recalled how they had used to dance in their youth on the autumn nights with the moon above them and his heart so full that it was like a bucket full of water, almost spilling over.

At last Janet sat down, as she was breathless.

And Murdo sat on a chair beside her.

'Well, well,' said he, 'we must do that oftener.'

'Oh the pan,' said his wife and she ran over to the cooker where the pan was boiling over.

The pan, said Murdo to himself, the old scarred pan. It also is dancing.

On its own fire.

Everything is dancing, said Murdo, if we only knew it. The whole world is dancing. The lion is dancing and the lamb is dancing. Good is dancing with Evil in an eternal reel in an invisible light. And he thought of them for a moment, Good and Evil, with their arms around each other on a fine autumn evening with the dew falling steadily and invisibly on the grass.

SOMETIMES JANET THOUGHT that Murdo was out of his mind. Once when they were in Glasgow they went into a café where there was a juke box which was playing 'Bridge over Troubled Water' and Murdo sat at the green, scarred, imitation marble-topped table. He was wearing a thick heavy black coat such as church elders wear and a hard black hat on his head.

When the music stopped he went over to the juke box, put money in the slot and the music started again, whereupon sitting at the table in his black coat and stiff black hat he swayed to the music, moving his head from side to side as if he were in a trance of happiness. A number of girls gazed at him with astonishment.

Also in Glasgow he went up to a policeman and asked him, 'Could you please direct me to Parnassus Street, officer. I think it's quite near Helicon Avenue, or so I was told.'

He bent his head as if he were listening carefully to what the policeman might say.

'Parnassus Street,' said the policeman, a large heavy man with a slow voice. 'What part of the city did you say it was in again?'

'I think, or so I was told, I don't know whether it's right or wrong, I'm a stranger in the city myself,' said Murdo, 'I'm sure someone said to me that it's very near Helicon Avenue.'

'Helicon Avenue?' said the policeman, gazing at Murdo and then at Murdo's wife and then down at his boots.

'It may be in one of the new schemes,' said Murdo helpfully, his head on one side like a bird's on a branch.

'That may be,' said the policeman. 'I'm very sorry but I can't inform you where the places you mention happen to be.'

'Oh that's all right,' said Murdo looking at a radiant clock which had stopped at three o'clock. 'There are so many places, aren't there?' (Muttering under his breath, 'Indonesia, Hong Kong, Kilimanjaro.')

'You're right,' said the policeman, and then turned away to direct the traffic, raising a white glove.

'I think that policeman is from the Highlands,' said Murdo. 'He's got a red neck. And red fists. Big red fists.'

But at other times Murdo would sit in the house completely silent like a spider putting out an invisible web. And Janet wasn't used to such silence. She came from a family that always had something to say, always had morsels of news to feed to each other.

And for a lot of the time she felt lonely even when Murdo was with her. Sometimes when they were sitting in the kitchen Murdo would come over to her with a piece of paper on which he had written some such word as BLOWDY

'What do you think that word means?' Murdo would say to her.

'Blowdy?' Janet would say. 'I never heard that word before.'

'Didn't you?' Murdo would say. Blowdy, he would say to himself again.

Blowdy, blowdy, among the chairs, the green walls.

Once when his mother-in-law was in drinking tea Murdo said to her quietly:

'It's a fine blowdy day today.'

'What did you say?' said his mother-in-law, the cup of tea in her lap and a crumb of bread on her lip.

'A fine blowdy day,' Murdo said, 'a fine windy bright blowdy day.'

'It's a windy day right enough,' said his mother-in-law, looking meaningfully at Janet.

'That's an Irish word,' said Murdo. 'The Irish people used it to give an idea of the kind of marbly clouds that you sometimes see in the sky on a windy day, and also when the wind is from the east.'

'Oh?' said his mother-in-law looking at him carefully.

When Murdo had gone back to his room she said to Janet:

'I don't think Murdo is all there. Do you think he is?'

'Well,' said Janet, 'he acts very funny at times.'

'He's worse than funny,' said her mother. 'Do you remember at the wedding when he took a paper ring from his pocket and he was wearing a piece of cabbage instead of a flower like everybody else?'

'I remember it well enough,' said her daughter. 'But he's very good at figures.'

'That's right enough,' said her mother, 'but a man should be more settled than he is. He should be indeed.'

After her mother had left Janet sat in her chair and began to laugh and she could hardly stop, but at the same time she felt frightened as if there was some strange unnatural being in the house with her.

FOR ABOUT THE seventh or the eighth time Murdo tried to write a story.

'There was a clerk once and he was working in a bank . . .'

When Murdo was working he used to go into the bank at nine in the morning and he would finish at five in the afternoon. And he had an hour for his lunch. There were another ten people working in the bank with him and Murdo would sit at a desk and add figures all day, at the back of the bank, in the half-dark.

Beside him there sat a small bald man who had been in the bank for thirty years and who was always wiping his nose as if there was something there that he wished continually to clean off. At last Murdo said to him, 'Why do you do that?'

'What?' said the man.

'Why do you wipe your nose all the time?' said Murdo.

'It's none of your business,' said the bald man and after that he wouldn't speak to Murdo. They would sit beside each other all day and they wouldn't speak to each other. They wouldn't even say Good morning to each other.

Murdo would begin to think about money. When he was in the bank he would see thousands and thousands of banknotes and it would occur to him:

What if I stole some money and went away to the Bahamas or some place like that? But actually the place he really wanted to go to was Rome and he imagined himself standing among these stony ruins wearing a red cloak while the sun was setting and he was gazing down at the city like a conqueror.

After a time, he would, in his imagination, enter a café and eat spaghetti and he would meet a girl in a mini-skirt and he would say to her:

'Is your name Beatrice?'

And they would stand in the sunset where red fires were burning and there would be a church behind her, a church with gigantic carvings by Michelangelo.

'Have you ever heard of Leonardo da Vinci?' he would say to her and she would look at him with dull pebbly eyes in which no soul was visible.

And in the morning Murdo would rise from his bed and he would see a new world in front of him, a bright clean world, a new morning, and he'd say:

'Where will we go today?'

And she would be asleep and he would leave her there like a corrupted angel with arms as white as those of Venus and a small discontented mouth, and he would go out and he would talk to the women with their long Italian noses and after that he would leave Rome and travel to Venice and sail on a gondola, his red cloak streaming from his shoulders.

And all around him there would be colours such as he had never seen before and his nose would twitch like a rabbit's.

And in an art gallery he would stand in front of a painting and the painting would show a man walking down a narrow road while ahead of him the sun was setting in a green light like the light of the sea.

And he would meet a priest and he would say to him, 'What is keeping you alive?'

And the priest would say to him, 'Come with me and I'll show you.'

And they would go into a small room in a small dirty house and there would be a child lying in bed there with a red feverish face, and beside the bed there would be a woman wearing a black snood. And she would be sitting there motionless while the child stirred restlessly in the bed. And the priest would say to Murdo:

'She has been sitting by that bed for nearly a week now.'

'Do you think,' Murdo would ask, 'that Leonardo had as much care for the Mona Lisa as this woman has for her child?'

And he would look around him, at the picture of the Virgin Mary and the candle that was burning in a corner of the room.

'I understand what you're saying,' the priest would say.

'I hope the child will recover,' Murdo would say.

'Exactly like that,' the priest would say, 'God keeps a watch over the world till the sun rises.'

Murdo would leave the priest and the woman and the child and walk down a street where he would be met by the two men who would attack him, beating him on the head and chest, and steal all the money he had except for the six thousand pounds that were tied round his pants.

'Well, well,' he'd say to the blank Italian sky, 'there is nothing here but troubles.'

He would then see a group of people standing beside a house that had fallen to the ground.

One of the women would say, 'My mother and father are in there dead. And what I want to know is, what is the government going to do about it?'

'I am from the government myself,' Murdo would say. 'And here are two hundred pounds for you.'

'Two hundred pounds isn't enough,' the woman would say, 'to compensate for all the love I felt for my father and mother. I would require five hundred pounds at least. But I'll take the two hundred pounds just now.'

'Right,' Murdo would say and he would run away, his red cloak streaming down his back and from his shoulders as if they were the wings of an angel or a devil.

He would hear sweet voices floating from the gondolas and his heart would be at peace.

When he would wake from his Italian dream the man beside him would be wiping his nose.

'I'm sorry,' Murdo would say to him, 'for what I said to you before.'

But the man wouldn't answer him.

After Murdo had resigned from the bank he sent the man a letter saying,

> I had nothing against your nose. But I'm certain that if you hope to get on in the world you must stop wiping your nose. Napoleon didn't wipe his nose continually. Or William Wallace. I'm sorry to tell you this but I'm only doing it for your own good.
>
> Yours sincerely,
> MURDO MACRAE

WHAT WAS MURDO like? Well, he was about five feet ten inches in height, thin, pale-faced (like the clerk he once had been) and blue-eyed. He shaved himself every morning at half-past eight, sometimes listening to the radio and sometimes whistling in a monotonous melancholy manner. He often cut himself with his razor blade and for this reason he bought sticks of styptic which he could never find and which, after being dipped in water, became soggy. He ate very little food and this worried Janet. He had a theory that too much food made his brain feel heavy, and that this was particularly the case with meat and soup, though not with fish. At nine o'clock he would go and sit at his desk, open the notebook in which he had been trying to write and look at it. He would then take out of his pocket the green pen which he had once found on the road near the house and chew it for a long while, still looking down at the paper. Now and again he would get up from his chair and walk about the room, stopping to study a purple bucket in the corner. He had a strong affection for this bucket: he thought that some day it would yield him some extraordinary vision.

Then he would go back to his chair and sit down again.

He would sometimes think that there was a crown on his head and that he was king of a country which did not yet exist but which would some day emerge with its own constitution. In this country poets and novelists, painters and ballet dancers, musicians and singers would be the most respected citizens. He would think to himself:

How did other writers work? It is said that Schiller (was it Schiller?) would keep a rotten apple in his desk and that he would take it out every morning, and its corrupt smell would arouse his imagination.

For this reason Murdo got an apple, and kept it in his desk till it was rotten, but one day Janet found it and threw it out. And some bird or other ate it.

After some time he might leave the house altogether and go for a walk.

No matter how cold the day was he never wore a coat.

One morning he was walking down the main street when he met the manager of the bank, a man called Maxwell. Maxwell always carried a rolled umbrella even if the day was perfectly fine with no sign of rain. He also wore thick black glasses.

'Imphm,' he said to Murdo.

'Good morning,' Murdo said.

'Imphm,' said Maxwell.

At last he recognised Murdo and he said to him, looking at him sideways all the time in a furtive manner.

'I'm sorry you felt you had to leave the bank. We needed you.'

'Imphm,' said Murdo.

'It's not easy to get work nowadays,' said Maxwell. 'What are you doing?'

'Imphm,' said Murdo.

He was afraid that if he told Maxwell that he didn't do anything, was in fact totally idle though committed to a blank sheet of paper, that Maxwell would fall dead in the road.

At last he said, 'I'm looking after my grandfather. There is no one in the house but myself and him and his old dog which he had in the Great War.'

'An old dog?' said Maxwell.

'Yes,' said Murdo. 'An old dog. He's very fond of my grandfather. He saved his life at Passchendaele. He picked him up between his teeth and took him back to the British lines after he had been very badly nay almost fatally wounded. Nay. He laid him down at the feet of a first lieutenant called Griffiths. From Ilfracombe.'

'Well, well,' said Maxwell, 'well, well.' Murdo was gazing directly at a point between Woolworths and the Italian café and Maxwell was gazing at a point between Lows and Templetons, and they stood like that for a long while in the cold morning. At last Maxwell said, 'I must go to the office. I'm glad I met you. Imphm.'

And he went away. Murdo looked after him in a vague negligent manner and then went into Woolworths.

He weighed himself and found that he was ten stone two pounds.

He walked from counter to counter. He picked up a book about vampires, glanced at it and then went up to a girl in a yellow dress who was paring her nails. On her breast the name *Lily* was written.

'Lily,' said he, 'have you any tins of Arragum? Lily. It's a kind of paint,' he added trying to be helpful.

'Arragum?'

'Yes,' said Murdo. 'It's for windows and doors and tables. It's used a lot in places where there is great cold and sometimes much rain. The Eskimos use it a great deal.'

'Arragum?' she said. 'I don't think that . . .'

'Well,' said Murdo, 'maybe it's called Arragul, I'm not sure. I saw it advertised in the *Observer* Colour Supplement.'

'Wait a minute,' she said, and she went and got another girl in the same yellow uniform as her own, except that instead of *Lily* the name *Mary* was written on the breast.

'Arragum?' said Mary. 'I never heard of that.'

'Well,' said Murdo, 'it doesn't matter. You can't have everything in the shop. But it just occurred to me that as I was passing anyway . . .'

'What was that name again?' said Mary, taking a pencil from her breast pocket.

'Arragum,' said Murdo. 'A-R-R-A-G-U-M. I think the Queen uses it.'

'Well, we can try and get it,' said Mary.

'All right,' said Murdo. 'I think there'll be a big demand for it after that article.'

And with that he left.

He was thinking of his grandfather and the dog that looked after him, and this imagined world became real to him. The dog was large and had gentle brown eyes and he would lie there on the rug in front of the fire gazing at his slightly damaged grandfather, who was thinking of Passchendaele and the Somme and the early sun glittering on the early bayonets. O those early days, those days of untarnished youth.

I could have gone to Vietnam myself, said Murdo, but I was too lazy. I didn't do anything about it, I stayed where I was in the bank reading about it in the papers. I did not set my breast against battle, no indeed. And why didn't I? Who knows the answer to that question? Because I believe in nothing, said Murdo to himself.

He saw a Pakistani a little ahead of him but did not go to speak to him.

For what could I say to him? He has come from another world, he belongs to another civilisation. I myself come from the civilisation of TV. He walked up the road and sat on a bench. After a while the town fool called Donnie came and sat beside him. He was carrying a brown paper parcel from which there came the smell of salt herring.

'Fine day,' said Donnie, his eyes blinking rapidly. 'Fine day.'

He was wearing a long brown dirty coat which trailed to his ankles. The smell of salt herring was in Murdo's nostrils.

'A fine day,' said Donnie again.

After a while he said, 'I don't suppose you could give me a penny. A penny so I can buy sweets.'

'No understand,' said Murdo. 'No understand. Me German. Tourist.'

The fool turned his head away slowly and gazed towards the farther shore, his large head like a cannon ball, his body like a dull rusty gun. His dirty brown hair streamed down the collar of his coat.

At last he turned to Murdo and said, 'I was wondering if you could spare a shilling for a man in poor circumstances.'

Murdo rose rapidly from his seat, and said, 'Me German. Me no understand your money. Me without pity. Have done enough for shrinking pound already. What fought war for, what sent Panzer divisions into civilised treasuries of the West for, if required to prop up currency now? Regard this as paradox of our time.' And he went away thinking of the fool.

He stood for a long time watching the children play in an adjacent park and then went slowly home.

A Letter to the Prime Minister

I am of the opinion that there is a strong conspiracy afoot to undermine this country of ours.

Why do people sit watching TV all the time? I am convinced that there are certain rays which come out of the TV set and that these rays are causing people to lose their commitment to the pure things of life.

Did you ever consider the possibility that John Logie Baird was a Communist?

Do you really believe that there is no connection between the rise of TV and the rise of Communism in the Western world?

Who controls TV? Let me ask you that. Let me put that question to you in all sincerity.

And if the Russians attacked this country what would our people be doing? I think they would continue to sit and watch the TV.

AND THEY WOULD NOT BELIEVE IT WAS AN ATTACK BY THE RUSSIANS AT ALL. THEY WOULD THINK IT WAS A TV DOCUMENTARY.

Did this ever occur to you?

And as well as that there are many people who do not believe that you yourself exist at all. They believe that you have been assembled on TV.

If this is false please answer this letter at once and establish your identity.

With great respect,
MURDO MACRAE

I nearly signed my letter PRO PUBLICO BONO but there has been such a decline in the use of the Latin language that I could not do so. And what is the cause of that? Is it not the TV?

NOW AND AGAIN Murdo would go and visit his father whose health was rather poor and who lived by himself since the death of his wife.

His father would be sitting by the fire on the cold winter's day and Murdo would think of the days when his father had been fit and strong and how when he himself was young his father would take him out fishing.

And now all he had was his pension and a moderately warm hearth. He wouldn't go and live with Murdo and Janet not because he didn't like them but because he didn't want to leave his own house.

Sometimes he would speak of Libya where he had fought in the war.

'There was this fellow from Newcastle beside me,' he would say, 'when we were in the trenches, and he was always saying that he wanted a quick death. Well, that happened right enough. One evening I looked down at him (he was beside me, you see) and he had no head. A shell had taken his head off. It was like a football.'

'Well, well, imagine that,' his visitors would say. 'Isn't that funny. Well well. Think of that, no head on him.'

'Ay, ay, that's the way it was,' Murdo's father would say. 'He had no head. The head was beside me in the sand there like a football.' And Murdo would see the naked head on the sand, the head without thought or imagination.

'And how are you today?' Murdo would say as he went into the house.

'Oh, no complaints, no complaints,' his father would answer. There would often be an open tin of Spam on the table.

'Is there anything to be done?'

'No, nothing, nothing at all.'

When Murdo was young his father would carry him on his shoulders and show him off to people and he would buy for him chocolate sweets in the shape of cats or dogs.

And he would teach him how to fish on red sunset evenings.

Murdo would sweep the floor or dry the dishes of which the sink was full. And his father would say to him, 'You don't need to do that. I'll do that myself.'

And at last Murdo would sit in front of the fire and his father would tell him a story.

'One time,' he said, 'we were in Libya and there was a man there from the islands and he was always reading the Bible. I don't know whether he was frightened or what. Anyway he was always reading the Bible any chance that he had. He knew it from end to end, I would think.

'Well, he once told me this story. One night, he told me, there was a great sandstorm and the sand was thick about the desert, so thick he said that he couldn't see hardly a yard in front of him, and he was afraid that the Germans would suddenly come out of the middle of it with their guns. Well, he said he was waiting there ready with his own gun and he was looking into the middle of the sandstorm with a handkerchief over his mouth. "Well," he said, "I don't know whether you'll believe this or not but about three in the morning out of the middle of the sandstorm there came this man with a beard and in a long white gown. He was like an Arab and some were saying that many of the Arabs were on the side of the Germans. Anyway," he said, "I raised my gun and I fired at this fellow in the long white gown. But he came straight on and there were no marks at all in his breast where I had hit him at point-blank range and he came right on in his long white gown and he went straight through me. He was smiling all the time and he went straight through me. Isn't that funny?"

'Think of that now,' said his father to Murdo. 'Eh? But he was a bit queer that same fellow right enough.'

These were the kinds of stories that Murdo's father would tell Murdo as they sat in front of the fire on a cold winter's day while now and again Murdo's father would light and relight his pipe. Nearly all his stories were about the war.

And Murdo would look out of the window and he would see the movement of the grass under the cold wind, and the world outside so dark and dull and sometimes stormy.

And he would think of his mother in her long blue apron with the red flowers on it as she walked about the house while his father would be quietly reading the paper. And he himself would be playing on the floor with a train which his father had bought for him.

What had his father been doing in Libya anyway disguised as a soldier? What good had his soldiership done for him, now as he sat by the fire and the wind blew coldly and endlessly round his house.

His father didn't know that Murdo was unemployed: he thought of him with pride as a clerk in a well-known and well-trusted bank.

Once his father had said to him, 'Do you know something? Your mother always said that you should have been a minister. Did you know that?'

'No, I didn't know that,' said Murdo, astonished by the absurdity of the statement.

'Ay,' said his father, 'she used to say that. She used to say that often to me. "Murdo should be a minister," she would say. "One day Murdo will be a minister. You mark my words. He's got the face of a minister."'

'Well, well,' said Murdo, 'well, well.'

And he would look into the red glowing fire as if he was seeing a pulpit there and he would hear himself saying, 'In the immortal words of our theologian De Sade . . .'

After a time he would get to his feet and he would say, 'I'll come again next week. Look after yourself.'

And his father would say, 'Don't worry about me. I'll do that all right.'

And Murdo would leave the house and look at the snow and test the thin roof of ice over the pools with the toe of his shoe delicately and elegantly as if he were thinking of some new ballet, and he would think of his father in Libya and his dead mother and Maxwell walking up and down the winter landscape with a rolled umbrella in his hand.

Here is another story that Murdo told little Colin:

In a country far away (he said), there once lived a little mouse and this mouse used to go to her work every day. She would sit at a desk and write in a big book. She even wore glasses. When her work in the office was over she would take the bus home and then she would make her tea and look at the TV and put her feet up on the sofa.

At eight o'clock at night she would make her supper, wash the dishes and watch the TV again. And after that she would go to bed.

At eight o'clock in the morning she would get up, listen to the radio for a little while, wash herself, eat her breakfast and then she would go to the office again. And she did this every day from Monday to Friday.

Sometimes on Friday night after the week's work was over she would have a party for the other mice in the neighbourhood, and they would eat a lot of cheese.

Well, one day, about twelve o'clock, she came out of the office and she took a walk down to a big quiet river that was quite near the place where she worked and she was eating her dinner on the bank of the river—a piece of bread and cheese—when she saw a large white swan swimming in the water. The swan was very beautiful and as white as snow and it had a large red beak which now and again it dipped into the water as if it was drinking. Now and again it would glance towards the bank of the river and stare as if it was seeing the mouse, but of course it couldn't have, as the mouse was so small.

That swan seems to have a very easy life of it, said the mouse to herself. All it does all day is swim about in the water and look at its own reflection and eat and drink. No wonder it looks so beautiful and clean. It doesn't have to cook its dinner or its supper or its breakfast; it doesn't have to wash and dry dishes: it doesn't have to sweep the floor: and it doesn't have to get up in the morning. That swan must be very happy.

And the swan looked so queenly, so calm, swimming in the river like a great white picture. And the mouse said to herself, wouldn't it be wonderful if I could lead the same sort of life? I too would be like a queen.

Well, one day the mouse's manager in the office was very angry with her because of a mistake she had made in her books, and he told her that she must come back and work late at five o'clock at night. When the mouse left the office she began to cry.

Look, she said to herself, at the life I lead. I try to do my best and look what happens to me. Tonight I was going to wash my clothes and now I have to go back to the office though I don't want to do that.

Some of the other mice in the office laugh at me and some of them steal my food.

And so she looked out at the swan that was swimming so calmly in the water.

'I'm just as good as you,' she said to the swan. 'I do more work than you. You never did any work in your life. What use are you to the country? You never do anything but admire yourself in the water. Well, it's high time I got some rest as well. I need it more than you do. Anyway in my own way I'm just as beautiful as you. And there were kings and queens in my family as well, I'm sure, in the past, though now I'm working in an office.'

She was so upset that she couldn't eat her food and later a crow came down from the sky and ate it.

Anyway the mouse jumped into the river thinking that she would swim just as well as the swan was doing.

But she slowly began to sink because she wasn't used to swimming and she was drowned in the river and the swan continued to swim round and round, dipping her throat now and again in the water, and then raising it and looking around her with her long neck and her blunt red beak.

MURDO SENT THE following to the local newspaper, but it was never printed.

> *Is Calvin Still Alive?*
>
> Many people think that Hitler is still alive and that he is living in South America with money that he stole from the Jews.
>
> But there is a rumour going about this island that Calvin is still alive. He is supposed to have been seen in a small house a little out of town on the road to Holm.
>
> He is a small hunchbacked man with spectacles, who speaks to no one, or if he does speak he speaks in very sloppy not to say ungrammatical Gaelic.
>
> He has a face like iron and he is said to sit at a table night and day studying a Bible almost as big as himself.
>
> He can't stand a candle in the same house.
>
> If he sees anyone drinking or smoking he rushes out of the house and shouts insults at him and dances up and down on the road, shaking his fist.
>
> He also has a strong aversion to cars.
>
> If he sees a woman approaching he shuts the door at once and sits at the window shaking his fist at her and mouthing inaudible words. If she looks at him he shuts his eyes and keeps them shut till she has gone past. After that he washes his face.

He wears black gloves on his hands. He hardly ever leaves the house in the summer but in the winter he goes on long walks.

Now a number of people in the village wonder if you can find a picture of Calvin so that they can establish his identity. It may be that this is a man who is impersonating Calvin for some reason of his own.

If anyone were to say that it would certainly be odd to find Calvin still alive, I would answer that stranger things have happened down the centuries.

What about for instance the man in the Bible who rose to heaven in a chariot?

And what about Nebuchadnezzar who lived on grass for many years?

It is also odd that this man won't go to any of our churches but that now and again on a Sunday he will be seen hanging about one of them though he won't actually go in.

I await your answer with much interest. I enclose a stamp.

Yours etc.,
MURDO MACRAE

ONE DAY MURDO visited the local library and he said to the thin bespectacled woman who was standing at the counter:

'I want the novel *War and Peace* written by Hugh Macleod.'

'Hugh Macleod?' she said.

'Yes,' he said, 'but if you don't happen to have *War and Peace* I'll take any other book by the same author, such as *The Brothers Karamazov*.'

'I thought,' she said doubtfully, 'I mean are you sure that . . .'

'I'm quite sure that the book is by Hugh Macleod,' said Murdo, 'and I often wonder why there aren't more of his books in the libraries.'

'Well,' she said, 'I think we have *War and Peace* but surely it was written by Tolstoy.'

'What's it about?' said Murdo. 'Is it about a family growing up in Harris at the time of Napoleon?'

'I thought,' she said, 'that the story is set in Russia,' looking at him keenly through her glasses.

'Bloody hell,' said Murdo under his breath and then aloud,

'Oh well I don't think we can be talking about the same Hugh Macleod. This man was never in Russia as far as I know. Is it a long book, about a thousand pages?'

'I think that's right,' said the woman, who was beginning to look rather wary.

'Uh huh,' said Murdo. 'This is a long book as well. It's about Napoleon in Harris in the eighteenth century. Hugh Macleod was an extraordinary man, you know. He had a long beard and he used to make his own shoes. A strange man. I don't really know much about his life except that he became a bit religious in his old age. But it doesn't matter. If you haven't got *War and Peace* maybe you could give me his other book *The Brothers Karamazov*. It's about three brothers and their struggle for a croft.'

'I don't think,' said the woman, 'that we have that one.'

'Well, isn't that damnable,' said Murdo. 'Here you have an author as distinguished as any that has ever come out of the Highlands and you don't have his books. And I can't get them in any other library. I think it's shameful. But I bet you if he was a Russian you would have all his books. I'm pretty sure that you'll have *Tramping through Siberia* by Gogol. Anyway it doesn't matter.

'But I was forgetting another reason for my call,' and he took a can out of his pocket. 'I'm collecting money for authors who can't write. A penny or two will do.'

'Authors who can't write?' said the woman looking suspiciously at the can as if it might explode in her face.

'That's right,' said Murdo. 'Poor people who sit at their desks every morning and find that they can't put a word to paper. Have you ever spared a thought for them? Those people who can write don't of course need help. But think,' he said, leaning forward, 'of those people who sit at their desks day after day while the sun rises and the sun sets and when they look at their paper they find that there isn't a word written on it. Do you not feel compassion for them? Aren't your bowels moved with pity? Doesn't it surprise you that in our modern society not enough is done for such people?'

'Well,' she said, 'to tell the truth . . .'

'Oh, I know what you're going to say,' said Murdo. 'Why should you give money for non-existent books? And that point of view is natural enough. There is a great deal in it. But has it ever occurred to you that the books that have never been written may be as good as, nay even better than, the ones that have? That there is in some heaven or other books as spotless as the angels themselves without a stain of ink on them? For myself, I can believe this quite easily as I put a lot of credence in the soul as I am sure you do also. Think,' he said, 'if this room were full of non-existent unwritten books how much easier your job would be.'

He saw her hand creeping steadily towards the phone that lay on her desk and said hurriedly,

'Perhaps that day will come though it hasn't come yet.'

He took the can in his hand and half-ran half-walked out of the library down the corridor with the white marble busts of Romans on each side of him.

Still half running he passed a woman laden with books and said, 'I'm sorry. Bubonic plague. Please excuse me. I'll be all right in a few minutes. Brucellosis,' and half crouching he ran down the brae among the bare trees and the snow.

Ahead of him he saw the white mountain and he shook his fist at it shouting

'Neil Munro. Neil Munro.'

After a while he took a black hat out of his bag and he went home limping, now and again removing his hat when he saw a child walking past him on the street.

'THE POTATO,' SAID Murdo to his wife one night, 'what is like the potato? What would we do without the potato especially in the islands? The potato is sometimes wet and sometimes dry. It is even said that the dry potato is "laughing" at you. Now that is a very odd thing, a laughing potato. But it could happen. And there are many people whose faces are like potatoes. If we had no potatoes we would have to eat the herring with our tea and that wouldn't be very tasty. In the spring we plant the potatoes and we pick them in the autumn. Now in spite of that no poet has made a poem for the humble potato. It didn't occur to William Ross or Alexander Macdonald—great poets though they were—to do so, and I am sure that they must have eaten a lot of potatoes in their poetic careers.

'There is a very big difference, when you think of it, between the potato and the herring. The herring moves, it travels from place to place in the ocean, and they say that there aren't many fish in the sea faster than the herring. But the potato lies in the dark till someone digs it up with a graip. We should therefore ask ourselves, Which is the happier of the two, the potato or the herring? That is a big philosophical question and it astonishes me that it hasn't been studied in greater depth. It is a very profound question. For the potato lies there in the dark, and it doesn't hear or see anything. But in spite of that we have no evidence that it is less happy than the herring. No indeed. And as well as that we have no evidence that the herring is either happy or unhappy. The herring journeys through the ocean meeting many other kinds of fish on its way, such as seals and mackerel.

'But the potato stays in the one place in the dark in its brown skin, without, we imagine, desire or hope. For what could a potato hope for? Or what could it desire? Now at a certain time, the potato and the herring come together on the one plate, say on a summer day or on an autumn day. It greatly puzzles me how they come together in that fashion. Was it predestined that that particular herring and that particular potato should meet—the herring that was roving the sea in its grey dress and the potato that was lying in the earth in its brown dress. That is a very deep question. And the herring cannot do without the potato, nor for that matter can the potato do without the herring. For they need each other.

'They are as closely related as the soul and the body. But is the herring the body or the soul?

'That is another profound question.

'And also you can roast a potato and you can roast a herring but I don't think they are as good when they are roasted. I myself think that the herring is better when it is salted and I may say the same about the potato.

'But no one has ever conjectured about the feelings of the potato or the feelings of the herring. The herring leaves its house and travels all over the world and it sees strange sights in the sea, but the potato sees nothing, it is lying in the darkness while the days and the weeks and the years pass. The potato doesn't move from the place in which it was planted.

'I must make a poem about this sometime,' said Murdo to his wife. 'I am very surprised that up till now no one has made a poem about it.'

And he stopped speaking and his wife looked at him and then got up and made some tea.

ONE NIGHT MURDO woke from sleep, his wife beside him in the bed, and he was sweating and trembling.

'Put on the light at once,' he shouted. His wife jumped out of bed and did as he had told her to do.

'What's wrong?' she said. 'What's wrong?' Murdo's face was as white as the sheet on the bed. He was sitting up in bed as if he was listening to some odd sound that only he was hearing: in the calmness they could hear the gurgling of the water from the stream that ran past their house among the undergrowth.

'A dream I had,' said Murdo. 'It was a dream I dreamed. In the dream I saw a witch and she was coming after me and she had a cup of blood in her hand as if it was a cup of tea. And her face . . . There's something wrong with this house.'

'There's nothing wrong with the house,' she said, and when he looked at her he began to tremble as if she herself might indeed be the witch.

'Her face was sharp and long,' he said, 'and she had a cup of blood in her hand and I was making the sign of the cross. The devil was in that dream, there was real evil in that dream. I never dreamed a dream like that before.' And his face was dead white, his teeth were chattering, and he was looking around him wildly.

He thought that the room was full of evil, of devils, that his wife's face was like the face of a witch among the evil.

'I never thought that evil existed till now,' he said. 'Leave the light on. Don't put it off.'

He was afraid to leave his bed or to walk about the house and he felt that there was some evil moving about the outside of the house in the darkness. He thought that there were devils clawing at the walls, trying to get in through the windows, perhaps even breaking the glass or tapping on it.

'Her face,' he said, 'was so sharp and so long, and her back was crooked and she had black wings.'

'You're all right now, aren't you?' said his wife and her blue eyes were gazing at him with what he thought was compassion. But he couldn't be sure. He thought again, What if she is a witch? What if I am a devil myself? What world have we come from, what evil world? What dark woods?

Sitting upright in bed it was as if he was a ghost rising from the grave.

'You're all right, you're all right,' said Janet again.

'Who lived in this house before us?' he asked. 'It was an old woman, wasn't it?'

'Not at all,' said Janet. 'You remember very well who lived here. It was a young family. Surely you remember.'

'You're right,' he said, 'you're right enough.'

Masks, he said to himself. Masks on all the faces, as happens on Hallowe'en. Masks that don't move. Stiff cardboard masks. A wolf's face, a bear's face.

And he felt as if the house were shaking in a storm of evil and the evil hitting it like a strong wind and light pouring out of the house.

'I'm sorry,' he said to Janet. 'I'm sorry I wakened you.'

'Do you want some tea?' she asked him.

'No,' he said. 'But leave the light on for a while.' He listened to the sound of the river flowing through the darkness. Directly underneath the window there was grass where he had buried the black dog when it had been killed on a summer's day by a motor car.

The bones rotting.

'I'm all right now,' he said. 'I'm all right. You can put the light off.'

And she rose and did that and he sat awake for a long time listening to his wife's breathing and he heard above her tranquil breathing the sound of the river flowing past.

At last he fell asleep and this time he had no frightening dreams.

But just before he fell asleep he had a vision of the house as a lighted shell moving through the darkness, and animals around it with red beaks and claws and red teeth, leaping and jumping venomously at the windows and walls to get at him.

'WHAT'S WRONG WITH that man of yours if he can be called a man at all?' said Janet's father to her one day. He was sitting in an easy chair, his face red with the light of the fire, like a cockerel about to crow.

'When I was young,' he said, 'I used to be at the fishing no matter what kind of weather it was.'

'You've told me,' said Janet. She was more familiar with her father's world than she was with Murdo's. She didn't understand what attraction the white mountain, of which he was continually speaking, had for him.

She herself was of the opinion that the mountain though beautiful was very cold. She much preferred the spring to winter or autumn. She liked to hang billowing clothes on a line in breezy spring and to watch the birds flying about the moorland.

'You don't even have any children,' her father said to her. They were alone together for her mother was at the midweek evening service in the church hall. Her father never went to church.

He was always wandering about in the open air with a hammer or a piece of wood or standing at the door studying the weather.

'It's easy enough to work in an office,' he said. 'Anyone can do that. Why did he leave his work?' In the days before Murdo left the office he used to write letters for his father-in-law about matters connected with the croft, which he couldn't understand but which he could transform into reasonably official English.

'Is he going to stay in that house forever?' said her father again. 'What does he do all day?'

In a way Janet was on her father's side for she couldn't really understand Murdo any more than he did. When she married him she had thought she understood him and that he was normal enough but now she wasn't so sure. He did such odd not to say abnormal things. Her father was not at all odd, he was the quintessence of normality: he was like stone on a moor. Murdo would sometimes come home from the office and he would say, 'I don't understand why I am in that office at all. Why do people work anyway? A sort of fog comes over my eyes when I look at Maxwell and the rest of them. They actually believe that what they are doing is important to the human race. They actually believe that by gathering in money and counting, and by adding figures in columns, they are contributing to the salvation of the world. It's really quite incredible. I mean, the absurdity of what they do has never occurred to them at all. They haven't even thought about it. They are so glad and so pleased that they can actually do the work they're doing, and they make a great mystery of it, as if it were of some immense secret importance. They don't realise at all the futility of what they're doing, and sometimes it takes me all my time to keep from bursting out laughing. If they all dropped dead with pens in their hands it wouldn't make the slightest difference to the world. They would be replaced by other people equally absurd absorbed in the same absurd work.'

'What are you talking about?' she would say to him. 'What do you mean?' She didn't understand clearly what he was saying.

'Well, the world would carry on in the same way as before, wouldn't it,' said Murdo. 'I only hope that Maxwell's umbrella is struck by lightning one of these days. It might teach him a lesson.'

Her father was saying, 'Many people would be happy with the work he's got. There are people I know who clean the roads, clever people too. And look at the warm dry job he had.'

He lifted a newspaper and laid it down again. He bought the paper every day but he never read it right through. He would glance at it now and again and then he would put it down.

'You would be as well to leave him,' said her father.

She had actually thought of leaving him but she knew that she would never go through with it. It wasn't that she was frightened to leave him but she really hoped that one morning he would suddenly leap out of bed and say, 'I'm going back to my work today.' She was hoping that this would happen. And also she thought that she should be loyal to him so long as he was being attacked by his strange sickness.

'No I won't leave him,' she said looking into the fire.

'Well, I hope you know what you're doing,' said her father.

Janet sometimes thought that everything would be all right if Murdo would find himself able to write something instead of staring at that white mountain which obsessed him so much.

Her father was so large and definite and red in his opinions: she actually thought of his opinions as red and bristly.

'I never thought much of him,' he said. 'There was a foolishness in his people. His grandfather was a daft bard. He used to write silly songs.'

And sometimes her father would pace about the room like a prisoner, his great red hands at his sides.

He raised his fist and said, 'What he needs is a good thump. That's what he needs.' And his face became a deep red with anger.

'You can make tea for yourself if you like,' he told Janet and he went to the door and looked out. 'The weather looks as if it's going to take a turn for the worse.' His round red head was like a tomato on top of his stocky body.

Poor Murdo, she said to herself. What are you going to do? Poor Murdo. And she felt a deep pity for him, in her very womb.

'No I don't want any tea,' she said. 'I have to go home.'

On the way home, she looked at the white mountain for a long time, but all she saw was the mountain itself. At last she turned her eyes away, for the glitter of the snow was dazzling her.

What am I going to do? she thought. There's no money coming into the house and the neighbours are laughing at me.

But in spite of that there was no one she knew as witty and lively as her own husband.

If only we had children, she thought. If only there was some money coming into the house I'd be happy enough.

But a small persistent voice was saying, 'Would you really? Would you really?' like a small winter bird with a small black beak.

'Would you? Would you?' twittered the small bird.

For every day now as she looked in the mirror she saw herself growing older all the time.

And Murdo also growing older.

And the chairs and tables closing in on her.

Last Will and Testament by Murdo Macrae

1. To my beloved wife I leave my shoes and clothes, my pencil and my pen and my papers (All my love such as it is).
2. To my mother-in-law I leave the newspapers that I've been collecting for many years. And my rubber nose.
3. To my father-in-law I leave a stone.
4. To tell the truth I haven't much else except for my bicycle and I leave that also to my mother-in-law. And I leave my watch to Maxwell.

I wish my wife to send the following letter through the post:

To Whomsoever it may Concern

If anyone can tell me why we are alive, I will give him TWO POUNDS, all my money.
For in the first place we are created of flesh and lightning.
And in the fullness of time the flesh and the lightning grow old.
And also we are working in a world without meaning.
Yesterday I looked at an egg and I couldn't understand why it was in the place where it was.
Now I should know the reason for its position in space. For that surely is not a mysterious thing. And I could say the same about butter. And salt. And Bovril. Now we have come out of the lightning, in our ragged clothes. And at last we arrived at Maxwell with his umbrella.
This is the problem that Newton never unravelled.
We kill each other.
For no reason at all.
These thoughts climb my head as if it were a staircase.
And that is why I am an idiot.

WE CANNOT LIVE WITHOUT SOME BELIEF.

I believe in my mother-in-law. She will live forever. She will be knitting in a country unknown to the Greeks.
I believe in my mother-in-law and in my father-in-law and also in Mrs Macleod.
They will all live forever.
For in their condition they are close to that of the animal.
They survive on dressers and sideboards.

Those who approach most closely to the conditions of the
animal are the ones most likely to survive.
And Woolworths.
Woolworths will live forever.
Too much intelligence is not good for one.
Too much of the spirit is not good for the body, but the
following are good for the body:
Bovril.
Sanatogen.
Butter.
Crowdie.
Eggs.
Water.
Bread.
Meat.
And the sun on a warm day.
And a girl's breast,
and
a spoonful of honey.

I am sending you this letter, nameless one, with much happiness and without a stamp.

MURDO MACRAE

MURDO'S FATHER WAS dying and Murdo and Janet were watching him. Now and again his father would ask for water so that he could wet his lips and his breath was going faster and faster. Janet was sitting on a chair beside the bed but Murdo was walking up and down restlessly, unceasingly. On a small table beside the bed he saw a letter that had come to his father and had not been opened: it was in a brown envelope and looked official. And the tears came unbidden to his eyes.

Why didn't I do more? he was saying to himself all the time. He couldn't sit down. Outside the window the darkness was falling quickly, and he felt cold. He was shaking as if he had a fever, and his teeth were chattering. Now and again he would look at his father's thin grey face as the head turned ceaselessly on the pillow.

Murdo nearly knelt and prayed. He nearly said, 'Save my father, save my father, and I will do anything You want me to do.' He thought of earlier days when his father used to tease him or carry him about on his shoulders. He thought of his father as a soldier in the war.

What did he get out of life? he asked himself. What did he get? Janet amazed him sitting there so serenely on her chair as if she were used to deaths, as if this room were her true element though in fact as far as he knew she had never seen anyone die before.

A voice was screaming in his head, 'I'm sorry. I'm sorry.' He knew that his father was dying, but he didn't know why he should feel so sorry.

The smell of death was in the room: death was an inevitability of the air.

In a strange way he had never thought that his father would die though he was old and frail.

He saw his father's pipe on the table and the tears again welled to his eyes. He was grinding his teeth together. 'I'm sorry, I'm sorry,' the voice was screaming silently like a voice that might be coming down from the sky, from some bleak planet without light.

His father's breath was accelerating all the time as if he were preparing himself: for a journey, as if he were in a hurry to go somewhere.

And Murdo paced restlessly up and down the room. Pictures flashed in front of his eyes.

His father with a spade, his father at the peat bank, his father reading the paper. And below each picture like an image in a dark pool was the thin grey face.

The stars, they are so far away, Murdo thought.

He was thinking of the other houses in the town with their lights, and they did not know what was going on in this room.

And all the time his body was shaking and shivering as if with the coldness of death itself.

He put his hand on his father's brow and it had the chillness of death on it. Like marble.

Janet rose and went for some more water. Once his father opened his eyes and looked around him but Murdo knew that he wasn't seeing either of them.

And his breath was going like an engine, fast, fast.

Murdo turned away and went to the window. He looked out but he could see nothing in the darkness.

Is this what we were born for? he was saying to himself over and over. He turned back to his father who was melting away before his eyes like snow.

He looked out of the window again.

When he turned round next time he felt a deep silence in the room.

The breath had ceased its frantic running.

His father's head had fallen on one side and the mouth was twisted. Murdo began to cry and he couldn't stop. He knew that his father was dead. He himself was crying and shivering at the same time.

He couldn't stop crying. Janet put her hand on his shoulder and he in turn put his face on her breast like a child, crying.

There was no sound in the room except his own weeping.

He rose abruptly and went outside. Through the darkness he could see the white mountain. Like a ghost.

It frightened him.

It looked so cold and distant and white.

Like a ghost staring at him.

He stayed there for a long time looking at it. He expected no help from it.

There was no happiness nor warning nor comfort nor sadness in that terrible cold whiteness.

It was just a mountain that rose in front of him out of the darkness.

I must climb it, he thought. I must do that now.

He went into the room again and said to Janet. 'I'll be all right now.' She looked at him with love in her eyes and her face was streaming with tears as if the snow had begun to melt in spring, for her face was so pale and tired and white.

'There are no angels,' said Murdo. 'There is only the white mountain.'

Janet looked at him with wonder.

'I'll be all right now,' said Murdo. He knew what he was going to write on white leaves.

A story about his father. At least one story, while he fought with the white mountain, wrestled with it, and after that if he couldn't defeat the white mountain he knew also what he would do.

He picked up his father's pipe and put it in his pocket.

Janet was looking from Murdo's face to his father's. Something was happening to Murdo but she didn't know what it was. His face was becoming more settled, white as snow, but at the same time the trembling life and vibrancy were leaving it.

He was like a tombstone above his father's body.

And she felt fear and happiness together.

For Murdo was growing more and more, minute by minute, like his father and her own father.

It was as if he was settling down into a huge heaviness.

But at the same time there was a terrible question in his face, a question without end, without boundary, a question without laughter.

Murdo took her by the hand and led her out of the house and he showed her the mountain.

'Soon,' he said, 'we shall have to climb it.'

And his face was as set as stone.

And her father-in-law's face was in front of her as well.

It glared gauntly out of the middle of the chairs and the table and the dresser.

That grey question.

That grey thin shrunken question.

Alasdair Gray

FIVE LETTERS FROM AN EASTERN EMPIRE

On separate occasions, Alasdair Gray (b.1934) has described himself as a Glaswegian who 'lived by painting and selling infrequent plays to broadcasting companies' or as 'a painter who lives by writing'. His first novel, *Lanark,* was published in 1981 and caused Anthony Burgess to hail Alisdair Gray as the best Scottish novelist since Sir Walter Scott. In form and content *Lanark* is certainly the most exuberant and inventive Scottish prose work since Sir Thomas Urquhart's *The Jewel.*

'Five Letters from an Eastern Empire' made its first appearance in *Words* magazine. It was written when Gray was Glasgow University's Writer in Residence and seems to be about the business of being a writer in residence at a Scottish university, where, by and large, no one has read anything you have written. Like many another with an office, financial security and time, Alasdair found the will was gone. He had nothing to write about and did what any sane man in a similar position would do; he read. And amongst Ezra Pound's Chinese Cantos he came across the line: 'Moping around the Emperor's court waiting for the order to write.'

Five Letters from an Eastern Empire

DESCRIBING ETIQUETTE
GOVERNMENT IRRIGATION
EDUCATION CLOGS KITES
RUMOUR POETRY JUSTICE
MASSAGE TOWN-PLANNING
SEX AND VENTRILOQUISM
IN AN OBSOLETE NATION

FIRST LETTER

DEAR MOTHER, DEAR FATHER, I like the new palace. It is all squares like a chessboard. The red squares are buildings, the white squares are gardens. In the middle of each building is a courtyard, in the middle of each garden is a pavilion. Soldiers, nurses, postmen, janitors and others of the servant-class live and work in the buildings. Members of the honoured-guest-class have a pavilion. My pavilion is small but beautiful, in the garden of evergreens. I don't know how many squares make up the palace but certainly more than a chessboard has. You heard the rumour that some villages and a small famous city were demolished to clear space for the foundation. The rumour was authorized by the immortal emperor yet I thought it exaggerated. I now think it too timid. We were ten days sailing upstream from the old capital, where I hope you are still happy. The days were clear and cool, no dust, no mist. Sitting on deck we could see the watchtowers of villages five or six miles away and when we stood up at nightfall we saw, in the sunset, the sparkle of the heliograph above cities, on the far side of the horizon. But after six days there was no sign of any buildings at all, just ricefields with here and there the tent of a waterworks inspector. If all this empty land feeds the new palace then several cities have been cleared from it. Maybe the inhabitants are inside the walls with me, going out a few days each year to plant and harvest, and working between times as gardeners of the servant-class.

You would have admired the company I kept aboard the barge. We were all members of the honoured-guest-class: accountants, poets and headmasters, many many headmasters. We were very jolly together and said many things we would not be able to say in the new palace under the new etiquette. I asked the headmaster of literature, 'Why are there so many headmasters and so few poets? Is it easier for you to train your own kind than ours?' He said, 'No. The emperor needs all the headmasters he can get. If a quarter of his people were headmasters he would be perfectly happy. But more than two poets would tear his kingdom apart.' I led the loud laughter which rewarded this deeply witty remark and my poor, glum little enemy and colleague Tohu had to go away and sulk. His sullen glances amuse me all the time. Tohu has been educated to envy and fear everyone, especially me, while I have been educated to feel serenely superior to everyone, especially him. Nobody knows this better than the headmaster of literature who taught us both. This does not mean he wants me to write better than Tohu, it shows he wants me to write with high feelings and Tohu with low ones. Neither of us have written yet but I expect I will be the best. I hope the emperor soon orders me to celebrate something grand and that I provide exactly what is needed. Then you will both be able to love me as much as you would like to do.

This morning as we breakfasted in the hold of the barge Tohu came down into it with so white a face that we all stared. He screamed, 'The emperor has tricked us! We have gone downstream instead of up! We are coming to the great wall round the edge of the kingdom, not to a palace in the middle! We are being sent into exile among the barbarians!' We went on deck. He was wrong of course. The great wall has towers with loopholes every half mile, and it bends in places. The wall which lay along the horizon before us was perfectly flat and windowless and on neither side could we see an end of it. Nor could we see anything behind it but the high tapering tops of two post-office towers, one to the east, one to the west, with the white flecks of messenger pigeons whirling toward them and away from them at every point of the compass. The sight made us all very silent. I raised a finger, summoned my entourage and went downstairs to dress for disembarking. They took a long time lacing me into the ceremonial cape and clogs and afterwards they found it hard lifting me back up to the deck again. Since I was now the tallest man aboard I had to disembark first. I advanced to the prow and stood there, arms rigid by my sides, hands gripping the topknot of the doctor, who supported my left thigh, and the thick hair of Adoda, my masseuse, who warmly clasped my right. Behind me the secretary and chef each held back a corner of the cape so that everyone could see, higher than a common man's head, the dark green kneebands of the emperor's tragic poet. Without turning I knew that behind my entourage the headmasters were ranged, the first of them a whole head shorter than me, then the accountants, then, last and least, the emperor's comic poet, poor Tohu. The soles of his ceremonial clogs are only ten inches thick and he has nearly no entourage at all. His doctor, masseuse, secretary and chef are all the same little nurse.

I had often pictured myself like this, tall upon the prow, the sublime tragedian arriving at the new palace. But I had imagined a huge wide-open gate or door, with policemen holding back crowds on each side, and maybe a balcony above with the emperor on it surrounded by the college of headmasters. But though the smooth wall was twice as high as most cliffs I could see no opening in it. Along the foot was a landing stage crowded with shipping. The river spread left and right along this in a wide moat, but the current of the stream seemed to come from under the stage. Among yelling dockers and heaped bales and barrels I saw a calm group of men with official gongs on their wrists, and the black clothes and scarlet kneebands of the janitors. They waited near an empty notch. The prow of our barge slid into this notch. Dockers bolted it there. I led the company ashore.

I recognized my janitor by the green shoes these people wear when guiding poets. He reminded us that the new etiquette was enforced within the palace walls and led us to a gate. The other passengers were led to other gates. I could now see hundreds of gates, all waist high and wide enough to roll a barrel through. My entourage helped me to my knees and I crawled in after the janitor. This was the worst part of the journey. We had to crawl a great distance, mostly uphill. Adoda and the doctor tried to help by alternately butting their heads against the soles of my clogs. The floor was carpeted with bristly stuff which pierced my kneebands and scratched the palms of my hands. After twenty minutes it was hard not to sob with pain and exhaustion, and when at last they helped me to my feet I sympathized with Tohu who swore aloud that he would never go through that wall again.

The new etiquette stops honoured guests from filling their heads with useless knowledge. We go nowhere without a janitor to lead us and look at nothing above the level of his kneebands. As I was ten feet tall I could only glimpse these slips of scarlet by leaning forward and pressing my chin into my chest. Sometimes in sunlight, sometimes in lamplight, we crossed wooden floors, brick pavements, patterned rugs and hard-packed gravel. But I mainly noticed the pain in my neck and calves, and the continual whine of Tohu complaining to his nurse. At last I feel asleep. My legs moved onward because Adoda and the doctor lifted them. The chef and secretary stopped me bending forward in the middle by pulling backward on the cape. I was wakened by the janitor striking his gong and saying, 'Sir. This is your home.' I lifted my eyes and saw I was inside the sunlit, afternoon, evergreen garden. It was noisy with birdsongs.

We stood near the thick hedge of cypress, holly and yew trees which hide all but some tiled roofs of the surrounding buildings. Triangular pools, square lawns and the grassy paths of a zig-zag maze are symmetrically placed round the pavilion in the middle. In each corner is a small pinewood with cages of linnets, larks and nightingales in the branches. From one stout branch hangs a trapeze where a servant dressed like a cuckoo sits imitating the call of that bird, which does not sing well in captivity. Many gardeners were discreetly trimming things or mounting ladders to feed the birds. They wore black clothes without kneebands, so they were socially invisible, and this gave the garden a wonderful air of privacy. The janitor struck his gong softly and whispered, 'The leaves which grow here never fade or die.' I rewarded this delicate compliment with a slight smile then gestured to a patch of moss. They laid me flat there and I was tenderly undressed. The doctor cleaned me. Adoda caressed my aching body till it breathed all over in the sun-warmed air. Meanwhile Tohu had flopped down in his nurse's arms and was snoring horribly. I had the couple removed and placed behind a hollybush out of earshot. Then I asked for the birds to be silenced, starting with the linnets and ending with the cuckoo. As the gardeners covered the cages the silence grew louder, and when the notes of the cuckoo faded there was nothing at all to hear and I slept once more.

Adoda caressed me awake before sunset and dressed me in something comfortable. The chef prepared a snack with the stove and the food from his satchel. The janitor fidgeted impatiently. We ate and drank and the doctor put something in the tea which made me quick and happy. 'Come!' I said, jumping up, 'Let us go straight to the pavilion!' and instead of following the path through the maze I stepped over the privet hedge bordering it which was newly planted and a few inches high. 'Sir!' called the janitor, much upset, 'Please do not offend the gardeners! It is not their fault that the hedge is still too small.'

I said, 'The gardeners are socially invisible to me.'

He said, 'But you are officially visible to them, and honoured guests do not offend the emperor's servants. That is not the etiquette?!'

I said, 'It is not a rule of the etiquette, it is convention of the etiquette, and the etiquette allows poets to be unconventional in their own home. Follow me Tohu.'

But because he is trained to write popular comedy Tohu dreads offending members of the servant class, so I walked straight to the pavilion all by myself.

It stands on a low platform with steps all round and is five sided, with a blue wooden pillar supporting the broad eaves at each corner. An observatory rises from the centre of the sloping green porcelain roof and each wall has a door in the middle with a circular window above. The doors were locked but I did not mind that. The air was still warm. A gardener spread cushions on the platform edge and I lay and thought about the poem I would be ordered to write. This was against all rules of education and etiquette. A poet cannot know his theme until the emperor orders it. Until then he should think of nothing but the sublime classics of the past. But I knew I would be commanded to celebrate a great act and the greatest act of our age is the building of the new palace. How many millions lost their homes to clear the ground? How many orphans were prostituted to keep the surveyors cheerful? How many captives died miserably quarrying its stone? How many small sons and daughters were trampled to death in the act of wiping sweat from the eyes of desperate, bricklaying parents who had fallen behind schedule? Yet this building which barbarians think a long act of intricately planned cruelty has given the empire this calm and solemn heart where honoured guests and servants can command peace and prosperity till the end of time. There can be no greater theme for a work of tragic art. It is rumoured that the palace encloses the place where the rivers watering the empire divide. If a province looks like rebelling, the headmasters of waterworks can divert the flow elsewhere and reduce it to drought, quickly or slowly, just as he pleases. This rumour is authorized by the emperor and I believe it absolutely.

While I was pondering the janitor led the little party through the maze, which seemed designed to tantalize them. Sometimes they were a few yards from me, then they would disappear behind the pavilion and after a long time reappear far away in the distance. The stars came out. The cuckoo climbed down from his trapeze and was replaced by a nightwatchman dressed like an owl. A gardener went round hanging paper boxes of glow-worms under the eaves. When the party reached the platform by the conventional entrance all but Adoda were tired, cross and extremely envious of my unconventional character. I welcomed them with a good-humoured chuckle.

The janitor unlocked the rooms. Someone had lit lamps in them. We saw the kitchen where the chef sleeps, the stationery office where the secretary sleeps, the lavatory where the doctor sleeps, and Adoda's room, where I sleep. Tohu and his nurse also have a room. Each room has a door into the garden and another into the big central hall where I and Tohu will make poetry when the order-to-write comes. The walls here are very white and bare. There is a thick blue carpet and a couple of punt-shaped thrones lined with cushions and divided from each other by a screen. The only other furniture is the ladder to the observatory above. The janitor assembled us here, struck the gong and made this speech in the squeaky voice the emperor uses in public.

'The emperor is glad to see you safe inside his walls. The servants will now cover their ears.

'The emperor greets Bohu, his tragic poet, like a long-lost brother. Be patient, Bohu. Stay at home. Recite the classics. Use the observatory. It was built to satisfy your craving for grand scenery. Fill your eyes and mind with the slow, sublime, eternally returning architecture of the stars. Ignore trivial flashes which stupid peasants call *falling* stars. It has been proved that these are not heavenly bodies but white-hot cinders fired out of volcanoes. When you cannot stay serene without talking to someone, dictate a letter to your parents in the old capital. Say anything you like. Do not be afraid to utter unconventional thoughts, however peculiar. Your secretary will not be punished for writing these down, your parents not punished for reading them. Be serene at all times. Keep a calm empty mind and you will see me soon.

'And now, a word for Tohu. Don't grovel so much. Be less glum. You lack Bohu's courage and dignity and don't understand people well enough to love them, as he does, but you might still be my best poet. My new palace contains many markets. Visit them with your chef when she goes shopping. Mix with the crowds of low, bustling people you must one day amuse. Learn their quips and catch-phrases. Try not to notice they stink. Take a bath when you get home and you too will see me soon.'

The janitor struck his gong then asked in his own voice if we had any polite requests. I looked round the hall. I stood alone, for at the sound of the emperor's voice all but the janitor and I had lain face down on the carpet and even the janitor had sunk to his knees. Tohu and the entourage sat up now and watched me expectantly. Adoda arose with her little spoon and bottle and carefully collected from my cheeks the sacred tears of joy which spring in the eyes of everyone the emperor addresses. Tohu's nurse was licking his tears off the carpet. I envied him, for he would see more of the palace than I would, and be more ready to write a poem about it when the order came. I did not want to visit the market but I ached to see the treasuries and reservoirs and grain-silos, the pantechnicons and pantheons and gardens of justice. I wondered how to learn about these and still stay at home. The new dictionary of etiquette says *All requests for knowledge will be expressed as requests for things.* So I said, 'May the bare walls of this splendid hall be decorated with a map of the new palace? It will help my colleague's chef to lead him about.'

Tohu shouted, 'Do not speak for me, Bohu! The emperor will send janitors to lead the chef who leads me. I need nothing more and nothing less than the emperor has already decided to give.'

The janitor ignored him and told me, 'I hear and respect your request.'

According to the new dictionary of etiquette this answer means *No* or *Maybe* or *Yes, after a very long time.*

The janitor left, I felt restless. The chef's best tea, the doctor's drugs, Adoda's caresses had no effect so I climbed into the observatory and tried to quieten myself by watching the stars as the emperor had commanded. But that did not work, as he foresaw, so I summoned my secretary and dictated this letter, as he advised. Don't be afraid to read it. You know what the emperor said. And the postman who re-writes letters before fixing them to the pigeons always leaves out dangerous bits. Perhaps he will improve my prose-style, for most of these sentences are too short and jerky. This is the first piece of prose I have ever composed, and as you know, I am a poet.

Goodbye. I will write to you again,
From the evergreen garden,
Your son,
Bohu

DICTATED ON THE 27TH LAST DAY
OF THE OLD CALENDAR.

SECOND LETTER

DEAR MOTHER, DEAR FATHER, I discover that I still love you more than anything in the world. I like my entourage, but they are servants and cannot speak to me. I like the headmaster of literature, but he only speaks about poetry. I like poetry, but have written none. I like the emperor, but have never seen him. I dictated the last letter because he said talking to you would cure my loneliness. It did, for a while, but it also brought back memories of the time we lived together before I was five, wild days full of happiness and dread, horrid fights and ecstatic picnics. Each of you loved and hated a different bit of me.

You loved talking to me, mother, we were full of playful conversation while you embroidered shirts for the police and I toyed with the coloured silks and buttons. You were small and pretty yet told such daring stories that your sister, the courtesan, screamed and covered her ears, while we laughed till the tears came. Yet you hated me going outside and locked me for an hour in the sewing-box because I wore my good clogs in the lane. These were the clogs father had carved with toads on the tips. You had given them many coats of yellow lacquer, polishing each one till a member of the honoured-guest-class thought my clogs were made of amber and denounced us to the police for extravagance. But the magistrate was just and all came right in the end.

Mother always wanted me to look pretty. You, father, didn't care how I looked and you hated talking, especially to me, but you taught me to swim before I was two and took me in the punt to the sewage ditch. I helped you sift out many dead dogs and cats to sell to the gardeners for dung. You wanted me to find a dead man, because corpse-handlers (you said) don't often die of infectious diseases. The corpse I found was not a man but a boy of my own age, and instead of selling him to the gardeners we buried him where nobody would notice. I wondered why, at the time, for we needed money for rent. One day we found the corpse of a woman with a belt and bracelet of coins. The old capital must have been a slightly mad place that year. Several corpses of the honoured-guest-class bobbed along the canals and the emperor set fire to the south-eastern slums. I had never seen you act so strangely. You dragged me to the nearest market (the smell of burning was everywhere) and rented the biggest possible kite and harness. You who hate talking carried that kite down the long avenue to the eastern gate, shouting all the time to the priest, your brother, who was helping us. You said all children should be allowed to fly before they were too heavy, not just children of the honoured-guest-class. On top of the hill I grew afraid and struggled as you tightened the straps, then uncle perched me on his shoulders under that huge sail, and you took the end of the rope, and you both ran downhill into the wind. I remember a tremendous jerk, but nothing else.

I woke on the sleeping-rug on the hearth of the firelit room. My body was sore all over but you knelt beside me caressing it, mother, and when you saw my eyes were open you sprang up, screamed and attacked father with your needles. He did not fight back. Then you loved each other in the firelight beside me. It comforted me to see that. And I liked watching the babies come, especially my favourite sister with the pale hair. But during the bad winter two years later she had to be sold to the merchants for money to buy firewood.

Perhaps you did not know you had given me exactly the education a poet needs, for when you led me to the civil service academy on my fifth birthday I carried the abacus and squared slate of an accountant under my arm and I thought I would be allowed to sleep at home. But the examiner knew his job and after answering his questions I was sent to the classics dormitory of the closed literature wing and you never saw me again. I saw you again, a week or perhaps a year later. The undergraduates were crossing the garden between the halls of the drum-master who taught us rhythms and the chess-master who taught us consequential logic. I lagged behind them then slipped into the space between the laurel bushes and the outside fence and looked through. On the far side of the fresh-water canal I saw a tiny distant man and woman standing staring. Even at that distance I recognized the pink roses on the scarlet sleeves of mother's best petticoat. You could not see me, yet for a minute or perhaps a whole hour you stood staring at the tall academy fence as steadily as I stared at you. Then the monitors found me. But I knew I was not forgotten, and my face never acquired the haunted, accusing look which stamped the face of the other scholars and most of the teachers too. My face displays the pained but perfectly real smile of the eternally hopeful. That glimpse through the fence enabled me to believe in love while living without it, so the imagination lessons, which made some of my schoolmates go mad or kill themselves, did not frighten me.

The imagination lessons started on my eleventh birthday after I had memorized all the classical literature and could recite it perfectly. Before that day only my smile showed how remarkable I was. The teachers put me in a windowless room with a ceiling a few inches above my head when I sat on the floor. The furniture was a couple of big shallow earthenware pans, one empty and one full of water. I was told to stay there until I had passed the water through my body and filled the empty pan with it. I was told that when the door was shut I would be a long time in darkness and silence, but before the water was drunk I would hear voices and imagine the bodies of strange companions, some of them friendly and others not. I was told that if I welcomed everyone politely even the horrible visitors would teach me useful things. The door was shut and the darkness which drowned me was surprisingly warm and familiar. It was exactly the darkness inside my mother's sewing-box. For the first time since entering the academy I felt at home.

After a while I heard your voices talking quietly together and thought you had been allowed to visit me at last, but when I joined the conversation I found we were talking of things I must have heard discussed when I was a few months old. It was very interesting. I learned later that other students imagined the voices and company of ghouls and madmen and gulped down the water so fast that they became ill. I sipped mine as slowly as possible. The worst person I met was the corpse of the dead boy I had helped father take from the canal. I knew him by the smell. He lay a long time in the corner of the room before I thought of welcoming him and asking his name. He told me he was not an ill-treated orphan, as father had thought, but the son of a rich waterworks inspector who had seen a servant stealing food and been murdered to stop him telling people. He told me many things about life among the highest kinds of honoured-guest-class, things I could never have learned from my teachers at the academy who belonged to the lower kind. The imagination lessons became, for me, a way of escaping from the drum, chess and recitation masters and of meeting in darkness everyone I had lost with infancy. The characters of classical literature started visiting me too, from the celestial monkey who is our ancestor to emperor Hyun who burned all the unnecessary books and built the great wall to keep out unnecessary people. They taught me things about themselves which classical literature does not mention. Emperor Hyun, for instance, was in some ways a petty, garrulous old man much troubled with arthritis. The best part of him was exactly like my father patiently dredging for good things in the sewage mud of the north-west slums. And the imperious seductive white demon in the comic creation myth turned out to be very like my aunt, the courtesan, who also transformed herself into different characters to interest strangers, yet all the time was determinedly herself. My aunt visited me more than was proper and eventually I imagined something impossible with her and my academic gown was badly stained. This was noted by the school laundry. The next day the medical inspector made small wounds at the top of my thighs which never quite healed and are still treated twice a month. I have never since soiled cloth in that way. My fifth limb sometimes stiffens under Adoda's caresses but nothing comes from it.

Soon after the operation the headmaster of literature visited the academy. He was a heavy man, as heavy as I am now. He said, 'You spend more days imagining than the other scholars, yet your health is good. What guests come to your dark room?'

I told him. He asked detailed questions. I took several days to describe everyone. When I stopped he was silent a while then said, 'Do you understand why you have been trained like this?'

I said I did not.

He said, 'A poet needs an adventurous, sensuous infancy to enlarge his appetites. But large appetites must be given a single direction or they will produce a mere healthy human being. So the rich infancy must be followed by a childhood of instruction which starves the senses, especially of love. The child is thus forced to struggle for love in the only place he can experience it, which is memory, and the only place he can practise it, which is imagination. This education, which I devised, destroys the minds it does not enlarge. You are my first success. Stand up.'

I did, and he stooped, with difficulty, and tied the dark green ribbons round my knees. I said, 'Am I a poet now?'

He said, 'Yes. You are now the emperor's honoured guest and tragic poet, the only modern author whose work will be added to the classics of world literature.' I asked when I could start writing. He said, 'Not for a long time. Only the emperor can supply a theme equal to your talent and he is not ready to do so. But the waiting will be made easy. The days of the coarse robe, dull teachers and dark room are over. You will live in the palace.'

I asked him if I could see my parents first. He said, 'No. Honoured guests only speak to inferior classes when asking for useful knowledge and your parents are no use to you now. They have changed. Perhaps your small pretty mother has become a brazen harlot like her sister, your strong silent father an arthritic old bore like the emperor Hyun. After meeting them you would feel sad and wise and want to write ordinary poems about the passage of time and fallen petals drifting down the stream. Your talent must be preserved for a greater theme than that.'

I asked if I would have friends at the palace. He said, 'You will have two. My system has produced one other poet, not very good, who may perhaps be capable of some second-rate doggerel when the order-to-write comes. He will share your apartment. But your best friend knows you already. Here is his face.'

He gave me a button as broad as my thumb with a small round hairless head enamelled on it. The eyes were black slits between complicated wrinkles; the sunk mouth seemed to have no teeth but was curved in a surprisingly sweet sly smile. I knew this must be the immortal emperor. I asked if he was blind.

'Necessarily so. This is the hundred-and-second year of his reign and all sights are useless knowledge to him now. But his hearing is remarkably acute.'

So I and Tohu moved to the palace of the old capital and a highly trained entourage distracted my enlarged mind from the work it was waiting to do. We were happy but cramped. The palace staff kept increasing until many honoured guests had to be housed in the city outside, which took away homes from the citizens. No new houses could be built because all the skill and materials in the empire were employed on the new palace upriver, so all gardens and graveyards and even several streets were covered with tents, barrels and packing-cases where thousands of families were living. I never used the streets myself because honoured guests there were often looked at very rudely, with glances of concealed dislike. The emperor arranged for the soles of our ceremonial clogs to be thickened until even the lowest of his honoured guests could pass through a crowd of common citizens without meeting them face-to-face. But after that some from the palace were jostled by criminals too far beneath them to identify, so it was ordered that honoured guests should be led everywhere by a janitor and surrounded by their entourage. This made us perfectly safe, but movement through the densely packed streets became very difficult. At last the emperor barred common citizens from the streets during the main business hours and things improved.

Yet these same citizens who glared and jostled and grumbled at us were terrified of us going away! Their trades and professions depended on the court; without it most of them would become unnecessary people.

The emperor received anonymous letters saying that if he tried to leave his wharves and barges would catch fire and the sewage ditches would be diverted into the palace reservoir. You may wonder how your son, a secluded poet, came to know these things. Well, the headmaster of civil peace sometimes asked me to improve the wording of rumours authorized by the emperor, while Tohu improved the unauthorized ones that were broadcast by the beggars' association. We both put out a story that citizens who worked hard and did not grumble would be employed as servants in the new palace. This was true, but not as true as people hoped. The anonymous letters stopped and instead the emperor received signed petitions from the workingmen's clubs explaining how long and well they had served him and asking to go on doing it. Each signatory was sent a written reply with the emperor's seal saying that his request had been heard and respected. In the end the court departed upriver quietly, in small groups, accompanied by the workingmen's leaders. But the mass of new palace servants come from more docile cities than the old capital. It is nice to be in a safe home with nobody to frighten us.

I am stupid to mention these things. You know the old capital better than I do. Has it recovered the bright uncrowded streets and gardens I remember when we lived there together so many years ago?

This afternoon is very sunny and hot, so I am dictating my letter on the observatory tower. There is a fresh breeze at this height. When I climbed up here two hours ago I found a map of the palace on the table beside my map of the stars. It seems my requests are heard with unusual respect. Not much of the palace is marked on the map but enough to identify the tops of some big pavilions to the north. A shining black pagoda rises from the garden of irrevocable justice where disobedient people have things removed which cannot be returned, like eardrums, eyes, limbs and heads. Half-a-mile away a similar but milkwhite pagoda marks the garden of revocable justice where good people receive gifts which can afterwards be taken back, like homes, wives, salaries and pensions. Between these pagodas but further off, is the court of summons, a vast round tower with a forest of bannerpoles on the roof. On the highest pole the emperor's scarlet flag floats above the rainbow flag of the headmasters, so he is in there today conferring with the whole college.

Shortly before lunch Tohu came in with a woodcut scroll which he said was being pinned up and sold all over the market, perhaps all over the empire. At the top is the peculiar withered-apple-face of the immortal emperor which fascinates me more each time I see it. I feel his blind eyes could eat me up and a few days later the sweet sly mouth would spit me out in a new, perhaps improved form. Below the portrait are these words:

Forgive me for ruling you but someone must. I am a small weak old man but have the strength of all my good people put together. I am blind, but your ears are my ears so I hear everything. As I grow older I try to be kinder. My guests in the new palace help me. Their names and pictures are underneath.

Then come the two tallest men in the empire. One of them is:

Fieldmarshal Ko who commands all imperial armies and police and defeats all imperial enemies. He has degrees in strategy from twenty-eight academies but leaves thinking to the emperor. He hates unnecessary people but says 'Most of them are outside the great wall.'

The other is:

Bohu, the great poet. His mind is the largest in the land. He knows the feelings of everyone from the poor peasant in the ditch to the old emperor on the throne. Soon his great poem will be painted above the door of every townhouse, school, barracks, post-office, law-court, theatre and prison in the land. Will it be about war? Peace? Love? Justice? Agriculture? Architecture? Time? Fallen apple-blossom in the stream? Bet about this with your friends.

I was pleased to learn there were only two tallest men in the empire. I had thought there were three of us. Tohu's face was at the end of the scroll in a row of twenty others. He looked very small and cross between a toe-surgeon and an inspector of chickenfeed. His footnote said:

Tohu hopes to write funny poems. Will he succeed?

I rolled up the scroll and returned it with a friendly nod but Tohu was uneasy and wanted conversation. He said 'The order-to-write is bound to come soon now.'

'Yes.'

'Are you frightened?'

'No.'

'Your work may not please.'

'That is unlikely.'

'What will you do when your great poem is complete?'

'I shall ask the emperor for death.'

Tohu leaned forward and whispered eagerly, 'Why? There is a rumour that when our poem is written the wounds at the top of our thighs will heal up and we will be able to love our masseuse as if we were common men!'

I smiled and said, 'That would be anticlimax.'

I enjoy astonishing Tohu.

Dear parents, this is my last letter to you. I will write no more prose. But laugh aloud when you see my words painted above the doors of the public buildings. Perhaps you are poor, sick or dying. I hope not.

But nothing can deprive you of the greatest happiness possible for a common man and woman. You have created an immortal.

Who lives in the evergreen garden,
Your son,
Bohu.

DICTATED ON THE 19TH LAST DAY
OF THE OLD CALENDAR.

THIRD LETTER

DEAR MOTHER, DEAR FATHER, I am full of confused feelings. I saw the emperor two days ago. He is not what I thought. If I describe everything very carefully, especially to you, perhaps I won't go mad.

I wakened that morning as usual and lay peacefully in Adoda's arms. I did not know this was my last peaceful day. Our room faces north. Through the round window above the door I could see the banners above the court of summons. The scarlet and the rainbow flags still floated on the highest pole but beneath them flapped the dark green flag of poetry. There was a noise of hammering and when I looked outside some joiners were building a low wooden bridge which went straight across the maze from the platform edge. I called in the whole household. I said 'Today we visit the emperor.'

They looked alarmed. I felt very gracious and friendly. I said, 'Only I and Tohu will be allowed to look at him but everyone will hear his voice. The clothes I and Tohu wear are chosen by the etiquette, but I want the rest of you to dress as if you are visiting a rich famous friend you love very much.'

Adoda smiled but the others still looked alarmed. Tohu muttered, 'The emperor is blind.'

I had forgotten that. I nodded and said 'His headmasters are not.'

When the janitor arrived I was standing ten feet tall at the end of the bridge. Adoda on my right wore a dress of dark green silk and her thick hair was mingled with sprigs of yew. Even Tohu's nurse wore something special. The janitor bowed, turned, and paused to let me fix my eyes on his kneebands; then he struck his gong and we moved toward the court.

The journey lasted an hour but I would not have wearied had it lasted a day. I was as incapable of tiredness as a falling stone on its way to the ground. I felt excited, strong, yet peacefully determined at the same time. The surfaces we crossed became richer and larger: pavements of marquetry and mosaic, thresholds of bronze and copper, carpets of fine tapestry and exotic fur. We crossed more than one bridge for I heard the lip-lapping of a great river or lake. The janitor eventually struck the gong for delay and I sensed the wings of a door expanding before us. We moved through a shadow into greater light. The janitor struck the end-of-journey note and his legs left my field of vision. The immortal emperor's squeaky voice said, 'Welcome, my poets. Consider yourselves at home.'

I raised my eyes and first of all saw the college of headmasters. They sat on felt stools at the edge of a platform which curved round us like the shore of a bay. The platform was so high that their faces were level with my own, although I was standing erect. Though I had met only a few of them I knew all twenty-three by their regalia. The headmaster of waterworks wore a silver drainpipe round his leg, the headmaster of civil peace held a ceremonial bludgeon, the headmaster of history carried a stuffed parrot on his wrist. The headmaster of etiquette sat in the very centre holding the emperor, who was two feet high. The emperor's head and the hands dangling out of his sleeves were normal size, but the body in the scarlet silk robe seemed to be a short wooden staff. His skin was papier mâché with lacquer varnish, yet in conversation he was quick and sprightly. He ran from hand to hand along the row and did not speak again until he reached the headmaster of vaudeville on the extreme left. Then he said, 'I shock you. Before we talk I must put you at ease, especially Tohu whose neck is sore craning up at me. Shall I tell a joke Tohu?'

'Oh yes sir, hahaha! Oh yes sir, hahaha!' shouted Tohu, guffawing hysterically.

The emperor said, 'You don't need a joke. You are laughing happily already!'

I realized that this was the emperor's joke and gave a brief appreciative chuckle. I had known the emperor was not human, but was so surprised to see he was not alive that my conventional tears did not flow at the sound of his voice. This was perhaps lucky as Adoda was too far below me to collect them. The emperor moved to the headmaster of history and spoke on a personal note: 'Ask me intimate questions, Bohu.'

I said, 'Sir, have you always been a puppet?'

He said, 'I am not, even now, completely a puppet. My skull and the bones of my hands are perfectly real. The rest was boiled off by doctors fifteen years ago in the operation which made me immortal.'

I said, 'Was it sore becoming immortal?'

He said, 'I did not notice. I had senile dementia at the time and for many years before that I was, in private life, vicious and insensitive. But the wisdom of an emperor has nothing to do with his character. It is the combined intelligence of everyone who obeys him.'

The sublime truth of this entered me with such force that I gasped for breath. Yes. The wisdom of a government is the combined intelligence of those who obey it. I gazed at the simpering dummy with pity and awe. Tears poured thickly down my cheeks but I did not heed them.

'Sir!' I cried, 'Order us to write for you. We love you. We are ready.'

The emperor moved to the headmaster of civil peace and shook the tiny imperial frock into dignified folds before speaking. He said, 'I order you to write a poem celebrating my irrevocable justice.'

I said, 'Will this poem commemorate a special act of justice?'

He said, 'Yes. I have just destroyed the old capital, and everyone living there, for the crime of disobedience.'

I smiled and nodded enthusiastically, thinking I had not heard properly. I said, 'Very good sir, yes, that will do very well. But could you suggest a particular event, a historically important action, which might, in my case, form the basis of a meditative ode, or a popular ballad, in my colleague's case? The action or event should be one which demonstrates the emperor's justice. Irrevocably.'

He said, 'Certainly. The old capital was full of unnecessary people. They planned a rebellion. Fieldmarshal Ko besieged it, burned it flat and killed everyone who lived there. The empire is peaceful again. That is your theme. Your pavilion is now decorated with information on the subject. Return there and write.'

'Sir!' I said, 'I hear and respect your order, I hear and respect your order!'

I went on saying this, unable to stop. Tohu was screaming with laughter and shouting, 'Oh my colleague is extremely unconventional, all great poets are, I will write for him, I will write for all of us hahahaha!'

The headmasters were uneasy. The emperor ran from end to end of them and back, never resting till the headmaster of moral philosophy forced him violently onto the headmaster of etiquette. Then the emperor raised his head and squeaked, 'This is not etiquette, I adjourn the college!'

He then flopped upside down on a stool while the headmasters hurried out.

I could not move. Janitors swarmed confusedly round my entourage. My feet left the floor, I was jerked one way, then another, then carried quickly backward till my shoulder struck something, maybe a doorpost. And then I was falling, and I think I heard Adoda scream before I became unconscious.

I woke under a rug on my writing-throne in the hall of the pavilion. Paper screens had been placed round it painted with views of the old capital at different stages of the rebellion, siege and massacre. Behind one screen I heard Tohu dictating to his secretary. Instead of taking nine days to assimilate his material the fool was composing already.

Postal pigeons whirl like snow from the new palace,

he chanted.

Trained hawks of the rebels strike them dead.
The emperor summons his troops by heliograph:
'Fieldmarshal Ko, besiege the ancient city.'
Can hawks catch the sunbeam flashed from silver mirror?
No, hahahaha. No, hahahaha. Rebels are ridiculous.

I held my head. My main thought was that you, mother, you, father, do not exist now and all my childhood is flat cinders. This thought is such pain that I got up and stumbled round the screens to make sure of it.

I first beheld a beautiful view of the old capital, shown from above like a map, but with every building clear and distinct. Pink and green buds on the trees showed this was springtime. I looked down into a local garden of justice where a fat magistrate fanned by a singing-girl sat on a doorstep. A man, woman, and child lay flat on the ground before him and nearby a policeman held a dish with two yellow dots on it. I knew these were clogs with toads on the tips, and that the family was being accused of extravagance and would be released with a small fine. I looked again and saw a little house by the effluent of a sewage canal. Two little women sat sewing on the doorstep, it was you, mother, and your sister, my aunt. Outside the fence a man in a punt, helped by a child, dragged a body from the mud. The bodies of many members of the honoured-guest-class were bobbing along the sewage canals. The emperor's cavalry were setting fire to the south-eastern slums and sabering families who tried to escape. The strangest happening of all was on a hill outside the eastern gate. A man held the rope of a kite which floated out over the city, a kite shaped like an eagle with parrot-coloured feathers. A child hung from it. This part of the picture was on a larger scale than the rest. The father's face wore a look of great pride, but the child was staring down on the city below, not with terror or delight, but with a cool, stern, assessing stare. In the margin of this screen was written *The rebellion begins*.

I only glanced at the other screens. Houses flamed, whole crowds were falling from bridges into canals to avoid the hooves and sabres of the cavalry. If I had looked closely I would have recognized your figures in the crowds again and again. The last screen showed a cindery plain scored by canals so clogged with ruin that neither clear nor foul water appeared in them. The only life was a host of crows and ravens as thick on the ground as flies on raw and rotten meat.

I heard an apologetic cough and found the headmaster of literature beside me. He held a dish with a flask and two cups on it. He said, 'Your doctor thinks wine will do you good.'

I returned to the throne and lay down. He sat beside me and said, 'The emperor has been greatly impressed by the gravity of your response to his order-to-write. He is sure your poem will be very great.' I said nothing. He filled the cups with wine and tasted one. I did not. He said, 'You once wanted to write about the building of the new palace. Was that a good theme for a poem?'

'Yes.'

'But the building of the new palace and the destruction of the old capital are the same thing. All big new things must begin by destroying the old. Otherwise they are a mere continuation.'

I said, 'Do you mean that the emperor would have destroyed the old capital even without a rebellion?'

'Yes. The old capital was linked by roads and canals to every corner of the empire. For more than nine dynasties other towns looked to it for guidance. Now they must look to us.'

I said, 'Was there a rebellion?'

'We are so sure there was one that we did not enquire about the matter. The old capital was a market for the empire. When the court came here we brought the market with us. The citizens left behind had three choices. They could starve to death, or beg in the streets of other towns, or rebel. The brave and intelligent among them must have dreamed of rebellion. They probably talked about it. Which is conspiracy.'

'Was it justice to kill them for that?'

'Yes. The justice which rules a nation must be more dreadful than the justice which rules a family. The emperor himself respects and pities his defeated rebels. Your poem might mention that.'

I said, 'You once said my parents were useless to me because time had changed them. You were wrong. As long as they lived I knew that though they might look old and different, though I might never see them again, I was still loved, still alive in ways you and your emperor can never know. And though I never saw the city after going to school I thought of it growing like an onion; each year there was a new skin of leaves and dung on the gardens, new traffic on the streets, new whitewash on old walls. While the old city and my old parents lived my childhood lived too. But the emperor's justice has destroyed my past, irrevocably. I am like a land without culture or history. I am now too shallow to write a poem.'

The headmaster said, 'It is true that the world is so packed with the present moment that the past, a far greater quantity, can only gain entrance through the narrow gate of a mind. But your mind is unusually big. I enlarged it myself, artificially. You are able to bring your father, mother and city to life and death again in a tragedy, a tragedy the whole nation will read. Remember that the world is one vast graveyard of defunct cities, all destroyed by the shifting of markets they could not control, and all compressed by literature into a handful of poems. The emperor only does what ordinary time does. He simply speeds things up. He wants your help.'

I said, 'A poet has to look at his theme steadily. A lot of people have no work because an emperor moves a market, so to avoid looking like a bad government he accuses them of rebelling and kills them. My stomach rejects that theme. The emperor is not very wise. If he had saved the lives of my parents perhaps I could have worked for him.'

The headmaster said, 'The emperor did consider saving your parents before sending in the troops, but I advised him not to. If they were still alive your poem would be an ordinary piece of political excuse-making. Anyone can see the good in disasters which leave their family and property intact. But a poet must feel the cracks in the nation splitting his individual heart. How else can he mend them?'

I said, 'I refuse to mend this cracked nation. Please tell the emperor that I am useless to him, and that I ask his permission to die.'

The headmaster put his cup down and said, after a while, 'That is an important request. The emperor will not answer it quickly.'

I said, 'If he does not answer me in three days I will act without him.'

The headmaster of literature stood up and said, 'I think I can promise an answer at the end of three days.'

He went away. I closed my eyes, covered my ears and stayed where I was. My entourage came in and wanted to wash, feed and soothe me but I let nobody within touching distance. I asked for water, sipped a little, freshened my face with the rest then commanded them to leave. They were unhappy, especially Adoda who wept silently all the time. This comforted me a little. I almost wished the etiquette would let me speak to Adoda. I was sure Tohu talked all the time to his nurse when nobody else could hear. But what good does talking do? Everything I could say would be as horrible to Adoda as it is to me. So I lay still and said nothing and tried not to hear the drone of Tohu dictating all through that night and the following morning. Toward the end half his lines seemed to be stylized exclamations of laughter and even between them he giggled a lot. I thought perhaps he was drunk, but when he came to me in the evening he was unusually dignified. He knelt down carefully by my throne and whispered 'I finished my poem today. I sent it to the emperor but I don't think he likes it.'

I shrugged. He whispered, 'I have just received an invitation from him. He wants my company tomorrow in the garden of irrevocable justice.'

I shrugged. He whispered, 'Bohu, you know my entourage is very small. My nurse may need help. Please let your doctor accompany us.'

I nodded. He whispered, 'You are my only friend,' and went away.

I did not see him next day till late evening. His nurse came and knelt at the steps of my throne. She looked smaller, older and uglier than usual and she handed me a scroll of the sort used for public announcements. At the top were portraits of myself and Tohu. Underneath it said:

> *The emperor asked his famous poets Bohu and Tohu to celebrate the destruction of the old capital. Bohu said no. He is still an honoured guest in the evergreen garden, happy and respected by all who know him. Tohu said yes and wrote a very bad poem. You may read the worst bits below. Tohu's tongue, right shoulder, arm and hand have now been replaced by wooden ones. The emperor prefers a frank confession of inability to the useless words of the flattering toad-eater.*

I stood up and said drearily 'I will visit your master.'

He lay on a rug in her room with his face to the wall. He was breathing loudly. I could see almost none of him for he still wore the ceremonial cape which was badly stained in places. My doctor knelt beside him and answered my glance by spreading the palms of his hands. The secretary, chef and two masseuses knelt near the door. I sighed and said, 'Yesterday you told me I was your only friend, Tohu. I can say now that you are mine. I am sorry our training has stopped us showing it.'

I don't think he heard me for shortly after he stopped breathing. I then told my entourage that I had asked to die and expected a positive answer from the emperor on the following day. They were all very pale but my news made them paler still. When someone more than seven feet tall dies of unnatural causes the etiquette requires his entourage to die in the same way. This is unlucky, but I did not make this etiquette, this palace, this empire which I shall leave as soon as possible, with or without the emperor's assistance. The hand of my secretary trembles as he writes these words. I pity him.

To my dead parents in the ash of the old capital,
From the immortal emperor's supreme nothing, Their son,
Bohu.

DICTATED ON THE 10TH LAST DAY
OF THE OLD CALENDAR.

FOURTH LETTER

DEAR MOTHER, DEAR FATHER, I must always return to you, it seems. The love, the rage, the power which fills me now cannot rest until it has sent a stream of words in your direction. I have written my great poem but not the poem wanted. I will explain all this.

On the evening of the third day my entourage were sitting round me when a common janitor brought the emperor's reply in the unusual form of a letter. He gave it to the secretary, bowed and withdrew. The secretary is a good ventriloquist and read the emperor's words in the appropriate voice.

The emperor hears and respects his great poet's request for death. The emperor grants Bohu permission to do anything he likes, write anything he likes, and die however, wherever, and whenever he chooses.

I said to my doctor, 'Choose the death you want for yourself and give it to me first.'

He said, 'Sir, may I tell you what that death is?'

'Yes.'

'It will take many words to do so. I cannot be brief on this matter.'

'Speak. I will not interrupt.'

He said, 'Sir, my life has been a dreary and limited one, like your own. I speak for all your servants when I say this. We have all been, in a limited way, married to you, and our only happiness was being useful to a great poet. We understand why you cannot become one. Our own parents have died in the ancient capital, so death is the best thing for everyone, and I can make it painless. All I need is a closed room, the chef's portable stove and a handful of prepared herbs which are always with me.

'But sir, need we go rapidly to this death? The emperor's letter suggests not, and that letter has the force of a passport. We can use it to visit any part of the palace we like. Give us permission to escort you to death by a flowery, roundabout path which touches on some commonplace experiences all men wish to enjoy. I ask this selfishly, for our own sakes, but also unselfishly, for yours. We love you sir.' Tears came to my eyes but I said firmly, 'I cannot be seduced. My wish for death is an extension of my wish not to move, feel, think or see. I desire *nothing* with all my heart. But you are different. For a whole week you have my permission to glut yourself on anything the emperor's letter permits.'

The doctor said, 'But sir, that letter has no force without your company. Allow yourself to be carried with us. We shall not plunge you into riot and disorder. All will be calm and harmonious, you need not walk, or stand, or even think. We know your needs. We can read the subtlest flicker of your eyebrow. Do not even say *yes* to this proposal of mine. Simply close your eyes in the tolerant smile which is so typical of you.'

I was weary, and did so, and allowed them to wash, feed and prepare me for sleep as in the old days. And they did something new. The doctor wiped the wounds at the top of my thighs with something astringent and Adoda explored them, first with her tongue and then with her teeth. I felt a pain almost too fine to be noticed and looking down I saw her draw from each wound a quivering silver thread. Then the doctor bathed me again and Adoda embraced me and whispered, 'May I share your throne?'

I nodded. Everyone else went away and I slept deeply for the first time in four days.

Next morning I dreamed my aunt was beside me, as young and lovely as in days when she looked like the white demon. I woke up clasping Adoda so insistently that we both cried aloud. The doors of the central hall were all wide open; so were the doors of the garden in the rooms beyond. Light flooded in on us from all sides. During breakfast I grew calm again but it was not my habitual calm. I felt adventurous under the waist. This feeling did not yet reach my head, which smiled cynically. But I was no longer exactly the same man.

The rest of the entourage came in wearing bright clothes and garlands. They stowed my punt-shaped throne with food, wine, drugs and instruments. It is a big throne and when they climbed in themselves there was no overcrowding even though Tohu's nurse was there too. Then a horde of janitors arrived with long poles which they fixed to the sides of the throne, and I and my entourage were lifted into the air and carried out to the garden. The secretary sat in the prow playing a mouth-organ while the chef and doctor accompanied him with zither and drum. The janitors almost danced as they trampled across the maze, and this was so surprising that I laughed aloud, staring freely up at the pigeon-flecked azure sky, the porcelain gables with their coloured flags, the crowded tops of markets, temples and manufactories. Perhaps when I was small I had gazed as greedily for the mere useless fun of it, but for years I had only used my eyes professionally, to collect poetical knowledge, or shielded them, as required by the etiquette. 'Oh, Adoda!' I cried, warming my face in her hair, 'All this new knowledge is useless and I love it.'

She whispered, 'The use of living is the taste it gives. The emperor has made you the only free man in the world. You can taste anything you like.'

We entered a hall full of looms where thousands of women in coarse gowns were weaving rich tapestry. I was fascinated. The air was stifling, but not to me. Adoda and the chef plied their fans and the doctor refreshed me with a fine mist of cool water. I also had the benefit of janitors without kneebands, so our party was socially invisible; I could stare at whom I liked and they could not see me at all. I noticed a girl with pale brown hair toiling on one side. Adoda halted the janitors and whispered, 'That lovely girl is your sister who was sold to the merchants. She became a skilled weaver so they resold her here.'

I said, 'That is untrue. My sister would be over forty now and that girl, though robust, is not yet sixteen.'

'Would you like her to join us?'

I closed my eyes in the tolerant smile and a janitor negotiated with an overseer. When we moved on the girl was beside us. She was silent and frightened at first but we gave her garlands, food and wine and she soon became merry.

We came into a narrow street with a gallery along one side on the level of my throne. Tall elegant women in the robes of the court strolled and leaned there. A voice squeaked 'Hullo, Bohu' and looking up I saw the emperor smiling from the arms of the most slender and disdainful. I stared at him. He said 'Bohu hates me but I must suffer that. He is too great a man to be ordered by a poor old emperor. This lady, Bohu, is your aunt, a very wonderful courtesan. Say hullo!'

I laughed and said 'You are a liar, sir.'

He said 'Nonetheless you mean to take her from me. Join the famous poet, my dear, he goes down to the floating world. Goodbye, Bohu. I do not just give people death. That is only half my job.'

The emperor moved to a lady nearby, the slender one stepped among us and we all sailed on down the street.

We reached a wide river and the janitors waded in until the throne rested on the water. They withdrew the poles, laid them on the thwarts and we drifted out from shore. The doctor produced pipes and measured a careful dose into each bowl. We smoked and talked; the men played instruments, the women sang. The little weaver knew many popular songs, some sad, some funny. I suddenly wished Tohu was with us, and wept. They asked why. I told them and we all wept together. Twilight fell and a moon came out. The court lady stood up, lifted a pole and steered us expertly into a grove of willows growing in shallow water. Adoda hung lanterns in the branches. We ate, clasped each other, and slept.

I cannot count the following days. They may have been two, or three, or many. Opium plays tricks with time but I did not smoke enough to stop me loving. I loved in many ways, some tender, some harsh, some utterly absent-minded. More than once I said to Adoda, 'Shall we die now? Nothing can be sweeter than this' but she said 'Wait a little longer. You haven't done all you want yet.'

When at last my mind grew clear about the order of time the weaver and court lady had left us and we drifted down a tunnel to a bright arch at the end. We came into a lagoon on a lane of clear water between beds of rushes and lily-leaves. It led to an island covered with spires of marble and copper shining in the sun. My secretary said, 'That is the poets' pantheon. Would you like to land, sir?'

I nodded.

We disembarked and I strolled barefoot on warm moss between the spires. Each had an open door in the base with steps down to the tomb where the body would lie. Above each door was a white tablet where the poet's great work would be painted. All the tombs and tablets were vacant, of course, for I am the first poet in the new palace and was meant to be the greatest, for the tallest spire in the centre was sheathed in gold with my name on the door. I entered. The room downstairs had space for us all with cushions for the entourage and a silver throne for me.

'To deserve to lie here I must write a poem,' I thought, and looked into my mind. The poem was there, waiting to come out. I returned upstairs, went outside and told the secretary to fetch paint and brushes from his satchel and go to the tablet. I then dictated my poem in a slow firm voice.

To The Emperor's Injustice

Scattered buttons and silks, a broken kite in the mud,
A child's yellow clogs cracked by the horses' hooves.
A land weeps for the head city, lopped by sabre, cracked by hooves,
The houses ash, the people meat for crows.

A week ago wind rustled dust in the empty market.
'Starve,' said the moving dust, 'Beg. Rebel. Starve. Beg. Rebel.'
We do not do such things. We are peaceful people.
We have food for six more days, let us wait.
The emperor will accommodate us, underground.

It is sad to be unnecessary.
All the bright mothers, strong fathers, raffish aunts,
Lost sisters and brothers, all the rude servants
Are honoured guests of the emperor, underground.

We sit in the tomb now. The door is closed, the only light is the red glow from the chef's charcoal stove. My entourage dreamily puff their pipes, the doctor's fingers sift the dried herbs, the secretary is ending my last letter. We are tired and happy. The emperor said I could write what I liked. Will my poem be broadcast? No. If that happened the common peole would rise and destroy that evil little puppet and all the cunning, straightfaced, pompous men who use him. Nobody will read my words but a passing gardener, perhaps, who will paint them out to stop them reaching the emperor's ear. But I have at last made the poem I was made to make. I lie down to sleep in perfect satisfaction.

Goodbye. I still love you.
Your son,
Bohu.

DICTATED SOMETIME SHORTLY BEFORE
THE LAST DAY
OF THE OLD CALENDAR.

LAST LETTER

A CRITICAL APPRECIATION OF THE POEM
BY THE LATE TRAGEDIAN BOHU
ENTITLED

THE EMPEROR'S INJUSTICE

DELIVERED
TO THE IMPERIAL COLLEGE OF HEADMASTERS,
NEW PALACE UNIVERSITY

My dear Colleagues, This is exactly the poem we require. Our patience in waiting for it till the last possible moment has been rewarded. The work is shorter than we expected, but that makes distribution easier. It had a starkness unusual in government poetry, but this starkness satisfies the nation's need much more than the work we hoped for. With a single tiny change the poem can be used at once. I know some of my colleagues will raise objections, but I will answer these in the course of my appreciation.

A noble spirit of pity blows through this poem like a warm wind. The destroyed people are not mocked and calumniated, we identify with them, and the third line:

A land weeps for the head city, lopped by sabre, cracked by hooves,

invites the whole empire to mourn. But does this wind of pity fan the flames of political protest? No. It presses the mind of the reader inexorably toward *nothing*, toward death. This is clearly shown in the poem's treatment of rebellion:

'Starve,' said the moving dust, 'Beg. Rebel. Starve. Beg. Rebel.'
We do not do such things. We are peaceful people.
We have food for six more days, let us wait.

The poem assumes that a modern population will find the prospect of destruction by their own government less alarming than action against it. The truth of this is shown in today's police report from the old capital. It describes crowds of people muttering at street corners and completely uncertain of what action to take. They have a little food left. They fear the worst, yet hope, if they stay docile, the emperor will not destroy them immediately. This state of things was described by Bohu yesterday in the belief that it had happened a fortnight ago! A poet's intuitive grasp of reality was never more clearly demonstrated.

At this point the headmaster of civil peace will remind me that the job of the poem is not to describe reality but to encourage our friends, frighten our enemies, and reconcile the middling people to the destruction of the old capital. The headmaster of moral philosophy will also remind me of our decision that people will most readily accept the destruction of the old capital if we accuse it of rebellion. That was certainly the main idea in the original order-to-write, but I would remind the college of what we had to do to the the poet who obeyed that order. Tohu knew exactly what we wanted and gave it to us. His poem described the emperor as wise, witty, venerable, patient, loving and omnipotent. He described the citizens of the old capital as stupid, childish, greedy, absurd, yet inspired by a vast communal lunacy which endangered the empire. He obediently wrote a popular melodrama which could not convince a single intelligent man and would only over-excite stupid ones, who are fascinated by criminal lunatics who attack the established order.

The problem is this. If we describe the people we kill as dangerous rebels they look glamorous; if we describe them as weak and silly we seem unjust. Tohu could not solve that problem. Bohu has done with startling simplicity.

He presents the destruction as a simple, stunning, inevitable fact. The child, mother and common people in the poem exist passively, doing nothing but weep, gossip, and wait. The active agents of hoof, sabre, and (by extension) crow, belong to the emperor, who is named at the end of the middle verse:

> *The emperor will accommodate us, underground.*

and at the end of the last:

> *Bright mothers, strong fathers . . . all the rude servants*
> *Are honoured guests of the emperor, underground.*

Consider the *weight* this poem gives to our immortal emperor! He is not described or analysed, he is presented as a final, competent, all-embracing force, as unarguable as the weather, as inevitable as death. This is how all governments should appear to people who are not in them.

To sum up, THE EMPEROR'S INJUSTICE will delight our friends, depress our enemies, and fill middling people with nameless awe. The only change required is the elimination of the first syllable in the last word of the title. I advise that the poem be sent today to every village, town and city in the land. At the same time Fieldmarshal Ko should be ordered to destroy the old capital. When the poem appears over doors of public buildings the readers will read of an event which is occurring simultaneously. In this way the literary and military sides of the attack will reinforce each other with unusual thoroughness. Fieldmarshal Ko should take special care that the poet's parents do not escape the general massacre, as a rumour to that effect will lessen the poignancy of the official biography, which I will complete in the coming year.

I remain your affectionate colleague,
Gigadib,
Headmaster of modern and classic literature.

DICTATED ON DAY 1 OF THE NEW CALENDAR

Saki

No one knows why Hector Hugh Munro (1870–1916), called himself Saki but he used the pseudonym when he published his first volume of Reginald stories in 1904 and continued to use it for his subsequent fictions.

He was born in Burma of Scottish parents, and although he is often referred to as an English writer, there are many Scottish themes, connections and most especially attitudes in his work. He went back to Burma at twenty-three, to work as a military policeman, but was invalided home to London within a year, and turned to writing to earn a living.

Munro had been raised in North Devon by two aunts after his mother died, and at times his work seems to speak for the period before the First World War when, for one class at least, life was slow, peaceful and well-mannered. Yet he is best remembered for his macabre or supernatural pieces and, better than anyone, he can use humour or a series of outrageous premises to make a serious point.

'Sredni Vashtar' is from his third collection of stories, *The Chronicles of Clovis* (1912). There may well be shades of his strict upbringing in North Devon in the tale, but he returns to the theme and develops it in later volumes, obviously warming to the idea of animals as agents of revenge against mankind.

Munro enlisted as a trooper in 1914 and two years later he was shot through the head while resting in a shallow crater somewhere in France.

Sredni Vashtar

CONRADIN WAS ten years old, and the doctor had pronounced his professional opinion that the boy would not live another five years. The doctor was silky and effete, and counted for little, but his opinion was endorsed by Mrs De Ropp, who counted for nearly everything. Mrs De Ropp was Conradin's cousin and guardian, and in his eyes she represented those three-fifths of the world that are necessary and disagreeable and real; the other two-fifths, in perpetual antagonism to the foregoing, were summed up in himself and his imagination. One of these days Conradin supposed he would succumb to the mastering pressure of wearisome necessary things—such as illnesses and coddling restrictions and drawn-out dullness. Without his imagination, which was rampant under the spur of loneliness, he would have succumbed long ago.

Mrs De Ropp would never, in her honestest moments, have confessed to herself that she disliked Conradin, though she might have been dimly aware that thwarting him 'for his good' was a duty which she did not find particularly irksome. Conradin hated her with a desperate sincerity which he was perfectly able to mask. Such few pleasures as he could contrive for himself gained an added relish from the likelihood that they would be displeasing to his guardian, and from the realm of his imagination she was locked out—an unclean thing, which should find no entrance.

In the dull, cheerless garden, overlooked by so many windows that were ready to open with a message not to do this or that, or a reminder that medicines were due, he found little attraction. The few fruit-trees that it contained were set jealously apart from his plucking, as though they were rare specimens of their kind blooming in an arid waste; it would probably have been difficult to find a market-gardener who would have offered ten shillings for their entire yearly produce. In a forgotten corner, however, almost hidden behind a dismal shrubbery, was a disused tool-shed of respectable proportions, and within its walls Conradin found a haven, something that took on the varying aspects of a playroom and a cathedral. He had peopled it with a legion of familiar phantoms, evoked partly from fragments of history and partly from his own brain, but it also boasted two inmates of flesh and blood. In one corner lived a ragged-plumaged Houdan hen, on which the boy lavished an affection that had scarcely another outlet. Further back in the gloom stood a large hutch, divided into two compartments, one of which was fronted with close iron bars. This was the abode of a large polecat-ferret, which a friendly butcher-boy had once smuggled, cage and all, into its present quarters, in exchange for a long-secreted hoard of small silver. Conradin was dreadfully afraid of the lithe, sharp-fanged beast, but it was his most treasured possession. Its very presence in the tool-shed was a secret and fearful joy, to be kept scrupulously from the knowledge of the Woman, as he privately dubbed his cousin. And one day, out of Heaven knows what material, he spun the beast a wonderful name, and from that moment it grew into a god and a religion. The Woman indulged in religion once a week at a church near by, and took Conradin with her, but to him the church service was an alien rite in the House of Rimmon. Every Thursday, in the dim and musty silence of the tool-shed, he worshipped with mystic and elaborate ceremonial before the wooden hutch where dwelt Sredni Vashtar, the great ferret. Red flowers in their season and scarlet berries in the winter-time were offered at his shrine, for he was a god who laid some special stress on the fierce impatient side of things, as opposed to the Woman's religion, which, as far as Conradin could observe, went to great lengths in the contrary direction. And on great festivals powdered nutmeg was strewn in front of his hutch, an important feature of the offering being that the nutmeg had to be stolen. These festivals were of irregular occurrence, and were chiefly appointed to celebrate some passing event. On one occasion, when Mrs De Ropp suffered from acute toothache for three days, Conradin kept up the festival during the entire three days, and almost succeeded in persuading himself that Sredni Vashtar was personally responsible for the toothache. If the malady had lasted for another day the supply of nutmeg would have given out.

The Houdan hen was never drawn into the cult of Sredni Vashtar. Conradin had long ago settled that she was an Anabaptist. He did not pretend to have the remotest knowledge as to what an Anabaptist was, but he privately hoped that it was dashing and not very respectable. Mrs De Ropp was the ground plan on which he based and detested all respectability.

After a while Conradin's absorption in the tool-shed began to attract the notice of his guardian. 'It is not good for him to be pottering down there in all weathers,' she promptly decided, and at breakfast one morning she announced that the Houdan hen had been sold and taken away overnight. With her short-sighted eyes she peered at Conradin, waiting for an outbreak of rage and sorrow, which she was ready to rebuke with a flow of excellent precepts and reasoning. But Conradin said nothing: there was nothing to be said. Something perhaps in his white set face gave her a momentary qualm, for at tea that afternoon there was toast on the table, a delicacy which she usually banned on the ground that it was bad for him; also because the making of it 'gave trouble', a deadly offence in the middle-class feminine eye.

'I thought you liked toast,' she exclaimed, with an injured air, observing that he did not touch it.

'Sometimes,' said Conradin.

In the shed that evening there was an innovation in the worship of the hutch-god. Conradin had been wont to chant his praises, tonight he asked a boon.

'Do one thing for me, Sredni Vashtar.'

The thing was not specified. As Sredni Vashtar was a god he must be supposed to know. And choking back a sob as he looked at that other empty corner, Conradin went back to the world he so hated.

And every night, in the welcome darkness of his bedroom, and every evening in the dusk of the tool-shed, Conradin's bitter litany went up: 'Do one thing for me, Sredni Vashtar.'

Mrs De Ropp noticed that the visits to the shed did not cease and one day she made a further journey of inspection.

'What are you keeping in that locked hutch?' she asked. 'I believe it's guinea-pigs. I'll have them all cleared away.'

Conradin shut his lips tight, but the Woman ransacked his bedroom till she found the carefully hidden key, and forthwith marched down to the shed to complete her discovery. It was a cold afternoon, and Conradin had been bidden to keep to the house. From the furthest window of the dining-room the door of the shed could just be seen beyond the corner of the shrubbery, and there Conradin stationed himself. He saw the Woman enter, and then he imagined her opening the door of the sacred hutch and peering down with her short-sighted eyes into the thick straw bed where his god lay hidden. Perhaps she would prod at the straw in her clumsy impatience. And Conradin fervently breathed his prayer for the last time. But he knew as he prayed that he did not believe. He knew that the Woman would come out presently with that pursed smile he loathed so well on her face, and that in an hour or two the gardener would carry away his wonderful god, a god no longer, but a simple brown ferret in a hutch. And he knew that the Woman would triumph always as she triumphed now, and that he would grow ever more sickly under her pestering and domineering and superior wisdom, till one day nothing would matter much more with him, and the doctor would be proved right. And in the sting and misery of his defeat, he began to chant loudly and defiantly the hymn of his threatened idol:

Sredni Vashtar went forth,
His thoughts were red thoughts and his teeth were white.
His enemies called for peace, but he brought them death.
Sredni Vashtar the Beautiful.

And then of a sudden he stopped his chanting and drew closer to the window-pane. The door of the shed still stood ajar as it had been left, and the minutes were slipping by. They were long minutes, but they slipped by nevertheless. He watched the starlings running and flying in little parties across the lawn; he counted them over and over again, with one eye always on that swinging door. A sour-faced maid came in to lay the table for tea, and still Conradin stood and waited and watched. Hope had crept by inches into his heart, and now a look of triumph began to blaze in his eyes that had only known the wistful patience of defeat. Under his breath, with a furtive exultation, he began once again the paean of victory and devastation. And presently his eyes were rewarded: out through the doorway came a long, low, yellow-and-brown beast, with eyes a-blink at the waning daylight, and dark wet stains around the fur of jaws and throat. Conradin dropped on his knees. The great polecat-ferret made its way down to a small brook at the foot of the garden, drank for a moment, then crossed a little plank bridge and was lost to sight in the bushes. Such was the passing of Sredni Vashtar.

'Tea is ready,' said the sour-faced maid; 'where is the mistress?'

'She went down to the shed some time ago,' said Conradin.

And while the maid went to summon her mistress to tea, Conradin fished a toasting fork out of the sideboard drawer and proceeded to toast himself a piece of bread. And during the toasting of it and the buttering of it with much butter and the slow enjoyment of eating it, Conradin listened to the noises and silences which fell in quick spasms beyond the dining-room door. The loud foolish screaming of the maid, the answering chorus of wondering ejaculations from the kitchen region, the scuttering footsteps and hurried embassies for outside help, and then, after a lull, the scared sobbings and the shuffling tread of those who bore a heavy burden into the house.

'Whoever will break it to the poor child? I couldn't for the life of me!' exclaimed a shrill voice. And while they debated the matter among themselves, Conradin made himself another piece of toast.

John Herdman

CLAPPERTON

John Herdman (b.1941), has made the exploration of a particular aspect of the Scottish psyche all his own. He approaches the small, insignificant incidents in our daily lives, then blows them into paranoic proportions and beyond. Taking all our previous national obsessions and concerns with duality for granted, he deals in anti-heroes, misfits, and grotesque characters plotting their own or someone else's downfall, while manically anxious about their appearance, or what others think of them. Yet we also find them questioning the morality of simple actions in a way that is surprisingly penetrating.

Far too crafty a writer to do more than nudge his readers, Herdman's main weapons in a considerably skilful armoury are irony and a humour whose serious undertones are only just below the surface. Born and educated in Edinburgh, with a spell at Cambridge, John Herdman has written a number of short stories, three novellas, *A Truth Lover*, *Pagan's Pilgrimage* and *Clapperton*, and a study of Bob Dylan's lyrics, *Voice Without Restraint*.

Clapperton

CLAPPERTON WOKE agreeably one December morning in a bed warmed down the middle by the heat of his extended body, and stretched out his feet towards the cool peripheries. Something was not quite right. His right foot felt somehow not entirely normal. The cold sensation of the sheet upon his skin was in some obscure and inexpressible way different from that in the left foot. This fact had registered itself as a shadow upon his consciousness, a slight draught playing upon the warmth of his well-being, even before he was properly awake.

From the beginning Clapperton had felt his body as a burden to him. His earliest reading matter being the Bible, he would, a child of seven, fearfully peruse the thirteenth and fourteenth chapters of Leviticus and examine his person for the marks of leprosy. 'And if, when the priest seeth it,' he read, 'behold, it *be* in sight lower than the skin, and the hair thereof turned white; the priest shall pronounce him unclean: it *is* a plague of leprosy broken out of the boil.' The most miniscule pluke was thereafter an object of terror, and he was seldom without his magnifying glass, in those days. Suffering from headaches from the first, he imagined the interior of his skull sprouting, like that of Schumann, stalactites of knife-sharp bone. If he cut his finger or scratched his knee, every twinge in his back presaged for him (since he disbelieved in growing pains) the arching of his body in the rigid bow of tetanus. Nipped once in the elbow by a dog, for six months he felt compelled to swallow endless glasses of water to confirm that hydrophobia had not closed his throat, and to cast nervous glances at naked light bulbs to see if convulsions would follow. Often in the wee small hours he felt the buboes of plague rising in his groins and oxters.

As he grew older his terrors grew less dramatic, more muted, but no less hideous. Harmless moles thickened before his eyes into black cancer, mouth ulcers seemed the sloughing lesions of leukaemia, the buzzing of his ears heralded the imminent explosion of aneurysms in his brain. He became a furtive prowler in medical bookshops; if an assistant looked at him curiously, propped weak and sweating in a corner, he would casually flick over the pages to examine the price. During all these years he had been the victim of nothing more deadly than varicose veins. A policy of reassurance, said the doctor, and he was endlessly reassured; yet always, after a month or two of buoyancy, another symptom would appear. He understood his madness, appreciated his near-perfect health, yet each new fear seemed a tempting of fate: I am a hypochondriac, I know, he said, but it is not impossible, after all, for even a hypochondriac to be, for once, genuinely ill. . . . His hypochondria was thus to Clapperton as his boulder to Sisyphus, a world of eternally repetitive misery.

So the strange sensation in his foot broke in upon his optimism and his peace of mind that morning like a stealthy enemy. His mood when he had gone to rest the previous night had been unusually benign, for he had been full of unexampled hopes for the morrow. The kernel of these hopes lay in his having secured for the coming evening, after long and taxing efforts, a date with Trudy Otter, the girl across the street. This was sufficient of a landmark in Clapperton's existence to lighten more than a little the accustomed murk of his dealings with a hostile world, and to infect him with an uncharacteristic and general optimism. His waking, then, had been entirely pleasurable, for once he had felt eager to rise and capable of confronting with defiance the day's realities. The feeling in his foot, a suppressed buzzing now it seemed to him, was like a mild chastening of such unwarranted presumption and confidence, a reminder that, Trudy Otter or no, he walked still upon the earth and was subject to the trials of the flesh. It was far from enough, however, to prevent him leaping energetically of a sudden from his bed, in two swift movements throwing back the covers and shutting the window, and moving precipitately towards the bathroom.

Clapperton was a man of indeterminate age, of whom Crazy Jane might have found it hard to say whether he was an old man young, or a young man old. Suffice it to observe that his youth, though surviving, was not in its first flush. The most striking feature of his physical appearance was its lack of self-consistency. His body seemed countlessly fractured, and its component parts—as if held together by no unitary principle but rather by an act of will upon which no absolute reliance might be placed—appeared anxious to hive off in independent directions. His movements consequently tended towards the erratic. He now lolloped shivering down the passage and gathered up the mail from the floor.

Clapperton's eye fell at once upon an envelope addressed in threatening red typescript, and he knew the letter it contained to be one which he had been awaiting for some days with eagerness and apprehension. He was by profession a zoologist, and at that date suspended on half-pay from his post as director of a small private zoo, a glorified menagerie it might better be termed, specialising in ungulates, and controlled by a committee presided over by a splenetic individual named Colonel Menteith Dudgeon. For several months a venomous correspondence had been passing to and fro between Clapperton and Colonel Dudgeon, rich in libels, slanders and defamations of character, in assertions and counter-assertions, in threats and calumnies, in bluff talk of lawsuits and interim interdicts and veiled hints of blackmail. The specific origin of the differences between Clapperton and the committee was now obscured by the mists of time and overlaid by impenetrable accretions of argument, but the long and short of it lay in this, that Clapperton believed he was being ousted by Colonel Dudgeon because of the latter's inchoate resentment of his innate superiority, whereas Colonel Dudgeon believed that Clapperton was an impudent young coxcomb who was exceeding the limits of his responsibilities and must be taught to know his place. Objectively, all that need be said is that Clapperton's face simply did not fit with the committee. That it should not have fitted was not perhaps altogether outrageous, for it had to be admitted that it was a singularly odd one. Clapperton knew, at any rate, that he was in the right in these matters, but at times he was assailed by doubts of a metaphysical nature. Was he, for instance, in the scrupulously intelligent refutations he had penned to the bombastic outpourings of Colonel Dudgeon, guilty of the sin of intellectual pride? Was he not positively exulting in his rightness? Was his concern motivated by the love of truth, or by the dictates of an assertive will? Such were the considerations which lifted this episode from the level of a squalid and petty local squabble to realms of lofty and impersonal moral grandeur. But they are boring considerations and we shall pass them over. Enough to note that Clapperton's last letter, an effusion of nine and a half sides of foolscap, had been a model of uncompromising clarity and concision, countering undisciplined abuse with remorseless and unremitting logic, and that he was breathless to learn its effect.

Recalled to a sense of proportion however by the knowledge that tonight he was to be the escort of Trudy Otter, he contemptuously laid the letter aside until he had thoroughly washed himself, cleaned his teeth, and shaved selected areas of his face. Only then did he wrap himself in his dressing-gown and return to his bedroom to read the letter. It proved to be from Colonel Dudgeon's private secretary and read as follows:

> Clapperton:
>
> I write on behalf of Colonel Menteith Dudgeon who is confined to a couch of sickness. As you know, though doubtless do not care, he has been ailing for some time: his improvement had recently been such that we had entertained high hopes of his early recovery, but on receipt of your infamous letter he suffered a relapse and has now taken to his bed once more.
>
> Clapperton! You are dealing with a highly sensitive man; just how sensitive, perhaps only those who come into close and daily contact with him can realise. As for you, you are a noted misanthropist, anglophobe and *malade imaginaire*; your

recent actions constitute a public scandal and fall not far short of criminal behaviour. You are a conceited and vain young fool and it would not surprise me to hear that you were guilty of self-abuse. Clapperton! If I were a man you would receive the thrashing you so richly deserve.

Edith Vole.

PS You are rotten in your soul.

Clapperton sat still upon the edge of his bed and gazed at this missive. His bedroom slipper seemed to be exerting an odd pressure upon the top of his right foot. He was at once outraged, vaguely amused, staggered at Miss Vole's immunity to logic, and nonplussed as to how to deal with such towering folly; but mainly he was hurt, deeply hurt, hurt to the quick and almost to the point of wanting to cry. Self-abuse! When he was seen walking down the streets with Trudy Otter resplendent upon his arm, they would see then whether he could be suspected of self-abuse. His face was red and his foot was buzzing. A blight had been cast upon his hopefulness and good humour.

He dressed quickly but meticulously in the raw cold of his bedroom, which was without a fire. That afternoon he would go to collect a small oil-heater which had long ago been promised him by his aged great-aunt. The visit was one which he had been postponing for weeks because of the considerable expenditure of his limited nervous resources which he knew that conversation with this old lady would involve. He reflected now that a price must be paid for everything enjoyed in this life, and that winter was approaching, and he began to prepare himself mentally for the ordeal ahead.

When he had dressed, Clapperton prepared and ate a light breakfast, his boiled egg exploding in the course of heating. Boiled eggs, or rather about-to-be-boiled eggs, almost always did that to Clapperton; they appeared to harbour a grudge against him. Having washed up he walked for an inordinate time in circles around his small sitting-room and up and down the passage, thinking about Trudy Otter, and occasionally looking cautiously out of the window towards the residence of the Otters on the other side of the street. For some months past he had been visiting this admirable family regularly once a fortnight in order to deliver a political newsletter and to drink a cup of hot chocolate.

Clapperton never tired of contemplating the beauty of the domestic arrangements which prevailed in that estimable household. There was no direct communication whatever, verbal or otherwise, between Mr Otter, a retired police sergeant of a chilling disposition, and his spouse. Their sense of each other's existence was registered instead by waves of palpable antipathy which passed to and fro from time to time between Mr Otter's straight-backed chair in the window, where he sat sullenly playing solitaire or reading such sections of his newspaper as had a bearing on law and order, and the corner of the sofa at the opposite end of the room, facing the television, where reposed Mrs Otter's weary limbs, the upper pair of which knitted compulsively throughout the evening. Such a wave of antipathy might be occasioned for instance by a vigorous rustle of the newspaper by Mr Otter, by a click from his false teeth as he drained his coffee cup, or by one of his frequent full-chested coughs. Whenever Mrs Otter spoke, to her son or daughter or to Clapperton, Mr Otter would begin to shake his head in an ostentatious fashion and affect a supercilious smile, perhaps at the same time emitting a humourless laughing noise, a performance intended to convey his contempt for his wife's supposed inanity. If Mrs Otter was watching television he would find occasion to go constantly in and out of the room in order to pass in front of her line of vision. The disruption of viewing which she suffered as a result of this behaviour was fully compensated for by the pleasure she derived from stonily ignoring it, staring expressionlessly ahead of her as if her husband were composed of thin air instead of all too solid flesh. The waves of antipathy were, however, very powerful at such times.

If Mr Otter found it necessary to make reference to members of his family in the course of the few sentences he might speak to Clapperton, he would always refer to them collectively as 'they', as if their individual personalities were submerged in the totality of a family unit which had its being in opposition to himself. Through Clapperton he could communicate to them without having to address them, which was useful. A certain hothouse quality could also be detected in the air around the area of the hearth, where the daughter Trudy was accustomed to sit at the feet of her brother Rex, but the cause of this lay not in the pleasures of hatred but in the pains of love, for their relationship was tragically incestuous. There existed in short in the Otter household an atmosphere which made Clapperton feel relaxed, confident and on top of the world.

The delectable Trudy spent these evenings flirting with Clapperton, but not of course out of any interest in his ridiculous person, but in order to induce a state of jealousy in Rex, with whom she had always had a tiff. So she would sit close to her brother but looking away from him, looking always at Clapperton but removed from him by distance, and thus she would flirt with Clapperton. She spoke to him but her words were all for Rex. The latter always succeeded in appearing to ignore her, looking steadfastly in the opposite direction as he listened intently, and only from time to time making a vicious gibe at Clapperton. He, though seething within, never made any outward reaction to these gibes, preferring to leave Otter in doubt as to whether he had taken the point, whether the admirable shafts had reached home. Rex on his part, learning to anticipate this disappointing response, would betray by no indication that his remark had been intended as a shaft. Stalemate, then; but occasionally Rex's colossal fists would clench and unclench, and it was clear that he was contemplating the voluptuous pleasure he would derive from beating Clapperton's odd features into some semblance of order. Clapperton rather enjoyed the experience of being a sufficiently substantial person to arouse in another the desire to smash his face in; besides he had something of a daring nature, Clapperton, he liked to take risks, if they were gentle risks, risks which could be approached with caution.

His pleasure on these occasions would be tempered only by the presence of a Persian blue cat, vast and relentless, its eyes full of a dull and stubborn malice, which would invariably leap up on his lap where it would keep up an unremitting vigil, a torpid burden upon the meagre stirrings of Clapperton's manhood. Whenever he got up he experienced great difficulty in removing this animal, for it would dig its claws into his clothing and hang on for grim death; sometimes, indeed, the scene could be witnessed of Clapperton proceeding doubled up on his way out of the room, a huge cat suspended from his person, until he got out of the door, when he would dislodge it with a restrained blow from a paperweight, or a modified karate chop which he had developed specially for the purpose.

During the course of these repeated visits Clapperton had become gradually but heavily smitten with Trudy Otter, to the extent indeed that he believed himself to be in love. Perhaps he was not mistaken in this, for it would be wrong to suppose that, ridiculous though he was, Clapperton was incapable of love. The unworthy object of his desires was a honey blonde with a peaches-and-cream complexion and green eyes, of middle height and a figure good but well-covered, inclining very slightly to the fleshy, but not to an objectionable degree. Her conversation revealed her to be adequately sensitive but not overly intelligent. All of these qualities added up more or less to Clapperton's ideal of female desirability, for he was a conventional soul, Clapperton, in some respects. At first he had accepted that Trudy was bound to her brother Rex by unspeakable and indissoluble ties; a situation to which he had readily reconciled himself, for Clapperton always preferred his loves to be hopeless and inaccessible: that forestalled the possibility of disappointment. A week previously, however, the situation had changed decisively.

It happened thus. In the local grocer's shop one morning Clapperton found himself standing behind Trudy in a queue, and as she bought her wares he began to be incommoded by the attentions of the Otter family dog, a Shetland collie with a delicate pointed muzzle of great length, called John. John had previously been standing placidly behind Trudy, but on a sudden impulse he now began to nuzzle and prod at Clapperton's crotch with his long nose. Backing rapidly away in the face of these unwelcome attentions, by ill fortune he first stepped heavily on the toes of a woman standing behind him, causing her to cry out in a petulant but refined agony, and then, retreating still before the advancing muzzle, walked sideways into a huge pile of soup tins awaiting their disposal on the shelves, and brought them to earth with a mighty roar. In the ensuing mêlee Clapperton came into exciting physical contact with a Trudy contrite for the effects of her dog's excesses, and sympathetically anxious to help Clapperton survive his acute and bitter embarrassment; and somehow it came about that they left the shop in each other's company. Clapperton offered to carry Trudy's groceries for her, having a vague idea that this was the sort of thing a gentleman did for a lady; and the lady was grateful, needing both hands to control the unruly John, for whom Clapperton's crotch was still exerting a horrid fascination. At the door of the Otter house, however, the fickle creature deserted him in favour of the railings, enabling the two humans to stand for some moments exchanging pleasantries, which gradually degenerated on Clapperton's side into tortured incoherencies as he realised with terror that he was facing an unrivalled opportunity to ask Trudy for a date. Just as he was about to take flight in panic before this challenge, Trudy, who had that morning had a severe altercation with Rex, came to his aid by inviting herself to dinner with him the following Wednesday. 'It would be better if you didn't pick me up here,' she said without waiting for his acquiescence, 'meet me at Scarlatti's at 7.30.' This Clapperton took as a reference to Rex, so he indicated his compliance with a grateful gulp. As he turned to say goodbye while stepping off the pavement he unluckily knocked down a bicycle propped against the kerb, and then avoided by inches an ignominious death beneath the wheels of a passing milk-float.

The week since these events had passed for Clapperton in a turmoil of nervous apprehension. It must be explained that our hero's experience of the opposite sex was somewhat limited. Some months previously, feeling perhaps that life was passing him by, he had belatedly entered upon the sexual life by commencing visits to a brothel. He had had to come to an arrangement with the madam whereby he agreed to pay three times the normal charge, because of the inordinate time it took him to attain the conditions necessary for the successful achievement of coitus. Great was his envy of the petty businessmen who drove down to the brothel every evening after work, left their cars double-parked, and in cold weather sometimes even with the engines running, in, in and out, and out again, and home in time for tea.

Leaving aside these commercial amours, his only previous encounter had been with a large girl at a party many years before. She had followed him into a small study whither he had retreated for solitude, and seating herself beside him on a sofa engaged him in conversation. This proved a taxing experience since conversation was not Clapperton's long suit. Finding him unresponsive she had begun to insult and vilify him in indirect ways. Clapperton was insufficiently experienced in affairs of the heart to understand that the behaviour of this large female had its origin not in disgust with his person or personality, well-founded though such disgust might have been, but in resentment at the lack of interest which he was exhibiting in hers. Great then had been his surprise when in spite of all her insults her hand had come to rest upon his thigh.

Worse was to come. Feeling it incumbent upon him to make some token response to this potent gesture, Clapperton had advanced his face an inch or two closer to hers, and allowed the corners of his mouth to twitch enigmatically. On this slight prompting and without warning she had plunged her tongue into his mouth to a great depth, to the region of his tonsils, or where they would have been had he retained them. He was rather taken aback, but in spite of his surprise—for he was always a quick learner—had responded promptly, energetically, and in kind. Not that he derived any vestige of pleasure from the exercise. On the contrary, during the course of this and subsequent embraces he had taken care so to position his head that he could, to relieve the boredom, study the titles of the books on the shelves opposite him, while his partner's eyes remained rapturously closed. Eventually he had taken advantage of a slight ebb in the tides of passion to excuse himself with the words, 'All that beer', and departed never to return.

Restless and unsettled, Clapperton set off about midday for an early lunch. When he reached the public house he found that his favourite table was occupied by a group of English business executives. That it was occupied was bad enough, that it was occupied by a group of English business executives was beyond endurance. Small things like that had a profound effect upon Clapperton; they became symbols, fraught with baleful significance. A pall of gloom settled upon his spirit, a sort of end-of-the-world feeling. A claustrophobic sensation seized him, impelling him to be off and on his way. Viciously he attacked his bridie and swilled it down half-chewed with great gulps of beer. Then he stormed out of the pub and began walking away from the city centre towards the western suburbs where his great-aunt lived. Clapperton was at his best when walking. Not that he was a pleasant sight for the eyes of man while engaged in that activity, but within himself he was at his best. He walked very fast with great loose strides, outstripping all rivals, his head craning forward and his eyes bent on the ground, often half-tripping as he stubbed his toe against some irregularity of the pavement, but surging on regardless. Only while walking could Clapperton keep at bay the threats which from all sides impinged upon him, the swift motion absorbing the excesses of his inner energy. It was some four miles to his great-aunt's house but he covered the ground rapidly. As he walked the world once more brightened for him a little, though the day was cold, raw, and overcast. He thought of Trudy and looked ahead with pleasure. Even his foot seemed to have settled down;

perhaps it was merely a circulatory disturbance, dispelled by exercise. For a time Clapperton even sang to himself a sonorous hymn tune. As he neared his destination however he had to suffer another affliction; a child who ran ahead of him then stopped, let him pass it then ran ahead again, and so on a great many times, until he thirsted for vengeance, and walked with fists clenched and grinding teeth.

At last Clapperton stood, ill at ease, at the front door of his great-aunt's house and rang the bell. There was no response, so he tried the handle: it turned, and he walked in. He had not taken two steps into the hallway before a Dutch barge-dog called Trixie, a cross between a tailless black rat and an animated prune, launched itself snarling and with bared teeth at his ankles. Clapperton's large and flat foot met it in full career, and it described a shrieking parabola through the fetid air. Landing at the far end of the hall it fled screaming into the kitchen. Clapperton then looked into various rooms but found no one about, so he stood at the foot of the stairs and shouted his great-aunt's name, without conviction or much hope of a reply. Aunt Hetty was ninety-six years old, 85% blind, 95% deaf, semi-paralysed and limitlessly incontinent. Far from dumb however. Her daily needs were attended to by one Bairnsfather, a respectable man in late middle age. At this juncture, as Clapperton stood uncertain how to proceed, Bairnsfather appeared descending the stairs, and doing up his fly-buttons. 'She's up the stair,' he observed laconically, with a jerk of his thumb in that direction, and disappeared into the kitchen.

Clapperton went up and entered Aunt Hetty's bedroom, where he found her sitting swathed in rugs and shawls beside her bed, a sordid monument amid the tasteless bric-à-brac. She was unaware of his presence and he stood there for a few moments observing her. She appeared to be in a state of suspended animation, though her mouth made damp movements from time to time, her dewlaps quivering peacefully. She had smeared her face with powder which lay there in clotted patches like flour. Clapperton did not like his great-aunt and his great-aunt did not like Clapperton, whom she considered an eccentric. All dealings and discourse with Aunt Hetty were dominated by the fact of her age, to the extent that she had ceased to be an individual and become a recalcitrant act of nature. It was impossible to speak with her without being aware that she was an old marvel, a living miracle, really wonderful, without considerations of her extraordinary mental alertness, her extreme touchiness, her indomitable will and so forth. Consequently she was accustomed to getting away with murder. Clapperton found her impossible to deal with, and now he had no idea how to begin conversation with her.

'Hello!' he bellowed from a few feet away.

Several seconds later Aunt Hetty gave a start and looked blindly in his direction. 'Is that you, James?' she asked in a piercing quaver. 'I thought I heard Trixie give a wee squeak.'

'No,' Clapperton shouted back at her, 'it's not James, it's Thomas, it's your great-nephew, Thomas Clapperton, and I have come for the oil-heater which you so kindly promised me.'

'Oh, it's you, Thomas,' came her muted scream, 'you never come and see me.'

Thinking of the oil-heater and of his neglect, Clapperton felt it expedient to kiss her and he bent down, holding his breath. When his hand took hold of her upper arm he felt through the layers of shawl a loosely-hanging pouch of skin with no flesh inside it. Kissing was not something which came easily to Clapperton, even under the most propitious circumstances, and these circumstances were not propitious. He aimed for a spot on her cheek free from the clogged patches of powder, but she turned her mouth to his and their moustaches mingled. Aunt Hetty laughed a quavering and humourless laugh as Clapperton extracted himself from this embrace.

'What have you come for?' she asked.

Clapperton was now well beyond the decencies of civilised discourse. 'Oil-heater!' he shrieked.

Her sightless eyes shone with complacent malice.

'Oh, the oil-heater,' she replied, 'I'm afraid I've given it away. I didn't think you were coming, so I gave it to Bairnsfather. Have you met my man Bairnsfather? A wonderful man, terribly strong. He's a great big Highlander, you know, six-foot-four and very handsome.'

The truth was that Bairnsfather was a Lowlander, a native in fact of Easthouses, Midlothian, five-foot-seven in height and unexceptional in features. Aunt Hetty's late husband, however, had been six-foot-one, moderately handsome and of distant Highland extraction. He remained her model of what a man should be, and, touchingly enough no doubt, she had recreated Bairnsfather in his image.

No oil-heater! Clapperton directed at his great-aunt a look of unadulterated hatred, and walked from the room without a word, fighting back the tears; distantly an angry peal of thunder rumbled, and outside large infrequent drops of rain began to splash on the pavement, for God had taken cognisance of Clapperton's discomfiture. He floundered down the stairs and through the hall, and rigid with rage and vexation began to stride down the garden path; the dog Trixie, who had ventured out to the front door, scuttled before him fouling the pathway in her terror, obliging Clapperton to stot gracelessly about the flagstones from foot to foot, sometimes so misjudging the distance that he landed, with a dull squelch, in that which he sought to avoid. In this manner he reached the garden gate and turned his face towards home.

So. Clapperton had the evening carefully planned. A leisurely aperitif or two, an intimate candle-lit dinner at Scarlatti's, good conversation, a little courtly dalliance, perhaps a brandy or a kümmel with the coffee; and then they would proceed to the Foggos' party. That was what he was really picturing to himself: his entry into the Foggos' drawing-room with Trudy Otter on his arm, and then Carmen's face when she saw them. At one time, it must be explained, Clapperton had hoped to marry Carmen. Objectively speaking, of course, he had no conceivable justification for any such aspiration; but we can all hope, can we not? And in youth it is all hope, our lives are but dazzling mosaics of giddy imaginings.

Well, then . . . that Carmen should have married someone else, that Clapperton could no doubt have accepted; but that she should have married Foghorn Foggo was beyond all endurance. But tonight, tonight she would appreciate what she had lost. She would understand, tonight, exactly what might have been. She would see him enter the room with Trudy Otter on his arm, her mouth would drop open just a little—not much, only a very little—perhaps her colour might change almost imperceptibly. She would fix him long and hard with her grey-blue eyes, she would hold out her elegant hand in greeting: then she would glance to her left and see Foggo, see the infamous and vulgar Foghorn ogling *his* young lady, and a wave of black despair would surge up in her soul. . . .

Inflated with such conjectures, at twenty-five past seven sharp Clapperton arrived scrubbed, shaven and smartly dressed at Scarlatti's Italian restaurant. He was nervous, but in full control of his faculties. He entered the cocktail bar, ordered a medium sherry, and settled himself comfortably to wait. At twenty-five to eight he looked at his watch. He knew that it was a lady's prerogative to be late. At twenty to eight he bought himself another sherry, and as its level dropped and no Trudy appeared his nervousness increased and he began to cross and uncross his legs too frequently and to peer anxiously at the door every time someone came in. He endeavoured, however, to maintain a casual pose for the benefit of the barman, before whom he was beginning to feel conspicuous. He did not want to buy another sherry before Trudy arrived, but his apprehension was making him drink faster than usual. At three minutes to eight he got up and went outside, and gazed up and down the street for some time. No Trudy Otter hove into sight. Then he went back to the bar and bought a third sherry. By five past eight the idea was establishing itself in his mind that he had been stood up, and at ten past he knew for certain that Trudy would not come. With this realisation his agitation began to leave him: things were returning to normal. Nevertheless he continued to wait on, reluctant to admit that it was all over, anxious to give Trudy every chance, determined that it should never be said that he had deserted his post. At eight-fifteen, however, he rose. Clapperton was not prepared to wait that length of time for anyone, certainly not for someone as fat as Trudy Otter.

Clapperton entered the restaurant and stood in painful embarrassment within the doorway, waiting to be shown to his table. He would have preferred, because of the obscenity of his head, to have been invisible, for the previous day he had had his hair cut. Clapperton was really satisfied with the state of his hair only for brief periods of ten days or so midway between haircuts, which took place at roughly monthly intervals. For any marked departure in either direction from the optimum desirable hair-length rendered his head obscene, in Clapperton's opinion. Could he not then have had his hair cut strictly to this optimum length, rather than shorter? No, because that would have necessitated its being cut more frequently, at fortnightly rather than monthly intervals, which would have been insupportable to him. Besides which it is almost impossible, if a short styling is desired, to persuade a barber not to crop the back of the neck; and in Clapperton's view the faculty of barbering, in a barber, came second, though a close second, to the faculty of silence. And in this world you can never have everything. Thus it was that always after a haircut Clapperton was for a time reluctant to exhibit the state of his head in public, until the passage of days had mitigated to some degree its obscenity.

A waiter at last appeared and Clapperton gave his name. The waiter however had difficulty in understanding it.

'Ah, yes, two, sir, no?' he said at last, after consulting his book.

'One now,' Clapperton replied rudely, and suffered the grim journey to his solitary table with set jaw and downcast eyes. He ordered Schnitzel Holstein and a bottle of Beaujolais, and as he waited the humiliation of his position began to stab at him. His first reaction to his jilting had been one of relief, as if he had been released from a taxing obligation, but Clapperton was not a man to be satisfied for long. It came upon him that once more he was alone, that he was the only lone diner in the restaurant, that most of the others indeed were couples, young couples in the main. His table was of course set for two, and it seemed to him that all the other diners had noticed this and were talking about him in whispers and giggles, making obscene cracks about him from behind their hands.

So rather than have to look upon the humanity assembled around him and suffer their insolent gaze in return, in a desperate attempt to seclude himself he drew from his pocket the letter from Edith Vole, and perused it with bitter distaste. Its ringing, confident phrases clanged in his ear, taunting him and vilifying him. 'You are a conceited and vain young fool and it would not surprise me to hear that you were guilty of self-abuse.' Every time he looked up some commonplace young man was leering towards him and whispering to his companion that Clapperton was a conceited and vain young fool who looked as if he were guilty of self-abuse, but not to look now, and after gazing with sheep's eyes at her lover the girl would crane her neck round adroitly towards Clapperton and quickly turn away again with a smothered snigger to her lover's eyes. Clapperton felt a profound hatred stir within him for the whole race of women.

Inflamed with anger and distress he fell to eating Schnitzel Holstein with voracious appetite and to swilling red wine at a high speed. His foot had begun buzzing again. As he ate he was made aware of the obtrusive presence, at a table a little distance to his left, of an Englishman. This yapping, yelping creature was making himself heard at no inconsiderable distance in giving an account to his party of guests of the events of his Highland tour. It was perhaps inevitable that the sum of Clapperton's pain, anger and annoyance should be gathered together into a pure and single hatred of this innocent and inoffensive personage, who remained oblivious of the emotion he was arousing even when Clapperton, having finished eating and being sufficiently drunk, swung his chair round to face him, and resting his elbow on the table and his chin on his hand, concentrated upon him a look of relentless malice.

What Clapperton stood in need of at this juncture was the restraining influence of a little woman, who would soothe him and ridicule him and cause him to regain a sense of proportion, perhaps even place a cooling hand on his brow and so on. Yet even should such a creature exist, and be sitting there, would Clapperton have been able to put up with her, or she with Clapperton? Probably not. However, that is by the way, and irrelevant, for Clapperton's only companion at this restaurant table was the hunch of bitterness within his breast, the hunch of endless longing and repeated failure and indescribable folly, suddenly rendered insupportable by the mindless yelping on his left. Accordingly, when he heard the phrase '. . . and then we came to a little place called Arrow-tchah,' he felt impelled to rise to his feet. By ill chance the table-cloth became entangled between his knees, and the wine bottle fell to the floor, but he pressed on regardless and soon found himself standing by the Englishman's table and enunciating rather distantly these sentiments:—

'I wish you to know that I detest and despise you. I do not propose to go into the rights and wrongs, the whys and wherefores, I am in no condition to do that; but I wish to make it abundantly clear to you that your presence here is a matter of offence to me.'

The man gaped at him without pain or comprehension; one or two of his companions emitted injured gasps; a waiter approached. A brief silence ensued, of which Clapperton could envisage no satisfactory break, so he moved with dimmed consciousness towards the door, scattering waitresses like chaff before him in his passage. He was about to plunge into the street when a hand fell on his shoulder. It was the head waiter, advising him that he had neglected to pay the bill. Clapperton looked at it vaguely, drew a number of notes from his wallet and handed them over. Then he walked out, leaving behind him a tip of some forty per cent.

Rage and shame in his heart, he made his way through the damp, foggy streets to the suburban flat of Stuart and Carmen Foggo. Trudy or no Trudy, he would show them, somehow, that he was not a person to be trifled with. When he arrived the little party was already in full swing. Just a few people, a dozen or so, not more, had been invited to meet Stuart and Carmen again. Stuart and Carmen were up for Christmas, up from London, where Stuart had been a merchant banker for the past six years. They had, of course, retained an Edinburgh residence—that, Clapperton thought, was typical. He knew only two other people present, namely his cousin and his cousin's wife: he no longer moved in such circles. Carmen greeted him warmly enough and said at once that they must have a long chat. Half an hour passed, however, then an hour, and the long chat had still not materialised. Carmen was now over by the fire on the far side of the room, in animated conversation with two or three young men, smoking incessantly, laughing every now and again that pealing, almost plangent laugh which never failed to assert its power over him. Edged into a corner by the door, no longer making any attempt to enter into the conversation of those around him, Clapperton watched her as she drank, her long slender fingers curled around the stem of her glass. When she glanced his way for a moment her eyes had a glassy, preoccupied look, and they flicked quickly away again.

Stuart's voice sounded above the other voices in the room, the words undifferentiated but the bray overriding. He could not pronounce his *R*s properly and for that reason exaggerated his drawl, in the hope that people would mistake this incapacity for affectation. Many did. He had patronised Clapperton when they had met on the latter's arrival, there was no room for doubt about that, and it rankled. Clapperton was determined not to let him get away with it, but time was passing and he was at a loss to think of a way to get even. Yes, time was short—only a moment or two before, Stuart had shown the first departures to the door. Not of course that Clapperton thought of him as Stuart. Foggo was his surname; 'Foghorn Foggo' they had called him at school, and this epithet described him more than adequately. Clapperton put down his glass and made his way to the cloakroom.

He stood for a moment looking at himself in the mirror, with distaste. It seemed to him that his face looked bloated, as if his collar were too tight. He padded up and down gloomily for a little, hands in pockets, sunk in thought. The air was redolent with Foggo's cigar.

Clapperton stood still and looked around him. The men's coats were hanging lumpishly from the too few pegs, one on top of the other. Checking nervously to make certain that his own coat was still there—for one can never be too sure—he found his hand entering by chance the useful inside pocket located in the lining, where he kept his wallet. A thought occurred to him, and he looked about him again. In a corner stood a tall, solid brass umbrella stand. Withdrawing his wallet,

Clapperton checked its contents, then after a moment's consideration laid it carefully on the floor between the umbrella stand and the wall, well into the shadow. He stood back and studied it: it was not easily visible, but from a certain angle the metal reinforcement on one corner glinted slightly. Not daring for an instant to examine his impulse more closely, he adjusted his tie, breathed deeply and returned immediately to the party. He walked straight up to Foggo, who smiled blandly and good-naturedly.

'Ah, Tom, we haven't had a chance . . .'

'Return my wallet to me, Foggo,' said Clapperton quietly, with controlled emotion, 'and we'll agree to forget it.' Only his cousin's wife, who had been talking to Foggo, heard what was said.

Foggo appeared genuinely puzzled. 'Come again?' he faltered.

'I think you understand me, Foggo,' said Clapperton more loudly, and very distinctly. 'If you give me back my property it will go no further.' This time Carmen had heard without a doubt—Clapperton could see from the corner of his eye that she had stiffened, and imagined with satisfaction the sudden falling-off of her interest in the young men; but she was too proud to turn her head.

'I take it you're not serious, Tom?' said Foggo, gathering himself together and retrieving his *sang-froid*, 'but I think you've a funny idea of a joke.'

'Yes, what on earth is all this about, Tom?' asked Isobel, the cousin's wife, her laughter shaking with unease.

'It's about this, Isobel,' said Clapperton, his temper rising. 'This man has purloined my wallet, and I want it back.'

'Oh, this is ridiculous!' gasped Foggo, now very white. His *r* was not quite a *w*, rather something between a *w* and a French *r*, but closer to the former. By this time everyone in the room was aware that something was happening.

'Oh, this is widiculous!' yelled Clapperton, now quite beside himself. 'Foghorn Foggo, Foghorn Foggo!' he brayed in jeering mimicry, like a child.

His cousin, who appeared to feel responsible for him, stared at his shoes in helpless embarrassment, but Isobel pluckily endeavoured to come to terms with the horror of it.

'What possible reason can you have for making such an accusation, Tom?' she pleaded with Clapperton.

'I shall try to keep calm,' he replied. 'My wallet was in the inside pocket of my overcoat fifteen minutes ago. It is no longer there. I have been standing beside the door, and since that time only one person has left this room—Stuart Foggo. I hope I make myself plain.'

'How much was in your wallet, Tom?' asked Carmen coolly, her velvety voice cutting.

Clapperton turned to her with a face of ice. 'Seven pounds,' he replied. 'One Bank of Scotland five pound note, one Royal Bank of Scotland pound note, one Bank of England pound note. Also my banker's card.'

She threw back her head and let out a long, slightly hysterical peal of laughter. 'And you really think that Stuart needs your seven pounds?'

'Oh, clever, clever,' Clapperton grimaced, snarling with malice. 'But they say that with some people, the more they get the more they want. . . . Search him! Search him!' he bellowed suddenly. 'Hold his arms!' And he made a dive at a side-pocket of Foggo's jacket.

'Whoa! Whoa there!' cried Clapperton's cousin, galvanised into action and leaping between them. 'This is getting beyond a joke!'

'It's outwageous!' shouted Foggo.

'Outwageous! Outwageous! Foghorn Foggo!' bawled Clapperton, foaming at the mouth. There was universal consternation.

'May I try to introduce an element of sanity into the proceedings?' asked a demure young lady, stepping forward. 'Before searching Stuart, might it not be an idea to search the house in case Mr Clapperton has *mislaid* his wallet?'

'I'm agreeable,' said Clapperton promptly, folding his arms, staring up at the ceiling and whistling affectedly under his breath. 'Search away.'

He remained in the room, striding up and down, while the others went out to search the passage and cloakroom; at first Foggo also remained sitting on the sofa with his head in his hands staring at the floor, visibly upset; but soon he too got up and went out without looking at Clapperton. Clapperton could hear the excited, low-toned voices buzzing away as the hunt went on, and presently the inevitable whoop of feminine triumph as the missing object was retrieved. It was inevitable, too, that it was Carmen who led the way back into the room, a fixed smile of heartless triumph splitting her face in two.

'Could this be yours?' she asked quietly, holding the wallet up between finger and thumb. Foggo was standing beside her, the tears rolling softly down his cheeks.

'I thought he was a fwiend,' he muttered brokenly.

Clapperton turned aside, his face suffused with shame.

'Your husband might have dropped it out there himself just now,' he stammered, as lamely and unconvincingly as possible.

At this a general moan, a kind of suppressed, mirthless guffaw arose from the entire company. Carmen cast the wallet at his feet without a word.

'It's unbelievable,' said somebody. Clapperton was aware of their hostile faces gazing at him now with undisguised contempt.

'Oh, God!' he said, taking a step forward, stopping, closing his eyes and making a gesture as if to wave reality away from before him. 'I've made a terrible mistake, a dreadful, disgraceful mistake. God forgive me.' He dropped to his knees before Carmen and bowed his head to the ground. 'Oh, God, the shame, the shame! Friends, I feel like disappearing beneath the floor. Oh, God, the shame!'

'Huh!' the same voice made itself heard.

Clapperton rose slowly to one knee and then to his feet. Bravely, but with dread, he looked around the company. With Carmen at their head and setting the tone, they were united in implacability. He bent again, picked up his wallet and put it in his pocket. Then an idea seemed to occur to him, he took it out again and impulsively held it out towards Foggo.

'Take it, Stuart—it's yours—it's the least I can do to make amends . . .'

Foggo let out a terrible sound, a sob contorted with hideous laughter, and waving him away with his left hand buried his face on Carmen's shoulder. Clapperton sighed deeply, nodding his head as if in acknowledgement of the justice of Foggo's reaction.

'Friends, I've ruined the party for all of you,' he said simply. 'Stuart, I've wronged a better man than myself. I can't ask you to forgive me, only God can do that. Please just let me go.'

With that he began to grope his way towards the door, and the crowd parted silently to let him pass. Someone spat on the floor. Shoulders hunched and head bowed, Clapperton went straight out of the front door, down the garden path and onto the street. He was breathing fast, sweating profusely and his knees were shaking with a violent tremor.

'I've done it! I've done it!' he whispered to himself with joy. 'What a humiliation! What a magnificent, astonishing humiliation! And in front of Carmen! Oh, to make myself do that, in front of Carmen, to carry it through, to stoop so low, I never believed I could do it! Oh, what glory!'

Soon he could no longer contain his excitement: he had to stop, and gripping hold of a lamp-post with both hands, he went into a kind of orgasm.

He stretched himself up slowly to his full height, and a great sigh, a weary, spent sigh issued from the depths of him. Instantly his exultation left him and a real shame, cold, clammy and all-pervasive, swept through his soul, and with it a sense of utter futility. He began to walk slowly on down the foggy street, in the raw, dank air, heavy as lead with fatigue. After a time his shame brought him to a halt. They would be talking about him back there even now, discussing with glee the extraordinary exhibition he had made of himself; Carmen by this time would be putting in a good word for him, saying that he must be under stress, that he was a very nice, kind chap in many ways, but odd, odd; heads would be nodding sagely, some would be barely hiding their smiles . . . he realised that he had left his coat behind. He must go back. Yes, he could not leave things the way they were, he would go back and put things right somehow, the coat would be his excuse.

Clapperton returned along the row of terraced houses, mocked as he went by lighted Christmas trees. He crept up the path, and from behind the gaily-coloured curtain of the front room, lit up from within, he could hear their laughter. He stole up to the window and he heard it louder, their relieved, exuberant mirth, their inextinguishable laughter at himself and his ludicrous, shameful performance. He rang the bell and waited. At length the door was opened by his cousin, the overcoat on his arm.

'Yes, you forgot your coat,' he said coldly, holding it out.

Clapperton took it but came on over the threshold, pushing past his cousin who offered no resistance. His eyes blinking against the light, he made his way once more into the drawing-room and paused wearily in the doorway. The guests had heard the bell and knew it was he; they seemed expectant, and at his appearance conversation was instantly silenced.

'I just wanted you all to know,' said Clapperton haltingly, holding his coat, 'that I am not quite such a fool as I appear to be.' He spoke with great sincerity. 'The whole thing was a practical joke—an ill-judged one, I admit, but nevertheless only a joke.' He hesitated, hoping for a response, but no one spoke; he saw that he had made a deplorable impression. Prominent before his eyes was the face of Foggo, utterly expressionless. Carmen, however, was close to tears, chewing her lower lip and staring at the wall. 'That's all I wanted to say,' blurted Clapperton, and turned to go.

As he did so, he heard that same malicious voice. 'It may not have been much of a joke,' it said clearly, 'but it was certainly practical!' A loud gust of tension-dispelling laughter rewarded these words.

In the hallway Clapperton found that Isobel, his cousin's wife, had followed him out, and his eyes filled with tears of gratitude for this act of kindness. He turned to say a word of thanks, and as he did so by ill fortune he tripped heavily over the cord of an electric radiator, and stumbled on into the outer lobby. Not looking back, he made his way into the street and set off aimlessly through the cold patchy fog. But he had no idea where he was heading, and soon he drifted to a halt and stood there vacantly, unaware of where he was or what he was doing. Three youths overtook him, talking loudly, and when they had passed they kept turning round every few paces to walk backwards staring at him standing there alone in the middle of the pavement. Eventually this mindless behaviour twisted his soul into uncontrollable fury. He threw his overcoat on the pavement and stamped his foot in rage.

'This is widiculous!' he screamed at them, the sounds of his hysteria echoing strangely fog-muffled through the calm of the suburb. 'This is outwageous! Foghorn Foggo! Foghorn Foggo! Foghorn Foggo!'

It was some time before Clapperton came fully to himself and began slowly to make his way home once more, moaning gently to himself as he drifted alone through the now deserted streets. When eventually he reached his small flat he spent some time meticulously re-arranging certain of his books on their shelves. It was bitterly cold, and he was without an oil-heater. Nonetheless he began slowly to undress, arranging his clothes with great care on a chair, brushed his suit and hung it away, brushed and polished his shoes. Then he washed with great thoroughness, brushed his teeth and brushed his hair, moaning all the while. Some time in the early hours he found himself once more in the bed from which he had arisen the previous morning with such sturdy hopes.

When a person weeps while lying flat on the back the tears do not descend down the front of the cheeks on either side of the nose, as might be supposed, but course sideways down into the ears. Thus it was that when sleep at last overtook Clapperton it found him with the cavities of his ears generously filled with salt tears, which he had not had the heart to mop away, for they seemed to sympathise with him and comfort him a little in his distress. Yet in the morning when a weak ray of sunshine alighted upon the waking Clapperton, it seemed the reflection of a meagre hope which stirred once more within his heart. Perhaps Trudy had been unavoidably detained somewhere, and even in a moment the phone would ring with her contrite apologies . . . Or Carmen, it might be, in an hour or two would call round, pathetically anxious to make amends for her unworthy misapprehension of his motives. . . . The previous night it had seemed to Clapperton that life might strike him down; but life could never strike him down, for it had never raised him up, and it never would raise him up, never. So Clapperton arose, meagrely sustained by his wretched hope, not briskly but resolutely enough, to live another day.

Hugh MacDiarmid

FIVE BITS OF MILLER

Hugh MacDiarmid (C. M. Grieve 1892–1978) was the son of a country postman. He began as a journalist and after service as a sergeant in the RAMC during the First World War, he returned to Scotland in the 1920s and in the space of six extraordinary years produced *Sangschaw*, *Penny Wheep* and *A Drunk Man Looks at the Thistle*, helping to found the Scottish Renaissance movement of which he was one of the leading figures.

MacDiarmid's reputation as a poet is assured, but his gift for polemic has tended to obscure his creative prose. In a letter to Neil Gunn in 1927 he admits to having made little headway with a novel in English (since lost), and says he has decided to concentrate on a collection of short stories. This project was rejected by Routledge, though some short fiction appeared in later anthologies.

MacDiarmid's prose lacks the reputation of his poetry, but he has a lively humour and a fine ironic turn of phrase. 'Five Bits of Miller' was written in 1934. It demonstrates the poet's delight in an older tradition of Scots grotesquerie and looks forward to the contemporary styles of Gray and Kelman.

Five Bits of Miller

FIRST OF all, there is my recollection of a certain fashion he had of blowing his nose: the effect of the sound mainly, and my appreciation of the physiology of the feat. A membraneous trumpeting. Fragments of a congested face, most of which was obliterated by the receptive handkerchief. Like an abortive conjuring trick in which, transiently, certain empurpled and blown-out facial data meaninglessly escaped (as if too soon) from behind the magic cloth which, whipped off immediately after, discovered to the astonished gaze not the expected rabbit or flower pot but only Miller's face as it had been before the so-called trick (the trick of remaining the same behind the snowy curtain when literally anything might have happened) or, rather, Miller's face practically unchanged, for the curious elements that had prematurely broken out of their customary association were to be seen in the act of reconciling themselves again, of disappearing into the physiognomical pool in which they usually moved so indetectibly.—I had invariably present in my mind on such occasions moreover a picture of the internal mechanism, the intricate tubing, as if Miller's clock-face had dropped off, disclosing the works. I never really liked the way his wheels went round; the spectacle offended some obscure sense of mechanical propriety in me; I felt that there should have been a great deal of simplification—that there was a stupid complexity, out of all proportion to the effects for which it was designed. I was in opposite case, regarding Miller, to the guest who took for a Cubist portrait of his host a plan of the drains that hung in the hall.

Then the condition in which this weird aggregation was kept revolted me. It was abominably clogged up. What should have been fine transparencies had become soggy and obtuse: bright blood pulsations had degenerated into viscid stagnancies; the tubes were twisted, ballooning or knotted in parts and taut or strangulated in others. Miller could never hoist his eupeptic cheeks with sufficient aplomb to hide this disgraceful chaos from me or dazzle my contemptuous eyes with that lardy effulgence of his brow from which his hair so precipitately retired. 'Yes, yes,' I would say to myself, 'a very fine and oedematous exterior, but if you were all right behind instead of being so horribly bogged—really lit-up from within, instead of disporting this false-facial animation—man!; if your works could only be completely overhauled and made to function freely and effectively, what a difference it would make!'

Then there was his throat. I hated to hear him clearing it. He was top-heavy as I have just shown. That appalling congestion behind his face consumed practically all his energy. The consequence was that any movement of his throat sounded remote and forlorn, a shuttle of phlegm sliding unaccountably in a derelict loom, the eerie cluck of a forgotten slot, trapping the casual sense that heard it in an oubliette of inconsequent sound. It was always like that; like the door of some little windowless room, into which one had stepped from sheer idle curiosity, implacably locking itself behind one. A fatal and inescapable sound, infinitesimally yet infinitely desolating. How many stray impulses of mine have been thus irrevocably trapped! I feel that a great portion of myself has been really buried alive, caught in subterranean passages of Miller's physical processes as by roof-falls, and skeletonising in the darkness there. Miller clearing his throat was really murdering me bit by bit; blowing bits off me with those subtle and unplaceable detonations of his, of which his over-occupied head behind that absurdly bland face must have been completely unaware—

Thirdly he had a way of twirling his little fingers, almost as if they had been corkscrews, in his ear-holes and withdrawing them with lumps of wax on the nail-ends. Uncorking himself by degrees. But his brain was never really opened: it remained blocked, or rather it had coagulated—his hearing never flowed clear into one. Just an opaque trickle devoid of the substance of his attention.—One felt always that one was receiving a very aloof incomplete audition. The wax itself was inhumanly stodgy and dull—not that bright golden vaseline-like stuff one sometimes sees, silky skeins of it netting the lights, flossily glistening, a fine live horripilating honey. But orts of barren comb that had never held honey; desiccated fragments of brown putty that made one sorry and ashamed.

Even yet I cannot trust myself to do more than suggest in the most elusive way the effect his cutting his fingernails had upon me. He did it so deliberately and his nails were so brittle and crackling. Dead shell. His finger-tips under them were dry and withered. Shaking hands with him was like touching dust and deepening reluctantly but helplessly into the cold clay of his palm.—But meanwhile I am speaking of his nails. They literally exploded. He affected to use scissors like the rest of us: but, watching him closely, I was never deceived. It was not by the scissors that he cut his nails. He blew them off with his eyes. I know that sounds absurd and impossible. But if you could only have seen the way in which he looked at his finger-tips while he was engaged in this operation, and the extraordinary crepitation and popping-off that ensued—

Lastly, there was the way in which he used to squeeze a black-head out of his chin. He was the sort of person who more or less surreptitiously permits a horde of these cattle to enjoy his cuticle for a certain length of time for the queer sport of killing them, and, at the appointed time, he slew them with amazing precaution and precision. I think this process gave him some strange dual effect of martyrdom and ceremonial purification. I cannot attempt to describe here the rites with which he was wont to sacrifice a black-head of the proper age on the altar of his complexion. For the outsider the ceremony was to a great extent masked by the fact that he only obliquely faced any congregation through the medium of a mirror. In a fragment of it that eluded the blocking back of his head and a thin slice of side-face decorated with a whorl of ear, one saw all that one might, heightened in effect by the liquid light in which such a reflection was steeped. The squeezing-out process was a delicate and protracted one. Black-heads do not squirt out under pressures like paint from a tube, but emerge by almost imperceptible degrees. A very slim yellow-white column (of the consistency of a ripe banana) that ascends perpendicularly and gradually curves over and finally, suddenly, relapses upon its base again.

Yes! I think that perhaps the most vivid recollection of Miller I still retain is that of some knobly fragment of his chin on which under the convergent pressure of two bloodless, almost leprous, finger-tips the stem of a black-head is waveringly ascending; and then of the collapse—lying there, thready, white, on a surface screwed and squeezed to a painful purple, like a worm on a rasp!

You remember the big toe-nail in one of Gogol's stories? Well, I have only these five somewhat analogous bits of Miller left—mucus, phlegm, wax, horn, and the parasitic worm—five unrelated and essentially unrepresentative bits of the jig-saw puzzle that I used to flatter myself I could put together with blasphemous expertise. All the rest are irretrievably lost. But see what you can make of these five.

Bernard MacLaverty

A TIME TO DANCE

Born in Belfast in 1942, Bernard MacLaverty moved to Scotland originally to teach and later to write, living in Edinburgh, Islay and now Glasgow. His beautifully constructed short stories and the novels *Lamb* and *Cal,* which took the thriller into new emotional and psychological territories, have been published in many languages, and adapted for radio, film and television by the author.

MacLaverty is undoubtedly at home with the short prose form. His clarity, economy and emotional precision are exemplary. The frailty of relationships, the intensity of chance meetings and the hidden vulnerabilities of his characters are vividly described. A child or adolescent is often his central figure, lending the sharpness of focus that new experience brings to the events he describes.

'A Time to Dance' reveals the risks of everyday life. MacLaverty creates a realistically warm yet ambivalent relationship between the single mother, her son and the world in an Edinburgh that will never find its way into a tourist brochure. The story is built over a network of understated tensions, especially Nelson's startling awareness of, and exposure to, a side of his mother he or the reader could never have imagined.

A Time to Dance

NELSON, WITH a patch over one eye, stood looking idly into Mothercare's window. The sun was bright behind him and made a mirror out of the glass. He looked at his patch with distaste and felt it with his finger. The Elastoplast was rough and dry and he disliked the feel of it. Bracing himself for the pain, he ripped it off and let a yell out of him. A woman looked down at him curiously to see why he had made the noise, but by that time he had the patch in his pocket. He knew without looking that some of his eyebrow would be on it.

He had spent most of the morning in the Gardens avoiding distant uniforms, but now that it was coming up to lunchtime he braved it on to the street. He had kept his patch on longer than usual because his mother had told him the night before that if he didn't wear it he would go 'stark, staring blind'.

Nelson was worried because he knew what it was like to be blind. The doctor at the eye clinic had given him a box of patches that would last for most of his lifetime. Opticludes. One day Nelson had worn two and tried to get to the end of the street and back. It was a terrible feeling. He had to hold his head back in case it bumped into anything and keep waving his hands in front of him backwards and forwards like windscreen wipers. He kept tramping on tin cans and heard them trundle emptily away. Broken glass crackled under his feet and he could not figure out how close to the wall he was. Several times he heard footsteps approaching, slowing down as if they were going to attack him in his helplessness, then walking away. One of the footsteps even laughed. Then he heard a voice he knew only too well.

'Jesus, Nelson, what are you up to this time?' It was his mother. She led him back to the house with her voice blaring in his ear.

She was always shouting. Last night, for instance, she had started into him for watching T.V. from the side. She had dragged him round to the chair in front of it.

'That's the way the manufacturers make the sets. They put the picture on the front. But oh no, that's not good enough for our Nelson. He has to watch it from the side. Squint, my arse, you'll just go blind—stark, staring blind.'

Nelson had then turned his head and watched it from the front. She had never mentioned the blindness before. Up until now all she had said was, 'If you don't wear them patches that eye of yours will turn in till it's looking at your brains. God knows, not that it'll have much to look at.'

His mother was Irish. That was why she had a name like Skelly. That was why she talked funny. But she was proud of the way she talked and nothing angered her more than to hear Nelson saying 'Ah ken' and 'What like is it?' She kept telling him that someday they were going back, when she had enough ha'pence scraped together. 'Until then I'll not let them make a Scotchman out of you.' But Nelson talked the way he talked.

His mother had called him Nelson because she said she thought that his father had been a seafaring man. The day the boy was born she had read an article in the *Reader's Digest* about Nelson Rockefeller, one of the richest men in the world. It seemed only right to give the boy a good start. She thought it also had the advantage that it couldn't be shortened, but she was wrong. Most of the boys in the scheme called him Nelly Skelly.

He wondered if he should sneak back to school for dinner then skive off again in the afternoon. They had good dinners at school—like a hotel, with choices. Chips and magic things like rhubarb crumble. There was one big dinner-woman who gave him extra every time she saw him. She told him he needed fattening. The only drawback to the whole system was that he was on free dinners. Other people in his class were given their dinner money and it was up to them whether they went without a dinner and bought Coke and sweets and stuff with the money. It was a choice Nelson didn't have, so he had to invent other things to get the money out of his mother. In Lent there were the Black Babies; library fines were worth the odd 10p, although, as yet, he had not taken a book from the school library—and anyway they didn't have to pay fines, even if they were late; the Home Economics Department asked them to bring in money to buy their ingredients and Nelson would always add 20p to it.

'What the hell are they teaching you to cook—sides of beef?' his mother would yell. Outdoor pursuits required extra money. But even though they had ended after the second term, Nelson went on asking for the 50p on a Friday—'to go horse riding'. His mother would never part with the money without a speech of some sort.

'Horse riding? Horse riding! Jesus, I don't know what sort of a school I've sent you to. Is Princess Anne in your class or something? Holy God, horse riding.'

Outdoor pursuits was mostly walking round museums on wet days and, when it was dry, the occasional trip to Portobello beach to write on a flapping piece of foolscap the signs of pollution you could see. Nelson felt that the best outdoor pursuit of the lot was what he was doing now. Skiving. At least that way you could do what you liked.

He groped in his pocket for the change out of his 50p and went into a shop. He bought a giant thing of bubble-gum and crammed it into his mouth. It was hard and dry at first and he couldn't answer the woman when she spoke to him.

'Whaaungh?'

'Pick the paper off the floor, son! Use the basket.'

He picked the paper up and screwed it into a ball. He aimed to miss the basket, just to spite her, but it went in. By the time he reached the bottom of the street the gum was chewy. He thrust his tongue into the middle of it and blew. A small disappointing bubble burst with a plip. It was not until the far end of Princes Street that he managed to blow big ones, pink and wobbling, that he could see at the end of his nose, which burst well and had to be gathered in shreds from his chin.

Then suddenly the crowds of shoppers parted and he saw his mother. In the same instant she saw him. She was on him before he could even think of running. She grabbed him by the fur of his parka and began screaming into his face.

'In the name of God, Nelson, what are you doing here? Why aren't you at school?' She began shaking him. 'Do you realise what this means? They'll put me in bloody jail. It'll be bloody Saughton for me, and no mistake.' She had her teeth gritted together and her mouth was slanting in her face. Then Nelson started to shout.

'Help! Help!' he yelled.

A woman with an enormous chest like a pigeon stopped. 'What's happening?' she said.

Nelson's mother turned on her. 'It's none of your bloody business.'

'I'm being kidnapped,' yelled Nelson.

'Young woman. Young woman . . .' said the lady with the large chest, trying to tap Nelson's mother on the shoulder with her umbrella, but Mrs Skelly turned with such a snarl that the woman edged away hesitatingly and looked over her shoulder and tut-tutted just loudly enough for the passing crowd to hear her.

'Help! I'm being kidnapped,' screamed Nelson, but everybody walked past looking the other way. His mother squatted down in front of him, still holding on to his jacket. She lowered her voice and tried to make it sound reasonable.

'Look Nelson, love. Listen. If you're skiving school, do you realise what'll happen to me? In Primary the Children's Panel threatened to send me to court. You're only at that Secondary and already that Sub-Attendance Committee thing wanted to fine me. Jesus, if you're caught again . . .'

Nelson stopped struggling. The change in her tone had quietened him down. She straightened up and looked wildly about her, wondering what to do.

'You've got to go straight back to school, do you hear me?'

'Yes.'

'Promise me you'll go.' The boy looked down at the ground. 'Promise?' The boy made no answer.

'I'll kill you if you don't go back. I'd take you myself only I've my work to go to. I'm late as it is.'

Again she looked around as if she would see someone who would suddenly help her. Still she held on to his jacket. She was biting her lip.

'Oh God, Nelson.'

The boy blew a flesh-pink bubble and snapped it between his teeth. She shook him.

'That bloody bubble-gum.'

There was a loud explosion as the one o'clock gun went off. They both leapt.

'Oh Jesus, that gun puts the heart sideways in me every time it goes off. Come on, son, you'll have to come with me. I'm late. I don't know what they'll say when they see you but I'm bloody taking you to school by the ear. You hear me?'

She began rushing along the street, Nelson's sleeve in one hand, her carrier bag in the other. The boy had to run to keep from being dragged.

'Don't you dare try a trick like that again. Kidnapped, my arse. Nelson, if I knew somebody who would kidnap you—I'd pay *him* the money. Embarrassing me on the street like that.'

They turned off the main road and went into a hallway and up carpeted stairs which had full-length mirrors along one side. Nelson stopped to make faces at himself but his mother chugged at his arm. At the head of the stairs stood a fat man in his shirtsleeves.

'What the hell is this?' he said. 'You're late, and what the hell is that?' He looked down from over his stomach at Nelson.

'I'll explain later,' she said. 'I'll make sure he stays in the room.'

'You should be on *now*,' said the fat man and turned and walked away through the swing doors. They followed him and Nelson saw, before his mother pushed him into the room, that it was a bar, plush and carpeted with crowds of men standing drinking.

'You sit here, Nelson, until I'm finished and then I'm taking you back to that school. You'll get nowhere if you don't do your lessons. I have to get changed now.'

She set her carrier bag on the floor and kicked off her shoes. Nelson sat down, watching her. She stopped and looked over her shoulder at him, biting her lip.

'Where's that bloody eyepatch you should be wearing?' Nelson indicated his pocket.

'Well, wear it then.' Nelson took the crumpled patch from his pocket, tugging bits of it unstuck to get it flat before he stuck it over his bad eye. His mother took out her handbag and began rooting about at the bottom of it. Nelson heard the rattle of her bottles of scent and tubes of lipstick.

'Ah,' she said and produced another eyepatch, flicking it clean. 'Put another one on till I get changed. I don't want you noseying at me.' She came to him, pulling away the white backing to the patch, and stuck it over his remaining eye. He imagined her concentrating, the tip of her tongue stuck out. She pressed his eyebrows with her thumbs, making sure that the patches were stuck.

'Now don't move, or you'll bump into something.'

Nelson heard the slither of her clothes and her small grunts as she hurriedly got changed. Then he heard her rustle in her bag, the soft pop and rattle as she opened her capsules. Her 'tantalisers' she called them, small black and red torpedoes. Then he heard her voice.

'Just you stay like that till I come back. That way you'll come to no harm. You hear me, Nelson? If I come back in here and you have those things off, I'll *kill* you. I'll not be long.'

Nelson nodded from his darkness.

'The door will be locked, so there's no running away.'

'Ah ken.'

Suddenly his darkness exploded with lights as he felt her bony hand strike his ear.

'You don't ken things, Nelson. You *know* them.'

He heard her go out and the key turn in the lock. His ear sang and he felt it was hot. He turned his face up to the ceiling. She had left the light on because he could see pinkish through the patches. He smelt the beer and stale smoke. Outside the room pop music had started up, very loudly. He heard the deep notes pound through to where he sat. He felt his ear with his hand and it *was* hot.

Making small *aww* sounds of excruciating pain, he slowly detached both eyepatches from the bridge of the nose outwards. In case his mother should come back he did not take them off completely, but left them hinged to the sides of his eyes. When he turned to look around him they flapped like blinkers.

It wasn't really a room, more a broom cupboard. Crates were stacked against one wall; brushes and mops and buckets stood near a very low sink; on a row of coat-hooks hung some limp raincoats and stained white jackets; his mother's stuff hung on the last hook. The floor was covered with tramped-flat cork tips. Nelson got up to look at what he was sitting on. It was a crate of empties. He went to the keyhole and looked out, but all he could see was a patch of wallpaper opposite. Above the door was a narrow window. He looked up at it, his eyepatches falling back to touch his ears. He went over to the sink and had a drink of water from the low tap, sucking noisily at the column of water as it splashed into the sink. He stopped and wiped his mouth. The water felt cold after the mint of the bubble-gum. He looked up at his mother's things, hanging on the hook; her tights and drawers were as she wore them, but inside out and hanging knock-kneed on top of everything. In her bag he found her blonde wig and tried it on, smelling the perfume of it as he did so. At home he liked noseying in his mother's room; smelling all her bottles of make-up; seeing her spangled things. He had to stand on the crate to see himself but the mirror was all brown measles under its surface and the eyepatches ruined the effect. He sat down again and began pulling at the bubble-gum, seeing how long he could make it stretch before it broke. Still the music pounded outside. It was so loud the vibrations tickled his feet. He sighed and looked up at the window again.

If his mother took him back to school, he could see problems. For starting St John the Baptist's she had bought him a brand new Adidas bag for his books. Over five pounds it had cost her, she said. On his first real skive he had dumped the bag in the bin at the bottom of his stair, every morning for a week, and travelled light into town. On the Friday he came home just in time to see the bin lorry driving away in a cloud of bluish smoke. He had told his mother that the bag had been stolen from the playground during break. She had threatened to phone the school about it but Nelson had hastily assured her that the whole matter was being investigated by none other than the headmaster himself. This threat put the notion out of his head of asking her for the money to replace the books. At that point he had not decided on a figure. He could maybe try it again some time when all the fuss had died down. But now it was all going to be stirred if his mother took him to school.

He pulled two crates to the door and climbed up but they were not high enough. He put a third one on top, climbed on again, and gingerly straightened, balancing on its rim. On tip-toe he could see out. He couldn't see his mother anywhere. He saw a crowd of men standing in a semicircle. Behind them were some very bright lights, red, yellow and blue. They all had pints in their hands which they didn't seem to be drinking. They were watching something which Nelson couldn't see. Suddenly the music stopped and the men all began drinking and talking. Standing on tip-toe for so long, Nelson's legs began to shake and he heard the bottles in the crate rattle. He rested for a moment. Then the music started again. He looked to see. The men now just stood looking. It was as if they were seeing a ghost. Then they all cheered louder than the music.

Nelson climbed down and put the crates away from the door so that his mother could get in. He closed his eyepatches over for a while, but still she didn't come. He listened to another record, this time a slow one. He decided to travel blind to get another drink of water. As he did so the music changed to fast. He heard the men cheering again, then the rattle of the key in the lock. Nelson, his arms rotating in front of him, tried to make his way back to the crate. His mother's voice said,

'Don't you dare take those eyepatches off.' Her voice was panting.

Then his hand hit up against her. It was her bare stomach, hot and damp with sweat. She guided him to sit down, breathing heavily through her nose.

'I'll just get changed and then you're for school right away, boy.' Nelson nodded. He heard her light a cigarette as she dressed. When she had finished she ripped off his right eyepatch.

'There now, we're ready to go,' she said, ignoring Nelson's anguished yells.

'That's the wrong eye,' he said.

'Oh shit,' said his mother and ripped off the other one, turned it upside down and stuck it over his right eye. The smoke from the cigarette in her mouth trickled up into her eye and she held it half shut. Nelson could see the bright points of sweat shining through her make-up. She still hadn't got her breath back fully yet. She smelt of drink.

On the way out, the fat man with the rolled-up sleeves held out two fivers and Nelson's mother put them into her purse.

'The boy—never again,' he said, looking down at Nelson.

They took the Number Twelve to St John the Baptist's. It was the worst possible time because, just as they were going in, the bell rang for the end of a period and suddenly the quad was full of pupils, all looking at Nelson and his mother. Some sixth-year boys wolf-whistled after her and others stopped to stare. Nelson felt a flush of pride that she was causing a stir. She was dressed in black satiny jeans, very tight, and her pink blouse was knotted, leaving her tanned midriff bare. They went into the office and a secretary came to the window.

'Yes?' she said, looking Mrs Skelly up and down.

'I'd like to see the Head,' she said.

'I'm afraid he's at a meeting. What's it about?'

'About him.' She waved her thumb over her shoulder at Nelson.

'What year is he?'

'What year are you, son?' His mother turned to him.

'First.'

'First Year. Oh, then you'd best see Mr MacDermot, the First Year Housemaster.' The secretary directed them to Mr MacDermot's office. It was at the other side of the school and they had to walk what seemed miles of corridors before they found it. Mrs Skelly's stiletto heels clicked along the tiles.

'It's a wonder you don't get lost in here, son,' she said as she knocked on the Housemaster's door. Mr MacDermot opened it and invited them in. Nelson could see that he too was looking at her, his eyes wide and his face smiley.

'What can I do for you?' he said when they were seated.

'It's him,' said Mrs Skelly. 'He's been skiving again. I caught him this morning.'

'I see,' said Mr MacDermot. He was very young to be a Housemaster. He had a black moustache which he began to stroke with the back of his hand. He paused for a long time. Then he said,

'Remind me of your name, son.'

'—Oh, I'm sorry,' said Mrs Skelly. 'My name is Skelly and this is my boy Nelson.'

'Ah, yes, Skelly.' The Housemaster got up and produced a yellow file from the filing cabinet. 'You must forgive me, but we haven't seen a great deal of Nelson lately.'

'Do you mind if I smoke?' asked Mrs Skelly.

'Not at all,' said the Housemaster, getting up to open the window.

'The trouble is, that the last time we were at the Sub-Attendance Committee thing they said they would take court action if it happened again. And it has.'

'Well, it may not come to that with the Attendance Sub-Committee. If we nip it in the bud. If Nelson makes an effort, isn't that right, Nelson?' Nelson sat silent.

'Speak when the master's speaking to you,' yelled Mrs Skelly.

'Yes,' said Nelson, making it barely audible.

'You're Irish too,' said Mrs Skelly to the Housemaster, smiling.

'That's right,' said Mr MacDermot. 'I thought your accent was familiar. Where do you come from?'

'My family come from just outside Derry. And you?'

'Oh, that's funny. I'm just across the border from you. Donegal.' As they talked, Nelson stared out the window. He had never heard his mother so polite. He could just see a corner of the playing fields and a class coming out with the Gym teacher. Nelson hated Gym more than anything. It was crap. He loathed the changing rooms, the getting stripped in front of others, the stupidity he felt when he missed the ball. The smoke from his mother's cigarette went in an arc towards the open window. Distantly he could hear the class shouting as they started a game of football.

'Nelson! Isn't that right?' said Mr MacDermot loudly.

'What?'

'That even when you are here you don't work hard enough.'

'Hmmm,' said Nelson.

'You don't have to tell me,' said his mother. 'It's not just his eye that's lazy. If you ask me the whole bloody lot of him is. I've never seen him washing a dish in his life and he leaves everything at his backside.'

'Yes,' said the Housemaster. Again he stroked his moustache. 'What is required from Nelson is a change of attitude. Attitude, Nelson. You understand a word like attitude?'

'Yes.'

'He's just not interested in school, Mrs Skelly.'

'I've no room to talk, of course. I had to leave at fifteen,' she said, rolling her eyes in Nelson's direction. 'You know what I mean? Otherwise I might have stayed on and got my exams.'

'I see,' said Mr MacDermot. 'Can we look forward to a change in attitude, Nelson?'

'Hm-hm.'

'Have you no friends in school?' asked the Housemaster.

'Naw.'

'And no interest. You see, you can't be interested in any subject unless you do some work at it. Work pays dividends with interest . . .' he paused and looked at Mrs Skelly. She was inhaling her cigarette. He went on. 'Have you considered the possibility that Nelson may be suffering from school phobia?'

Mrs Skelly looked at him. 'Phobia, my arse,' she said. 'He just doesn't like school.'

'I see. Does he do any work at home then?'

'Not since he had his bag with all his books in it stolen.'

'Stolen?'

Nelson leaned forward in his chair and said loudly and clearly, 'I'm going to try to be better from now on. I am. I am going to try, sir.'

'That's more like it,' said the Housemaster, also edging forward.

'I am not going to skive. I am going to try. Sir, I'm going to do my best.'

'Good boy. I think, Mrs Skelly, if I have a word with the right people and convey to them what we have spoken about, I think there will be no court action. Leave it with me, will you? And I'll see what I can do. Of course it all depends on Nelson. If he is as good as his word. One more truancy and I'll be forced to report it. And he must realise that he has three full years of school to do before he leaves us. You must be aware of my position in this matter. You understand what I'm saying, Nelson?'

'Ah ken,' he said. 'I know.'

'You go off to your class now. I have some more things to say to your mother.'

Nelson rose to his feet and shuffled towards the door. He stopped.

'Where do I go, sir?'

'Have you not got your timetable?'

'No sir. Lost it.'

The Housemaster, tut-tutting, dipped into another file, read a card and told him that he should be at R.K. in Room 72. As he left, Nelson noticed that his mother had put her knee up against the Housemaster's desk and was swaying back in her chair, as she took out another cigarette.

''Bye, love,' she said.

When he went into Room 72 there was a noise of oos and ahhs from the others in the class. He said to the teacher that he had been seeing Mr

MacDermot. She gave him a Bible and told him to sit down. He didn't know her name. He had her for English as well as R.K. She was always rabbiting on about poetry.

'You, boy, that just came in. For your benefit, we are talking and reading about organisation. Page 667. About how we should divide our lives up with work and prayer. How we should put each part of the day to use, and each part of the year. This is one of the most beautiful passages in the whole of the Bible. Listen to its rhythms as I read.' She lightly drummed her closed fist on the desk in front of her.

'"There is an appointed time for everything, and a time for every affair under the heavens. A time to be born and a time to die; a time to plant and a time to uproot . . ."'

'What page did you say, Miss?' asked Nelson.

'Six-six-seven,' she snapped and read on, her voice trembling, '"A time to kill and a time to heal; a time to wear down and a time to build. A time to weep and a time to laugh; a time to mourn and a time to dance . . ."'

Nelson looked out of the window, at the tiny white H of the goal posts in the distance. He took his bubble-gum out and stuck it under the desk. The muscles of his jaw ached from chewing the now flavourless mass. He looked down at page 667 with its microscopic print, then put his face close to it. He tore off his eyepatch, thinking that if he was going to become blind then the sooner it happened the better.

Alan Spence

Alan Spence was born in Glasgow in 1948, and now lives in Edinburgh where he and his wife run the Sri Chinmoy Meditation Centre. He has published one collection of short stories, *Its Colours They Are Fine* (1977), and two collections of poetry. He has also adapted some stories for stage and television.

Its Colours They Are Fine became an immediate classic, showing us Glasgow tenement life from a boy's point of view as he learns unwritten rules of territorial and sectarian behaviour. Spence's view of adult Glasgow is divided between the fictional and the autobiographical, but he maintains the telling details and the human scale we have come to expect. Life may be dangerous, violent and bleak, but there is a fierce hope running through his descriptions of what might otherwise be dead-end jobs or dead-end lives.

Tinsel

THE SWING-DOORS of the steamie had windows in them but even when he stood on tiptoe he couldn't reach up to see out. If he held the doors open, the people queuing complained about the cold and anyway the strain would make his arms ache. So he had to be content to peer out through the narrow slit between the doors, pressing his forehead against the brass handplate. He could see part of the street and the grey buildings opposite, everything covered in snow. He tried to see more by moving a little sideways, but the gap wasn't wide enough. He could smell the woodandpaint of the door and the clean bleachy smell from the washhouse. His eye began to sting from the draught so he closed it tight and put his other eye to the slit, but he had to jump back quickly as a woman with a pramful of washing crashed open the doors. When the doors had stopped swinging and settled back into place he noticed that the brass plate was covered with fingermarks. He wanted to see it smooth and shiny so he breathed up on it, clouding it with his breath, and rubbed it with his sleeve. But he only managed to smear the greasy marks across the plate leaving it streaky and there was still a cluster of prints near the top that he couldn't reach at all.

He went over and sat down on the long wooden bench against the wall. His feet didn't quite reach the ground and he sat swinging his legs. It felt as if his mother had been in the washhouse for hours.

Waiting.

People passed in and out. The queue was just opposite the bench. They queued to come in and wash their clothes or to have a hot bath or a swim. The way to the swimming baths was through an iron turnstile, like the ones at Ibrox Park. When his father took him to the match he lifted him over the turnstile so he didn't have to pay.

Unfastening his trenchcoat, he rummaged about in his trouser pocket and brought out a toy Red Indian without a head, a pencil rubber, a badge with a racing car, a yellow wax crayon and a foreign coin. He pinned the badge on to his lapel and spread the other things out on the bench. The crayon was broken in the middle but because the paper cover wasn't torn the two ends hadn't come apart. It felt wobbly. He bent it in half, tearing the paper. Now he had two short crayons instead of one long one. There was nothing to draw on except the green-tiled wall so he put the pieces back in his pocket.

The coin was an old one, from Palestine, and it had a hole in the middle. He'd been given it by his uncle Andy who had been a soldier there. Now he was a policeman in Malaya. He would be home next week for Christmas. Jesus's birthday. Everybody gave presents then so that Jesus would come one day and take them to Heaven. That was where he lived now, but he came from Palestine. Uncle Andy had been to see his house in Bethlehem. At school they sang hymns about it. Come all ye faithful. Little Star of Bethlehem.

He scraped at the surface of the bench with his coin, watching the brown paint flake and powder, blowing the flakings away to see the mark he'd made.

The woman at the pay-desk shouted at him.

'Heh! Is that how ye treat the furniture at hame? Jist chuck it!'

He sat down again.

Two boys and two girls aged about fifteen came laughing and jostling out of the baths, red faced, their hair still damp. One of the boys was flicking his wet towel at the girls who skipped clear, just out of reach. They clattered out into the street, leaving the doors swinging behind them. He heard their laughter fade, out of his hearing. For the moment again he was alone.

He stood his headless Indian on the bench. If he could find the head he'd be able to fix it back on again with a matchstick. He pushed the Indian's upraised arm through the hole in the coin, thinking it would make a good shield, but it was too heavy and made the Indian fall over.

He shoved his things back into his pocket and went over to the doorway of the washhouse. The place was painted a grubby cream and lightgreen and the stone floor was wet.

Clouds of steam swishing up from faraway metaltub machines. Lids banging shut. Women shouting above the throbbing noise.

He couldn't see his mother.

He went back and climbed on to the bench, teetering, almost falling as he stood carefully up.

A woman came in with a little girl about his own age. He was glad he was standing on the bench and he knew she was watching him.

He ignored her and pretended to fight his way along the bench, hacking aside an army of unseen cut-throats, hurling them over the immense drop from the perilous bench-top ridge. He kept looking round to make sure she was still watching him, not looking directly at her but just glancing in her direction then looking past her to the pay-box and staring at that with fixed interest and without seeing it at all.

The woman had taken her bundle into the washhouse and the little girl sat down on the far end of the bench, away from him.

His mother came out of the washhouse pushing her pram. He jumped down noisily and ran to her. As they left he turned and over his shoulder stuck out his tongue at the girl.

Once outside, his mother started fussing over him, buttoning his coat, straightening his belt, tucking in his scarf.

'There yar then, ah wasn't long, was ah?' Gentle voice. Her breath was wheezy.

She was wearing the turban she wore to work in the bakery. Today was Saturday and she only worked in the morning, coming home at dinnertime with cakes and pies. He'd gone with her to the steamie because his father was out at the doctor's and he couldn't find any of his friends. They'd probably gone to the pictures.

He had to walk very quickly, sometimes trotting, to keep up with the pram. The snow under his feet made noises like a catspurr at every step. The pramwheels creaked. In the pram was a tin tub full of damp washing which was already starting to stiffen in the cold. It was the same pram he'd been carried in when he was a baby. His mother's two other babies had been carried in it too. They would have been his big brothers but they'd both died. They would be in Heaven. He wondered if they were older than him now or if they were still babies. He was six years and two weeks old. His wellington boots were folded down at the top like pirate boots. His socks didn't reach up quite far enough and the rims of the boots had rubbed red stinging chafe-marks round his legs.

They rounded the corner into their own street and stopped outside the Dairy.

'You wait here son. Ah'll no be a minnit.'

Waiting again.

Out of a close came a big loping longhaired dog. The hair on its legs looked like a cowboy's baggy trousers. Some boys were chasing it and laughing. All its fur was clogged with dirt and mud.

His mother came out of the shop with a bottle of milk.

There was a picture of the same kind of dog in his Wonder Book of The World. It was called an Afghan Hound. But the one in the book looked different. Again the steady creak of the pram. The trampled snow underfoot was already grey and slushy.

They reached their close and he ran on up ahead. They lived on the top landing and he was out of breath when he reached the door. He leaned over the banister. Down below he could hear his mother bumping the pram up the stairs. Maybe his father was home from the doctor's.

He kicked the door.

'O-pen. O-pen.'

His father opened the door and picked him up.

'H'Hay! Where's yer mammy?'

'She's jist comin up.'

His father put him down and went to help her with the pram.

He went into the kitchen and sat down by the fire.

Dusty, their cat, jumped down from the sink and slid quietly under the bed. The bed was in a recess opposite the window and the three of them slept there in winter. Although they had a room, the kitchen was easier to keep warm. The room was bigger and was very cold and damp. His father said it would cost too much to keep both the room and the kitchen heated.

He warmed his hands till they almost hurt. He heard his mother and father coming in. They left the pram in the lobby. His father was talking about the doctor.

'Aye, e gave me a prescription fur another jar a that ointment.' He had to put the ointment all over his body because his skin was red and flaky and he had scabby patches on his arms and legs. That was why he didn't have a job. He'd had to give up his trade in the shipyards because it was a dirty job and made his skin disease worse.

'An ah got your pills as well, when ah wis in the Chemist's.'

His mother had to take pills to help her breathing. At night she had to lie on her back, propped up with pillows.

'Never mind hen. When ah win the pools . . .'

'Whit'll ye get ME daddy?' This was one of their favourite conversations.

'Anythin ye like sun.'

'Wull ye get me a pony, daddy? Lik an Indian.'

'Ah'll get ye TWO ponies.' Laughing. 'An a wigwam as well!'

He could see it. He'd ride up to school, right up the stairs and into the classroom and he'd scalp Miss Heather before she could reach for her belt.

He'd keep the other pony for Annie. She was his friend. She wasn't his girlfriend. That was soft. She was three weeks older than him and she lived just round the corner. They were in the same class at school. She had long shiny black hair and she always wore bright clean colours. (One night in her back close—showing bums—giggling—they didn't hear the leerie coming in to light the gas-lamp—deep loud voice somewhere above them—sneering laugh—Annie pulling up her knickers and pulling down her dress in the same movement—scramble into the back—both frightened to go home in case the leerie had told, but he hadn't.)

The memory of it made him blush. He ripped off a piece of newspaper and reached up for the toilet key from the nail behind the door where it hung.

'Jist goin t' the lavvy.'

From the lobby he heard the toilet being flushed so he waited in the dark until he heard the slam of the toilet door then the flop of Mrs Dolan's feet on the stairs. The Dolans lived in the single end, the middle door of the three on their landing. The third house, another room and kitchen, was empty for the moment because the Andersons had emigrated to Canada.

When he heard Mrs Dolan closing the door he stepped out on to the landing and slid down the banister to the stairhead. In the toilet there was only one small window very high up, and he left the door slightly open to let light seep in from the stairhead.

A pigeon landed on the window-ledge and sat there gurgling and hooing, its feathers ruffled up into a ball. To pull the plug he climbed up on to the seat and swung on the chain, squawking out a Tarzan-call. The pigeon flurried off, scared by the noise, and he dropped from his creeperchain, six inches to the floor.

He looked out through the stairhead window. Late afternoon. Out across the back and a patch of wasteground, over factory roofs and across a railway line stood Ibrox Stadium. He could see a patch of terracing and the roof of the stand. The pressbox on top looked like a little castle. When Rangers were playing at home you could count the goals and near misses just by listening to the roars. Today there was only a reserve game and the noise could hardly be heard. Soon it would be dark and they'd have to put on the floodlights.

For tea they had sausages and egg and fried bread. After they'd eaten he sat down in his own chair at the fire with his Wonder Book of the World. The chair was wooden and painted bright blue.

His father switched on the wireless to listen to the football results and check his pools.

The picture of the Afghan Hound had been taken in a garden on a sunny day. The dog was running and its coat shone in the sun.

'Four draws,' said his father. 'Ach well, maybe next week . . .'

'There's that dog, mammy.' He held up the book.

'So it is.'

'Funny tae find a dog lik that in Govan,' said his father.

'Right enough,' said his mother. 'Expect some'dy knocked it.'

Nothing in the book looked like anything he had ever seen. There were pictures of cats but none of them looked like Dusty. They were either black and white or striped and they all looked clean and sleek. Dusty was a grubby grey colour and he spat and scratched if anyone tried to pet him. His mother said he'd been kept too long in the house. There was a section of the book about the weather with pictures of snow crystals that looked like flowers and stars. He thought he'd like to go out and play in the snow and he asked his mother if he could.

'Oh well, jist for a wee while then. Ah'll tell ye what. If ye come up early enough we kin put up the decorations before ye go tae bed.'

He'd forgotten about the decorations. It was good to have something special like that to come home for. It was the kind of thing he'd forget about while he was actually playing, then there would be moments when he'd remember, and feel warm and comforted by the thought.

He decided he'd get Joe and Jim and Annie and they'd build a snowman as big as a midden.

Joe was having his tea and Jim felt like staying in and Annie's mother wouldn't let her out.

He stood on the pavement outside the paper-shop, peering in through the lighted window at the Christmas annuals and selection boxes. The queue for the evening papers reached right to the door of the shop. The snow on the pavement was packed hard and greybrown, yellow in places under the streetlamps. He scraped at the snow with the inside of his boot, trying to rake up enough to make a snowball, but it was too powdery and it clung to the fingers of his woollen gloves, making his hands feel clogged and uncomfortable. He took off his gloves and scooped up some slush from the side of the road but the cold made his bare fingers sting, red. It felt as if he'd just been belted by Miss Heather.

Annie's big brother Tommy was clattering his way across the road, trailing behind him a sack full of empty bottles. He'd gathered them on the terracing at Ibrox and he was heading for the Family Department of the pub to cash in as many as he could. Every time the pub door opened the noise and light seeped out. It was a bit like pressing your hands over your ears then easing off then pressing again. If you did that again and again people's voices sounded like mwah . . . mwah . . . mwah . . . mwah . . .

He looked closely at the snow still clogging his gloves. It didn't look at all like the crystals in his book. Disgusted, he slouched towards his close.

Going up the stairs at night he always scurried or charged past each closet for fear of what might be lurking there ready to leap out at him. Keeping up his boldness, he whistled loudly. Little Star of Bethlehem. He was almost at the top when he remembered the decorations.

The kitchen was very bright after the dimness of the landing with its sputtering gas light.

'Nob'dy wis coming out tae play,' he explained.

His mother wiped her hands. 'Right! What about these decorations!'

The decorations left over from last year were in a cardboard box under the bed. He didn't like it under there. It was dark and dirty, piled with old rubbish—books, clothes, boxes, tins. Once he'd crawled under looking for a comic, dust choking him, and he'd scuttled back in horror from bugs and darting silverfish. Since then he'd had bad dreams about the bed swarming with insects that got into his mouth when he tried to breathe.

His father rummaged in the sideboard drawer for a packet of tin tacks and his mother brought out the box.

Streamers and a few balloons and miracles of coloured paper that opened out into balls or long concertina snakes. On the table his mother spread out some empty cake boxes she'd brought home from work and cut them into shapes like Christmas trees and bells, and he got out his painting box and a saucerful of water and he coloured each one and left it to dry—green for the trees and yellow for the bells, the nearest he could get to gold.

His father had bought something special.

'Jist a wee surprise. It wis only a coupla coppers in Woollies.'

From a cellophane bag he brought out a length of shimmering rustling silver.

'What dis that say daddy?' He pointed at the label.

'It says UNTARNISHABLE TINSEL GARLAND.'

'What dis that mean?'

'Well that's what it is. It's a tinsel garland. Tinsel's the silvery stuff it's made a. An a garland's jist a big long sorta decoration, for hangin up. An untarnishable means . . . well . . . how wid ye explain it hen?'

'Well,' said his mother, 'it jist means it canny get wasted. It always steys nice an shiny.'

'Aw Jesus!' said his father. 'Ther's only three tacks left!'

'Maybe the paper-shop'll be open.'

'It wis open a wee minnit ago!'

'Ah'll go an see,' said his father, putting on his coat and scarf. 'Shouldnae be very long.'

The painted cut-out trees and bells had long since dried and still his father hadn't come back. His mother had blown up the balloons and she'd used the three tacks to put up some streamers. Then she remembered they had a roll of sticky tape. It was more awkward to use than the tacks so the job took a little longer. But gradually the room was transformed, brightened; magical colours strung across the ceiling. A game he liked to play was lying on his back looking up at the ceiling and trying to imagine it was actually the floor and the whole room was upside down. When he did it now it looked like a toy garden full of swaying paper plants.

Round the lampshade in the centre of the room his mother was hanging the tinsel coil, standing on a chair to reach up. When she'd fixed it in place she climbed down and stood back and they watched the swinging lamp come slowly to rest. Then they looked at each other and laughed.

When they heard his father's key in the door his mother shooshed and put out the light. They were going to surprise him. He came in and fumbled for the switch. They were laughing and when he saw the decorations he smiled but he looked bewildered and a bit sad.

He put the box of tacks on the table.

'So ye managed, eh,' he said. He smiled again, his eyes still sad. 'Ah'm sorry ah wis so long. The paper-shop wis shut an ah had tae go down nearly tae Govan Road.'

Then they understood. He was sad because they'd done it all without him. Because they hadn't waited. They said nothing. His mother filled the kettle. His father took off his coat.

'Time you were in bed malad!' he said.

'Aw bit daddy, themorra's Sunday!'

'Bed!'

'Och!'

He could see it was useless to argue so he washed his hands and face and put on the old shirt he slept in.

'Mammy, ah need a pee.'

Rather than make him get dressed again to go out and down the stairs, she said he could use the sink. She turned on the tap and lifted him up to kneel on the ledge.

When he pressed his face up close to the window he could see the back court lit here and there by the light from a window, shining out on to the yellow snow from the dark bulk of the tenements. There were even one or two Christmas trees and, up above, columns of palegrey smoke, rising from chimneys. When he leaned back he could see the reflection of their own kitchen. He imagined it was another room jutting out beyond the window, out into the dark. He could see the furniture, the curtain across the bed, his mother and father, the decorations and through it all, vaguely, the buildings, the night. And hung there, shimmering, in that room he could never enter, the tinsel garland that would never ever tarnish.

Fred Urquhart

ROBERT / HILDA

Fred Urquhart (b.1912), is the author of several novels and some well-loved collections of short stories, notably *The Dying Stallion* (1967), and *The Ploughing Match* (1968). His impact on Scottish literature is equally felt in the many collections of short fiction which he has edited. He has worked in a bookshop, was Literary Editor of the *Tribune*, a reader for MGM, a scout for Walt Disney and a literary agent, (he has even had a hand in a cartoon biography of Winston Churchill) spent almost twenty years as a reader and editor for a London publisher and has latterly lived in Ashdown Forest in Sussex.

Urquhart shows an understanding of human nature with its dreams, pretensions and physical needs. When faced with the incredible, he is able to use the homely and outlandish to reinforce each other. 'Robert / Hilda' explores what is still for many an unapproachable subject with intelligence, sensitivity and humour.

Robert / Hilda

ONE

AFTER SHE DIED Robert Greenlees took to dressing up in his wife's clothes. It started when he had driven himself to go through Hilda's belongings to see what he could give away to her friends or to a jumble sale. He knew his daughter-in-law wouldn't even consider them. Alison had been scarcely civil when he'd asked her if she'd sort them out for him. 'Not at the moment, Father,' she had said. 'I'm very busy just now. Later on, maybe, if I can be of any help I'll give you what advice I can.'

He would never ask her again. So, one evening, he pulled out a drawer in Hilda's mahogany chest and took out a few folded garments: a blouse, three night-dresses, some silk scarves, a couple of cardigans. Hilda had been a great knitter; she'd been a dab hand at cardigans for herself and pullovers for him and Donny. She had sold them, too, to many of his customers in the Lothian and Borders villages within a radius of thirty to forty miles around Curlerscuik. Sold them at a profit: Hilda in her way had been as good a businessman as her husband. Robert rifled through the drawers and counted the cardigans, but he stopped when he got to seventeen. It was a wonder how Hilda had managed to wear them all turn about, but of course she'd liked a change. And she'd been fond of bright colours: orange, scarlet, emerald green, magenta, cherry, as well as more sedate heliotrope, powder blue, shell pink and the occasional striped ones, and she'd tried to outdo the fairisle knitting folk of Shetland with elaborate designs. He didn't fancy seeing them on any of Hilda's friends, and they were miles too good to send to a jumble.

Hilda had been a big woman. Not as big as him, but big enough. A pity to keep the cardigans in the drawers when he might be wearing one himself. They'd keep him warm. He could wear one in bed maybe, over his pyjamas. He needed something now he couldn't cuddle up against Hilda. Poor lass, lying in that cold old kirkyard at Otterheath, all on her own, waiting for his box to come and lie on top of hers. Though that, he hoped, would not be for a good while yet.

And so he put on a pink and grey cardigan to try it. It fitted better than he'd expected. He kept it on for the rest of the evening. Next night he put on one of the fairisles and stood for a long time admiring himself in the mirror, smoothing the cardigan down over his hips. And then one night he thought he'd try on another kind of garment. And so it wasn't long before he had a great desire to go out to see and be seen. He was desperate to talk to somebody and what's more to talk dressed like this. He was fed up sitting on his own night after night. Of course he went out during the day dressed as he'd always been dressed, for a walk along the back roads in the afternoon when he wasn't likely to meet anybody, and to the village shop sometimes in the morning.

He hated the visit to the shop, for there were always women there who'd almost throttle him with sympathy, talking about Hilda and offering to help; some wanted to do his housework, some went the length of making meals and bringing them to his door just when he'd made a nice simple meal for himself, so that he was forced to eat the neighbour's meal, to show good faith, and often waste his own. Though he'd become cunning enough now and never made a meal that would spoil after a few hours in the fridge or the pantry safe. But what irked him most about these women was the fact that several were widows, and he knew fine they were after him. There was Mrs Nairn who'd been a widow for only two years since poor David got himself killed by the tractor that was the darling of his life, the tractor he'd christened *Peg o' my Heart*. Robert knew Peggy Nairn was after him like a game hunter in Africa with a rifle.

He didn't want to marry again. He didn't need a helping hand from any of these women. He'd been dominated enough all his life by women, and he wanted a change.

Robert was gregarious. When he was a travelling packman and a draper he had been used to meeting people, talking and laughing with them. He loved a good-going clash, sharing other folk's opinions, hopes and experiences. He never read books. He skipped through the newspapers, and he only half-listened to what he still called the wireless. They had been getting on in years when Hilda and he bought a television, and now that she was gone he hardly ever switched on the set, and when he did he often sat with his eyes shut, half-asleep. In the old days Hilda and he had gone to the cinema once a week, but he had not watched a film on television for a very long time. In his first years in Curlerscuik he got to know everybody in the village: every man, woman and child was his friend. When Donny was young Robert had gone to the pub, *The Stag*, one or two evenings a week and always on Saturday nights. He was well known as 'one of our regulars' until, after several years, he cast out with the landlord and his lady, Dan and Effie Moffat, over the affair of the pissy professor, and Robert never darkened *The Stag*'s door again. Sometimes he regretted it, yet he still felt, though it was many years ago now, that he'd been right to take the stand he did.

The pissy professor was a gentle unassuming little fat man who had retired from one of the great universities and come to live in a fine stone-built late Victorian mansion about half a mile from the village. The professor was an alcoholic, though that was not the description used about him then. The villagers said he was a nice auld gentleman that was fond of his dram. He was so fond of it that every night at six o'clock he came into *The Stag*'s saloon bar, laid a pound note on the counter and asked in a quiet voice that was almost a whisper for 'A double whisky, please.' By closing time he'd had many double whiskies, and he'd also bought many other double whiskies, pints of beer, sherries and gins and tonics for many other inhabitants of Curlerscuik. He was fair game for the avaricious, the mean, the bold and the brash.

After about six months of observing the pissy professor and the locals who hung around, always ready to swallow quickly and thrust out empty glasses at his invitation, and sometimes himself accepting the professor's 'What's yours, Mr Greenlees?'—though he always made sure he returned the compliment immediately—Robert talked forcibly to Mr and Mrs Moffat. He accused them of helping to rook the professor by aiding and abetting the villagers who battened on him for drinks. 'He may be a rich man for all I know,' Robert said. 'He may be well able to afford to fling his money around like he does on a pack of scrounging buggers, but I don't hold with it. I don't approve, and what's more I don't approve of you letting him do it. You encourage him, and you've no right to do it. He's your best customer, but if you go on like this you're going to kill the goose that lays the golden eggs.'

Robert had never gone near *The Stag* again. He'd stamped out of the door with Effie Moffat shouting after him: 'You'll live to regret this, Greenlees, you big fat shite that lets your wife sit on you. You'll come back here crawling one o' thae days.'

He remembered it all as he put on a pair of Hilda's silk stockings and then a skirt of fawn and brown checks that had been one of her favourites. It was a pity he couldn't dander along to *The Stag* and have a whisky and a nice wee gossip with old friends. But he daren't do it. The Moffats had retired a while back, and their daughter and son-in-law, Nell and Jock Jackson, had taken over, but any time Robert had seen either of the Jacksons in the shop or the village street he'd known by their sour looks that the time wasn't ripe yet for returning to his old haunts. It was a great pity, for he'd like fine to get a breath of fresh air. He was desperate to get out of the house for an hour, so to hell with anybody who saw him.

TWO

'A big change this morning, Mrs Fletcher,' Mrs Nairn shouted across the garden fence to her neighbour. 'It's turned very cauld.'

'Has it?' Mrs Fletcher said. 'I cannie say I've noticed. I'm a bit ahint this mornin' and I've been hurrying to make up.'

'Oh ay, it's much caulder,' Peggy Nairn said. 'It was quite warm last night, but there's a nip in the air the day. It was that warm last night I had to open our front door and stand out on the step for a while to get a breather.'

'Rather you than me, dear,' Mrs Fletcher said. 'I'm no keen on lookin' out at the dark.'

'Ay, but it's wonderful the things you see in the dark,' Mrs Nairn said. 'Fabulous things. I've had my eyes opened many's a time. One thing I've seen lately is that Greenlees has got a fancy woman.'

'Aw no, Mrs Nairn, I don't believe it.'

'It's gospel,' Peggy Nairn said. 'I've seen her with my own eyes. Not once, but at least half a dozen times. It's aye late at night she visits him. After I saw her the first time by accident, I've watched for her. She's very furtive-like. Very furtive. She sneaks past my gate and into his like a sleekit tabby cat. And little wonder. I wouldn't like to swear to it—after all, it was in the dark—but I think she was wearing Hilda's green tweed coat. It's dreadful. Giving away the poor woman's clothes and her not dead six months yet.'

'Are you sure?'

'Of course I'm sure,' Mrs Nairn said. 'I've got good eyesight, haven't I? Oh yes, she just scuttled past. A right sleekit scuttle. Just like a tabby that's stolen the cream.'

'Fancy that now,' Mrs Fletcher said. 'It just goes to show, doesn't it?' If there's anything sleekit it's that Robert Greenlees. I've aye thought he was two-faced. I could never be doing with him. It was her I liked. Hilda was a fine woman and too good for him. Mind you, he's a good enough neighbour. He minds his own business. But there's something about him I've never taken to. He's a real salesman. Very smarmy, and full o' gush. He'll gas away like an auld wife until he has your head fair birling.'

'It hasn't taken him long, has it, to forget poor Hilda?' Mrs Nairn said. 'After all the roaring and greeting there was at her funeral. Will you ever forget the fuss he made? He had the cheek to choose yon hymn *O Love that Wilt not let me go* for the service and then he grat like a bairn in the middle of it. I saw him with my own eyes and was fair ashamed of the spectacle he made. I saw the minister looking at him very funny-like. No wonder. A man that is a man would never greet like that. Greenlees should think black burning shame. And now he's got this woman and Hilda hardly cauld in her grave.'

'Ay, she's been soon forgotten, poor lass,' Mrs Fletcher said. 'I'll tell you something that I was going to keep to myself, but now you've told me about this fancy woman it's high time I aired my views, I made it my business last Sunday to go to Otterheath kirkyard and have a wee keek at her grave. And it was neglected. Shamefully neglected. Only a few withered flowers in a jar full o' stinking water. They'd been there for weeks.'

'Ah well, he'll not get away with it if I have my way,' Peggy Nairn said. 'I'll soon let the whole village know what a monster we've got in our midst.'

'I wonder who she is, Peggy?' Mrs Fletcher said. 'Did you get a good look at her?'

'I tell you it was dark every time. So I saw nothing, though it wasn't for the want of trying. I even went out to my gate to get a better look. I think she must be a stranger. I didn't ken her walk. But one thing I will swear to, and that is that she was wearing one of Hilda's head-scarfs—yon bonnie one with the Chinese figures—forby her green coat. I made no mistake about that.'

Peggy Nairn pursed her lips, tossed her head, growing squint-eyed with spleen, and added: 'You and me must get to the bottom of this, Mrs Fletcher, and then it's our duty to let Donny and his wife ken what a snake in the grass their father is.'

THREE

Robert Greenlees was born in the small Midlothian town of Otterheath. Like his father before him, he was an only child. His mother was nearly forty when he was born. She had only one relative, her sister Bertha who was ten years older. Robert had no other near relatives. Auntie Bertha had been housekeeper and companion to an old lady who had left her some money and a cottage in the village of Curlerscuik, five miles from Otterheath. The money not being enough to keep her in idleness, Bertha had become the District Nurse, cycling around the countryside and making herself both a blessing and a nuisance.

Auntie Bertha was the bane of Robert's life when he was a child. Every Sunday, unless she had an urgent nursing case, she cycled to Otterheath and spent the afternoon with the Greenlees. Bertha was a big domineering woman, always interfering in other folks' affairs. She never stopped telling her sister about her brother-in-law's faults and how she wasn't bringing up Robert in the proper manner. Even when he was a grown boy, fifteen or sixteen, Auntie Bertha would seize him by the ear and say: 'Your lugs are dirty and you've got a tidemark round your neck. If you were mine, my lad, I'd make you fonder of soap and water and I'd fairly ginger you up.'

'But he's not yours, Bertha,' his mother would say. 'He's mine and I'm quite satisfied with him.'

When he was fourteen Robert went to work in the Otterheath paper mill. Before he had time to look around and become pals with one of his workmates he was taken under the wing of Hilda Wishart, a typist in the office, a dark-haired determined young woman with plain heavy features. Hilda had been one of the big girls when Robert was at school and she had never spoken to him. She made up for this as soon as she got him into her clutches in the mill. She smothered him in her engulfing wings, and he never had a chance to seek other company. They went together to the pictures twice a week. She was waiting for him every night when the mill stopped work, and she walked home with him, and they stood for half an hour, daffing and chaffing, until Robert's mother called out of the window that it was time he came in for his high tea.

On Sundays in summer they went for long walks over the Pentland Hills, always avoiding contact with other young people hiking in pairs and quartets; they wanted no company but their own. In the winter Robert played cards after tea with Hilda and her parents, then he stayed to supper, going home always just before half past ten when his mother often opened the door before he had time to put his key in the lock.

Hilda was twenty-two when she decided it was time they got married. Neither lot of parents objected, though Auntie Bertha, who thoroughly approved of Hilda, said she didn't think Robert should settle down quite so quickly: 'He's only nineteen, and he must ha'e more wild oats to sow yet.'

They could not get a house, so they rented two rooms from old Mrs Pendreich, a friend of Hilda's mother. Seeing she had no housework to contend with, Hilda kept on her job, and every night, as usual, she met Robert at the paper mill gates, cleeked arms, and they walked home together. They still went to the pictures twice a week, and on Sundays they had high tea at the Greenlees' home and then went to play cards and have supper with the Wisharts.

At twenty-five Robert left the paper mill and became a travelling packman. This change was caused by the death of Auntie Bertha. She got knocked off her bike by a runaway horse dragging an empty coal-lorry, and she died two days later in the infirmary in Edinburgh. She left her cottage in Curlerscuik to Robert.

By this time the young Greenlees had moved to other lodgings; they had got tired of Mrs Pendreich dogging their footsteps and always asking if Hilda was expecting. They could not find an empty house at a reasonably cheap rent in Otterheath, and they were tired of being lodgers in nosey old women's houses, so Auntie Bertha's death was a great blessing. But the five miles stretch between Curlerscuik and Otterheath was not.

Robert did not fancy cycling back and forrit every day to the paper mill, and Hilda did not fancy spending her days cleaning and dusting a four-roomed cottage in a village where she knew nobody. As luck would have it, there was a sudden and unexpected solution. Old Jimmy Nairn, the travelling packman, whose cottage with its adjoining field and roughly-built stable was next door to Auntie Bertha's, decided to pack up for good and sell his stock and the goodwill of his many customers within a forty-mile radius of the Lothians and Borders. Hilda said it was just the very job that would suit Robert to perfection; the dust and the din of machinery in the paper mill were bad for his health. Having endured them for over ten years, Robert was ready enough to agree with her, and he liked the idea of a life travelling from place to place in a pony-and-trap, selling his haberdashery to women customers in outlying cottages, farms and villages, the very thing the doctor had ordered. And so they bought

Jimmy Nairn's business and set forth together to make it a good paying one.

Hilda did her housework in the morning while Robert was grooming the pony and getting his wares packed into the trap. Then about eleven o'clock they'd set out at a spanking pace along the village street waving to any neighbour wifie who happened to be at her door or had her head stuck out of a window. They drove a different route every day, for the main point of the business was a weekly visit to each customer. On this visit Robert would take his pack or packs into the house after his customer had greeted him at the door and she'd exchanged a few words with Hilda, who always sat in the trap and knitted while her husband was inside. Hilda always said she did not want to interfere with what, after all, was Robert's own business, but she made an exception whenever it was raining or if the customer invited her in for a cup of tea.

Whether Hilda came into the house or not, Robert's procedure was always the same. He would chaff the cottar wifie and then he'd spread out his wares—camisoles, scarves, knickers, petticoats, men's underwear, shirts, blouses, sheets, cushion-covers, bedspreads and the like—and the customer would finger her way through them while she talked about her family and her neighbours. Then, after she'd made her choice of the articles she wanted, Robert would get out his notebook and say: 'Well now, Mrs Nisbet, if we add this to what you're owing me, it comes to fourteen pounds, nine and sixpence. Is that all right with you? And what can you afford to pay me this week? Five bob or ten bob?'

Sometimes she said: 'I think I'll manage a pound this week, Mr Greenlees. My man had a nice wee win on the Grand National.' But more often she said: 'I can only afford to give ye four shillings, Mr Greenlees. I'm awful short at the moment. But I hope to give ye more next week. In fact, I think I can promise ye ten bob. My youngest laddie starts a new job on Monday, and he's going to give me twenty-five shillings a week for his keep. That pair of pants and the semmit are for him, so I'll see that he pays for them.'

And so the transaction would go down in Robert's notebook, and he and Hilda would depart, waving gaily to Mrs Nisbet or whoever it was, on their way to another customer in the next village or isolated cottage or farmhouse. In this way Robert and Hilda, for he always repeated the gist of the conversation to her as they clopperty-clopped along, got to know the history of all members of the family of each customer.

Robert was a good salesman. He was always good-natured, and the women knew his cheeriness was not just put on for their benefit. He was reasonable, too, about bad debts, and always willing to stretch a point and not press for payment when he knew the women's pleas for more time were genuine. Many a customer got herself into debt just by listening to banter, and most of them were susceptible to his flow of words and often bought things they hadn't thought of or didn't need. 'You could sell sunglasses to a blind man at the North Pole, Mr Greenlees,' said one old woman after he gave her what she called his 'patter' when showing her sheets she had not asked for.

'Ach away with your flattery, Mrs Bruce,' Robert said, laughing. 'These are the best and cheapest sheets you're ever likely to get, so be a devil and lash out. I ken you're not needing new sheets at the moment, but be a devil and buy a couple of pairs to put away. I tell you, woman, in another couple of years you'll have to pay double the price for sheets like these. Look at the quality. That's no cheap cotton. That's as near as dammit to good old Irish linen from Belfast.'

'Ye're an awful man, Mr Greenlees. You'd worm a body's false teeth out of her.' Mrs Bruce tee-heeheed and gave him a dig with a bony elbow. 'I'll buy a pair,' she said, opening her purse. 'They can aye be kept. They'll come in handy for my winding sheet.'

'Ach, you're not likely to need a winding sheet for a long time yet, Mrs Bruce. These sheets are too good for a shroud. If you want a shroud, if you want to put it by for your future like, I've got a nice line in cheap shrouds. Might as well buy one now, Mrs Bruce, when they're going a-begging as wait ten, twenty years when you need it and have to pay ten times the price.'

'Oh, ye're a shameless crature, Mr Greenlees, wheelin' an auld woman's life blood out of her like that.'

The packman's business prospered. In 1936 it was flourishing so well that Hilda and Robert decided to sell the pony and trap and buy a car. The pony was old and ought to be retired, and the trap was too slow a means of travel. But they were dilatory about making the decisive move, for Robert was fond of the old pony and didn't like to think what might happen after it was sold; he didn't want it to end in a slaughterhouse. And then Hilda became pregnant, so the idea was allowed to lapse.

Hilda had a miscarriage, and after a lot of talk they bought a car in 1938. They were helped in their decision by Jimmy Nairn's son David, who was anxious to buy back the field and the old stable where the pony was housed; David had plans to set up as a smallholder producing necessary foodstuffs if the war with Hitler came. He also agreed to teach Robert to drive. It was an uphill struggle, though. Robert did not have a mechanical mind, and he could not get his feet, eyes and hands to coordinate. In the long run, after Robert had rammed the car into a stone wall and done quite a bit of damage and David had grabbed the wheel from him before he did more, David cried: 'You silly stupid bugger, you'll never be able to drive, so give it up before you kill yourself or somebody else.'

Robert was glad to give up the struggle; he would willingly have bought back the pony and trap. But Hilda was not to be downfaced by

David Nairn or anybody else. She asked David to teach her, and in no time she was driving the car as if she'd been driving for years and had, actually, been born in a car.

For the next two years Robert and Hilda ignored the coming and then the outbreak of war. Five days a week they set forth at eleven o'clock every morning, Hilda driving the fawn-coloured Austin, and in no time they had extended their territory and their profit. While Robert was gossiping with his customers, encouraging them to forget the war and their men being in the army, Hilda sat in the car and knitted steadily. This way of Greenlees life was interrupted for a short time in 1940 when Hilda became pregnant again and gave birth to their only child Donald. For a few weeks Robert had to hire another driver, an elderly man who nearly drove him daft by his monologues about the merits and demerits of different Scottish football teams. In a few weeks, however, Hilda was back in the driving seat and they had a passenger, baby Donny, in a wicker basket amongst the packs of haberdashery.

After the war trade started to fall off. It was a gradual decline, not very noticeable at first. The war was really responsible. Many families had become more prosperous during it, owing to women doing well paid work while drawing their husband's army allowances. People have always put by money for a rainy day, but in the years 1939–45 many families saved more money and spent more than heretofore. A large number of Robert Greenlees' customers had never been so well off. At the same time their ideas and ambitions widened. Many, far enough away from bombing and death, had a very good time and enjoyed themselves with new found prosperity. And so they were dissatisfied with the type and quality of the goods Robert provided. They wanted to go to Edinburgh to stravaig through the classy shops in Princes Street, Leith Walk and The Bridges to look at the greater variety of jumpers, blouses, frocks and knickers and choose what appealed most to them rather than accept the kind of things Robert brought in his packs. And because their newly-affluent sons and daughters were buying cars instead of bicycles many country-women were able to go forth on a shopping spree whenever they felt like it rather than having to wait for the packman. Old women who distrusted cars and never ventured on public transport stayed at home as they'd always done, but the younger generation was only too delighted to get into the family car and go to Edinburgh.

As soon as Hilda noticed the decline in trade—for Hilda, after all, kept the account books—she said it was time to make a change. They had made money with the packman business, had put it in the bank and had invested their profits. No sense in losing what they had gained, and they were too young to retire yet. They would get a shop. The decline had never really dawned on Robert, although he'd seen that many old customers weren't buying as much as usual. Some, in fact, were not buying at all; instead, every week they paid only a few shillings towards what they owed him, and spent the rest of his visit gossiping. Robert did not want a shop. 'It would tie us down too much,' he told Hilda. 'I don't want to spend the rest of my life being behind a counter either. You'd miss travelling from place to place, woman. We'd both miss it, and we'd miss the fine fresh country air. I couldn't thole looking through a window and watching folk walk by. I'd miss clashing with the likes of Mrs Nisbet and Mrs Stoddart and auld Jessie Finlayson. And you'd miss all the titbits of gossip I get from them.'

Hilda ignored his arguments. She read advertisements and went to see estate agents. She surveyed several shops in the small towns round about, but none satisfied her. Meantime she nagged away at Robert, trying to make him see reason. But he saw this and decided to give up only when an old customer, Mrs Gibson, a woman nearly fifty and a poor payer, always in arrears, said: 'Well, that's the last of what I owe ye, Mr Greenlees. Paid up to the last shilling. I've always enjoyed your company and many's the good laugh we've had thegither, but I don't think ye need come here again. It would be a waste of my time and yours, for I'll no' be buyin' any more from ye. Yer goods are no' fashionable enough. And my auldest laddie has just bocht a car, so I can gang further afield now and get what I want.'

In less than a week after Mrs Gibson's valediction, Hilda found a shop for sale in Otterheath. It would make a grand draper's, which Otterheath badly needed, and there was a house above it, which would suit them fine and save travelling. She told Robert to bid for it, and after Hilda had haggled about the price, getting it for a few hundreds less than the asking-price, it was theirs. Robert wasn't keen about going back to Otterheath; his parents were dead, and he hardly ever thought about the days of his youth. But Donny was growing, and he needed a better school than the Curlerscuik village one.

The draper's shop did even better than Hilda had prophesied. It was a busy life and not as entertaining as a packman's, but the profits mounted and Donny did well at the Otterheath school. Robert was content. Hilda wanted to sell the Curlerscuik cottage, but for once in his life Robert put down his foot; it had belonged to Auntie Bertha, she'd left it to him, and he was going to hold on to it. Then Hilda said they'd let it at a high rent, but Robert wouldn't have that either. There was no knowing what kind of tenants they'd get and what damage they might do; it was better to leave it as it was and allow it to idle; it wasn't eating up anything, and it was always there for them to bide in at weekends and holidays. Not that there were many free weekends, though they always went to Curlerscuik on Sundays, and there were no holidays. The only kind of holiday they ever got was to have two or three evenings out each week at a restaurant or a pub. Hilda liked eating out; it saved her making an evening meal and it gave them an opportunity to see people other than their shop customers. They went far afield on many evenings, visiting villages where they met old customers: women who, in the packman's time, had never ventured far from home but who now, with prosperity, liked to eat out and see and be seen. It was often around midnight when the Greenlees got home, but no matter how late Hilda always drove with calm deliberation. Hilda often got tipsy, but she never got drunk. She drove the car without fear or favour, and never once did she have an accident.

Like his father before him, Donny got married at nineteen. Like Robert, he'd been taken in tow by a very determined and domineering young woman. Except that Alison was younger than Hilda when she popped the question. Alison was two years younger than Donny. She was a little sharp-faced blonde with a precise polite voice that became shrill when she lost her temper.

Robert had hoped that Donny might be clever enough to go to Edinburgh University; Robert had a great respect for learning though he had no pretence to any himself. Robert still remembered the pissy professor with admiration. He and the professor had had many an interesting talk, and Robert often wondered what happened to the old man after he left Curlerscuik. Donny, however, had no desire to be academic. As soon as he left school at fourteen, he got a job in a garage. He soon became so proficient about the mechanism of cars, as well as the selling of them, that he was able to persuade his father to buy him into the business, and he took over the garage when his former boss retired.

When Donny married Alison they could not find a house that Alison considered suitable for a couple of their status, so Hilda and Robert gave them the house above the shop and themselves returned to Curlerscuik. In this way it was as if they'd gone back to their early years as packmen. Hilda drove Robert to Otterheath every day, and this helped to change their view of the draper's and its customers. At last Robert realised that instead of dealing with the friendly cottage wifies of pre-war days he was dealing with small town women who imagined they were sophisticated and, therefore, threw their weight around when choosing garments. He often had to choke down his pride in his goods and his salesmanship. Hilda, on the other hand, was not prepared to be sat on by women she disliked on sight, so she often gave vent to acid-tinged remarks and lost sales. Not that either she or Robert cared about that. They were counting the days until they retired and handed over the business to Alison, who spent a few hours every day learning the trade and bossing her father-in-law.

Their retirement was delayed because Alison had a baby. No sooner had she produced her son than she became pregnant again. It was another son. As soon as the two little boys were old enough for Alison to take over the shop, Hilda and Robert retired. But they had only two years of peace and happiness together in the Curlerscuik cottage before Hilda died. She'd had cancer for a long time without ever telling Robert.

The Greenlees car was taken over by Alison who said: 'You'll have no further use for it now, Father. Donny is always here to take you wherever you want to go.'

Not that Donny was. Donny was too busy in his garage, buying and selling second-hand cars and making money, to have time to take his father for jaunts in the car. Every Saturday night, though, he drove to Curlerscuik and took his father on a pub crawl while Alison stayed at home and looked after the children. She kept telling Donny and Robert how unselfish it was of her to do this after a hard week's work in the shop. 'Very few wives would let you go out on your own gallivanting like this,' she said. 'I should get a medal.' She always succeeded in making Donny feel guilty, though he knew that as soon as she'd got rid of him she hustled the children to bed and then sat down and watched television until he came home about midnight.

FOUR

One Saturday night when Donny came to take Robert out for their weekly spree at two or three or more pubs, he found his father wearing a skirt and blouse, his mother's best green tweed coat with the mink collar and cuffs, and a green velour toque that Hilda had kept for best. Robert's lips were well encarmined with lipstick, and there was powder on his face.

'What in God's name are you doing, Dad?' Donny said. 'Have you gone cuckoo?'

''No, I thought I'd wear this,' Robert said. 'I thought we might go to *The Stag* tonight. It'll save petrol.'

'I'm not going into *The Stag* with you dressed like that,' Donny said. 'It's all very well for a laugh in our own house, but I'm not setting one foot outside the door with you.'

'Why not?'

'Ach, be your age, Dad. What do you think the folks in the village would say if you walked in like that in Mother's clothes? They'd send for the police and the doctor. Anyway, I thought you didn't like *The Stag*. You haven't been in it for years to the best of my knowledge.'

'I'm not keen on it,' Robert said. 'I used to like it before I had yon barney with the Moffats and said I'd never enter it again. But the Moffats have been retired for years, and their son-in-law and daughter hardly know me.'

'They'd know you soon enough if you go in dressed like that. What do you think it is? Hallowe'en? And you're a guiser?'

'I'm not guising, son,' Robert said. 'I'm very serious. However, if you don't want to go to *The Stag*, we'll go somewhere else. Let's go into the car and then we can make up our minds where we're going.'

'I've made up my mind already, Dad. We're not going any place with you dressed like that.'

'We're going to *The Red Lion* at Lasswade,' Robert said. 'Nobody there will ken me. They'll think I'm your mother. Remember to call me "Ma".'

'I'll do no such thing,' Donny said. 'I like a laugh as well as the next one, but I draw the line at capers like this.'

'It's not a caper, son. I don't see anything funny about it. I like wearing your Ma's clothes. They do something to me.'

'They do something to me, too,' Donny said. 'What would my mother say if she saw you? She wouldn't like it.'

'Your mother would've loved it,' Robert said. 'She'd have laughed fit to burst. I can just hear her saying: "What'll you get up to next, you silly auld kipper?"'

'I don't believe it. She'd say you'd turned kinky.'

'Well, maybe I have,' Robert said. 'It's something that happens sometimes to men of my age. I'm androgynous.'

Donny said: 'Androg what?'

'Androgynous.'

'Where did you learn a word like that?' Donny said. 'I thought you never read the papers, Dad?'

'I don't, but I saw this in one that was wrapped round a packet of soap powder I got from the village shop. I had nothing else to do, so I read this article about what happens often to both old men and old women. They begin to look like each other. You must surely have noticed how a lot of old women look like old men.'

'You're pulling my leg, Dad. You're no more androg-whatever-it-is than I am.'

'It's a change of personality in old people,' Robert said. 'I'm not alone in this. Just you wait till you get to my age. Maybe you'll become androgynous too.'

'Not on your nelly,' Donny said. 'Nobody will believe it. Folk'll just laugh and say you've gone off your rocker.'

'Let them laugh,' Robert said.

'That's all very well,' Donny said. 'But they'll think you should be put away. Some bright spark is sure to call the police and have you put in the loony bin.'

'Let them think what they like,' his father said, going to the mirror and prissing his lips to see if the lipstick was staying on all right. He gave his toque a little tweak, giggled and said: 'It's still my car, y'know, and if I like I can just get into it and drive away on my own. But seeing I don't want to quarrel with you . . . and I'm sure you don't want to quarrel with me . . .'

'You don't want to break your neck, you mean,' Donny cried. 'Now Dad, be reasonable. Don't you dare try to drive that car. I'll take you, only . . .'

'All right,' Robert said. 'I'll be good. I tell you what. I'll sit in the car and nobody will see me in the dark, and you can bring the drinks out to me.'

They argued about this all the way to Lasswade, but Donny's argument got weaker and weaker. Once in the car and he'd started to drive, a sideways glance at his father reminded him so strongly of his mother that he began to think maybe they could pull it off. But not in Lasswade, where Hilda and Robert had been well known to many throughout the years. Donny drove past *The Red Lion* and said: 'I've just had a good idea, Dad—I mean Ma. There's a very good pub I know in Gorekeith where we can have a nice supper and you're not likely to be recognised.'

Donny took great care not to risk this when they walked into the pub. He took his father by the elbow and steered him to a table in a corner. The saloon bar-cum-dining room was only dimly lit, so that helped to cloak Robert's appearance, though he cursed the dim lights later on when they were eating.

But all went well at first. Donny went to the bar to get the drinks and the menu. He stood beside a tall well-built man of about his father's age, with broad shoulders, a head of thick white hair worn fairly long, and a brown still-goodlooking face. The man said something that Donny didn't catch, but they got into conversation. Donny carried a large gin and tonic to his father, and then went back to the bar to talk to the white-headed man.

Robert sipped his gin, opened the green tweed coat, felt to see that his toque was on at a suitable angle but was not revealing his ears, crossed his legs, admired the silken sheen of his stockings, and then looked around the saloon. Not a soul that he even knew by sight. He recrossed his legs and settled back to enjoy his drink. He was just about to drain it when the white-headed man who, Robert realised, had been looking steadily at him for several minutes, winked and then grinned at him.

Robert winked back in a very ladylike way, and he gave his lips a little twist.

The man said to Donny in a tone Robert heard clearly: 'Will your lady mother accept a gin and tonic with my compliments?'

'Tell him I'd rather have a pint of heavy,' Robert whispered to Donny when he came to the table and repeated the message. But it was a double gin and tonic that he got. He looked at it, gave his lips a lick, and then raised his glass and bowed to the man. 'Here's looking at you, kind sir,' he said.

The white haired man winked again. So did Robert. A second or two later the white haired man came to the table with Donny. 'My name's George Carnie,' he said, putting out his hand.

'This is my mother, Mrs Greenlees,' Donny said.

George Carnie was a retired sea captain. He had been all over the world. Now he'd come back to live at Newtongrange, where he'd been born. He ate supper with them and insisted on paying the bill. At closing time they said cordial goodnights without mention of ever meeting again.

'What a performance, Dad—I mean Ma.' Donny said when they were in the car. 'You should've been on the stage. You'd be smashing on TV.'

Robert giggled and said: 'I didn't do that bad, did I? I daresay George thought I was really Charlie's aunt from Brazil—where the nuts come from, y'know!'

'You're a nut all right,' Donny said. 'And so is he to be taken in by you.'

'We're all taken in by somebody,' Robert said. 'It's a part of life. You're being taken in yourself if it comes to that.'

'Ay, I daresay,' Donny laughed. 'Oh, Dad, you were a right scream when you said: "My hubby passed on a while back." I nearly laughed out loud, though I know it's not funny.'

'Of course it's not funny. I'm the one that knows that. I miss your Ma, and I miss her more when I'm wearing her clothes. But I felt I had to say something to George. To explain matters, like.'

'You did it fine,' Donny said. 'You were that good I could've kissed you.'

'Well, why don't you kiss me now?' Robert said.

'I'm not that soppy,' Donny said.

FIVE

Five or six months after that Donny had influenza, so he telephoned his father on the Saturday afternoon and told him there was no hope of their usual weekly outing. Robert said it was okay, he'd be quite pleased not to go out for once, he'd watch television instead, and he hoped Donny would be better soon.

In the evening, without telling Donny who was fast asleep, Alison left him and the two little boys in charge of a babysitter and drove to Curlerscuik. She had no intention of taking her father-in-law out for a drive and a few drinks—she regarded such outings as 'common'. She wanted to see him only because she wanted him to agree to handing over the Otterheath shop and house as a gift to her and Donny, and she had in her handbag a paper all ready for him to sign—'To save death duties, Father. It's something that should be done now, and it'll save money and prevent a lot of trouble later on.'

Alison had it all rehearsed, but she never got a chance to make her speech. She went into the cottage by the back door without knocking, and she gave a startled yelp when she saw what her father-in-law was doing.

Robert hadn't had his hair cut for over six months, and now it was hanging over his ears and down the back of his neck. He was combing it before the mirror in the sitting-room and arranging curls over his cheeks when Alison opened the door. His face was well painted and powdered, and he wore an evening dress that Hilda had admired but seldom wore: a stylish creation of primrose and gold silk with a high neckline and flowing sleeves of chiffon.

'What are you doing, Father?' Alison cried. 'What do you mean being dressed up like this?'

'What do you think I'm doing?' Robert said. 'Getting ready for my beau to take me out on the ran-dan, of course. Will you have a drink?'

He picked up a half-empty glass of whisky and toasted her before draining the glass. 'Would you like whisky or gin?'

'Father, I'm fair ashamed of you,' Alison yelped. 'You're a disgrace. Behaving like something in *The News of the World*. If this is what you get up to when you're on your own it's high time a stop was put to it. I'll have a word with the doctor about such outrageous behaviour.'

'I'll behave as I want to behave,' Robert said. 'And I'll have none of your bloody jaw, my girl.'

'Get thae claes off at once,' Alison shouted. 'I'll take them and all the rest of Mother's things to Oxfam before you get into any more mischief.'

'I'll do no such thing,' Robert said, taking another gulp of whisky. 'You've interfered in my life far too often, my girl. Don't think I haven't seen all you're doing to get the business completely under your control. But you're not going to succeed. I've made a watertight will—though I've no intention of dying for a while yet. I'm going to enjoy myself first.'

'Take off thae claes at once,' she shouted. 'Or I'll get a real man to do it for you. I'll get the bobby here in a jiffy.'

'Are you taking the name of our local policeman in vain by any chance?' Robert poured a fresh drink. 'Constable Paddy Fairbairn himself, do you mean? Paddy Fairbairn that couldn't take the clothes off a scabbit cat, far less a grown man. Even an old one!'

'Get thae claes off,' Alison screamed.

'You're forgetting your posh voice, aren't you?' Robert said. 'You self-centred, pug-nosed cow. You hooked our Donny before he had a chance to look around and see what he could make out of life and what fun he might have got. Well, you won't be so full of pride and highpan notions by the time I've finished with you. So there's the door. Clear out before I clash my whisky in your face—and it would be a waste of good whisky! Get out, and don't come back!'

'You auld bastard,' Alison screamed in her high thin bloodless voice. 'I'll make you pay for this.'

She was in such a temper flouncing into the car that she never noticed another car drawing up behind hers. As she drove off with much sound and fury a tall man got out of the other car, opened the door she had just banged and went inside.

Alison woke Donny out of a deep sleep and ordered him never to go near Curlerscuik again and to have nothing more to do with his father except through a solicitor. They argued about it for a fortnight. Then on the Saturday night Donny told her he was going to visit his father and was taking the two little boys with him.

Alison slapped Donny's face and stood with her back against the door, saying: 'You don't move one foot out of this house, Donald Greenlees, or I'll know the reason why.'

Donald said: 'I give you two seconds to get away from that door, woman, or I'll give you such a sock on the jaw you'll not be the better of it for a week.'

Two minutes later Alison was holding her face and yelling: 'You're a pervert like your father,' while Donny herded the two frightened little boys out in front of him. 'That'll maybe teach you to keep your trap shut in future,' he said, closing the door behind him.

The boys sat quietly in the car all the way to Curlerscuik. Donny was silent, too upset to try to explain. He felt that would come when they got to their grandfather's. William, the eldest, was a sedate boy of seven, selfpossessed and self-sufficient. He was named after Alison's father, and he had all Alison's ways. Bobby was six, wide-eyed with curiosity. He ran ahead of them into the Curlerscuik cottage.

'What've you got on a skirt for, Grandpa?' Bobby cried, gazing at his grandfather's silk-stockinged legs.

'I'm not your Grandpa tonight, Bobby,' Robert said. 'I'm your Granny.'

'But Mammy says Granny's with the angels.'

'Granny is not with the angels, no matter what your Mammy says. Granny is here right now, I'm your Grandpa some days, your Granny other days. I'm your Granny at the top, but I'm your Grandpa at the bottom.'

Watching the child's puzzled face, Robert said: 'I'm A/C one day, D/C the next. Do you ken what that means?'

'He doesn't know anything about electricity, Dad,' Donny said. 'I mean Ma. You'll have to teach him, and he'll learn in time.'

'I'm really androgynous, Bobby,' his grandfather said.

'It's too big a word for the bairn,' said another man's voice.

George Carnie came into the sitting-room from the kitchen, carrying a tray of bottles and glasses. 'We thought you might come tonight, Donny,' he said. 'We were hoping you would, anyway. So we're well prepared.'

'I ken androgynous is a big word, Bobby,' Robert said. 'But you'll learn what it means as you grow older. I hope you'll learn it quicker than I did.'

'Now Dad—er—Ma,' Donny warned. 'Let him stick to electricity in the meantime. Maybe you and George between you will teach him and William all about direct current and alternating current. I would do it, but I don't think my explanations would be as good as yours.'

He turned to the white haired sea captain who was wearing one of Hilda's scarlet cardigans. 'How did you get here George? I don't remember us giving you this address yon night at Gorekeith.'

'I gave him the phone number when you were away to the gents,' Robert said. 'I wasn't going to miss the chance of seeing him again.'

'I'd have found you all right,' George Carnie said. 'I'm very good at hunting out things and solving puzzles. I enjoy a bit of jiggerypokery.'

He poured out orange drinks for the two solemn-faced small boys, then he said to Donny: 'And what're you wanting to drink to our future happiness, Donny m'lad? Whisky, gin, or plain beer?'

'Well, if it's your future happiness it had better be the best and most expensive drink you've got.'

'That'll be champagne then,' George said. 'I'm glad we have a bottle. I bought it in case we had a wedding.'

'George and me are thinking of setting up house together,' Robert said.

'But—' Donny looked from one old man to the other. 'Does he know about things?'

'Of course he knows,' his father said. 'Would he be here tonight if he didn't? Him and me are in the same boat. Don't you worry about us, son. We'll be all right together. A/C one day, and D/C the next. I think we'll be very happy, and we'll give the neighbours something to talk about.'

A. L. Kennedy

DIDACUS

There is something heartening in the way writing manages to survive and develop.

Everyone agrees on its importance, yet the provision for new writing in this country leaves a lot to be desired. New voices are forced to compete for a diminishing share of the available space in periodicals whose reputation and importance is seldom justified by their performance. Publishers and potential sponsors are usually interested in people who have been published before, so that many new writers take matters into their own hands by issuing small circulation magazines, usually based around a writers' group. The quality of work they are producing continues to improve.

Alison Kennedy is the product of a writers' group. Her work has appeared in the Dundee Writers' Group publication *Samizdat* as well as other magazines based in England. She was born in Dundee in 1965, and has lived in Arbroath and Coventry, while studying for a degree in theatre studies and dramatic arts at Warwick University. She now lives in Glasgow and is a community arts worker in Clydebank, describing herself as 'without pets, dependents or houseplants, single, with few hobbies apart from writing and playing the banjo'. This story was written when she was twenty-one.

Didacus

THESE ARE a small people. On the whole, on the average, on the pavements, the people here are small.

Small in the body.

And we are speaking of a time here when small things were thought unimportant and the figures who now fill our bus stops were withered by lack of belief. In the larger world they were steadily forgotten and they woke up every morning, lost in their beds.

This is an early evening, run in the teeth of a frost. October or later. In a graveyard to the West of the city a woman turns from the street and walks away. The cemetery has no lights and she is alone, but she thinks she wouldn't care, whatever happens. Just now, she is looking for silence and somewhere dark to speak.

Please, God, be with us.

Help us to be good to each other.

The sky is clean and open and she feels she has a chance of getting through. On cloudy nights she doesn't bother and there's no point praying in the flat. There are seven other families above them and she doesn't have the energy to talk her way through that; she is, after all, a small woman.

They dug the older graves into the hillside, marking them with marble and sandstone. The woman is lost between monuments and the incline hurts her legs. When the path evens out a little she can see the car, parked beneath the yew tree. Inside, a cigarette blinks alight.

I've brought the mud in with me.

That's alright.

He waits while she closes the door and settles herself in the seat.

Kiss me, Jean.

No. No kissing.

He sighs and throws his cigarette out of the window.

Fine, then: just give me your hand.

Jean helps unfasten the trousers and he rolls the seat back. Ready.

At least you could tell me you want to.

Would I be here if I didn't.

Oh, Jean.

She stares from behind his shoulder. A twist in the path leaves one stone out apart and she tries to fix her eyes on that. It belongs to a man called Didacus McGlone; she looked to find the name once in daylight and now she can remember it in the dark.

He takes her hand again.

Did you?

Yes.

I didn't hear you.

Sometimes I don't make a noise.

If you want us to stop, you only have to tell me. You wouldn't lose your job—it isn't like that. I could move you up on the pay scale: get you an assistant for the lifting.

No.

O.K. Jean, O.K. There's Kleenex in the glove compartment.

Thankyou.

Will you let me drive you back?

No. What if Brian saw you?

What if?

You can't drive me back.

Do I really make you unhappy? You know you're free to do whatever you want . . .

She opens the door and steps out; sleet is falling.

Jean? Have a safe journey home. We'll see you on Monday morning.

The small woman walks below the weather and feels the chill of the slurry underfoot. She wants to be back with her husband and this will make her late.

Please, God, let us be good for each other.

Brian is lying on the sofa and making machine tools in his head. He watches them turning and threading and smoothing; the swarf curls up towards him; perfect; like wax. It carries the eye clear away.

At one time he saved up his future and put it in the cupboard at the end of the hall. He changed it into drill bits; micrometers; wonderful pieces of metal; heavy and precise. Their weight was a power in his hand.

His cupboard had been a place to be impatient, he would look at the piles of containers and lick his lips. Now when he passed it he smelt oil and disappointment. Jean's cleaning stuff was in there, and other types of nonsense. He didn't mind.

Jean has a photograph of Brian. She keeps it in her handbag but she knows it off by heart. It was taken in the first year they met.

He stands in his overalls, both hands in the pockets, smile at an angle and the weight on one leg. Behind him is the wooden fence from the bottom of her mother's garden and she knows from his face that the sun is bright and shining in his eyes.

Nothing has survived but the image.

The clock in the police station window is jerking towards half past ten. She wishes there were still buses running. The walk leaves her too much time to think.

The process of confinement and decay has been so gentle that their present situation still comes as a surprise. They are not without hope. Brian folds the sofa open, fetches out the sheets and knows that he can lie in in the morning. Both of them are free every Sunday: at liberty to talk and sleep together.

That can't be bad.

He separates the pages of this evening's paper, then rolls them up and twists them for the fire. This way they burn slowly. He feeds on the first one to keep the glow alive. The rest can wait for Jean. He doesn't want to go to sleep without her, not tonight, but his hands are like dead things already and his eyes are letting go of the room.

Over Jean, the sky has turned the colour of yellow milk so the praying will be over for tonight. The city is going to work, filling up the loans with footsteps and breathing. Maybe the year before there would have been conversation; room for a voice in the mouth. It's too late now for that.

Jean turns down the home street and tucks herself close to the wall. When she closes the door she wakes him.

I'm sorry.

Jean?

Who else would it be?

You don't know who I'm expecting.

Yes I do. Did you have what I left you to eat?

No. I was too tired. Will it keep?

He moves to start the fire again and she takes off her coat.

There's no room in here with the bed down. It's like a padded cell.

Brian throws the box of matches into the burning paper and the flare throws his shadow to the ceiling.

You stupid,

He sits on the mattress in the way that he sits when she knows that she has to go and hold him.

Oh God,

She would finish, but she knows there's no one near enough to hear.

I kept them nice. I used to have nice hands. They were softer than yours. Always. Once we had the business started, no one would have known I'd ever worked.

His face is different from the photograph but the eyes are almost the same. She pulls him to the side and takes his head on her lap. He keeps his fists curled to his stomach and the firelight swells the shadow, then the bone, then the shadow.

Do they hurt you?

There's all metal in them again. I can't get it out.

I can, with a needle. I'll get all the pieces out; it's just you've got big fingers; you should leave it to me.

You never deserved this.

The streets around them flatten under the wind as it rises and the final doors are locked until morning. Low voices murmur; calling after dreams while in other places, small people run amongst machinery, their faces closed.

Jean and Brian hold each other and whisper, awake to taste the opening of the day.

They consider the freedom ahead.

Naomi Mitchison

A MATTER OF BEHAVIOUR

A friend and contemporary of writers like Aldous Huxley, W.H. Auden and Wyndham Lewis, Naomi Mitchison (b.1897), was at one time considered a decidedly racy author. Her novel *We Have Been Warned* was refused publication more than once. It dealt with contraception and, as she said later, 'I don't suppose any reputable writer before my time had mentioned the unpleasantness of the touch of rubber'.

In no way salacious, her straight-forward approach to sex, and her honest and vivid evocations of women's awareness of their own physicality, combined to shock her early publishers. Today they make her a woman writer of undeniable stature.

Naomi Mitchison has written over seventy books covering novels, stories, diaries, autobiography and poetry and her artistry has always been linked to her deeply held social and political beliefs.

A Matter of Behaviour is a recent story which takes what has almost become a traditional subject, the relationship of a tinker with a scaldie, and places it in the modern context of unemployment and social deprivation; implying that today's urban unemployed, who travel to find work where they can, have become contemporary tinkers. The narrator tells a tale of subtle violence and ultimate despair in a voice of gentle understatement which makes the brutal climax all the more shocking and hopeless.

A Matter of Behaviour

I AM NOT one for making distinctions between one sort of person and another. And besides, there are matters of behaviour which I myself, as a teacher, have tried to establish. You see, Elsie was a Tinker—that made her different. It was no use talking about regulations. The fact was that mostly all the tinker children came to my school in winter, maybe two terms, but then they would be on the road again, all summer, everything they had learned from me forgotten. Then in August, when it came to a new start, away behind all their own age. It was hard for the tinker children, right enough, though they were healthy apart from scratches and rashes that their mothers were not bothering themselves about, and maybe they were learning another set of things on the roads the travellers took, deer and birds, a fox or maybe a pair of weasels running the road, what's called wild-life these days. But could they put it in writing? Not they, so they'd be laughed at. Not by me, but by the other children, for no child is kind by nature.

But as for wee Elsie, her mother was dead and her Dadda only wanted the boys off on the roads with him when it came to the end of April and the good weather calling at them. So Elsie stayed with an old auntie that had the use of a shed and a row of kale and two cats. She barely missed a day off school. When I saw she could read to herself I gave her a few old picture books that I was throwing out and soon enough there was a tink reading the best in the class.

More than that, she was trying to keep herself clean, which was more than the old tinker wifie did. The way it was, my children would never sit next the tinks. It was the smell off them, you understand, wood smoke and little washing, with no soap. But if you lived the way the travelling folk used to, you'd not have much chance of looking a bath in the face. Mind you, it is different today; many of them with the smart caravans, the same size and make as the tourists' or better. You'll not see a woman lugging away between two barrow handles the way I'd seen them when I first took on a single teacher school with a roll of twenty dropping to fifteen, away in the west. No, it was different altogether in those days.

But Elsie managed to wash herself and her school clothes, though they were nothing great. But I found her bits of decent cloth she could work with in the sewing class. She learned to knit and I unravelled an old jersey of my own, a New Year's present, but too bright altogether for me. But for all that Elsie was slow at her writing. She persevered, yes that she did, and she picked up arithmetic, so long as it was about real things, and indeed that's how I feel about it myself. Once she was in Standard Two she made friends with a few her own age, two from the Forestry houses and one, Linda that was, from the Post Office. Respectable families and they'd ask her for tea, or rather their mothers did, maybe three or four times in the year, and pleasing themselves to feel they'd been good. But all the same they never let it drift out of their minds that wee Elsie was just a tinker.

She grew up to be a handsome figure of a girl, so she did, with that bright hair that most of the travellers have, and bright blue eyes to match it. I'd seen less of her once she went on to the Grammar School at Oban, and left on the stroke of fifteen, for the old woman was getting less able to do even the bit of cleaning she used to do and when her father and the boys were around it was Elsie who had to wash and mend their clothes and see to their dirty heads and all that. So it was hard on her. She would come over to me an odd evening and I could see she'd been crying.

Well, the years went by and, as you know, I married and we moved around, first to Dumbarton, then to Glasgow itself. But I'd enough friends around the village that would be pleased to see us both, and my own wee Ian when he came. So I kept up with the old families I'd known and I saw Elsie turn into a fine young woman, even if she had no time for anything beyond what she had to do, and then suddenly she was married.

This would have been in the early sixties, with things brightening up and all of us sure the bad times were past. There were only a few at the wedding and the old wifie was safe in the kirk-yard, but Elsie's father had smartened himself up with a red rose in his coat and so had the one brother who was still about. I liked the look of the bridegroom. His mother and sister were there and doubtless wondering what like of a lass was coming into the family. Truly, I was afraid the two tinks might make a scene and that would be hard on Elsie, but they were scared to say much. They were fou drunk by the evening, but the others were well away by then.

I went to the wedding myself. I thought it would have been kind of nice if one of her school mates, Linda or Jessie perhaps, had been there to see how bonny she looked, poor Elsie, but none of them came. (Linda was courting at that same time and married the next year. I was at her wedding too, but it was a bigger affair, with a two-tier cake.) It was only strangers or part strangers in the church, come just for the taste of a wedding. Elsie was wearing high-necked white and I wondered was it a bought dress. Her hair showed flaming under her veil and I didn't wonder a man would fall for her.

He seemed a very decent man, a welder from a steel works, and his folk pleased that I had come and at my present of a set of cups, the same I'd give to any one of my old pupils if I'd been to the wedding. They went back to one of those small towns that were springing up, Edinburgh way, but not for long. The year after they moved to Corby in England. She wrote to me from there. I think she was a wee bit scared to be out of Scotland and not always understanding what people said to her. I was kind of surprised to hear from her, but all the same I wrote back and the next year she wrote again, asking me if ever I was in the south could I not come over and see her.

I thought this hardly likely, but as things turned out my husband was sent south to a branch his firm was setting up in Kettering and that was only a bus ride from Corby. I remember it well, a beautiful, rich countryside, parts of it Bucceleugh land, so what were the Buccleughs doing this far south was beyond me. There were well-doing villages, pretty old cottages and gardens packed to the gate with rose bushes. But Corby itself was given over to steel, rows and crescents and long streets of workers' houses and all that was left of the old village not knowing itself in the middle of them. There was a great chimney, alight with flames from the furnaces below; you could see it for miles. They called it the Corby Candle.

There was a Scots club and pleasant enough to be among ken'd folk, even if they were from the far ends of Scotland. They would have concerts and that; time and again there'd be a hundred folk standing to sing Auld Lang Syne. But some were terrible home-sick, worst the ones who had come from towns along the coasts, whether it was Peterhead or Campbeltown. They missed the sea sorely, here in the very middle of England. But the fishing had gone down and the money was away better down here. There were others from Wales or Cornwall or anywhere at all, but it was the Scots there were most of, and who made up the best part of the clubs, the Labour club as well.

So Elsie met me and took me back to her house, talking all the way. It was a modern house, in one of the crescents, two bedrooms and a smart bathroom. And almost all the furnishing bought: a lounge suite, the kind you'd see advertised, a table with a pot plant, new kitchen stuff, only she'd brought her old kettle and her griddle, for you'd not get one in England. But she had an electric iron and there were my tea cups, not a chip out of them. Everything was kept shining and a biscuit jar, I mind that, which they'd won in a Labour Party lottery. She showed it all to me, piece by piece, and told me not one bit of furnishing, not even the suite, was on the never-never, but all paid for. 'And nobody knows I'm a tinker!' she said and when I laughed and said she shouldn't be ashamed of that, she clutched my hand and said 'You'll not tell!'

So I said no, no, and laughed a bittie and then she took me out to her wee garden in front of the house, all newly planted with small rose bushes that still had their labels on. They'd a drill of potatoes and a few cabbages at the back. Her wee girl was at play-school—yes, they had that and all—but there was a baby boy in a pram out among the rose bushes, asleep, with a soft fuzz of orange. I said to her, laughing 'I see he has your colour of hair' and I can still hear her saying back 'I could wish it was black!' And her husband, just coming back from work, had dark hair. They were that friendly, both of them, and I went over there from time to time, with my Ian who was about the age of her wee girl. She talked sometimes of the days she'd been at school—she'd still got the books I'd given her—but not much about the other girls, only a mention of Miss McSporran who had been the infant teacher and well liked by all my pupils.

But then, as you know, my husband was moved back to Scotland and we settled down in Hillhead. I remember the last time I saw her she had a big stomach, but full of content and looking forward. So the years went by and I sometimes thought of Kettering and Corby and wondered how the friends we'd made were doing and sometimes we'd send cards. But mostly I was glad to be back in Scotland with my husband and my own two, both shooting up taller than myself, and Ian talking of what he'd be doing after University. For my own part I was doing supply teaching, but I had begun to lose touch with my profession. And indeed, teaching in Glasgow is away different from teaching in a village.

And then, in the late seventies and eighties, the bad times came on us, with the yards closing down all along Clydeside and where to turn, and all the anger breaking. And not us alone, but industry everywhere, what our forebears worked for and built up, coal, steel, shipping, the great companies that had seemed to be there forever. It seemed strange to me, since we had won the bitter war with Japan and tried and executed their Generals, that now they could be the ones who had all the factories, or else it was the Germans who had them, while our men who had fought, the older ones, in that war, were now thrown out with nothing but their old medals and the dole. What had gone wrong?

At first it did not hit us and our friends just so hard, though salary rises that my husband had expected just didn't come through. What we felt most was the terrible price that everything was, the way you had to pay a whole pound for something that was only worth what used to be half a crown in the old days. And then, well, everything got worse. But you'll know that. At least I had my two educated.

The works of Corby went. The steel industry was cut down so that it was hardly there; we didn't know what worse would follow. How had it happened? It seemed we couldn't make steel as cheaply as other countries, or it was not the kind that was wanted. We couldn't understand. Only we knew it was a matter of money, not of men working. And when money talks there's no place for people, for ordinary men and women, the like of Elsie and her man.

Well, it seemed that there could be small industries starting up here or there, maybe taking over premises in a small town and not doing too badly, at least for a few years. You've heard of TT and MCV? Yes, well they started up somewhere west of Bathgate, on some waste ground there was, and it seemed there were jobs going. A few of the Corby men heard of it. It was nothing like what they were used to and you wouldn't see the furnace men going, but those who'd been on the lighter side and willing to take training, they might have a chance. At least they'd be nearer home. The wages were nothing near Corby, but better than the dole. Yes, it had come to that. They cursed the Tory Government and this man MacGregor—but no Scot!—who'd been put in charge of the steel industry, but they went up to the new place for interview, remembered to say Sir, and were taken on. Elsie waited to hear. They sold most of the furniture, the best bits, the ones they'd been proud of, the lounge suite, the Hoover, the washing machine.

Well, I know the rest of the story by hearsay. He started work. For a while they were in one room, not easy to keep decent. And then they got half an old house, a bike ride away. The two older children, the girl and the boy, started at the new school; the girl was well up in Secondary by now and promising well. But the third child, another wee boy, was still at home. There was no kind of pre-school in those parts. The nearest was a bus-drive away and most likely full up, let alone she couldn't afford the bus fare. She tried to feed the children well and her man best; that's the way it is for most of us women.

Well, she went to a jumble sale. The children kept growing and had to be clothed. Some of the jumbles were away better than you'd get at the shops, anyway the shops where Elsie could go. The wee one was with her of course, he was a red-head the same as his brother, though it's not a true red but more of an orange. You'll know it, I'm sure. There's always a bit of snatching at the jumbles, and so it was this time. It was just bad luck that she met with an old school mate and they knew one another. Yes, they met across a boy's jacket and Linda—for it was her—said 'Ah, it's you—you dirty tink!' and a man behind said 'What, playing tinkers' tricks on us!' And poor Elsie ran out of the sale with nothing, just hauling the wee one, pulling him along crying, and maybe the good folk walking past would have stopped and scolded her, and when she got back in she saw that her purse was gone out of her pocket.

So she put the wee boy into the bedroom with what toys they had and half an orange, and herself went to the kitchen, turned on the gas and put her head in the oven.

That was how the two children back from school found her and had the sense for the boy to run to the corner ring the police—and lucky the 'phone was working. The ambulance men found the two children practising the artificial respiration they'd learned at school—and they'd turned the gas off. And it all came in the evening paper and I happened to read it. It was only a small piece and I only read as far as the name because I was waiting for my Peggy to come home before I'd put the kettle on and I wondered could it be Elsie. But the next morning there was a photo in the paper of the two children and I could see that the girl looked like her mother. I knew they'd been in trouble, that the man had lost his job in Corby, but she hadn't written to say where she was. No, she'd have been ashamed. But now the shame was worse. And now I was ashamed too, that I hadn't got round to writing and finding out how my old pupil was doing.

I rang the paper and got her address, saying I was a friend, and the very next day I made my way over. I remember once when I'd visited at Corby, my own Peggy asking me 'Is she really a tink?' and I said 'Yes, and I'm telling you who the tinkers were. It was they who made the weapons for the High Kings of Ireland that came over to the west of Scotland: all those beautiful swords and shields!' For that's one of the Tinker stories, though who's to know what's true and what's not? But I felt I had to get another picture told and believed, even if it wasn't the right one. Maybe it is and would account for a lot; in the old days, before my time, the tinkers really made and mended all kinds of metal things and were more welcome then than they've ever been since.

So off I went and found poor Elsie lying on a lumpy old sofa they had, wrapped in blankets and the big girl, allowed off from school, making tea and keeping an eye on the wee boy. I'd brought some cakes and we all took our tea together. I could tell from what the girl said that her father had been in a terrible taking, coming back from work to find his wife carried off to hospital and the two children, though they'd done well and the paper said so afterwards, all to bits and no tea made.

The next time I went over she was getting on fine and ashamed of what she had done, but she told me how that name that Linda had thrown at her had been that sore on her, she had just felt that nothing else she could ever do would be any good. Nothing would ever get the bad name off her back and it came out that the boy had been called a tink at school. Nobody at Corby had ever said anything against them, but now when they came back to Scotland—and she burst into tears, the poor thing. I could have sorted that Linda who had thrown it at her, and both of them my pupils. Sure as I'm a living soul, Linda would have seen that story in the papers, but not a cheep from her. Most like she'll have forgotten Elsie's married name, so there she'll be sitting at her ease. And me forgetting Linda's married name, I'm not able to get at her! But I'm hoping that someone calls her something worse than a tink, this side of Judgement Day.

Rosa Macpherson

One of the most encouraging trends in Scotland and elsewhere in the last few years is the number of women writers who have been appearing in magazines and anthologies. It would be fair to say that most would prefer to be known as women who write, rather than as women writers, and though it is too early to make any major claims the old themes are being treated in a new way and certainly given a fresh approach.

Rosa Macpherson's story is typical of this development, concentrating on a woman's relationship with her mother and on the writer's own role as a parent. Born in Alloa in 1955 Rosa Macpherson is married and writes in her spare time. She is also a product of the writers' circuit and is herself now a tutor in the Alloa Writers' Group.

The Boiled Egg

THE BOILED egg's face is blank and unseeing, although the eyes are pretty enough. The lashes are long and curled; the green eye-shadow below the arched brows is expertly applied. The black, crayonned hair falls between the eyes, careless, but deliberately so.

The nose, it can be admitted, is drawn haphazardly; misshapen and unlifelike.

But it is not the nose, the wrong nose, which makes the eyes blank and unseeing. No, not that.

The mouth is full and red, sensuous even. It wears an expression that is not quite a smile, not at all a frown. It is poised. Yes, poised. For a camera? For an audience? For me?

None of these things matter.

It's the hat. It is the green hat, perched suavely on top of the egg's head, which troubles me. No, it is not the hat, not even the hat, but the slant of the hat. The jaunty slant of the green hat over the eyes. Over the blank unseeing eyes. It is the jaunt; the angle of the hat which torments me so. Which makes my soul weep.

The hat is crayon-green. It is an eggbox hat, torn out and coloured harshly, bluntly. A single strip of sellotape keeps it securely in place, on the smooth hard-boiled head. On the back of the head, so that it does not interfere with the jaunt of the hat.

It does not, even although I know it is there.

The rim of the hat starts just at the edge of the eye, the left eye. It slants upwards towards the right, right over the right eye, then falls, slightly, relaxing above the right ear.

My mother made the hat. My mother made the hat with the angle that is jaunty. My mother, who is not too old, but old enough for me never to have seen her like that. Jaunty. Never to have seen her as poised, as ready, as sure, as expecting, as the boiled egg in the green jaunty hat.

Yet it was my mother who made the hat. It was she who tore the cardboard eggbox at just such an angle so that it would slant; jauntily.

The egg in the green hat makes me sad. It makes me sad for something I do not know.

My mother made the boiled-egg lady for Easter. For my son. At Easter. It is a tradition she has always followed. For me, for my sisters, for my brother, when we were the age of my son.

She does it for him now.

You must take it and roll it and then when the shell is cracked, you must peel off the face and eat what is left.

The priest blessed the egg; you must eat what is left.

My mother gets God into me any way she can.

When I was as young as my son I read Bible stories and when my mother made me a painted boiled-egg head, I would take it and roll it. When the shell was cracked, I would peel off the face and eat what was left.

My son will not do it. My son loves the face and the green hat. He does not want it cracked. So he keeps it, perched on the window-sill, near the television set, and it is still there. Long after Easter.

My mother frowns on this.

She will not understand that things can come in the way of what should be done.

She has always eaten the egg.

Even an egg which has borne such a jaunty hat. Even an egg which has borne such a jaunty hat that she has made.

When she was a young woman and not an old one, she had a son. She called him Mikhaila and she clothed him in girls' dresses. It was all she had. And when the war came and she had to leave her Ukranian home and her Ukranian son, she dressed him in a dress. A pretty white dress, she said, that covered his chubby white knees.

And she walked the length of the dusty road three times before she said goodbye to Mikhaila.

It was a long road, she said.

After the war she came back for Mikhaila but Mikhaila was gone. The godless Russians had taken him and he was gone.

Now my mother is an old woman, and when a Russian leader dies, she laughs. My Christian mother laughs because a godless power has died. But her now Russian son is still godless. She left him on the road, and he is godless.

But my son will not eat the egg and she frowns at him.

I let him be, although I too would rather he ate the egg.

The jaunty hat disturbs me and fills all of my head. As long as it is there I can have no life in me, except for the hat. It overbrims my consciousness.

How could my mother make a hat like that and hide her soul so well? Before the hat I knew my mother. Now she is dangerous, a dangerous sighing stranger and when I am with her she makes me breathless. I try to look behind her eyes; behind the layers of aching years and swallowed self.

I cannot see. My eyes are blank and unseeing. They are distorted by my mother's face. I cannot see the Julia for the mother who has nothinged her.

We have eroded the Julia, the jaunty hat-maker, and I would never even have glimpsed her had it not been for the hat. The jaunty angle of the green hat.

My mother once tried to tell me about herself; when she was Julia.

She was in Germany, during the war, and she worked for a farmer. There were four girls altogether. My mother, Julia, was their protector. They feared the farmer but my mother was a giant to him. Anna, she said, was terrified of him. He called them lazy Polish dogs and he would kick them. In the mornings Anna was always up first; ready and terrified. He would kick my mother and the others because they were not as quick as Anna.

Anna slept in her clothes, my mother said, because she was afraid. She did not waste time washing herself, because she was afraid.

My mother, Julia, always undressed herself and she always washed.

My mother, Julia, the giant, took the German farmer to a people's court and she lifted her torn dress and she showed them her black and bleeding legs. Where he kicked her.

In Germany, during the war, my mother, Julia, took the German farmer to a people's court and she showed them her black and bleeding legs, where he kicked her.

My mother was a giant. Only she was not my mother then. She was Julia.

My mother painted the egg with the blank unseeing eyes.

But it was Julia who made the hat. The green hat with the jaunty slant.

Dorothy K. Haynes

Dorothy Haynes's (1918–87) first anthology, 'Thou Shalt Not Suffer a Witch', put her amongst Scotland's foremost writers of short fiction. Her haunting, atmospheric pieces have been widely published, broadcast, and included in several genre-based collections of horror writing. But her stories cannot be confined within categories. They range from evocations of childhood and Scottish urban life around the turn of the century, to stark mediaeval scenes, or they mingle everyday reality with dark, surprising, and even bloody undercurrents. As well as two collections of short stories she published three novels, a book on New Lanark and a volume of autobiography. Her stories inspired charming, yet slightly disturbing illustrations from her friend and fellow author Mervyn Peake.

'Thou Shalt Not Suffer a Witch', fully justifies the uncompromising tone of its title. Dorothy Haynes shows us figures from the past full of poverty, ignorance and superstition, who are painfully aware of the narrow margin between acceptance and ostracism, life and death. She illuminates the daily pressures and fears which can drive whole communities to find protection behind the bigotry and violence of a mob. Who is to say that such forces are unknown in modern times?

Thou shalt not suffer a witch

THE CHILD sat alone in her bedroom, weaving the fringe of the counterpane in and out of her fingers. It was a horrible room, the most neglected one of the house. The grate was narrow and rusty, cluttered up with dust and hair combings, and the floor-boards creaked at every step. When the wind blew, the door rattled and banged, but the windows were sealed tight, webbed, fly-spotted, a haven for everything black and creeping.

In and out went her fingers, the fringe pulled tight between nail and knuckle. Outside the larches tossed and flurried, brilliant green under a blue sky. Sometimes the sun would go in, and rain would hit the window like a handful of nails thrown at the glass; then the world would lighten suddenly, the clouds would drift past in silver and white, and the larches would once more toss in sunshine.

'Jinnot! Jinnot!' called a voice from the yard. 'Where've you got to, Jinnot?'

She did not answer. The voice went farther away, still calling. Jinnot sat on the bed, hearing nothing but the voice which had tormented her all week.

'You'll do it, Jinnot, eh? Eh, Jinnot? An' I'll give you a sixpence to spend. We've always got on well, Jinnot. You like me better than her. She never gave you ribbons for your hair, did she? She never bought you sweeties in the village? It's not much to ask of you, Jinnot, just to say she looked at you, an' it happened. It's not as if it was telling lies. It has happened before; it has, eh, Jinnot?'

She dragged herself over to the mirror, the cracked sheet of glass with the fawn fly-spots. The door on her left hand, the window on her right, neither a way of escape. Her face looked back at her, yellow in the reflected sunlight. Her hair was the colour of hay, her heavy eyes had no shine in them. Large teeth, wide mouth, the whole face was square and dull. She went back to the bed, and her fingers picked again at the fringe.

Had it happened before? Why could she not remember properly? Perhaps it was because they were all so kind to her after it happened, trying to wipe it out of her memory. 'You just came over faint, lassie. Just a wee sickness, like. Och, you don't need to cry, you'll be fine in a minute. Here's Minty to see to you . . .'

But Minty would not see to her this time.

The voice went on and on in her head, wheedling, in one ear and out of the other.

'Me and Jack will get married, see, Jinnot? And when we're married, you can come to see our house whenever you like. You can come in, and I'll bake scones for you, Jinnot, and sometimes we'll let you sleep in our wee upstairs room. You'll do it, Jinnot, will you not? For Jack as well as for me. You like Jack. Mind he mended your Dolly for you? And you'd like to see us married thegither, would you not?

'He'd never be happy married to her, Jinnot. You're a big girl now, you'll soon see that for yourself. She's good enough in her way, see, but she's not the right kind for him. She sits and sews and works all day, but she's never a bit of fun with him, never a word to say. But he's never been used to anyone better, see, Jinnot, and he'll not look at anybody else while she's there. It's for his own good, Jinnot, and for her sake as well. They'd never be happy married.

'And Jinnot, you're not going to do her any harm. Someday you'll get married yourself, Jinnot, and you'll know. So it's just kindness . . . and she *is* like that, like what I said. Mebbe she's been the cause of the trouble you had before, you never know. So you'll do it, Jinnot, eh? You'll do it?'

She did not want to. The door rattled in the wind, and the sun shone through the dirt and the raindrops on the window. Why did she want to stay here, with the narrow bed, the choked grate, the mirror reflecting the flaked plaster of the opposite wall? The dust blew along the floor, and the chimney and the keyhole howled together. 'Jinnot! Jinnot!' went the voice again. She paid no attention. Pulling back the blankets, she climbed fully dressed into the bed, her square, suety face like a mask laid on the pillows. 'Jinnot! Jinnot!' went the voice, calling, coaxing through the height of the wind. She whimpered, and curled herself under the bedclothes, hiding from the daylight and the question that dinned at her even in the dark. 'You'll do it, Jinnot, eh? Will you? Eh, Jinnot?'

Next day, the weather had settled. A quiet, spent sun shone on the farm, the tumbledown dykes and the shabby thatch. Everything was still as a painting, the smoke suspended blue in the air, the ducks so quiet on the pond that the larches doubled themselves in the water. Jinnot stood at the door of the byre, watching Jack Hyslop at work. His brush went swish swish, swirling the muck along to the door. He was a handsome lad. No matter how dirty his work, he always looked clean. His boots were bright every morning, and his black hair glistened as he turned his head. He whistled as his broom spattered dung and dirty water, and Jinnot turned her face away. The strong, hot smell from the byre made something grip her stomach with a strong, relentless fist.

Now Minty came out of the kitchen, across the yard with a basin of pig-swill. With her arm raised, pouring out the slops, she looked at the byre door for a long minute. To the child, the world seemed to stop in space. The byreman's broom was poised in motion, his arms flexed for a forward push; his whistle went on on the same note, high and shrill; and Minty was a statue of mute condemnation, with the dish spilling its contents in a halted stream.

A moment later, Jinnot found that Jack Hyslop was holding her head on his knee. Minty had run up, her apron clutched in both hands. Beatrice, the dairymaid, was watching too, bending over her. There was a smell of the dairy on her clothes, a slight smell of sourness, of milk just on the turn, and her hair waved dark under her cap. 'There now,' she said. 'All right, dearie, all right! What made you go off like that, now?'

The child's face sweated all over, her lips shivered as the air blew cold on her skin. All she wanted now was to run away, but she could not get up to her feet. 'What was it, Jinnot?' said the voice, going on and on, cruel, kind, which was it? 'Tell me, Jinnot. Tell me.'

She could not answer. Her tongue seemed to swell and press back on her throat, so that she vomited. Afterwards, lying in bed, she remembered it all, the sense of relief when she had thrown up all she had eaten, and the empty languor of the sleep which followed. Beatrice had put her to bed, and petted her and told her she was a good girl. 'It was easy done, eh, Jinnot? You'd have thought it was real.' She gave a high, uneasy laugh. 'Aye, you're a good wee thing, Jinnot. All the same, you fair frichted me at the beginning!'

She was glad to be left alone. After her sleep, strangely cold, she huddled her knees to her shoulders, and tried to understand. Sometime, in a few months or a few years, it did not seem to matter, Minty and Jack Hyslop were to be married. Minty was kind. Since Jinnot's mother had died, she had been nurse and foster mother, attending to clothes and food and evening prayers. She had no time to do more. Her scoldings were frequent, but never unjust. Jinnot had loved her till Beatrice came to the dairy, handsome, gay, and always ready with bribes.

'You're a nice wee girl, Jinnot. Look—will you do something for Jack and me—just a wee thing? You've done it before; I know you have. Some time, when Minty's there . . .'

And so she had done it, for the sake of sixpence, and the desire to be rid of the persistent pleading; but where she had meant to pretend to fall in a fit at Minty's glance, just to pretend, she had really lost her senses, merely thinking about it. She was afraid now of what she had done . . . was it true then, about Minty, that the way she looked at you was enough to bring down a curse?

It could not be true. Minty was kind, and would make a good wife. Beatrice was the bad one, with her frightening whispers—and yet, it wasn't really badness; it was wisdom. She knew all the terrible things that children would not understand.

Jinnot got up and put on her clothes. Down in the kitchen, there was firelight, and the steam of the evening meal. Her father was eating heartily, his broad shoulders stooped over his plate. 'All right again, lassie?' he asked, snuggling her to him with one arm. She nodded, her face still a little peaked with weakness. At the other side of the room, Minty was busy at the fireside, but she did not turn her head. Jinnot clung closer to her father.

All the air seemed to be filled with whispers.

From nowhere at all, the news spread that Jinnot was bewitched. She knew it herself. She was fascinated by the romance of her own affliction, but she was frightened as well. Sometimes she would have days with large blanks which memory could not fill. Where had she been? What had she done? And the times when the world seemed to shrivel to the size of a pin-head, with people moving like grains of sand, tiny, but much, much clearer, the farther away they seemed—who was behind it all? When had it all started?

In time, however, the trouble seemed to right itself. But now, Jack Hyslop courted Beatrice instead of Minty. Once, following them, Jinnot saw them kiss behind a hayrick. They embraced passionately, arms clutching, bodies pressed together. It had never been like that with Minty, no laughter, no sighs. Their kisses had been mere respectful tokens, the concession to their betrothal.

Minty said nothing, but her sleek hair straggled, her once serene eyes glared under their straight brows. She began to be abrupt with the child. 'Out the road!' she would snap. 'How is it a bairn's aye at your elbow?' Jinnot longed for the friendliness of the young dairymaid. But Beatrice wanted no third party to share her leisure, and Jinnot was more lonely than ever before.

Why had she no friends? She had never had young company, never played games with someone of her own age. Her pastimes were lonely imaginings, the dark pretence of a brain burdened with a dull body. She made a desperate bid to recover her audience. Eyes shut, her breathing hoarse and ragged, she let herself fall to the ground, and lay there until footsteps came running, and kind hands worked to revive her.

So now she was reinstated, her father once more mindful of her, and the household aware of her importance, a sick person in the house. The voices went on whispering around her, 'Sshh! It's wee Jinnot again. Fell away in a dead faint. Poor lassie, she'll need to be seen to . . . Jinnot—Jinnot . . . wee Jinnot . . .'

But this time, there was a difference. They waited till she waked, and then questioned her. Her father was there, blocking out the light from the window, and the doctor sat by the bedside, obviously displeased with his task. Who was to blame? Who was there when it happened? She knew what they wanted her to say; she knew herself what to tell them. 'Who was it?' pressed her father. 'This has been going on too long.' 'Who was it?' said the doctor. 'There's queer tales going around, you know, Jinnot!' 'You know who it was,' said the voice in her mind. 'You'll do it, Jinnot, eh?'

'I—I don't know,' she sighed, her eyes drooping, her mouth hot and dry. 'I . . . only . . .' she put her hand to her head, and sighed. She could almost believe she was really ill, she felt so tired and strange.

After that, the rumours started again. The voice came back to Jinnot, the urgent and convincing warning—'She *is* like that, like what I said . . .' For her own peace of mind, she wanted to *know*, but there was no one she could ask. She could not trust her own judgement.

It was months before she found out, and the days had lengthened to a queer tarnished summer, full of stale yellow heat. The larches had burned out long ago, and their branches drooped in dull fringes over the pond. The fields were tangled with buttercups and tall moon daisies, but the flowers dried and shrivelled as soon as they blossomed. All the brooks were silent; and the nettles by the hedges had a curled, thirsty look. Jinnot kept away from the duckpond these days. With the water so low, the floating weeds and mud gave off a bad, stagnant smell.

Over the flowers, the bees hovered, coming and going endlessly, to and from the hives. One day, a large bumble, blundering home, tangled itself in the girl's collar, and stung her neck. She screamed out, running into the house, squealing that she had swallowed the insect, and that something with a sting was flying round in her stomach, torturing her most cruelly. They sent for the doctor, and grouped round her with advice. Later, they found the bee, dead, in the lace which had trapped it; but before that, she had vomited up half her inside, with what was unmistakably yellow bees' bodies, and a quantity of waxy stuff all mixed up with wings and frail, crooked legs.

She looked at the watchers, and knew that the time had come. 'It was Minty Fraser!' she wailed. 'It was her! She *looked* at me!' She screamed, and hid her face as the sickness once more attacked her in heaving waves.

They went to the house, and found Minty on her knees, washing over the hearthstone. One of the farm-men hauled her to her feet, and held her wrists together. 'Witch! Witch! Witch!' shouted the crowd at the door.

'What—What—'

'Come on, witch! Out to the crowd!'

'No! No, I never—'

'Leave her a minute,' roared Jack Hyslop. 'Mebbe she—give her a chance to speak!' His mouth twitched a little. At one time, he was thinking, he had been betrothed to Minty, before Beatrice told him . . .

he faltered at the thought of Beatrice. 'Well, don't be rough till you're sure,' he finished lamely, turning away and leaving the business to the others. Those who sympathized with witches, he remembered, were apt to share their fate.

The women were not so blate. 'Witch! Witch!' they shrilled. 'Burn the witch! Our bairns are no' safe when folks like her is let to live!'

She was on the doorstep now, her cap torn off, her eye bleeding, her dress ripped away at the shoulder. Jinnot's father, pushing through the mob, raised his hand for the sake of order. 'Look, men! Listen, there! This is my house; there'll be no violence done on the threshold.'

'Hang her! Burn her! A rope, there!'

'No hanging till you make sure. Swim her first. If the devil floats—'

'Jinnot! Here's Jinnot!'

The girl came through a lane in the throng, Beatrice holding her hand, clasping her round the waist. She did not want to see Minty, but her legs forced her on. Then she looked up. A witch . . . she saw the blood on the face, the torn clothes, the look of horror and terrible hurt. That was Minty, who cooked her meals and looked after her and did the work of a mother. She opened her mouth and screamed, till the foam dripped over her chin.

Her father's face was as white as her own spittle. 'Take the beast away,' he said, 'and if she floats, for God's sake get rid of her as quick as you can!'

It was horrible. They all louped at her, clutching and tearing and howling as they plucked at her and trussed her for ducking. She was down on the ground, her clothes flung indecently over her head, her legs kicking as she tried to escape. 'It wasna me!' she skirled. 'It wasna me! I'm no' a witch! Ah-ah!' The long scream cut the air like a blade. Someone had wrenched her leg and snapped the bone at the ankle, but her body still went flailing about in the dust, like a kitten held under a blanket.

They had her trussed now, wrists crossed, legs crossed, her body arched between them. She was dragged to the pond, blood from her cuts and grazes smearing the clothes of those who handled her. Her hair hung over her face and her broken foot scraped the ground. 'No! No!' she screamed. 'Ah, God . . .!' and once, 'Jinnot! Tell them it wasna me—'

A blow over the mouth silenced her, and she spat a tooth out with a mouthful of blood. She shrieked as they swung and hurtled her through the air. There was a heavy splash, and drops of green, slimy water spattered the watching faces. If Minty was a witch, she would float; and then they would haul her out and hang her, or burn her away, limb by limb.

She sank; the pond was shallow, but below the surface, green weed and clinging mud drew her down in a deadly clutch. The crowd on the bank watched her, fascinated. It was only when her yammering mouth was filled and silenced that they realised what had happened, and took slow steps to help her. By that time, it was too late.

What must it be like to be a witch? The idea seeped into her mind like ink, and all her thoughts were tinged with the black poison. She knew the dreadful aftermath; long after, her mind would be haunted by the sight she had seen. In her own nostrils, she felt the choke and snuffle of pond slime; but what must it feel like, the knowledge of strange power, the difference from other people, the danger? Her imagination played with the thrilling pain of it, right down to the last agony.

She asked Beatrice about it. Beatrice was married now, with a baby coming, and Jinnot sat with her in the waning afternoons, talking with her, woman to woman.

'I didn't like to see them set on her like yon. She never done me any harm. If it hadn't been for me—'

'Are you sure, Jinnot? Are you sure? Mind the bees, Jinnot, an' yon time at the barn door? What about them?'

'I—I don't know.'

'Well, I'm telling you. She was a witch, that one, if anybody was.'

'Well, mebbe she couldn't help it.'

'No, they can't help the power. It just comes on them. Sometimes they don't want it, but it comes, just the same. It's hard, but you know what the Bible says: "Thou shalt not suffer a witch . . ."'

She had a vision of Minty, quiet, busy, struggling with a force she did not want to house in her body. Beside this, her own fits and vomitings seemed small things. She could forgive knowing that. 'How . . . how do they first know they're witches?' she asked.

'Mercy, I don't know! What questions you ask, Jinnot! How would I know, eh? I daresay they find out soon enough.'

So that was it; they knew themselves. Her mind dabbled and meddled uncomfortably with signs and hints. She wanted to curse Beatrice for putting the idea into her head; she would not believe it; but once there, the thought would not be removed. What if she was a witch? 'I'm not,' she said to herself. 'I'm too young,' she said; but there was no conviction in it. Long before she had been bewitched, she had known there was something different about her. Now it all fell into place. No wonder the village children would not call and play with her. No wonder her father was just rather than affectionate, shielding her only because she was his daughter. And no wonder Beatrice was so eager to keep in with her, with the incessant 'Eh, Jinnot?' always on her lips.

Well, then, she was a witch. As well to know it sooner as later, to accept the bothers with the benefits, the troubles and trances with the newfound sense of power. She had never wanted to kill or curse, never in her most unhappy moments, but now, given the means, would it not be as well to try? Did her power strengthen by being kept, or did it spring up fresh from some infernal reservoir? She did not know. She was a very new witch, uncertain of what was demanded of her. Week after week passed, and she was still no farther forward.

She continued her visits to Beatrice, though the thought of it all made her grue. It angered her to see the girl sitting stout and placid at the fireside, unhaunted, unafraid. 'You'll come and see the baby when it's born, eh, Jinnot?' she would say. 'Do you like babies? Do you?' Nothing mattered to her now, it seemed, but the baby. In the dark winter nights, Jinnot made a resolve to kill her. But for Beatrice, she might never have discovered this terrible fact about herself. Beatrice was to blame for everything, but a witch has means of revenge, and one witch may avenge another.

She had no idea how to cast a spell, and there was no one to help her. What had Minty done? She remembered the moment at the byre-door, the upraised arm, and the long, long look. It would be easy. Bide her time, and Beatrice would die when the spring came.

She sat up in the attic, twining her fingers in the fringe of the bedcover, in and out, under and over. Beatrice was in labour. It had been whispered in the kitchen, spreading from mouth to mouth. Now, Jinnot sat on the bed, watched the larches grow black in the dusk. She was not aware of cold, or dirt, or darkness. All her senses were fastened on the window of Beatrice's cottage, where a light burned, and women gathered round the bed. She fixed her will, sometimes almost praying in her effort to influence fate. 'Kill her! Kill her! Let her die!' Was she talking to God, or to the devil? The thoughts stared and screamed in her mind. She wanted Beatrice to suffer every agony, every pain, and wrench, to bear Minty's pain, and her own into the bargain. All night she sat, willing pain and death, and suffering it all in her own body. Her face was grey as the ceiling, her flesh sweated with a sour smell. Outside, an owl shrieked, and she wondered for a moment if it was Beatrice.

Suddenly, she knew that it was all over. The strain passed out of her body, the lids relaxed over her eyes, her body seemed to melt and sprawl over the bed. When she woke, it was morning, and the maids were beaming with good news. 'Did you hear?' they said. 'Beatrice has a lovely wee boy! She's fair away wi' herself!'

Jinnot said nothing. She stopped her mouth and her disappointment with porridge. It did not cross her mind that perhaps, after all, she was no witch. All she thought was that the spell had not worked, and Beatrice was still alive. She left the table, and hurried over to the cottage. The door was ajar, the fire bright in the hearth, and Beatrice was awake in bed, smiling, the colour already flushing back into her cheeks.

'He's a bonny baby, Jinnot. He's lovely, eh? Eh, Jinnot?'

She crept reluctantly to the cradle. Why, he was no size at all, so crumpled, so new, a wee sliver of flesh in a bundle of white wool. She stared for a long time, half sorry for what she had to do. The baby was snuffling a little, its hands and feet twitching under the wrappings. He was so young, he would not have his mother's power to resist a witch.

She glared at him for a long minute, her eyes fixed, her lips firm over her big teeth. His face, no bigger than a lemon, turned black, and a drool of foam slavered from the mouth. When the twitching stopped, and the eyes finally uncrossed themselves, she walked out, and left the door again on the latch. She had not spoken one word.

It seemed a long time before they came for her, a long time of fuss and running about while she sat on the bed, shivering in the draught from the door. When she crossed to the window, her fingers probing the webs and pressing the guts from the plumpest insects, she saw them arguing and gesticulating in a black knot. Jack Hyslop was there, his polished hair ruffled, his face red. The women were shaking their heads, and Hyslop's voice rose clear in the pale air.

'Well, that's what she said. The wee thing had been dead for an hour. An' it was that bitch Jinnot came in an' glowered at it.'

'Och, man, it's a sick woman's fancy! A wee mite that age can easy take convulsions.'

'It wasna convulsions. My wife said Jinnot was in and out with a face like thunder. She was aye askin' about witches too, you can ask Beatrice if you like.'

'Well, she was in yon business o' Minty Fraser. Ye cannie blame her, a young lassie like that . . . mind, we sympathise about the bairn, Jacky, but—'

They went on placating him, mindful of the fact that Jinnot was the farmer's daughter. It would not do to accuse *her*; but one of the women went into the cottage, and came out wiping her eyes. 'My, it would make anybody greet. The wee lamb's lying there like a flower, that quiet! It's been a fair shock to the mother, poor soul. She's gey faur through . . .'

They muttered, then, and drifted towards the house. Jinnot left the window, and sat again on the bed. She was not afraid, only resigned, and horribly tired of it all.

When they burst into her room, clumping over the bare boards, her father was with them. They allowed him to ask the questions. Was he angry with them, or with her? She could not guess.

'Jinnot,' he said sternly, 'what's this? What's all this?'

She stared at him.

'What's all this? Do you know what they're saying about you? They say you killed Beatrice Hyslop's bairn. Is that true, Jinnot?'

She did not answer. Her father held up his hand as the men began to growl.

'Come now, Jinnot, enough of this sulking! It's for your own good to answer, and clear yourself. Mind of what happened to Minty Fraser! Did you do anything to the baby?'

'I never touched it. I just looked at it.'

'Just looked?'

'Yes.'

A rough cry burst from Jack Hyslop. 'Is that not what Minty Fraser said? Was that not enough from her?'

'Hyslop, hold your tongue, or you lose your job.'

'Well, by God, I lose it then! There's been more trouble on this bloody farm—'

'Aye! Leave this to us!'

'We'll question the wench. If she's no witch, she's nothing to fear.'

The women had come in now, crowding up in angry curiosity. The farmer was pushed back against the wall. 'One word, and you'll swim along with her,' he was warned, and he knew them well enough to believe them. They gathered round Jinnot, barking questions at her, and snatching at the answers. Every time she paused to fidget with the fringe, they lammed her across the knuckles till her hands were swollen and blue.

'Tell the truth now; are you a witch?'

'No. No, I'm not!'

'Why did you kill the baby this morning?'

'I—I never. I can't kill folk. I—'

'You hear that? She can't kill folk! Have you ever tried?'

She cowered back from them, the faces leering at her like ugly pictures. She would tell the truth, as her father said, and be done with all this dreamlike horror. 'Leave me alone!' she said. 'Leave me, and I'll tell!'

'Hurry then. Out with it! Have you ever tried to kill anybody?'

'Yes. I tried, and—and I couldn't. It was her, she started telling me I was bewitched—'

'Who?'

'Beatrice—Mistress Hyslop.'

'My God!' said Jack and her father, starting forward together.

'Hold on, there! Let her speak.'

'She said I was bewitched, an' I thought I was. I don't know if it was right . . . it was all queer, and I didn't know . . . and then, when she said about witches, she put it in my head, and it came over me I might be one. I *had* to find out—'

'There you are. She's admitting it!'

'No!' She began to shout as they laid hold of her, screaming in fright and temper till her throat bled. 'No! *Leave* me alone! I never; I tried, and I couldn't do it! I couldn't, I tell you! She *wouldn't* die. She'd have died if I'd been a witch, wouldn't she? She's a witch herself; I don't care, Jack Hyslop, she is! It was her fault Minty Fraser—oh God, no! NO!'

She could not resist the rope round her, the crossing of her limbs, the tight pull of cord on wrists and ankles. When she knew it was hopeless, she dared not resist, remembering Minty's broken leg, her cuts and blood and bruises, the tooth spinning out in red spittle. She was not afraid of death, but she was mortally afraid of pain. Now, if she went quietly, there would only be the drag to the pond, the muckle splash, and the slow silt and suffocation in slime. . .

She had no voice left to cry out when they threw her. Her throat filled with water, her nose filled, and her ears. She was tied too tightly to struggle. Down, down she went, till her head sang, and her brain nearly burst; but the pond was full with the spring rains, and her body was full-fleshed and buoyant. Suddenly, the cries of the crowd burst upon her again, and she realised that she was floating. Someone jabbed at her, and pushed her under again with a long pole, but she bobbed up again a foot away, her mouth gulping, her eyes bulging under her dripping hair. The mob on the bank howled louder.

'See, see! She's floating!'

'Witch! Burn her! Fish her out and hang her!'

'There's proof now. What are you waiting for? What are you waiting for? Out with her. See, the besom'll *no'* sink!'

So now they fished her out, untied her, and bound her again in a different fashion, hands by her side, feet together. She was too done to protest, or to wonder what they would do. She kept her eyes shut as they tied her to a stake, and she ignored the tickle of dead brushwood being piled round feet and body. She could hardly realise that she was still alive, and she was neither glad nor sorry.

They were gentle with her now, sparing her senses for the last pain. At first, she hardly bothered when the smoke nipped her eyes and her nostrils; she hardly heard the first snap of the twin twigs. It was only when the flames lapped her feet and legs that she raised her head and tried to break free. As the wood became red hot, and the flames mounted to bite her body, she screamed and writhed and bit her tongue to mincemeat. When they could not see her body through the fire, the screams still went on.

The crowd drifted away when she lost consciousness. There was no more fun to be had; or perhaps, it wasn't such fun after all. The men went back to the fields, but they could not settle to work. Jinnot's father was gnawing his knuckles in the attic, and they did not know what would happen when he came down. Beatrice tossed in a muttering, feverish sleep; and beside the pond, a few veins and bones still sizzled and popped in the embers.

John Galt

John Galt (1779–1838), felt his important fictions should be regarded as theoretical histories, observations or sketches rather than novels. They outline a provincial society's manners and changes, often through a single character, while the subtlety and irony of his first person writing are a delight.

Born in Irvine and raised in Greenock, Galt went to London when he was twenty-five. After his business plans collapsed he spent a couple of years travelling on the Continent, where he met and became friendly with Byron, writing a biography of him in later years. Galt married in 1813 and became a full time author, producing poems, plays, historical novels, travel books and text books. Success eluded him till *Blackwood's* serialised *The Ayrshire Legatees* in 1820. This was followed by *Annals of the Parish* which had been turned down by Constable when it was offered just after Galt's marriage. *The Provost, The Entail* and *The Member*, complete Galt's sequence of major Scottish novels.

Following the stroke that forced his departure from London, Galt settled into writing short stories. There is more to these than the yarns and anecdotes he scattered through his novels, and 'The Gudewife' is a splendid example of his comic and satirical technique.

The Gudewife

I AM inditing the good matter of this book for the instruction of our only daughter when she comes to years of discretion, as she soon will, for her guidance when she has a house of her own, and has to deal with the kittle temper of a gudeman in so couthy a manner as to mollify his sour humour when anything out of doors troubles him. Thanks be and praise I am not ill qualified! indeed, it is a clear ordinance that I was to be of such a benefit to the world; for it would have been a strange thing if the pains taken with my education had been purposeless in the decrees of Providence.

Mr Desker, the schoolmaster, was my father; and, as he was reckoned in his day a great teacher, and had a pleasure in opening my genie for learning, it is but reasonable to suppose that I in a certain manner profited by his lessons, and made a progress in parts of learning that do not fall often into the lot of womankind. This much it behoves me to say, for there are critical persons in the world that might think it very upsetting of one of my degree to write a book, especially a book which has for its end the bettering of the conjugal condition. If I did not tell them, as I take it upon me to do, how well I have been brought up for the work, they might look down upon my endeavours with a doubtful eye; but when they read this, they will have a new tout to their old horn, and reflect with more reverence of others who may be in some things their inferiors, superiors, or equals. It would not become me to say to which of these classes I belong, though I am not without an inward admonition on the head.

It fell out, when I was in my twenties, that Mr Thrifter came, in the words of the song of Auld Robin Gray, 'a-courting to me'; and, to speak a plain matter of fact, in some points he was like that bald-headed carle. For he was a man considering my juvenility, well stricken in years; besides being a bachelor, with a natural inclination (as all old bachelors have) to be dozened, and fond of his own ayes and nays. For my part, when he first came about the house, I was as dawty as Jeanie—as I thought myself entitled to a young man, and did not relish the apparition of him coming in at the gloaming, when the day's darg was done, and before candles were lighted. However, our lot in life is not of our own choosing. I will say—for he is still to the fore—that it could not have been thought he would have proved himself such a satisfactory gudeman as he has been. To be sure, I put my shoulder to the wheel, and likewise prayed to Jupiter; for there never was a rightful head of a family without the concurrence of his wife. These are words of wisdom that my father taught, and I put in practice.

Mr Thrifter, when he first came about me, was a bein man. He had parts in two vessels, besides his own shop, and was sponsible for a nest-egg of lying money; so that he was not, though rather old, a match to be, as my father thought, discomfited with a flea in the lug instanter. I therefore, according to the best advice, so comported myself that it came to pass in the course of time that we were married; and of my wedded life and experience I intend to treat in this book.

ONE

Among the last words that my sagacious father said when I took upon me to be the wedded wife of Mr Thrifter were, that a man never throve unless his wife would let, which is a text that I have not forgotten; for though in a way, and in obedience to the customs of the world, women acknowledge men as their head, yet we all know in our hearts that this is but diplomatical. Do not we see that men work for us, which shews that they are our servants? do we not see that men protect us, are they not therefore our soldiers? do we not see that they go hither and yon at our bidding, which shews that they have that within their nature that teaches them to obey? and do not we feel that we have the command of them in all things, just as they had the upper hand in the world till woman was created? No clearer proof do I want that, although in a sense for policy we call ourselves the weaker vessels—and in that very policy there is power—we know well in our hearts that, as the last made creatures, we necessarily are more perfect, and have all that was made before us, by hook or crook, under our thumb. Well does Robin Burns sing of this truth in the song where he has—

Her 'prentice hand she tried on man,
And syne she made the lassies oh!

Accordingly, having a proper conviction of the superiority of my sex, I was not long of making Mr Thrifter, my gudeman, to know into what hands he had fallen, by correcting many of the bad habits of body to which he had become addicted in his bachelor loneliness. Among these was a custom that I did think ought not to be continued after he had surrendered himself into the custody of a wife, and that was an usage with him in the morning before breakfast to toast his shoes against the fender and forenent the fire. This he did not tell me till I saw it with my own eyes the morning after we were married, which, when I beheld, gave me a sore heart, because, had I known it before we were everlastingly made one, I will not say but there might have been a dubiety as to the paction; for I have ever had a natural dislike to men who toasted their shoes, thinking it was a hussie fellow's custom. However, being endowed with an instinct of prudence, I winked at it for some days; but it could not be borne any longer, and I said in a sweet manner, as it were by and by,

'Dear Mr Thrifter, that servant lass we have gotten has not a right notion of what is a genteel way of living. Do you see how the misleart creature sets up your shoes in the inside of the fender, keeping the warmth from our feet? really I'll thole this no longer; it's not a custom in a proper house. If a stranger were accidently coming in and seeing your shoes in that situation, he would not think of me as it is well known he ought to think.'

Mr Thrifter did not say much, nor could he; for I had judiciously laid all the wyte and blame of the thing to the servant; but he said, in a diffident manner, that it was not necessary to be so particular.

'No necessary! Mr Thrifter, what do you call a particularity, when you would say that toasting shoes is not one? It might do for you when you were a bachelor, but ye should remember that you're so no more, and it's a custom I will not allow.'

'But,' replied he with a smile, 'I am the head of the house; and to make few words about it, I say, Mrs Thrifter, I will have my shoes warmed anyhow, whether or no.'

'Very right, my dear,' quo' I; 'I'll ne'er dispute that you are the head of the house; but I think that you need not make a poor wife's life bitter by insisting on toasting your shoes.'

And I gave a deep sigh. Mr Thrifter looked very solemn on hearing this, and as he was a man not void of understanding, he said to me:

'My dawty,' said he, 'we must not stand on trifles; if you do not like to see my shoes within the parlour fender, they can be toasted in the kitchen.'

I was glad to hear him say this; and, ringing the bell, I told the servant-maid at once to take them away and place them before the kitchen fire, well pleased to have carried my point with such debonair suavity; for if you get the substance of a thing, it is not wise to make a piece of work for the shadow likewise. Thus it happened I was conqueror in the controversy; but Mr Thrifter's shoes have to this day been toasted every morning in the kitchen; and I daresay the poor man is vogie with the thoughts of having gained a victory; for the generality of men have, like parrots, a good conceit of themselves, and cry 'Pretty Poll!' when everybody sees they have a crooked neb.

TWO

But what I have said was nothing to many other calamities that darkened our honeymoon. Mr Thrifter having been a long-keepit bachelor, required a consideration in many things besides his shoes; for men of that stamp are so long accustomed to their own ways that it is not easy to hammer them into docility, far less to make them obedient husbands. So that although he is the best of men, yet I cannot say on my conscience that he was altogether free from an ingrained temper, requiring my canniest hand to manage properly. It could not be said that I suffered much from great faults; but he was fiky, and made more work about trifles that didna just please him than I was willing to conform to. Some excuse, however, might be pleaded for him, because he felt that infirmities were growing upon him, which was the cause that made him think of taking a wife; and I was not in my younger days quite so thoughtful, maybe, as was necessary: for I will take blame to myself, when it would be a great breach of truth in me to deny a fault that could be clearly proven.

Mr Thrifter was a man of great regularity; he went to the shop and did his business there in a most methodical manner; he returned to the house and ate his meals like clockwork; and he went to bed every night at half-past nine o'clock, and slept there like a door nail. In short, all he did and said was as orderly as commodities on chandler pins; but for all that he was at times of a crunkly spirit, fractiously making faults about nothing at all: by which he was neither so smooth as oil nor so sweet as honey to me, whose duty it was to govern him.

At the first outbreaking of the original sin that was in him, I was vexed and grieved, watering the plants in the solitude of the room, when he was discoursing on the news of the day with customers in the shop. At last I said to myself, 'This will never do; one of two must obey: and it is not in the course of nature that a gudeman should rule a house, which is the province of a wife and becomes her nature to do.'

So I set a stout heart to the stey brae, and being near my time with our daughter, I thought it would be well to try how he would put up with a little sample of womanhood. So that day when he came in to his dinner, I was, maybe, more incommoded with my temper than might be, saying to him, in a way as if I could have fought with the wind, that it was very unsettled weather.

'My dawty,' said he, 'I wonder what would content you! we have had as delightful a week as ever made the sight of the sun heartsome.'

'Well, but,' said I, 'good weather that is to you may not be so to me; and I say again, that this is most ridiculous weather.'

'What would you have, my dawty? Is it not known by a better what is best for us?'

'Oh,' cried I, 'we can never speak of temporal things but you haul in the grace of the Maker by the lug and the horn. Mr Thrifter, ye should set a watch on the door of your lips; especially as ye have now such a prospect before you of being the father of a family.'

'Mrs Thrifter,' said he, 'what has that to do with the state of the weather?'

'Everything,' said I. 'Isn't the condition that I am in a visibility that I cannot look after the house as I should do? which is the cause of your having such a poor dinner to-day; for the weather wiled out the servant lass, and she has in consequence not been in the kitchen to see to her duty. Doesn't that shew you that, to a woman in the state that I am, fine sunshiny weather is no comfort?'

'Well,' said he, 'though a shower is at times seasonable, I will say that I prefer days like this.'

'What you, Mr Thrifter, prefer, can make no difference to me; but I will uphold, in spite of everything you can allege to the contrary, that this is not judicious weather.'

'Really now, gudewife,' said Mr Thrifter, 'what need we quarrel about the weather? neither of us can make it better or worse.'

'That's a truth,' said I, 'but what need you maintain that dry weather is pleasant weather, when I have made it plain to you that it is a great affliction? And how can you say the contrary? does not both wet and dry come from Providence? Which of them is the evil?—for they should be in their visitations both alike.'

'Mrs Thrifter,' said he, 'what would you be at, summering and wintering on nothing?'

Upon which I said, 'Oh, Mr Thrifter, if ye were like me, ye would say anything; for I am not in a condition to be spoken to. I'll not say that ye're far wrong, but till my time is a bygone ye should not contradict me so; for I am no in a state to be contradicted: it may go hard with me if I am. So I beg you to think, for the sake of the baby unborn, to let me have my way in all things for a season.'

'I have no objection,' said he, 'if there is a necessity for complying; but really, gudewife, ye're at times a wee fashous just now; and this house has not been a corner in the kingdom of heaven for some time.'

Thus, from less to more, our argolbargoling was put an end to; and from that time I was the ruling power in our domicile, which has made it the habitation of quiet ever since; for from that moment I never laid down the rod of authority, which I achieved with such a womanly sleight of hand.

THREE

Though from the time of the conversation recorded in the preceding chapter I was, in a certain sense, the ruling power in our house, as a wedded wife should be, we did not slide down a glassy brae till long after. For though the gudeman in a compassionate manner allowed me to have my own way till my fullness of time was come, I could discern by the tail of my eye that he meditated to usurp the authority again, when he saw a fit time to effect the machination. Thus it came to pass, when I was delivered of our daughter, I had, as I lay on my bed, my own thoughts anent the evil that I saw barming within him; and I was therefore determined to keep the upper hand, of which I had made a conquest with such dexterity, and the breaking down of difficulties.

So when I was some days in a recumbent posture, but in a well-doing way, I said nothing; it made me, however, often grind my teeth in a secrecy when I saw from the bed many a thing that I treasured in remembrance should never be again. But I was very thankful for my deliverance, and assumed a blitheness in my countenance that was far from my heart. In short, I could see that the gudeman, in whose mouth you would have thought sugar would have melted, had from day to day a stratagem in his head subversive of the regency that I had won in my tender state; and as I saw it would never do to let him have his own will, I had recourse to the usual diplomaticals of womankind.

It was a matter before the birth that we settled, him and me, that the child should be baptized on the eighth day after, in order that I might be up and a partaker of the ploy; which, surely, as the mother, I was well entitled to. But from what I saw going on from the bed and jaloused, it occurred to me that the occasion should be postponed, and according as Mr Thrifter should give his consent, or withhold it, I should comport myself; determined, however, I was to have the matter postponed, just to ascertain the strength and durability of what belonged to me.

On the fifth day I, therefore, said to him, as I was sitting in the easy chair by the fire, with a cod at my shoulders and my mother's fur cloak about me—the baby was in a cradle close by, but not rocking, for the keeper said it was yet too young—and sitting, as I have said, Mr Thrifter forenent me, 'My dear,' said I, 'it will never do to have the christening on the day we said.'

'What for no?' was the reply; 'isn't it a very good day?'

So I, seeing that he was going to be upon his peremptors, replied, with my usual meekness, 'No human being, my dear, can tell what sort of day it will be; but be it good or it bad, the christening is not to be on that day.'

'You surprise me!' said he, 'I considered it a settled point, and have asked Mr Sweetie, the grocer, to come to his tea.'

'Dear me!' quo' I; 'ye should not have done that without my consent; for although we set the day before my time was come, it was not then in the power of man to say how I was to get through; and therefore it was just a talk we had on the subject, and by no manner of means a thing that could be fixed.'

'In some sort,' said Mr Thrifter, 'I cannot but allow that you are speaking truth; but I thought that the only impediment to the day was your illness. Now you have had a most blithe time o't, and there is nothing in the way of an obstacle.'

'Ah, Mr Thrifter!' said I, 'it's easy for you, who have such a barren knowledge of the nature of women, so to speak, but I know that I am in no condition to have such a handling as a christening; and besides, I have a scruple of conscience well worth your attention concerning the same—and it's my opinion, formed in the watches of the night, when I was in my bed, that baby should be christened in the kirk on the Lord's day.'

'Oh,' said he, 'that's but a fashion, and you'll be quite well by the eighth; the howdie told me that ye had a most pleasant time o't, and cannot be ill on the eighth day.'

I was just provoked into contumacy to hear this; for to tell a new mother that childbirth is a pleasant thing, set me almost in a passion; and I said to him that he might entertain Mr Sweetie himself, for that I was resolved the christening should not be as had been set.

In short, from less to more, I gained my point; as, indeed, I always settled it in my own mind before broaching the subject: first, by letting him know that I had latent pains, which made me very ill, though I seemed otherwise; and, secondly, that it was very hard, and next to a martyrdom, to be controverted in religion, as I would be if the bairn was baptized anywhere but in the church.

FOUR

In due time the christening took place in the kirk, as I had made a point of having; and for some time after we passed a very happy married life. Mr Thrifter saw that it was of no use to contradict me, and in consequence we lived in great felicity, he never saying nay to me; and I, as became a wife in the rightful possession of her prerogatives, was most condescending. But still he shewed, when he durst, the bull-horn; and would have meddled with our householdry, to the manifest detriment of our conjugal happiness, had I not continued my interdict in the strictest manner. In truth, I was all the time grievously troubled with nursing Nance, our daughter, and could not take the same pains about things that I otherwise would have done; and it is well known that husbands are like mice, that know when the cat is out of the house or her back turned, they take their own way: and I assure the courteous reader, to say no ill of my gudeman, that he was one of the mice genus.

But at last I had a trial that was not to be endured with such a composity as if I had been a black snail. It came to pass that our daughter was to be weaned, and on the day settled—a Sabbath day—we had, of course, much to do, for it behoved in this ceremony that I should keep out of sight; and keeping out of sight it seemed but reasonable, considering his parentage to the wean, that Mr Thrifter should take my place. So I said to him in the morning that he must do so, and keep Nance for that day; and, to do the poor man justice, he consented at once, for he well knew that it would come to nothing to be contrary.

So I went to the kirk, leaving him rocking the cradle and singing hush, ba! as he saw need. But oh, dule! scarcely had I left the house when the child screamed up in a panic, and would not be pacified. He thereupon lifted it out of the cradle, and with it in his arms went about the house; but it was such a roaring buckie that for a long time he was like to go distracted. Over what ensued I draw the curtain, and must only say that, when I came from the church, there he was, a spectacle, and as sour as a crab apple, blaming me for leaving him with such a devil.

I was really woeful to see him, and sympathised in the most pitiful manner with him, on account of what had happened; but the more I condoled with him the more he would not be comforted, and for all my endeavours to keep matters in a propriety, I saw my jurisdiction over the house was in jeopardy, and every now and then the infant cried out, just as if it had been laid upon a heckle. Oh! such a day as that was for Mr Thrifter, when he heard the tyrant bairn shrieking like mad, and every now and then drumming with its wee feetie like desperation, he cried:

'For the love of God, give it a drop of the breast! or it will tempt me to wring off its ankles or its head.'

But I replied composedly that it could not be done, for the wean must be speant, and what he advised was evendown nonsense.

'What has come to pass, both my mother and other sagacious carlines told me I had to look for; and so we must bow the head of resignation to our lot. You'll just,' said I, 'keep the bairn this afternoon; it will not be a long fashery.'

He said nothing, but gave a deep sigh.

At this moment the bells of the kirk were ringing for the afternoon's discourse, and I lifted my bonnet to put it on and go; but ere I knew where I was, Mr Thrifter was out of the door and away, leaving me alone with the torment in the cradle, which the bells at that moment wakened: and it gave a yell that greatly discomposed me.

Once awa and aye awa, Mr Thrifter went into the fields, and would not come back when I lifted the window and called to him, but walked faster and faster, and was a most demented man; so that I was obligated to stay at home, and would have had my own work with the termagant baby if my mother had not come in and advised me to give it sweetened rum and water for a pacificator.

FIVE

Mr Thrifter began in time to be a very complying husband, and we had, after the trial of the weaning, no particular confabulation; indeed he was a very reasonable man, and had a rightful instinct of the reverence that is due to the opinion of a wife of discernment. I do not think, to the best of my recollection, that between the time Nance was weaned till she got her walking shoes and was learning to walk, that we had a single controversy; nor can it be said that we had a great ravelment on that occasion. Indeed, saving our daily higling about trifles not worth remembering, we passed a pleasant life. But when Nance came to get her first walking shoes, that was a catastrophe well worthy of being rehearsed for her behoof now.

It happened that for some months before, she had, in place of shoes, red worsted socks; but as she began, from the character of her capering, to kithe that she was coming to her feet, I got a pair of yellow slippers for her; and no mother could take more pains than I did to learn her how to handle her feet. First, I tried to teach her to walk by putting a thimble or an apple beyond her reach, at least a chair's breadth off, and then I endeavoured to make the cutty run from me to her father, across the hearth, and he held out his hands to catch her.

This, it will be allowed, was to us pleasant pastime. But it fell out one day, when we were diverting ourselves by making Nance run to and fro between us across the hearth, that the glaiket baudrons chanced to see the seal of her father's watch glittering, and, in coming from him to me, she drew it after her, as if it had been a turnip. He cried, 'Oh, Christal and—' I lifted my hands in wonderment; but the tottling creature, with no more sense than a sucking turkey, whirled the watch—the Almighty knows how!—into the fire, and giggled as if she had done an exploit.

'Take it out with the tongs,' said I.

'She's an ill-brought-up wean,' cried he.

The short and the long of it was, before the watch could be got out, the heat broke the glass and made the face of it dreadful; besides, he wore a riband chain—that was in a blaze before we could make a redemption.

When the straemash was over, I said to him that he could expect no better by wearing a watch in such a manner.

'It is not,' said he, 'the watch that is to blame, but your bardy bairn that ye have spoiled in the bringing up.'

'Mr Thrifter,' quo' I, 'this is not a time for upbraiding; for if ye mean to insinuate anything to my disparagement, it is what I will not submit to.'

'E'en as you like, my dawty,' said he; 'but what I say is true—that your daughter will just turn out a randy like her mother.'

'What's that ye say?' quo' I, and I began to wipe my eyes with the corner of my shawl—saying in a pathetic manner, 'If I am a randy, I ken who has made me one.'

'Ken,' said he, 'Ken! everybody kens that ye are like a clubby foot, made by the hand of God, and passed the remede of doctors.'

Was not this most diabolical to hear? Really my corruption rose at such blasphemy; and starting from my seat, I put my hands on my haunches, and gave a stamp with my foot that made the whole house dirl; 'What does the man mean?' said I.

But he replied with a composity as if he had been in liquor, saying, with an ill-faured smile, 'Sit down, my dawty; you'll do yourself a prejudice if ye allow your passion to get the better of you.'

Could mortal woman thole the like of this; it stunned me speechless, and for a time I thought my authority knocked on the head. But presently the spirit that was in my nature mustered courage, and put a new energy within me, which caused me to say nothing, but to stretch out my feet, and stiffen back, with my hands at my sides, as if I was a dead corpse. Whereupon the good man ran for a tumbler of water to jaup on my face; but when he came near me in this posture, I dauded the glass of water in his face, and drummed with my feet and hands in a delirious manner, which convinced him that I was going by myself. Oh, but he was in an awful terrification! At last, seeing his fear and contrition, I began to moderate, as it seemed; which made him as softly and kindly as if I had been a true frantic woman; which I was not, but a practiser of the feminine art, to keep the ruling power.

Thinking by my state that I was not only gone daft, but not without the need of soothing, he began to ask my pardon in a proper humility, and with a most pitiful penitence. Whereupon I said to him, that surely he had not a rightful knowledge of my nature: and then he began to confess a fault, and was such a dejected man that I took the napkin from my eyes and gave a great guffaw, telling him that surely he was silly daft and gi'en to pikery, if he thought he could daunton me. 'No, no, Mr Thrifter,' quo' I, 'while I live, and the iron tongs are by the chumly leg, never expect to get the upper hand of me.'

From that time he was as bidable a man as any reasonable woman could desire; but he gave a deep sigh, which was a testificate to me that the leaven of unrighteousness was still within him, and might break out into treason and rebellion if I was not on my guard.

George Mackay Brown

CELIA

'I write this book not as a booster for Albany, which I am, nor as an apologist for the city, which I sometimes am, but as a person whose imagination has become fused with a single place, and in that place finds all the elements that a man ever needs for the life of the soul.'—That is the first sentence of *O Albany* by William Kennedy in which he explores his native town as a state of mind. I believe it is a statement George Mackay Brown would understand and empathise with entirely.

Brown was born in Orkney in 1921 and has lived there for most of his life. His stories, poems, plays and novels give the impression that Stromness, his Hamnavoe, has all that any writer could need or want, and he has always portrayed a clear and uniform picture of Orkney life. His style, based on that of the ballads and sagas, is pared to essentials, so that the dignity of labour and the small communities of town or croft become a model for the world and the values he upholds.

Brown's poetry is terse with clear, pure images and he brings a poet's eye for detail and description to his stories. The stories in turn bring him back into contact with the world and are, I believe, his finest achievement. 'Celia' comes from his second collection, *A Time to Keep* (1967), where he is closest to contemporary life, though the loneliness and the desperate pain he finds in 'Celia' is a timeless human condition.

Celia

THE NORWEGIAN whaler *Erika* tied up at the pier in the middle of Monday afternoon, and when the pubs opened at five o'clock all six of the crew went into the Hamnavoe Bar. Per Bjorling the skipper was with them, but about seven o'clock he bought a full bottle of vodka and left them drinking their whiskies and lagers and went outside. It was getting dark. He walked along the street till he came to an opening that descended step by step to a small pier with a house on it. From inside the house came the thwack of a hammer driving nails into leather. One room of the house had a lamp burning in the window but the other room next the sea was dark. Per Bjorling was about to knock at the door when it was opened from inside. He smiled and raised his sailor's cap and went in.

'What kind of a man is it this time?' shouted a voice from the lighted room. 'Is it that bloody foreigner? . . .' All the people in the neighbouring houses could hear what was being said. Maisie Ness came to the end of her pier and stood listening, her head cocked to one side.

The hammer smacked on leather, a rapid tattoo.

The seaward room remained dark; or rather, the window flushed a little as if a poker had suddenly woken flames from the coal.

'Yes,' yelled the shoemaker, 'a bloody drunken foreign sailor.'

Then silence returned to the piers and one by one the lights went on in all the houses round about.

TWO

The *Erika* and three other Norwegian whalers caught the morning tide on Tuesday and it was quiet again in the harbour. In the house on the small pier the shoe-repairing began early, the leisurely smack of the hammer on the moulded leather in between periods of quiet stitching. At ten o'clock Maisie Ness from the next close came with a pair of shoes to be soled. She walked straight in through the open door and turned into the room on the left next the street. The shoemaker sat on his stool, his mouth full of tacks. Maisie laid her shoes on the bench, soles upward.

'Celia isn't up yet, surely. I don't hear her,' she said.

'Celia's a good girl,' said the shoemaker.

'I don't believe you've had your breakfast,' cried Maisie Ness, 'and it's past ten o'clock. You need your food, or you'll be ill same as you were in the winter-time.'

'I'll get my breakfast,' said the shoemaker. 'Just leave the shoes on the bench. All they need is rubber soles and a protector or two in the right heel to keep it level. You're an impudent woman. Ignorant too. Could you read the deep books that Celia reads? I don't believe you can sign your name. I'll get my breakfast all right. Celia's a good girl. Just keep your tongue off her.'

Maisie Ness went up the steps of the pier shaking her head. She managed to look pleased and outraged at the same time.

'Celia,' the shoemaker called out, 'I'll make you a cup of tea. Just you lie in bed for an hour or two yet.'

THREE

It was early spring. Darkness was still long but the light was slowly encroaching and the days grew colder. The last of the snow still scarred the Orphir hills. One sensed a latent fertility; under the hard earth the seeds were awake and astir; their long journey to blossom and ripeness was beginning. But in Hamnavoe, the fishermen's town, the lamps still had to be lit early.

On Tuesday night every week Mr Spence the jeweller paid his visit. He would hesitate at the head of the close, look swiftly right and left along the street, then quickly descend the steps.

The shoemaker heard his precise footsteps on the flagstones outside and immediately took down from the shelf the draught-board and the set of draughtsmen. He had the pieces arranged on the board before Mr Spence was at the threshold.

'Come in, Mr Spence,' he shouted, 'come in. I heard your feet.'

And Mr Spence, without a single glance at the dark seaward window, went straight into the work-room on the left, bending his head under the lintel and smiling in the lamplight. 'Well, Thomas,' he said.

They always played for about an hour, best of three games. Mr Spence generally lost. Perhaps he was a poor player; perhaps he was nervous (he shuffled and blinked and cleared his throat a good deal); perhaps he genuinely liked to give the shoemaker the pleasure of winning; perhaps he was anxious to get this empty ritual over with. They played this night without speaking, the old man in his leather apron and the middle-aged bachelor in his smart serge tailor-made suit. The shoemaker won two games right away, inside half an hour, so that there was no need that night to play a decider.

'You put up a very poor show tonight,' said the shoemaker.

'I'm not in the same class as you, Thomas,' said Mr Spence.

He went over to his coat hanging on a peg and brought a half-bottle of whisky out of the pocket. 'Perhaps, Thomas,' he said, 'you'd care for a drink.'

'You know fine,' said the shoemaker, 'I never drink that filthy trash. The poison!'

'Then,' said Mr Spence, 'perhaps I'll go and see if Miss Celia would care to have a little drink. A toddy, seeing it's a cold night.'

'No,' said the shoemaker anxiously, 'I don't think you should do that. Or if you do, only a very small drop.'

But Mr Spence was already tiptoeing along the lobby towards the dark room, carrying the half-bottle in his hand. He tapped on the door, and opened it gently. The girl was bending over the black range, stabbing the coal with a poker. At once the ribs were thronged with red and yellow flames, and the shadow of the girl leapt over him before she herself turned slowly to the voice in the doorway.

'My dear,' said Mr Spence.

FOUR

'How are you, Thomas?' said Dr Wilson on the Wednesday morning, sitting down on the bench among bits and scrapings of leather.

'I'm fine,' said the shoemaker.

'The chest all right?'

'I still get a bit of a wheeze when the wind's easterly,' said the shoemaker, 'but I'm not complaining.'

There was silence in the room for a half-minute.

'And Celia?' said Dr Wilson.

'Celia's fine,' said the shoemaker. 'I wish she would eat more and get more exercise. I'm a nuisance to her, I keep her tied to the house. But she keeps her health. She's fine.'

'I'm glad to hear it,' said Dr Wilson.

'Celia's a good girl,' said the shoemaker.

'I know she's a good girl,' said Dr Wilson. Then his voice dropped a tone. 'Thomas,' he said, 'I don't want to worry you, but there are complaints in the town.'

'She's a good girl,' said the old man, 'a very good girl to me.'

'Complaints,' said Dr Wilson quietly, 'that this is a house of bad repute. I'm not saying it, for I know you're both good people, you and Celia. But the scandal-mongers are saying it along the street. You know the way it is. I've heard it twenty times this past week if I've heard it once. That all kinds of men come here, at all hours of the night, and there's drinking and carrying-on. I don't want to annoy you, Thomas, but I think it's right you should know what they're saying in the public, Maisie Ness and the other women. All this worry is not good for your lungs.'

'*I* don't drink,' said the shoemaker. 'How do I know who comes and goes in the night? That Maisie Ness should have her tongue cut out. Celia has a sweetheart, Ronald Leask of Clett, and she's applied to be a member of the Kirk. The minister's coming to see her Friday evening. She's a good girl.'

'Perhaps I could see Celia for a minute?' said Dr Wilson and got to his feet.

'No,' said the shoemaker, 'she's sleeping. She needs her rest. She's sleeping late. Celia is a very good girl to me. If it wasn't for Celia I know I'd have died in the winter-time.'

'Good morning, Thomas,' said Dr Wilson. 'I'll be back next Wednesday. You have plenty of tablets to be getting on with. Tell Celia I'm asking for her. Send for me if you need me, any time.'

FIVE

'Go away,' said the shoemaker to Mr William Snoddy the builder's clerk. 'Just you go away from this house and never come back, never so much as darken the door again. I know what you're after. I'm not a fool exactly.'

'I want you to make me a pair of light shoes for the summer,' said Mr Snoddy. 'That's all I want.'

'Is it?' said the shoemaker. 'Then you can go some other place, for I have no intention of doing the job for you.'

They were standing at the door of the house on the pier. It was Wednesday evening and the lamp was burning in the work-room but the room next the sea was in darkness.

'Last Saturday,' said Mr Snoddy, 'at the pier-head, you promised to make me a pair of light shoes for the summer.'

'I didn't know then,' said the shoemaker, 'what I know now. You and your fancy-women. Think shame of yourself. You have a wife and three bairns waiting for you in your house at the South End. And all you can do is run after other women here, there and everywhere. I'm making no shoes for whore-mastering expeditions. You can take that for sure and certain.'

'You've been listening,' said Mr Snoddy, 'to cruel groundless gossip.'

'And I believe the gossip,' said the shoemaker. 'I don't usually believe gossip but I believe this particular piece of gossip. You're an immoral man.'

'There's such a thing as a court of law,' said Mr Snoddy, 'and if ever I hear of these slanders being repeated again, I'll take steps to silence the slanderers.'

'You'll have your work cut out,' said the shoemaker, 'because you've been seen going to this house and that house when the men have been away at the fishing. I've seen you with my own two eyes. And if you want names I'll supply them to you with pleasure.'

'Let's go inside,' said Mr Snoddy in a suddenly pleasant voice, 'and we'll talk about something else. We'll have a game of draughts.'

The shoemaker stretched out foot and arm and blocked the door.

'Stay where you are,' he said. 'Just bide where you are. What's that you've got in the inside pocket of your coat, eh?'

'It's my wallet,' said Mr Snoddy, touching the bulge at his chest.

'It's drink,' said the shoemaker, 'it's spirits. I'm not exactly so blind or so stupid that I can't recognise the shape of a half-bottle of whisky. I allow no drink into this house. Understand that.'

'Please, Thomas,' said Mr Snoddy. 'It's a cold night.'

'Forby being a whore-master,' said the shoemaker, 'you're a drunkard. Never a day passed that you aren't three or four times in the pub. Just look in the mirror when you get home and see how red your nose is getting. I'm sorry for your wife and children.'

'I mind my own business,' said Mr Snoddy.

'That's fine,' said the shoemaker. 'That's very good. Just mind your own business and don't come bothering this house. There's one thing I have to tell you before you go.'

'What's that?' said Mr Snoddy.

'Celia is not at home,' shouted the old man. He suddenly stepped back into the lobby and slammed the door shut. Mr Snoddy stood alone in the darkness, his mouth twitching. Then he turned and began to walk up the pier slowly.

From inside the house came the sound of steel protectors being hammered violently into shoes.

Mr Snoddy's foot was on the first step leading up to the street when a hand tugged at his sleeve. He turned round. It was Celia. She had a grey shawl over her head and her hair was tucked into it. Her face in the darkness was an oval oblique shadow.

'Celia,' said Mr Snoddy in a shaking voice.

'Where are you off to so soon, Billy boy?' said Celia. 'Won't you stop and speak for a minute to a poor lonely girl?'

Mr Snoddy put his hands round her shoulders. She pushed him away gently.

'Billy,' she said, 'if you have a little drink on you I could be doing with it.'

The loud hammering went on inside the house.

Mr Snoddy took the flask from his inside pocket. 'I think, dear,' he said, 'where we're standing we're a bit in the public eye. People passing in the street. Maybe if we move into that corner . . .'

Together they moved to the wall of the watchmaker's house, into a segment of deeper darkness.

'Dear Celia,' muttered Mr Snoddy.

'Just one little mouthful,' said Celia. 'I believe it's gin you've gone and bought.'

SIX

Ronald Leask closed the door of the tractor shed. The whole field on the south side of the hill was ploughed now, a good day's work. He looked round him, stretched his aching arms, and walked slowly a hundred yards down to the beach. The boat was secure. There had been south-westerly winds and high seas for two days, but during that afternoon the wind had veered further west and dropped. He thought he would be able to set his lobster-creels the next morning, Friday, under the Hoy crags. The *Celia* rocked gently at the pier like a furled sea bird.

Ronald went back towards his house. He filled a bucket with water from the rain barrel at the corner. He stripped off his soiled jersey and shirt and vest and washed quickly, shuddering and gasping as the cold water slapped into his shoulders and chest. He carried the pail inside and kicked off his boots and trousers and finished his washing. Then he dried himself at the dead hearth and put on his best clothes—the white shirt and tartan tie, the dark Sunday suit, the pigskin shoes. He combed his wet fair hair till it clung to both sides of his head like bronze wings. His face looked back at him from the square tarnished mirror on the mantelpiece, red and complacent and healthy. He put on his beret and pulled it a little to one side.

Ronald wheeled his bicycle out of the lobby on to the road, mounted, and cycled towards Hamnavoe.

He passed three cars and a county council lorry and a young couple out walking. It was too dark to see their faces. As he freewheeled down into the town there were lights here and there in the houses. It would be a dark night, with no moon.

Ronald Leask left his bicycle at the head of the shoemaker's close and walked down the steps to the house. The lamp was lit in the old man's window but Celia's room, as usual, was dark. He knocked at the outer door. The clob-clob-clobbering of hammer against leather stopped. 'Who's that?' cried the old man sharply.

'It's me, Ronald.'

'Ronald,' said the shoemaker. 'Come in, Ronald.' He appeared at the door. 'I'm glad to see thee, Ronald.' He took Ronald's arm and guided him into the workroom. 'Come in, boy, and sit down.'

'How are you keeping, Thomas?' said Ronald.

'I'm fine, Ronald,' said the shoemaker, and coughed.

'And Celia?' said Ronald.

'Celia's fine,' said the shoemaker. 'She's wanting to see thee, I know that. It's not much of a life for a girl, looking after a poor old thing like me. She'll be glad of your company.'

'Last time I came, last Thursday, I didn't get much of a reception,' said Ronald.

'Celia wasn't well that day,' said the shoemaker. 'She likes thee more than anybody, I can assure thee for that.' He went over to the door and opened it and shouted across the lobby, 'Celia, Ronald's here.'

There was no answer from the other room.

'She's maybe sleeping,' said the shoemaker. 'Poor Celia, she works too hard, looking after me. What she needs is a long holiday. We'll go and see her.'

The old man crossed the lobby on tiptoe and opened the door of Celia's room gently. 'Celia,' he said, 'are you all right?'

'Yes,' said Celia's voice from inside.

'Ronald's here,' said the shoemaker.

'I know,' said Celia. 'I heard him.'

'Well,' said the shoemaker sharply, 'he wants to speak to you. And I'm taking him in now, whether you want it or not. And I'm coming in too for a minute.'

The two men went into the room. They could just make out the girl's outline against the banked-up glow of the fire. They groped towards chairs and sat down.

'Celia,' said the shoemaker, 'light your lamp.'

'No,' said Celia, 'I like it best this way, in the darkness. Besides, I have no money for paraffin. I don't get many shillings from you to keep the house going, and bread and coal and paraffin cost dear.'

'Speak to her, Ronald,' said the shoemaker.

'I can't be bothered to listen to him,' said Celia. 'I'm not well.'

'What ails you?' said the shoemaker.

'I don't know,' said Celia. 'I'm just not well.'

'Celia,' said Ronald earnestly, 'there's an understanding between us. You know it and I know it and the whole of Hamnavoe knows it. Why are you behaving this way to me?'

'That's true,' said the shoemaker. 'You're betrothed to one another.'

'Not this again,' said Celia, 'when I'm sick.' Then she said in a low voice, 'I need something to drink.'

'Drink!' said the old man angrily. 'That's all your mind runs on, drink. Just you listen to Ronald when he's speaking to you.'

'Celia,' said Ronald, 'it's a year come April since I buried my mother and the croft of Clett has stood there vacant ever since, except for me and the dog.'

'And a fine croft it is,' said the shoemaker. 'Good sandy soil and a tractor in the shed and a first-rate boat in the bay.'

'I'm not listening,' said Celia.

'It needs a woman about the place,' said Ronald. 'I can manage the farm work and the fishing. But inside the house things are going to wrack and ruin. That's the truth. Celia, you promised six months ago to come to Clett.'

'So that's all you want, is it?' said Celia. 'A housekeeper.'

'No,' said Ronald, 'I want you for my wife. I love you.'

'He does love you,' said the shoemaker. 'And he's a good man. And he has money put by. And he works well at the farming and the fishing. He's a good fellow any girl would be proud to have for a man.'

'I'm not well tonight,' said Celia. 'I would be the better of a glass of brandy.'

'And what's more,' said the shoemaker, 'you love him, because you told me with your own lips not a fortnight ago.'

'I do not,' said Celia.

Ronald turned to the shoemaker and whispered to him and put something in his hand. The shoemaker rose up at once and went out. He banged the outer door shut behind him.

'Celia,' said Ronald.

'Leave me alone,' said Celia.

They sat in the growing darkness. The only light in the room was the dull glow from the range. Ronald could see the dark outline of the girl beside the fire. For ten minutes they neither moved nor spoke.

At last the door opened again and the old man came back. He groped his way to the table and put a bottle down on it. 'That's it,' he said to Ronald and laid down some loose coins beside the bottle. 'And that's the change.'

'Celia,' said Ronald, 'I'm sorry to hear you aren't well. I've got something here that'll maybe help you. A little brandy.'

'That's kind of you,' said Celia.

She picked up the poker and drove it into the black coal on top of the range. The room flared wildly with lights and shadows. The three dark figures were suddenly sitting in a warm rosy flickering world.

Celia took two cups from the cupboard and set them on the table and poured brandy into them.

'That's enough for me,' said Ronald, and put his hand over the cup next to him.

Celia filled the other cup to the top. Then she lifted it to her mouth with both hands and gulped it like water.

'Good health,' said the shoemaker. 'I'm saying that and I mean it though I'm not a drinking man myself. The very best of luck to you both.'

Ronald raised his cup and drank meagrely from it and put it down again on the table. 'Cheers,' he said.

Celia took another mouthful and set down her empty cup beside the bottle.

'Are you feeling better now, Celia?' said the shoemaker.

'A wee bit,' said Celia. She filled up her cup again. 'I'm very glad to see you,' she said to Ronald.

'That's better,' said the shoemaker, 'that's the way to speak.'

Celia took a drink and said, 'Ronald, supposing I come to live at Clett what's going to become of Thomas?'

'I'll be all right,' said the shoemaker, 'don't worry about me. I'll manage fine.'

'He'll come and live with us,' said Ronald. 'There's plenty of room.

'No,' said Celia, 'but who's going to walk a mile and more to Clett to get their boots mended? We must think of that. He'll lose trade.

'Don't drink so fast,' said the shoemaker.

'And besides that,' said Celia, 'he'll miss his friends, all the ones that come and visit him here and play draughts with him. What would he do without his game of draughts? Clett's a long distance away. I'm very pleased, Ronald, that you've come to see me.'

'I'm pleased to be here,' said Ronald.

'Light the lamp,' said the shoemaker happily.

'I love you both very much,' said Celia. 'You're the two people that I love most in the whole world.'

Celia filled up her cup again. This time half the brandy spilled over the table.

'I don't know whether I'll come to Clett or not,' said Celia. 'I'll have to think about it. I have responsibilities here. That's what makes me feel ill, being torn this way and that. I can't be in two places, can I? I love you both very much. I want you to know that, whatever happens.'

She suddenly started to cry. She put her hands over her face and her whole body shook with grief. She sat down in her chair beside the fire and sobbed long and bitterly.

The two men looked at each other, awed and awkward.

'I'll put a match to the lamp,' said the shoemaker. 'Then we'll see what's what.'

Celia stopped crying for a moment and said, 'Leave the bloody lamp alone.' Then she started to sob again, louder than ever.

Ronald got to his feet and went over to Celia. He put his arm across her shoulder. 'Poor Celia,' he said, 'tell me what way I can help thee?'

Celia rose to her feet and screamed at him. 'You go away from here, you bastard,' she shouted. 'Just go away! I want never to see you again! Clear off!'

'Celia,' pleaded the old man.

'If that's what you want, Celia,' said Ronald. He picked up his beret from the chair and stood with his back to the cupboard. 'Good night, Thomas,' he said.

'Come back, Ronald,' said the shoemaker. 'Celia isn't herself tonight. She doesn't mean a word of what she says.'

The flames were dying down in the range. Celia and Ronald and the shoemaker moved about in the room, three unquiet shadows.

'Good night, Celia,' said Ronald from the door.

'I hate you, you bastard,' she shrieked at him.

The last flame died. In the seething darkness the girl and the old man heard the bang of the outer door closing. Celia sat down in her chair and began to cry again, a slow gentle wailing.

Half-way up the steps of the close the shoemaker caught up with Ronald. 'This is the worst she's ever been,' he said. 'You know the way it is with her—she drinks heavily for a week or so, after that she's as peaceable as a dove. But this is the worst she's ever been. God knows what will come of her.'

'God knows,' said Ronald.

'It started on Monday night,' said the shoemaker. 'That Norsky was here with foreign hooch.'

'Don't worry, Thomas,' said Ronald. 'It'll turn out all right, like you say.'

'She'll be fine next time you come back,' said the shoemaker. 'Just you wait and see.'

Ronald got on to his bicycle at the head of the close.

The shoemaker went back slowly into the house. As he opened the door Celia's low voice came out of the darkness. 'God forgive me,' she was saying gently and hopelessly, 'O God forgive me.'

SEVEN

'No,' said Celia to the minister, 'I don't believe in your God. It's no good. You're wasting your time. What the Hamnavoe folk are saying is true, I'm a bad woman. I drink. Men come about the place all hours of the night. It isn't that I want them fumbling at me with their mouths and their hands. That sickens me. I put up with it for the drink they have in their pockets. I must drink.

'You're not a drinking man, Mr Blackie. I know that. I *had* to buy this bottle of wine from the licensed grocer's. It give me courage to speak to you. Try to understand that. And we're sitting here in the half darkness because I can speak to you better in this secrecy. Faces tell lies to one another. You know the way it is. The truth gets buried under smiles.

'I drink because I'm frightened. I'm so desperately involved with all the weak things, lonely things, suffering things I see about me. I can't bear the pity I feel for them, not being able to help them at all. There's blood everywhere. The world's a torture chamber, just a sewer of pain. That frightens me.

'Yesterday it was a gull and a water rat. They met at the end of this pier. I was pinning washing to the line when I saw it. The gull came down on the rat and swallowed it whole the way it would gulp a crust of bread, then with one flap of its wing it was out over the sea again. I could see the shape of the rat in the blackback's throat, a kind of fierce twist and thrust. The bird broke up in the air. It screamed. Blood and feathers showered out of it. The dead gull and the living rat made separate splashes in the water.

'It seems most folk can live with that kind of thing. Not me—I get all caught up in it . . .'

Stars slowly thickened and brightened in the window that looked over the harbour. The rising tide began to lap against the gable ends of the houses.

'Mr Blackie,' said Celia, 'an earthquake ruined a town in Serbia last week. The ground just opened and swallowed half the folk. Did your God in his mercy think up that too? The country folk in Vietnam, what kind of vice is it they're gripped in, guns and lies and anger on both sides of them, a slowly tightening agony? Is your God looking after them? They never harmed anybody, but the water in the rice fields is red now all the time. Black men and white men hate each other in Chicago and Cape Town. God rules everything. He knew what was going to happen before the world was made. So we're told. If that's goodness, I have another name for it. Not the worst human being that ever lived would do the things God does. Tell me this, was God in the Warsaw ghetto too? I just want to know. I was reading about it last week in a book I got out of the Library.

'I know you don't like this darkness and the sound of wine being poured in the glass. It's the only way I can speak to you and be honest . . .

'I remember my mother and my father. They were like two rocks in the sea. Life might be smooth or rough for me—there was hunger every now and then when the fishing was poor—but the two rocks were always there. I knew every ledge and cranny. I flew between them like a young bird.

'We were poor, but closer together because of that. We gave each other small gifts. I would take shells and seapinks into the house for them. My father always had a special fish for me when he came in from the west, a codling or a flounder as small as my hand. Then my mother would bake a small bannock for me to eat with it at teatime, when I was home from school.

'I was twelve years old. One morning when I got up for school my mother was standing in the door looking out over the harbour. The fire was dead. She told me in a flat voice I wasn't to go to school that day, I was to go back to my room and draw the curtain and stay there till she called me. An hour later I heard feet on the pier. I looked through the edge of the curtain. Four fishermen were carrying something from the boat into the house. The thing was covered with a piece of sail and there was a trail of drops behind it. My father was in from his creels for the last time.

'We knew what real poverty was after that. My mother was too proud to take anything from the Poor Fund. "Of course not," she said, "my grandfather was schoolmaster in Hoy." . . . But in the middle of February she swallowed her pride and went to the Poor Inspector. One night I woke up and heard voices and came downstairs and I saw Thomas Linklater the shoemaker having supper beside the fire. A month after that my mother married him in the registry office. He came and sat in my father's chair and slept in my father's bed. He carried a new smell into our house, leather and rosin, like an animal of a different species.

'I hated him. Of course I smiled and spoke. But in my room, in the darkness, I hated the stranger.

'Three years went past. Then it was my mother's turn. I watched her changing slowly. I didn't know what the change was, nor why Dr Wilson should trouble to come so often. Then I heard Maisie Ness saying "cancer" to the watchmaker's wife at the end of the close. My mother was a good-looking woman. She was a bit vain and she'd often look long in the mirror, putting her hair to rights and smiling to her reflection. The change went on in her all that summer. She looked in the mirror less and less. Every day though she did her housework. The room had to be swept and the dishes put away before Dr Wilson called. Half a ghost, she knelt at the unlit fire and struck a match. That last morning she laid three bowls of porridge on the table. She looked at her withered face in the mirror. Then she groped for her chair and sank into it. She was dead before I could put down my spoon. The shoemaker hurried away to find Dr Wilson. The body slowly turned cold in the deep straw chair.

'I heard the shoemaker crying in his room the day before the funeral.

'"Blessed are the dead which die in the Lord"—that's what you said at the graveside. It was a poor way to die. It was ugly and degrading and unblessed, if anything ever was.

'We were alone in the house together then, a girl and an old cobbler. It was the beginning of winter. We spoke to each other only when it was needful. He gave me the housekeeping money every Friday and it was never enough. "There'll be more soon," he would say, "It's hard times, a depression all over the country. So-and-so owes five pounds for two pairs of shoes and I had a bill from the wholesale leather merchant for twenty pounds odds." . . . I wanted cakes on the table at the week-end but there was never anything but the usual bread and oatcakes and margarine.

'Christmas came. I wanted a few decorations about the house, a tree, paper bells, some tinsel, a dozen cards to send to my special friends—you know the way it is with young girls. "We can't afford nonsense like that," the shoemaker said. "We should be thankful to God for a roof over our heads." . . . And so the walls remained bare.

'That Christmas I hated him worse than ever.

'"Celia," he said at Hogmanay, just before it struck midnight, "I'm not a drinking man. But it's bad luck not to drink a health to the house at this time of year. We'll take one small dram together."

'He brought a half-bottle of whisky out of the cupboard.

'The clock struck twelve. We touched glasses. I shuddered as the whisky went down. It burned my mouth and my stomach and it took tears to my eyes. "He's doing this deliberately to hurt me," I thought. My eyes were still wet when the door opened and Mr Spence the jeweller came in. He had a bottle of whisky in his hand to wish us a good New Year. He poured three glasses and we toasted each other. The cobbler merely wet his lips. I drank my whisky down quickly to get it over with.

'It's hard to explain what happened next. I knew who I was before I took that drink—a poor girl in an ordinary house on a fisherman's pier. I stood there holding an empty glass in my hand. A door was opening deep inside me and I looked through it into another country. I stood between the two places, confused and happy and excited. I still wore Celia's clothes but the clothes were all a disguise, bits of fancy dress, a masquerade. You know the ballad about the Scottish King who went out in the streets of Edinburgh in bonnet and tradesman's apron? I wore the clothes of a poor girl but I was wise, rich, great, gentle, good.

Then doon he let his duddies fa',
And doon he let them fa'
And he glittered a' in gold
For abune them a'.

The world was all mine and I longed to share it with everybody. Celia was a princess in her little house on the pier. She pretended to be poor but she had endless treasures in her keeping, and it was all a secret, nobody knew about it but Celia. A wild happiness filled the house.

'I bent down and kissed the old shoemaker.

'Mr Spence, I remember, was pouring another whisky into my glass. The confusion and the happiness increased. I felt very tired then, I remember. I went to bed wrapped in silks and swan's feathers.

'It was Celia the poor girl who woke up next morning. There was a hard grey blanket up at her face. She had a mouth like ashes. The wireless when she switched it on downstairs told of people dying of hunger in the streets of Calcutta, drifting about like wraiths and lying down on the burning pavements. And a plane had fallen from the sky in Kansas and forty people were dead on a hillside.

'She cried, the poor princess, beside the dead fire.

'The next Friday out of the housekeeping money I bought a bottle of cheap wine.

'That's all there is to tell, really. You've heard the confession of an alcoholic, or part of it, for the bad fairy tale isn't over yet.

'Once a month, maybe every six weeks, the fisher girl craves for news of the lost country, the real world, what she calls her kingdom. For a week or more I enchant myself away from the town and the pier and the sound of cobbling. When I have no more money left I encourage men to come here with drink. I'm shameless about it now. Everybody who has a bottle is welcome, even Mr Snoddy. At the end of every bout I'm in deeper exile than the time before. Every debauch kills a piece of Celia—I almost said, kills a part of her soul, but of course I don't believe in that kind of thing any more.

'And so the bad fairy tale goes on and the fisher girl who thinks that somehow she's a princess is slowly fitted with the cold blood and leathery skin and the terrible glittering eye of a toad.

'This kingdom I've had a glimpse of, though—what about that? It *seemed* real and precious. It seemed like an inheritance we're all born for, something that belongs to us by right.

'If that's true, it should be as much *there* as this pier is in the first light of morning. Why do we have to struggle towards it through fogs of drink? What's the good of all this mystery? The vision should be like a loaf or a fish, simple and real, something given to nourish the whole world.

'I blame God for that too.'

There was no sound for a while but the lapping of harbour water against stone as the tide rose slowly among the piers and slipways. The huge chaotic ordered wheel of stars tilted a little westward on its axis.

'The bottle's nearly empty,' said Celia, 'and I haven't said what I meant to say at all. I wonder if the licensed grocer would sell me another bottle? No, it's too late. And besides, I don't think I have enough money in my purse. And besides, you don't want to listen to much more of this bad talk.

'All the same, you can see now why I could never be a member of your church. All I could bring to it is this guilt, shame, grief for things that happen, a little pity, a sure knowledge of exile.

'Will Christ accept that?'

There was another longer silence in the room.

'Celia,' said the Reverend Andrew Blackie, a little hopelessly, 'you must try to have faith.'

The girl's window was full of stars. The sky was so bright that the outlines of bed and chair and cupboard could be dimly seen, and the shapes of an empty bottle and a glass on the table.

'I want to have faith,' said Celia. 'I want that more than anything in the world.'

EIGHT

Ronald Leask worked his creels with Jock Henryson all that Saturday afternoon along the west coast. They hauled eighty creels under Marwick Head and Yesnaby. In the late afternoon the wind shifted round to the north-west and strengthened and brought occasional squalls of rain. They decided to leave their remaining score of creels under the Black Crag till morning and make for home before it got dark. They had a box of lobsters and half a basket of crabs, a fair day's work. As Ronald turned the *Celia* into Hoy Sound he saw three Norwegian whalers racing for the shelter of Hamnavoe on the last of the flood tide. Another squall of rain hit them. Ronald put on his sou'wester and buttoned his black oilskin up to the chin. Jock Henryson was at the wheel now, in the shelter of the cabin.

'It's going to be a dirty night,' said Jock.

They delivered their lobsters and crabs at the Fishermen's Society pier. Then Jock said he must go home for his supper. 'You come too,' he said to Ronald. 'The wife'll have something in the pot.'

'No,' said Ronald, 'I think I'll go along for a drink.'

It was raining all the time now. The flagstones of the street shone. Ronald stopped for a few seconds at the head of the shoemaker's close, then he walked on more quickly until he came to the lighted window of the Hamnavoe Bar. He pushed open the door. Bill MacIsaac the boatbuilder was at the bar drinking beer with Thorfinn Vik the farmer from Helliar. Sammy Flett the drunk was in too—he was half stewed and he was pestering the barman to give him a pint, and Drew the barman was refusing him patiently but firmly. A half-empty bottle of cheap wine stuck out of Sammy Flett's pocket.

'Here's Ronald Leask, a good man,' said Sammy Flett, going up to Ronald unsteadily. 'Ronald, you're a good friend of mine and I ask you to accept a cigarette out of my packet, and I'm very glad of your offer to furnish me with a glass of beer for old time's sake.'

'A glass of whisky,' said Ronald to Drew the barman.

'Absolutely delighted, old friend,' said Sammy Flett.

'It's not for you,' said Drew the barman to Sammy Flett. 'You're getting nothing, not a drop. The police sergeant was here this morning and your father with him and I know all about the trouble you're causing at home, smashing the chairs and nearly setting fire to the bed at the week-end. This place is out of bounds to you, sonny boy. I promised the sergeant and your old man. You can push off any time you like.'

'That's all lies,' said Sammy Flett. 'Just give me one pint of ordinary beer. That's not much for a man to ask.'

'No,' said Drew the barman.

'I demand to see the manager,' said Sammy Flett.

Ronald Leask drank his whisky at one go and put down his empty glass and nodded to Drew. The barman filled it up again.

'No water?' said Bill MacIsaac the boatbuilder, smiling across at Ronald.

'No,' said Ronald, 'no water.'

'Men in love,' said Thorfinn Vik of Helliar, 'don't need water in their drink.' Vik was in one of his dangerous insulting moods.

Sammy Flett went into the toilet. They heard the glug-glug of wine being drunk, then a long sigh.

The door opened and Mr William Snoddy the builder's clerk came in out of the rain. He looked round the bar nervously. 'A small whisky,' he said to Drew the barman, 'and put a little soda in it, not too much, and a bottle of export, if you please.' . . . He wiped his spectacles with his handkerchief and owled the bar with bulging naked eyes and put his spectacles on again. Then he recognised the man he was standing beside.

'Why, Ronald,' he said. 'It isn't often we see you in the bar. It's a poor night, isn't it?'

Ronald stared straight ahead at the rank of bottles under the bar clock. He put back his head and drank the remains of his second glass of whisky.

'Ronald, have a glass of whisky with me,' said Mr Snoddy, taking his wallet out of his inside pocket. 'It'll be a pleasure.'

'Same again,' said Ronald to the barman. 'And I'll pay for my own drink with my own money.'

Mr Snoddy flushed till his brow was almost as pink as his nose. Then he put his wallet back in his inside pocket.

Sammy Flett emerged from the toilet, smiling.

Bill MacIsaac and Thorfinn Vik began to play darts at the lower end of the bar.

'O well,' said Mr Snoddy, 'I don't suppose you can force a person to speak to you if he doesn't want to.' He drank his whisky down quickly and took a sip of beer.

Suddenly Sammy Flett came up behind Mr Snoddy and threw his arm round his neck. 'If it isn't my dear friend Mr Snoddy,' said Sammy Flett. 'Mr Snoddy, accept a cigarette, with my compliments.'

'Go away,' cried Mr Snoddy. 'Go away. Just leave me alone.'

'Mr Snoddy,' said Sammy Flett, 'I'll take the whisky that Mr Leask refused to accept for reasons best known to himself.'

'I come in here for a quiet drink,' said Mr Snoddy to the barman, trying to disengage his neck from Sammy Flett's arm.

'And you shall have it, dear Mr Snoddy,' said Sammy Flett. 'Accompany me to the gentleman's toilet. We shall have a drink of wine together. Mr Snoddy is always welcome to have a drink from Sammy.'

'Leave Mr Snoddy alone,' said Drew the barman.

The door opened and six Norwegian fishermen came in. 'Six double scotches, six Danish lagers,' Per Bjorling said to the barman. The Norwegians shook the rain from their coats and leaned against the bar counter. A row of six blond heads shone with wetness under the lamps.

'I know what they're saying about you, Mr Snoddy,' said Sammy Flett. 'They say you're going with other women. They say you're unfaithful to Mrs Snoddy. It's an evil world and they'll say anything but their prayers. But I don't believe that, Mr Snoddy. You and me, we're old friends, and I wouldn't believe such a thing about you. Not Sammy. Never.'

Mr Snoddy looked about him, angry and confused. He left his half-empty glass standing on the counter and went out quickly, clashing the door behind him.

'Mr Snoddy is a very fine man,' said Sammy Flett to the Norwegians.

'Is so?' said one of the Norwegians, smiling.

'Yes,' said Sammy Flett, 'and he's a very clever man too.'

'Interesting,' said another Norwegian.

'I'm no fool myself,' said Sammy Flett. 'I didn't sail up Hoy Sound yesterday in a banana skin. Sammy knows a thing or two.'

Dod Isbister the plumber came in and Jimmy Gold the postman and Andrew Thomson the crofter from Knowe. They went to the upper-end of the bar and ordered beer. They emptied a box of dominoes on the counter and began to play.

The dart players finished their game and stuck their darts in the cork rim of the board. Thorfinn Vik was a bit drunk. He came over and stood beside Ronald Leask and began to sing:

I was dancing with my darling at the Tennessee waltz
When an old friend I happened to see,
Introduced him to my sweetheart and while they were dancing
My friend stole my sweetheart from me.

'No singing,' said Drew the barman sternly. 'No singing in this bar. There's guests in the lounge upstairs.'

Thorfinn Vik turned to Ronald Leask. 'That's a song that you'll appreciate, Mr Leask,' he said. 'I sang it specially for you. A song about disappointed love.'

'Same again,' said Sammy Flett from the middle of the Norwegian group. He had a glass of whisky in one hand and a glass of lager in the other that one of the whalers had bought for him. 'Very delightfully sung. Have you got songs in Norway as good as that? I daresay you have. Silence now for a Norwegian love song.'

'No singing,' said Drew.

'We sing only on our boat,' said Per Bjorling. 'We respect your rules. Please to give us seven double scotches and seven Danish lagers.' . . . To Sammy Flett he said, 'There will be singings later on the *Erika*—how you say?—a sing-song.'

'You are the true descendants of Vikings,' said Sammy Flett.

'No,' said a young Norwegian, 'they were cruel men. It is best to forget such people, no? We are peaceable fishermen.'

'Such is truthfully what we are,' said another Norwegian.

The door opened quietly and Mr Spence the jeweller tiptoed in. He shook his umbrella close and went up to the bar. 'One half-bottle of the best whisky, to carry out,' he murmured to Drew the barman. He laid two pound notes discreetly on the counter.

'Mr Spence,' cried Sammy Flett from the centre of the Norwegian group. 'My dear friend.'

'Leave Mr Spence alone,' said Drew. 'He doesn't want anything about you.'

'I am content where I am,' said Sammy Flett, 'in the midst of our

Scandinavian cousins. But there's nothing wrong in greeting my old friend Mr Spence.'

Mr Spence smiled and picked up his change and slid the half-bottle into his coat pocket.

'I think I know where you're off to with that,' said Sammy Flett, wagging a finger at him.

Mr Spence smiled again and went out as quietly and quickly as he had come in.

'Yes,' said Thorfin Vik of Helliar, 'we all know where he's going . . .' He winked across at the domino players. 'Mr Leask knows too.'

'I want no trouble in here,' said Drew the barman.

'Same again,' said Ronald Leask and pushed his empty glass at the barman. His face was very red.

'Is clock right? said Per Bjorling.

'Five minutes fast,' said Drew. 'It's twenty minutes to ten.'

Sammy Flett drank first his whisky and then his lager very quickly. The huge adams-apple above his dirty collar wobbled two or three times. He sighed and said, 'Sammy is happy now. Sammy asks nothing from life but a wee drink now and then.'

'I am happy for you,' said the Norwegian boy. 'I will now buy you other drink.'

'No,' said Sammy Flett, 'not unless you all promise to partake of a little wine with me later in the gentlemen's toilet. At closing time Sammy knows all the places.'

'Here is pleasures enough,' said the oldest Norwegian, 'in the pub.'

'No,' said Sammy, 'but I will take you to girls.'

'Girls,' said the old man. 'Oh no no. I am grandfather.'

'I have little sweetheart outside of Hammerfest,' said the boy. 'Gerd. She is milking the cattle and makes butter, also cheese from goats.'

'Also I am married,' said another Norwegian, 'and also is Paal and Magnus and Henrik. No girls. All are committed among us but Per.'

'Is true,' said Per Bjorling gravely.

'Per is liberty to find a girl where he likes,' said the old man. 'Per is goodlooking, is handsome, there is no trouble that Per our skipper will find a beautiful girl.'

The other Norwegians laughed.

'He's like a film star,' said Sammy Flett. 'Thank you most kindly, I'll have a glass of whisky and a bottle of beer. No offence. Per has a profile like a Greek hero.'

'Has found a beautiful girl already,' said the boy, smiling, 'in Hamnavoe.'

'One bottle of vodka,' said Per Bjorling to Drew, 'for outside drinking.'

Drew the barman took down a bottle of vodka from the shelf and called out, 'Last orders, gentlemen.'

'Double whisky,' said Ronald Leask.

Sammy Flett said to Per Bjorling, 'Are you going to visit this young lady now with your bottle of vodka?'

'A gift to her,' said Per Bjorling. 'Is a good girl. Is kind. Is understanding, intelligent. I like her very much.'

'What is the name of this fortunate young lady, if I might make so bold as to ask?' said Sammy Flett. 'Listen, Ronald. Per Bjorling is just going to tell us the name of his Hamnavoe sweetheart.'

Per Bjorling said, 'Celia.'

For about five seconds there was no sound in the bar but the click of dominoes on the counter.

Then Ronald Leask turned and hit Per Bjorling with his fist on the side of the head. The lager glass fell from Per Bjorling's hand and smashed on the floor. The force of the blow sent him back against the wall, his hands up at his face. He turned to Ronald Leask and said, 'Is not my wish to cause offence to any man present.'

'Cut it out,' cried Drew the barman. 'That's enough now.'

Ronald Leask stepped forward and hit Per Bjorling again, on the mouth. A little blood ran down Per Bjorling's jaw and his cap fell on the floor. He turned and hit Ronald Leask in the stomach and Ronald Leask flapped against the counter like a shiny black puppet. A score of glasses fell and smashed and a rapid pool of whisky and beer formed on the floor. Ronald Leask and Per Bjorling splintered and splashed through it, wrestling with each other. Ronald Leask clubbed down his fist on Per Bjorling's eye and Per Bjorling thrashed him across the jaw with the back of his hand. Ronald Leask went down on all fours among the beer and the broken glass.

'I am sorry for this,' said Per Bjorling and held out his hand.

Ronald Leask got slowly to his feet. His trouser knees were sopping wet and the palms of his hands cut and bleeding. A small bubble of blood grew and burst at his right nostril.

'Get out of here,' said Drew the barman, taking Ronald Leask by the sleeve of his oilskin, 'and never come back again. That applies to you too,' he said to Per Bjorling.

'So this is your Scotch hospitality,' said the Norwegian called Paal, 'to strike a man without reason. This we will not forget.'

'Remember this too,' said Thorfinn Vik, and struck Paal on the ear. 'This is our bar where we come to enjoy ourselves and this is our town and our women live in it.'

Drew picked up the telephone and his forefinger juggled in the dial.

'This is cowardice,' said the Norwegian boy. He stepped forward and took Thorfinn Vik by the throat. They lurched violently, locked together, between the seats and the bar counter. Half a dozen more glasses went over and smashed. Bill MacIsaac the boatbuilder tried to prise Thorfinn Vik and the young Norwegian apart. Andrew Thomson of Knowe put down his dominoes and began to take off his jacket slowly. 'I don't like fighting,' he said, 'but I'll fight if there's fighting to be done.'

'Gentlemen, gentlemen,' piped Sammy Flett from the fringe of the fight. Then he noticed an unattended glass of whisky on the bar counter and made for it. He was hidden behind a welter of heaving backs.

'You are bad man,' said the old Norwegian to Ronald Leask and slapped him magisterially across the face.

'Enough,' cried Per Bjorling.

Two policemen stood in the door.

Dod Isbister with a bottle in his hand and the Norwegian called Magnus with a glass in his hand were circling each other at the top end of the bar. Ronald Leask lashed out at Paal with his foot and missed and kicked Henrik on the elbow. Thorfinn Vik and the young Norwegian went over on the floor with a thud that made the bottles reel and rattle and clink. Dod Isbister threw the bottle he was holding and it missed Magnus's head and smashed into the lamp bulb. The light went out. The pub was a twilight full of grunting, breathing, slithering, cursing shadows.

'All right, gentlemen,' said the voice of Drew the barman, 'you can break it up. The law is here.'

The two policemen beamed their torches slowly over the wreckage. The fighters disengaged themselves. One by one they got to their feet.

'So this is the way it is,' said the sergeant. 'You'll have to come along to the station. We have accommodation for gentry like you. You haven't heard the last of this, I'm afraid. The sheriff will be wanting to see you all next Tuesday.'

'Not me, sergeant,' said Sammy Flett. 'Sammy never laid a finger on anybody.'

'You too,' said the sergeant. 'I wouldn't be surprised if you weren't at the bottom of this, Flett.'

Later, in the Black Maria going to the police station, Sammy Flett said, 'That was the best fight since the Kirkwall men threw Clarence Shaw into the harbour last carnival week.'

'Shut up, drunkard,' said Thorfinn Vik sleepily from the corner of the van.

'No, Thorfinn,' said Sammy Flett, 'but I want to reassure everyone, especially our Norwegian guests. The beds in the lock-up are very comfortable. The sergeant's wife will give us a cup of tea and toast in the morning. I know, because I've had bed and breakfast at Her Majesty's expense on twenty-two occasions—no, this makes it twenty-three. Everybody is very nice.'

'The little Gerd,' said the young Norwegian miserably. 'I am thinking of her so very much.'

The Black Maria jolted to a stop. They had arrived.

NINE

In the shoemaker's room the lamp was turned down low. It threw a feeble pool of light in one corner. The shoemaker was in his iron bed; he leaned back on three pillows and struggled for breath. Every inhalation was hard-won and shallow; the slack strings of his throat grew taut to force a passage for it, and his whole torso laboured to expel it again. His breathing slowly thickened and roughened, came in a quick spasm, and then he turned over on the pillows in a storm of feeble importunate coughing.

Celia came quickly through from the other room. She sat down on the edge of the bed and took the shoemaker's damp hand in both hers. 'You'll be all right,' she said. 'Just take it easy.'

The coughing stopped and the old man lay back on his pillows with his mouth open. Celia wiped his face with her apron. Then she lifted a small brown bottle from the table and shook a tablet out and poured some water in a cup. 'You've to take a tablet every four hours, Dr Wilson says,' she said. 'It stops the coughing.' She put the tablet in his mouth and raised his head and gave him a sip of water.

'If only I could sleep,' whispered the shoemaker. He lay back on the pillows with his eyes shut. 'I'm a very poor old sick man.'

'I won't leave you,' said Celia.

'Tell me one thing,' said the shoemaker, 'then maybe I can get to sleep. Is there any man or drink in the room next door?'

'No,' said Celia.

'Tell me the truth,' he whispered sternly. 'The truth, mind. I heard someone at the door.'

'Snoddy came at half-past eight,' said Celia. 'I sent him away. I told him you were ill. What's more, I told him I didn't want his drink.'

'Till the next time,' said the shoemaker.

'I suppose so,' said Celia.

The shoemaker's breath slowly roughened as new threads of phlegm spun themselves into a thick cord in his chest. Then suddenly he was possessed by spasm after spasm of futile coughing. He drew himself up in the bed and Celia put her arms round his thin body and held him close to her until the tough cord of phlegm broke and the coughing stopped. She took a bowl from the bedside chair and he managed to spit into it. The effort exhausted him. Celia laid him back on his pillows. Then she wiped his face in her apron.

'If only I could sleep,' said the shoemaker. 'I was dropping off to sleep an hour and more ago and then I was wakened first by Snoddy and then by a terrible noise along the street.'

'There was fighting in the Hamnavoe Bar,' said Celia. 'So Snoddy said. That's what you heard. Drew had to get the police.'

'It sounded like an earthquake,' said the shoemaker.

Celia stroked his chest outside his grey flannel shirt. 'Try to sleep now,' she said. 'I'll stay beside you till you go to sleep.' . . . After a time she felt his chest grow quiet under her hand. His eyes were shut and his breath came deep and even through slightly parted lips. Celia knew that he wasn't asleep, but he was pretending to sleep so that she could get back to her bed.

Outside the rain slanted darkly. A sudden gust of wind caught the downpour and threw it against the window till all the panes surged and throbbed. Through the onset Celia heard a discreet tapping at the outside door.

'Don't let him in,' said the shoemaker, opening his eyes.

It was Mr Spence the jeweller. 'Celia,' he said.

'The old man isn't well,' said Celia in a low voice. 'The doctor was here in the afternoon. I'll have to be up with him all night.'

'Perhaps if I could just come in,' said Mr Spence.

'No,' said Celia.

'I'm very wet, my dear,' said Mr Spence.

'Please go home,' said Celia, 'Please.'

Mr Spence took a flask of whisky from his coat pocket. 'We will just have one little toddy,' he said. 'Thomas won't mind me being in the house. He tells me I can come whenever I like. You know that. A little dram for a damp night, eh?'

'Not tonight,' said Celia, 'I'm sorry.'

The rain slanted all about Mr Spence, a diagonal bright-dark nagging susurration on the flagstones of the pier. The gutters bubbled. Celia could smell the wetness from his clothes.

'Celia,' said Mr Spence in a hurt voice, 'I am a very lonely man.'

'Everybody is lonely,' said Celia gently. 'We're all prisoners. We must try to find out a way to be pardoned.'

She shut the door and drew the bar across it. She was just about to turn into her own seaward room when she heard the shoemaker speaking aloud to himself in the room with the dim light and the noise of rain in it. She stood in the lobby and listened.

'And so it'll be all right once we're settled in Clett. Ronald has a small room I can bide in. It doesn't matter about me. I won't live that long. But Celia, she'll be happy at last. She'll soon learn to look after the cow and the few hens, yes, he'll get a pot of soup when he comes in cold from the fishing. She'll be a good wife to Ronald. And I tell you this, Ronald won't allow all them bottles in his cupboard, no, and no bloody foreigners'll get within a stone's throw of the place, and as for Snoddy, the dog of Clett'll tear the arse off the likes of him. Mr Spence, he can come as usual twice a week for a game of draughts, I'm sure Ronald won't object to that. We'll be fine once we're settled in Clett. Not that Ronald Leask's conferring any favour on Celia, not a bit of it, he's a lucky chap to be getting the likes of Celia for a wife. She can cook and sew and wash as well as any woman in Hamnavoe. I'll maybe be a burden to them for a winter or two, but Ronald said I could come, and by that time they'll likely have another burden, a bairn in the cradle, but a sweet burden, not an old done man. Once Celia's settled in Clett she'll have a new life entirely, there'll be no more drink and no more poverty and no more stray men in the night. An end to this darkness.'

Celia went softly into the room. The shoemaker closed his eyes quickly and pretended to be asleep. But another rope of phlegm was beginning to rasp in his chest. There was a smell too, all about the bed. Celia sat beside him and wiped his face with her apron. He opened his eyes and said, 'I'm sorry. I think I've messed the bed up.' He was ashamed and his eyes were wet.

'I know,' said Celia. 'Don't worry. I'll get you cleaned up before anything else. There's a kettle of hot water on the range. Plenty of clean sheets in the cupboard.'

She opened the window to let the smell out. Rain and wind swirled in and the shoemaker began to cough. She closed the window again quickly.

For the next twenty minutes Celia washed the old man and dried him and put a clean shirt on him and stripped the bed and put clean sheets on it and set the soiled stinking sheets in a tub of disinfected water in the lobby.

'You'll feel better now,' said Celia. 'I'm going to make a cup of tea for the two of us.'

The shoemaker was racked with a violent spasm of coughing. She held him till the tough cord of phlegm shore in his throat and he spat it out. She laid him back exhausted on the pillows.

'Fighting along the street a while ago,' said the shoemaker wearily. 'It's always them foreigners.'

'It's all quiet now,' said Celia. 'Time you had another tablet though.'

She took a yellow tablet out of the bottle on to her hand and put it on his tongue. She laid her arm round his shoulders and raised him and put the cup of water to his mouth.

'They don't seem to help me, them tablets,' said the shoemaker.

'They will,' said Celia. 'Give them time. Dr Wilson's tablets always work, you know that.'

'Maybe I'll get a sleep now,' said the shoemaker.

'Try,' said Celia.

But the hoarseness was in his chest again. He coughed and spat out thick phlegm. But as always when this sickness was on him, he had hardly torn the purulent fungus from his bronchial tree when a new growth rose about it, blocking and strangling his breath.

'I'm a terrible nuisance to you,' he said, 'a silly awkward old man.'

'You're not,' said Celia, 'and you'll be better tomorrow. And there's a fine shed at Clett where you can mend boots. I'll ask Ronald to put a stove in it.'

The shoemaker was suddenly asleep, the way sleep comes to the very young and the very old. His cheeks flushed like two withered apples. He breathed as quietly as a child.

'Thank God,' said Celia.

She drew the blankets up to his chin and kissed him on the forehead.

The window paled with the end of the night.

The rain had stopped, as it often does before dawn. Celia closed the door of the shoemaker's room softly and unbarred the outer door and went out on to the pier. The first seagulls were screaming along the street, scavenging in the bins. She breathed the clean air of early morning. She stood at the pier wall and watched the sea moving darkly against the weeded steps and slipways. A rat in the seaweed squinnied at her and twitched its whiskers and went into the water with a soft plop. The sun had not yet risen, but light was assembling in broken colours over the Orphir hills. The first blackbird in the fuchsia bush under the watchmaker's wall faltered into song and then was silent again. Celia could see the boats in the harbour now and at the farm across the harbour black ploughed squares among the green grass and brown heather. It would be a beautiful morning.

Then the sun rose clear of the Orphir hills and folded the girl in the light of a new day.

Alexander Reid

WHAT'S IT ALL ABOUT

Alexander Reid (1914–82) is still strongly associated with the Glasgow Citizen's Theatre where his best known play, *The Lass wi' the Muckle Mou*, was first produced in 1950.

His plays were mostly written in Scots and he relied on a generation of actors like Roddy Macmillan and Duncan Macrae (famous for his part in *The World's Wonder*), to give his lines the understanding and wry rhythmic delivery they deserved. Sadly, the brief vogue for quality Scots in Scottish theatre and the performers who could do it justice seem to have disappeared, along with the vitality and variety they offered.

'What's It All About?' is as much a monologue as a short story and as such gives a fine illustration of Reid's skills as a dramatist. In the space of a few hundred words his narrator locates the action in a precisely defined time and place almost without the reader noticing.

Reid also takes the opportunity to play with our preconceptions. He explores the meaning of life using the language of the street and lets us see a working man experiencing the kind of existential angst thought to be the preserve of the intellectual. In a piece which cries out to be read aloud, Alex Reid carefully lends dignity and significance to the commonplace, while democratising philosophy with an infectious humour and humanity.

What's it All About?

WHAT'S IT all about? That's what I want to know. What's it all for? I've thought and I've thought but I just can't make sense of it. And I can't find anyone else who can either. What's it mean? I ask them. What's it all about? But if anyone knows I haven't found them yet.

The beginning of it was a night about a year ago when Bell Brown and me were on our way to see *Angels in Ashcloth* at the New Tiv. Bell's my girl—at least she was then; I haven't seen much of her lately. She works in the wireworks where I do, but in the office. A secretary, she got three O-levels so she must be bright I suppose. But she hadn't any answer either. In fact I don't think she knew what I was speaking about when I asked her.

As the Tiv's on the other side from the scheme we're in we took the Circular to save changing buses. It takes longer that way, but it's interesting for the road runs for part of the way along the embankment of the old suburban railway, close up to hulking great tenements and the backyards of factories that you didn't know existed. And on this night I'm speaking about our bus drew up between stops on this stretch just opposite one of these tenements.

'Must be an accident,' I said hauling down the window. But I couldn't see anything but a line of cars and lorries stretching up to a bend not far ahead.

'I hope we're not going to be held up long,' said Bell. 'I hate going in in the middle of a film.'

'Me too,' I said. But I wasn't really worrying. I was looking at the windows of the houses just opposite. There were lights on in most of the houses and where the curtains weren't drawn you could look right in and see the folk living—as if you were looking at a tower of TV sets all tuned into different channels. In one house you could see a family having their tea—a man in shirt sleeves, a woman with her hair in curlers and three kids, all crowded at three sides of the table so's they could watch the telly while they were eating, and in the next house a plump chick was struggling to get into a black dress that was far too tight for her and had got stuck over her head. Below that a birthday party was going on—kids and adults of all ages, all wearing paper hats and on the table among a regiment of bottles and glasses a huge cake with one big candle. To the right of that a fat woman was washing a kid's hair at the sink under the window and in another house you could see an old man propped up in bed reading a huge book with black covers—a bible maybe. But the show of the week was further along to the right where a bloke and a dame were locked in a clinch like Elizabeth Taylor and Richard Burton between divorces. Maybe that isn't funny, but the thing is this guy was wearing a long black coat, high boots and a fur hat, as if he had just come in from Siberia, while the woman, so far as I could see, hadn't a stitch on!

'Take a look at this, Bell,' I said. 'It's as good as a film.'

But Bell wouldn't budge.

'It's vulgar to look into windows,' she sniffed.

'Oh, come off it,' I said. 'If they don't want folk to look in they should draw the curtains.' However I shoved up the window and sat down and just then the bus began to move on again and as we were in time for the big feature that was all right.

But I couldn't forget these windows. The thought of them kept coming back to me all through the show that night, and afterwards when I got to bed, and they keep coming to me now. I mean . . . so many houses, so many rooms, so many people, and every man-Jack and girl-Jill of them thinking: This is the world—this man, this woman, these kids! This is what matters! This is special! And in fact we're all doing much the same things, aren't we? I mean, getting up in the morning and going off to factories, shops and offices, going to the flicks now and then, or watching telly; dropping in for a drink at the pub, going to sleep when the night comes; hoping our coupons come up, wishing for Friday, wishing for happiness. Being born, living and dying. In Leningrad like Leith, in Tokyo like Chicago. Millions and millions of us. Thousands of millions! Where are we all going? What's it all for? What's it about? I keep on asking folk about it, but if anyone knows I haven't met them. I even asked the old man one night.

'What do you think it's about?' I asked him, casual like.

When he understood what I was after, he didn't know either.

'Come to think of it,' he said, scratching behind his ear with his pipe like he does sometimes when he's filling up his football coupon. 'Come to think of it, it *is* a queer business and I can't say I ever made sense of it.'

But for the most part when you ask anybody, all you get is a blank stare as if they thought you'd gone nuts or a: 'Forget it! Where's it get you thinking that way? Where's it get you?'

But the truth is that I don't want to forget it. It's important. I don't know why it's important but I'm sure that it's important. Anyway, it keeps coming back on me. At work; at the pub; at Mac's in the middle of a snooker angle.

I'll be bending over the table to pot a nice pink, maybe, when suddenly I'll see those windows and everything around me, the coloured balls, the green table, the chaps standing round in their shirt sleeves waiting to play their shots, will look queer—oh queerer than anything you ever saw on a film! And then I'll ask myself once again: What's it all about?—and foozle the shot likely! And it won't matter! That's another funny thing. It won't matter!

All the same I wish I could find somebody who had the answer. Or does nobody know? Is it all a big con—I mean those blokes in universities, in the government, who write books and all that. Does nobody know, I mean *really* know what's underneath it all? This room now . . . this fag smoke . . . me here . . . Jo nipping an end there . . . this light . . . those shadows . . . chaps coming in . . . going out . . . What's the point exactly? What's it all about?

Arthur Conan Doyle

Sherlock Holmes is one of fiction's most popular and enduring characters. Fragments of his speech have entered the language and people who have never read a Sherlock story know what he looks like, indeed the bent pipe, deerstalker and violin, along with his liking for opium, his deductive powers and the foil of Watson have transferred so successfully to film and television that the actual stories almost take second place.

Conan Doyle (1859–1930), wrote many books, including *The Exploits of Brigadier Gerard*, *The White Company* and *The Lost World*, but Sherlock has become a legend, spawning a new breed of fictional hero. Doyle based Holmes on Dr Joseph Bell, a teacher at Edinburgh University's medical faculty, and although he belongs to Baker Street and Victorian London, it has been pointed out that Holmes's stamping ground is remarkably like last century's Edinburgh.

Holmes first appeared in *Study in Scarlet* in 1887 and thereafter in the pages of *Strand Magazine*, which is where 'The Reigate Squires' was published. It highlights the elements Conan Doyle used to make Holmes a Victorian anti-hero. With an intelligence derived as much from genius as education, Holmes's capacity for deception and nervous excitement was definitely 'not cricket'. As a thief, a play actor and a drug addict he may well have been more of a threat to existing social order than Moriarty ever could be.

The Reigate Squires

IT WAS some time before the health of my friend, Mr Sherlock Holmes, recovered from the strain caused by his immense exertions in the spring of '87. The whole question of the Netherlands-Sumatra Company and of the colossal schemes of Baron Maupertuis is too recent in the minds of the public, and too intimately concerned with politics and finance, to be a fitting subject for this series of sketches. It led, however, in an indirect fashion to a singular and complex problem, which gave my friend an opportunity of demonstrating the value of a fresh weapon among the many with which he waged his life-long battle against crime.

On referring to my notes, I see that it was on the 14th of April that I received a telegram from Lyons, which informed me that Holmes was lying ill in the Hotel Dulong. Within twenty-four hours I was in his sick-room, and was relieved to find that there was nothing formidable in his symptoms. His iron constitution, however, had broken down under the strain of an investigation which had extended over two months, during which period he had never worked less than fifteen hours a day, and had more than once, as he assured me, kept to his task for five days at a stretch. The triumphant issue of his labours could not save him from reaction after so terrible an exertion, and at a time when Europe was ringing with his name and when his room was literally ankle-deep with congratulatory telegrams, I found him a prey to the blackest depression. Even the knowledge that he had succeeded where the police of three countries had failed, and that he had outmanoeuvred at every point the most accomplished swindler in Europe, was insufficient to rouse him from his nervous prostration.

Three days later we were back in Baker Street together, but it was evident that my friend would be much the better for a change, and the thought of a week of springtime in the country was full of attractions to me also. My old friend, Colonel Hayter, who had come under my professional care in Afghanistan, had now taken a house near Reigate, in Surrey, and had frequently asked me to come down to him upon a visit. On the last occasion he had remarked that if my friend would only come with me, he would be glad to extend his hospitality to him also. A little diplomacy was needed, but when Holmes understood that the establishment was a bachelor one, and that he would be allowed the fullest freedom, he fell in with my plans, and a week after our return from Lyons we were under the Colonel's roof. Hayter was a fine old soldier, who had seen much of the world, and he soon found, as I had expected, that Holmes and he had plenty in common.

On the evening of our arrival we were sitting in the Colonel's gun-room after dinner, Holmes stretched upon the sofa, while Hayter and I looked over his little armoury of firearms.

'By the way,' said he, suddenly, 'I'll take one of these pistols upstairs with me in case we have an alarm.'

'An alarm!' said I.

'Yes, we've had a scare in this part lately. Old Acton, who is one of our county magnates, had his house broken into last Monday. No great damage done, but the fellows are still at large.'

'No clue?' asked Holmes, cocking his eye at the Colonel.

'None as yet. But the affair is a petty one, one of our little county crimes which must seem too small for your attention, Mr Holmes, after this great international affair.'

Holmes waved away the compliment, though his smile showed that it had pleased him.

'Was there any feature of interest?'

'I fancy not. The thieves ransacked the library, and got very little for their pains. The whole place was turned upside down, drawers burst open and presses ransacked, with the result that an odd volume of Pope's "Homer", two plated candlesticks, an ivory letter-weight, a small oak barometer, and a ball of twine are all that have vanished.'

'What an extraordinary assortment!' I exclaimed.

'Oh, the fellows evidently grabbed hold of anything they could get.'

Holmes grunted from the sofa.

'The county police ought to make something of that,' said he. 'Why, it is surely obvious that—'

But I held up a warning finger.

'You are here for a rest, my dear fellow. For Heaven's sake, don't get started on a new problem when your nerves are all in shreds.'

Holmes shrugged his shoulders with a glance of comic resignation towards the Colonel, and the talk drifted away into less dangerous channels.

It was destined, however, that all my professional caution should be wasted, for next morning the problem obtruded itself upon us in such a way that it was impossible to ignore it, and our country visit took a turn which neither of us could have anticipated. We were at breakfast when the Colonel's butler rushed in with all his propriety shaken out of him.

'Have you heard the news, sir?' he gasped. 'At the Cunninghams', sir!'

'Burglary?' cried the Colonel, with his coffee cup in mid-air.

'Murder!'

The Colonel whistled. 'By Jove!' said he, 'who's killed, then? The J.P., or his son?'

'Neither, sir. It was William, the coachman. Shot through the heart, sir, and never spoke again.'

'Who shot him, then?'

'The burglar, sir. He was off like a shot and got clean away. He'd just broke in at the pantry window when William came on him and met his end in saving his master's property.'

'What time?'

'It was last night, sir, somewhere about twelve.'

'Ah, then, we'll step over presently,' said the Colonel, coolly settling down to his breakfast again. 'It's a baddish business,' he added, when the butler had gone. 'He's our leading squire about here, is old Cunningham, and a very decent fellow, too. He'll be cut up over this, for the man has been in his service for years, and was a good servant. It's evidently the same villains who broke into Acton's.'

'And stole that very singular collection?' said Holmes, thoughtfully.

'Precisely.'

'Hum! It may prove the simplest matter in the world; but, all the same, at first glance this is just a little curious, is it not? A gang of burglars acting in the country might be expected to vary the scene of their operations, and not to crack two cribs in the same district within a few days. When you spoke last night of taking precautions, I remember that it passed through my mind that this was probably the last parish in England to which the thief or thieves would be likely to turn their attention; which shows that I have still much to learn.'

'I fancy it's some local practitioner,' said the Colonel. 'In that case, of course, Acton's and Cunningham's are just the places he would go for, since they are far the largest about here.'

'And richest?'

'Well, they ought to be; but they've had a lawsuit for some years which has sucked the blood out of both of them, I fancy. Old Acton has some claim on half Cunningham's estate, and the lawyers have been at it with both hands.'

'If it's a local villain, there should not be much difficulty in running him down,' said Holmes, with a yawn. 'All right, Watson, I don't intend to meddle.'

'Inspector Forrester, sir,' said the butler, throwing open the door.

The official, a smart, keen-faced young fellow, stepped into the room. 'Good morning, Colonel,' said he. 'I hope I don't intrude, but we hear that Mr Holmes, of Baker Street, is here.'

The Colonel waved his hand towards my friend, and the Inspector bowed.

'We thought that perhaps you would care to step across, Mr Holmes.'

'The Fates are against you, Watson,' said he, laughing. 'We were chatting about the matter when you came in, Inspector. Perhaps you can let us have a few details.' As he leaned back in his chair in the familiar attitude, I knew that the case was hopeless.

'We had no clue in the Acton affair. But here we have plenty to go on, and there's no doubt it is the same party in each case. The man was seen.'

'Ah!'

'Yes, sir. But he was off like a deer after the shot that killed poor William Kirwan was fired. Mr Cunningham saw him from the bedroom window, and Mr Alec Cunningham saw him from the back passage. It was a quarter to twelve when the alarm broke out. Mr Cunningham had just got into bed, and Mister Alec was smoking a pipe in his dressing-gown. They both heard William, the coachman, calling for help, and Mister Alec he ran down to see what was the matter. The back door was open, and as he came to the foot of the stairs he saw two men wrestling together outside. One of them fired a shot, the other dropped, and the murderer rushed across the garden and over the hedge. Mr Cunningham, looking out of his bedroom window, saw the fellow as he gained the road, but lost sight of him at once. Mister Alec stopped to see if he could help the dying man, and so the villain got clean away. Beyond the fact that he was a middle-sized man, and dressed in some dark stuff, we have no personal clue, but we are making energetic inquiries, and if he is a stranger we shall soon find him out.'

'What was this William doing there? Did he say anything before he died?'

'Not a word. He lives at the lodge with his mother, and as he was a very faithful fellow, we imagine that he walked up to the house with the intention of seeing that all was right there. Of course, this Acton business has put everyone on their guard. The robber must have just burst open the door—the lock has been forced—when William came upon him.'

'Did William say anything to his mother before going out?'

'She is very old and deaf, and we can get no information from her. The shock has made her half-witted, but I understand that she was never very bright. There is one very important circumstance, however. Look at this!'

He took a small piece of torn paper from a notebook and spread it out upon his knee.

'This was found between the finger and thumb of the dead man. It appears to be a fragment torn from a larger sheet. You will observe that the hour mentioned upon it is the very time at which the poor fellow met his fate. You see that his murderer might have torn the rest of the sheet from him or he might have taken this fragment from the murderer. It reads almost as though it was an appointment.'

Holmes took up the scrap of paper, a facsimile of which is here reproduced.

'Presuming that it is an appointment,' continued the Inspector, 'it is, of course, a conceivable theory that this William Kirwan, although he had the reputation of being an honest man, may have been in league with the thief. He may have met him there, may even have helped him to break in the door, and then they may have fallen out between themselves.'

at quarter to twelve
learn what
maybe

'This writing is of extraordinary interest,' said Holmes, who had been examining it with intense concentration. 'These are much deeper waters than I had thought.' He sank his head upon his hands, while the Inspector smiled at the effect which his case had had upon the famous London specialist.

'Your last remark,' said Holmes, presently, 'as to the possibility of there being an understanding between the burglar and the servant, and this being a note of appointment from one to the other, is an ingenious and not entirely an impossible supposition. But this writing opens up—' he sank his head into his hands again and remained for some minutes in the deepest thought. When he raised his face I was surprised to see that his cheek was tinged with colour, and his eyes as bright as before his illness. He sprang to his feet with all his old energy.

'I'll tell you what!' said he. 'I should like to have a quiet little glance into the details of this case. There is something in it which fascinates me extremely. If you will permit me, Colonel, I will leave my friend, Watson, and you, and I will step round with the Inspector to test the truth of one or two little fancies of mine. I will be with you again in half an hour.'

An hour and a half had elapsed before the Inspector returned alone.

'Mr Holmes is walking up and down in the field outside,' said he. 'He wants us all four to go up to the house together.'

'To Mr Cunningham's?'

'Yes, sir.'

'What for?'

The Inspector shrugged his shoulders. 'I don't quite know, sir. Between ourselves, I think Mr Holmes has not quite got over his illness yet. He's been behaving very queerly, and he is very much excited.'

'I don't think you need alarm yourself,' said I. 'I have usually found that there was method in his madness.'

'Some folk might think there was madness in his method,' muttered the Inspector. 'But he's all on fire to start, Colonel, so we had best go out, if you are ready.'

We found Holmes pacing up and down in the field, his chin sunk upon his breast, and his hands thrust into his trouser pockets.

'The matter grows in interest,' said he. 'Watson, your country trip has been a distinct success. I have had a charming morning.'

'You have been up to the scene of the crime, I understand?' said the Colonel.

'Yes; the Inspector and I have made quite a little reconnaissance together.'

'Any success?'

'Well, we have seen some very interesting things. I'll tell you what we did as we walk. First of all we saw the body of this unfortunate man. He certainly died from a revolver wound, as reported.'

'Had you doubted it, then?'

'Oh, it is as well to test everything. Our inspection was not wasted. We then had an interview with Mr Cunningham and his son, who were able to point out the exact spot where the murderer had broken through the garden hedge in his flight. That was of great interest.'

'Naturally.'

'Then we had a look at this poor fellow's mother. We could get no information from her, however, as she is very old and feeble.'

'And what is the result of your investigations?'

'The conviction that the crime is a very peculiar one. Perhaps our visit now may do something to make it less obscure. I think that we are both agreed, Inspector, that the fragment of paper in the dead man's hand, bearing, as it does, the very hour of his death written upon it, is of extreme importance.'

'It should give a clue, Mr Holmes.'

'It *does* give a clue. Whoever wrote that note was the man who brought William Kirwan out of his bed at that hour. But where is the rest of that sheet of paper?'

'I examined the ground carefully in the hope of finding it,' said the Inspector.

'It was torn out of the dead man's hand. Why was someone so anxious to get possession of it? Because it incriminated him. And what would he do with it? Thrust it into his pocket most likely, never noticing that a corner of it had been left in the grip of the corpse. If we could get the rest of that sheet, it is obvious that we should have gone a long way towards solving the mystery.'

'Yes, but how can we get at the criminal's pocket before we catch the criminal?'

'Well, well, it was worth thinking over. Then there is another obvious point. The note was sent to William. The man who wrote it could not have taken it, otherwise of course he might have delivered his own message by word of mouth. Who brought the note, then? Or did it come through the post?'

'I have made inquiries,' said the Inspector. 'William received a letter by the afternoon post yesterday. The envelope was destroyed by him.'

'Excellent!' cried Holmes, clapping the Inspector on the back. 'You've seen the postman. It is a pleasure to work with you. Well, here is the lodge, and if you will come up, Colonel, I will show you the scene of the crime.'

We passed the pretty cottage where the murdered man had lived, and walked up an oak-lined avenue to the fine old Queen Anne house, which bears the date of Malplaquet upon the lintel of the door. Holmes and the Inspector led us round it until we came to the side gate, which is separated by a stretch of garden from the hedge which lines the road. A constable was standing at the kitchen door.

'Throw the door open, officer,' said Holmes. 'Now it was on those stairs that young Mr Cunningham stood and saw the two men struggling just where we are. Old Mr Cunningham was at that window—the second on the left—and he saw the fellow get away just to the left of that bush. So did the son. They are both sure of it on account of the bush. Then Mister Alec ran out and knelt beside the wounded man. The ground is very hard, you see, and there are no marks to guide us.'

As he spoke two men came down the garden path, from round the angle of the house. The one was an elderly man, with a strong, deep-lined, heavy-eyed face; the other a dashing young fellow, whose bright, smiling expression and showy dress were in strange contrast with the business which had brought us there.

'Still at it, then?' said he to Holmes. 'I thought you Londoners were never at fault. You don't seem to be so very quick after all.'

'Ah! you must give us a little time,' said Holmes good-humouredly.

'You'll want it,' said young Alec Cunningham. 'Why, I don't see that we have any clue at all.'

'There's only one,' answered the Inspector. 'We thought that if we could only find—Good heavens! Mr Holmes, what is the matter?'

My poor friend's face had suddenly assumed the most dreadful expression. His eyes rolled upwards, his features writhed in agony, and with a suppressed groan he dropped on his face upon the ground. Horrified at the suddenness and severity of the attack, we carried him into the kitchen, where he lay back in a large chair and breathed heavily for some minutes. Finally, with a shamefaced apology for his weakness, he rose once more.

'Watson would tell you that I have only just recovered from a severe illness,' he explained. 'I am liable to these sudden nervous attacks.'

'Shall I send you home in my trap?' asked old Cunningham.

'Well, since I am here there is one point on which I should like to feel sure. We can very easily verify it.'

'What is it?'

'Well, it seems to me that it is just possible that the arrival of this poor fellow William was not before but after the entrance of the burglar into the house. You appear to take it for granted that although the door was forced the robber never got in.'

'I fancy that is quite obvious,' said Mr Cunningham gravely. 'Why, my son Alec had not yet gone to bed, and he would certainly have heard anyone moving about.'

'Where was he sitting?'

'I was sitting smoking in my dressing-room.'

'Which window is that?'

'The last on the left, next my father's.'

'Both your lamps were lit, of course?'

'Undoubtedly.'

'There are some very singular points here,' said Holmes, smiling. 'Is it not extraordinary that a burglar—and a burglar who had had some previous experience—should deliberately break into a house at a time when he could see from the lights that two of the family were still afoot?'

'He must have been a cool hand.'

'Well, of course, if the case were not an odd one we should not have been driven to ask you for an explanation,' said Mister Alec. 'But as to your idea that the man had robbed the house before William tackled him, I think it a most absurd notion. Shouldn't we have found the place disarranged and missed the things which he had taken?'

'It depends on what the things were,' said Holmes. 'You must remember that we are dealing with a burglar who is a very peculiar fellow, and who appears to work on lines of his own. Look, for example, at the queer lot of things which he took from Acton's—what was it?—a ball of string, a letter-weight, and I don't know what other odds and ends!'

'Well, we are quite in your hands, Mr Holmes,' said old Cunningham. 'Anything which you or the Inspector may suggest will most certainly be done.'

'In the first place,' said Holmes, 'I should like you to offer a reward—coming from yourself, for the officials may take a little time before they would agree upon the sum, and these things cannot be done too promptly. I have jotted down the form here, if you would not mind signing it. Fifty pounds was quite enough, I thought.'

'I would willingly give five hundred,' said the J.P., taking the slip of paper and the pencil which Holmes handed to him. 'This is not quite correct, however,' he added, glancing over the document.

'I wrote it rather hurriedly.'

'You see you begin: "Whereas, at about a quarter to one on Tuesday morning, an attempt was made"—and so on. It was at a quarter to twelve, as a matter of fact.'

I was pained at the mistake, for I knew how keenly Holmes would feel any slip of the kind. It was his speciality to be accurate as to fact, but his recent illness had shaken him, and this one little incident was enough to show me that he was still far from being himself. He was obviously embarrassed for an instant, while the Inspector raised his eyebrows and Alec Cunningham burst into a laugh. The old gentleman corrected the mistake, however, and handed the paper back to Holmes.

'Get it printed as soon as possible,' he said. 'I think your idea is an excellent one.'

Holmes put the slip of paper carefully away in his pocket-book.

'And now,' said he, 'it would really be a good thing that we should all go over the house together, and make certain that this rather erratic burglar did not, after all, carry anything away with him.'

Before entering, Holmes made an examination of the door which had been forced. It was evident that a chisel or strong knife had been thrust in, and the lock forced back with it. We could see the marks in the wood where it had been pushed in.

'You don't use bars, then?' he asked.

'We have never found it necessary.'

'You don't keep a dog?'

'Yes; but he is chained on the other side of the house.'

'When do the servants go to bed?'

'About ten.'

'I understand that William was usually in bed also at that hour?'

'Yes.'

'It is singular that on this particular night he should have been up. Now, I should be very glad if you would have the kindness to show us over the house, Mr Cunningham.'

A stone-flagged passage, with the kitchens branching away from it, led by a wooden staircase directly to the first floor of the house. It came out upon the landing opposite to a second more ornamental stair which led up from the front hall. Out of this landing opened the drawing-room and several bedrooms, including those of Mr Cunningham and his son. Holmes walked slowly, taking keen note of the architecture of the house. I could tell from his expression that he was on a hot scent, and yet I could not in the least imagine in what direction his inferences were leading him.

'My good sir,' said Mr Cunningham, with some impatience, 'this is surely very unnecessary. That is my room at the end of the stairs, and my son's is the one beyond it. I leave it to your judgement whether it was possible for the thief to have come up here without disturbing us.'

'You must try round and get on a fresh scent, I fancy,' said the son, with a rather malicious smile.

'Still, I must ask you to humour me a little further. I should like, for example, to see how far the windows of the bedrooms commanded the front. This, I understand, is your son's room'—he pushed open the door—'and that, I presume, is the dressing-room in which he sat smoking when the alarm was given. Where does the window of that look out to?' He stepped across the bedroom, pushed open the door, and glanced round the other chamber.

'I hope you are satisfied now?' said Mr Cunningham testily.

'Thank you; I think I have seen all that I wished.'

'Then, if it is really necessary, we can go into my room.'

'If it is not too much trouble.'

The J.P. shrugged his shoulders, and led the way into his own chamber, which was a plainly furnished and commonplace room. As we moved across it in the direction of the window, Holmes fell back until he and I were the last of the group. Near the foot of the bed was a small square table, on which stood a dish of oranges and a carafe of water. As we passed it, Holmes, to my unutterable astonishment, leaned over in front of me and deliberately knocked the whole thing over. The glass smashed into a thousand pieces, and the fruit rolled about into every corner of the room.

'You've done it now, Watson,' said he coolly. 'A pretty mess you've made of the carpet.'

I stooped in some confusion and began to pick up the fruit, understanding that for some reason my companion desired me to take the blame upon myself. The others did the same, and set the table on its legs again.

'Hallo!' cried the Inspector, 'where's he got to?'

Holmes had disappeared.

'Wait here an instant,' said young Alec Cunningham. 'The fellow is off his head, in my opinion. Come with me, father, and see where he has got to!'

They rushed out of the room, leaving the Inspector, the Colonel, and me, staring at each other.

''Pon my word, I am inclined to agree with Mister Alec,' said the official. 'It may be the effect of this illness, but it seems to me that—'

His words were cut short by a sudden scream of 'Help! Help! Murder!' With a thrill I recognised the voice as that of my friend. I rushed madly from the room on to the landing. The cries, which had sunk down into a hoarse, inarticulate shouting, came from the room which we had first visited. I dashed in, and on into the dressing-room beyond. The two Cunninghams were bending over the prostrate figure of Sherlock Holmes, the younger clutching his throat with both hands, while the elder seemed to be twisting one of his wrists. In an instant the three of us had torn them away from him, and Holmes staggered to his feet, very pale, and evidently greatly exhausted.

'Arrest these men, Inspector!' he gasped.

'On what charge?'

'That of murdering their coachman, William Kirwan!'

The Inspector stared about him in bewilderment. 'Oh, come now, Mr Holmes,' said he at last; 'I am sure you don't really mean to—'

'Tut, man; look at their faces!' cried Holmes curtly.

Never, certainly, have I seen a plainer confession of guilt upon human countenances. The older man seemed numbed and dazed, with a heavy, sullen expression upon his strongly-marked face. The son, on the other hand, had dropped all that jaunty, dashing style which had characterised him, and the ferocity of a dangerous wild beast gleamed in his dark eyes and distorted his handsome features. The Inspector said nothing, but, stepping to the door, he blew his whistle. Two of his constables came at the call.

'I have no alternative, Mr Cunningham,' said he. 'I trust that this may all prove to be an absurd mistake; but you can see that—Ah, would you? Drop it!' He struck out with his hand, and a revolver, which the younger man was in the act of cocking, clattered down upon the floor.

'Keep that,' said Holmes, quickly putting his foot upon it. 'You will find it useful at the trial. But this is what we really wanted.' He held up a little crumpled piece of paper.

'The remainder of the sheet?' cried the Inspector.

'Precisely.'

'And where was it?'

'Where I was sure it must be. I'll make the whole matter clear to you presently. I think, Colonel, that you and Watson might return now, and I will be with you again in an hour at the furthest. The Inspector and I must have a word with the prisoners; but you will certainly see me back at luncheon time.'

Sherlock Holmes was as good as his word, for about one o'clock he rejoined us in the Colonel's smoking-room. He was accompanied by a little, elderly gentleman, who was introduced to me as the Mr Acton whose house had been the scene of the original burglary.

'I wished Mr Acton to be present while I demonstrated this small matter to you,' said Holmes, 'for it is natural that he should take a keen interest in the details. I am afraid, my dear Colonel, that you must regret the hour that you took in such a stormy petrel as I am.'

'On the contrary,' answered the Colonel warmly, 'I consider it the greatest privilege to have been permitted to study your methods of working. I confess that they quite surpass my expectations, and that I am utterly unable to account for your result. I have not yet seen the vestige of a clue.'

'I am afraid that my explanation may disillusionise you, but it has always been my habit to hide none of my methods, either from my friend Watson or from anyone who might take an intelligent interest in them. But first, as I am rather shaken by the knocking about which I had in the dressing-room, I think that I shall help myself to a dash of your brandy, Colonel. My strength has been rather tried of late.'

'I trust you had no more of those nervous attacks.'

Sherlock Holmes laughed heartily. 'We will come to that in its turn,' said he. 'I will lay an account of the case before you in its due order, showing you the various points which guided me in my decision. Pray interrupt me if there is any inference which is not perfectly clear to you.

'It is of the highest importance in the art of detection to be able to recognise out of a number of facts which are incidental and which vital. Otherwise your energy and attention must be dissipated instead of being concentrated. Now, in this case there was not the slightest doubt in my mind from the first that the key of the whole matter must be looked for in the scrap of paper in the dead man's hand.

'Before going into this I would draw your attention to the fact that if Alec Cunningham's narrative were correct, and if the assailant after shooting William Kirwan had *instantly* fled, then it obviously could not be he who tore the paper from the dead man's hand. But if it was not he, it must have been Alec Cunningham himself, for by the time the old man had descended several servants were upon the scene. The point is a simple one, but the Inspector had overlooked it because he had started with the supposition that these county magnates had had nothing to do with the matter. Now, I make a point of never having any prejudices and of following docilely wherever fact may lead me, and so in the very first stage of the investigation I found myself looking a little askance at the part which had been played by Mr Alec Cunningham.

'And now I made a very careful examination of the corner of paper which the Inspector had submitted to us. It was at once clear to me that it formed part of a very remarkable document. Here it is. Do you not now observe something very suggestive about it?'

'It has a very irregular look,' said the Colonel.

'My dear sir,' cried Holmes, 'there cannot be the least doubt in the world that it has been written by two persons doing alternate words. When I draw your attention to the strong t's of "at" and "to" and ask you to compare them with the weak ones of "quarter" and "twelve", you will instantly recognise the fact. A very brief analysis of those four words would enable you to say with the utmost confidence that the "learn" and the "maybe" are written in the stronger hand, and the "what" in the weaker.'

'By Jove, it's as clear as day!' cried the Colonel. 'Why on earth should two men write a letter in such a fashion?'

'Obviously the business was a bad one, and one of the men who distrusted the other was determined that, whatever was done, each should have an equal hand in it. Now, of the two men it is clear that the one who wrote the "at" and "to" was the ringleader.'

'How do you get at that?'

'We might deduce it from the mere character of the one hand as compared with the other. But we have more assured reasons than that for supposing it. If you examine this scrap with attention you will come to the conclusion that the man with the stronger hand wrote all his words first, leaving blanks for the other to fill up. These blanks were not always sufficient, and you can see that the second man had a squeeze to fit his "quarter" in between the "at" and the "to", showing that the latter were already written. The man who wrote all his words first is undoubtedly the man who planned this affair.'

'Excellent!' cried Mr Acton.

'But very superficial,' said Holmes. 'We come now, however, to a point which is of importance. You may not be aware that the deduction of a man's age from his writing is one which has been brought to considerable accuracy by experts. In normal cases one can place a man in his true decade with tolerable confidence. I say normal cases, because ill-health and physical weakness reproduce the signs of old age, even when the invalid is a youth. In this case, looking at the bold, strong hand of the one, and the rather broken-backed appearance of the other, which still retains its legibility, although the t's have begun to lose their crossings, we can say that the one was a young man, and the other was advanced in years without being positively decrepit.'

'Excellent!' cried Mr Acton again.

'There is a further point, however, which is subtler and of greater interest. There is something in common between these hands. They belong to men who are blood-relatives. It may be most obvious to you in the Greek e's, but to me there are many smaller points which indicate the same thing. I have no doubt at all that a family mannerism can be traced in these two specimens of writing. I am only, of course, giving you the leading results now of my examination of the paper. There were twenty-three other deductions which would be of more interest to experts than to you. They all tended to deepen the impression upon my mind that the Cunninghams, father and son, had written this letter.

'Having got so far, my next step was, of course, to examine into the details of the crime and to see how far they would help us. I went up to the house with the Inspector, and saw all that was to be seen. The wound upon the dead man was, as I was able to determine with absolute confidence, caused by a shot from a revolver fired at a distance of something over four yards. There was no powder-blackening on the clothes. Evidently, therefore, Alec Cunningham had lied when he said that the two men were struggling when the shot was fired. Again, both father and son agreed as to the place where the man escaped into the road. At that point, however, as it happens, there is a broadish ditch, moist at the bottom. As there were no indications of boot-marks about this ditch, I was absolutely sure not only that the Cunninghams had again lied, but that there had never been any unknown man upon the scene at all.

'And now I had to consider the motive of this singular crime. To get at this I endeavoured first of all to solve the reason of the original burglary at Mr Acton's. I understood from something which the Colonel told us that a lawsuit had been going on between you, Mr Acton, and the Cunninghams. Of course, it instantly occurred to me that they had broken into your library with the intention of getting at some document which might be of importance in the case.'

'Precisely so,' said Mr Acton; 'there can be no possible doubt as to their intentions. I have the clearest claim upon half their present estate, and if they could have found a single paper—which, fortunately, was in the strong-box of my solicitors—they would undoubtedly have crippled our case.'

'There you are!' said Holmes, smiling. 'It was a dangerous, reckless attempt, in which I seem to trace the influence of young Alec. Having found nothing, they tried to divert suspicion by making it appear to be an ordinary burglary, to which end they carried off whatever they could lay their hands upon. That is all clear enough, but there was much that was still obscure. What I wanted above all was to get the missing part of that note. I was certain that Alec had torn it out of the dead man's hand, and almost certain that he must have thrust it into the pocket of his dressing-gown. Where else could he have put it? The only question was whether it was still there. It was worth an effort to find out, and for that object we all went up to the house.

'The Cunninghams joined us, as you doubtless remember, outside the kitchen door. It was, of course, of the very first importance that they should not be reminded of the existence of this paper, otherwise they would naturally destroy it without delay. The Inspector was about to tell them the importance which was attached to it when, by the luckiest chance in the world, I tumbled down in a sort of fit and so changed the conversation.'

'Good heavens!' cried the Colonel, laughing. 'Do you mean to say all our sympathy was wasted and your fit an imposture?'

'Speaking professionally, it was admirably done,' cried I, looking in amazement at this man who was for ever confounding me with some new phase of his astuteness.

'It is an art which is often useful,' said he. 'When I recovered I managed by a device, which had, perhaps, some little merit of ingenuity, to get old Cunningham to write the word "twelve" so that I might compare it with the "twelve" upon the paper.'

'Oh, what an ass I have been!' I exclaimed.

'I could see that you were commiserating with me over my weakness,' said Holmes, laughing. 'I was sorry to cause you the sympathetic pain which I know that you felt. We then went upstairs together, and having entered the room and seen the dressing-gown hanging up behind the door, I contrived by upsetting a table to engage their attention for the moment and slipped back to examine the pockets. I had hardly got the paper, however, which was as I had expected, in one of them, when the two Cunninghams were on me, and would, I verily believe, have murdered me then and there but for your prompt and friendly aid. As it is, I feel that young man's grip on my throat now, and the father has twisted my wrist round in the effort to get the paper out of my hand. They saw that I must know all about it, you see, and the sudden change from absolute security to complete despair made them perfectly desperate.

'I had a little talk with old Cunningham afterwards as to the motive of the crime. He was tractable enough, though his son was a perfect demon, ready to blow out his own or anybody else's brains if he could have got to his revolver. When Cunningham saw that the case against him was so strong he lost all heart, and made a clean breast of everything. It seems that William had secretly followed his two masters on the night when they made their raid upon Mr Acton's, and, having thus got them into his power, proceeded under threats of exposure to levy blackmail upon them. Mister Alec, however, was a dangerous man to play games of that sort with. It was a stroke of positive genius on his part to see in the burglary scare, which was convulsing the countryside, an opportunity of plausibly getting rid of the man whom he feared. William was decoyed up and shot and, had they only got the whole of the note, and paid a little more attention to detail in their accessories, it is very possible that suspicion might never have been aroused.'

'And the note?' I asked.

Sherlock Holmes placed the subjoined paper before us.

If you will only come round at quarter to twelve
to the east gate you will learn what
will very much surprise you and maybe
be of the greatest service to you and also
to Annie Morrison. But say nothing to anyone
upon the matter

'It is very much the sort of thing that I expected,' said he. 'Of course, we do not yet know what the relations may have been between Alec Cunningham, William Kirwan, and Annie Morrison. The result shows that the trap was skilfully baited. I am sure that you cannot fail to be delighted with the traces of heredity shown in the p's and in the tails of the g's. The absence of the i-dots in the old man's writing is also most characteristic. Watson, I think our quiet rest in the country has been a distinct success, and I shall certainly return, much invigorated, to Baker Street tomorrow.'

Robert Louis Stevenson

THE BOTTLE IMP

Stevenson continues to surprise us. His popular books have remained in print and have been frequently filmed. Yet for many years the critical attention given to his work has been obscured by the adventurous life which took him from his birth in Edinburgh in 1850, to death at forty-four on the Island of Somoa, in the South Seas. And then there was his apparent refusal to take writing seriously: 'Fiction is to grown men what play is to the child,' he said.

His writing can be light, but it is often filled with apprehension and suffering. The *Doppelganger* is a recurring theme and he prefers anti-heroes. Many stories have the same convincing belief in the Devil that we find in Hogg, and they may well spring from the same oral roots. He is also a master of atmosphere and the sense of place, which he uses to add an eerie depth and surprising subtlety to what could be little more than a fairy tale.

The author wrote his own introductory note: 'Any student of that very unliterary product, the English drama of the early part of the century, will here recognise the name and the root idea of a piece once rendered popular by the redoubtable O. Smith. The root idea is there, and identical, and yet I hope I have made it a new thing. And the fact that the tale has been designed and written for a Polynesian audience may lend it some extraneous interest nearer home.'

The Bottle Imp

THERE WAS a man of the Island of Hawaii, whom I shall call Keawe; for the truth is, he still lives, and his name must be kept secret; but the place of his birth was not far from Honaunau, where the bones of Keawe the Great lie hidden in a cave. This man was poor, brave, and active; he could read and write like a schoolmaster; he was a first-rate mariner besides, sailed for some time in the island steamers, and steered a whaleboat on the Hamakua coast. At length it came in Keawe's mind to have a sight of the great world and foreign cities, and he shipped on a vessel bound to San Francisco.

This is a fine town, with a fine harbour, and rich people uncountable; and, in particular, there is one hill which is covered with palaces. Upon this hill Keawe was one day taking a walk with his pocket full of money, viewing the great houses upon either hand with pleasure. 'What fine houses these are!' he was thinking, 'and how happy must those people be who dwell in them, and take no care for the morrow!' The thought was in his mind when he came abreast of a house that was smaller than some others, but all finished and beautified like a toy; the steps of that house shone like silver, and the borders of the garden bloomed like garlands, and the windows were bright like diamonds; and Keawe stopped and wondered at the excellence of all he saw. So stopping, he was aware of a man that looked forth upon him through a window so clear that Keawe could see him as you see a fish in a pool upon the reef. The man was elderly, with a bald head and a black beard; and his face was heavy with sorrow, and he bitterly sighed. And the truth of it is, that as Keawe looked in upon the man, and the man looked out upon Keawe, each envied the other.

All of a sudden the man smiled and nodded, and beckoned Keawe to enter, and met him at the door of the house.

'This is a fine house of mine,' said the man, and bitterly sighed. 'Would you not care to view the chambers?'

So he led Keawe all over it, from the cellar to the roof, and there was nothing there that was not perfect of its kind, and Keawe was astonished.

'Truly,' said Keawe, 'this is a beautiful house; if I lived in the like of it I should be laughing all day long. How comes it, then, that you should be sighing?'

'There is no reason,' said the man, 'why you should not have a house in all points similar to this, and finer, if you wish. You have some money, I suppose?'

'I have fifty dollars,' said Keawe; 'but a house like this will cost more than fifty dollars.'

The man made a computation. 'I am sorry you have no more,' said he, 'for it may raise you trouble in the future; but it shall be yours at fifty dollars.'

'The house?' asked Keawe.

'No, not the house,' replied the man; 'but the bottle. For I must tell you, although I appear to you so rich and fortunate, all my fortune, and this house itself and its garden, came out of a bottle not much bigger than a pint. This is it.'

And he opened a lockfast place, and took out a round-bellied bottle with a long neck; the glass of it was white like milk, with changing rainbow colours in the grain. Withinsides something obscurely moved, like a shadow and a fire.

'This is the bottle,' said the man; and, when Keawe laughed, 'You do not believe me?' he added. 'Try, then, for yourself. See if you can break it.'

So Keawe took the bottle up and dashed it on the floor till he was weary; but it jumped on the floor like a child's ball, and was not injured.

'This is a strange thing,' said Keawe. 'For by the touch of it, as well as by the look, the bottle should be of glass.'

'Of glass it is,' replied the man, sighing more heavily than ever; 'but the glass of it was tempered in the flames of hell. An imp lives in it, and that is the shadow we behold there moving; or so I suppose. If any man buy this bottle the imp is at his command; all that he desires—love, fame, money, houses like this house, ay, or a city like this city—all are his at the word uttered. Napoleon had this bottle, and by it he grew to be the king of the world; but he sold it at last, and fell. Captain Cook had this bottle, and by it he found his way to so many islands; but he, too, sold it, and was slain upon Hawaii. For, once it is sold, the power goes and the protection; and unless a man remain content with what he has, ill will befall him.'

'And yet you talk of selling it yourself?' Keawe said.

'I have all I wish, and I am growing elderly,' replied the man. 'There is one thing the imp cannot do—he cannot prolong life; and, it would not be fair to conceal from you, there is a drawback to the bottle; for if a man die before he sells it, he must burn in hell for ever.'

'To be sure, that is a drawback and no mistake,' cried Keawe. 'I would not meddle with the thing. I can do without a house, thank God; but there is one thing I could not be doing with one particle, and that is to be damned.'

'Dear me, you must not run away with things,' returned the man. 'All you have to do is to use the power of the imp in moderation, and then sell it to someone else, as I do to you, and finish your life in comfort.'

'Well, I observe two things,' said Keawe. 'All the time you keep sighing like a maid in love, that is one; and, for the other, you sell this bottle very cheap.'

'I have told you already why I sigh,' said the man. 'It is because I fear my health is breaking up; and, as you said yourself, to die and go to the devil is a pity for any one. As for why I sell so cheap, I must explain to you there is a peculiarity about the bottle. Long ago, when the devil brought it first upon earth, it was extremely expensive, and was sold first of all to Prester John for many millions of dollars; but it cannot be sold at all, unless sold at a loss. If you sell it for as much as you paid for it, back it comes to you again like a homing pigeon. It follows that the price has kept falling in these centuries, and the bottle is now remarkably cheap. I bought it myself from one of my great neighbours on this hill, and the price I paid was only ninety dollars. I could sell it for as high as eighty-nine dollars and ninety-nine cents, but not a penny dearer, or back the thing must come to me. Now, about this there are two bothers. First, when you offer a bottle so singular for eighty odd dollars, people do not suppose you to be jesting. And second—but there is no hurry about that—and I need not go into it. Only remember it must be coined money that you sell it for.'

'How am I to know that this is all true?' asked Keawe.

'Some of it you can try at once,' replied the man. 'Give me your fifty dollars, take the bottle, and wish your fifty dollars back into your pocket. If that does not happen, I pledge you my honour I will cry off the bargain and restore your money.'

'You are not deceiving me?' said Keawe.

The man bound himself with a great oath.

'Well, I will risk that much,' said Keawe, 'for that can do no harm.' And he paid over his money to the man, and the man handed him the bottle.

'Imp of the bottle,' said Keawe, 'I want my fifty dollars back.' And sure enough he had scarce said the word before his pocket was as heavy as ever.

'To be sure this is a wonderful bottle,' said Keawe.

'And now good-morning to you, my fine fellow, and the devil go with you for me!' said the man.

'Hold on,' said Keawe, 'I don't want any more of this fun. Here, take your bottle back.'

'You have bought it for less than I paid for it,' replied the man, rubbing his hands. 'It is yours now; and, for my part, I am only concerned to see the back of you.' And with that he rang for his Chinese servant, and had Keawe shown out of the house.

Now, when Keawe was in the street, with the bottle under his arm, he began to think. 'If all is true about this bottle, I may have made a losing bargain,' thinks he. 'But perhaps the man was only fooling me.' The first thing he did was to count his money; the sum was exact—forty-nine dollars American money, and one Chili piece. 'That looks like the truth,' said Keawe. 'Now I will try another part.'

The streets in that part of the city were as clean as a ship's decks, and though it was noon, there were no passengers. Keawe set the bottle in the gutter and walked away. Twice he looked back, and there was the milky round-bellied bottle where he left it. A third time he looked back, and turned a corner; but he had scarce done so, when something knocked upon his elbow, and behold! it was the long neck sticking up; and as for the round belly, it was jammed into the pocket of his pilotcoat.

'And that looks like the truth', said Keawe.

The next thing he did was to buy a corkscrew in a shop, and go apart into a secret place in the fields. And there he tried to draw the cork, but as often as he put the screw in, out it came again, and the cork as whole as ever.

'This is some new sort of cork,' said Keawe, and all at once he began to shake and sweat, for he was afraid of that bottle.

On his way back to the port-side he saw a shop where a man sold shells and clubs from the wild islands, old heathen deities, old coined money, pictures from China and Japan, and all manner of things that sailors bring in their sea-chests. And here he had an idea. So he went in and offered the bottle for a hundred dollars. The man of the shop laughed at him at the first, and offered him five; but, indeed, it was a curious bottle—such glass was never blown in any human glassworks, so prettily the colours shone under the milky white, and so strangely the shadow hovered in the midst; so, after he had disputed a while after the manner of his kind, the shopman gave Keawe sixty silver dollars for the thing, and set it on a shelf in the midst of his window.

'Now,' said Keawe, 'I have sold that for sixty which I bought for fifty—or, to say truth, a little less, because one of my dollars was from Chili. Now I shall know the truth upon another point.'

So he went back on board his ship, and, when he opened his chest, there was the bottle, and had come more quickly than himself. Now Keawe had a mate on board whose name was Lopaka.

'What ails you?' said Lopaka, 'that you stare in your chest?'

They were alone in the ship's forecastle, and Keawe bound him to secrecy, and told all.

'This is a very strange affair,' said Lopaka; 'and I fear you will be in trouble about this bottle. But there is one point very clear—that you are sure of the trouble, and you had better have the profit in the bargain. Make up your mind what you want with it; give the order, and if it is done as you desire, I will buy the bottle myself; for I have an idea of my own to get a schooner, and go trading through the islands.'

'That is not my idea,' said Keawe; 'but to have a beautiful house and garden on the Kona Coast, where I was born, the sun shining in at the door, flowers in the garden, glass in the windows, pictures on the walls, and toys and fine carpets on the tables, for all the world like the house I was in this day—only a story higher, and with balconies all about like the King's palace; and to live there without care and make merry with my friends and relatives.'

'Well,' said Lopaka, 'let us carry it back with us to Hawaii; and if all comes true, as you suppose, I will buy the bottle, as I said, and ask a schooner.'

Upon that they were agreed, and it was not long before the ship returned to Honolulu, carrying Keawe and Lopaka, and the bottle. They were scarce come ashore when they met a friend upon the beach, who began at once to condole with Keawe.

'I do not know what I am to be condoled about,' said Keawe.

'Is it possible you have not heard,' said the friend, 'your uncle—that good old man—is dead, and your cousin—that beautiful boy—was drowned at sea?'

Keawe was filled with sorrow, and, beginning to weep and to lament, he forgot about the bottle. But Lopaka was thinking to himself, and presently, when Keawa's grief was a little abated, 'I have been thinking,' said Lopaka. 'Had not your uncle lands in Hawaii, in the district of Kaü?'

'No,' said Keawe, 'not in Kaü; they are on the mountain side—a little way south of Hookena.'

'These lands will now be yours?' asked Lopaka.

'And so they will,' says Keawe, and began again to lament for his relatives.

'No,' said Lopaka, 'do not lament at present. I have a thought in my mind. How if this should be the doing of the bottle? For here is the place ready for your house.'

'If this be so,' cried Keawe, 'it is a very ill way to serve me by killing my relatives. But it may be indeed; for it was in just such a station that I saw the house with my mind's eye.'

'The house, however, is not yet built,' said Lopaka.

'No, nor like to be!' said Keawa; 'for though my uncle has some coffee and ava and bananas, it will not be more than will keep me in comfort; and the rest of that land is the black lava.'

'Let us go to the lawyer,' said Lopaka; 'I have still this idea in my mind.'

Now, when they came to the lawyer's, it appeared Keawe's uncle had grown monstrous rich in the last days, and there was a fund of money.

'And here is the money for the house!' cried Lopaka.

'If you are thinking of a new house,' said the lawyer, 'here is the card of a new architect, of whom they tell me great things.'

'Better and better !' cried Lopaka. 'Here is all made plain for us. Let us continue to obey orders.'

So they went to the architect, and he had drawings of houses on his table.

'You want something out of the way,' said the architect. 'How do you like this?' and he handed a drawing to Keawe.

Now, when Keawe set eyes on the drawing, he cried out aloud, for it was the picture of his thought exactly drawn.

'I am in for this house,' thought he. 'Little as I like the way it comes to me, I am in for it now, and I may as well take the good along with the evil.'

So he told the architect all that he wished, and how he would have that house furnished, and about the pictures on the wall and the knickknacks on the tables; and he asked the man plainly for how much he would undertake the whole affair.

The architect put many questions, and took his pen and made a computation; and when he had done he named the very sum that Keawe had inherited.

Lopaka and Keawe looked at one another and nodded.

'It is quite clear,' thought Keawe, 'that I am to have this house, whether or no. It comes from the devil, and I fear I will get little good by that; and of one thing I am sure, I will make no more wishes as long as I have this bottle. But with the house I am saddled, and I may as well take the good along with the evil.'

So he made his terms with the architect, and they signed a paper; and Keawe and Lopaka took ship again and sailed to Australia; for it was concluded between them they should not interfere at all, but leave the architect and the bottle imp to build and adorn that house at their own pleasure.

The voyage was a good voyage, only all the time Keawe was holding in his breath, for he had sworn he would utter no more wishes, and take no more favours from the devil. The time was up when they got back. The architect told them that the house was ready, and Keawe and Lopaka took a passage in the *Hall*, and went down Kona way to view the house, and see if all had been done fitly according to the thought that was in Keawe's mind.

Now, the house stood on the mountain side, visible to ships. Above, the forest ran up into the clouds of rain; below, the black lava fell in cliffs, where the kings of old lay buried. A garden bloomed about that house with every hue of flowers; and there was an orchard of papaia on the one hand and an orchard of bread-fruit on the other, and right in front, toward the sea, a ship's mast had been rigged up and bore a flag. As for the house, it was three stories high, with great chambers and broad balconies on each. The windows were of glass, so excellent that it was as clear as water and as bright as day. All manner of furniture adorned the chambers. Pictures hung upon the wall in golden frames: pictures of ships, and men fighting, and of the most beautiful women, and of singular places; nowhere in the world are there pictures of so bright a colour as those Keawe found hanging in his house. As for the knickknacks, they were extraordinary fine; chiming clocks and musical boxes filled with pictures, weapons of price from all quarters of the world, and the most elegant puzzles to entertain the leisure of a solitary man. And as no one would care to live in such chambers, only walk through and view them, the balconies were made so broad that a whole town might have lived upon them in delight; and Keawe knew not which to prefer, whether the back porch, where you got the land-breeze, and looked upon the orchards and the flowers, or the front balcony, where you could drink the wind of the sea, and look down the steep wall of the mountain and see the *Hall* going by once a week or so between Hookena and the hills of Pele, or the schooners plying up the coast for wood and ava and bananas.

When they had viewed all, Keawe and Lopaka sat on the porch.

'Well,' asked Lopaka, 'is it all as you designed ?'

'Words cannot utter it,' said Keawe. 'It is better than I dreamed, and I am sick with satisfaction.'

'There is but one thing to consider,' said Lopaka; 'all this may be quite natural, and the bottle imp have nothing whatever to say to it. If I were to buy the bottle, and got no schooner after all, I should have put my hand in the fire for nothing. I gave you my word, I know; but yet I think you would not grudge me one more proof.'

'I have sworn I would take no more favours,' said Keawe. 'I have gone already deep enough.'

'This is no favour I am thinking of,' replied Lopaka. 'It is only to see the imp himself. There is nothing to be gained by that, and so nothing to be ashamed of; and yet, if I once saw him, I should be sure of the whole matter. So indulge me so far, and let me see the imp; and, after that, here is the money in my hand, and I will buy it.'

'There is only one thing I am afraid of,' said Keawe. 'The imp may be very ugly to view and if you once set eyes upon him you might be very undesirous of the bottle.'

'I am a man of my word,' said Lopaka. 'And here is the money betwixt us.'

'Very well,' replied Keave. 'I have a curiosity myself.— So, come, let us have one look at you, Mr Imp.'

Now as soon as that was said the imp looked out of the bottle, and in again, swift as a lizard; and there sat Keawe and Lopaka turned to stone. The night had quite come, before either found a thought to say or voice to say it with ; and then Lopaka pushed the money over and took the bottle.

'I am a man of my word,' said he, 'and had need to be so, or I would not touch this bottle with my foot. Well, I shall get my schooner, and a dollar or two for my pocket; and then I will be rid of this devil as fast as I can. For to tell you the plain truth, the look of him has cast me down.'

'Lopaka,' said Keawe, 'do not you think any worse of me than you can help; I know it is night, and the roads bad, and the pass by the tombs an ill place to go by so late, but I declare since I have seen that little face, I cannot eat or sleep or pray till it is gone from me. I will give you a lantern, and a basket to put the bottle in, and any picture or fine thing in all my house that takes your fancy;—and be gone at once, and go sleep at Hookena with Nahinu.'

'Keawe,' said Lopaka, 'many a man would take this ill ; above all, when I am doing you a turn so friendly as to keep my word and buy the bottle; and for that matter, the night, and the dark, and the way by the tombs, must be all tenfold more dangerous to a man with such a sin upon his conscience, and such a bottle under his arm. But for my part, I am so extremely terrified myself, I have not the heart to blame you. Here I go then; and I pray God you may be happy in your house, and I fortunate with my schooner, and both get to heaven in the end in spite of the devil and his bottle.'

So Lopaka went down the mountain; and Keawe stood in his front balcony, and listened to the clink of the horse's shoes, and watched the lantern go shining down the path, and along the cliff of caves where the old dead are buried; and all the time he trembled and clasped his hands, and prayed for his friend, and gave glory to God that he himself was escaped out of that trouble.

But the next day came very brightly, and that new house of his was so delightful to behold that he forgot his terrors. One day followed another, and Keawe dwelt there in perpetual joy. He had his place on the back porch; it was there he ate and lived, and read the stories in the Honolulu newspapers; but when any one came by they would go in and view the chambers and the pictures. And the fame of the house went far and wide; it was called *Ka-Hale Nui*—the Great House—in all Kona; and sometimes the Bright House, for Keawe kept a Chinaman, who was all day dusting and furbishing; and the glass and the gilt, and the fine stuffs, and the pictures, shone as bright as the morning. As for Keawe himself, he could not walk in the chambers without singing, his heart was so enlarged; and when ships sailed by upon the sea, he would fly his colours on the mast.

So time went by, until one day Keawe went upon a visit as far as Kailua to certain of his friends. There he was well feasted; and left as soon as he could the next morning, and rode hard, for he was impatient to behold his beautiful house; and, besides, the night then coming on was the night in which the dead of old days go abroad in the sides of Kona; and having already meddled with the devil, he was the more chary of meeting with the dead. A little beyond Honaunau, looking far ahead, he was aware of a woman bathing in the edge of the sea; and she seemed a well-grown girl, but he thought no more of it. Then he saw her white shift flutter as she put it on, and then her red holoku;

and by the time he came abreast of her she was done with her toilet, and had come up from the sea, and stood by the track side in her red holoku, and she was all freshened with the bath, and her eyes shone and were kind. Now Keawe no sooner beheld her than he drew rein.

'I thought I knew every one in this country,' said he. 'How comes it that I do not know you ?'

'I am Kokua, daughter of Kiano,' said the girl, 'and I have just returned from Oahu. Who are you?'

'I will tell you who I am in a little,' said Keawe, dismounting from his horse, 'but not now. For I have a thought in my mind, and if you knew who I was, you might have heard of me, and would not give me a true answer. But tell me, all, one thing: Are you married?'

At this Kokua laughed out aloud. 'It is you who ask questions,' she said. 'Are you married yourself?'

'Indeed, Kokau, I am not,' replied Keawe, 'and never thought to be until this hour. But here is the plain truth. I have met you here at the roadside, and I saw your eyes, which are like the stars, and my heart went to you as swift as a bird. And so now, if you want none of me, say so, and I will go on to my own place; but if you think me no worse than any other young man, say so, too, and I will turn aside to your father's for the night, and tomorrow I will talk with the good man.'

Kokua said never a word, but she looked at the sea and laughed.

'Kokua,' said Keawe, 'if you say nothing, I will take that for the good answer; so let us be stepping to your father's door.'

She went ahead of him, still without speech; only sometimes she glanced back and glanced away again, and she kept the strings of her hat in her mouth.

Now, when they had come to the door, Kiano came out on his verandah, and cried out and welcomed Keawe by name. At that the girl looked over, for the fame of the great house had come to her ears; and, to be sure, it was a great temptation. All that evening they were very merry together; and the girl was as bold as brass under the eyes of her parents, and made a mock of Keawe, for she had a quick wit. The next day he had a word with Kiano, and found the girl alone.

'Kokua', said he, 'you made a mock of me all the evening; and it is still time to bid me go. I would not tell you who I was, because I have so fine a house, and I feared you would think too much of that house, and too little of the man that loves you. Now you know all, and if you wish to have seen the last of me, say so at once.'

'No,' said Kokua; but this time she did not laugh, nor did Keawe ask for more.

This was the wooing of Keawe; things had gone quickly; but so an arrow goes, and the ball of a rifle swifter still, and yet both may strike the target. Things had gone fast, but they had gone far also, and the thought of Keawe rang in the maiden's head; she heard his voice in the breach of the surf upon the lava, and for this young man that she had seen but twice she would have left father and mother in her native islands. As for Keawe himself, his horse flew up the path of the mountain under the cliff of tombs, and the sound of the hoofs, and the sound of Keawe singing to himself for pleasure, echoed in the caverns of the dead. He came to the Bright House, and still he was singing. He sat and ate in the broad balcony, and the Chinaman wondered at his master, to hear how he sang between the mouthfuls. The sun went down into the sea, and the night came; and Keawe walked the balconies by lamplight, high on the mountains, and the voice of his singing startled men on ships.

'Here am I now upon my high place,' he said to himself. 'Life may be no better; this is the mountain top; and all shelves about me toward the worse. For the first time I will light up the chambers, and bathe in my fine bath with the hot water and the cold, and sleep alone in the bed of my bridal chamber.'

So the Chinaman had word, and he must rise from sleep and light the furnaces; and as he wrought below, beside the boilers, he heard his master singing and rejoicing above him in the lighted chambers. When the water began to be hot the Chinaman cried to his master; and Keawe went into the bathroom; and the Chinaman heard him sing as he filled the marble basin; and heard him sing, and the singing broken, as he undressed; until of a sudden the song ceased. The Chinaman listened, and listened; he called up the house to Keawe to ask if all were well, and Keawe answered him 'Yes', and bade him go to bed; but there was no more singing in the Bright House; and all night long the Chinaman heard his master's feet go round and round the balconies without repose.

Now the truth of it was this; as Keawe undressed for his bath, he spied upon his flesh a patch like a patch of lichen on a rock, and it was then that he stopped singing. For he knew the likeness of that patch, and knew that he was fallen in the Chinese Evil.*

Now, it is a sad thing for any man to fall into this sickness. And it would be a sad thing for any one to leave a house so beautiful and so commodious, and depart from all his friends to the north coast of Molokai between the mighty cliff and the sea-breakers. But what was that to the case of the man Keawe, he who had met his love but yesterday, and won her but that morning, and now saw all his hopes break, in a moment, like a piece of glass?

A while he sat upon the edge of the bath; then sprang, with a cry, and ran outside; and to and fro, to and fro, along the balcony, like one despairing.

'Very willingly could I leave Hawaii, the home of my fathers,' Keawe was thinking. 'Very lightly could I leave my house, the high-placed, the many-windowed, here upon the mountains. Very bravely could I go to

* Leprosy [R. L. S.]

Molokai, to Kalaupapa by the cliffs, to live with the smitten and to sleep there, far from my fathers. But what wrong have I done, what sin lies upon my soul, that I should have encountered Kokua coming cool from the seawater in the evening? Kokua, the soul-ensnarer! Kokua, the light of my life! Her may I never wed, her may I look upon no longer, her may I no more handle with my loving hand; and it is for this, it is for you, O Kokua! that I pour my lamentations!'

Now you are to observe what sort of man Keawe was, for he might have dwelt there in the Bright House for years, and no one been the wiser of his sickness; but he reckoned nothing of that, if he must lose Kokua. And again, he might have wed Kokua even as he was; and so many would have done, because they have the souls of pigs; but Keawe loved the maid manfully, and he would do her no hurt and bring her in no danger.

A little beyond the midst of the night, there came in his mind the recollection of the bottle. He went round to the back porch, and called to memory the day when the devil had looked forth; and at the thought ice ran in his veins.

'A dreadful thing is the bottle,' thought Keawe, 'and dreadful is the imp, and it is a dreadful thing to risk the flames of hell. But what other hope have I to cure my sickness or to wed Kokua? What!' he thought, 'would I beard the devil once, only to get me a house, and not face him again to win Kokua?'

Thereupon he called to mind it was the next day the *Hall* went by on her return to Honolulu. 'There must I go first,' he thought, 'and see Lopaka. For the best hope that I have now is to find that same bottle I was so pleased to be rid of.'

Never a wink could he sleep; the food stuck in his throat; but he sent a letter to Kiano, and, about the time when the steamer would be coming, rode down beside the cliff of the tombs. It rained; his horse went heavily; he looked up at the black mouths of the caves, and he envied the dead that slept there and were done with trouble; and called to mind how he had galloped by the day before, and was astonished. So he came down to Hookena, and there was all the country gathered for the steamer as usual. In the shed before the store they sat and jested and passed the news; but there was no matter of speech in Keawe's bosom, and he sat in their midst and looked without on the rain falling on the houses, and the surf beating among the rocks, and the sighs arose in his throat.

'Keawe of the Bright House is out of spirits,' said one to another. Indeed, and so he was, and little wonder.

Then the *Hall* came, and the whaleboat carried him on board. The after-part of the ship was full of Haoles,* who had been to visit the volcano, as their custom is; and the midst was crowded with Kanakas,

* Whites [R. L. S.]

and the forepart with wild bulls from Hilo and horses from Kaü; but Keawe sat apart from all in his sorrow, and watched for the house of Kiano. There it sat, low upon the shore in the black rocks, and shaded by the cocoa palms, and there by the door was a red holoku, no greater than a fly, and going to and from with a fly's busyness. 'Ah, queen of my heart,' he cried, 'I'll venture my dear soul to win you!'

Soon after, darkness fell, and the cabins were lit up, and the Haoles sat and played at the cards and drank whisky as their custom is; but Keawe walked the deck all night; and all the next day, as they steamed under the lee of Maui or of Molokai, he was still pacing to and fro like a wild animal in a menagerie.

Towards evening they passed Diamond Head, and came to the pier of Honolulu. Keawe stepped out among the crowd and began to ask for Lopaka. It seemed he had become the owner of a schooner—none better in the islands—and was gone upon an adventure as far as Pola-Pola or Kahiki; so there was no help to be looked for from Lopaka. Keawe called to mind a friend of his, a lawyer in the town (I must not tell his name), and inquired of him. They said he was grown suddenly rich, and had a fine new house upon Waikiki shore; and this put a thought in Keawe's head, and he called a hack and drove to the lawyer's house.

The house was all brand new, and the trees in the garden no greater than walking-sticks, and the lawyer, when he came, had the air of a man well pleased.

'What can I do to serve you?' said the lawyer.

'You are a friend of Lopaka's,' replied Keawe, 'and Lopaka purchased from me a certain piece of goods that I thought you might enable me to trace.'

The lawyer's face became very dark. 'I do not profess to misunderstand you, Mr Keawe,' said he, 'though this is an ugly business to be stirring in. You may be sure I know nothing, but yet I have a guess, and if you would apply in a certain quarter I think you might have news.'

And he named the name of a man, which, again, I had better not repeat. So it was for days, and Keawe went from one to another, finding everywhere new clothes and carriages, and fine new houses, and men everywhere in great contentment, although, to be sure, when he hinted at his business their faces would cloud over.

'No doubt I am upon the track,' thought Keawe. 'These new clothes and carriages are all the gifts of the little imp, and these glad faces are the faces of men who have taken their profit and got rid of the accursed thing in safety. When I see pale cheeks and hear sighing, I shall know I am near the bottle.'

So it befell at last that he was recommended to a Haole in Beritania Street. When he came to the door, about the hour of the evening meal, there were the usual marks of the new house, and the young garden, and the electric light shining in the windows; but when the owner came, a shock of hope and fear ran through Keawe; for here was a young man, white as a corpse, and black about the eyes, the hair shedding from his head, and such a look in his countenance as a man may have when he is waiting for the gallows.

'Here it is, to be sure,' thought Keawe, and so with this man he noways veiled his errand. 'I am come to buy the bottle,' said he.

At the word the young Haole of Beritania Street reeled against the wall.

'The bottle!' he gasped. 'To buy the bottle!' Then he seemed to choke, and seizing Keawe by the arm carried him into a room and poured out wine in two glasses.

'Here is my respects,' said Keawe, who had been much about with Haoles in his time. 'Yes,' he added, 'I am come to buy the bottle. What is the price by now?'

At that word the young man let his glass slip through his fingers, and looked upon Keawe like a ghost.

'The price,' says he; 'the price! You do not know the price?'

'It is for that I am asking you,' returned Keawe. 'But why are you so much concerned? Is there anything wrong about the price?'

'It has dropped a great deal in value since your time, Mr Keawe,' said the young man, stammering.

'Well, well, I shall have the less to pay for it,' says Keawe. 'How much did it cost you?'

The young man was as white as a sheet. 'Two cents,' said he.

'What!' cried Keawe, 'two cents? Why, then, you can only sell it for one. And he who buys it—' The words died upon Keawe's tongue; he who bought it could never sell it again, the bottle and the bottle imp must abide with him until he died, and when he died must carry him to the red end of hell.

The young man of Beritania Street fell upon his knees. 'For God's sake, buy it !' he cried. 'You can have all my fortune in the bargain. I was mad when I bought it at that price. I had embezzled money at my store; I was lost else; I must have gone to jail.'

'Poor creature,' said Keawe, 'you would risk your soul upon so desperate an adventure, and to avoid the proper punishment of your own disgrace; and you think I could hesitate with love in front of me. Give me the bottle, and the change, which I make sure you have all ready. Here is a five-cent piece.'

It was as Keawe supposed; the young man had the change ready in a drawer; the bottle changed hands, and Keawe's fingers were no sooner clasped upon the stalk than he had breathed his wish to be a clean man. And, sure enough, when he got home to his room, and stripped himself before a glass, his flesh was whole like an infant's. And here was the strange thing: he had no sooner seen this miracle than his mind changed within him, and he cared naught for the Chinese Evil, and little enough for Kokua; and had but the one thought, that here he was bound to the bottle imp for time and for eternity, and had no better hope but to be a cinder for ever in the flames of hell. Away ahead of him he saw them blaze with his mind's eye, and his soul shrank, and darkness fell upon the light.

When Keawe came to himself a little, he was aware it was the night when the band played at the hotel. Thither he went, because he feared to be alone; and there, among happy faces, walked to and fro, and heard the tunes go up and down, and saw Berger beat the measure, and all the while he heard the flames crackle, and saw the red fire burning in the bottomless pit. Of a sudden the band played *Hiki-ao-ao*; that was a song that he had sung with Kokua, and at the strain courage returned to him.

'It is done now,' he thought, 'and once more let me take the good along with the evil.'

So it befell that he returned to Hawaii by the first steamer, and as soon as it could be managed he was wedded to Kokua, and carried her up the mountain side to the Bright House.

Now it was with these two, that when they were together, Keawe's heart was stilled; but so soon as he was alone he fell into a brooding horror, and heard the flames crackle, and saw the red fire burn in the bottomless pit. The girl, indeed, had come to him wholly; her heart leapt in her side at the sight of him, her hand clung to his; and she was so fashioned from the hair upon her head to the nails upon her toes that none could see her without joy. She was pleasant in her nature. She had the good word always. Full of song she was, and went to and fro in the Bright House, the brightest thing in its three stories, carolling like the birds. And Keawe beheld and heard her with delight, and then must shrink upon the side, and weep and groan to think upon the price that he had paid for her; and then he must dry his eyes, and wash his face, and go and sit with her on the broad balconies, joining in her songs, with a sick spirit, answering her smiles.

There came a day when her feet began to be heavy and her songs more rare; and now it was not Keawe only that would weep apart, but each would sunder from the other and sit in opposite balconies with the whole width of the Bright House betwixt. Keawe was so sunk in his despair he scarce observed the change, and was only glad he had more hours to sit alone and brood upon his destiny, and was not so frequently condemned to pull a smiling face on a sick heart. But one day, coming softly through the house, he heard the sound of a child sobbing, and there was Kokua rolling her face upon the balcony floor, and weeping like the lost.

'You do well to weep in this house, Kokua,' he said. 'And yet I would give the head off my body that you (at least) might have been happy.'

'Happy!' she cried. 'Keawe, when you lived alone in your Bright House you were the word of the island for a happy man; laughter and song were in your mouth, and your face was as bright as the sunrise. Then you wedded poor Kokua; and the good God knows what is amiss in her—but from that day you have not smiled. O!' she cried, 'what ails me? I thought I was pretty, and I knew I loved him. What ails me that I throw this cloud upon my husband?'

'Poor Kokua,' said Keawe. He sat down by her side, and sought to take her hand; but that she plucked away. 'Poor Kokua!' he said again. 'My poor child—my pretty. And I had thought all this while to spare you! Well, you shall know all. Then, at least, you will pity poor Keawe; then you will understand how much he loved you in the past—that he dared hell for your possession—and how much he loves you still (the poor condemned one), that he can yet call up a smile when he beholds you.'

With that he told her all, even from the beginning.

'You have done this for me?' she cried. 'Ah, well, then what do I care!'—and she clasped and wept upon him.

'Ah, child!' said Keawe, 'and yet, when I consider of the fire of hell, I care a good deal!'

'Never tell me,' said she; 'no man can be lost because he loved Kokua, and no other fault. I tell you, Keawe, I shall save you with these hands, or perish in your company. What! you loved me, and gave your soul, and you think I will not die to save you in return?'

'Ah, my dear! you might die a hundred times, and what difference would that make?' he cried, 'except to leave me lonely till the time comes of my damnation?'

'You know nothing,' said she. 'I was educated in a school in Honolulu; I am no common girl. And I tell you, I shall save my lover. What is this you say about a cent? But all the world is not American. In England they have a piece they call a farthing, which is about half a cent. Ah! sorrow!' she cried, 'that makes it scarcely better, or the buyer must be lost, and we shall find none so brave as my Keawe! But then, there is France: they have a small coin there which they call a centime, and these go five to the cent, or thereabout. We could not do better. Come, Keawe, let us go to the French islands; let us go to Tahiti as fast as ships can bear us. There we have four centimes, three centimes, two centimes, one centime; four possible sales to come and go on; and two of us to push the bargain. Come, my Keawe! kiss me, and banish care. Kokua will defend you.'

'Gift of God!' he cried. 'I cannot think that God will punish me for desiring aught so good! Be it as you will, then; take me where you please: I put my life and my salvation in your hands.'

Early the next day Kokua was about her preparations. She took Keawe's chest that he went with sailoring; and first she put the bottle in a corner; and then packed it with the richest of their clothes and the bravest of the knickknacks in the house. 'For,' said she, 'we must seem to be rich folks, or who will believe in the bottle?' All the time of her preparation she was as gay as a bird; only when she looked upon Keawe the tears would spring in her eye, and she must run and kiss him. As for Keawe, a weight was off his soul; now that he had his secret shared, and some hope in front of him, he seemed like a new man, his feet went lightly on the earth, and his breath was good to him again. Yet was terror still at his elbow ; and ever and again, as the wind blows out a taper, hope died in him, and he saw the flames toss and the red fire burn in hell.

It was given out in the country they were gone pleasuring to the States, which was thought a strange thing, and yet not so strange as the truth, if any could have guessed it. So they went to Honolulu in the *Hall*, and thence in the *Umatilla* to San Francisco with a crowd of Haoles, and at San Francisco took their passage by the mail brigantine, the *Tropic Bird*, for Papeete, the chief place of the French in the south islands. Thither they came, after a pleasant voyage, on a fair day of the Trade Wind, and saw the reef with the surf breaking, and Motuiti with its palms, and the schooner riding withinside, and the white houses of the town low down along the shore among green trees, and overhead the mountains and the clouds of Tahiti, the wise island.

It was judged the most wise to hire a house, which they did accordingly, opposite the British Consul's, to make a great parade of money, and themselves conspicuous with carriages and horses. This it was easy to do, so long as they had the bottle in their possession; for Kokua was more bold than Keawe, and, whenever she had a mind, called on the imp for twenty or a hundred dollars. At this rate they soon grew to be remarked in the town; and the strangers from Hawaii, their riding and their driving, the fine holokus and the rich lace of Kokua, became the matter of much talk.

They got on well after the first with the Tahitian language, which is indeed like to the Hawaiian, with a change of certain letters; and as soon as they had any freedom of speech, began to push the bottle. You are to consider it was not an easy subject to introduce; it was not easy to persuade people you were in earnest, when you offered to sell them for four centimes the spring of health and riches inexhaustible. It was necessary besides to explain the dangers of the bottle; and either people disbelieved the whole thing and laughed, or they thought the more of the darker part, became overcast with gravity, and drew away from Keawe and Kokua, as from persons who had dealings with the devil. So far from gaining ground, these two began to find they were avoided in the town; the children ran away from them screaming, a thing intolerable to Kokua; Catholics crossed themselves as they went by; and all persons began with one accord to disengage themselves from their advances.

Depression fell upon their spirits. They would sit at night in their new house, after a day's weariness, and not exchange one word, or the silence would be broken by Kokua bursting suddenly into sobs. Sometimes they would pray together; sometimes they would have the bottle out upon the floor, and sit all evening watching how the shadow hovered in the midst. At such times they would be afraid to go to rest. It was long ere slumber came to them, and, if either dozed off, it would be to wake and find the other silently weeping in the dark, or, perhaps, to wake alone, the other having fled from the house and the neighbourhood of that bottle, and to pace under the bananas in the little garden, or to wander on the beach by moonlight.

One night it was so when Kokua awoke. Keawe was gone. She felt in the bed, and his place was cold. Then fear fell upon her, and she sat up in bed. A little moonshine filtered through the shutters. The room was bright, and she could spy the bottle on the floor. Outside it blew high, the great trees of the avenue cried aloud, and the fallen leaves rattled in the verandah. In the midst of this Kokua, was aware of another sound; whether of a beast or of a man she could scarce tell, but it was as sad as death, and cut her to the soul. Softly she arose, set the door ajar, and looked forth into the moonlit yard. There, under the bananas, lay Keawe, his mouth in the dust, and as he lay he moaned.

It was Kokua'a first thought to run forward and console him; her second potently withheld her. Keawe had borne himself before his wife like a brave man; it became her little in the hour of weakness to intrude upon his shame. With the thought she drew back into the house.

'Heaven!' she thought, 'how careless have I been—how weak! It is he, not I, that stands in this eternal peril; it was he, not I, that took the curse upon his soul. It is for my sake and for the love of a creature of so little worth and such poor help, that he now beholds so close to him the flames of hell-ay, and smells the smoke of it, lying without there in the wind and moonlight. Am I so dull of spirit that never till now I have surmised my duty or have I seen it before and turned aside? But now, at least, I take up my soul in both the hands of my affection; now I say farewell to the white steps of heaven and the waiting faces of my friends. A love for a love, and let mine be equalled with Keawe's! A soul for a soul, and be it mine to perish!'

She was a deft woman with her hands, and was soon apparelled. She took in her hands the change—the precious centimes they kept ever at their side; for this coin is little used, and they had made provision at a Government office. When she was forth in the avenue clouds came on the wind, and the moon was blackened. The town slept, and she knew not whither to turn till she heard one coughing in the shadow of the trees.

'Old man,' said Kokua, 'what do you here abroad in the cold night?'

The old man could scarce express himself for coughing, but she made out that he was old and poor, and a stranger in the island.

'Will you do me a service?' said Kokua. 'As one stranger to another, and as an old man to a young woman, will you help a daughter of Hawaii?'

'Ah,' said the old man. 'So you are the witch from the Eight Islands, and even my old soul you seek to entangle. But I have heard of you, and defy your wickedness.'

'Sit down here,' said Kokua, 'and let me tell you a tale.' And she told him the story of Keawe from the beginning to the end.

'And now,' said she, 'I am his wife, whom he bought with his soul's welfare. And what should I do? If I went to him myself and offered to buy it, he would refuse. But if you go, he will sell it eagerly; I will await you here; you will buy it for four centimes, and I will buy it again for three. And the Lord strengthen a poor girl!'

'If you meant falsely,' said the old man, 'I think God would strike you dead.'

'He would!' cried Kokua. 'Be sure he would. I could not be so treacherous—God would not suffer it.'

'Give me the four centimes and await me here,' said the old man.

Now, when Kokua stood alone in the street, her spirit died. The wind roared in the trees, and it seemed to her the rushing of flames of hell; the shadows tossed in the light of the street lamp, and they seemed to her the snatching hands of evil ones. If she had had the strength, she must have run away, and if she had had the breath she must have screamed aloud; but in truth she could do neither, and stood and trembled in the avenue, like an affrighted child.

Then she saw the old man returning, and he had the bottle in his hand.

'I have done your bidding,' said he. 'I left your husband weeping like a child; tonight he will sleep easy.' And he held the bottle forth.

'Before you give it me,' Kokua panted, 'take the good with the evil—ask to be delivered from your cough.'

'I am an old man,' replied the other, 'and too near the gate of the grave to take a favour from the devil.—But what is this? Why do you not take the bottle? Do you hesitate?'

'Not hesitate!' cried Kokua. 'I am only weak. Give me a moment. It is my hand resists, my flesh shrinks back from the accursed thing. One moment only!'

The old man looked upon Kokua kindly. 'Poor child!' said he, 'you fear; your soul misgives you. Well, let me keep it. I am old, and can never more be happy in this world, and as for the next—'

'Give it me!' gasped Kokua. 'There is your money. Do you think I am so base as that? Give me the bottle.'

'God bless you, child,' said the old man.

Kokua concealed the bottle under her holoku. said farewell to the old man, and walked off along the avenue, she cared not whither. For all roads were now the same to her, and led equally to hell. Sometimes she walked, and sometimes ran; sometimes she screamed out loud in the night, and, sometimes lay by the wayside in the dust and wept. All that she had heard of hell came back to her; she saw the flames blaze, and she smelt the smoke, and her flesh withered on the coals.

Near day she came to her mind again, and returned to the house. It was even as the old man said—Keawe slumbered like a child. Kokua stood and gazed upon his face.

'Now, my husband,' said she, 'it is your turn to sleep. When you wake it will be your turn to sing and laugh. But for poor Kokua, alas! that meant no evil—for poor Kokua, no more sleep, no more singing, no more delight, whether in earth or heaven.'

With that she lay down in the bed by his side, and her misery was so extreme that she fell in a deep slumber instantly.

Late in the morning her husband woke her and gave her the good news. It seemed he was silly with delight, for he paid no heed to her distress, ill though she dissembled it. The words stuck in her mouth, it mattered not; Keawe did the speaking. She ate not a bite, but who was to observe it? for Keawe cleared the dish. Kokua saw and heard him, like some strange thing in a dream; there were times when she forgot or doubted, and put her hands to her brow; to know herself doomed and hear her husband babble seemed so monstrous.

All the while Keawe was eating and talking, and planning the time of their return, and thanking her for saving him, and fondling her, and calling her the true helper after all. He laughed at the old man that was fool enough to buy that bottle.

'A worthy old man he seemed,' Keawe said. 'But no one can judge by appearances. For why did the old reprobate require the bottle?'

'My husband,' said Kokua humbly, 'his purpose may have been good.'

Keawe laughed like an angry man.

'Fiddle-de-dee!' cried Keawe. 'An old rogue, I tell you, and an old ass to boot. For the bottle was hard enough to sell at four centimes; and at three it will be quite impossible. The margin is not broad enough, the thing begins to smell of scorching—brrr!' said he, and shuddered. 'It is true I bought it myself at a cent, when I knew not there were smaller coins. I was a fool for my pains; there will never be found another: and whoever has that bottle now will carry it to the pit.'

'O my husband!' cried Kokua. 'Is it not a terrible thing to save oneself by the eternal ruin of another? It seems to me I could not laugh. I would be humbled. I would be filled with melancholy. I would pray for the poor holder.'

Then Keawe, because he felt the truth of what she said, grew the more angry. 'Heighty-teighty!' cried he. 'You may be filled with melancholy if you please. It is not the mind of a good wife. If you thought at all of me you would sit shamed.'

Thereupon he went out, and Kokua was alone.

What chance had she to sell that bottle at two centimes? None, she perceived. And if she had any, here was her husband hurrying her away to a country where there was nothing lower than a cent. And here—on the morrow of her sacrifice—was her husband leaving her and blaming her.

She would not even try to profit by what time she had, but sat in the house, and now had the bottle out and viewed it with unutterable fear, and now, with loathing, hid it out of sight.

By and by Keawe came back, and would have her take a drive.

'My husband, I am ill,' she said. 'I am out of heart. Excuse me, I can take no pleasure.'

Then was Keawe more wroth than ever. With her, because he thought she was brooding over the case of the old man; and with himself, because he thought she was right, and was ashamed to be so happy.

'This is your truth,' cried he, 'and this your affection! Your husband is just saved from eternal ruin, which he encountered for the love of you—and you can take no pleasure! Kokua, you have a disloyal heart.'

He went forth again furious, and wandered in the town all day. He met friends, and drank with them; they hired a carriage and drove into the country, and there drank again. All the time Keawe was ill at ease, because he was taking this pastime while his wife was sad, and because he knew in his heart that she was more right than he; and the knowledge made him drink the deeper.

Now there was an old brutal Haole drinking with him, one that had been a boatswain of a whaler, a runaway, a digger in gold mines, a convict in prisons. He had a low mind and a foul mouth; he loved to drink and to see others drunken; and he pressed the glass upon Keawe. Soon there was no more money in the company.

'Here, you!' says the boatswain, 'you are rich, you have been always saying. You have a bottle or some foolishness.'

'Yes,' says Keawe, 'I am rich; I will go back and get some money from my wife, who keeps it.'

'That's a bad idea, mate,' said the boatswain. 'Never you trust a petticoat with dollars. They're all false as water; you keep an eye on her.'

Now this word stuck in Keawe's mind; for he was muddled with what he had been drinking.

'I should not wonder but she was false, indeed,' thought he. 'Why else should she be so cast down at my release? But I will show her I am not the man to be fooled. I will catch her in the act.'

Accordingly, when they were back in town, Keawe bade the boatswain wait for him at the corner, by the old calaboose, and went forward up the avenue alone to the door of his house. The night had come again; there was a light within, but never a sound; and Keawe crept about the corner, opened the back-door softly, and looked in.

There was Kokua on the floor, the lamp at her side; before her was a milk-white bottle, with a round belly and a long neck; and as she viewed it, Kokua wrung her hands.

A long time Keawe stood and looked in the doorway. At first he was struck stupid; and then fear fell upon him that the bargain had been made amiss, and the bottle had come back to him as it came at San Francisco; and at that his knees were loosened, and the fumes of the wine departed from his head like mists off a river in the morning. And then he had another thought; and it was a strange one, that made his cheeks to burn.

'I must make sure of this,' thought he.

So he closed the door, and went softly round the corner again, and then came noisily in, as though he were but now returned. And, lo! by the time he opened the front door no bottle was to be seen; and Kokua sat in a chair and started up like one awakened out of sleep.

'I have been drinking all day and making merry,' said Keawe. 'I have been with good companions, and now I only come back for money, and return to drink and carouse with them again.'

Both his face and voice were as stern as judgment, but Kokua was too troubled to observe.

'You do well to use your own, my husband,' said she, and her words trembled.

'O, I do well in all things,' said Keawe, and he went straight to the chest and took out money. But he looked besides in the corner where they kept the bottle, and there was no bottle there.

At that the chest heaved upon the floor like a sea-billow, and the house span about him like a wreath of smoke, for he saw he was lost now, and there was no escape. 'It is what I feared,' he thought. 'It is she who has bought it.'

And then he came to himself a little and rose up; but the sweat streamed on his face as thick as the rain and as cold as the well-water.

'Kokua,' said he, 'I said to you today what ill became me. Now I return to carouse with my jolly companions,' and at that he laughed a little quietly. 'I will take more pleasure in the cup if you forgive me.'

She clasped his knees in a moment; she kissed his knees with flowing tears.

'O,' she cried, 'I asked but a kind word!'

'Let us never one think hardly of the other,' said Keawe, and was gone out of the house.

Now, the money that Keawe had taken was only some of that store of centime pieces they had laid in at their arrival. It was very sure he had no mind to be drinking. His wife had given her soul for him, now he must give his for hers; no other thought was in the world with him.

At the corner, by the old calaboose, there was the boatswain waiting.

'My wife has the bottle,' said Keawe, 'and, unless you help me to recover it, there can be no more money and no more liquor tonight.'

'You do not mean to say you are serious about that bottle?' cried the boatswain.

'There is the lamp,' said Keawe. 'Do I look as if I was jesting?'

'That is so,' said the boatswain. 'You look as serious as a ghost.'

'Well, then,' said Keawe, 'here are two centimes; you must go to my wife in the house, and offer her these for the bottle, which (if I am not much mistaken) she will give you instantly. Bring it to me here, and I will buy it back from you for one; for that is the law with this bottle, that it still must be sold for a less sum. But whatever you do, never breathe a word to her that you come from me.'

'Mate, I wonder are you making a fool of me?' asked the boatswain.

'It will do you no harm if I am,' returned Keawe.

'That is so, mate,' said the boatswain.

'And if you doubt me,' added Keawe, 'you can try. As soon as you are clear of the house, wish to have your pocket full of money, or a bottle of the best rum, or what you please, and you will see the virtue of the thing.'

'Very well, Kanaka,' says the boatswain. 'I will try; but if you are having your fun out of me, I will take my fun out of you with a belaying-pin.'

So the whaler-man went off up the avenue; and Keawe stood and waited. It was near the same spot where Kokua had waited the night before; but Keawe was more resolved, and never faltered in his purpose; only his soul was bitter with despair.

It seemed a long time he had to wait before he heard a voice singing in the darkness of the avenue. He knew the voice to be the boatswain's; but it was strange how drunken it appeared upon a sudden.

Next, the man himself came stumbling into the light of the lamp. He had the devil's bottle buttoned in his coat; another bottle was in his hand; and even as he came in view he raised it to his mouth and drank.

'You have it,' said Keawe. 'I see that.'

'Hands off!' cried the boatswain, jumping back. 'Take a step near me and I'll smash your mouth. You thought you could make a cat's-paw of me, did you?'

'What do you mean?' cried Keawe.

'Mean?' cried the boatswain, 'This is a pretty good bottle, this is; that's what I mean. How I got it for two centimes I can't make out; but I'm sure you shan't have it for one.'

'You mean you won't sell it?' gasped Keawe.

'No, *sir*!' cried the boatswain. 'But I'll give you a drink of the rum, if you like.'

'I tell you,' said Keawe, 'the man who has that bottle goes to hell.'

'I reckon I'm going anyway,' returned the sailor; 'and this bottle's the best thing to go with I've struck yet. No, sir!' he cried again, 'this is my bottle now, and you can go and fish for another.'

'Can this be true?' Keawe cried. 'For your own sake, I beseech you, sell it me!'

'I don't value any of your talk,' replied the boatswain. 'You thought I was a flat; now you see I'm not; and there's an end. If you won't have a swallow of the rum I'll have one myself. Here's your health, and good-night to you!'

So off he went down the avenue towards town, and there goes the bottle out of the story.

But Keawe ran to Kokua light as the wind; and great was their joy that night; and great, since then, has been the peace of all their days in the Bright House.

Robert McLellan

THE CAT

Robert McLellan's 'Linmill' stories are named after the place where he was born in 1907 at Kirkfieldbank in Lanarkshire. Brought up on a farm, McLellan has captured the living dialect of the rural West of Scotland in poetry, prose and drama. His plays are now largely neglected as the taste for historical Scots dialogue has waned. Even for the original production of his most famous work, *Jamie the Saxt* (1937), it was difficult to cast actors sufficiently fluent in the old language.

With strong Arran connections, McLellan wrote several books on the island and its history. His poems include 'Arran Burn', written for television, and a radio piece for seven voices, called 'Sweet Largie Bay'. In fact many of his short stories were broadcast on radio and 'The Cat', taken from *Linmill and Other Stories* (1977), has a strong, relaxed style which is ideal for live reading. McLellan allows his chosen language to extend across its full musical range as the narrator offers what seems' at first, to be a nostalgic tale from a happy rural boyhood.

The Cat

THERE WERE three grocers' shops in Kirkfieldbank, but I was best acquant wi Mistress Yuill's. It had been a guid shop at ae time, clean as a new preen and weill stockit, and when I was a laddie haurdly auld eneuch for the schule I could hae thocht o naething better than the chance o cawin in wi a bawbee. It wasna juist for what ye could buy, but for the sicht and smell o it. She selt gey nearly everything ye could think o, frae paraffin and cheese to weekly papers and tacketty buits, and ye could hae spent a haill efteernune peerin into aw the odd neuks at the faur end o the coonter, sniffin yer fill.

As time gaed bye, though, Mistress Yuill grew less able, and syne began to turn blin, and the last time I had cawed in the shop had been a fair disgrace, though the puir auld craitur couldna help it, nae dout. My first look at the winnock had gart me woner, for at ae end there was an auld grey cat sittin on a box o kippers, and at the tither a wheen sticks a gundie that the sun had meltit into ae big stickie mess.

I had come that day to Linmill for my simmer holiday, though, and Mistress Yuill's had aye been pairt o it, sae I didna let the winnock keep me oot. I liftit the sneck and pusht the door open.

The bell didna ping, and that was new tae. It gied a clatter like a pat lid. It was lood eneuch, for aw that, to hae brocht her forrit, but for a while there was nae sign o her, and I had rowth o time to hae a guid look roun.

It wasna plaisint. The flair was dirty and the coonter a fair clutter. Naething was fresh. The butter stank and the cheese was mouldie, and there was an auld ham-end aside the scales sae thick wi big blue flees that ye could haurdly see it. The papers, weeks auld by the look o them, were aw markit. At first I thocht the cat had dune it, and the marks o its pads were on them shair eneuch, but on a closer look I foun finger-marks, hunders o them; and no juist on the papers. Aw over the coonter, aw ower the haill shop, there were fingermarks, creeshie, flourie and aw sorts; and there was a look aboot them that wasna cannie.

The auld grey cat rase aff the kippers and cam in frae the winnock, slinkin alang wi its tail up, rubbin its backside on everything it passed and purrin like a kettle on the beyl. I followed its een and a cauld shiver cam ower me. Mistress Yuill had come forrit, hoo I dinna ken, and was feelin her wey alang the coonter, layin her hands on this and that, sweeties, puddens, papers and aw, and her blank blae een were like the shutters o a toom hoose.

'Ay?'

I stude like a gommeril. I could think o naething to ask for. The cat pat its back up and spat in my face.

'Ay?'

'A pair o whangs.'

It was aw I could think that wadna be foustie. They wad dae for my grandfaither.

The whangs were hinging frae a nail on a post that took the wecht o the upstairs flair. She felt alang the coonter for her knife, pawin the papers, and syne for the post, pawin the sweeties and puddens again. She ran her fingers ower the wangs to fin the ends o them. She cut aff twa.

'A penny.'

I pat the penny on the coonter and turnt to rin.

'Haud on,' she said.

She fingert the penny and let it drap on the coonter, listenin for the ring. It was a guid ane, nearly new. She felt for it, foun it, and haundit me the whangs.

'What is it?

I couldna speak. Her een didna alter, but she soundit gey bitter.

'Ye're gey blate the day, Rab. Did ye think I wadna ken ye?'

Still I could say naething.

'Whan did ye stert usin whangs?'

'They're for my grandfaither.'

'Ay ay. Ye arena the first o the laddies to stop buyin sweeties.'

I backit and fell ower a pail. The cat lowpit doun aff the coonter and spat in my face again. I ran for the door.

I gied her shop the bye frae that day on, though whan my grandfaither drave me to Kirkfieldbank I couldna help but pass it, and ilka time I spied the winnock I grued at the sicht o the cat.

It was aboot twa months efter, whan the strawberries were bye and the blae plooms were turnin ripe, that I drave wi my grandfaither to Lanark to the Cattle Show. On oor wey through Kirkfieldbank he lat me haud the reyns, sae I didna look roun muckle except mebbe to see if the folk were watchin me, but as we passed Mistress Yuill's I gied a keek for the cat, for I couldna get it oot o my mind. I lay wauken aw nicht, whiles, thinkin o it, and aye whaun I foun mysell alane in the daurk I could see the wee nerra slits o its glintin green een.

The cat wasna there, or if it was it couldna be seen, for the shop was shuttert.

'Is it the hauf day, grandfaither?'

'Na.'

'Mistress Yuill's shop's shut.'

'Ay.'

'Is she no weill?'

'That's richt.'

'What's wrang wi her?'

'Naething.'

'There maun be something wrang if she's no weill.'

'Ay, there's something.'

'What is it?'

'She's deid, but dinna speak aboot it.'

'What wey that?'

'Dinna heed. Keep yer ee on the horse or I'll hae to tak the reyns mysell.'

That was eneuch. I didna press him. But the neist day, whan I was doun at the fute o the bottom orchard haein a look at the blae plooms, I met my kizzen Jockie, and he telt me his wey o it.

Aboot a fortnicht syne Mistress Yuill had grown sae desperate that she had peyed a laddie to come in and help her. I kent the laddie weill, for his mither had poued strawberries at Linmill. She didna pey him muckle, Mistress Yuill, but aw he had to dae was soop the flair and redd things up, and watch that naebody gied her a penny for a hauf-croun. He ran errands, tae, but there couldna hae been mony, for up to that she had sent oot the messages by a laddie frae the schule, efter fower o'clock.

Noo this laddie, Will MacPherson was his name, had watchit Mistress Yuill, day in day oot, till he foun oot whaur she hid the till key. She didna tak it hame, for she had a son bidin wi' her, a deil for drink.

Then, ae daurk wat windy nicht, whan the Kirkfieldbank folk were sleepin, and there was nae soun bune the blatter o the wind and rain and the swish o Clyde watter, he had creepit roun to the shop back and sclimmed up on to a shed there. Frae the shed rufe he was able to wriggle up the sclaits o the shop itsell, and in the end he won to the skylicht abune the flair upstairs. There was a gey drap doun, but he maun hae managed it, for he foun the till key and filled his pooches wi siller, as muckle as there was, and syne wi cigarettes and sweeties, though hoo he could hae stamacked the sweeties I dinna ken. Then he tried to fin his wey oot.

The skylicht was ower heich to grip frae the flair, sae he stude a chair aneth it and sclimmed up on to that. Still he couldna grip it, it seems, and he sclimmed up on to the chair back. It fell whan he tried that, as ye wad hae thocht, but it maun hae served his turn, for he was able to pou himsell pairtly through. That was as faur as he gat, for to mak room for himsell he had putten the skylicht richt back on the sclaits, whaur it couldna be fastened.

The wind brocht it bash ower his heid.

The neist mornin Mistress Yuill gaed alang to the shop, and likely she missed him, and whether she gaed up the stair for something she keepit there, or whether she had second sicht like the lave o blin folk, naebody could say, but up the stair she gaed. She couldna hae seen the laddie, that was certain, sae she maun hae felt him wi her haunds.

He was hingin by the chin frae the skylicht, wi his airms stickin up oot through it.

She didna gang hame that nicht at her richt time, and her son didna bother, but a neibor that aye had her kettle beylin gat worrit, and gaed alang to the shop. The meenit she opened the door the cat flew at her. She gat aff wi a scart or twa and gaed for Galbraith, the polis. They had to throw a tattie bag ower it afore they could win in, and whan they gaed upstairs they foun Will MacPherson, wi Mistress Yuill on the flair at his feet. The shock had been ower muckle for her.

That was the story I heard frae my kizzen Jockie, but it wasna the trith. He hadna been telt richt himsell.

I gat the trith frae my faither, whan I was aulder, at Tam Baxter's funeral. Tam Baxter had been ane o the men to gang in wi Galbraith.

The laddie hadna filled his pooches wi siller at aw. He hadna haen the chance. Whan they had foun him hingin they had haurdly kent him. His claes were aw bluid and his face was like butcher-meat.

The cat had gaen for him the meenit he had landit on the flair.

Sir Walter Scott

Though Walter Scott (1771–1832) is not primarily remembered as a short story writer, two of his stories are as satisfying as anything he wrote.

His novels and poems have popped in and out of literary, social and political fashion, but critics and readers have remained unanimous in their praise and admiration for 'The Two Drovers' and 'Wandering Willie's Tale'. 'These we can praise without reservation,' wrote David Cecil. 'They are the only two perfect things Scott ever wrote, they are among the glories of English literature. Considered in any of its three aspects, "Wandering Willie's Tale" is equally a masterpiece.'

'Wandering Willie's Tale' takes up most of Letter 11 in *Redgauntlet*, written between March and early June of 1824. It joins 'Tam O'Shanter' as a *tour de force* of Scots black art and mystery, which was one of the three aspects referred to by David Cecil. (The others were Scott's strong characterisation and the story's sense of historical evocation.) It is also unique by being entirely in vernacular. In fact his 'glory of English, literature' uses a memorable and vigorous Scots, skilfully matching the force and rhythms of a story told by a blind musician:

'When I am tired of scraping thairm or singing ballants, I whiles mak a tale serve the turn among the country bodies; . . . But this that I am gaun to tell you was a thing that befell in our ain house in my father's time. . . .'

He commenced his tale accordingly. . . .

Wandering Willie's Tale

Ye maun have heard of Sir Robert Redgauntlet of that Ilk, who lived in these parts before the dear years. The country will lang mind him; and our fathers used to draw breath thick if ever they heard him named. He was out wi' the Hielandmen in Montrose's time; and again he was in the hills wi' Glencairn in the saxteen hundred and fifty-twa; and sae when King Charles the Second came in, wha was in sic favour as the Laird of Redgauntlet? He was knighted at Lonon court, wi' the king's ain sword; and being a red-hot prelatist, he came down here, rampauging like a lion, with commissions of lieutenancy (and of lunacy, for what I ken) to put down a' the Whigs and Covenanters in the country. Wild wark they made of it; for the Whigs were as dour as the Cavaliers were fierce, and it was which should first tire the other. Redgauntlet was ay for the strong hand; and his name is kend as wide in the country as Claverhouse's or Tam Dalyell's. Glen, nor dargle, nor mountain, nor cave, could hide the puir hill-folk when Redgauntlet was out with bugle and bloodhound after them, as if they had been sae mony deer. And troth when they fand them, they didna mak muckle mair ceremony than a Hielandman wi' a roebuck—it was just, 'Will ye tak the test?'—if not, 'Make ready—present—fire!'—and there lay the recusant.

Far and wide was Sir Robert hated and feared. Men thought he had a direct compact with Satan—that he was proof against steel—and that bullets happed aff his buff-coat like hailstanes from a hearth—that he had a mear that would turn a hare on the side of Carrifra-gawns*—and muckle to the same purpose, of whilk mair anon. The best blessing they wared on him was, 'Deil scowp wi' Redgauntlet!' He wasna a bad master to his ain folk, though, and was weel aneugh liked by his tenants; and as for the lackies and troopers that raid out wi' him to the persecutions, as the Whigs caa'd those killing times, they wad hae drunken themsells blind to his health at ony time.

Now you are to ken that my gudesire lived on Redgauntlet's grund—they ca' the place Primrose Knowe. We had lived on the grund, and under the Redgauntlets, since the riding days, and lang before. It was a pleasant bit; and I think the air is callerer and fresher there than onywhere else in the country. It's a' deserted now; and I sat on the broken door-cheek three days since, and was glad I couldna see

* A precipitous side of a mountain in Moffatdale.

the plight the place was in; but that's a' wide o' the mark. There dwelt my gudesire, Steenie Steenson, a rambling, rattling chiel' he had been in his young days, and could play weel on the pipes; he was famous at 'Hoopers and Girders'—a' Cumberland couldna touch him at 'Jockie Lattin'—and he had the finest finger for the back-lilt between Berwick and Carlisle. The like o' Steenie wasna the sort that they made Whigs o'. And so he became a Tory, as they ca' it, which we now ca' Jacobites, just out of a kind of needcessity, that he might belang to some side or other. He had nae ill will to the Whig bodies, and liked little to see the blude rin, though, being obliged to follow Sir Robert in hunting and hoisting, watching and warding, he saw muckle mischief, and maybe did some, that he couldna avoid.

Now Steenie was a kind of favourite with his master, and kend a' the folks about the castle, and was often sent for to play the pipes when they were at their merriment. Auld Dougal MacCallum, the butler, that had followed Sir Robert through gude and ill, thick and thin, pool and stream, was specially fond of the pipes, an ay gae my gudesire his gude word wi' the laird; for Dougal could turn his master round his finger.

Weel, round came the Revolution, and it had like to have broken the hearts baith of Dougal and his master. But the change was not a'thegether sae great as they feared, and other folk thought for. The Whigs made an unco crawing what they wad do with their auld enemies, and in special wi' Sir Robert Redgauntlet. But there were ower mony great folks dipped in the same doings, to make a spick and span new warld. So Parliament passed it a' ower easy; and Sir Robert, bating that he was held to hunting foxes instead of Covenanters, remained just the man he was.* His revel was as loud, and his hall as weel lighted, as ever it had been, though maybe he lacked the fines of the nonconformists, that used to come to stock his larder and cellar; for it is certain he began to be keener about the rents than his tenants used to find him before, and they behoved to be prompt to the rent-day, or else the laird wasna pleased. And he was sic an awsome body, that naebody cared to anger him; for the oaths he swore, and the rage that he used to get into, and the looks that he put on, made men sometimes think him a devil incarnate.

Weel, my gudesire was nae manager—no that he was a very great misguider—but he hadna the saving gift, and he got twa terms' rent in arrear. He got the first brash at Whitsunday put ower wi' fair word and piping; but when Martinmas came, there was a summons

* The caution and moderation of King William III, and his principles of unlimited toleration, deprived the Cameronians of the opportunity they ardently desired, to retaliate the injuries which they had received during the reign of prelacy, and purify the land, as they called it, from the pollution of blood. They esteemed the Revolution, therefore, only a half measure, which neither comprehended the rebuilding the Kirk in its full splendour, nor the revenge of the death of the Saints on their persecutors.

from the grund-officer to come wi' the rent on a day preceese, or else Steenie behoved to flit. Sair wark he had to get the siller; but he was weel-freended, and at last he got the haill scraped thegether—a thousand merks—the maist of it was from a neighbour they ca'd Laurie Lapraik—a sly tod. Laurie had walth o' gear—could hunt wi' the hound and rin wi' the hare—and be Whig or Tory, saunt or sinner, as the wind stood. He was a professor in this Revolution warld, but he liked an orra sough of this warld, and a tune on the pipes weel aneugh at a bytime; and abune a', he thought he had gude security for the siller he lent my gudesire ower the stocking at Primrose Knowe.

Away trots my gudesire to Redgauntlet Castle wi' a heavy purse and a light heart, glad to be out of the laird's danger. Weel, the first thing he learned at the castle was, that Sir Robert had fretted himsell into a fit of the gout, because he did not appear before twelve o'clock. It wasna a'thegether for sake of the money, Dougal thought; but because he didna like to part wi' my gudesire aff the grund. Dougal was glad to see Steenie, and brought him into the great oak parlour, and there sat the laird his leesome lane, excepting that he had beside him a great, ill-favoured jackanape, that was a special pet of his; a cankered beast it was, and mony an ill-natured trick it played—ill to please it was, and easily angered—ran about the haill castle, chattering and yowling, and pinching, and biting folk, specially before ill weather, or disturbances in the state. Sir Robert caa'd it Major Weir, after the warlock that was burnt;* and few folk liked either the name or the conditions of the creature—they thought there was something in it by ordinar—and my gudesire was not just easy in mind when the door shut on him, and he saw himself in the room wi' naebody but the laird, Dougal Mac Callum, and the major, a thing that hadna chanced to him before.

Sir Robert sat, or, I should say, lay, in a great armed chair, wi' his grand velvet gown, and his feet on a cradle; for he had baith gout and gravel, and his face looked as gash and ghastly as Satan's. Major Weir sat opposite him, in a red laced coat, and the laird's wig on his head; and ay as Sir Robert girned wi' pain, the jackanape girned too, like a sheep's-head between a pair of tangs—an ill-faur'd, fearsome couple they were. The laird's buff-coat was hung on a pin behind him, and his broadsword and his pistols within reach; for he keepit up the auld fashion of having the weapons ready, and a horse saddled day and night, just as he used to do when he was able to loup on horseback, and away after ony of the hill-folk he could get speerings of. Some said it was for fear of the Whigs taking vengeance, but I judge it was just his auld custom—he wasna gien to fear onything. The rental-book, wi' its black cover and brass clasps, was lying beside him; and a book of sculduddry sangs was put betwixt the leaves, to keep it open at the place where it

* A celebrated wizard, executed at Edinburgh for sorcery and other crimes.

bore evidence against the Goodman of Primrose Knowe as behind the hand with his mails and duties. Sir Robert gave my gudesire a look, as if he would have withered his heart in his bosom. Ye maun ken he had a way of bending his brows, that men saw the visible mark of a horseshoe in his forehead, deep dinted, as if it had been stamped there.

'Are ye come light-handed, ye son of a toom whistle?' said Sir Robert. 'Zounds! if you are—'

My gudesire, with as gude a countenance as he could put on, made a leg, and placed the bag of money on the table wi' a dash, like a man that does something clever. The laird drew it to him hastily—'Is it all here, Steenie, man?'

'Your honour will find it right,' said my gudesire.

'Here, Dougal,' said the laird, 'gie Steenie a tass of brandy downstairs, till I count the siller and write the receipt.'

But they werena weel out of the room, when Sir Robert gied a yelloch that garr'd the castle rock. Back ran Dougal—in flew the livery-men—yell on yell gied the laird, ilk ane mair awfu' than the ither. My gudesire knew not whether to stand or flee, but he ventured back into the parlour, where a' was gaun hirdy-girdie—naebody to say 'come in', or 'gae out.' Terribly the laird roared for cauld water to his feet, and wine to cool his throat; and Hell, hell, hell, and its flames, was ay the word in his mouth. They brought him water, and when they plunged his swollen feet into the tub, he cried out it was burning; and folk say that it *did* bubble and sparkle like a seething cauldron. He flung the cup at Dougal's head, and said he had given him blood instead of burgundy; and, sure aneugh, the lass washed clotted blood aff the carpet the neist day. The jackanape they caa'd Major Weir, it jibbered and cried as if it was mocking its master; my gudesire's head was like to turn—he forgot baith siller and receipt, and downstairs he banged; but as he ran, the shrieks came faint and fainter; there was a deep-drawn shivering groan, and word gaed through the castle that the laird was dead.

Weel, away came my gudesire, wi' his finger in his mouth, and his best hope was that Dougal had seen the money-bag, and heard the laird speak of writing the receipt. The young laird, now Sir John, came from Edinburgh, to see things put to rights. Sir John and his father never gree'd weel. Sir John had been bred an advocate, and afterwards sat in the last Scots Parliament and voted for the Union, having gotten, it was thought, a rug of the compensations—if his father could have come out of his grave, he would have brained him for it on his awn hearthstane. Some thought it was easier counting with the auld rough knight than the fair-spoken young ane—but mair of that anon.

Dougal MacCallum, poor body, neither grat nor grained, but gaed about the house looking like a corpse, but directing, as was his duty, a' the order of the grand funeral. Now, Dougal looked ay waur and waur when night was coming, and was ay the last to gang to his bed, whilk was in a little round just opposite the chamber of dais, whilk his master occupied while he was living, and where he now lay in state, as they caa'd it, weel-a-day! The night before the funeral, Dougal could keep his awn counsel nae langer; he came doun with his proud spirit, and fairly asked auld Hutcheon to sit in his room with him for an hour. When they were in the round, Dougal took ae tass of brandy to himsell, and gave another to Hutcheon, and wished him all health and lang life, and said that, for himsell, he wasna lang for this world; for that, every night since Sir Robert's death, his silver call had sounded from the state chamber, just as it used to do at nights in his lifetime, to call Dougal to help to turn him in his bed. Dougal said that being alone with the dead on that floor of the tower (for naebody cared to wake Sir Robert Redgauntlet like another corpse) he had never daured to answer the call, but that now his conscience checked him for neglecting his duty; for, 'though death breaks service,' said MacCallum, 'it shall never break my service to Sir Robert; and I will answer his next whistle, so be you will stand by me, Hutcheon.'

Hutcheon had nae will to the wark, but he had stood by Dougal in battle and broil, and he wad not fail him at this pinch; so down the carles sat ower a stoup of brandy, and Hutcheon, who was something of a clerk, would have read a chapter of the Bible; but Dougal would hear naething but a blaud of Davie Lindsay, whilk was the waur preparation.

When midnight came, and the house was quiet as the grave, sure enough the silver whistle sounded as sharp and shrill as if Sir Robert was blowing it, and up got the twa auld serving-men, and tottered into the room where the dead man lay. Hutcheon saw aneugh at the first glance; for there were torches in the room, which showed him the foul fiend, in his ain shape, sitting on the laird's coffin! Ower he cowped as if he had been dead. He could not tell how lang he lay in a trance at the door, but when he gathered himself, he cried on his neighbour, and getting nae answer, raised the house, where Dougal was found lying dead within twa steps of the bed where his master's coffin was placed. As for the whistle, it was gaen anes and ay; but mony a time was it heard at the top of the house on the bartizan, and amang the auld chimneys and turrets where the howlets have their nests. Sir John hushed the matter up, and the funeral passed over without mair bogle-wark.

But when a' was ower, and the laird was beginning to settle his affairs, every tenant was called up for his arrears, and my gudesire for the full sum that stood against him in the rental-book. Weel, away he trots to the castle, to tell his story, and there he is introduced to Sir John, sitting in his father's chair, in deep mourning, with weepers and hanging cravat, and a small walking rapier by his side, instead of the auld broadsword that had a hundredweight of steel about it, what with blade, chape, and basket-hilt. I have heard their communing so often tauld over, that I almost think I was there myself, though I couldna be born at the time. (In fact, Alan, my companion mimicked, with a good deal of humour, the flattering, conciliating tone of the tenant's address, and the hypocritical melancholy of the laird's reply. His grandfather, he said, had, while he spoke, his eye fixed on the rental-book, as if it were a mastiff-dog that he was afraid would spring up and bite him.)

'I wuss ye joy, sir, of the head seat, and the white loaf, and the braid lairdship. Your father was a kind man to friends and followers; muckle grace to you, Sir John, to fill his shoon—his boots, I suld say, for he seldom wore shoon, unless it were muils when he had the gout.'

'Aye, Steenie,' quoth the laird, sighing deeply, and putting his napkin to his een, 'his was a sudden call, and he will be missed in the country; no time to set his house in order—weel prepared Godward, no doubt, which is the root of the matter—but left us behind a tangled hesp to wind, Steenie. Hem! hem! We maun go to business, Steenie; much to do, and little time to do it in.'

Here he opened the fatal volume. I have heard of a thing they call Doomsday Book—I am clear it has been a rental of back-ganging tenants.

'Stephen,' said Sir John, still in the same soft, sleekit tone of voice—'Stephen Stevenson, or Steenson, ye are down here for a year's rent behind the hand—due at last term.'

Stephen. 'Please your honour, Sir John, I paid it to your father.'

Sir John. 'Ye took a receipt, then, doubtless, Stephen; and can produce it?'

Stephen. 'Indeed I hadna time, an it like your honour; for nae sooner had I set doun the siller, and just as his honour, Sir Robert, that's gaen, drew it till him to count it, and write out the receipt, he was ta'en wi' the pains that removed him.'

'That was unlucky,' said Sir John, after a pause. 'But ye maybe paid it in the presence of somebody. I want but a *talis qualis* evidence, Stephen. I would go ower strictly to work with no poor man.'

Stephen. 'Troth, Sir John, there was naebody in the room but Dougal MacCallum the butler. But, as your honour kens, he has e'en followed his auld master.'

'Very unlucky again, Stephen,' said Sir John, without altering his voice a single note. 'The man to whom ye paid the money is dead—and the man who witnessed the payment is dead too—and the siller, which should have been to the fore, is neither seen nor heard tell of in the repositories. How am I to believe a' this?'

Stephen. 'I dinna ken, your honour; but there is a bit memorandum note of the very coins; for, God help me! I had to borrow out of twenty purses; and I am sure that ilka man there set down will take his grit oath for what purpose I borrowed the money.'

Sir John. 'I have little doubt ye *borrowed* the money, Steenie. It is the *payment* to my father that I want to have some proof of.'

Stephen. 'The siller maun be about the house, Sir John. And since your honour never got it, and his honour that was canna have taen it wi' him, maybe some of the family may have seen it.'

Sir John. 'We will examine the servants, Stephen; that is but reasonable.'

But lackey and lass, and page and groom, all denied stoutly that they had ever seen such a bag of money as my gudesire described. What was waur, he had unluckily not mentioned to any living soul of them his purpose of paying his rent. Ae quean had noticed something under his arm, but she took it for the pipes.

Sir John Redgauntlet ordered the servants out of the room, and then said to my gudesire, 'Now, Steenie, ye see ye have fair play; and, as I have little doubt ye ken better where to find the siller than ony other body, I beg, in fair terms, and for your own sake, that you will end this fasherie; for, Stephen, ye maun pay or flit.'

'The Lord forgie your opinion,' said Stephen, driven almost to his wit's end—'I am an honest man.'

'So am I, Stephen,' said his honour; 'and so are all the folks in the house, I hope. But if there be a knave amongst us, it must be he that tells the story he cannot prove.' He paused, and then added, mair sternly, 'If I understand your trick, sir, you want to take advantage of some malicious reports concerning things in this family, and particularly respecting my father's sudden death, thereby to cheat me out of the money, and perhaps take away my character, by insinuating that I have received the rent I am demanding. Where do you suppose this money to be? I insist upon knowing.'

My gudesire saw everything look so muckle against him, that he grew nearly desperate—however, he shifted from one foot to another, looked to every corner of the room, and made no answer.

'Speak out, sirrah,' said the laird, assuming a look of his father's, a very particular ane, which he had when he was angry—it seemed as if the wrinkles of his frown made that selfsame fearful shape of a horse's shoe in the middle of his brow—'Speak out, sir! I *will* know your thoughts;—do you suppose that I have this money?'

'Far be it frae me to say so,' said Stephen.

'Do you charge any of my people with having taken it?'

'I wad be laith to charge them that may be innocent,' said my gudesire; 'and if there be any one that is guilty, I have nae proof.'

'Somewhere the money must be, if there is a word of truth in your story,' said Sir John; 'I ask where you think it is—and demand a correct answer?'

'In hell, if you *will* have my thoughts of it,' said my gudesire, driven to extremity, 'in hell! with your father, his jackanape, and his silver whistle.'

Down the stairs he ran (for the parlour was nae place for him after such a word) and he heard the laird swearing blood and wounds behind him, as fast as ever did Sir Robert, and roaring for the bailie and the baron-officer.

Away rode my gudesire to his chief creditor (him they ca'd Laurie Lapraik) to try if he could make onything out of him; but when he tauld his story, he got but the worst word in his wame—thief, beggar and dyvour, were the saftest terms; and to the boot of these hard terms, Laurie brought up the auld story of his dipping his hand in the blood of God's saunts, just as if a tenant could have helped riding with the laird, and that a laird like Sir Robert Redgauntlet. My gudesire was, by this time, far beyond the bounds of patience, and, while he and Laurie were at deil speed the liars, he was wanchancie aneugh to abuse Lapraik's doctrine as weel as the man, ond said things that garr'd folks' flesh grue that heard them;—he wasna just himsell, and he had lived wi' a wild set in his day.

At last they parted, and my gudesire was to ride hame through the wood of Pitmurkie, that is a' fou of black firs, as they say. I ken the wood, but the firs may be black or white for what I can tell. At the entry of the wood there is a wild common, and on the edge of the common, a little lonely change-house, that was keepit then by an ostler-wife, they suld hae caa'd her Tibbie Faw, and there puir Steenie cried for a mutchkin of brandy, for he had had no refreshment the haill day. Tibbie was earnest wi' him to take a bite of meat, but he couldna think o't, nor would he take his foot out of the stirrup, and took off the brandy wholely at twa draughts, and named a toast at each:—the first was the memory of Sir Robert Redgauntlet, and might he never lie quiet in his grave till he had righted his poor bond-tenant; and the second was a health to Man's Enemy, if he would but get him back the pock of siller or tell him what came o't, for he saw the haill world was like to regard him as a thief and a cheat, and he took that waur than even the ruin of his house and hauld.

On he rode, little caring where. It was a dark night turned, and the trees made it yet darker, and he let the beast take its ain road through the wood; when all of a sudden, from tired and wearied that it was before, the nag began to spring and flee, and stend, that my gudesire could hardly keep the saddle. Upon the whilk, a horseman, suddenly riding up beside him, said, 'That's a mettle beast of yours, freend; will you sell him?' So saying, he touched the horse's neck with his riding-wand, and it fell into its auld neigh-ho of a stumbling trot. 'But his spunk's soon out of him, I think,' continued the stranger, 'and that is like mony a man's courage, that thinks he wad do great things till he come to the proof.'

My gudesire scarce listened to this, but spurred his horse, with 'Gude e'en to you, freend.'

But it's like the stranger was ane that doesna lightly yield his point; for, ride as Steenie liked, he was ay beside him at the selfsame pace. At last my gudesire, Steenie Steenson, grew half angry, and, to say the truth, half feared.

'What is it that ye want with me, freend?' he said. 'If ye be a robber, I have nae money; if ye be a leal man, wanting company, I have nae heart to mirth or speaking; and if ye want to ken the road, I scarce ken it mysell.'

'If you will tell me your grief,' said the stranger, 'I am one that, though I have been sair miscaa'd in the world, am the only hand for helping my freends.'

So my gudesire, to ease his ain heart, mair than from any hope of help, told him the story from beginning to end.

'It's a hard pinch,' said the stranger; 'but I think I can help you.'

'If you could lend the money, sir, and take a lang day—I ken nae other help on earth,' said my gudesire.

'But there may be some under the earth,' said the stranger. 'Come, I'll be frank wi' you; I could lend you the money on bond, but you would maybe scruple my terms. Now, I can tell you, that your auld laird is disturbed in his grave by your curses, and the wailing of your family, and if ye daur venture to go to see him, he will give you the receipt.'

My gudesire's hair stood on end at this proposal, but he thought his companion might be some humoursome chield that was trying to frighten him, and might end with lending him the money. Besides, he was bauld wi' brandy, and desperate wi' distress; and he said he had courage to go to the gate of hell, and a step farther, for that receipt. The stranger laughed.

Weel, they rode on through the thickest of the wood, when, all of a sudden, the horse stopped at the door of a great house; and, but that he knew the place was ten miles off, my father would have thought he was at Redgauntlet Castle. They rode into the outer courtyard, through the muckle faulding yetts and aneath the auld portcullis; and the whole front of the house was lighted, and there were pipes and fiddles, and as much dancing and deray within as used to be at Sir Robert's house at Pace and Yule, and such high seasons. They lap off, and my gudesire, as seemed to him, fastening his horse to the very ring he had tied him to that morning, when he gaed to wait on the young Sir John.

'God!' said my gudesire, 'if Sir Robert's death be but a dream!'

He knocked at the ha' door just as he was wont and his auld acquaintance, Dougal MacCallum—just after his wont, too—came to open the door, and said, 'Piper Steenie, are ye there, lad? Sir Robert has been crying for you.'

My gudesire was like a man in a dream—he looked for the stranger, but he was gane for the time. At last he just tried to say, 'Ha! Dougal Driveower, are ye living? I thought ye had been dead.'

'Never fash yoursell wi' me,' said Dougal, 'but look to yoursell; and see ye tak naething frae ony body here, neither meat, drink, or siller, except just the receipt that is your ain.'

So saying, he led the way out through halls and trances that were weel kend to my gudesire, and into the auld oak parlour; and there was as much singing of profane sangs, and birling of red wine, and speaking blasphemy and sculduddry, as had ever been in Redgauntlet Castle when it was at the blithest.

But, Lord take us in keeping, what a set of ghastly revellers they were that sat around that table! My gudesire kend mony that had long before gane to their place, for often had he piped to the most part in the hall of Redgauntlet. There was the fierce Middleton, and the dissolute Rothes, and the crafty Lauderdale; and Dalyell, with his bald head and a beard to his girdle; and Earlshall, with Cameron's blude on his hand; and wild Bonshaw, that tied blessed Mr Cargill's limbs till the blude sprung; and Dunbarton Douglas, the twice-turned traitor baith to country and king. There was the Bluidy Advocate MacKenyie, who, for his worldly wit and wisdom had been to the rest as a god. And there was Claverhouse, as beautiful as when he lived, with his long, dark, curled locks streaming down over his laced buff-coat, and his left hand always on his right spule-blade, to hide the wound that the silver bullet had made. He sat apart from them all, and looked at them with a melancholy, haughty countenance; while the rest hallooed, and sang, and laughed, that the room rang. But their smiles were fearfully contorted from time to time; and their laugh passed into such wild sounds as made my gudesire's very nails grow blue, and chilled the marrow in his banes.

They that waited at the table were just the wicked serving-men and troopers, that had done their work and cruel bidding on earth. There was the Lang Lad of the Nethertown, that helped to take Argyle; and the bishop's summoner, that they called the Deil's Rattle-bag; and the wicked guardsmen in their laced coats; and the savage Highland Amorites, that shed blood like water; and many a proud serving-man, haughty of heart and bloody of hand, cringing to the rich, and making them wickeder than they would be; grinding the poor to powder, when the rich had broken them to fragments. And mony, mony mair were coming and ganging, a' as busy in their vocation as if they had been alive.

Sir Robert Redgauntlet, in the midst of a' this fearful riot, cried, wi' a voice like thunder, on Steenie Piper to come to the board-head where he was sitting; his legs stretched out before him, and swathed up with flannel, with his holster pistols aside him, while the great broadsword rested against his chair, just as my gudesire had seen him the last time upon earth—the very cushion for the jackanape was close to him, but the creature itself was not there—it wasna its hour, it's likely; for he heard them say as he came forward, 'Is not the major come yet?' And another answered, 'The jackanapes will be here betimes the morn.' And when my gudesire came forward, Sir Robert, or his ghaist, or the deevil in his likeness, said, 'Weel, piper, hae ye settled wi' my son for the year's rent?'

With much ado my father gat breath to say that Sir John would not settle without his honour's receipt.

'Ye shall hae that for a tune of the pipes, Steenie,' said the appearance of Sir Robert—'Play us up "Weel hoddled, Luckie".'

Now this was a tune my gudesire learned frae a warlock, that heard it when they were worshipping Satan at their meetings, and my gudesire had sometimes played it at the ranting suppers in Redgauntlet Castle, but never very willingly; and now he grew cauld at the very name of it, and said, for excuse, he hadna his pipes wi' him.

'MacCallum, ye limb of Beelzebub,' said the fearfu' Sir Robert, 'bring Steenie the pipes that I am keeping for him!'

MacCallum brought a pair of pipes which might have served the piper of Donald of the Isles. But he gave my gudesire a nudge as he offered them; and looking secretly and closely, Steenie saw that the chanter was of steel, and heated to a white heat; so he had fair warning not to trust his fingers with it. So he excused himself again, and said he was faint and frightened, and had not wind aneugh to fill the bag.

'Then ye maun eat and drink, Steenie,' said the figure; 'for we do little else here; and it's ill speaking between a fou man and a fasting.'

Now these were the very words that the bloody Earl of Douglas said to keep the king's messenger in hand while he cut the head off MacLellan of Bombie, at the Threave Castle, and that put Steenie mair and mair on his guard. So he spoke up like a man, and said he came neither to eat, or drink, or make minstrelsy; but simply for his ain—to ken what was come o' the money he had paid, and to get a discharge for it; and he was so stout-hearted by this time that he charged Sir Robert for conscience-sake (he had no power to say the holy name) and as he hoped for peace and rest, to spread no snares for him, but just to give him his ain.

The appearance gnashed its teeth and laughed, but it took from a large pocket-book the receipt, and handed it to Steenie. 'There is your receipt, ye pitiful cur; and for the money, my dog-whelp of a son may go look for it in the Cat's Cradle.'

My gudesire uttered many thanks, and was about to retire when Sir Robert roared aloud, 'Stop, though, thou sack-doudling son of a whore! I am not done with thee. HERE we do nothing for nothing; and you must return on this very day twelvemonth, to pay your master the homage that you owe me for my protection.'

My father's tongue was loosed of a suddenty, and he said aloud, 'I refer mysell to God's pleasure, and not to yours.'

He had no sooner uttered the word than all was dark around him;

and he sank on the earth with such a sudden shock, that he lost both breath and sense.

How lang Steenie lay there, he could not tell; but when he came to himsell, he was lying in the auld kirkyard of Redgauntlet parochine just at the door of the family aisle, and the scutcheon of the auld knight, Sir Robert, hanging over his head. There was a deep morning fog on grass and gravestane around him, and his horse was feeding quietly beside the minister's twa cows. Steenie would have thought the whole was a dream, but he had the receipt in his hand, fairly written and signed by the auld laird; only the last letters of his name were a little disorderly, written like one seized with sudden pain.

Sorely troubled in his mind, he left that dreary place, rode through the mist to Redgauntlet Castle, and with much ado he got speech of the laird.

'Well, you dyvour bankrupt,' was the first word, 'have you brought me my rent?'

'No,' answered my gudesire, 'I have not; but I have brought your honour Sir Robert's receipt for it.'

'How, sirrah? Sir Robert's receipt! You told me he had not given you one.'

'Will your honour please to see if that bit line is right?'

Sir John looked at every line, and at every letter, with much attention; and at last, at the date, which my gudesire had not observed—'*From my appointed place*,' he read, '*this twenty-fifth of November*.'—'What!—That is yesterday!—Villain, thou must have gone to hell for this!'

'I got it from your honour's father—whether he be in heaven or hell, I know not,' said Steenie.

'I will delate you for a warlock to the Privy Council!' said Sir John, 'I will send you to your master, the devil, with the help of a tar-barrel and a torch!'

'I intend to delate mysell to the Presbytery,' said Steenie, 'and tell them all I have seen last night, whilk are things fitter for them to judge of than a borrel man like me.'

Sir John paused, composed himsell, and desired to hear the full history; and my gudesire told it him from point to point, as I have told it you—word for word, neither more nor less.

Sir John was silent again for a long time, and at last he said, very composedly, 'Steenie, this story of yours concerns the honour of many a noble family besides mine; and if it be a leasing-making, to keep yourself out of my danger, the least you can expect is to have a redhot iron driven through your tongue, and that will be as bad as scaulding your fingers wi' a redhot chanter. But yet it may be true, Steenie; and if the money cast up, I shall not know what to think of it. But where shall we find the Cat's Cradle? There are cats enough about the old house, but I think they kitten without the ceremony of bed or cradle.'

'We were best ask Hutcheon,' said my gudesire; 'he kens a' the odd corners about as weel as—another serving-man that is now gane, and that I wad not like to name.'

Aweel, Hutcheon, when he was asked, told them, that a ruinous turret, lang disused, next to the clock-house, only accessible by a ladder, for the opening was on the outside, and far above the battlements, was called of old the Cat's Cradle.

'There will I go immediately,' said Sir John; and he took (with what purpose, Heaven kens) one of his father's pistols from the hall-table, where they had lain since the night he died, and hastened to the battlements.

It was a dangerous place to climb, for the ladder was auld and frail, and wanted ane or twa rounds. However, up got Sir John, and entered at the turret-door, where his body stopped the only little light that was in the bit turret. Something flees at him wi' a vengeance, maist dang him back ower—bang gaed the knight's pistol, and Hutcheon, that held the ladder, and my gudesire that stood beside him, hears a loud skelloch. A minute after, Sir John flings the body of the jackanape down to them, and cries that the siller is fund, and that they should come up and help him. And there was the bag of siller sure aneugh, and mony orra things besides, that had been missing for mony a day. And Sir John, when he had riped the turret weel, led my gudesire into the dining-parlour, and took him by the hand and spoke kindly to him, and said he was sorry he should have doubted his word and that he would hereafter be a good master to him to make amends.

'And now, Steenie,' said Sir John, 'although this vision of yours tend, on the whole, to my father's credit, as an honest man, that he should, even after his death, desire to see justice done to a poor man like you, yet you are sensible that ill-dispositioned men might make bad constructions upon it, concerning his soul's health. So, I think, we had better lay the haill dirdum on that ill-deedie creature, Major Weir, and say naething about your dream in the wood of Pitmurkie. You had taken ower muckle brandy to be very certain about onything; and, Steenie, this receipt' (his hand shook while he held it out)—'it's but a queer kind of document, and we will do best, I think, to put it quietly in the fire.'

'Od, but for as queer as it is, it's a' the voucher I have for my rent,' said my gudesire, who was afraid, it may be, of losing the benefit of Sir Robert's discharge.

'I will bear the contents to your credit in the rental-book, and give you a discharge under my own hand,' said Sir John, 'and that on the spot. And, Steenie, if you can hold your tongue about this matter, you shall sit, from this term downward, at an easier rent.'

'Mony thanks to your honour,' said Steenie, who saw easily in what corner the wind was; 'doubtless I will be conformable to all your honour's commands; only I would willingly speak wi' some powerful minister on the subject, for I do not like the sort of soumons of appointment whilk your honour's father—'

'Do not call the phantom my father!' said Sir John, interrupting him.

'Weel, then, the thing that was so like him,' said my gudesire; 'he spoke of my coming back to see him this time twelvemonth, and it's a weight on my conscience.'

'Aweel, then,' said Sir John, 'if you be so much distressed in mind, you may speak to our minister of the parish; he is a douce man, regards the honour of our family, and the mair that he may look for some patronage from me.'

Wi' that, my father readily agreed that the receipt should be burnt, and the laird threw it into the chimney with his ain hand. Burn it would not for them, though; but away it flew up the lum, wi' a lang train of sparks at its tail, and a hissing noise like a squib.

My gudesire gaed down to the Manse, and the minister, when he had heard the story, said it was his real opinion that though my gudesire had gaen very far in tampering with dangerous matters, yet, as he had refused the devil's arles (for such was the offer of meat and drink) and had refused to do homage by piping at his bidding, he hoped, that if he held a circumspect walk hereafter, Satan could take little advantage by what was come and gane. And, indeed, my gudesire, of his ain accord, lang foreswore baith the pipes and the brandy—it was not even till the year was out, and the fatal day past, that he would so much as take the fiddle, or drink usquebaugh or tippeny.

Sir John made up his story about the jackanape as he liked himsell; and some believe till this day there was no more in the matter than the filching nature of the brute. Indeed, ye'll no hinder some to threap that it was nane o' the auld Enemy that Dougal and my gudesire saw in the laird's room, but only that wanchancy creature, the major, capering on the coffin; and that, as to the blawing on the laird's whistle that was heard after he was dead, the filthy brute could do that as weel as the laird himsell, if no better. But Heaven kens the truth, whilk first came out by the minister's wife, after Sir John and her ain gudeman were baith in the moulds. And then my gudesire, wha was failed in his limbs, but not in his judgement or memory—at least nothing to speak of—was obliged to tell the real narrative to his friends, for the credit of his good name. He might else have been charged for a warlock.

The shades of evening were growing thicker around us as my conductor finished his long narrative with this moral—'Ye see, birkie, it is nae chancy thing to tak a stranger traveller for a guide, when you are in an uncouth land.'

'I should not have made that inference,' said I. 'Your grandfather's adventure was fortunate for himself, whom it saved from ruin and distress; and fortunate for his landlord also, whom it prevented from committing a gross act of injustice.'

'Aye, but they had baith to sup the sauce o't sooner or later,' said Wandering Willie—'what was fristed wasna forgiven. Sir John died before he was much over threescore; and it was just like of a moment's illness. And for my gudesire, though he departed in fullness of life, yet there was my father, a yauld man of forty-five, fell down betwixt the stilts of his pleugh, and rase never again, and left nae bairn but me, a puir sightless, fatherless, motherless creature, could neither work nor want. Things gaed weel aneugh at first; for Sir Redwald Redgauntlet, the only son of Sir John, and the oye of auld Sir Robert, and, waes me! the last of the honourable house, took the farm aff our hands, and brought me into his household to have care of me. He liked music, and I had the best teachers baith England and Scotland could gie me. Mony a merry year was I wi' him; but waes me! he gaed out with other pretty men in the Forty-five—I'll say nae mair about it—My head never settled weel since I lost him; and if I say another word about it, deil a bar will I have the heart to play the night. 'Look out, my gentle chap,' he resumed in a different tone, 'ye should see the lights at Brokenburn Glen by this time.'

R. B. Cunninghame Graham

Joseph Conrad said, 'When I think of Cunninghame Graham, I feel as though I have lived all my life in a dark hole without seeing or knowing anything.' In George Bernard Shaw's opinion, 'He is an incredible personage. There are moments when I do not myself believe in his existence.'

Robert Bontine Cunninghame Graham (1852–1936), led a life which annoyed his contemporaries and friends alike. Amongst other things, he was a descendent of Robert the Bruce, a South American revolutionary, a Member of Parliament and a founder member of both the Independent Labour Party and the Scottish National Party, as well as an early supporter of the American Indians. He was beaten by the police in Trafalgar Square for asserting the right of free speech and frequently suspended from Parliament for demanding free education, a better deal for women, stronger trade unions, higher wages and a shorter working week.

'Don Roberto' travelled extensively through Europe, North Africa and the Americas, writing prolifically about his adventures as well as producing biography, eleven histories of Latin America and fourteen collections of short stories and sketches.

Cunninghame Graham's stories use a variety of locations and although his work often falls between story, sketch and reminiscence, his sense of irony and humanity control the narratives and allow both character and plot to develop naturally.

The Gold Fish

OUTSIDE THE little straw-thatched café in a small courtyard trellised with vines, before a miniature table painted in red and blue, and upon which stood a dome-shaped pewter teapot and a painted glass half filled with mint, sat Amarabat, resting and smoking hemp. He was of those whom Allah in his mercy (or because man in the Blad-Allah has made no railways) has ordained to run. Set upon the road, his shoes pulled up, his waistband tightened, in his hand a staff, a palm-leaf wallet at his back, and in it bread, some hemp, a match or two (known to him as el spiritus), and a letter to take anywhere, crossing the plains, fording the streams, struggling along the mountain-paths, sleeping but fitfully, a burning rope steeped in saltpetre fastened to his foot, he trotted day and night—unitiring as a camel, faithful as a dog. In Rabat as he sat dozing, watching the greenish smoke curl upwards from his hemp pipe, word came to him from the Khalifa of the town. So Amarabat rose, paid for his tea with half a handful of defaced and greasy copper coins, and took his way towards the white palace with the crenelated walls, which on the cliff, hanging above the roaring tide-rip, just inside the bar of the great river, looks at Salee. Around the horseshoe archway of the gate stood soldiers, wild, fierce-eyed, armed to the teeth, descendants, most of them, of the famed warriors whom Sultan Muley Ismail (may God have pardoned him!) bred for his service, after the fashion of the Carlylean hero Frederic; and Amarabat walked through them, not aggressively, but with the staring eyes of a confirmed hemp-smoker, with the long stride of one who knows that he is born to run, and the assurance of a man who waits upon his lord. Sometime he waited whilst the Khalifa dispensed what he thought justice, chaffered with Jewish pedlars for cheap European goods, gossiped with friends, looked at the antics of a dwarf, or priced a Georgian or Circassian girl brought with more care than glass by some rich merchant from the East. At last Amarabat stood in the presence, and the Khalifa, sitting upon a pile of cushions, playing with a Waterbury watch, a pistol and a Koran by his side, addressed him thus:

'Amarabat, son of Bjorma, my purpose is to send thee to Tafilet, where our liege lord the Sultan lies with his camp. Look upon this glass bowl made by the Kaffir, but clear as is the crystal of the rock; see how the light falls on the water, and the shifting colours that it makes, as when the Bride of the Rain stands in the heavens, after a shower in spring. Inside are seven gold fish, each scale as bright as letters in an Indian book. The

Christian from whom I bought them said originally they came from the Far East where the Djin-descended Jawi live, the little yellow people of the faith. That may be, but such as they are, they are a gift for kings. Therefore, take thou the bowl. Take it with care, and bear it as it were thy life. Stay not, but in an hour start from the town. Delay not on the road, be careful of the fish, change not their water at the muddy pool where tortoises bask in the sunshine, but at running brooks; talk not to friends, look not upon the face of woman by the way, although she were as a gazelle, or as the maiden who when she walked through the fields the sheep stopped feeding to admire. Stop not, but run through day and night, pass through the Atlas at the Glaui; beware of frost, cover the bowl with thine own haik; upon the other side shield me the bowl from the Saharan sun, and drink not of the water if thou pass a day athirst when toiling through the sand. Break not the bowl, and see the fish arrive in Tafilet, and then present them, with this letter, to our lord. Allah be with you, and his Prophet; go, and above all things see thou breakest not the bowl.' And Amarabat, after the manner of his kind, taking the bowl of gold fish, placed one hand upon his heart and said: 'Inshallah, it shall be as thou hast said. God gives the feet and lungs. He also gives the luck upon the road.'

So he passed out under the horeshoe arch, holding the bowl almost at arms' length so as not to touch his legs, and with the palmetto string by which he carried it, bound round with rags. The soldiers looked at him, but spoke not, and their eyes seemed to see far away, and to pass over all in the middle distance, though no doubt they marked the smallest detail of his gait and dress. He passed between the horses of the guard all standing nodding under the fierce sun, the reins tied to the cantles of their high red saddles, a boy in charge of every two or three: he passed beside the camels resting by the well, the donkeys standing dejected by the firewood they had brought: passed women, veiled white figures going to the baths; and passing underneath the lofty gateway of the town, exchanged a greeting with the half-mad, half-religious beggar just outside the walls, and then emerged upon the sandy road, between the aloe hedges, which skirts along the sea. So as he walked, little by little he fell into his stride; then got his second wind, and smoking now and then a pipe of hemp, began, as Arabs say, to eat the miles, his eyes fixed on the horizon, his stick stuck down between his shirt and back, the knob protruding over the left shoulder like the hilt of a two-handed sword. And still he held the precious bowl from Franquestan in which the golden fish swam to and fro, diving and circling in the sunlight, or flapped their tails to steady themselves as the water danced with the motion of his steps. Never before in his experience had he been charged with such a mission, never before been sent to stand before Allah's vicegerent upon earth. But still the strangeness of his business was what preoccupied him most. The fish like molten gold, the water to be changed only at running streams, the fish to be preserved from frost and sun; and then the bowl: had not the Khalifa said at the last, 'Beware, break not the bowl'? So it appeared to him that most undoubtedly a charm was in the fish and in the bowl, for who sends common fish on such a journey through the land? Then he resolved at any hazard to bring them safe and keep the bowl intact, and trotting onward, smoked his hemp, and wondered why he of all men should have had the luck to bear the precious gift. He knew he kept his law, at least as far as a poor man can keep it, prayed when he thought of prayer, or was assailed by terror in the night alone upon the plains; fasted in Ramadan, although most of his life was one continual fast; drank of the shameful but seldom, and on the sly, so as to give offence to no believer, and seldom looked upon the face of the strange women, Daughters of the Illegitimate, whom Sidna Mohammed himself has said, avoid. But all these things he knew were done by many of the faithful, and so he did not set himself up as of exceeding virtue, but rather left the praise to God, who helped his slave with strength to keep his law. Then left off thinking, judging the matter was ordained, and trotted, trotted over the burning plains, the gold fish dancing in the water as the miles melted and passed away.

Duar and Kasbah, castles of the Caids, Arabs' black tents, suddra zaribas, camels grazing—antediluvian in appearance—on the little hills, the muddy streams edged all along the banks with oleanders, the solitary horsemen holding their long and brass-hooped guns, like spears, the white-robed noiseless-footed travellers on the roads, the chattering storks upon the village mosques, the cow-birds sitting on the cattle in the fields—he saw, but marked not, as he trotted on. Day faded into night, no twilight intervening, and the stars shone out, Soheil and Rigel with Betelgeuse and Aldebaran, and the three bright lamps which the cursed Christians know as the Three Maries—called, he supposed, after the mother of their Prophet; and still he trotted on. Then by the side of a lone palm-tree springing up from a cleft in a tall rock, an island on the plain, he stopped to pray; and sleeping, slept but fitfully, the strangeness of the business making him wonder; and he who cavils over matters in the night can never rest, for thus the jackal and the hyena pass their nights talking and reasoning about the thoughts which fill their minds when men die with their faces covered in their haiks, and after prayer sleep. Rising after an hour or two and going to the nearest stream, he changed the water of his fish, leaving a little in the bottom of the bowl, and dipping with his brass drinking-cup into the stream for fear of accidents. He passed the Kasbah of el Daudi, passed the land of the Rahamna, accursed folk always in 'siba', saw the great snowy wall of Atlas rise, skirted Marakesh, the Kutubieh, rising first from the plain and sinking last from sight as he approached the mountains and left the great white city sleeping in the plain.

Little by little the country altered as he ran: cool streams for muddy rivers, groves of almond-trees, ashes and elms, with grape-vines binding them together as the liana binds the canella and the urunday in the dark forests of Brazil and Paraguay. At midday when the sun was at its height, when locusts, whirring through the air, sank in the dust as flying-fish sink in the waves, when palm-trees seem to nod their heads, and lizards are abroad drinking the heat and basking in the rays, when the dry air shimmers, and sparks appear to dance before the traveller's eye, and a thin, reddish dust lies on the leaves, on clothes of men, and upon every hair of horses' coats, he reached a spring. A river springing from a rock, or issuing after running underground, had formed a little pond. Around the edge grew bulrushes, great catmace, water-soldiers, tall arums and metallic-looking sedge-grass, which gave an air as of an outpost of the tropics lost in the desert sand. Fish played beneath the rock where the stream issued, flitting to and fro, or hanging suspended for an instant in the clear stream, darted into the dark recesses of the sides; and in the middle of the pond enormous tortoises, horrid and antediluvian-looking, basked with their backs awash or raised their heads to snap at flies, and all about them hung a dark and fetid slime.

A troop of thin brown Arab girls filled their tall amphoræ whilst washing in the pond. Placing his bowl of fish upon a jutting rock, the messenger drew near. 'Gazelles,' he said, 'will one of you give me fresh water for the Sultan's golden fish?' Laughing and giggling, the girls drew near, looked at the bowl, had never seen such fish. 'Allah is great; why do you not let them go in the pond and play a little with their brothers?' And Amarabat with a shiver answered, 'Play, let them play! and if they come not back my life will answer for it.' Fear fell upon the girls, and one advancing, holding the skirt of her long shift between her teeth to veil her face, poured water from her amphora upon the fish.

Then Amarabat, setting down his precious bowl, drew from his wallet a pomegranate and began to eat, and for a farthing buying a piece of bread from the women, was satisfied, and after smoking, slept, and dreamed he was approaching Tafilet; he saw the palm-trees rising from the sand; the gardens; all the oasis stretching beyond his sight; at the edge the Sultan's camp, a town of canvas, with the horses, camels, and the mules picketed, all in rows, and in the midst of the great 'duar' the Sultan's tent, like a great palace all of canvas, shining in the sun. All this he saw, and saw himself entering the camp, delivering up his fish, perhaps admitted to the sacred tent, or at least paid by a vizier as one who has performed his duty well. The slow match blistering his foot, he woke to find himself alone, the 'gazelles' departed, and the sun shining on the bowl, making the fish appear more magical, more wondrous, brighter, and more golden than before.

And so he took his way along the winding Atlas paths, and slept at Demnats, then, entering the mountains, met long trains of travellers going to the south. Passing through groves of chestnuts, walnut-trees, and hedges thick with blackberries and travellers' joy, he climbed through vineyards rich with black Atlas grapes, and passed the flat mud-built Berber villages nestling against the rocks. Eagles flew by and moufflons gazed at him from the peaks, and from the thickets of lentiscus and dwarf arbutus wild boars appeared, grunted, and slowly walked across the path, and still he climbed, the icy wind from off the snow chilling him in his cotton shirt, for his warm Tadla haik was long ago wrapped round the bowl to shield the precious fish. Crossing the Wad Ghadat, the current to his chin, his bowl of fish held in one hand, he struggled on. The Berber tribesmen at Tetsula and Zarkten, hard-featured, shaved but for a chin-tuft, and robed in their 'achnifs' with the curious eye woven in the skirt, saw he was a 'rekass', or thought the fish not worth their notice, so gave him a free road. Night caught him at the stone-built, antediluvian-looking Kasbah of the Glaui, perched in the eye of the pass, with the small plain of Teluet two thousand feet below. Off the high snow-peaks came a whistling wind, water froze solid in all the pots and pans, earthenware jars and bottles throughout the castle, save in the bowl which Amarabat, shivering and miserable, wrapped in his haik and held close to the embers, hearing the muezzin at each call to prayers; praying himself to keep awake so that his fish might live. Dawn saw him on the trail, the bowl wrapped in a woollen rag, and the fish fed with breadcrumbs, but himself hungry and his head swimming with want of sleep, with smoking 'kief', and with the bitter wind which from El Tisi N'Glaui flagellates the road. Right through the valley of Teluet he still kept on, and day and night still trotting, trotting on, changing his bowl almost instinctively from hand to hand, a broad leaf floating on the top to keep the water still, he left Agurzga, with its twin castles, Ghresat and Dads, behind. Then rapidly descending, in a day reached an oasis between Todghra and Ferkla, and rested at a village for the night. Sheltered by palm-trees and hedged round with cactuses and aloes, either to keep out thieves or as a symbol of the thorniness of life, the village lay, looking back on the white Atlas gaunt and mysterious, and on the other side towards the brown Sahara, land of the palm-tree (Belad-el-Jerid), the refuge of the true Ishmaelite; for in the desert, learning, good faith, and hospitality can still be found—at least, so Arabs say.

Orange and azofaifa trees, with almonds, sweet limes and walnuts, stood up against the waning light, outlined in the clear atmosphere almost so sharply as to wound the eye.

Around the well goats and sheep lay, whilst a girl led a camel round the Noria track; women sat here and there and gossiped with their tall earthenware jars stuck by the point into the ground, and waited for their turn, just as they did in the old times, so far removed from us, but which in Arab life is but as yesterday, when Jacob cheated Esau, and the whole scheme of Arab life was photographed for us by the writers of the Pentateuch. In fact, the self-same scene which has been acted every evening for two thousand years throughout North Africa, since the adventurous ancestors of the tribesmen of to-day left Hadrumut or Yemen, and upon which Allah looks down approvingly, as recognising that the traditions of his first recorded life have been well kept. Next day he trotted through the barren plain of Seddat, the Jibel Saghra making a black line on the horizon to the south. Here Berber tribes sweep in their razzias like hawks; but who would plunder a rekass carrying a bowl of fish? Crossing the dreary plain and dreaming of his entry into Tafilet, which now was almost in his reach not two days distant, the sun beating on his head, the water almost boiling in the bowl, hungry and footsore, and in the state betwixt waking and sleep into which those who smoke hemp on journeys often get, he branched away upon a trail leading towards the south. Between the oases of Todghra and Ferkla, nothing but stone and sand, black stones of yellow sand; sand, and yet more sand, and then again stretches of blackish rocks with a suddra bush or two, and here and there a colocynth, bitter and beautiful as love or life, smiling up at the traveller from amongst the stones. Towards midday the path led towards a sandy tract all overgrown with sandrac bushes and crossed by trails of jackals and hyenas, then it quite disappeared, and Amarabat waking from his dream saw he was lost. Like a good shepherd, his first thought was for his fish; for he imagined the last few hours of sun had made them faint, and one of them looked heavy and swam sideways, and the rest kept rising to the surface in an uneasy way. Not for a moment was Amarabat frightened, but looked about for some known landmark, and finding none started to go back on his trail. But to his horror the wind which always sweeps across the Sahara had covered up his tracks, and on the stony paths which he had passed his feet had left no prints. Then Amarabat, the first moments of despair passed by, took a long look at the horizon, tightened his belt, pulled up his slipper heels, covered his precious bowl with a corner of his robe, and started doggedly back upon the road he thought he traversed on the deceitful path. How long he trotted, what he endured, whether the fish died first, or if he drank, or faithful to the last, thirsting met death, no one can say. Most likely wandering in the waste of sandhills and of suddra bushes he stumbled on, smoking his hashish while it lasted, turning to Mecca at the time of prayer, and trotting on more feebly (for he was born to run), till he sat down beneath the sundried bushes where the Shinghiti on his Mehari found him dead beside the trail. Under a stunted sandarac tree, the head turned to the east, his body lay, swollen and distorted by the pangs of thirst, the tongue protruding rough as a parrot's, and beside him lay the seven golden fish, once bright and shining as the pure gold when the goldsmith pours it molten from his pot, but now turned black and bloated, stiff, dry, and dead. Life the mysterious, the mocking, the inscrutable, unseizable, the uncomprehended essence of nothing and of everything, had fled, both from the faithful messenger and from his fish. But the Khalifa's parting caution had been well obeyed, for by the tree, unbroken, the crystal bowl still glistened beautiful as gold, in the fierce rays of the Saharan sun.

James Hogg

At first sight James Hogg (1770–1835) would have seemed an unlikely rival for James Galt, Sir Walter Scott or any of the fashionable Edinburgh literati of their day. Unlettered until his early twenties, Hogg spent his youth labouring or shepherding on Border farms. Yet by the time he died at sixty-five his poetry, prose and essays had formed a body of work whose influence can still be felt in modern Scottish writing.

Born into an oral tradition, Hogg seems to have had a phenomenal capacity for remembering events, anecdotes and storytelling in general. His literary career began at the age of thirty-one, when he sent traditional ballads he had collected to Scott. Six years later he published a collection of his own ballads, and six years after that the appearance of *The Queen's Wake* meant that Hogg had arrived as a poet of stature.

He continued to work in verse, but also began to produce prose, drawing on a wealth of tales from his Border surroundings. He is best known today for his novel, *Confessions of a Justified Sinner* (1824), and although it was not well received in Scotland at the time, it remains one of the seminal works of European literature.

'Seeking the Houdy' first appeared in *Forget Me Not*, a fashionable literary London annual for women, and it finds Hogg once again adopting his deceptively ingenuous stance as narrator. Finding it difficult to sustain the language necessary to appeal to his polite lady readers, Hogg lapses into Scots mid-way through the story. The pace increases with the hero's confusion and while Hogg is in his element with such fantastic happenings, we should not miss the story's subtler implications of this tale of a man at odds with a world of female mysteries which he cannot understand.

Seeking the Houdy

THERE WAS a shepherd on the lands of Meggat-dale, who once set out riding with might and main, under cloud of night, for that most important and necessary personage in a remote and mountainous country, called by a different name in every country of the world, excepting perhaps Egypt and England; but by the Highlanders most expressively termed *bean-glhuine*, or *te the toctor*.

The mare that Robin rode was a black one, with a white face like a cow. She had a great big belly, a switch tail, and a back, Robin said, as sharp as a knife; but perhaps this part of the description was rather exaggerated. However, she was laziness itself personified, and the worst thing of all, her foal was closed in at home; for Robin had wiled the mare and foal into the bire with a piece of bread, which he did not give her after all, but put in his pocket in case of farther necessity: he then whipped a hair halter on the mare's head, and the straw sunks on her back, these being the only equipment within his reach; and it having cost Robin a great deal of trouble to get the foal into the bire, he now eyed him with an exulting, and at the same time a malicious, look. 'Ye mischievous rascal,' said he, 'I think I have you now; stand you there an' chack flees till I come back to teach you better manners.'

Robin then hurried out the mare to the side of the kail-yard dike, and calling out to Jean his wife not to be in ower grit a hurry, and to exercise all the patience she was mistress of, he flew on the yaud's back, and off he went at full gallop.

The hair halter that Robin rode with had a wooden snibbelt upon the end of it, as all hair halters had erewhile, when there were no other bridles in Meggat, saving branks and hair halters annexed; consequently with the further end of this halter one could hit an exceeding hard stroke. Indeed, I never saw anything in my life that hurt so sore as a hair halter and wooden snibbelt at the end of it; and I may here mention, as an instance of its efficacy, that there was once a boy at Hartwood mines, near Selkirk, who killed with a snibbelt two Highland soldiers, who came to press his horses in *the forty-five*.

Well, to this halter and snibbelt Robin had trusted for a rod, there being no wood in Meggat-dale, not so much as a tree; and a more unlucky and dangerous goad he could scarcely have possessed, and that the black mare, with a white face like a cow, felt to her experience. Robin galloped by the light of the full moon down by the Butt-haugh and Glengaber-foot about as fast as a good horse walks; still he was galloping, and could make no more of it, although he was every now and then lending the yaud a yerk on the flank with the snibbelt. But when he came to Henderland, to which place the mare was accustomed to go every week to meet the eggler, then Robin and the mane split in their opinions. Robin thought it the most natural and reasonable thing in the world that the mare should push on to the Sandbed, about eight miles further, to bring home the wise woman to his beloved wife's assistance. The mare thought exactly the reverse, being inwardly convinced that the most natural and reasonable path she could take was the one straight home again to her foal; and without any farther ceremony, save giving a few switches with her long illshapen tail, she set herself with all her might to dispute the point with Robin.

Then there was such a battle commenced as never was fought at the foot of Henderland-bank at midnight either before or since. O my beloved and respected editor and readers! I wish I could make you understand the humour of this battle as well as I do. The branks were two sticks hung by a headsteel, which, when one drew the halter hard, nipped the beast's nose most terribly; but when they were all made in one way, and could only turn the beast to the near side. Now the black mare did not, or could not, resist this agency of the branks; she turned round as often as Robin liked, but not one step farther would she proceed on the road to Sandbed. So roundabout and roundabout the two went; and the mare, by a very clever expedient, contrived at every circle to work twice her own length nearer home. Saint Sampson! how Robin did lay on with the halter and snibbelt whenever he got her head round towards the way he wanted her to go! No—round she came again! He cursed her, he flattered her, he reminded her of the precarious state of her mistress, who had so often filled her manger; but all would not do: she thought only of the precarious state of her foal, closed in an old void smearing-house.

Robin at last fell upon a new stratagem, which was this, that as the mane wheeled round whenever her head reached the right point, he hit her a yerk with the wooden snibbelt on the near cheek, to stop that millstone motion of hers. This occasioned some furious plunges, but no advancement the right way, till at length he hit her such a pernicious blow somewhere near about the ear, that he brought her smack to the earth in a moment; and so much was he irritated, that he laid on her when down, and nodding like ane falling asleep. After two or three prolonged groans, she rose again, and, thus candidly admonished, made no further resistance for the present, but moved on apace to the time of the halter and the snibbelt. On reaching a ravine called Capper Cleuch, the mare, coming again in some degree to her senses, perceived that she was not where she ought to have been, at least where it was her interest, and the interest of her foal, that she should have been; and, raising her white face, she uttered a tremendous neigh. The hills to the left are there steep and rocky; and the night being calm and frosty, first one fine echo neighed out of the hill, then another, and then another. 'There are plenty of foals here,' thought the old mare; and neighing again even louder than before, she was again answered in the same way; and, perceiving an old crabbed thorn tree among the rocks, in the direction whence the echo proceeded, it struck her obtuse head that it was her great lubber of a foal standing on very perilous ground; and off she set at a right angle from the road, or rather a left one, with her utmost speed, braying as she went, while every scream was returned by her shaggy colt with interest. It was in vain that Robin pulled by the hair halter, and smote her on the cheek with the wooden snibbelt: away she ran, through long heath and large stones, with a tremendous and uncultivated rapidity, neighing as she flew. 'Wo! ye jaud! Hap-wo! chywooo!' shouted Robin; 'Hap-wo! hap-wo! Devil confound the beast, for I'm gone!'

Nothing would stay her velocity till she stabled herself against a rock over which she could not win, and then Robin lost no time in throwing himself from her back. Many and bitter were the epithets he there bestowed on his old mare, and grievous was the lamentation he made for his wife, as endeavouring to lead back the mare from the rocky hill into the miserable track of a road. No; the plague o' one foot would the mare move in that direction! She held out her long nose, with her white muslin face, straight up to heaven, as if contemplating the moon. She weened that her foal was up among the crags, and put on a resolution not to leave him a second time for any man's pleasure. After all, Robin confessed that he had some excuse for her, for the shadow of the old thorn was so like a colt, that he could scarcely reason himself out of the belief that it was one.

Robin was now hardly set indeed, for the mare would not lead a step; and when he came back to her side to leather her with the snibbelt, she only galloped round him and round him, and neighed. 'O plague on you for a beast that ever you were foaled!' exclaimed Robin; 'I shall lose a dearly beloved wife, and perhaps a couple of babies at least, and all owing to your stupidity and obstinacy! I could soon run on foot to the Sandbed, but then I cannot carry the midwife home on my back; and could I once get you there, you would not be long in bringing us both home again. Plague on you for a beast, if I winna knock your brains out!'

Robin now attacked the mare's white face with the snibbelt, yerk for yerk, so potently, that the mare soon grew madly crazed, and came plunging and floundering from the hill at a great rate. Robin thus found out a secret not before known in this country, on which he acted till the day of his death; namely, 'that the best way to make a horse spring forward is to strike it on the face.'

Once more on the path, Robin again mounted, sparing neither the mare nor the halter; while the mare, at every five or six paces, entertained him with a bray so loud, with its accompanying nicker, that every one made the hills ring again.

There is scarcely any thing a man likes worse than this constant neighing of the steed he rides upon, especially by night. It makes him start as from a reverie, and puts his whole frame in commotion. Robin did not like it more than other men. It caused him inadvertently to utter some imprecations on the mare, that he confessed he should not have uttered; but it also caused him to say some short prayers for preservation; and to which of these agencies he owed the following singular adventure he never could divine.

Robin had got only about half a mile farther on his road, when his mare ceased her braying, and all at once stood stone still, cocking her large ears, and looking exceedingly frightened. 'Oho, madam! what's the matter now?' said Robin; 'is this another stratagem to mar my journey, for all the haste that you see me in? Get on, my fine yaud, get on! There is nothing uncanny there.'

Robin coaxed thus, as well to keep up his own spirits, as to encourage his mare; for the truth is, that his hair began to stand on end with affright. The mare would neither ride, lead, nor drive, one step further; but there she stood, staring, snuffing the wind, and snorting so loud, that it was frightsome to hear as well as to see her. This was the worst dilemma of all. What was our forlorn shepherd to do now? He averred that the mare *would not* go on either by force or art; but I am greatly deceived, if by this time he durst for his life have gone on, even though the mare could have been induced to proceed. He took the next natural expedient, which was that of shouting out as loud as he could bellow, 'Hilloa! who's there? Be ye devils, be ye witches, or be ye Christian creatures, rise an' shaw yoursels. I say, hilloa! who's there?'

Robin was at this time standing hanging by the mare's hair halter with both his hands, for she was capering and flinging up her white face with such violence, that she sometimes made him bob off the ground; when, behold! at his last call, a being like a woman rose from among some deep heather bushes about twenty yards before him. She was like an elderly female, dressed in a coarse country garb, tall and erect; and there she stood for a space, with her pale face, on which the moon shone full, turned straight towards Robin. He then heard her muttering something to herself; and, with a half-stifled laugh, she stooped down, and lifted something from among the heath, which Robin thought resembled a baby. 'There the gipsy yaud has been murdering that poor bairn!' thought Robin to himself: 'it was nae wonder my auld yaud was frighted! she kens what's what for as contrarysome as she is. And murderess though the hizzy be, it is out o' my power to pursue her wi' this positive auld hack, for no another foot nearer her will she move.'

Robin never thought but that the mysterious being was to fly from him, or at least go off the road to one side; but in place of that she rolled her baby, or bundle, or whatever it was, deliberately up in a blanket, fastened it between her shoulders, and came straight up to the place where Robin stood hanging by his mare's head. The mare was perfectly mad. She reared, snorted, and whisked her long ill-shaped tail; but Robin held her, for he was a strong young man, and the hair halter must have been proportionably so, else it never could have stood the exercise of that eventful night.

Though I have heard Robin tell the story oftener than once when I was a boy, there was always a confusion here which I never understood. This may be accounted for, in some measure, by supposing that Robin was himself in such perplexity and confusion, that he neither knew well what passed, nor remembered it afterwards. As far as I recollect, the following was the dialogue that passed between the two.

'Wha's this?'

'What needye speer, goodman? kend fo'k, gin it war daylight.'

'I think I'm a wee bit at a loss. I dinna ken ye.'

'May be no, for ye never saw me afore. An' yet it is a queer thing for a father no to ken his ain daughter.'

'Ay, that wad be a queer thing indeed. But where are you gaun at this time o' the night?'

'Where am I gaun? where but up to the Craigyrigg, to get part o' my ain blithemeat. But where are you riding at sic a rate?'

'Why, I'm just riding my whole might for the houdy: an' that's very true, I hae little need to stand claverin here wi' you.'

'Ha, ha, ha, ha! daddy Robin! It is four hours sin' ye came frae hame, an' ye're no won three miles yet. Why, man, afore ye get to the Sandbed an' hame again, your daughter will be ready for spaining.'

'Daughter! what's a' this about a daughter! Has my dear Jean really a daughter?'

'You may be sure she has, else I could not have been here.'

'An' has she only ane? for, od! ye maun ken wifie that I expectit twa at the fewest. But I dinna understand you. I wish ye may be canny enough, for my white-faced yaud seems to jalouse otherwise.'

'Ye dinna ken me, Robin, but ye will ken me. I am Helen Grieve. I was weel brought up, and married to a respectable farmer's son; but he turned out a villain, and, among other qualifications, was a notorious thief; so that I have been reduced to this that you see, to travel the country with a pack, and lend women a helping hand in their hour o' need. An', Robin, when you and I meet here again, you may be preparing for another world.'

'I dinna comprehend ye at a', wifie. No; a' that I can do, I canna comprehend ye. But I understand thus far. It seems ye are a houdy, or a meedwife, as the grit fo'ks will ca' you. Now that's the very thing I want at present, for your helping hand may be needfu' yonder. Come on ahint me, and we'll soon be hame.'

I must give the expedition home in Robin's own words.

'Weel, I forces my yaud into the Cleuch-brae, contrary as she was, wi' her white face, for she had learned by this time to take a wee care o' the timmer snibbelt. I was on her back in a jiffey; an', to say truth, the kerling wi' the pale round face, and the bit lang bundle on her back, wasna slack; for she was on ahint me, bundle an' a', ere ever I kend I was on mysel. But, Gude forgie us! sickan a voyage as we gat! I declare my yaud gae a snore that gart a' the hills ring, an' the verra fire flew frae her snirls. Out o' the Cleuch-brae she sprang, as there hadna been a bane or a joint within her hide, but her hale carcass made o' steel springs; an' ower bush, ower breer, ower stock, an' ower stane she flew, I declare, an' so be it, faster than ever an eagle flew through the firmament of the heavens.

'I kend then that I had either a witch or a mermaid on ahint me; but how was I now to get quit o' her? The hair halter had lost a' power, an' I had no other shift left, than to fix by instinct on the mare wi' baith hands, an' cry out to the mare to stop. "Wo ye auld viper o' the pit! wo, ye beast o' Bashan!" I cries in outer desperation; but ay the louder I cried, the faster did the glyde flee. She snored, an' she grained, an' she reirdit baith ahint an' afore; an' on she dashed, regardless of a' danger.

'I soon lost sight o' the ground—off gaed my bonnet, an' away i' the wind—off gaed my plaid, an' away i' the wind; an' there was I sitting lootching forret, cleaving the wind like an arrow out of a bow, an' my een rinning pouring like streams of water from the south. At length we came to the Birk-bush Lin! and alangst the very verge of that awsome precipice there was my dementit beast scouring like a fiery dragon. "Lord preserve me!" cried I loud out; an' I hadna weel said the word, till my mare gae a tremendous plunge ower something, I never kend what it was, and then down she came on her nose. No rider could stand this concussion, an' I declare, an' so be it, the meed-wife lost her haud, and ower the precipice she flew head foremost. I just gat ae glisk o' her as she was gaun ower the top o' the birk-bush like a shot stern, an' I heard her gie a waw like a cat; an' that was the last sight I saw o' her.

'I was then hanging by the mare an' the right hough; an', during the moment that my mare took to gather hersel' up, I recovered my seat, but only on the top o' the shoulder, for I couldna win to the right place. The mare flew on as madly as ever; and frae the shoulder I came on to the neck, an' forret, an' forret, piecemeal, till, just as I came to my ain door, I had gotten a grip o' baith the lugs. The foal gae a screed of a nicher; on which the glyde threw up her white face wi' sic a vengeance, that she gart me play at pitch-an'-toss up in the air. The foal nichered, an' the mare nichered, an' out camme the kirmmers; an' I declare, an' so be it, there was I lying in the gutter senseless, wanting the plaid, an' wanting the bonnet, an' nae meedwife at a'; an' that's the truth, sir, I declare, an' so be it.

'Then they carried me in, an' they washed me, an' they bathed me, an' at last I came to mysel'; an', to be sure, I had gotten a bonny doughter, an' a' things war gaun on *as weel as could be expectit*. "What hae ye made o' your plaid, Robin?" says ane. "Whare's your bonnet, Robin?" says another. 'But, gudeness guide us! what's come o' the houdy, Robin? Whare's the meedwife, Robin?' cried they a' at aince. I trow this question gart me glower as I had seen a ghaist. "Och! huh!" cried the wives, an' held up their hands; "something has happened! something has happened! We see by his looks!—Robin! what has happened Whare's the meedwife?

' "Haud your tongue, Janet Reive; an' haud ye your tongue too, Eppie Dickson," says I, "an' dinna speer that question at me again; for the houdy is where the Lord will, an' where my white-faced yaud was pleased to pit her, and that's in the howe o' the Birk-bush Lin. Gin she be a human creature, she's a' dashed to pieces: but an she be nae a human creature she may gang where she like for me; an' that's true, I declare, an' so be it." '

Now it must strike every reader, as it did me at first and for many years afterwards, that this mysterious nocturnal wanderer gave a most confused and unintelligible account of herself. She was Robin's daughter; her name was Helen Grieve; she was married to such and such a man; and had now become a pedlar, and acted occasionally as a midwife: and finally, when they two met there again, it would be time for Robin to be preparing for another state of existence. Now, in the first place, Robin never had a daughter till that very hour and instant when the woman rose out of the heather bush and accosted him. All the rest appeared to him like a confused dream, of which he had no comprehension, save that he could never again be prevailed on to pass that way alone at night; for he had an impression that at some time or other he should meet with her again.

But by far the most curious part of this story is yet to come, and it shall be related in few words. Robin went with some others, as soon as it was day, to the Birk-bush Lin, but there was neither body nor blood to be seen, nor any appearance of a person having been killed or hurt. Robin's daughter was christened by the name of Helen, after her maternal grandmother, so that her name was actually Helen Grieve: and from the time that Robin first saw his daughter, there never was a day on which some of her looks did not bring the mysterious midwife to his mind. Thus far the story had proceeded when I heard it related; for I lived twelve months in the family, and the girl was then only about seven years of age. But, strange to relate, the midwife's short history of herself has turned out the exact history of this once lovely girl's life; and Robin, a few days before his death, met her at the Kirk Cleuch, with a bundle on her back, and recognized his old friend in every lineament and article of attire. He related this to his wife as a secret, but added, that 'he did not know whether it was his *real* daughter whom he met or not.'

Many are the traditions remaining in the country, relative to the seeking of midwives, or houdies, as they are universally denominated all over the south of Scotland; and strange adventures are related as having happened in these precipitate excursions, which were proverbially certain to happen by night. Indeed it would appear, that there hardly ever was a midwife brought, but some incident occurred indicative of the fate or fortunes of the little forthcoming stranger; but, amongst them all, I have selected this as the most remarkable.

I am exceedingly grieved at the discontinuance of midwifery, that primitive and original calling, in this primitive and original country; for never were there such merry groups in Scotland as the mdwives and their kimmers in former days, and never was there such store of capital stories and gossip circulated as on these occasions. But those days are over! and alack, and wo is me! no future old shepherd shall tell another tale of SEEKING THE HOUDY!

Betsy Whyte

THE MAN IN THE BOAT

When Betsy Whyte first came to the attention of the School of Scottish Studies in 1973, she had a wealth of stories, songs and lore, collected over decades spent as a traveller. From then until her death, she was a regular contributor to *Tocher* magazine and to readings and ceilidhs around Scotland. Her storytelling, transcribed for wider audience, links the modern reader with the living oral tradition of Scotland. Her humanity and sense of history put us in touch with a common heritage, beyond the reach of more formal records.

Betsy, or Bessie, Whyte (1919–88) was born into a travelling family in Blairgowrie. In her autobiography *The Yellow On The Broom* she recalls a childhood spent around Perthshire, either camping out, working and travelling, or spending grinding winters, confined in a house. Her memoirs have the warmth, accuracy and sensitivity which shine through all her tales. Betsy gave up travelling when she married and began a family, and the way of life she grew up with has now changed beyond all recognition, yet her stories still keep that past alive, and the past of generations before her.

In 'The Man In The Boat', Betsy combines plain story telling with the relation of historical fact and brings to question where history stops and the folk tale begins, for the borders in between the two are not always clear. But tales have always fuelled the imagination to consider the enduring sources of both pleasure and pain; in this example, the difference between the sexes.

The Man in the Boat

THIS STORY is aboot a laird awa in the Heilands . . . and he had the Black Art . . . but every year he used to gie a big ceilidh for aa the workers on his estate, an aa the fairm folk an aa the fairm hands, an he used tae had this ceilidh in a big barn. There wis a fire in this barn, an they'd put on a big pot of sowens. (Ye ken whit sowens are? No? Well Scotland, it's always been a very poor country, and no that very long ago, jist aboot a hundred years ago, they used to soak . . . the husks o the grain . . . until they were soor, and then they strained it an boiled up the liquid an this made a sort of porridge, and a lot o them had to exist on that.) So this big pot o sowens wis boilin away anywey, and everybody wis doin their thing: ye hed tae

Tell a story,
Sing a sang,
Show yir bum
Or oot ye gang!

They hed other things as well as singin an tellin stories an that: they hed sort of games, they'd games of strength an guesses an that sort o thing, and one o the things wis to see who could tell the biggest lie. So everybody wis gaun their roond and gaun their roond, but every time it came tae this cattleman he would ay say, 'Ye ken fine I cannae dae nothing, yet shouldnae ask me! Ye ken I cannae dae it.'

So this laird says, 'Look, ye can surely tell a lie.'

He says, 'No, A cannae.' Sandy wis a bit simple, ye ken, and he wisnae very good at nothin but lookin efter the coos.

So the laird says, 'Sandy, look, try an tell a story, or tell us a lie o some kind.'

He says, 'A cannae, I dinnae ken how tae.'

'Well,' the laird says, 'if ye dinnae ken how tae ye're no gaunnae be here. Awa ye go an mak yirsel useful some other place.'

He says, 'What am I gaunnae dae?'

He says, 'I'll tell ye what tae dae. Awa ye go doon tae the water an clean my boat, because A'll be usin it shortly.' He says, 'Awa ye go.' So Sandy's away, tramp, tramp, tramp, doon through the gutters [mud] tae this river, this big river. And he scraped aa the moss an dirt aff the boat, scrapin it oot, and there wis a baler lyin in the boat an he wis balin oot the water an balin oot the water, an he steps inside the boat so that he could finish balin it oot, ye see?

But didn't this boat take off wi him, an there's no wey he could stop it! An before he could get time to think, even, they're away in the middle o the water, and he couldnae swim. So he ays, 'Ach, A'll jist sit an let it go wherever it wants tae go.' So he jist sat like this lookin up at the birds an things.

But he glanced doon again, and there he saw the loveliest wee green satin slippers; pure silk stockins; taffeta dress—he says, 'Whit's this? Whit's this?' an he felt his sel ower—oh! pappies [breasts] an everything! 'Oh!' he says. 'Whit's happenin?' Curls an everything. As he looked . . . ower the side o the boat, an there wis the bonniest lassie that ye ever saw lookin back at him. 'What's happened?' he says, 'What's happened? [higher voice] *What's Happened?*' His voice changed all of a sudden. Oh! So he says, 'Oh, my God!'—he was so stunned he jist sat there, and this boat, it got tae the other side, an he felt . . . it was the boat scrapin the bottom that brought him back tae himsel, ye see—but he was a she now!

So she stands up in this lovely green claes, an she looked—she wondered how she wis gaunnae get oot o the boat withoot makin a mess o her shoes an everything. Now there wis a young man walkin alang the bank o the river, and when he looked doon an sa this young lassie in this boat, 'course he would run doon an help her oot. So he ran doon and he cairried her oot o the boat till he got her on dry land, an he says, 'Where are ye goin?'

'I don't know,' she says. 'I don't really know where I'm goin.'

He says, 'Well, where did ye come from?'

'Oh, I came from the other side o the water.'

'Are ye goin tae anybody?'

'I don't know.'

He says, 'Lassie, I think you must have fell an bumped yir heid. I think you've lost yir memory wi aa this "Don't knows, don't knows".'

She says, 'Well, mebbe something like that happened.' She says, 'I jist don't know where A'm goin here. Ye see, A know where A'm goin when A'm at the other side o the water, but A don't know where A'm goin here.'

'Well,' he says, 'A think A'll take ye home tae ma mother, an get her tae look after ye, see if ye get yir memory back.' So he took her home tae his mother, and she helped his mother in the hoose an did this an that. But in time he got aafae fond o her, in fact he fell in love wi her, and the two o them got married. And within a couple o year they had two o the bonniest wee bairns ye ever saw, a wee toddler and one in the pram.

So one day, when they were oot walkin wi the bairns, an he was pushin his pram, quite proud o this wee laddie he got, ye see . . . she says, 'Ye know, I think we'll go a walk down the river today.' She says, 'A haven't been back down that way since the day A came here.'

He says, 'Well, that's a good idea.' He says, 'It might bring back yir memory,' he says, 'if nothing else has all this time.'

She says, 'That's right.' So away they go down the riverside, and, sure enough, the wee boat wis still sittin there. 'Aw,' she says, 'look at it! It's all covered wi moss an lichen an aa kinds o dirt: A must go doon an clean it.'

So she ran doon the bank: she says, 'You keep the bairns here an A'll run doon the bank an clean it.' Down she goes, an she's scrapin away at it, an the baler wis still lyin in it, an she startit to bale oot the water. And in the end she stepped intae the boat to bale oot the last, an ye can guess whit happen't! This boat's away wi her again, and it kept goin an kept goin, and the fella—there wis no wey he could stop it, it went so fast, an he couldnae swim efter it, so he jist had to stand there and let it go.

Now half way across the water, when she lookit doon, there wis the auld tackety boots, auld moleskin troosers covered wi coo shairn [dung], whiskers an baird an . . . this auld sleeved waistcoat, an he looked ower intae the water an there wis this cattleman . . . wi his teeth all broon wi tobacco juice an everything. 'Oh my God!' He started to roar an greet, an howl an greet, 'Oh, ma man an ma bairns! Ma man an ma bairns! Ma man an ma bairns . . .' and he jist sat like this and the tears trippin him, until the boat scraped the other side: an the boat took him right back tae where it had started aff.

Then Sandy jumpit oot the boat, an he ran and ran greetin and sobbin an sobbin an greetin. An when he ran up tae the fairm, this ceilidh's still gaun on, see? an the pot o sowens is still on the fire! An he cam in howlin an greetin an sobbin, an the laird says tae him, 'Whit's adae wi ye, Sandy?'

'Oh, dinnae speak tae me, dinnae speak tae me,' he says. 'Wheesht, leave me alane—wid ye leave me alane? Ma man an ma bairns! Ma man an ma bairns!'

'Man an bairns?' the laird says. 'Whit are ye speakin aboot?'

'Oh, would you wheesht?' he says.

'Sandy, come in here. Come on an sit doon beside . . . me here an tell us aa aboot it!' So Sandy came in an he sat doon beside the laird, an between sobbin an greetin he tellt them aa aboot his man an his bairns. An the laird says, 'Well, Sandy, that's the biggest lee we've heard the nicht, so you've won the golden guinea!'

* * *

That's the end o that one. Ye see the laird had pit a glamourie ower him, so that he thought aa this had happen't tae him, but actually he'd only been awa aboot twenty minutes.

As told by the late Mrs Betsy Whyte to students at the School of Scottish Studies in November 1981.

Neil Gunn

THE MOOR

In 1937 Neil Miller Gunn resigned his post with His Majesty's Custom and Excise to become a full time writer. He had already published several successful novels and, with the early encouragement of Hugh MacDiarmid, his stories had found a home in many magazines. By 1948, when Gunn was awarded an LLD by Edinburgh University, he was at the height of his powers after highly acclaimed novels such as *Highland River* and *The Silver Darlings*. But his popularity began to wane and it was not until the 60s and 70s that he was to find his place again, helping and encouraging a generation of young writers, as his work began to reappear in fresh editions.

Born in Dunbeath, Caithness in 1891, Neil Gunn was the son of a fisherman. While working for the Customs and Excise he began to write poetry and then prose. He produced more than twenty novels, along with short stories, documentaries, drama and pieces for radio. This productivity may have compensated a little for personal grief. He and his wife Daisy were unable to have children. Despite their sometimes strained relations, Gunn never really recovered after her death in 1963. A year later his closest friend, the Irish author Maurice Walsh, was also gone. On 15 January 1973, after a period of failing health, Gunn died in hospital.

Neil Gunn had a natural interest in the mystic and spiritual and became drawn towards Zen Buddhism. 'The Moor' contains a characteristic blend of powerful natural description and a deeper, elusive symbolism. The action takes place as much in imagination as in real life and this duality of substance is built into a narrative that might have come from the old ballads themselves.

The Moor

A FEW MILES back it had looked like a sea-anemone on a vast tidal ledge, but now, at hand, it rose out of the moor's breast like a monstrous nipple. The scarred rock, heather tufted, threw a shadow to his aching feet, and because he was young enough to love enchantment in words, he savoured slowly, 'like the shadow of a great rock in a weary land.' With a nameless shudder of longing he passed his tongue between his sticky lips. The wide Sutherland moor under the August sun was silent as a desert.

At a little pool by the rock-base he drank and then dipped his face.

From the top of the rocky outcrop the rest of his tramp unrolled before him like a painted map. The earth fell away to the far sea, with cottages set here and there upon it like toys, and little cultivated strips, green and brown, and serpentine dark hollows.

He kept gazing until the sandwich in his mouth would not get wet enough to swallow. Then his eyes rested on the nearest cottage of all.

The loneliness of that cottage was a thing to catch the heart. Its green croft was snared in the moor's outflung hand. In the green stood a red cow. Creaming in upon his mind stole the seductive thought of milk. Tasting it made a clacking sound in his mouth and he stopped eating.

As he neared the cottage the red cow stared at him, unmoving save for the lifeless switch of her tail. The cottage itself, with its grey curved thatch and pale gable-end, made no move. The moor's last knuckle shut off the world.

The heather had not yet stirred into bloom and, far as the eye could see, lay dark under the white sun. He listened for a sound . . . and in that moment of suspense it came upon him that the place was bewitched.

A dog barked and every sense leapt. The tawny brute came out at the front door, showing half-laughing teeth, twisting and twining, and in no time was at his back. He turned round, but still kept moving towards the door, very careful not to lift his eyes from those eyes, so that he nearly tumbled backwards over the doorstep . . . and was aware, with the beginnings of apologetic laughter, that he was in the presence of a woman. When he looked up, however, the laugh died.

Her eyes were gipsy dark. Perhaps she was twenty. Sunk in the darkness of her eyes were golden sun motes. Madonna of the adder-haunted moor. His confusion stared speechless. A tingling trepidation beset his skin. A tight drawn bodice just covered and repressed her breasts. Her beauty held the still, deep mesmerism of places at the back of beyond. She was shy, yet gazed at him.

The dry cup of his flesh filled with wine. Then his eyes flickered, shifted quickly; he veiled them, smiling, as though the rudeness of his bared emotion had gone forth unpardonably and touched her skin.

To his stammered request for milk, she smiled faintly, almost automatically, and disappeared.

Then he heard the beating his heart. Through the warmth of his tired body swept a distinct heat. Excitement broke in spindrift. He smiled secretly to himself, absorbed.

When he caught himself listening at the door, however, he immediately bespoke the dog, inviting its approach with such a sudden snapping hand that the brute leapt back, surprised into a short growl. He awaited her appearance so alive and happy that he was poised in apprehension.

She brought the milk in a coarse tumbler. He barely looked at her face, as if good manners could not trust his instinct; but the last grain of thanks he concentrated in a glance, a word or two, a smile breaking into a laugh. She had covered somewhat the wide V gleam of her breast, had swept back her hair; but the rents, the burst seam under an arm, the whole covering for her rich young body was ragged as ever, ragged and extraordinarily potent, as if it sheathed the red pulse at white beauty's core. He said he would drink the milk sitting outside if she didn't mind. She murmured, smiled, withdrew.

He ate his lunch excitedly, nibbling at the sandwiches to make them last, throwing crusts to the dog. His mind moved in its bewilderment as in coloured spindrift, but underneath were eyes avid for the image of her body, only he would not let their stare fix. Not yet. Not now . . . Living here at the back of beyond . . . this secret moor . . . Extraordinary! The wave burst in happy excited spindrift. . . . But underneath he felt her like a pulse and saw her like a flame—a flame going to waste—in the dark of the moor, this hidden moor. Attraction and denial became a tension of exquisite doubt, of possible cunning, of pain, of desire. His soul wavered like a golden jet.

As the last drop of the milk slid over, he heard a sound and turned—and stared.

A withered woman was looking at him, eyes veiled in knowingness. She said, 'It's a fine day that's in it.'

'Yes. isn't it!' He got to his feet.

She slyly looked away from him to the moor, the better to commune with her subtle thought. A wisp of grey hair fell over an ear. Her neck was sinewy and stretched, her chin tilted level from the stoop of her shoulders. The corners of her eyes returned to him. Just then the girl came to the door.

'It's waiting here, Mother.' Through a veiled anxiety quietly, compellingly, she eyed the old woman.

'Are ye telling me?'

'Come on in.'

'Oh, I'm coming.' She turned to the young man and gave a little husky laugh, insanely knowing. The daughter followed her within, and he found himself with the thick glass in his hand staring at the empty doorway. '*She leuch*' rose a ballad echo, like a sunless shudder. A sudden desire to tiptoe away from that place seized him. My God! he thought. The blue of heaven trembled.

But he went to the door and knocked.

'This is the glass—' he began.

She smiled shyly, politely, and, taking the glass from his outstretched hand, smoothly withdrew.

His hand fell to his side. He turned away, going quietly.

Down between the cottages, the little cultivated strips green and brown, the serpentine dark hollows, he went jerkily, as though the whole place were indeed not earth, but a painted map, and he himself a human toy worked by one spring. Only it was a magic spring that never got unwound. Even in the hotel that overlorded the final cluster of cottages, the spring seemed wound up tighter than ever.

For privacy he went up and sat on his bed. 'Lord, I cannot get over it!' he cried silently. He got off his bed and walked about the floor. This was the most extraordinary thing that had ever happened to him . . . without, as it were, quite happening to him.

Inspiration had hitherto thrilled from within. This was from without, and so vast were its implications that he could not feel them all at once in a single spasm of creation. He got lost in them and wandered back to his bed, whereon he lay full length, gazing so steadily that he sank through his body into a profound sleep.

He awoke to a stillness in his room so intense that he held his breath, listening. His eyes slowly turned to the window where the daylight was not so much fading as changing into a glimmer full of a moth-pale life, invisible and watchful. Upon his taut ear the silence began to vibrate with the sound of a small tuning fork struck at an immense distance.

His staring eyes, aware of a veiled face . . . focused the face of the girl on the moor. The appeal of her sombre regard was so great that he began to tremble; yet far back in him cunningly he willed body and mind to an absolute suspense so that the moment might remain transfixed. Footsteps on the corridor outside smashed it, and all at once he was listening acutely to perfectly normal voices.

'Well, Mr Morrison—you here? What's up now?'

'Nothing much. The old woman up at Albain—been certified.'

'So I heard. Poor old woman. When are you lifting her?'

'To-morrow.'

'There's no doubt, of course, she is . . . ay, ay, very sad.'

'Yes. There's the girl, too—her daughter. You'll know her?'

'Well—yes. But she's right enough. I mean there's nothing—there. A bit shy, maybe . . . like the heather. You know.'

'I was wondering what could be done for her.'

'Oh, the neighbours will look after her, I'm sure. She'll just have to go into service. We're fixed up for the season here now, or I . . .'

The footsteps died away, and the light in the bedroom withdrew itself still more, like a woman withdrawing her dress, her eyes, but on a lingering watchfulness more critical than ever, and now faintly ironic.

His body snapped into action and began restlessly pacing the floor, irony flickering over the face. Suddenly he paused . . . and breathed aloud—'The auld mither!' His eyes gleamed in a profound humour.

The exclamation made him walk as it were more carefully, and presently he came to the surface of himself some distance from the hotel and realised where he was going.

But now he cunningly avoided the other cottages and in a roundabout way came in over the knuckle of moor in the deepening dusk. The cow was gone and the cottage seemed more lonely than ever. Indeed, it crouched to the earth with rounded shoulders drawing its grey thatch about its awful secret. Only the pale gable-end gloomed in furtive watchfulness.

Grey-green oasis, dark moor, and huddled cottage were privy to the tragedy of their human children, and, he felt, inimical to any interference from without. Never before had he caught this living secretive intensity of background, although, as a young painter believing in vision, it had been his business to exploit backgrounds of all sorts.

The girl herself walked out from the end of the house, carrying two empty pitchers. On the soft turf her feet made no sound. Unlike her background she was not inimical but detached. And, as her slave, her background spread itself in quiet ecstasy under her feet.

By the time he joined her at the well she had her buckets full, and as he offered to carry them she lifted one in each hand. He pursued his offer, stooping to take them. The little operation brought their bodies into contact and their hands, so that there was a laughing tremble in his voice as he walked beside her, carrying the water. But at the doorway, which was reached in a moment, he set down the buckets and raised his cap.

As he went on into the moor, still smiling warmly as though she were beside him, he kept saying to himself that to have dallied or hesitated would have been unpardonable . . . yet not quite believing it . . . yet knowing it to be true.

He sat down on the moor, his heart aflame. The moor lost its hostility and became friendly. Night drew about them her dim purple skin. Silence wavered like the evening smoke of a prehistoric fire. The sense of translation grew in him . . . until the girl and himself went walking on the moor, on the purple, the rippled skin, their faces set to mountain crests and far dawns.

He tore his vision with a slow humour and, getting to his feet, shivered. As he returned by the cottage he saw her coming out of the byre-door and on a blind impulse went up to her and asked:

'Are you not lonely here?'

'No,' she answered, with a smile that scarcely touched her still expression.

'Well—it does seem lonely—doesn't it?'

Her eyes turned to the moor and only by a luminous troubling of their deeps could he see that his words were difficult. She simply did not speak, and for several seconds they stood perfectly silent.

'I can understand,' he broke through, 'that it's not lonely either.' But his awkwardness rose up and clutched him. If the thickening dusk saved his colour, it heightened her beauty in a necromantic way. Mistrust had not touched her, if tragedy had. A watchfulness, a profound instinct young and artless—yet very old.

The front door opened and her mother came peering on to the doorstep. In low quick tones he said:

'I'll come—to-morrow evening.'

Her eyes turned upon his with a faint fear, but found a light deeper than sympathy.

By the time he got back to the hotel, his companion, Douglas Cunningham, had arrived, round about, with the motor-cycle combination.

'Sorry I'm so late. The beastly clutch kept slipping. I had the devil's own time of it.'

'Had you?'

'Yes. We'll have to get down to it to-morrow. . . . What happened?' Douglas looked at Evan shrewdly. 'Seems to have lit you up a bit, anyhow!'

'Does it?'

Then Evan told him.

Douglas met his look steadily.

'You can't see?' probed Evan, finally. 'The moor, the lonely cottage, the mad mother, and the daughter. . . . My God, what a grouping! Can't you see—that it transcends chance? It has overwhelmed me.'

'My dear chap, if you'd been in the ditch with a burst clutch and umpteen miles from nowhere you would have been, by analogy, completely pulverised.'

Their friendly arguments frequently gathered a mocking hostility.

'You show me the clutch of your tinny motor bike,' thrust Evan. 'I show you the clutch of eternal or infernal life. I'm not proving or improving anything: I'm only showing you. But you can't see. Lord, you are blind. Mechanism, clutch, motor bike . . . these are the planets wheeling about your Cyclops glassy eye. You are the darling of evolution, the hope of your country, the proud son of your race. You are the *thing* we have arrived at! . . . By the great Cuchulain, is it any wonder that your old mother is being taken to a mad-house?'

'By which I gather that you have found the daughter's mechanism —fool-proof?'

Evan took a slow turn about the floor, then with hands in pockets stood glooming satanically. 'I suppose,' he said, 'we have sunk as low as that.'

Douglas eyed him warningly.

'Easy, Evan.'

Evan nodded. 'Whatever I do I must not go in off the deep end!' He suddenly sat down and over his closed fist on the table looked Douglas in the face. 'Why shouldn't I go in off the deep end?'

Douglas turned from the drawn lips and kicked off his boots.

'You can go in off any damned end you like,' he said.

And in bed, Evan could not sleep. To the pulse of his excitement parable and symbol danced with exquisite rhythm and to a pattern set upon the grey-green oasis of the croft, centring in the cottage . . . fertile matrix of the dark moor.

Vision grew and soon wholly obsessed him. He found in it a reality at once intoxicating and finally illuminating. A pagan freedom and loveliness, a rejuvenation, an immense hope . . . and, following after, the moods of reflection, of beauty, of race . . . to go into the moor not merely to find our souls but to find life itself—and to find it more abundantly.

But the following evening the little cottage presented quite another appearance. He came under its influence at the very first glance from the near moor crest. It had the desolate air of having had its heart torn out, of having been raped. A spiritless shell, its dark-red door pushed back in an imbecile gape. One could hear the wind in its emptiness. A sheer sense of its desolation overcame him. He could not take his eyes off it.

And presently an elderly woman came to the door, followed by the girl herself. They stood on the doorstep for a long time, then began slowly to walk up to the ridge beyond which lay the neighbours' cottages. But before they reached the ridge they stopped and again for a long time stood in talk. At last the elderly woman put out her hand and caught the girl's arm. But the girl would not go with her. She released herself and stepped back a pace, her body bending and swaying sensitively. The elderly woman stood still and straight, making her last appeal. The girl swayed away from that appeal also, turned and retreated. With hooded shawl her elder remained looking after her a moment, then like a woman out of the ages went up over the crest of the moor.

From his lair in the heather, Evan saw the door close, heard, so still the evening was, the clash and rattle of the latch. And with the door closed and the girl inside, the house huddled emptier than ever. His heart listened so intently that it caught the dry sound of her desolate thought . . . she was not weeping . . . her arms hung so bare that her empty hands kept plucking down her sleeves. . . .

She came at his knock. The pallor of her face deepened the dark of her eyes. Their expressionlessness was troubled and she stood aside to let him in. Only when they were by the fire in the gloom of the small-windowed kitchen did she realise what had happened.

But Evan did not feel awkward. He knew what he had to do like a man who might have imaginatively prepared himself for the test. He placed her chair at the other side of the fire but did not ask her to sit down. He sat down himself, however, and looking into the fire began to speak.

Sometimes he half turned with a smile, but for the most part kept his eyes on the burning peat, with odd silences that were pauses in his thought. He was not eager nor hurried; yet his gentleness had something fatal in it like the darkness of her mood. Sensitiveness that was as exquisite as pain transmuted pain to a haunted monotone.

She stood so still on the kitchen floor that in the end he dared not look at her. Nor did his immobility break when he heard her quietly sit down in the opposite chair, though the core of the fire quickened before his gaze.

Without moving, he started talking again. He did not use words that might appeal to a primitive intelligence. He spoke in the highest—the simplest—way he could to himself.

He looked at himself as a painter desiring to paint the moor. Why? He found himself dividing the world into spirit and mechanism. Both might be necessary, but spirit must be supreme. Why? Even if from no other point than this that it afforded the more exquisite delight. And the more one cultivated it the more varied and interesting life became, the deeper, the more charming, and yes, the more tragical. Yes, the more tragical, thereby drawing spirit to spirit in a communion that was the only known warmth in all the coldness of space. And we needed that particular warmth; at moments one needed it more than anything else. Man's mechanism was a tiny flawed toy in the vast flawless mechanism of the universe. But this warmth of his was a thing unique; it was his own special creation . . . and in a way—who could say?—perhaps a more significant, more fertile, thing than even the creation of the whole mechanical universe. . . .

As he thought over this idea for a time, he felt her eyes on his face. The supreme test of spirit would be that while not knowing his words it would yet understand him perfectly—*if it was there.*

'I do not know,' he said at last, and repeated it monotonously. 'Coming in over the moor there I saw you and the woman. Then there was the moor itself. And you in the cottage. I wish I could understand that. But I cannot understand it, any more than you—or the woman. Yet we understand it, too. And the woman could have helped you. Only you didn't want to be helped in her way yet.' He paused, then went on slowly: 'I can see that. It's when I go beyond that to my sitting here that it becomes difficult. For what I see is you who are the moor, and myself with the moor about me, and in us there is dawn, and out of the moor comes more of us. . . . That sounds strange, but perhaps it is truer than if I said it more directly. For you and I know that we cannot speak to each other yet—face to face.'

Then he turned his face and looked at her.

Her dark eyes were alight with tears that trickled in slow beads down her cheeks.

He gave his face to the fire again. *It was there.*

Quietly he got to his feet. 'I'll make a cup of tea.'

She also arose. 'I'll make it.'

It had grown quite dark in the kitchen. They stood very still facing the unexpected darkness. Caught by something in the heart of it, they instinctively drew together. He turned her face from it.

In the morning Douglas arrived at the cottage on the heels of the woman with the shawl. The woman had tried the door and found it locked. But here quick consternation lessened when she found the key under the thatch.

Douglas, grown oddly curious, waited for her to come out. She came, with a face as grey as the wall.

'She hasn't slept in her bed at all.'

'Oh!' His lips closed.

The woman looked at him.

'Do you know . . . ?'

'Not a thing,' said Douglas. 'Must have gone over the hills and far away. They've got a fine morning for it.' And he turned and left her, his scoffing sanity sticking in his throat like a dry pellet.

John Buchan

The adventure novels of John Buchan (1875–1940), follow naturally from the historical fiction of Neil Munro and R.L. Stevenson. The action has been transposed to a contemporary setting, his characterisation is simple and there is always a series of cross-country chases where the landscape is lovingly evoked.

This sense of place is equally strong in Buchan's short fictions, and his early stories in particular have a special freshness. There is a sense of inquisitiveness in them, as of a young man trying to understand himself and his country, and especially the language of his country. There is hardly an early story where he doesn't use dialect, as if trying to pin to the page the language he hears around him.

'The Herd of Standlan' was written when Buchan was an Oxford undergraduate and shows his love for the people and places of the Tweed valley. The tale uses national events as the backdrop to a local incident, which allows Buchan the freedom to develop its political, comic and cosmic elements, always with an eye on the Calvinist doctrines which underline the Herd of Standlan's thinking.

The Herd of Standlan

When the wind is nigh and the moon is high
   And the mist on the riverside,
Let such as fare have a very good care
   Of the Folk who come to ride.
For they may meet with the riders fleet
   Who fare from the place of dread;
And hard it is for a mortal man
   To sort at ease with the Dead.

The Ballad of Grey Weather

WHEN STANDLAN BURN leaves the mosses and hags which gave it birth, it tumbles over a succession of falls into a deep, precipitous glen, whence in time it issues into a land of level green meadows, and finally finds its rest in the Gled. Just at the opening of the ravine there is a pool shut in by high, dark cliffs, and black even on the most sunshiny day. The rocks are never dry but always black with damp and shadow. There is scarce any vegetation save stunted birks, juniper bushes, and draggled fern; and the hoot of owls and the croak of hooded crows is seldom absent from the spot. It is the famous Black Linn where in winter sheep stray and are never more heard of, and where more than once an unwary shepherd has gone to his account. It is an Inferno on the brink of a Paradise, for not a stone's throw off is the green, lawn-like turf, the hazel thicket, and the broad, clear pools, by the edge of which on that July day the Herd of Standlan and I sat drowsily smoking and talking of fishing and the hills. There he told me this story, which I here set down as I remember it, and as it bears repetition.

'D'ye mind Airthur Morrant?' said the shepherd, suddenly.

I did remember Arthur Mordaunt?' Ten years past he and I had been inseparables, despite some half-dozen summers difference in age. We had fished and shot together, and together we had tramped every hill within thirty miles. He had come up from the South to try sheep-farming, and as he came of a great family and had no need to earn his bread, he found the profession pleasing. Then irresistible fate had swept me southward to college, and when after two years I came back to the place, his father was dead and he had come into his own. The next I heard of him was that in politics he was regarded as the most promising of the younger men, one of the staunchest and ablest upstays of the Constitution. His name was rapidly rising into prominence, for he seemed to exhibit that rare phenomenon of a man of birth and culture in direct sympathy with the wants of the people.

'You mean Lord Brodakers?' I said.

'Dinna call him by that name,' said the shepherd, darkly. 'I hae nae thocht o' him now. He's a disgrace to his country, servin' the Deil wi' baith hands. But nine year syne he was a bit innocent callant wi' nae Tory deevilry in his heid. Well, as I was sayin', Airthur Morrant has cause to mind that place till his dying day;' and he pointed his finger to the Black Linn.

I looked up the chasm. The treacherous water, so bright and joyful at our feet, was like ink in the great gorge. The swish and plunge of the cataract came like the regular beating of a clock, and though the weather was dry, streams of moisture seamed the perpendicular walls. It was a place eerie even on that bright summer's day.

'I don't think I ever heard the story,' I said casually.

'Maybe no,' said the shepherd. 'It's no yin I like to tell;' and he puffed sternly at his pipe, while I awaited the continuation.

'Ye see it was like this,' he said, after a while. 'It was just the beginning o' the back-end, and that year we had an awfu' spate o' rain. For near a week it poured hale water, and a' doon by Drumeller and the Mossfennan haughs was yae muckle loch. Then it stopped, and an awfu' heat came on. It dried the grund in nae time, but it hardly touched the burns; and it was rale queer to be pourin' wi' sweat and the grund aneath ye as dry as a potato-sack, and a' the time the water neither to haud nor bind. A' the waterside fields were clean stripped o' stooks, and a guid wheen hay-ricks gaed doon tae Berwick, no to speak o' sheep and nowt beast. But that's anither thing.

'Weel, ye'll mind that Airthur was terrible keen on fishing. He wad gang oot in a' weather, and he wasna feared for only mortal or naitural thing. Dod, I've seen him in Gled wi' the water rinnin' ower his shouthers yae cauld March day playin' a saumon. He kenned weel aboot the fishing, for he had traivelled in Norroway and siccan outlandish places, where there's a heap o' big fish. So that day—and it was a Setterday tae and far ower near the Sabbath—he maun gang awa' up Standlan Burn wi' his rod and creel to try his luck.

'I was bidin' at that time, as ye mind, in the wee cot-house at the back o' the faulds. I was alane, for it was three years afore I mairried Jess, and I wasna begun yet to the coortin'. I had been at Gledsmuir that day for some o' the new stuff for killing sheep-mawks, and I wasna very fresh on my legs when I gaed oot after my tea that night to hae a look at the hill-sheep. I had had a bad year on the hill. First the lambin'-time was snaw, snaw ilka day, and I lost mair than I wad like to tell. Syne the grass a' summer was so short wi' the drought that the puir beasts could scarcely get a bite and were as thin as pipe-stapples. And then, to crown a', auld Will Broun, the man that helpit me, turned ill wi' his back, and had to bide at hame. So I had twae man's work on yae man's shouthers, and was nane so weel pleased.

'As I was saying, I gaed oot that nicht, and after lookin' a' the Dun Rig and the Yellow Mire and the back o' Cramalt Craig, I cam down the burn by the road frae the auld faulds. It was geyan dark, being about seven o'clock o' a September nicht, and I keepit weel back frae that wanchancy hole o' a burn. Weel, I was comin' kind o' quick, thinkin' o' supper and a story-book that I was readin' at the time, when just abune that place there, at the foot o' the Linn, I saw a man fishing. I wondered what ony body in his senses could be daein' at that time o' nicht in sic a dangerous place, so I gae him a roar and bade him come back. He turned his face round and I saw in a jiffey that it was Mr Airthur.

'"O, sir," I cried, "What for are ye fishing there? The water's awfu' dangerous, and the rocks are far ower slid."

'"Never mind, Scott," he roars back cheery-like. "I'll take care o' mysel'."

'I lookit at him for two-three meenutes, and then I saw by his rod he had yin on, and a big yin tae. He ran it up and doon the pool, and he had uncommon wark wi' 't, for it was strong and there was little licht. But bye and bye he got it almost tae his feet, and was just about to lift it oout when a maist awfu' thing happened. The tackets o' his boots maun hae slithered on the stane, for the next thing I saw was Mr Airthur in the muckle hungry water.

'I dinna exactly ken what happened after that, till I found myself on the very stone he had slipped off. I maun hae come doon the face o' the rocks, a thing I can scarcely believe when I look at them, and a thing no man ever did afore. At ony rate I ken I fell the last fifteen feet or sae, and lichted on my left airm, for I felt it crack like a rotten branch, and an awfu' sairness ran up it.

'Now, the pool is a whirlpool as ye ken, and if anything fa's in, the water first smashes it against the muckle rock at the foot, then it brings it round below the fall again, and syne at the second time it carries it doon the burn. Weel, that was what happened to Mr Airthur. I heard his heid gang dunt on the stane wi' a sound that made me sick. This must hae dung him clean senseless, and indeed it was a wonder it didna knock his brains oot. At ony rate there was nae mair word o' swimming, and he was whirled round below the fa' just like a corp.

'I kenned fine that nae time was to be lost, for if he once gaed doun the burn he wad be in Gled or ever I could say a word, and nae wad ever see him mair in life. So doon I got on my hunkers on the stane, and waited for the turnin'. Round he came, whirling in the foam, wi' a lang line o' blood across his brow where the stane had cut him. It was a terrible meenute. My heart fair stood still. I put out my airm, and as he passed I grippit him and wi' an awfu' pu' got him out o' the current into the side.

'But now I found that a waur thing still was on me. My left airm was broken, and my richt sae numbed and weak wi' my fall that, try as I micht,

I couldnae raise him ony further. I thocht I wad burst a blood-vessel i' my face and my muscles fair cracked wi' the strain, but I would make nothing o' 't. There he stuck wi' his heid and shouthers abune the water, pu'd close until the edge of a rock.

'What was I to dae? If I once let him slip he wad be into the stream and lost forever. But I couldna hang on here a' nicht, and as far as I could see there wad be naebody near till the mornin', when Ebie Blackstock passed frae the Head o' the Hope. I roared wi' a' my power; but I got nai answer, naething but the rummle o' the water and the whistling o' some whaups on the hill.

'Then I turned very sick wi' terror and pain and weakness and I kenna what. My broken airm seemed a great lump o' burnin' coal. I maun hae given it some extra wrench when I hauled him out, for it was sae sair now that I thocht I could scarcely thole it. Forbye, pain and a', I could hae gone off to sleep wi' fair weariness. I had heard tell o' men sleepin' on their feet, but I never felt it till then. Man, if I hadna warstled wi' myself, I wad hae dropped off as deid's a peery.

'There there was the awfu' strain o' keepin' Mr Airthur up. He was a great big man, twelve stone I'll warrant, and weighing a terrible lot mair wi' his fishing togs and things. If I had had the use o' my ither airm I micht hae taen off his jacket and creel and lichtened the burden, but I could do naething. I scarcely like to tell ye how I was tempted in that hour. Again and again I says to mysel, "Gidden Scott," say I, "what do ye care for this man? He's no a drap's bluid to you, and forbye ye'll never be able to save him. Ye micht as weel let him gang. Ye've dune a' ye could. Ye're a brave man, Gidden Scott, and ye've nae cause to be ashamed o' givin' up the fecht." But I says to mysel again: "Gidden Scott, ye're a coward. Wad ye let a man die, when there's a breath in your body? Think shame o' yoursel, man." So I aye kept haudin' on, although I was very near bye wi' 't. Whenever I lookit at Mr Airthur's face, as white's death and a' blood, and his een sae stelled-like, I got a kind o' groo and felt awfu' pitiful for the bit laddie. Then I thocht on his faither, the auld Lord, wha was sae built up in him, and I couldna bear to think o' his son droonin' in that awfu' hole. So I set myself to the wark o' keepin' him up a' nicht, though I had nae hope in the matter. It wasna what ye ca' bravery that made me dae't, for I had nae ither choice. It was just kind o' dourness that runs in my folk, and a kind o' vexedness for sae young a callant in sic an ill place.

'The nicht was hot and there was scarcely a sound o' wind. I felt the sweat standin' on my face like frost on tatties, and abune me the sky was a' misty and nae mune visible. I thocht very likely that it micht come a thunder-shower and I kind o' lookit forrit tae 't. For I was aye feared at lichtning, and if it came that nicht I was bound to get clean dazed and likely tummle in. I was a lonely man wi' nae kin to speak o', so it wouldna maitter muckle.

'But now I come to tell ye about the queer side o' that nicht's wark, while I never telled to nane but yoursel, though a' the folk about here ken the rest. I maun hae been geyan weak, for I got into a kind o' doze, no sleepin', ye understand, but awfu' like it. And then a' sort o' daft things began to dance afore my een. Witches and bogles and brownies and things oot o' the Bible, and leviathans and brazen bulls—a' cam fleerin' and flauntin' on the top o' the water straucht afore me. I didna pay muckle heed to them, for I half kenned it was a' nonsense, and syne they gaed awa'. Then an aulf wife wi' a mutch and a hale procession o' auld wives passed, and just about the last I saw yin I thocht I kenned.

'"Is that you, grannie?" says I.

'"Ay, it's me, Gidden," says she; and as shure as I'm a leevin' man, it was my auld grannie, whae had been deid thae sax year. She had on the same mutch as she aye wore, and the same auld black stickie in her hand, and, Dod, she had the same snuff-box I made for her out o' a sheep's horn when I first took to the herdin'. I thocht she was lookin' rale weel.

'"Losh, Grannie," says I, "Where in the warld hae ye come frae? It's no canny to see ye danderin' about there."

'"Ye've been badly brocht up," she says, "and ye ken nocht about it. Is't no a decent and comely thing that I should get a breath o' air yince in a while?"

'"Deed," said I, "I had forgotten. Ye were sae like yoursel I never had a mind ye were deid. And how d' ye like the Guid Place?"

'"Wheesht, Gidden," says she, very solemn-like, "I'm no there."

'Now at this I was fair flabbergasted. Grannie had aye been a guid contentit auld wumman, and to think that they hadna let her intil Heeven made me think ill o' my ain chances.

'"Help us, ye dinna mean to tell me ye're in Hell?" I cries.

'"No exactly," says she, "But I'll trouble ye, Gidden, to speak mair respectful about holy things. That's a name ye uttered the noo whilk we dinna daur to mention."

'"I'm sorry, Grannie," says I, "but ye maun allow it's an astonishin' thing for me to hear. We aye counted ye shure, and ye died wi' the Buik in your hands."

'"Weel," she says, "it was like this. When I gaed up till the gate o' Heeven a man wi' a long white robe comes and says, 'Wha may ye be?' Says I, 'I'm Elspeth Scott.' He gangs awa' and consults a wee and then he says, 'I think, Elspeth my wumman, ye'll hae to gang doon the brae a bit. Ye're no quite guid eneuch for this place, but ye'll get a very comfortable doonsittin' whaur I tell ye. 'So off I gaed and cam' to a place whaur the air was like the inside of the glass-houses at the Lodge. They took me in wi'oot a word and I've been rale comfortable. Ye see they keep the bad part o' the Ill Place for the reg'lar bad folk, but they've a very nice half-way house where the likes o' me stop."

'"And what kind o' company hae ye?"

'"No very select," says she. "There's maist o' the ministers o' the countryside and a pickle fairmers, tho' the maist o' them are further ben. But there's my son Jock, your ain faither, Gidden, and a heap o' folk from the village, and oh, I'm nane sae bad."

'"Is there naething mair ye wad like then, Grannie?"

'"Oh aye," says she, "we've each yae thing which we canna get. It's a' the punishment we hae. Mine's butter. I canna get fresh butter for my bread, for ye see it winna keep, it just melts. So I've to take jeely to ilka slice, whilk is rale sair on the teeth. Ye'll no hae ony wi' ye?"

'"No," I says, "I've naething but some tobaccy. D' ye want it? Ye were aye fond o' 't."

'"Na, na," says she. "I get plenty o' tobaccy doon bye. The pipe's never out o' the folks' mouth there. But I'm no speakin' about yoursel, Gidden. Ye're in a geyan ticht place."

'"I'm a' that," I said. "Can ye no help me?"

'"I micht try." And she raxes out her hand to grip mine. I put out mine to take it, never thinkin' that that wasna the richt side, and that if Grannie grippit it she wad pu' the broken airm and haul me into the water. Something touched my fingers like a hot poker; I gave a great yell; and ere ever I kenned I was awake, a' but off the rock, wi' my left airm aching like hell-fire. Mr Airthur I had let slunge ower the heid and my ain legs were in the water.

'I gae an awfu' whammle and edged my way back though it was near bye my strength. And now anither thing happened. For the cauld water roused Mr Airthur frae his dwam. His een opened and he gave a wild look around him. "Where am I?" he cries, "Oh God!" and he gaed off intil anither faint.

'I can tell ye, sir, I never felt anything in this warld and I hope never to feel anything in anither sae bad as the next meenutes on that rock. I was fair sick wi' pain and weariness and a kind o' fever. The lip-lap o' the water, curling round Mr Airthur, and the great *crush* o' the Black Linn itsel dang me fair silly. Then there was my airm, which was bad eneuch, and abune a' I was gotten into sic a state that I was fleyed as ilka shadow just like a bairn. I felt fine I was gaun daft, and if the thing had lasted anither score o' meenutes I wad be in a madhouse this day. But soon I felt the sleepiness comin' back, and I was off again dozin' and dreamin'.

'This time it was nae auld wumman but a muckle black-avised man that was standin' in the water glowrin' at me. I kenned him fine by the bandy-legs o' him and the broken nose (whilk I did mysel), for Dan Kyle the poacher deid thae twae year. He was a man, as I remembered him weel, wi' a great black beard and een that were stuck sae far in his heid that they looked like twae wull-cats keekin' oot o' a hole. He stands and just stares at me, and never speaks a word.

'"What d'ye want?" I yells, for by this time I had lost a' grip o' mysel. "Speak, man, and dinna stand there like a dummy."

'"I want naething," he says in a mournfu' sing-song voice, "I'm just thinkin'."

'"Whaur d' ye come frae?" I asked, "and are ye keepin' weel?"

'"Weel," he says bitterly. "In this warld I was ill to my wife, and two-three times I near killed a man, and I stole like a pyet, and I was never sober. How d'ye think I should be weel in the next?"

'I was sorry for the man. "D'ye ken I'm vexed for ye, Dan," says I; "I never likit ye when ye were here, but I'm wae to think ye're sae ill off yonder."

'"I'm no alane," he says. "There's Mistress Courhope o' the Big House, she's waur. Ye mind she was awfu' fond o' gum-flowers. Weel, she canna keep them Yonder, for they a' melt wi' the heat. She's in an ill way about it, puir body." Then he broke off. "Whae's that ye've got there? Is't Airthur Morrant?"

'"Ay, it's Airthur Morrant," I said.

'"His family's weel kent doon bye," says he. "We've maist o' his forebears, and we're expectin' the auld Lord every day. May be we'll sune get the lad himsel."

'"That's a damned lee," says I, for I was angry at the man's presumption.

'Dan lookit at me sorrowfu'-like. "We'll be gettin' you tae, if ye swear that gate," says he, "and then ye'll ken what it's like."

'Of a sudden I fell into a great fear. "Dinna say that, Dan," I cried; "I'm better than ye think. I'm a deacon, and 'll maybe sune be an elder, and I never swear except at my dowg."

'"Tak care, Gidden," said the face afore me. "Where I am, a' things are taken into account."

'"Then they'll hae a gey big account for you," says I. "What-like do they treat you, may be?"

'The man groaned.

'"I'll tell ye what they dae to ye doon there," he said. "They put ye intil a place a' paved wi' stanes and wi' four square walls around. And there's naething in 't, nae grass, nae shadow. And abune you there's a sky like brass. And sune ye get terrible hot and thirsty, and your tongue sticks to your mouth, and your eyes get blind wi' lookin' on the white stane. Then ye gang clean fey, and dad your heid on the ground and the walls to try and kill yoursel. But though ye dae 't till a' eternity ye couldna feel pain. A' that ye feel is just the awfu' devourin' thirst, and the heat and the weariness. And if ye lie doon the ground burns ye and ye're fain to get up. And ye canna lean on the walls for the heat, and bye and bye when ye're fair perished wi' the thing, they tak ye out to try some ither ploy."

'"Nai mair," I cried, "nae mair, Dan!"

'But he went on malicious-like,—

'"Na, na, Gidden, I'm no dune yet. Syne they tak you to a fine room but awfu' warm. And there's a big fire in the grate and thick woollen rugs on the floor. And in the corner there's a braw feather bed. And they lay ye down on 't, and then they pile on the tap o' ye mattresses and blankets and sacks and great rolls o' woollen stuff miles wide. And then ye see what they're after, tryin' to suffocate ye as they dae to folk that a mad dowg has bitten. And ye try to kick them off, but they're ower heavy, and ye canna move your feet nor your airms nor gee your heid. Then ye gang clean gyte and skirl to yoursel, but your voice is choked and naebody is near. And the warst o' 't is that ye canna die and get it ower. It's like death a hundred times and yet ye're aye leevin'. Bye and bye when they think ye've got eneuch they tak you out and put ye somewhere else."

'"Oh," I cries, "stop, man, or you'll ding me silly."

'But he says never a word, just glowrin' at me.

'"Aye, Gidden, and waur than that. For they put ye in a great loch wi' big waves just like the sea at the Pier o' Leith. And there's nae chance o' soomin', for as sune as ye put out your airms a billow gulfs ye down. Then ye swallow water and your heid dozes round and ye're chokin'. But ye canna die, ye must just thole. And down ye gang, down, down, in the cruel deep, till your heid's like to burst and your een are fu' o' bluid. And there's 'a kind o' fearfu' monsters about, muckle slimy things wi' blind een and white scales, that claw at ye wi' claws just like the paws o' a drooned dog. And ye canna get away though ye fecht and fleech, and bye and bye ye're fair mad wi' horror and choking and the feel o' thae awfu' things. Then—"

'But now I think something snapped in my heid, and I went daft in doonricht earnest. The man before me danced about like a lantern's shine on a windy nicht and then disappeared. And I woke yelling like a pig at a killing, fair wud wi' terror, and my skellochs made the rocks ring. I found mysel in the pool a' but yae airm—the broken yin—which had hankit in a crack o' rock. Nae wonder I had been dreaming o' deep waters among the torments o' the Ill Place, when I was in them mysel. The pain in my airm was sae fearsome and my heid was gaun round sae wi' horror that I just skirled on and on, shrieking and groaning wi'oot a thocht what I was daein'. I was as near death as ever I will be, and as for Mr Airthur he was on the very nick o' 't, for by this time he was a' in the water, though I still kept a grip o' him.

'When I think ower it often I wonder how it was possible that I could be here the day. But the Lord's very gracious, and he works in a queer way. For it so happened that Ebie Blackstock, whae had left Gledsmuir an hour afore me and whom I thocht by this time to be snorin' in his bed at the Head o' the Hope, had gone intil the herd's house at the Waterfit, and had got sae muckle drink there that he was sweered to start for hame till about half-past twal i' the night. Weel, he was comin' up the burnside, gae happy and contentit, for he had nae wife at hame to speir about his ongaeings, when, as he's telled me himsel, he heard sic an uproar doon by the Black Linn that made him turn pale and think that the Deil, whom he had long served, had gotten him at last. But he was a brave man, was Ebie, and he thinks to himsel that some fellow-creature micht be perishin'. So he gangs forrit wi' a' his pith, trying to think on the Lord's Prayer and last Sabbath's sermon. And, lookin' ower the edge, he saw naething for a while, naething but the black water wi' the awfu' yells coming out o' 't. Then he made out something like a heid near the side. So he rins doon by the road, no ower the rocks as I had come, but round by the burnside road, and soon he gets to the pool, where the crying was getting aye fainter and fainter. And then he saw me. And he grips me by the collar, for he was a sensible man, was Ebie, and hauls me oot. If he hadna been geyan strong he couldna hae dune it, for I was a deid wecht, forbye having a heavy man hanging on to me. When he got me up, what was his astonishment to find anither man at the end o' my airm, a man like a crop a' bloody about the heid. So he got us baith out, and we wae baith senseless; and he laid us in a safe bit back frae the water, and syne gaed off for help. So bye and bye we were baith got home, me to my house and Mr Airthur up to the Lodge.'

'And was that the end of it?' I asked.

'Na,' said the shepherd. 'I lay for twae month there raving wi' brain fever, and when I cam to my senses I was as weak as a bairn. It was many months ere I was mysel again, and my left airm to this day is stiff and no muckle to lippen to. But Mr Airthur was far waur, for the dad he had gotten on the rock was thocht to have broken his skull, and he lay long atween life and death. And the warst thing was that his faither was sae vexed about him that he never got ower the shock, but dee'd afore Airthur was out o' bed. And so when he cam out again he was My Lord, and a monstrously rich man.'

The shepherd puffed meditatively at his pipe for a few minutes.

'But that's no a' yet. For Mr Airthur wad take nae refusal but that I maun gang awa' doon wi' him to his braw house in England and be a land o' factor or steward or something like that. And I had a rale fine cottage a' to mysel, wi' a very bonny gairden and guid wages, so I stayed there maybe sax month and then I gaed up till him. "I canna bide nae longer," says I. "I canna stand this place. It's far ower laigh, and I'm fair sick to get hills to rest my een on. I'm awfu' gratefu' to ye for your kindness, but I maun gie up my job." He was very sorry to lose me, and was for giein' me a present o' money or stockin' a fairm for me, because he said that it was to me he owed his life. But I wad hae nane o' his gifts. "It wad be a terrible thing," I says, "to take siller for daein' what ony body wad hae dune out o' pity." So I cam awa' back to Standlan, and I maun say I'm rale contentit here. Mr Airthur used whiles to write to me and ca' in and see me when he cam North for the shooting; but since he's gane sae far wrang wi' the Tories, I've had naething mair to dae wi' him.'

I made no answer, being busy pondering in my mind on the depth of the shepherd's political principles, before which the ties of friendship were as nothing.

'Aye,' said he, standing up, 'I did what I thocht my duty at the time and I was rale glad I saved the callant's life. But now, when I think on a' the ill he's daein' to the country and the Guid Cause, I whiles think I wad hae been daein' better if I had just drappit him in.

'But whae kens? It's a queer warld.' And the shepherd knocked the ashes out of his pipe.

Duncan Williamson

DEATH IN A NUT

Duncan Williamson (b.1928) is a living exponent of the Scots and Celtic story telling traditions as they remain preserved within the surviving traveller families. The stories he brings to life have links with Gaelic and international tales which can in turn trace their origins back to the earliest myths and storytellers.

In his fifty years amongst the travelling people of Scotland, Williamson developed a formidable reputation for his skills and the range of his repertoire. He now lives with his wife Linda, who transcribes his stories for publication. These stories are rendered in a vibrant Scots travellers' dialect which has a remarkable richness and immediacy even in print.

These tales are now available to a wider audience and have since been acknowledged as a fundamental part of Scotland's social and literary heritage. When Duncan Williamson first heard them, in the tent where he was born on the shores of Loch Fyne, they were a natural source of education and entertainment to all traveller children.

Death in a Nut

JACK LIVED with his mother in a little cottage by the shoreside, an his mother kept some ducks an some hens. Jack cuid barely remember his father because his father had died long before he wis born. An they had a small kin o croft, Jack cut a little hay fir his mother's goats. When dher wur no hay tae collect, he spent most of his time along the shoreside as a beach-comber collecting everything that cam in bi the tide, whatever it wad be—any auld drums, any auld cans, pieces of driftwood, something that wis flung off a boat—Jack collectit all these things an brought them in, put them biside his mother's cottage an said, 'Some day they might come in useful.' But the mos thing that Jack ever collected fir his mother was firewood. An Jack wis very happy, he wis jist a young man, his early teens, and he dearly loved his mother. He used tae some days take duck eggs tae the village (his mother wis famed fir er duck eggs) an hen eggs to the village forbyes, they helped them survive, and his mother wad take in a little sewin fir the local people in the village; Jack and his mother lived quite happy. Till one particular day, it wis around about the wintertime, about the month o January, this time o the year now.

Jack used tae always get up early in the mornin an make a cup o tea, he always gev his mother a cup o tea in bed every mornin. An one particular mornin he rose early because he want't tae catch the in-comin tide tae see what it wad bring in fir him. He brought a cup o tea into his mother in her own little bed in a little room, it wis only a two-room little cottage they had.

He says, 'Mother, I've brought you a cup o' tea.'

She says, 'Son, I don't want any tea.'

'Mother,' he says, 'why? What's wrong, are you not feelin—'

She says, 'Son, I'm not feelin' very well this morning, I'm not feelin very well. I don't think I cuid even drink a cup of tea if ye gev it to me.'

'Oh, Mother,' he says, 'try an take a wee sip,' an he leaned over the bed, held the cup to his mother's mooth an tried to get her . . .

She took two-three sips, 'That's enough, laddie,' she says, 'I don't feel very well.'

He says, 'What's wrong with you, Mother? Are you in pain or somethin?'

'Well, so an no so, Jack, I dinnae ken what's wrong wi me,' she says, 'I'm an ill woman, Jack, an ye're a young man an I cannae go on for ever.'

'But, Mother,' he says, 'you cannae dee an leave me masel! What am

I gaunnae dae? I've nae freends, nae naebody in this worl but you, Mother! Ye cannae dee an lea me!'

'Well,' she says, 'Jack, I think I'm no long fir this worl. In fact, I think he'll be comin fir me some o these days . . . soon.'

'Wha, Mother, ye talking about "comin fir me"?'

She says, 'Jack, ye ken wha he is, Jack. Between me an you, we dinna share nae secrets—I'm an auld woman an I'm gaunna dee—Death's gaunna come fir me, Jack, I can see it in ma mind.'

'Oh, Mother, no, Mother,' he says, an he held her hand.

'But,' she says, 'never mind, laddie, ye'll manage to take care o yirsel. Yir mother has saved a few shillins fir ye an I'm sure some day ye'll meet a nice wee wife when I'm gone, ye'll prob'ly get on in the world.'

'No, Mother,' he says, 'I cuidna get on withoot you.'

She says, 'Laddie, leave me an I'll try an get a wee sleep.'

Bi this time it was daylight as the sun begint tae get up, an Jack walkit up along the shoreway jist in the grey-dark in the mornin, gettin clear. It must hae been about half-past eight-nine o'clock, (in the wintertime it took a long while tae get clear in the mornins) when the tide was comin in. Jack walked along the shoreway an lo an behold, the first thing he seen comin a-walkin the shoreway was an auld man with a long grey beard, skinny legs and a ragged coat o'er his back an a scythe on his back. His two eyes were sunk inta his heid, sunk back intae his skull, an he wis the most uglies'-luikin creature that Jack ever seen in his life. But he had on his back a *brand new scythe* an hit was shinin in the light fae the mornin.

Noo, his mother hed always tellt Jack what like Deith luikit an Jack says tae his ainsel, 'That's Deith come fir my auld mother! He's come tae take on'y thing that I love awa fae me, but,' he said, 'he's no gettin awa wi it! He's no gettin away wi hit!' So Jack steps oot aff the shoreside, an up he comes an meets this Auld Man—bare feet, lang ragged coat, lang ragged beard, high cheek bones an his eyes sunk back in his heid, two front teeth sticking out like that—an a shinin scythe on his back, the morning sun wis glitterin on the blade—ready to cut the people's throats an take them away to the Land o Death.

Jack steps up, says, 'Good morning, Auld Man.'

'Oh,' he said, 'good morning, young man! Tell me, is it far tae the next cottage?'

Jack said, 'Ma mother lives i the next cottage just along the shoreway a little bit.'

'Oh,' he says, 'that's her I want to visit.'

'Not this mornin,' says Jack, 'ye're not gaunna visit her! I know who you are—you're Death—an you've come tae take my aul mother, kill her an tak her awa an lea me masel.'

'Well,' Death says, 'it's natural. Yir mother, ye know, she's an auld wumman an she's reacht a certain age, I'll no be doin her any harm, I'll jist do her a guid turn—she's sufferin in pain.'

'You're no takin my aul mither!' says Jack. And he ran forward, he snappit the scythe aff the Aul Man's back an he walkit tae a big stane, he smashed the scythe against the stane.

An the Auld Man got angrier an angrier an angrier an ugly-luikin, 'My young man,' he says, 'you've done that—but that's not the end!'

'Well,' Jack says, 'it's the end fir you!' An Jack dived o top o him, Jack got a haud o him an Jack pickit a bit stick up the shoreside, he beat him an he weltit him an he weltit him an he beat him an he weltit him. He fought wi Death an Death wis as strong as what Jack was, but finally Jack conquered him! An Jack beat im with a bit stick, and lo an behold the funny thing happened: the more Jack beat him the wee-er he got, an Jack beat him an Jack beat him an Jack beat him—no blood cam fae him or nothing—Jack beat him wi the stick till he got barely the size o that! An Jack catcht im in his hand, 'Now,' he said, 'I got ye! Ye'll no get my aul mither!'

Noo Jack thought in his ainsel, 'What in the worl am I gaunna do wi him? A hev him here, I canna let him go, A beat him, I broke his scythe an I conquered him. But what in the world am I gaunna do wi him? I canna hide him bilow a stane because he'll creep oot an he'll come back tae his normal size again.' An Jack walkit along the shore an he luikit—comin in by the tide was a big hazelnut, that size! But the funny thing about this hazelnut, a squirrel had dug a hole in the nut cause squirrels always dig holes in the nuts—they have sharp teeth—an he eats the kernel oot inside an leas the empty case. An Jack pickit up the hazelnut, he luikit, says, 'The very thing!' An Jack crushed Death in through the wee hole—inta the nut! An squeezed him in heid fist, an his wee feet, put him in there, shoved him in. An he walkit aboot, he got a wee plug o stick and he plugged the hole fae the outside. 'Now,' he says, 'Death, you'll never get ma mither.' An he catcht him in his hand, he threw im oot inta the tide! An the heavy waves wis 'whoosh-an-whoosh-an-whoosh-an, whoosh-an-whoosh-in' in an back an forward. An Jack watched the wee nut, hit went a-sailin, floatin an back an forward away wi the tide. 'That's hit!' says Jack, 'that's the end o Death. He'll never bother my mother again, or naebody else forbyes my mither.'

Jack got two-three sticks under his arm an he walkit back. Whan he landed back he seen the reek wis comin fae the chimney, he says, 'My mother must be up, she must be feelin a wee bit better.' Lo an behold he walks in the hoose, there wis his auld mother up, her sleeves rolled up, her face full o flooer, her apron on an she's busy makin scones.

He said, 'How ye feelin, Mother?'

She says, 'Jack, I'm feelin great, I never feelt better in ma life! Laddie, I dinna ken what happened to me, but I wis lyin there fir a minute in pain an torture, and all in a minute I feelt liek someone hed come an rumbled all the pains an tuik everything oot o my body, an made me . . . I feel like a lassie again, Jack! I made some scones fir yir breakfast.'

Jack never mentioned to his mother aboot Deith, never said a word. His mother fasselt roon the table, she's pit up her hair . . . Jack never seen his mother in better health in her life! Jack sit doon bi the fire, his mother made some scones. He had a wee bit scone, he says, 'Mother, is that all you've got tae eat?'

'Well,' she says, 'Jack, the're no much, jist a wee puckle flooer an I thocht I'd mak ye a wee scone fir yir breakfast. Go on oot tae the hen house an get a couple eggs, I'll mak ye a couple eggs alang wi yir scone an that'll fill ye up, laddie.'

Jack walks oot to the hen hoose as usual, wee shed beside his mother's hoose. Oh, every nest is full o eggs, hens' eggs, duck eggs, the nests is all full. Jack picks up four o the big beautiful broon eggs oot o the nest, gaes back in an 'Here, Mother, the're fowr,' he said, 'two tae you, two to me.'

De aul wumman says, 'I'll no be a minute, Jack.' It was an open fire they had. The wumman pulled the sway oot, put the fryin pan on, pit a wee bit fat i the pan. She waitit an she waitit an she watcht, but the wee bit fat wadna melt. She poked the fire with the poker but the wee bit fat wadna melt. 'Jack,' she says, 'fire's no kindlin very guid, laddie, it'll no even melt that wee bit fat.'

'Well, pit some mair sticks on, Mother,' he said, 'pit some mair wee bits o sticks on.' Jack pit the best o sticks on, but na! The wee bit o fat sut in the middle o the pan, but it wouldna melt, he says, 'Mother, never mind, pit the egg in an gie it a rummle roon, it'll dae me the way it is. Jis pit it in the pan.'

Aul mother tried—'crack'—na. She hut the egg again—na. An s'pose she cuid hae take a fifty-pun hammer an hut the egg, *that egg would not break!* She says, 'Jack, I cannae break these eggs.'

'An, Mother,' he said, 'I thought ye said ye were feelin weel an feelin guid, an you cannae break an egg! Gie me the egg, I'll break hit!' Jack tuik the egg, went in his big hand, ye ken, Jack big young laddie, catcht the egg one hand—'clank' on the side o the pan—na! Ye're as well tae hit a stane on the side o the pan, *the egg would not break* in no way in this worl! 'Ah, Mother,' he says, 'I dinna ken what's wrong, I dinna ken whit's wrong, Mother, wi these eggs, I don't know. Prob'ly they're no richt eggs, I better go an get another two.'

He walkit oot to the shed again, he brung in two duck eggs. But he tried the same—na, they wadna break, the eggs jist would not break in any way in the worl. 'Mother,' he says, 'pit them in a taste o water an bring them a-boil!'

She says, 'That's right, Jack, I never thocht about that.' The aul wumman got a wee pan an the fir wis goin well bi this time of bonnie shore sticks. She pit the pan on an within seconds the water wis boilan, she poppit the two eggs in. An it bubbled an bubbled an bubbled an bubbled an bubbled, an bubbled, she said, 'They're ready noo, Jack.' She tuik them oot—'crack'—na. As suppose they hed hae tried fir months, they cuidna crack that two eggs.

'Ah, Mother,' he says, 'the're something wrong. Mither, the're something wrong, the're enchantment upon us, that eggs'll no cook. We're gaunna dee wi hunger.'

'Never mind, Jack,' she says, 'eat yir wee bit scone. I'll mak ye a wee drop soup, I'll mak ye a wee pot o soup. Go oot tae the gairden, Jack, an get me a wee taste o vegetables, leeks an a few carrots.'

'Noo Jack had a guid garden he passes all his time makkin a guid garden tae his mother. Ot he goes, he pulls two carrots, a leek, bit parsley an a neep an he brings it tae his mother. Aul wumman washes the pots, pits some water in, pits it on the fire. But she goes tae the table with the knife, but na—every time she touches the carrot, the knife jist skates aff hit. She toucht the leek—it skates aff it an aa. The auld wumman tried her best, an Jack tried his best—there's no way in the world—Jack said, 'That knife's blunt, Mother.'

An Jack had a wee bit o shairpen stane he'd fand in the shoreside, he took the stane an he shairpit the knife, but no way in the world wad hit ever look at the carrots or the neep or the wee bit parsley tae mak a wee pot o soup. She says, 'Jack, the're somethin wrang wi my vegetables, Jack, they must be frozen solid.'

'But,' he said, 'Mother, the're been nae frost tae freeze them! Hoo in the world can this happen?'

'Well,' she says, 'Jack, luik, ye ken I've an awfa cockerels this year, we have an awfa cockerels an we'll no need them aa, Jack. Wad ye gae oot to the shed an pull a cockerel's neck, and A'll pit it in the pot, boil hit for wir supper?'

'Ay,' says Jack. Noo the aul wumman kep a lot o hens. Jack went oot an all i the shed dher wur dozens o them sittin i a raa, cockerels o all description. Jack luikit ti he seen a big fat cockerel sittin on a perch, he put his hand up, catcht hit an he feel'd it, it wis fat. 'Oh,' he says, 'Mother'll be pleased wi this yin.' Jack pullt the neck—na! Pulled again—*no way*. He pullt it, he shakit it, he swung it roond his heid three-five times. He tuik a stick and he battert it i the heid, there's no way—he cuidna touch the cockerel in any way! He pit it bilow his oxter an he walks inta his mother.

She said, 'Ye get a cockerel, Jack?'

'Oh, Mother,' he said, 'I got a cockerel aa right, I got a cockerel. But, Mother, you may care!'*

She says, 'What do you mean, laddie?'

'You may care,' he says, 'I cannae kill hit.'

*you may care—there's nothing you can do about it

'Ah, Jack,' she says, 'ye cannae kill a cockerel! I ken, ye killt dozens tae me afore, the hens an ducks an aa.'

'Mother,' he said, 'I cannae kill this one—it'll no dee!'

She says, 'Gie me it ower here, gie me it over here!' An the auld woman had a wee hatchet fir splittin sticks, she kep it by the fire. She says, 'Gie it tae me, Jack, I'll show ye the way tae kill it ricth!' She pit it doon the top o the block an she hut it wi the hatchet, chop its heid aff. She hut it with the hatchet seventeen times, but no—every time the heid jumpit aff—heid jumpit back on! 'Na, Jack,' she says, 'it's nae good. There's something wrang here, the're something terrible gaun a-wrong. Nethin seems tae be richt aboot the place. Here—go out to my purse, laddie, run up tae the village to the butcher! I'm savin this fir a rainy day,' an she tuik a half-croon oot o her purse. 'Jack, gae up tae the butcher an get a wee bit o meat fae the butcher, I'll mak ye a wee bite when ye come back.'

Noo, it wisna far fae the wee hoose to the village, about a quarter o mile Jack hed tae walk. When Jack walkit up the village, all the people were gaithert in the middle o the town square. They're all bletherin an they're chattin and they're bletherin an they're chattin, speakin tae each other. One was sayin, 'A've sprayed ma garden an it's overrun wi caterpillars! An I've tried tae spray hit, it's no good.'

The butcher wis oot wi his apron, he said, 'Three times I tried tae kill a bullock this mornin an three times I killed it, three times it jumpit back on its feet. I don't know what's wrong. The villagers run out o meat! I got a quota o hens in this mornin, ducks, an every time I pull their necks their heads jumps back on. There's somethin terrible is happenin!'

Jack went up to the butcher's, he says, 'Gie me a wee bit o meat fir ma mother.'

He says, 'Laddie, the're no a bit o meat in the shop. Dae ye no ken what I'm tryi' tae tell the people in the village: I've tried ma best this mornin to kill a young bullock tae supply the village an I cannae kill hit!'

'Well,' Jack said, 'the same thing happen to me. I tried tae boil an egg an I cannae boil an egg, I tried tae kill a cockerel—'

'I tried tae kill ten cockerels,' says the butcher, 'but *they'll no dee!*'

'Oh dear-dear,' says Jack, 'we must be in some kin o trouble. Is hit happenin tae other places forbyes this?'

'Well, I jist hed word,' says the butcher, 'the next village up two mile awa an the same thing's happened tae them. Folk cannae even eat an apple—when they sink their teeth inta it, it'll no even bite. They cannae cook a vegetable, they cannae boil water, they cannae dae nothin! The hale worl's gaunna come tae a standstill, the're something gaen terrible wrong—*nothing seems to die anymore.*'

An then Jack thought in his head, he said, 'It's my fault, I'm the cause o't.' He walkit back an he tellt his mother the same story I'm tellin you. He says, 'Mother, there's nae butcher meat fir ye.'

She says, 'Why, laddie, why no?'

He says, 'Luik, the butcher cannae kill nae beef, because hit'll no dee.'

'But Jack,' she says, 'why no—it'll no dee? What's wrang with the country, what's wrang with the world?'

He says, 'Mother, it's all my fault!'

'Your fault,' she says, 'Jack?'

'Ay, Mither, it's my fault,' he says. 'Listen, Mother: this morning when you were no feeling very well, I walkit along the shore tae gather some sticks fir the fire an I met Death comin tae tak ye awa. An I took his scythe fae him an I broke his scythe, I gi'n him a beatin, Mither, an I put him in a nut! An I flung him in the tide an I plugged the nut so's he canna get oot, Mither. An God knows where he is noo. He's floatin in the sea, Mother, firever an ever an ever, an nothing'll dee—the worl is overrun with caterpillars an worms an everything—Mither, the're nothing can dee! But Mither, I wad rather die with starvation than loss you.'

'Jack, Jack, Jack, laddie,' she says, 'dae ye no ken what ye've done? Ye've destroyed the only thing that keeps the world alive.'

'What do you mean, Mother, "keeps the world alive"? Luik, if I hedna killed him, I hedna hae beat im, Mother, an pit him in that nut—you'd be dead bi this time!'

'I wad be dead, Jack,' she says, 'probably, but the other people would be gettin food, an the worl'd be gaun on—the way it shuid be—only fir you, laddie!'

'But, Mother,' he says, 'what am I gaunna dae?'

She says, 'Jack, there's only thing ye can dae . . . ye're a beach-comber like yir faither afore ye—'

'Aye, Mother,' he says, 'I'm a beach-comber.'

'Well, Jack,' she says, 'there's only thing I can say: ye better gae an get im back an set him free! Because if ye dinnae, ye're gaunna put the whole worl tae a standstill. *Bithout Death there is no life* . . . fir nobody.'

'But, Mother,' he says, 'if I set him free, he's gaunna come fir you.'

'Well, Jack, if he comes fir me,' she said, 'I'll be happy, and go inta another world an be peaceful! But you'll be alive an so will the rest o the world.'

'But Mother,' he says, 'I cuidna live bithoot ye.'

'But,' she says, 'Jack, if ye dinnae set him free, *both* o hus'll suffer, an I cannae stand tae see you suffer fir the want o something to eat: because the're nothing in the world will die unless you set him free, because you cannae eat nothing until it's dead.'

Jack thought in his mind fir a wee while. 'Aa right, Mother,' he says, 'if that's the way it shuid be, that's the way it shuid be. Prob'ly I wis wrong.'

'Of course, Jack,' she says, 'you were wrong.'

'But,' he says, 'Mother, I only done it fir yir sake.'

'Well,' she says, 'Jack, fir *my* sake, wad ye search fir that hazelnut an set him free?'

So the next mornin true tae his word, Jack walks the tide an walks the tide fir miles an miles an miles, day out an day in fir three days an fir three days more. He hedna nothin tae eat, he only hed a drink water. They cuidna cook anything, they cuidna eat any eggs, they couldna fry nothing in the pan if they had it, they cuidna make any soup, they cuidna get nothin. The caterpillars an the worms crawled out o the garden in thousands, an they ett every single vegetable that Jack had. An the're nothing in the world—Jack went out an tried to teem hot water on them but it wis nae good. When he teemed hot water on them it just wis the same as he never poored nothing—no way. At last Jack said, 'I must go an find that nut!' So he walkit an he walkit, an he walkit day an he walkit night mair miles than he ever walked before, but no way cuid Jack fin' this nut! Till Jack was completely exhaustit an fed up an completely sick, an he cuidna walk another mile. He sat doon bi the shoreside right infront o his mother's hoose to rest, an wonderit, he pit his hand on his jaw an he said tae his ainsel, 'What have I done? I've ruint the world, I've destroyed the world. People disna know,' he said, 'what Death has so good, at Death is such a guid person. I wis wrong tae beat him an put him in a nut.'

An he's luikin all over—an lo and behold he luikit doon—there at his feet he seen a wee nut, an a wee bit o stick stickin oot hit. He liftit hit up in his hand, an Jack wis happy, happier an he'd ever been in his life before! And he pulled the plug an a wee head poppit oot. Jack held im in his two hands and Death spoke tae him, 'Now, Jack,' he said, 'are ye happy?'

'No,' Jack said, 'I'm no happy.'

He said, 'You thought if you beat me an conquered me an killed me—because I'm jist Death—that that wad be the end, everything be all right. Well, Jack, ma laddie, ye've got a lot to learn, Jack. Without me,' he said, 'there's no life.'

An Jack tuik him oot.

'But,' he says, 'Jack, thank you fir settin me free,' an jist like that, after Jack opent the nut, he cam oot an like that, he cam full strength again an stude before Jack—the same Auld Man with the long ragged coat an the sunken eyes an the two teeth in the front an the bare feet. He says, 'Jack, ye broke my scythe.'

Jack said, 'I'll tell ye somethin, while I wis searchin fir you ma mother made me mend it. An I have it in the hoose fir ye, come wi me!' An Jack led him up to the hoose. Lo an behold sure enough, sittin on the front o the porch wis the scythe that Jack broke. Jack had tuik it an he'd mend't it, he sortit it an made it as guid as ever.

Death cam to the door an he ran his hand doon the face o the scythe, he sput on his thumb and he run it up the face o the scythe, an he says tae Jack, 'I see you've sharpened it, Jack, and ye made a good job o it. Well, I hev some people to see in the village, Jack. But remember, I'll come back fir yir mother someday, but seein you been guid to me I'll make it a wee while!' An Death walkit away.

Jack an his mother lived happy till his mother wis about a hundred years of age! An then one day Death cam back tae take his aul mother away, but Jack never saw him. But Jack was happy fir he knew *there is no life bithout Death*. An that is the end o my story.

George MacDonald

THE GOLDEN KEY

George MacDonald (1824–1905), was raised on a farm in Aberdeenshire, from where he went to Aberdeen University to take an Arts degree. As a Congregationalist minister in Arundel, Sussex he got into trouble for expressing the belief that heathens could find salvation and that animals might go to heaven. He resigned and set out to support his wife and eleven children by writing and lecturing. He was the friend of many late Victorian writers and became known as a poet, a popular preacher, and the author of numerous novels. Many of these have banal, melodramatic plots and cardboard villains, but he uses them to assess his own background and argues that everyone needs to discover an unrestrained divine and human love which is free from Calvinism. Writing for an English market, MacDonald used Scots dialect self-consciously and helped establish the Kailyard School with several novels set in his native North East. When writing from his imagination, however, he seems to inhabit a country of the mind which is his own and his work has been praised by C.S.Lewis among others for its understanding of the language and symbolism of dreams.

'The Golden Key' is his best story. It is an allegory, a sort of pilgrim's progress which stresses the need for love and charity. The Golden Key broadly represents faith and the Grandmother represents a religion beyond dogma or creed. Mossy and Tangle seem to climb up a scale of being whose stages are marked by Sea, Earth and Fire, where the Devil and Hell hardly seem to apply: MacDonald makes his own oblique comment on the mainstream of Scottish supernatural fiction.

The Golden Key

THERE WAS a boy who used to sit in the twilight and listen to his great-aunt's stories.

She told him that if he could reach the place where the end of the rainbow stands he would find there a golden key.

'And what is the key for?' the boy would ask. 'What is it the key of? What will it open?'

'That nobody knows,' his aunt would reply. 'He has to find that out.'

'I suppose, being gold,' the boy once said, thoughtfully, 'that I could get a good deal of money for it if I sold it.'

'Better never find it than sell it,' returned his aunt.

And then the boy went to bed and dreamed about the golden key.

Now all that his great-aunt told the boy about the golden key would have been nonsense, had it not been that their little house stood on the borders of Fairyland. For it is perfectly well known that out of Fairyland nobody ever can find where the rainbow stands. The creature takes such good care of its golden key, always flitting from place to place, lest any one should find it! But in Fairyland it is quite different. Things that look real in this country look very thin indeed in Fairyland, while some of the things that here cannot stand still for a moment, will not move there. So it was not in the least absurd of the old lady to tell her nephew such things about the golden key.

'Did you ever know anybody find it?' he asked, one evening.

'Yes. Your father, I believe, found it.'

'And what did he do with it, can you tell me?'

'He never told me.'

'What was it like?'

'He never showed it to me.'

'How does a new key come there always?'

'I don't know. There it is.'

'Perhaps it is the rainbow's egg.'

'Perhaps it is. You will be a happy boy if you find the nest.'

'Perhaps it comes tumbling down the rainbow from the sky.'

'Perhaps it does.'

One evening, in summer, he went into his own room, and stood at the lattice-window, and gazed into the forest which fringed the outskirts of Fairyland. It came close up to his great-aunt's garden, and, indeed, sent some straggling trees into it. The forest lay to the east, and the sun, which was setting behind the cottage, looked straight into the dark wood with his level red eye. The trees were all old, and had few branches below, so that the sun could see a great way into the forest and the boy, being keen-sighted, could see almost as far as the sun. The trunks stood like rows of red columns in the shine of the red sun, and he could see down aisle after aisle in the vanishing distance. And as he gazed into the forest he began to feel as if the trees were all waiting for him, and had something they could not go on with till he came to them. But he was hungry, and wanted his supper. So he lingered.

Suddenly, far among the trees, as far as the sun could shine, he saw a glorious thing. It was the end of a rainbow, large and brilliant. He could count all the seven colours, and could see shade after shade beyond the violet; while before the red stood a colour more gorgeous and mysterious still. It was a colour he had never seen before. Only the spring of the rainbow-arch was visible. He could see nothing of it above the trees.

'The golden key!' he said to himself, and darted out of the house, and into the wood.

He had not gone far before the sun set. But the rainbow only glowed the brighter. For the rainbow of Fairyland is not dependent upon the sun, as ours is. The trees welcomed him. The bushes made way for him. The rainbow grew larger and brighter; and at length he found himself within two trees of it.

It was a grand sight, burning away there in silence, with its gorgeous, its lovely, its delicate colours, each distinct, all combining. He could now see a great deal more of it. It rose high into the blue heavens, but bent so little that he could not tell how high the crown of the arch must reach. It was still only a small portion of a huge bow.

He stood gazing at it till he forgot himself with delight—even forgot the key which he had come to seek. And as he stood it grew more wonderful still. For in each of the colours, which was as large as the column of a church, he could faintly see beautiful forms slowly ascending as if by the steps of a winding stair. The forms appeared irregularly—now one, now many, now several, now none—men and women and children—all different, all beautiful.

He drew nearer to the rainbow. It vanished. He started back a step in dismay. It was there again, as beautiful as ever. So he contented himself with standing as near it as he might, and watching the forms that ascended the glorious colours towards the unknown height of the arch, which did not end abruptly, but faded away in the blue air; so gradually that he could not say where it ceased.

When the thought of the golden key returned, the boy very wisely proceeded to mark out in his mind the space covered by the foundation of the rainbow, in order that he might know where to search, should the rainbow disappear. It was based chiefly upon a bed of moss.

Meantime it had grown quite dark in the wood. The rainbow alone was visible by its own light. But the moment the moon rose the rainbow vanished. Nor could any change of place restore the vision to the boy's eyes. So he threw himself down upon the mossy bed, to wait till the sunlight would give him a chance of finding the key. There he fell fast asleep.

When he woke in the morning the sun was looking straight into his eyes. He turned away from it, and the same moment saw a brilliant little thing lying on the moss within a foot of his face. It was the golden key. The pipe of it was of plain gold, as bright as gold could be. The handle was curiously wrought and set with sapphires. In a terror of delight he put out his hand and took it, and had it.

He lay for a while, turning it over and over, and feeding his eyes upon its beauty. Then he jumped to his feet, remembering that the pretty thing was of no use to him yet. Where was the lock to which the key belonged? It must be somewhere, for how could anybody be so silly as make a key for which there was no lock? Where should he go to look for it? He gazed about him, up into the air, down to the earth, but saw no keyhole in the clouds, in the grass, or in the trees.

Just as he began to grow disconsolate, however, he saw something glimmering in the wood. It was a mere glimmer that he saw, but he took it for a glimmer of rainbow, and went towards it.—And now I will go back to the borders of the forest.

Not far from the house where the boy had lived, there was another house, the owner of which was a merchant, who was much away from home. He had lost his wife some years before, and had only one child, a little girl, whom he left to the charge of two servants, who were very idle and careless. So she was neglected and left untidy, and was sometimes ill-used besides.

Now it is well known that the little creatures commonly called fairies, though there are many different kinds of fairies in Fairyland, have an exceeding dislike to untidiness. Indeed, they are quite spiteful to slovenly people. Being used to all the lovely ways of the trees and flowers, and to the neatness of the birds and all woodland creatures, it makes them feel miserable, even in their deep woods and on their grassy carpets, to think that within the same moonlight lies a dirty, uncomfortable, slovenly house. And this makes them angry with the people that live in it, and they would gladly drive them out of the world if they could. They want the whole earth nice and clean. So they pinch the maids black and blue, and play them all manner of uncomfortable tricks.

But this house was quite a shame, and the fairies in the forest could not endure it. They tried everything on the maids without effect, and at last resolved upon making a clean riddance, beginning with the child. They ought to have known that it was not her fault, but they have little principle and much mischief in them, and they thought that if they got rid of her the maids would be sure to be turned away.

So one evening, the poor little girl having been put to bed early, before the sun was down, the servants went off to the village, locking the door behind them. The child did not know she was alone, and lay contentedly looking out of her window towards the forest, of which, however, she could not see much, because of the ivy and other creeping plants which had straggled across her window. All at once she saw an ape making faces at her out of the mirror, and the heads carved upon a great old wardrobe grinning fearfully. Then two old spider-legged chairs came forward into the middle of the room, and began to dance a queer, old-fashioned dance. This set her laughing, and she forgot the ape and the grinning heads. So the fairies saw they had made a mistake, and sent the chairs back to their places. But they knew that she had been reading the story of Silverhair all day. So the next moment she heard the voices of three bears upon the stairs, big voice, middle voice, and little voice, and she heard their soft, heavy tread, as if they had stockings over their boots, coming nearer and nearer to the door of her room, till she could bear it no longer. She did just as Silverhair did, and as the fairies wanted her to do: she darted to the window, pulled it open, got up on the ivy, and so scrambled to the ground. She then fled to the forest as fast as she could run.

Now, although she did not know it, this was the very best way she could have gone; for nothing is ever so mischievous in its own place as it is out of it; and, besides, these mischievous creatures were only the children of Fairyland, as it were, and there are many other beings there as well; and if a wanderer gets in among them, the good ones will always help him more than the evil ones will be able to hurt him.

The sun was now set, and the darkness coming on, but the child thought of no danger but the bears behind her. If she had looked round, however, she would have seen that she was followed by a very different creature from a bear. It was a curious creature, made like a fish, but covered, instead of scales, with feathers of all colours, sparkling like those of a humming-bird. It had fins, not wings, and swam through the air as a fish does through the water. Its head was like the head of a small owl.

After running a long way, and as the last of the light was disappearing, she passed under a tree with drooping branches. It dropped its branches to the ground all about her, and caught her as in a trap. She struggled to get out, but the branches pressed her closer and closer to the trunk. She was in great terror and distress, when the air-fish, swimming into the thicket of branches, began tearing them with its beak. They loosened their hold at once, and the creature went on attacking them, till at length they let the child go. Then the air-fish came from behind her, and swam on in front, glittering and sparkling all lovely colours; and she followed.

It led her gently along till all at once it swam in at a cottage-door. The child followed still. There was a bright fire in the middle of the floor, upon which stood a pot without a lid, full of water that boiled and bubbled furiously. The air-fish swam straight to the pot and into the boiling water, where it lay quiet. A beautiful woman rose from the opposite side of the fire and came to meet the girl. She took her up in her arms, and said,—

'Ah, you are come at last! I have been looking for you a long time.'

She sat down with her on her lap, and there the girl sat staring at her. She had never seen anything so beautiful. She was tall and strong, with white arms and neck, and a delicate flush on her face. The child could not tell what was the colour of her hair, but could not help thinking it had a tinge of dark green. She had not one ornament upon her, but she looked as if she had just put off quantities of diamonds and emeralds. Yet here she was in the simplest, poorest little cottage, where she was evidently at home. She was dressed in shining green.

The girl looked at the lady, and the lady looked at the girl.

'What is your name?' asked the lady.

'The servants always called me Tangle.'

'Ah, that was because your hair was so untidy. But that was their fault, the naughty women! Still it is a pretty name, and I will call you Tangle too. You must not mind my asking you questions, for you may ask me the same questions, every one of them, and any others that you like. How old are you?'

'Ten,' answered Tangle.

'You don't look like it,' said the lady.

'How old are you, please?' returned Tangle.

'Thousands of years old,' answered the lady.

'You don't look like it,' said Tangle.

'Don't I? I think I do. Don't you see how beautiful I am?'

And her great blue eyes looked down on the little Tangle, as if all the stars in the sky were melted in them to make their brightness.

'Ah! but,' said Tangle, 'when people live long they grow old. At least I always thought so.'

'I have no time to grow old,' said the lady. 'I am too busy for that. It is very idle to grow old.—But I cannot have my little girl so untidy. Do you know I can't find a clean spot on your face to kiss?'

'Perhaps,' suggested Tangle, feeling ashamed, but not too much so to say a word for herself—'perhaps that is because the tree made me cry so.'

'My poor darling!' said the lady, looking now as if the moon were melted in her eyes, and kissing her little face, dirty as it was, 'the naughty tree must suffer for making a girl cry.'

'And what is your name, please?' asked Tangle.

'Grandmother,' answered the lady.

'Is it really?'

'Yes, indeed. I never tell stories, even in fun.'

'How good of you!'

'I couldn't if I tried. It would come true if I said it, and then I should be punished enough.'

And she smiled like the sun through a summer-shower.

'But now,' she went on, 'I must get you washed and dressed, and then we shall have some supper.'

'Oh! I had supper long ago,' said Tangle.

'Yes, indeed you had,' answered the lady—'three years since you ran away from the bears. You don't know that it is three years since you ran away from the bears. You are thirteen and more now.'

Tangle could only stare. She felt quite sure it was true.

'You will not be afraid of anything I do with you—will you?' said the lady.

'I will try very hard not to be; but I can't be certain, you know,' replied Tangle.

'I like your saying so, and I shall be quite satisfied,' answered the lady.

She took off the girl's night-gown, rose with her in her arms, and going to the wall of the cottage, opened a door. Then Tangle saw a deep tank, the sides of which were filled with green plants, which had flowers of all colours. There was a roof over it like the roof of the cottage. It was filled with beautiful clear water, in which swam a multitude of such fishes as the one that had led her to the cottage. It was the light their colours gave that showed the place in which they were.

The lady spoke some words Tangle could not understand, and threw her into the tank.

The fishes came crowding about her. Two or three of them got under her head and kept it up. The rest of them rubbed themselves all over her, and with their wet feathers washed her quite clean. Then the lady, who had been looking on all the time, spoke again; whereupon some thirty or forty of the fishes rose out of the water underneath Tangle, and so bore her up to the arms the lady held out to take her. She carried her back to the fire, and, having dried her well, opened a chest, and taking out the finest linen garments, smelling of grass and lavender, put them upon her, and over all a green dress, just like her own, shining like hers, and soft like hers, going into just such lovely folds from the waist, where it was tied with a brown cord, to her bare feet.

'Won't you give me a pair of shoes too, grandmother?' said Tangle.

'No, my dear; no shoes. Look here. I wear no shoes.'

So saying, she lifted her dress a little, and there were the loveliest white feet, but no shoes. Then Tangle was content to go without shoes too. And the lady sat down with her again, and combed her hair, and brushed it, and then left it to dry while she got the supper.

First she got bread out of one hole in the wall; then milk out of another; then several kinds of fruit out of a third; and then she went to the pot on the fire, and took out the fish now nicely cooked, and, as soon as she had pulled off its feathered skin, ready to be eaten.

'But,' exclaimed Tangle. And she stared at the fish, and could say no more.

'I know what you mean,' returned the lady. 'You do not like to eat the messenger that brought you home. But it is the kindest return you can make. The creature was afraid to go until it saw me put the pot on, and heard me promise it should be boiled the moment it returned with you. Then it darted out of the door at once. You saw it go into the pot of itself the moment it entered, did you not?'

'I did,' answered Tangle, 'and I thought it very strange; but then I saw you, and forgot all about the fish.'

'In Fairyland,' resumed the lady, as they sat down to the table, 'the ambition of the animals is to be eaten by the people; for that is their highest end in that condition. But they are not therefore destroyed. Out of that pot comes something more than the dead fish, you will see.'

Tangle now remarked that the lid was on the pot. But the lady took no further notice of it till they had eaten the fish, which Tangle found nicer than any fish she had ever tasted before. It was as white as snow, and as delicate as cream. And the moment she had swallowed a mouthful of it, a change she could not describe began to take place in her. She heard a murmuring all about her, which became more and more articulate, and at length, as she went on eating, grew intelligible. By the time she had finished her share, the sounds of all the animals in the forest came crowding through the door to her ears; for the door still stood wide open, though it was pitch dark outside; and they were no longer sounds only; they were speech, and speech that she could understand. She could tell what the insects in the cottage were saying to each other too. She had even a suspicion that the trees and flowers all about the cottage were holding midnight communications with each other; but what they said she could not hear.

As soon as the fish was eaten, the lady went to the fire and took the lid off the pot. A lovely little creature in human shape, with large white wings, rose out of it, and flew round and round the roof of the cottage; then dropped, fluttering, and nestled in the lap of the lady. She spoke to it some strange words, carried it to the door, and threw it out into the darkness. Tangle heard the flapping of its wings die away in the distance.

'Now have we done the fish any harm?' she said, returning.

'No,' answered Tangle, 'I do not think we have. I should not mind eating one every day.'

'They must wait their time, like you and me too, my little Tangle.'

And she smiled a smile which the sadness in it made more lovely.

'But,' she continued, 'I think we may have one for supper to-morrow.'

So saying she went to the door of the tank, and spoke; and now Tangle understood her perfectly.

'I want one of you,' she said,—'the wisest.'

Thereupon the fishes got together in the middle of the tank, with their heads forming a circle above the water, and their tails a larger circle beneath it. They were holding a council, in which their relative wisdom should be determined. At length one of them flew up into the lady's hand, looking lively and ready.

'You know where the rainbow stands?' she asked.

'Yes, mother, quite well,' answered the fish.

'Bring home a young man you will find there, who does not know where to go.'

The fish was out of the door in a moment. Then the lady told Tangle it was time to go to bed; and, opening another door in the side of the cottage, showed her a little arbour, cool and green, with a bed of purple heath growing in it, upon which she threw a large wrapper made of the feathered skins of the wise fishes, shining gorgeous in the firelight. Tangle was soon lost in the strangest, loveliest dreams. And the beautiful lady was in every one of her dreams.

In the morning she woke to the rustling of leaves over her head, and the sound of running water. But, to her surprise, she could find no door—nothing but the moss-grown wall of the cottage. So she crept through an opening in the arbour, and stood in the forest. Then she bathed in a stream that ran merrily through the trees, and felt happier; for having once been in her grandmother's pond, she must be clean and tidy ever after; and, having put on her green dress, felt like a lady.

She spent that day in the wood, listening to the birds and beasts and creeping things. She understood all that they said, though she could not repeat a word of it; and every kind had a different language, while there was a common though more limited understanding between all the inhabitants of the forest. She saw nothing of the beautiful lady, but she felt that she was near all the time; and she took care not to go out of sight of the cottage. It was round, like a snow-hut or a wigwam; and she could see neither door nor window in it. The fact was, it had no windows, and though it was full of doors, they all opened from the inside, and could not even be seen from the outside.

She was standing at the foot of a tree in the twilight, listening to a quarrel between a mole and a squirrel, in which the mole told the squirrel that the tail was the best of him, and the squirrel called the mole Spade-fists, when, the darkness having deepened around her, she became aware of something shining in her face, and looking round, saw that the door of the cottage was open, and the red light of the fire flowing from it like a river through the darkness. She left Mole and Squirrel to settle matters as they might, and darted off to the cottage. Entering, she found the pot boiling on the fire, and the grand, lovely lady sitting on the other side of it.

'I've been watching you all day,' said the lady. 'You shall have something to eat by-and-by, but we must wait till our supper comes home.'

She took Tangle on her knee, and began to sing to her—such songs as made her wish she could listen to them for ever. But at length in rushed the shining fish, and snuggled down in the pot. It was followed by a youth who had outgrown his worn garments. His face was ruddy with health, and in his hand he carried a little jewel, which sparkled in the firelight.

The first words the lady said were,—

'What is that in your hand, Mossy?'

Now Mossy was the name his companions had given him, because he had a favourite stone covered with moss, on which he used to sit whole days reading; and they said the moss had begun to grow upon him too.

Mossy held out his hand. The moment the lady saw that it was the golden key, she rose from her chair, kissed Mossy on the forehead, made him sit down on her seat, and stood before him like a servant. Mossy could not bear this, and rose at once. But the lady begged him, with tears in her beautiful eyes, to sit, and let her wait on him.

'But you are a great, splendid, beautiful lady,' said Mossy.

'Yes, I am. But I work all day long—that is my pleasure; and you will have to leave me so soon!'

'How do you know that, if you please, madam?' asked Mossy.

'Because you have got the golden key.'

'But I don't know what it is for. I can't find the key-hole. Will you tell me what to do?'

'You must look for the key-hole. That is your work. I cannot help you. I can only tell you that if you look for it you will find it.'

'What kind of box will it open? What is there inside?'

'I do not know. I dream about it, but I know nothing.'

'Must I go at once?'

'You may stop here to-night, and have some of my supper. But you must go in the morning. All I can do for you is to give you clothes. Here is a girl called Tangle, whom you must take with you.'

'That *will* be nice,' said Mossy.

'No, no!' said Tangle. 'I don't want to leave you, please, grandmother.'

'You must go with him, Tangle. I am sorry to lose you, but it will be the best thing for you. Even the fishes, you see, have to go into the pot, and then out into the dark. If you fall in with the Old Man of the Sea, mind you ask whether he has not got some more fishes ready for me. My tank is getting thin.'

So saying, she took the fish from the pot, and put the lid on as before. They sat down and ate the fish, and then the winged creature rose from the pot, circled the roof, and settled on the lady's lap. She talked to it, carried it to the door, and threw it out into the dark. They heard the flap of its wings die away in the distance.

The lady then showed Mossy into just such another chamber as that of Tangle; and in the morning he found a suit of clothes laid beside him. He looked very handsome in them. But the wearer of Grandmother's clothes never thinks about how he or she looks, but thinks always how handsome other people are.

Tangle was very unwilling to go.

'Why should I leave you? I don't know the young man,' she said to the lady.

'I am never allowed to keep my children long. You need not go with him except you please, but you must go some day; and I should like you to go with him, for he has the golden key. No girl need be afraid to go with a youth that has the golden key. You will take care of her, Mossy, will you not?'

'That I will,' said Mossy.

And Tangle cast a glance at him, and thought she should like to go with him.

'And,' said the lady, 'if you should lose each other as you go through the—the—I never can remember the name of that country,—do not be afraid, but go on and on.'

She kissed Tangle on the mouth and Mossy on the forehead, led them to the door, and waved her hand eastward. Mossy and Tangle took each other's hand and walked away into the depth of the forest. In his right hand Mossy held the golden key.

They wandered thus a long way, with endless amusement from the talk of the animals. They soon learned enough of their language to ask them necessary questions. The squirrels were always friendly, and gave them nuts out of their own hoards; but the bees were selfish and rude, justifying themselves on the ground that Tangle and Mossy were not subjects of their queen, and charity must begin at home, though indeed they had not one drone in their poorhouse at the time. Even the blinking moles would fetch them an earth-nut or a truffle now and then, talking as if their mouths, as well as their eyes and ears, were full of cotton wool, or their own velvety fur. By the time they got out of the forest they were very fond of each other, and Tangle was not in the least sorry that her grandmother had sent her away with Mossy.

At length the trees grew smaller, and stood farther apart, and the ground began to rise, and it got more and more steep, till the trees were all left behind, and the two were climbing a narrow path with rocks on each side. Suddenly they came upon a rude doorway, by which they entered a narrow gallery cut in the rock. It grew darker and darker, till it was pitch-dark, and they had to feel their way. At length the light began to return, and at last they came out upon a narrow path on the face of a lofty precipice. This path went winding down the rock to a wide plain, circular in shape, and surrounded on all sides by mountains. Those opposite to them were a great way off, and towered to an awful height, shooting up sharp, blue, ice-enamelled pinnacles. An utter silence reigned where they stood. Not even the sound of water reached them.

Looking down, they could not tell whether the valley below was a grassy plain or a great still lake. They had never seen any space look like it. The way to it was difficult and dangerous, but down the narrow path they went, and reached the bottom in safety. They found it composed of smooth, light-coloured sandstone, undulating in parts, but mostly level. It was no wonder to them now that they had not been able to tell what it was, for this surface was everywhere crowded with shadows. It was a sea of shadows. The mass was chiefly made up of the shadows of leaves innumerable, of all lovely and imaginative forms, waving to and fro, floating and quivering in the breath of a breeze whose motion was unfelt, whose sound was unheard. No forests clothed the mountain-sides, no trees were anywhere to be seen, and yet the shadows of the leaves, branches, and stems of all various trees covered the valley as far as their eyes could reach. They soon spied the shadows of flowers mingled with those of the leaves, and now and then the shadow of a bird with open beak, and throat distended with song. At times would appear the forms of strange, graceful creatures, running up and down the shadow-boles and along the branches, to disappear in the wind-tossed foliage. As they walked they waded knee-deep in the lovely lake. For the shadows were not merely lying on the surface of the ground, but heaped up above it like substantial forms of darkness, as if they had been cast upon a thousand different planes of the air. Tangle and Mossy often lifted their heads and gazed upwards to descry whence the shadows came; but they could see nothing more than a bright mist spread above them, higher than the tops of the mountains, which stood clear against it. No forests, no leaves, no birds were visible.

After a while, they reached more open spaces, where the shadows were thinner; and came even to portions over which shadows only flitted, leaving them clear for such as might follow. Now a wonderful form, half bird-like half human, would float across on outspread sailing pinions. Anon an exquisite shadow group of gambolling children would be followed by the loveliest female form, and that again by the grand stride of a Titanic shape, each disappearing in the surrounding press of shadowy foliage. Sometimes a profile of unspeakable beauty or grandeur would appear for a moment and vanish. Sometimes they seemed lovers that passed linked arm in arm, sometimes father and son, sometimes brothers in loving contest, sometimes sisters entwined in gracefullest community of complex form. Sometimes wild horses would tear across, free, or bestrode by noble shadows of ruling men. But some of the things which pleased them most they never knew how to describe.

About the middle of the plain they sat down to rest in the heart of a heap of shadows. After sitting for a while, each, looking up, saw the other in tears: they were each longing after the country whence the shadows fell.

'We *must* find the country from which the shadows come,' said Mossy.

'We must, dear Mossy,' responded Tangle. 'What if your golden key should be the key to *it*?'

'Ah! that would be grand,' returned Mossy. 'But we must rest here for a little, and then we shall be able to cross the plain before night.'

So he lay down on the ground, and about him on every side, and over his head, was the constant play of wonderful shadows. He could look through them, and see the one behind the other, till they mixed in a mass of darkness. Tangle, too, lay admiring, and wondering, and longing for the country whence the shadows came. When they were rested they rose and pursued their journey.

How long they were in crossing this plain I cannot tell; but before night Mossy's hair was streaked with grey, and Tangle had got wrinkles on her forehead.

As evening drew on, the shadows fell deeper and rose higher. At length they reached a place where they rose above their heads, and made all dark around them. Then they took hold of each other's hand, and walked on in silence and in some dismay. They felt the gathering darkness, and something strangely solemn besides, and the beauty of the shadows ceased to delight them. All at once Tangle found that she had not a hold of Mossy's hand, though when she lost it she could not tell.

'Mossy, Mossy!' she cried aloud in terror.

But no Mossy replied.

A moment after, the shadows sank to her feet, and down under her feet, and the mountains rose before her. She turned towards the gloomy region she had left, and called once more upon Mossy. There the gloom lay tossing and heaving, a dark, stormy, foamless sea of shadows, but no Mossy rose out of it, or came climbing up the hill on which she stood. She threw herself down and wept in despair.

Suddenly she remembered that the beautiful lady had told them, if they lost each other in a country of which she could not remember the name, they were not to be afraid, but to go straight on.

'And besides,' she said to herself, 'Mossy has the golden key, and so no harm will come to him, I do believe.'

She rose from the ground, and went on.

Before long she arrived at a precipice, in the face of which a stair was cut. When she had ascended half-way, the stair ceased, and the path led straight into the mountain. She was afraid to enter, and turning again towards the stair, grew giddy at sight of the depth beneath her, and was forced to throw herself down in the mouth of the cave.

When she opened her eyes, she saw a beautiful little creature with wings standing beside her, waiting.

'I know you,' said Tangle. 'You are my fish.'

'Yes. But I am a fish no longer. I am an aëranth now.'

'What is that?' asked Tangle.

'What you see I am,' answered the shape. 'And I am come to lead you through the mountain.'

'Oh, thank you, dear fish—aëranth I mean,' returned Tangle, rising.

Thereupon the aëranth took to his wings, and flew on through the long narrow passage, reminding Tangle very much of the way he had swum on before when he was a fish. And the moment his white wings moved, they began to throw off a continuous shower of sparks of all colours, which lighted up the passage before them.—All at once he vanished, and Tangle heard a low, sweet sound, quite different from the rush and crackle of his wings. Before her was an open arch, and through it came light, mixed with the sound of sea-waves.

She hurried out, and fell, tired and happy, upon the yellow sand of the shore. There she lay, half asleep with weariness and rest, listening to the low plash and retreat of the tiny waves, which seemed ever enticing the land to leave off being land, and become sea. And as she lay, her eyes were fixed upon the foot of a great rainbow standing far away against the sky on the other side of the sea. At length she fell fast asleep.

When she awoke, she saw an old man with long white hair down to his shoulders, leaning upon a stick covered with green buds, and so bending over her.

'What do you want here, beautiful woman?' he said.

'Am I beautiful? I am so glad!' answered Tangle, rising. 'My grandmother is beautiful.'

'Yes. But what do you want?' he repeated, kindly.

'I think I want you. Are not you the Old Man of the Sea?'

'I am.'

'Then grandmother says, have you any more fishes ready for her?'

'We will go and see, my dear,' answered the old man, speaking yet more kindly than before. 'And I can do something for you, can I not?'

'Yes—show me the way up to the country from which the shadows fall,' said Tangle.

For there she hoped to find Mossy again.

'Ah! indeed, that would be worth doing,' said the old man. 'But I cannot, for I do not know the way myself. But, I will send you to the Old Man of the Earth. Perhaps he can tell you. He is much older than I am.'

Leaning on his staff, he conducted her along the shore to a steep rock, that looked like a petrified ship turned upside down. The door of it was the rudder of a great vessel, ages ago at the bottom of the sea. Immediately within the door was a stair in the rock, down which the old man went, and Tangle followed. At the bottom the old man had his house, and there he lived.

As soon as she entered it, Tangle heard a strange noise, unlike anything she had ever heard before. She soon found that it was the fishes talking. She tried to understand what they said; but their speech was so old-fashioned, and rude, and undefined, that she could not make much of it.

'I will go and see about those fishes for my daughter,' said the Old Man of the Sea.

And moving a slide in the wall of his house, he first looked out, and then tapped upon a thick piece of crystal that filled the round opening. Tangle came up behind him, and peeping through the window into the heart of the great deep green ocean, saw the most curious creatures, some very ugly, all very odd, and with especially queer mouths, swimming about everywhere, above and below, but all coming towards the window in answer to the tap of the Old Man of the Sea. Only a few could get their mouths against the glass; but those who were floating miles away yet turned their heads towards it. The Old Man looked through the whole flock carefully for some minutes, and then turning to Tangle, said,—

'I am sorry I have not got one ready yet. I want more time than she does. But I will send some as soon as I can.'

He then shut the slide.

Presently a great noise arose in the sea. The Old Man opened the slide again, and tapped on the glass, whereupon the fishes were all as still as sleep.

'They were only talking about you,' he said. 'And they do speak such nonsense!—To-morrow,' he continued, 'I must show you the way to the Old Man of the Earth. He lives a long way from here.'

'Do let me go at once,' said Tangle.

'No. That is not possible. You must come this way first.'

He led her to a hole in the wall, which she had not observed before. It was covered with the green leaves and white blossoms of a creeping plant.

'Only white-blossoming plants can grow under the sea,' said the Old Man. 'In there you will find a bath, in which you must lie till I call you.'

Tangle went in, and found a smaller room or cave, in the further corner of which was a great basin hollowed out of a rock, and half-full of the clearest sea-water. Little streams were constantly running into it from cracks in the wall of the cavern. It was polished quite smooth inside, and had a carpet of yellow sand in the bottom of it. Large green leaves and white flowers of various plants crowded up and over it, draping and covering it almost entirely.

No sooner was she undressed and lying in the bath, than she began to feel as if the water were sinking into her, and she were receiving all the good of sleep without undergoing its forgetfulness. She felt the good coming all the time. And she grew happier and more hopeful than she had been since she lost Mossy. But she could not help thinking how very sad it was for a poor old man to live there all alone, and have to take care of a whole seaful of stupid and riotous fishes.

After about an hour, as she thought, she heard his voice calling her, and rose out of the bath. All the fatigue and aching of her long journey had vanished. She was as whole, and strong, and well as if she had slept for seven days.

Returning to the opening that led into the other part of the house, she started back with amazement, for through it she saw the form of a grand man, with a majestic and beautiful face, waiting for her.

'Come,' he said; 'I see you are ready.'

She entered with reverence.

'Where is the Old Man of the Sea?' she asked, humbly.

'There is no one here but me,' he answered smiling. 'Some people call me the Old Man of the Sea. Others have another name for me, and are terribly frightened when they meet me taking a walk by the shore. Therefore I avoid being seen by them, for they are so afraid, that they never see what I really am. You see me now.—But I must show you the way to the Old Man of the Earth.'

He led her into the cave where the bath was, and there she saw, in the opposite corner a second opening in the rock.

'Go down that stair, and it will bring you to him,' said the Old Man of the Sea.

With humble thanks Tangle took her leave. She went down the winding-stair, till she began to fear there was no end to it. Still down and down it went, rough and broken, with springs of water bursting out of the rocks and running down the steps beside her. It was quite dark about her, and yet she could see. For after being in that bath, people's eyes always give out a light they can see by. There were no creeping things in the way. All was safe and pleasant, though so dark and damp and deep.

At last there was not one step more, and she found herself in a glimmering cave. On a stone in the middle of it sat a figure with its back towards her—the figure of an old man bent double with age. From behind she could see his white beard spread out on the rocky floor in front of him. He did not move as she entered, so she passed round that she might stand before him and speak to him. The moment she looked in his face, she saw that he was a youth of marvellous beauty. He sat entranced with the delight of what he beheld in a mirror of something like silver, which lay on the floor at his feet, and which from behind she had taken for his white beard. He sat on, heedless of her presence, pale with the joy of his vision. She stood and watched him. At length, all trembling, she spoke. But her voice made no sound. Yet the youth lifted up his head. He showed no surprise, however, at seeing her—only smiled a welcome.

'Are you the Old Man of the Earth?' Tangle had said.

And the youth answered, and Tangle heard him, though not with her ears:

'I am. What can I do for you?'

'Tell me the way to the country whence the shadows fall.'

'Ah! That I do not know. I only dream about it myself. I see its shadows sometimes in my mirror: the way to it I do not know. But I think the Old Man of the Fire must know. He is much older than I am. He is the oldest of all.'

'Where does he live?'

'I will show you the way to his place. I never saw him myself.'

So saying, the young man rose, and then stood for a while gazing at Tangle.

'I wish I could see that country too,' he said. 'But I must mind my work.'

He led her to the side of the cave, and told her to lay her ear against the wall.

'What do you hear?' he asked.

'I hear,' answered Tangle, 'the sound of a great water running inside the rock.'

'That river runs down to the dwelling of the oldest man of all—the Old Man of the Fire. I wish I could go to see him. But I must mind my work. The river is the only way to him.'

Then the Old Man of the Earth stooped over the floor of the cave, raised a huge stone from it, and left it leaning. It disclosed a great hole that went plumb-down.

'That is the way,' he said.

'But there are no stairs.'

'You must throw yourself in. There is no other way.'

She turned and looked him full in the face—stood so for a whole minute, as she thought: it was a whole year—then threw herself headlong into the hole.

When she came to herself, she found herself gliding down fast and deep. Her head was underwater, but that did not signify, for, when she thought about it, she could not remember that she had breathed once since her bath in the cave of the Old Man of the Sea. When she lifted up her head a sudden and fierce heat struck her, and she sank it again instantly, and went sweeping on.

Gradually the stream grew shallower. At length she could hardly keep her head under. Then the water could carry her no farther. She rose from the channel, and went step for step down the burning descent. The water ceased altogether. The heat was terrible. She felt scorched to the bone, but it did not touch her strength. It grew hotter and hotter. She said, 'I can bear it no longer.' Yet she went on.

At the long last, the stair ended at a rude archway in an all but glowing rock. Through this archway Tangle fell exhausted into a cool mossy cave.

The floor and walls were covered with moss—green, soft, and damp. A little stream spouted from a rent in the rock and fell into a basin of moss. She plunged her face into it and drank. Then she lifted her head and looked around. Then she rose and looked again. She saw no one in the cave. But the moment she stood upright she had a marvellous sense that she was in the secret of the earth and all its ways. Everything she had seen, or learned from books; all that her grandmother had said or sung to her; all the talk of the beasts, birds, and fishes; all that had happened to her on her journey with Mossy, and since then in the heart of the earth with the Old man and the Older man—all was plain: she understood it all, and saw that everything meant the same thing though she could not have put it into words again.

The next moment she descried, in a corner of the cave, a little naked child, sitting on the moss. He was playing with balls of various colours and sizes, which he disposed in strange figures upon the floor beside him. And now Tangle felt that there was something in her knowledge which was not in her understanding. For she knew there must be an infinite meaning in the change and sequence and individual forms of the figures into which the child arranged the balls, as well as in the varied harmonies of their colours, but what it all meant she could not tell.* He went on busily, tirelessly, playing his solitary game, without looking up, or seeming to know that there was a stranger in his deep-withdrawn cell. Diligently as a lace-maker shifts her bobbins, he shifted and arranged his balls. Flashes of meaning would now pass from them to Tangle, and now again all would be not merely obscure, but utterly dark. She stood looking for a long time, for there was fascination in the sight; and the longer she looked the more an indescribable vague intelligence went on rousing itself in her mind. For seven years she had stood there watching the naked child with his coloured balls, and it seemed to her like seven hours, when all at once the shape the balls took, she knew not why, reminded her of the Valley of Shadows, and she spoke:—

'Where is the Old Man of the Fire?' she said.

'Here I am,' answered the child, rising and leaving his balls on the moss. 'What can I do for you?'

There was such an awfulness of absolute repose on the face of the child that Tangle stood dumb before him. He had no smile, but the love in his large grey eyes was deep as the centre. And with the repose there lay on his face a shimmer as of moonlight, which seemed as if any moment it might break into such a ravishing smile as would cause the beholder to weep himself to death. But the smile never came, and the moonlight lay there unbroken. For the heart of the child was too deep for any smile to reach from it to his face.

* I think I must be indebted to Novalis for these geometrical figures. G. MACDONALD.

'Are you the oldest man of all?' Tangle at length, although filled with awe, ventured to ask.

'Yes, I am. I am very, very old. I am able to help you, I know. I can help everybody.'

And the child drew near and looked up in her face so that she burst into tears.

'Can you tell me the way to the country the shadows fall from?' she sobbed.

'Yes. I know the way quite well. I go there myself sometimes. But you could not go my way; you are not old enough. I will show you how you can go.'

'Do not send me out into the great heat again,' prayed Tangle.

'I will not,' answered the child.

And he reached up, and put his little cool hand on her heart.

'Now,' he said, 'you can go. The fire will not burn you. Come.'

He led her from the cave, and following him through another archway, she found herself in a vast desert of sand and rock. The sky of it was of rock, lowering over them like solid thunderclouds; and the whole place was so hot that she saw, in bright rivulets, the yellow gold and white silver and red copper trickling molten from the rocks. But the heat never came near her.

When they had gone some distance, the child turned up a great stone, and took something like a egg from under it. He next drew a long curved line in the sand with his finger, and laid the egg on it. He then spoke something Tangle could not understand. The egg broke, a small snake came out, and, lying in the line in the sand, grew and grew till he filled it. The moment he was thus full grown, he began to glide away, undulating like a sea-wave.

'Follow that serpent,' said the child. 'He will lead you the right way.'

Tangle followed the serpent. But she could not go far without looking back at the marvellous Child. He stood alone in the midst of the glowing desert, beside a fountain of red flame that had burst forth at his feet, his naked whiteness glimmering a pale rosy red in the torrid fire. There he stood, looking after her, till, from the lengthening distance, she could see him no more. The serpent went straight on, turning neither to the right nor left.

Meantime Mossy had got out of the lake of shadows, and, following his mournful, lonely way, had reached the sea-shore. It was a dark, stormy evening. The sun had set. The wind was blowing from the sea. The waves had surrounded the rock within which lay the Old Man's House. A deep water rolled between it and the shore, upon which a majestic figure was walking alone.

Mossy went up to him and said,—

'Will you tell me where to find the Old Man of the Sea?'

'I am the Old Man of the Sea,' the figure answered.

'I see a strong kingly man of middle age,' returned Mossy.

Then the Old Man looked at him more intently, and said,—

'Your sight, young man, is better than that of most who take this way. The night is stormy: come to my house and tell me what I can do for you.'

Mossy followed him. The waves flew from before the footsteps of the Old Man of the Sea, and Mossy followed upon dry sand.

When they had reached the cave, they sat down and gazed at each other.

Now Mossy was an old man by this time. He looked much older than the Old Man of the Sea, and his feet were very weary.

After looking at him for moment, the Old Man took him by the hand and led him into his inner cave. There he helped him to undress, and laid him in the bath. And he saw that one of his hands Mossy did not open.

'What have you in that hand?' he asked.

Mossy opened his hand, and there lay the golden key.

'Ah!' said the Old Man, 'that accounts for your knowing me. And I know the way you have to go.'

'I want to find the country whence the shadows fall,' said Mossy.

'I dare say you do. So do I. But meantime, one thing is certain —What is that key for, do you think?'

'For a keyhole somewhere. But I don't know why I keep it. I never could find the keyhole. And I have lived a good while, I believe,' said Mossy, sadly. 'I'm not sure that I'm not old. I know my feet ache.'

'Do they?' said the Old Man, as if he really meant to ask the question; and Mossy, who was still lying in the bath, watched his feet for a moment before he replied.

'No, they do not,' he answered. 'Perhaps I am not old either.'

'Get up and look at yourself in the water.'

He rose and looked at himself in the water, and there was not a grey hair on his head or a wrinkle on his skin.

'You have tasted of death now,' said the Old Man. 'It is good?'

'It is good,' said Mossy. 'It is better than life.'

'No,' said the Old Man: 'it is only more life.—Your feet will make no holes in the water now.'

'What do you mean?'

'I will show you that presently.'

They returned to the outer cave, and sat and talked together for a long time. At length the Old Man of the Sea rose, and said to Mossy,—

'Follow me.'

He led him up the stair again, and opened another door. They stood on the level of the raging sea, looking towards the east. Across the waste of waters, against the bosom of a fierce black cloud, stood the foot of a rainbow, glowing in the dark.

'This indeed is my way,' said Mossy, as soon as he saw the rainbow, and stepped out upon the sea. His feet made no holes in the water. He fought the wind, and clomb the waves, and went on towards the rainbow.

The storm died away. A lovely day and a lovelier night followed. A cool wind blew over the wide plain of the quiet ocean. And still Mossy journeyed eastward. But the rainbow had vanished with the storm.

Day after day he held on, and he thought he had no guide. He did not see how a shining fish under the waters directed his steps. He crossed the sea, and came to a great precipice of rock, up which he could discover but one path. Nor did this lead him farther than half-way up the rock, where it ended on a platform. Here he stood and pondered.—It could not be that the way stopped here, else what was the path for? It was a rough path, not very plain, yet certainly a path.—He examined the face of the rock. It was smooth as glass. But as his eyes kept roving hopelessly over it, something glittered, and he caught sight of a row of small sapphires. They bordered a little hole in the rock.

'The keyhole!' he cried.

He tried the key. It fitted. It turned. A great clang and clash, as of iron bolts on huge brazen caldrons, echoed thunderously within. He drew out the key. The rock in front of him began to fall. He retreated from it as far the breadth of the platform would allow. A great slab fell at his feet. In front was still the solid rock, with this one slab fallen forward out of it. But the moment he stepped upon it, a second fell, just short of the edge of the first, making the next step of a stair, which thus kept dropping itself before him as he ascended into the heart of the precipice. It led him into a hall fit for such an approach—irregular and rude in formation, but floor, sides, pillars, and vaulted roof, all of one mass of shining stones of every colour that light can show. In the centre stood seven columns, ranged from red to violet. And on the pedestal of one of them sat a woman, motionless, with her face bowed upon her knees. Seven years had she sat there waiting. She lifted her head as Mossy drew near. It was Tangle. Her hair had grown to her feet, and was rippled like the windless sea on broad sands. Her face was beautiful, like her grandmother's and as still and peaceful as that of the Old Man of the Fire. Her form was tall and noble. Yet Mossy knew her at once.

'How beautiful you are, Tangle!' he said, in delight and astonishment.

'Am I?' she returned. 'Oh, I have waited for you so long! But you, you are like the Old Man of the Sea. No. You are like the Old Man of the Earth. No, no. You are like the oldest man of all. You are like them all. And yet you are my own old Mossy. How did you come here? What did you do after I lost you? Did you find the keyhole? Have you got the key still?'

She had a hundred questions to ask him, and he a hundred more to ask her. They told each other all their adventures, and were as happy as man and woman could be. For they were younger and better, and stronger and wiser, than they had ever been before.

It began to grow dark. And they wanted more than ever to reach the country whence the shadows fall. So they looked about them for a way out of the cave. The door by which Mossy entered had closed again, and there was half a mile of rock between them and the sea. Neither could Tangle find the opening in the floor by which the serpent had led her thither. They searched till it grew so dark that they could see nothing, and gave it up.

After a while, however, the cave began to glimmer again. The light came from the moon, but it did not look like moonlight, for it gleamed through those seven pillars in the middle, and filled the place with all colours. And now Mossy saw that there was a pillar beside the red one, which he had not observed before. And it was of the same new colour that he had seen in the rainbow when he saw it first in the fairy forest. And on it he saw a sparkle of blue. It was the sapphires round the keyhole.

He took his key. It turned in the lock to the sounds of Æolian music. A door opened upon slow hinges, and disclosed a winding stair within. The key vanished from his fingers. Tangle went up. Mossy followed. The door closed behind them. They climbed out of the earth; and, still climbing, rose above it. They were in the rainbow. Far abroad, over ocean and land, they could see through its transparent walls the earth beneath their feet. Stairs beside stairs wound up together, and beautiful beings of all ages climbed along with them.

They knew that they were going up to the country whence the shadows fall.

And by this time I think they must have got there.

Margaret Oliphant

THE LIBRARY WINDOW

Margaret Oliphant (1828–97) was born in Wallyford, outside Edinburgh. In 1852 she married her cousin Frank, whose early death made it necessary for her to support their two sons and a daughter. She turned to writing and managed to send her sons to Eton and Oxford. Her responsibilities did not end there, for soon she was supporting her two brothers and their families as well. She wrote well over a hundred books and innumerable articles for many magazines. 'I must work or die' she told her publisher, William Blackwood, and indeed she was correcting the proofs of her last book, a history of Blackwood's publishing house, on her deathbed.

Among ninety-three novels of varying quality, *The Chronicles of Carlingford* series pleased Mrs Oliphant's English readers best. They are set in a small town outside London and sweep their way through society, from tradesfolk to the aristocracy, with a sharply funny eye. None of this prepares us for her exploration of supernatural fiction, in three novels and a dozen stories from the last seventeen years of her life. Although many are marred to today's taste by her attempts to formulate a theology, the strongest influences in these books go back to James Hogg and the Scottish ballad tradition.

'The Library Window' was published in *Blackwood's* in 1896 and is the last of Mrs Oliphant's supernatural tales to deal with an earthbound spirit. It is unique in having no obvious religious overtones and strong sexual and psychological dimension which is almost Jamesian in its exploration of a young girl's sensibility.

The Library Window

A STORY OF THE SEEN AND UNSEEN

ONE

I WAS NOT aware at first of the many discussions which had gone on about that window. It was almost opposite one of the windows of the large old-fashioned drawing-room of the house in which I spent that summer, which was of so much importance in my life. Our house and the library were on opposite sides of the broad High Street of St Rule's, which is a fine street, wide and ample, and very quiet, as strangers think who come from noisier places; but in a summer evening there is much coming and going, and the stillness is full of sound—the sound of footsteps and pleasant voices, softened by the summer air. There are even exceptional moments when it is noisy: the time of the fair, and on Saturday nights sometimes, and when there are excursion trains. Then even the softest sunny air of the evening will not smooth the harsh tones and the stumbling steps; but at these unlovely moments we shut the windows, and even I, who am so fond of that deep recess where I can take refuge from all that is going on inside, and make myself a spectator of all the varied story out of doors, withdraw from my watch-tower. To tell the truth, there never was very much going on inside. The house belonged to my aunt, to whom (she says, Thank God!) nothing ever happens. I believe that many things have happened to her in her time; but that was all over at the period of which I am speaking, and she was old, and very quiet. Her life went on in a routine never broken. She got up at the same hour every day, and did the same things in the same rotation, day by day the same. She said that this was the greatest support in the world, and that routine is a kind of salvation. It may be so; but it is a very dull salvation, and I used to feel that I would rather have incident, whatever kind of incident it might be. But then at that time I was not old, which makes all the difference.

At the time of which I speak the deep recess of the drawing-room window was a great comfort to me. Though she was an old lady (perhaps because she was so old) she was very tolerant, and had a kind of feeling for me. She never said a word, but often gave me a smile when she saw how I had built myself up, with my books and my basket of work. I did very little work, I fear—now and then a few stitches when the spirit moved me, or when I had got well afloat in a dream, and was more tempted to follow it out than to read my book, as sometimes happened. At other times, and if the book were interesting, I used to get through volume after volume sitting there, paying no attention to anybody. And yet I did pay a kind of attention. Aunt Mary's old ladies came in to call, and I heard them talk, though I very seldom listened; but for all that, if they had anything to say that was interesting, it is curious how I found it in my mind afterwards, as if the air had blown it to me. They came and went, and I had the sensation of their old bonnets gliding out and in, and their dresses rustling; and now and then had to jump up and shake hands with some one who knew me, and asked after my papa and mamma. Then Aunt Mary would give me a little smile again, and I slipped back to my window. She never seemed to mind. My mother would not have let me do it, I know. She would have remembered dozens of things there were to do. She would have sent me up-stairs to fetch something which I was quite sure she did not want, or down-stairs to carry some quite unnecessary message to the housemaid. She liked to keep me running about. Perhaps that was one reason why I was so fond of Aunt Mary's drawing-room, and the deep recess of the window, and the curtain that fell half over it, and the broad window-seat, where one could collect so many things without being found fault with for untidiness. Whenever we had anything the matter with us in these days, we were sent to St Rule's to get up our strength. And this was my case at the time of which I am going to speak.

Everybody had said, since ever I learned to speak, that I was fantastic and fanciful and dreamy, and all the other words with which a girl who may happen to like poetry, and to be fond of thinking, is so often made uncomfortable. People don't know what they mean when they say fantastic. It sounds like Madge Wildfire or something of that sort. My mother thought I should always be busy, to keep nonsense out of my head. But really I was not at all fond of nonsense. I was rather serious than otherwise. I would have been no trouble to anybody if I had been left to myself. It was only that I had a sort of second-sight, and was conscious of things to which I paid no attention. Even when reading the most interesting book, the things that were being talked about blew in to me; and I heard what the people were saying in the streets as they passed under the window. Aunt Mary always said I could do two or indeed three things at once—both read and listen, and see, I am sure that I did not listen much, and seldom looked out, of set purpose—as some people do who notice what bonnets the ladies in the street have on; but I did hear what I couldn't help hearing, even when I was reading my book, and I did see all sorts of things, though often for a whole half-hour I might never lift my eyes.

This does not explain what I said at the beginning, that there were many discussion about that window. It was, and still is, the last window in the High Street. Yet it is not exactly opposite, but a little to the west, so that I could see it best from the left side of my recess. I took it calmly for granted that it was a window like any other till I first heard the talk about it which was going on in the drawing-room. "Have you ever made up your mind,

Mrs Balcarres," said old Mr Pitmilly, "whether that window opposite is a window or no?" He said Mistress Balcarres—and he was always called Mr Pitmilly, Morton: which was the name of his place.

"I am never sure of it, to tell the truth," said Aunt Mary, "all these years."

"Bless me!" said one of the old ladies, "and what window may that be?"

Mr Pitmilly had a way of laughing as he spoke, which did not please me; but it was true that he was not perhaps desirous of pleasing me. He said, "Oh, just the window opposite," with his laugh running through his words; "our friend can never make up her mind about it, though she has been living opposite it since—"

"You need never mind the dare," said another, "the Leebrary window! Dear me, what should it be but a window? up at that height it could not be a door."

"The question is," said my aunt, "if it is a real window with glass in it, or if it is merely painted, or if it once was a window, and has been built up. And the oftener people look at it, the less they are able to say."

"Let me see this window," said old Lady Carnbee, who was very active and strong-minded; and then they all came crowding upon me—three or four old ladies, very eager, and Mr Pitmilly's white hair appearing over their heads, and my aunt sitting quiet and smiling behind.

"I mind the window very well," said Lady Carnbee; "ay; and so do more than me. But in its present appearance it is just like any other window; but has not bee cleaned, I should say, in the memory of man."

"I see what ye mean," said one of the others. "It is just a very dead thing without any reflection in it; but I've seen as bad before."

"Ay, it's dead enough," said another, "but that's not rule; for these hizzies of women-servants in this ill age—"

"Nay, the women are well enough," said the softest voice of all, which was Aunt Mary's. "I will never let them this risk their lives cleaning the outside of mine. And there are no women-servants in the Old Library; there is maybe something more in it than that."

They were all pressing into my recess, pressing upon me, a row of old faces, peering into something they could not understand. I had a sense in my mind how curious it was, the wall of old ladies in their old satin gowns all glazed with age. Lady Carnbee with her lace about her head. Nobody was loking at me or thinking of me; but I felt unconsciously the contrast of my youngness to their oldness, and stared at them as they stared over my head at the Library window. I had given it no attention up to this time. I was more taken up with the old laides than with the thing they were looking at.

"The framework is all right at least, I can see that, and pented black—"

"And the panes are pented black too. It's no window, Mrs Balcarres.

It has been filled in, in the days of the window duties you will mind, Leddy Carnbee."

"Mind!" said that oldest lady. "I mind when your mother was marriet, Jeanie; and that's neither the day nor yesterday. But as for the window, it's just a delusion: and that is my opinion of the matter, if you ask me."

"There's a great want of light in that muckle room at the college," said another. "If it was a window, the Leebrary would have more light."

"One thing is clear," said one of the younger ones, "it cannot be a window to see through. It may be filled in or it may be built up, but it is not a window to give light."

"And whoever heard of a window that was to see through?" Lady Carnbee said. I was fascinated by the look on her face, which was a curious scornful look as of one who knew more than she chose to say: and then my wandering fancy was caught by her hand as she held it up, throwing back the lace that dropped over it. Lady Carnbee's lace was the chief thing about her—heavy black Spanish lace with large flowers. Everything she wore was trimmed with it. A large veil of it hung over her old bonnet. But her hand coming out of this heavy lace was a curious thing to see. She had very long fingers, very taper, which had been much admired in her youth; and her hand was very white, or rather more than white, pale, bleached, and bloodless, with large blue veins standing up upon the back; and she wore some fine rings, among others a big diamond in an ugly old claw seting. They were too big for her, and were wound round and round with yellow silk to make them keep on: and this little cushion of silk, turned brown with long wearing, had twisted round so that it was more conspicuous than the jewels; while the big diamond blazed underneath in the hollow of her hand, like some dangerous thing hiding and sending out darts of light. The hand, which seemed to come almost to a point, with this strange ornament underneath, clutched at my half-terrified imagination. It too seemed to mean far more than was said. I felt as if it might clutch me with sharp claws, and the lurking, dazzling creature bite—with a sting that would go to the heart.

Presently, however, the circle of the old faces broke up, the old ladies returned to their seats, and Mr Pitmilly, small but very erect, stood up in the midst of them, talking with mild authority like a little oracle among the ladies. Only Lady Carnbee always contradicted the neat, little, old gentleman. She gesticulated, when she talked, like a Frenchwoman, and darted forth that hand of hers with the lace hanging over it, so that I always caught a glimpse of the lurking diamond. I thought she looked like a witch among the comfortable little group which gave such attention to everything Mr Pitmilly said.

'For my part, it is my opinion there is no window there at all,' he said. 'It's very like the thing that's called in scientific language an optical illusion. It arises generally, if I may use such a word in the presence of ladies, from a liver that is not just in the perfitt order and balance that organ demands—and then you will see things—a blue dog, I remember, was the thing in one case, and in another—'

'The man has gane gyte,' said Lady Carnbee; 'I mind the windows in the Auld Leebrary as long as I mind anything. Is the Leebray itself an optical illusion too?'

'Na, na,' and 'No, no,' said the old ladies; 'a blue dogue would be a strange vagary: but the Library we have all kent from our youth,' said one. 'And I mind when the Assemblies were held there one year when the Town Hall was building,' another said.

'It is just a great divert to me,' said Aunt Mary: but what was strange was that she paused there, and said in a low tone, 'now': and then went on again, 'for whoever comes to my house, there are aye discussions about that window. I have never just made up my mind about it myself. Sometimes I think it's a case of these wicked window duties, as you said, Miss Jeanie, when half the windows in our houses were blocked up to save the tax. And then, I think, it may be due to that blank kind of building like the great new buildings on the Earthen Mound in Edinburgh, where the windows are just ornaments. And then whiles I am sure I can see the glass shining when the sun catches it in the afternoon.'

'You could so easily satisfy yourself, Mrs Balcarres, if you were to—'

'Give a laddie a penny to cast a stone, and see what happens,' said Lady Carnbee.

'But I am not sure that I have any desire to satisfy myself,' Aunt Mary said. And then there was a stir in the room, and I had to come out from my recess and open the door for the old ladies and see them down-stairs, as they all went away following one another. Mr Pitmilly gave his arm to Lady Carnbee, though she was always contradicting him; and so the tea-party dispersed. Aunt Mary came to the head of the stairs with her guests in an old-fashioned gracious way, while I went down with them to see that the maid was ready at the door. When I came back Aunt Mary was still standing in the recess looking out. Returning to my seat she said, with a kind of wistful look, 'Well, honey: and what is your opinion?'

'I have no opinion. I was reading my book all the time,' I said.

'And so you were, honey, and no' very civil; but all the same I ken well you heard every word we said.'

TWO

It was a night in June; dinner was long over, and had it been winter the maids would have been shutting up the house, and my Aunt Mary preparing to go upstairs to her room. But it was still clear daylight, that daylight out of which the sun has been long gone, and which has no longer any rose reflections, but all has sunk into a pearly neutral tint—a light which is daylight yet is not day. We had taken a turn in the garden after dinner, and now we had returned to what we called our usual occupations. My aunt was reading. The English post had come in, and she had got her 'Times,' which was her great diversion. The 'Scotsman' was her morning reading, but she liked her 'Times' at night.

As for me, I too was at my usual occupation, which at that time was doing nothing. I had a book as usual, and was absorbed in it: but I was conscious of all that was going on all the same. The people strolled along the broad pavement, making remarks as they passed under the open window which came up into my story or my dream, and sometimes made me laugh. The tone and the faint sing-song, or rather chant, of the accent, which was 'a wee Fifish', was novel to me, and associated with holiday, and pleasant; and sometimes they said to each other something that was amusing, and often something that suggested a whole story; but presently they began to drop off, the footsteps slackened, the voices died away. It was getting late, though the clear soft daylight went on and on. All through the lingering evening, which seemed to consist of interminable hours, long but not weary, drawn out as if the spell of the light and the outdoor life might never end, I had now and then, quite unawares, cast a glance at the mysterious window which my aunt and her friends had discussed, as I felt, though I dared not say it even to myself, rather foolishly. It caught my eye without any intention on my part, as I paused, as it were, to take breath, in the flowing and current of undistinguishable thoughts and things from without and within which carried me along. First it occurred to me, with a little sensation of discovery, how absurd to say it was not a window, a living window, one to see through! Why, then, had they never *seen* it, these old folk? I saw as I looked up suddenly the faint greyness as of visible space within—a room behind, certainly—dim, as it was natural a room should be on the other side of the street—quite indefinite: yet so clear that if some one were to come to the window there would be nothing surprising in it. For certainly there was a feeling of space behind the panes which these old half-blind ladies had disputed about whether they were glass or only fictitious panes marked on the wall. How silly! when eyes that could see could make it out in a minute. It was only a greyness at present, but it was unmistakable, a space that went back into gloom, as every room does when you look into it across a street. There were no curtains to show whether it was inhabited or not; but a room—oh, as distinctly as ever room was! I was pleased with myself, but said nothing, while Aunt Mary rustled her paper, waiting for a favourable moment to announce a discovery which settled her problem at once. Then I was carried away upon the stream again, and forgot the window, till somebody threw unawares a word from the outer world, 'I'm goin' hame; it'll soon be dark.' Dark! what was the fool thinking of? it never would be dark if one waited out, wandering in the soft air for hours longer; and then my eyes, acquiring easily that new habit, looked across the way again.

Ah, now! nobody indeed had come to the window; and no light had been lighted, seeing it was still beautiful to read by—a still, clear, colourless light; but the room inside had certainly widened. I could see the grey space and air a little deeper, and a sort of vision, very dim, of a wall, and something against it; something dark, with the blackness that a solid article, however indistinctly seen, takes in the lighter darkness that is only space—a large, black, dark thing coming out into the grey. I looked more intently, and made sure it was a piece of furniture, either a writing-table or perhaps a large bookcase. No doubt it must be the last, since this was part of the old library. I never visited the old College Library, but I had seen such places before, and I could well imagine it to myself. How curious that for all the time these old people had looked at it, they had never seen this before!

It was more silent now, and my eyes, I suppose, had grown dim with gazing, doing my best to make it out, when suddenly Aunt Mary said, 'Will you ring the bell, my dear? I must have my lamp.'

'Your lamp?' I cried, 'when it is still daylight.' But then I gave another look at my window, and perceived with a start that the light had indeed changed: for now I saw nothing. It was still light, but there was so much change in the light that my room, with the grey space and the large shadowy bookcase, had gone out, and I saw them no more: for even a Scotch night in June, though it looks as if it would never end, does darken at the last. I had almost cried out, but checked myself, and rang the bell for Aunt Mary, and made up my mind I would say nothing till next morning, when to be sure naturally it would be more clear.

Next morning I rather think I forgot all about it—or was busy: or was more idle than usual: the two things meant nearly the same. At all events I thought no more of the window, though I still sat in my own, opposite to it, but occupied with some other fancy. Aunt Mary's visitors came as usual in the afternoon; but their talk was of other things, and for a day or two nothing at all happened to bring back my thoughts into this channel. It might be nearly a week before the subject came back, and once more it was old Lady Carnbee who set me thinking; not that she said anything upon that particular theme. But she was the last of my aunt's afternoon guests to go away, and when she rose to leave she threw up her hands, with those lively gesticulations which so many old Scotch ladies have. 'My faith!' said she, 'there is that bairn there still like a dream. Is the creature bewitched, Mary Balcarres? and is she bound to sit there by night and by day for the rest of her days? You should mind that there's things about, uncanny for women of our blood.'

I was too much startled at first to recognise that it was of me she was speaking. She was like a figure in a picture, with her pale face the colour of ashes, and the big pattern of the Spanish lace hanging half over it, and her hand held up, with the big diamond blazing at me from the inside of her uplifted palm. It was held up in surprise, but it looked as if it were raised in malediction; and the diamond threw out darts of light and glared and twinkled at me. If it had been in its right place it would not have mattered; but there, in the open of the hand! I started up, half in terror, half in wrath. And then the old lady laughed, and her hand dropped. 'I've wakened you to life, and broke the spell,' she said, nodding her old head at me, while the large black silk flowers of the lace waved and threatened. And she took my arm to go down-stairs, laughing and bidding me be steady, and no' tremble and shake like a broken reed. 'You should be as steady as a rock at your age. I was like a young tree,' she said, leaning so heavily that my willowy girlish frame quivered—'I was a support to virtue, like Pamela, in my time.'

'Aunt Mary, Lady Carnbee is a witch!' I cried, when I came back.

'Is that what you think, honey? well: maybe she once was,' said Aunt Mary, whom nothing surprised.

And it was that night once more after dinner, and after the post came in, and the 'Times', that I suddenly saw the Library window again. I had seen it every day—and noticed nothing; but to-night, still in a little tumult of mind over Lady Carnbee and her wicked diamond which wished me harm, and her lace which waved threats and warnings at me, I looked across the street, and there I saw quite plainly the room opposite, far more clear than before. I saw dimly that it must be a large room, and that the big piece of furniture against the wall was a writing-desk. That in a moment, when first my eyes rested upon it, was quite clear: a large old-fashioned escritoire, standing out into the room: and I knew by the shape of it that it had a great many pigeon-holes and little drawers in the back, and a large table for writing. There was one just like it in my father's library at home. It was such a surprise to see it all so clearly that I closed my eyes, for the moment almost giddy, wondering how papa's desk could have come here—and then when I reminded myself that this was nonsense, and that there were many such writing-tables besides papa's, and looked again—lo! it had all become quite vague and indistinct as it was at first; and I saw nothing but the blank window, of which the old ladies could never be certain whether it was filled up to avoid the window-tax, or whether it had ever been a window at all.

This occupied my mind very much, and yet I did not say anything to Aunt Mary. For one thing, I rarely saw anything at all in the early part of the day; but then that is natural: you can never see into a place from the outside, whether it is an empty room or a looking-glass, or people's eyes, or anything else that is mysterious, in the day. It has, I suppose, something to do with the light. But in the evening in June in Scotland—then is the time to see. For it is daylight, yet it is not day, and there is a quality in it which I cannot describe, it is so clear, as if every object was a reflection of itself.

I used to see more and more of the room as the days went on. The large escritoire stood out more and more into the space: with sometimes white glimmering things, which looked like papers, lying on it: and once or twice I was sure I saw a pile of books on the floor close to the writing-table, as if they had gilding upon them in broken specks, like old books. It was always about the time when the lads in the street began to call to each other that they were going home, and sometimes a shriller voice would come from one of the doors, bidding somebody to 'cry upon the laddies' to come back to their suppers. That was always the time I saw best, though it was close upon the moment when the veil seemed to fall and the clear radiance became less living, and all the sounds died out of the street, and Aunt Mary said in her soft voice, 'Honey! will you ring for the lamp?' She said honey as people say darling: and I think it is a prettier word.

Then finally, while I sat one evening with my book in my hand, looking straight across the street, not distracted by anything, I saw a little movement within. It was not any one visible—but everybody must know what it is to see the stir in the air the little disturbance—you cannot tell what it is, but that it indicates some one there, even though you can see no one. Perhaps it is a shadow making just one flicker in the still place. You may look at an empty room and the furniture in it for hours, and then suddenly there will be the flicker, and you know that something has come into it. It might only be a dog or a cat; it might be, if that were possible, a bird flying across; but it is some one, something living, which is so different, so completely different, in a moment from the things that are not living. It seemed to strike quite through me, and I gave a little cry. Then Aunt Mary stirred a little, and put down the huge newspaper that almost covered her from sight, and said, 'What is it, honey?' I cried 'Nothing,' with a little gasp, quickly, for I did not want to be disturbed just at this moment when somebody was coming! But I suppose she was not satisfied, for she got up and stood behind to see what it was, putting her hand on my shoulder. It was the softest touch in the world, but I could have flung it off angrily: for that moment everything was still again, and the place grew grey and I saw no more.

'Nothing,' I repeated, but I was so vexed I could have cried. 'I told you it was nothing, Aunt Mary. Don't you believe me, that you come to look—and spoil it all!'

I did not mean of course to say these last words; they were forced out of me. I was so much annoyed to see it all melt away like a dream: for it was no dream, but as real as—as real as—myself or anything I ever saw.

She gave my shoulder a little pat with her hand. 'Honey,' she said, 'were you looking at something? Is't that? is't that?' 'Is it what?' I wanted to say, shaking off her hand, but something in me stopped me: for I said nothing at all, and she went quietly back to her place. I suppose she must have rung the bell herself, for immediately I felt the soft flood of the light behind me, and the evening outside dimmed down, as it did every night, and I saw nothing more.

It was next day, I think, in the afternoon that I spoke. It was brought on by something she said about her fine work. 'I get a mist before my eyes,' she said; 'you will have to learn my old lace stitches, honey—for I soon will not see to draw the threads.'

'Oh, I hope you will keep your sight,' I cried, without thinking what I was saying. I was then young and very matter-of-fact. I had not found out that one may mean something, yet not half or a hundredth part of what one seems to mean: and even then probably hoping to be contradicted if it is anyhow against one's self.

'My sight!' she said, looking up at me with a look that was almost angry; 'there is no question of losing my sight—on the contrary, my eyes are very strong. I may not see to draw fine threads, but I see at a distance as well as ever I did—as well as you do.'

'I did not mean any harm, Aunt Mary,' I said. 'I thought you said— But how can your sight be as good as ever when you are in doubt about that window? I can see into the room as clear as—' My voice wavered, for I had just looked up and across the street, and I could have sworn that there was no window at all, but only a false image of one painted on the wall.

'Ah!' she said, with a little tone of keenness and of surprise: and she half rose up, throwing down her work hastily, as if she meant to come to me: then, perhaps seeing the bewildered look on my face, she paused and hesitated— 'Ay, honey!' she said, 'have you got so far ben as that?'

What did she mean? Of course I knew all the old Scotch phrases as well as I knew myself; but it is a comfort to take refuge in a little ignorance, and I know I pretended not to understand whenever I was put out. 'I don't know what you mean by "far ben",' I cried out, very impatient. I don't know what might have followed, but some one just then came to call, and she could only give me a look before she went forward, putting out her hand to her visitor. It was a very soft look, but anxious, and as if she did not know what to do: and she shook her head a very little, and I thought, though there was a smile on her face, there was something wet about her eyes. I retired into my recess, and nothing more was said.

But it was very tantalising that it should fluctuate so; for sometimes I saw that room quite plain and clear—quite as clear as I could see papa's library, for example, when I shut my eyes. I compared it naturally to my father's study, because of the shape of the writing-table, which, as I tell you, was the same as his. At times I saw the papers on the table quite plain, just as I had seen his papers many a day. And the little pile of books on the floor at the foot—not ranged regularly in order, but put down one above the other, with all their angles going different ways, and a speck of the old gilding shining here and there. And then again at other times I saw nothing, absolutely nothing, and was no better than the old ladies who had peered over my head, drawing their eyelids together, and arguing that the window had been shut up because of the old long-abolished window tax, or else that it had never been a window at all. It annoyed me very much at those dull moments to feel that I too puckered up my eyelids and saw no better than they.

Aunt Mary's old ladies came and went day after day while June went on. I was to go back in July, and I felt that I should be very unwilling indeed to leave until I had quite cleared up—as I was indeed in the way of doing—the mystery of that window which changed so strangely and appeared quite a different thing, not only to different people, but to the same eyes at different times. Of course I said to myself it must simply be an effect of the light. And yet I did not quite like that explanation either, but would have been better pleased to make out to myself that it was some superiority in me which made it so clear to me, if it were only the great superiority of young eyes over old—though that was not quite enough to satisfy me, seeing it was a superiority which I shared with every little lass and lad in the street. I rather wanted, I believe, to think that there was some particular insight in me which gave clearness to my sight—which was a most impertinent assumption, but really did not mean half the harm it seems to mean when it is put down here in black and white. I had several times again, however, seen the room quite plain, and made out that it was a large room, with a great picture in a dim gilded frame hanging on the farther wall, and many other pieces of solid furniture making a blackness here and there, besides the great escritoire against the wall, which had evidently been placed near the window for the sake of the light. One thing became visible to me after another, till I almost thought I should end by being able to read the old lettering on one of the big volumes which projected from the others and caught the light; but this was all preliminary to the great event which happened about Midsummer Day—the day of St John, which was once so much thought of as a festival, but now means nothing at all in Scotland any more than any other of the saints' days: which I shall always think a great pity and loss to Scotland, whatever Aunt Mary may say.

THREE

It was about midsummer, I cannot say exactly to a day when, but near that time, when the great event happened. I had grown very well acquainted by this time with that large dim room. Not only the escritoire, which was very plain to me now, with the papers upon it, and the books at its foot, but the great picture that hung against the farther wall, and various other shadowy pieces of furniture, especially a chair which one evening I saw had been moved into the space before the escritoire,—a little change which made my heart beat, for it spoke so distinctly of some one who must have been there, the some one who had already made me start, two or three times before, by some vague shadow of him or thrill of him which made a sort of movement in the silent space: a movement which made me sure that next minute I must see something or hear something which would explain the whole—if it were not that something always happened outside to stop it, at the very moment of its accomplishment. I had no warning this time of movement or shadow. I had been looking into the room very attentively a little while before, and had made out everything almost clearer than ever; and then had bent my attention again on my book, and read a chapter or two at a most exciting period of the story: and consequently had quite left St Rule's, and the High Street, and the College Library, and was really in a South American forest, almost throttled by the flowery creepers, and treading softly lest I should put my foot on a scorpion or a dangerous snake. At this moment something suddenly calling my attention to the outside, I looked across, and then, with a start, sprang up, for I could not contain myself. I don't know what I said, but enough to startle the people in the room, one of whom was old Mr Pitmilly. They all looked round upon me to ask what was the matter. And when I gave my usual answer of 'Nothing,' sitting down again shamefaced but very much excited, Mr Pitmilly got up and came forward, and looked out, apparently to see what was the cause. He saw nothing, for he went back again, and I could hear him telling Aunt Mary not to be alarmed, for Missy had fallen into a doze with the heat, and had startled herself waking up, at which they all laughed: another time I could have killed him for his impertinence, but my mind was too much taken up now to pay any attention. My head was throbbing and my heart beating. I was in such high excitement, however, that to restrain myself completely, to be perfectly silent, was more easy to me then than at any other time of my life. I waited until the old gentleman had taken his seat again, and then I looked back. Yes, there he was! I had not been deceived. I knew then, when I looked across, that this was what I had been looking for all the time—that I had known he was there, and had been waiting for him, every time there was that flicker of movement in the room—him and no one else. And there at last, just as I had expected, he was. I don't know that in reality I ever had expected him, or any one: but this was what I felt when, suddenly looking into that curious dim room, I saw him there.

He was sitting in the chair, which he must have placed for himself, or which some one else in the dead of night when nobody was looking must have set for him, in front of the escritoire—with the back of his head towards me, writing. The light fell upon him from the left hand and therefore upon his shoulders and the side of his head, which, however, was too much turned away to show anything of his face. Oh, how strange that there should be some one staring at him as I was doing, and he never to turn his head, to make a movement! If any one stood and looked at me, were I in the soundest sleep that ever was, I would wake, I would jump up, I would feel it through everything. But there he sat and never moved. You are not to suppose, though I said the light fell upon him from the left hand, that there was very much light. There never is in a room you are looking into like that across the street; but there was enough to see him by—the outline of his figure dark and solid, seated in the chair, and the fairness of his head visible faintly, a clear spot against the dimness. I saw this outline against the dim gilding of the frame of the large picture which hung on the farther wall.

I sat all the time the visitors were there, in a sort of rapture, gazing at this figure. I knew no reason why I should be so much moved. In an ordinary way, to see a student at an opposite window quietly doing his work might have interested me a little, but certainly it would not have moved me in any such way. It is always interesting to have a glimpse like this of an unknown life—to see so much and yet know so little, and to wonder, perhaps, what the man is doing, and why he never turns his head. One would go to the window—but not too close, lest he should see you and think you were spying upon him—and one would ask, Is he still there? is he writing, writing always? I wonder what he is writing! And it would be a great amusement: but no more. This was not my feeling at all in the present case. It was a sort of breathless watch, an absorption. I did not feel that I had eyes for anything else, or any room in my mind for another thought. I no longer heard, as I generally did, the stories and the wise remarks (or foolish) of Aunt Mary's old ladies or Mr Pitmilly. I heard only a murmur behind me, the interchange of voices, one softer, one sharper; but it was not as in the time when I sat reading and heard every word, till the story in my book, and the stories they were telling (what they said almost always shaped into stories), were all mingled into each other, and the hero in the novel became somehow the hero (or more likely heroine) of them all. But I took no notice of what they were saying now. And it was not that there was anything very interesting to look at, except the fact that he was there. He did nothing to keep up the absorption of my thoughts. He moved just so much as a man will do when he is very busily writing, thinking of nothing else. There was a faint turn of his head as he went from one side to another of the page he was writing; but it appeared to be a long long page which never wanted turning. Just a little inclination when he was at the end of the line, outward, and then a little inclination inward when he began the next. That was little enough to keep one gazing. But I suppose it was the gradual course of events leading up to this, the finding out of one thing after another as the eyes got accustomed to the vague light: first the room itself, and then the writing-table, and then the other furniture, and last of all the human inhabitant who gave it all meaning. This was all so interesting that it was like a country which one had discovered. And then the extraordinary blindness of the other people who disputed among themselves whether it was a window at all! I did not, I am sure, wish to be disrespectful, and I was very fond of my Aunt Mary, and I liked Mr Pitmilly well enough, and I was afraid of Lady Carnbee. But yet to think of the—I know I ought not to say stupidity—the blindness of them, the foolishness, the insensibility! discussing it as if a thing that your eyes could see was a thing to discuss! It would have been unkind to think it was because they were old and their faculties dimmed. It is so sad to think that the faculties grow dim, that such a woman as my Aunt Mary should fail in seeing, or hearing, or feeling, that I would not have dwelt on it for a moment, it would have seemed so cruel! And then such a clever old lady as Lady Carnbee, who could see through a millstone, people said—and Mr Pitmilly, such an old man of the world. It did indeed bring tears to my eyes to think that all those clever people, solely by reason of being no longer young as I was, should have the simplest things shut out from them; and for all their wisdom and their knowledge be unable to see what a girl like me could see so easily. I was too much grieved for them to dwell upon that thought, and half ashamed, though perhaps half proud too, to be so much better off than they.

All those thoughts flitted through my mind as I sat and gazed across the street. And I felt there was so much going on in that room across the street! He was so absorbed in his writing, never looked up, never paused for a word, never turned round in his chair, or got up and walked about the room as my father did. Papa is a great writer, everybody says: but he would have come to the window and looked out, he would have drummed with his fingers on the pane, he would have watched a fly and helped it over a difficulty, and played with the fringe of the curtain, and done a dozen other nice, pleasant, foolish things, till the next sentence took shape. 'My dear, I am waiting for a word,' he would say to my mother when she looked at him, with a question why he was so idle, in her eyes; and then he would laugh, and go back again to his writing-table. But He over there never stopped at all. It was like a fascination. I could not take my eyes from him and that little scarcely perceptible movement he made, turning his head. I trembled with impatience to see him turn the page, or perhaps throw down his finished sheet on the floor, as somebody looking into a window like me once saw Sir Walter do, sheet after sheet. I should have cried out if this Unknown had done that. I should not have been able to help myself, whoever had been present; and gradually I got into such a state of suspense waiting for it to be done that my head grew hot and my hands cold. And then, just when there was a little movement of his elbow, as if he were about to do this, to be called away by Aunt Mary to see Lady Carnbee to the door! I believe I did not hear her till she had called me three times, and then I stumbled up, all flushed and hot, and nearly crying. When I came out from the recess to give the old lady my arm (Mr Pitmilly had gone away some time before), she put up her hand and stroked my cheek. 'What ails the bairn?' she said; 'she's fevered. You must not let her sit her lane in the window, Mary Balcarres. You and me know what comes of that.' Her old fingers had a strange touch, cold like something not living, and I felt that dreadful diamond sting me on the cheek.

I do not say that this was not just a part of my excitement and suspense; and I know it is enough to make any one laugh when the excitement was all about an unknown man writing in a room on the other side of the way, and my impatience because he never came to an end of the page. If you think I was not quite as well aware of this as any one could be! but the worst was that this dreadful old lady felt my heart beating against her arm that was within mine. 'You are just in a dream,' she said to me, with her old voice close at my ear as we went down-stairs. 'I don't know who it is about, but it's bound to be some man that is not worth it. If you were wise you would think of him no more.'

'I am thinking of no man!' I said, half crying. 'It is very unkind and dreadful of you to say so, Lady Carnbee. I never thought of—any man, in all my life!' I cried in a passion of indignation. The old lady clung tighter to my arm, and pressed it to her, not unkindly.

'Poor little bird,' she said, 'how it's strugglin' and flutterin'! I'm not saying but what it's more dangerous when it's all for a dream.'

She was not at all unkind; but I was very angry and excited, and would scarcely shake that old pale hand which she put out to me from her carriage window when I had helped her in. I was angry with her, and I was afraid of the diamond, which looked up from under her finger as if it saw through and through me; and whether you believe me or not, I am certain that it stung me again—a sharp malignant prick, oh full of meaning! She never wore gloves, but only black lace mittens, through which that horrible diamond gleamed.

I ran up-stairs—she had been the last to go—and Aunt Mary too had gone to get ready for dinner, for it was late. I hurried to my place, and looked across, with my heart beating more than ever. I made quite sure I should see the finished sheet lying white upon the floor. But what I gazed at was only the dim blank of that window which they said was no window. The light had changed in some wonderful way during that five minutes I had been gone, and there was nothing, nothing, not a reflection, not a glimmer. It looked exactly as they all said, the blank form of a window painted on the wall. It was too much: I sat down in my excitement and cried as if my heart would break. I felt that they had done something to it, that it was not natural, that I could not bear their unkindness—even Aunt Mary. They thought it not good for me! not good for me! and they had done something—even Aunt Mary herself—and that wicked diamond that hid itself in Lady Carnbee's hand. Of course I knew all this was ridiculous as well as you could tell me; but I was exasperated by the disappointment and the sudden stop to all my excited feelings, and I could not bear it. It was more strong that I.

I was late for dinner, and naturally there were some traces in my eyes that I had been crying when I came into the full light in the dining-room, where Aunt Mary could look at me at her pleasure, and I could not run away. She said, 'Honey, you have been shedding tears. I'm loth, loth that a bairn of your mother's should be made to shed tears in my house.'

'I have not been made to shed tears,' cried I; and then, to save myself another fit of crying, I burst out laughing and said, 'I am afraid of that dreadful diamond on old Lady Carnbee's hand. It bites—I am sure it bites! Aunt Mary, look here.'

'You foolish lassie,' Aunt Mary said; but she looked at my cheek under the light of the lamp, and then she gave it a little pat with her soft hand. 'Go away with you, you silly bairn. There is no bite; but a flushed cheek, my honey, and a wet eye. You must just read out my paper to me after dinner when the post is in: and we'll have no more thinking and no more dreaming for tonight.'

'Yes, Aunt Mary,' said I. But I knew what would happen; for when she opens up her 'Times', all full of the news of the world, and the speeches and things which she takes an interest in, though I cannot tell why—she forgets. And as I kept very quiet and made not a sound, she forgot to-night what she had said, and the curtain hung a little more over me than usual, and I sat down in my recess as if I had been a hundred miles away. And my heart gave a great jump, as if it would have come out of my breast; for he was there. But not as he had been in the morning—I suppose the light, perhaps, was not good enough to go on with his work without a lamp or candles—for he had turned away from the table and was fronting the window, sitting leaning back in his chair, and turning his head to me. Not to me—he knew nothing about me. I thought he was not looking at anything; but with his face turned my way. My heart was in my mouth: it was so unexpected, so strange! though why it should have seemed strange I know not, for there was no communication between him and me that it should have moved me; and what could be more natural than that a man, wearied of his work, and feeling the want perhaps of more light, and yet that it was not dark enough to light a lamp, should turn round in his own chair, and rest a little, and think—perhaps of nothing at all? Papa always says he is thinking of nothing at all. He says things blow through his mind as if the doors were open, and he has no responsibility. What sort of things were blowing through this man's mind? or was he thinking, still thinking, of what he had been writing and going on with it still? The thing that troubled me most was that I could not make out his face. It is very difficult to do so when you see a person only through two windows, your own and his. I wanted very much to recognise him afterwards if I should chance to meet him in the street. If he had only stood up and moved about the room, I should have made out the rest of his figure, and then I should have known him again; or if he had only come to the window (as papa always did), then I should have seen his face clearly enough to have recognised him. But, to be sure, he did not see any need to do anything in order that I might recognise him, for he did not know I existed; and probably if he had known I was watching him, he would have been annoyed and gone away.

But he was as immovable there facing the window as he had been seated at the desk. Sometimes he made a little faint stir with a hand or a foot, and I held my breath, hoping he was about to rise from his chair—but he never did it. And with all the efforts I made I could not be sure of his face. I puckered my eyelids together as old Miss Jeanie did who was shortsighted, and I put my hands on each side of my face to concentrate the light on him: but it was all in vain. Either the face changed as I sat staring, or else it was the light that was not good enough, or I don't know what it was. His hair seemed to me light—certainly there was no dark line about his head, as there would have been had it been very dark—and I saw, where it came across the old gilt frame on the wall behind, that it must be fair: and I am almost sure he had no beard. Indeed I am sure that he had no beard, for the outline of his face was distinct enough; and the daylight was still quite clear out of doors, so that I recognised perfectly a baker's boy who was on the pavement opposite, and whom I should have known again whenever I had met him: as if it was of the least importance to recognise a baker's boy! There was one thing however, rather curious about this boy. He had been throwing stones at something or somebody. In St Rule's they have a great way of throwing stones at each other, and I suppose there had been a battle. I suppose also that he had one stone in his hand left over from the battle, and his roving eye took in all the incidents of the street to judge where he could throw it with most effect and mischief. But apparently he found nothing worthy of it in the street, for he suddenly turned round with a flick under his leg to show his cleverness, and aimed it straight at the window. I remarked without remarking that it struck with a hard sound and without any breaking glass, and fell straight down on the pavement. But I took no notice of this even in my mind, so intently was I watching the figure within, which moved not nor took the slightest notice, and remained just as dimly clear, as perfectly seen, yet as undistinguishable, as before. And then the light began to fail a little, not diminishing the prospect within, but making it still less distinct than it had been.

Then I jumped up, feeling Aunt Mary's hand upon my shoulder. 'Honey,' she said, 'I asked you twice to ring the bell; but you did not hear me.'

'Oh, Aunt Mary!' I cried in great penitence, but turning again to the window in spite of myself.

'You must come away from there: you must come away from there,' she said, almost as if she were angry: and then her soft voice grew softer, and she gave me a kiss: 'never mind about the lamp, honey: I have rung myself, and it is coming; but, silly bairn, you must not aye be dreaming—your little head will turn.'

All the answer I made, for I could scarcely speak, was to give a little wave with my hand to the window on the other side of the street.

She stood there patting me softly on the shoulder for a whole minute or more, murmuring something that sounded like, 'She must go away, she must go away.' Then she said, always with her hand soft on my shoulder, 'Like a dream when one awaketh.' And when I looked again, I saw the blank of an opaque surface and nothing more.

Aunt Mary asked me no more questions. She made me come into the room and sit in the light and read something to her. But I did not know what I was reading, for there suddenly came into my mind and took possession of it, the thud of the stone upon the window, and its descent straight down, as if from some hard substance that threw it off: though I had myself seen it strike upon the glass of the panes across the way.

FOUR

I am afraid I continued in a state of great exaltation and commotion of mind for some time. I used to hurry through the day till the evening came, when I could watch my neighbour through the window opposite. I did not talk much to any one, and I never said a word about my own questions and wonderings. I wondered who he was, what he was doing, and why he never came till the evening (or very rarely); and I also wondered much to what house the room belonged in which he sat. It seemed to form a portion of the old College Library, as I have often said. The window was one of the line of windows which I understood lighted the large hall; but whether this room belonged to the library itself, or how its occupant gained access to it, I could not tell. I made up my mind that it must open out of the hall, and that the gentleman must be the Librarian or one of his assistants, perhaps kept busy all the day in his official duties, and only able to get to his desk and do his own private work in the evening. One has heard of so many things like that—a man who had to take up some other kind of work for his living, and then when his leisure-time came, gave it all up to something he really loved—some study or some book he was writing. My father himself at one time had been like that. He had been in the Treasury all day, and then in the evening wrote his books, which made him famous. His daughter, however little she might know of other things, could not but know that! But it discouraged me very much when somebody pointed out to me one day in the street an old gentleman who wore a wig and took a great deal of snuff, and said, That's the Librarian of the old College. It gave me a great shock for a moment; but then I remembered that an old gentleman has generally assistants, and that it must be one of them.

Gradually I became quite sure of this. There was another small window above, which twinkled very much when the sun shone, and looked a very kindly bright little window, above that dullness of the other which hid so much. I made up my mind this was the window of his other room, and that these two chambers at the end of the beautiful hall were really beautiful for him to live in, so near all the books, and so retired and quiet, that nobody knew of them. What a fine thing for him! and you could see what use he made of his good fortune as he sat there, so constant at his writing for hours together. Was it a book he was writing, or could it be perhaps Poems? This was a thought which made my heart beat; but I concluded with much regret that it could not be Poems, because no one could possibly write Poems like that, straight off, without pausing for a word or a rhyme. Had they been Poems he must have risen up, he must have paced about the room or come to the window as papa did—not that papa wrote Poems: he always said, 'I am not worthy even to speak of such prevailing mysteries,' shaking his head—which gave me a wonderful admiration and almost awe of a Poet, who was thus much greater even than papa. But I could not believe that a poet could have kept still for hours and hours like that. What could it be then? perhaps it was history; that is a great thing to work at, but you would not perhaps need to move nor to stride up and down, or look out upon the sky and the wonderful light.

He did move now and then, however, though he never came to the window. Sometimes, as I have said, he would turn round in his chair and turn his face towards it, and sit there for a long time musing when the light had begun to fail, and the world was full of that strange day which was night, that light without colour, in which everything was so clearly visible, and there were no shadows. 'It was between the night and the day, when the fairy folk have power.' This was the after-light of the wonderful, long, long summer evening, the light without shadows. It had a spell in it, and sometimes it made me afraid: and all manner of strange thoughts seemed to come in, and I always felt that if only we had a little more vision in our eyes we might see beautiful folk walking about in it, who were not of our world. I thought most likely he saw them from the way he sat there looking out: and this made my heart expand with the most curious sensation, as if of pride that, though I could not see, he did, and did not even require to come to the window, as I did, sitting close in the depth of the recess, with my eyes upon him, and almost seeing things through his eyes.

I was so much absorbed in these thoughts and in watching him every evening—for now he never missed an evening, but was always there—that people began to remark that I was looking pale and that I could not be well, for I paid no attention when they talked to me, and did not care to go out, nor to join the other girls for their tennis, nor to do anything that others did; and some said to Aunt Mary that I was quickly losing all the ground I had gained, and that she could never send me back to my mother with a white face like that. Aunt Mary had begun to look at me anxiously for some time before that, and, I am sure, held secret consultations over me, sometimes with the doctor, and sometimes with her old ladies, who thought they knew more about young girls than even the doctors. And I could hear them saying to her that I wanted diversion, that I must be diverted, and that she must take me out more, and give a party, and that when the summer visitors began to come there would perhaps bea ball or two, or Lady Carnbee would get up a picnic. 'And there's my young lord coming home,' said the old lady whom they called Miss Jeanie, 'and I never knew the young lassie yet that would not cock up her bonnet at the sight of a young lord.'

But Aunt Mary shook her head. 'I would not lippen much to the young lord,' she said. 'His mother is sore set upon siller for him; and my poor bit honey has no fortune to speak of. No, we must not fly so high as the young lord; but I will gladly take her about the country to see the old castles and towers. It will perhaps rouse her up a little.'

'And if that does not answer we must think of something else,' the old lady said.

I heard them perhaps that day because they were talking of me, which is always so effective a way of making you hear—for latterly I had not been paying any attention to what they were saying; and I thought to myself how little they knew, and how little I cared about even the old castles and curious houses, having something else in my mind. But just about that time Mr Pitmilly came in, who was always a friend to me, and, when he heard them talking, he managed to stop them and turn the conversation into another channel. And after a while, when the ladies were gone away, he came up to my recess, and gave a glance right over my head. And then he asked my Aunt Mary if ever she had settled her question about the window opposite, 'that you thought was a window sometimes, and then not a window, and many curious things,' the old gentleman said.

My Aunt Mary gave me another very wistful look; and then she said, 'Indeed, Mr Pitmilly, we are just where we were, and I am quite as unsettled as ever; and I think my niece she has taken up my views, for I see her many a time looking across and wondering, and I am not clear now what her opinion is.'

'My opinion!' I said, 'Aunt Mary.' I could not help being a little scornful, as one is when one is very young. 'I have no opinion. There is not only a window but there is a room, and I could show you—' I was going to say, 'show you the gentleman who sits and writes in it,' but I stopped, not knowing what they might say, and looked from one to another. 'I could tell you—all the furniture that is in it,' I said. And then I felt something like a flame that went over my face, and that all at once my cheeks were burning. I thought they gave a little glance at each other, but that may have been folly. 'There is a great picture, in a big dim frame,' I said, feeling a little breathless, 'on the wall opposite the window—'

'Is there so?' said Mr Pitmilly, with a little laugh. And he said, 'Now I will tell you what we'll do. You know that there is a conversation party, or whatever they call it, in the big room to-night, and it will be all open and lighted up. And it is a handsome room, and two-three things well worth looking at. I will just step along after we have all got our dinner, and take you over to the pairty, madam—Missy and you—'

'Dear me!' said Aunt Mary. 'I have not gone to a pairty for more years than I would like to say—and never once to the Library Hall.' Then she gave a little shiver, and said quite low, 'I could not go there.'

'Then you will just begin again to-night, madam,' said Mr Pitmilly, taking no notice of this, 'and a proud man will I be leading in Mistress Balcarres that was once the pride of the ball!'

'Ah, once!' said Aunt Mary, with a low little laugh and then a sigh. 'And we'll not say how long ago;' and after that she made a pause, looking always at me: and then she said, 'I accept your offer, and we'll put on our braws; and I hope you will have no occasion to think shame of us. But why not take your dinner here?'

That was how it was settled, and the old gentleman went away to dress, looking quite pleased. But I came to Aunt Mary as soon as he was gone, and besought her not to make me go. 'I like the long bonnie night and the light that lasts so long. And I cannot bear to dress up and go out, wasting it all in a stupid party. I hate parties, Aunt Mary!' I cried, 'and I would far rather stay here.'

'My honey,' she said, taking both my hands, 'I know it will maybe be a blow to you,—but it's better so.'

'How could it be a blow to me?' I cried; 'but I would far rather not go.'

'You'll just go with me, honey, just this once: it is not often I go out. You will go with me this one night, just this one night, my honey sweet.'

I am sure there were tears in Aunt Mary's eyes, and she kissed me between the words. There was nothing more that I could say; but how I grudged the evening! A mere party, a conversazione (when all the College was away, too, and nobody to make conversation!), instead of my enchanted hour at my window and the soft strange light, and the dim face looking out, which kept me wondering and wondering what was he thinking of, what was he looking for, who was he? all one wonder and mystery and question, through the long, long, slowly fading night!

It occurred to me, however, when I was dressing—though I was so sure that he would prefer his solitude to everything—that he might perhaps, it was just possible, be there. And when I thought of that, I took out my white frock—though Janet had laid out my blue one—and my little pearl necklace which I had thought was too good to wear. They were not very large pearls, but they were real pearls, and very even and lustrous though they were small; and though I did not think much of my appearance then, there must have been something about me—pale as I was but apt to colour in a moment, with my dress so white, and my pearls so white, and my hair all shadowy—perhaps, that was pleasant to look at: for even old Mr Pitmilly had a strange look in his eyes, as if he was not only pleased but sorry too, perhaps thinking me a creature that would have troubles in this life, though I was so young and knew them not. And when Aunt Mary looked at me, there was a little quiver about her mouth. She herself had on her pretty lace and her white hair very nicely done, and looking her best. As for Mr Pitmilly, he had a beautiful fine French cambric frill to his shirt, plaited in the most minute plaits, and with a diamond pin in it which sparkled as much as Lady Carnbee's ring; but this was a fine frank kindly stone, that looked you straight in the face and sparkled, with the light dancing in it as if it were pleased to see you, and to be shining on that old gentleman's honest and faithful breast: for he had been one of Aunt Mary's lovers in their early days, and still thought there was nobody like her in the world.

I had got into quite a happy commotion of mind by the time we set out across the street in the soft light of the evening to the Library Hall. Perhaps, after all, I should see him, and see the room which I was so well acquainted with, and find out why he sat there so constantly and never was seen abroad. I thought I might even hear what he was working at, which would be such a pleasant thing to tell papa when I went home. A friend of mine at St Rule's—oh, far, far more busy than you ever were, papa!—and then my father would laugh as he always did, and say he was but an idler and never busy at all.

The room was all light and bright, flowers wherever flowers could be, and the long lines of the books that went along the walls on each side, lighting up wherever there was a line of gilding or an ornament, with a little response. It dazzled me at first all that light: but I was very eager, though I kept very quiet, looking round to see if perhaps in any corner, in the middle of any group, he would be there. I did not expect to see him among the ladies. He would not be with them,—he was too studious, too silent: but, perhaps among that circle of grey heads at the upper end of the room—perhaps—

No: I am not sure that it was not half a pleasure to me to make quite sure that there was not one whom I could take for him, who was at all like my vague image of him. No: it was absurd to think that he would be here, amid all that sound of voices, under the glare of that light. I felt a little proud to think that he was in his room as usual, doing his work, or thinking so deeply over it, as when he turned round in his chair with his face to the light.

I was thus getting a little composed and quiet in my mind, for now that the expectation of seeing him was over, though it was a disappointment, it was a satisfaction too—when Mr Pitmilly came up to me, holding out his arm. 'Now,' he said, 'I am going to take you to see the curiosities.' I thought to myself that after I had seen them and spoken to everybody I knew, Aunt Mary would let me go home, so I went very willingly, though I did not care for the curiosities. Something, however, struck me strangely as we walked up the room. It was the air, rather fresh and strong, from an open window at the east end of the hall. How should there be a window there? I hardly saw what it meant for the first moment, but it blew in my face as if there was some meaning in it, and I felt very uneasy without seeing why.

Then there was another thing that startled me. On that side of the wall which was to the street there seemed no windows at all. A long line of bookcases filled it from end to end. I could not see what that meant either, but it confused me. I was altogether confused. I felt as if I was in a strange country, not knowing where I was going, not knowing what I might find out next. If there were no windows on the wall to the street, where was my window? My heart, which had been jumping up and calming down again all this time, gave a great leap at this, as if it would come out of me—but I did not know what it could mean.

Then we stopped before a glass case, and Mr Pitmilly showed me some things in it. I could not pay much attention to them. My head was going round and round. I heard his voice going on, and then myself speaking with a queer sound that was hollow in my ears; but I did not know what I was saying or what he was saying. Then he took me to the very end of the room, the east end, saying something that I caught—that I was pale, that the air would do me good. The air was blowing full on me, lifting the lace of my dress, lifting my hair, almost chilly. The window opened into the pale daylight, into the little lane that ran by the end of the building. Mr Pitmilly went on talking, but I could not make out a word he said. Then I heard my own voice, speaking through it, though I did not seem to be aware that I was speaking. 'Where is my window?—where, then, is my window?' I seemed to be saying, and I turned right round, dragging him with me, still holding his arm. As I did this my eye fell upon something at last which I knew. It was a large picture in a broad frame, hanging against the farther wall.

What did it mean? Oh, what did it mean? I turned round again to the open window at the east end, and to the daylight, the strange light without any shadow, that was all round about this lighted hall, holding it like a bubble that would burst, like something that was not real. The real place was the room I knew, in which that picture was hanging, where the writing-table was, and where he sat with his face to the light. But where was the light and the window through which it came? I think my senses must have left me. I went up to the picture which I knew, and then I walked straight across the room, always dragging Mr Pitmilly, whose face was pale, but who did not struggle but allowed me to lead him, straight across to where the window was—where the window was not;—where there was no sign of it. 'Where is my window?—where is my window?' I said. And all the time I was sure that I was in a dream, and these lights were all some theatrical illusion, and the people talking; and nothing real but the pale, pale, watching, lingering day standing by to wait until that foolish bubble should burst.

'My dear,' said Mr Pitmilly, 'my dear! Mind that you are in public. Mind where you are. You must not make an outcry and frighten your Aunt Mary. Come away with me. Come away, my dear young lady! and you'll take a seat for a minute or two and compose yourself; and I'll get you an ice or a little wine.' He kept patting my hand, which was on his arm, and looking at me very anxiously. 'Bless me! bless me! I never thought it would have this effect,' he said.

But I would not allow him to take me away in that direction. I went to the picture again and looked at it without seeing it: and then I went across the room again, with some kind of wild thought that if I insisted I should find it. 'My window—my window!' I said.

There was one of the professors standing there, and he heard me. 'The window!' said he. 'Ah, you've been taken in with what appears outside. It was put there to be in uniformity with the window on the stair. But it never was a real window. It is just behind that bookcase. Many people are taken in by it,' he said.

His voice seemed to sound from somewhere far away, and as if it would go on for ever; and the hall swam in a dazzle of shining and of noises round me; and the daylight through the open window grew greyer, waiting till it should be over, and the bubble burst.

FIVE

It was Mr Pitmilly who took me home; or rather it was I who took him, pushing him on a little in front of me, holding fast to his arm, not waiting for Aunt Mary or any one. We came out into the daylight again outside, I, without even a cloak or a shawl, with my bare arms, and uncovered head, and the pearls round my neck. There was rush of the people about, and a baker's boy, that baker's boy, stood right in my way and cried, 'Here's a braw ane!' shouting to the others: the words struck me somehow, as his stone had struck the window, without any reason. But I did not mind the people staring, and hurried across the street, with Mr Pitmilly half a step in advance. The door was open, and Janet standing at it, looking out to see what she could see of the ladies in their grand dresses. She gave a shriek when she saw me hurrying across the street; but I brushed past her, and pushed Mr Pitmilly up the stairs, and took him breathless to the recess, where I threw myself down on the seat, feeling as if I could not have gone another step farther, and waved my hand across to the window. 'There! There!' I cried. Ah! there it was—not that senseless mob—not the theatres and the gas, and the people all in a murmur and clang of talking. Never in all these days had I seen that room so clearly. There was a faint tone of light behind, as if it might have been a reflection from some of those vulgar lights in the hall, and he sat against it, calm, wrapped in his thoughts, with his face turned to the window. Nobody but must have seen him. Janet could have seen him had I called her up-stairs. It was like a picture, all the things I knew, and the same attitude, and the atmosphere, full of quietness, not disturbed by anything. I pulled Mr Pitmilly's arm before I let him go,—'You see, you see!' I cried. He gave me the most bewildered look, as if he would have liked to cry. He saw nothing! I was sure of that from his eyes. He was an old man, and there was no vision in him. If I had called up Janet, she would have seen it all. 'My dear!' he said. 'My dear!' waving his hands in a helpless way.

'He has been there all these nights,' I cried, 'and I thought you could tell me who he was and what he was doing; and that he might have taken me in to that room, and showed me, that I might tell papa. Papa would understand, he would like to hear. Oh, can't you tell me what work he is doing, Mr Pitmilly? He never lifts his head as long as the light throws a shadow, and then when it is like this he turns round and thinks, and takes a rest!'

Mr Pitmilly was trembling, whether it was with cold or I know not what. He said, with a shake in his voice, 'My dear young lady—my dear—' and then stopped and looked at me as if he were going to cry. 'It's peetiful, it's peetiful,' he said; and then in another voice, 'I am going across there again to bring your Aunt Mary home; do you understand, my poor little thing, my—I am going to bring her home—you will be better when she is here.' I was glad when he went away, as he could not see anything: and I sat alone in the dark which was not dark, but quite clear light—a light like nothing I ever saw. How clear it was in that room! not glaring like the gas and the voices, but so quiet, everything so visible, as if it were in another world. I heard a little rustle behind me, and there was Janet, standing staring at me with two big eyes wide open. She was only a little older than I was. I called to her, 'Janet, come here, come here, and you will see him,—come here and see him!' impatient that she should be so shy and keep behind. 'Oh, my bonnie young leddy!' she said, and burst out crying. I stamped my foot at her, in my indignation that she would not come, and she fled before me with a rustle and swing of haste, as if she were afraid. None of them, none of them! not even a girl like myself, with the sight in her eyes, would understand. I turned back again, and held out my hands to him sitting there, who was the only one that knew. 'Oh,' I said, 'say something to me! I don't know who you are, or what you are: but you're lonely and so am I; and I only—feel for you. Say something to me!' I neither hoped that he would hear, nor expected any answer. How could he hear, with the street between us, and his window shut, and all the murmuring of the voices and the people standing about? But for one moment it seemed to me that there was only him and me in the whole world.

But I gasped with my breath, that had almost gone from me, when I saw him move in his chair! He had heard me, though I knew not how. He rose up, and I rose too, speechless, incapable of anything but this mechanical movement. He seemed to draw me as if I were a puppet moved by his will. He came forward to the window, and stood looking across at me. I was sure that he looked at me. At last he had seen me: at last he had found out that somebody, though only a girl, was watching him, looking for him, believing in him. I was in such trouble and commotion of mind and trembling, that I could not keep on my feet, but dropped kneeling on the window-seat, supporting myself against the window, feeling as if my heart were being drawn out of me. I cannot describe his face. It was all dim, yet there was a light on it: I think it must have been a smile; and as closely as I looked at him he looked at me. His hair was fair, and there was a little quiver about his lips. Then he put his hands upon the window to open it. It was stiff and hard to move; but at last he forced it open with a sound that echoed all along the street. I saw that the people heard it, and several looked up. As for me, I put my hands together, leaning with my face against the glass, drawn to him as if I could have gone out of myself, my heart out of my bosom, my eyes out of my head. He opened the window with a noise that was heard from the West Port to the Abbey. Could any one doubt that?

And then he leaned forward out of the window, looking out. There was not one in the street but must have seen him. He looked at me first, with a little wave of his hand, as if it were a salutation—yet not exactly that either, for I thought he waved me away; and then he looked up and down in the dim shining of the ending day, first to the east, to the old Abbey towers, and then to the west, along the broad line of the street where so many people were coming and going, but so little noise, all like enchanted folk in an enchanted place. I watched him with such a melting heart, with such a deep satisfaction as words could not say; for nobody could tell me now that he was not there,—nobody could say I was dreaming any more. I watched him as if I could not breathe—my heart in my throat, my eyes upon him. He looked up and down, and then he looked back at me. I was the first, and I was the last, though it was not for long: he did know, he did see, who it was that had recognised him and sympathised with him all the time. I was in a kind of rapture, yet stupor too; my look went with his look, following it as if I were his shadow; and then suddenly he was gone, and I saw him no more.

I dropped back again upon my seat, seeking something to support me, something to lean upon. He had lifted his hand and waved it once again to me. How he went I cannot tell, nor where he went I cannot tell; but in a moment he was away, and the window standing open, and the room fading into stillness and dimness, yet so clear, with all its space, and the great picture in its gilded frame upon the wall. It gave me no pain to see him go away. My heart was so content, and I was so worn out and satisfied—for what doubt or question could there be about him now? As I was lying back as weak as water, Aunt Mary came in behind me, and flew to me with a little rustle as if she had come on wings, and put her arms round me, and drew my head on to her breast. I had begun to cry a little, with sobs like a child. 'You saw him, you saw him!' I said. To lean upon her, and feel her so soft, so kind, gave me a pleasure I cannot describe, and her arms round me, and her voice saying 'Honey, my honey!'—as if she were nearly crying too. Lying there I came back to myself, quite sweetly, glad of everything. But I wanted some assurance from them that they had seen him too. I waved my hand to the window that was still standing open, and the room that was stealing away into the faint dark. 'This time you saw it all?' I said, getting more eager. 'My honey!' said Aunt Mary, giving me a kiss: and Mr Pitmilly began to walk about the room with short little steps behind, as if he were out of patience. I sat straight up and put away Aunt Mary's arms. 'You cannot be so blind, so blind!' I cried. 'Oh, not to-night, at least not to-night!' But neither the one nor the other made any reply. I shook myself quite free, and raised myself up. And there, in the middle of the street, stood the baker's boy like a statue, staring up at the open window, with his mouth open and his face full of wonder—breathless, as if he could not believe what he saw. I darted forward, calling to him, and beckoned him to come to me. 'Oh, bring him up! bring him, bring him to me!' I cried.

Mr Pitmilly went directly, and got the boy by the shoulder. He did not want to come. It was strange to see the little old gentleman, with his beautiful frill and his diamond pin, standing out in the street, with his hand upon the boy's shoulder, and the other boys round, all in a little crowd. And presently they came towards the house, the others all following, gaping and wondering. He came in unwilling, almost resisting, looking as if we meant him some harm. 'Come away, my laddie, come and speak to the young lady,' Mr Pitmilly was saying. And Aunt Mary took my hands to keep me back. But I would not be kept back.

'Boy,' I cried, 'you saw it too: you saw it: tell them you saw it! It is that I want, and no more.'

He looked at me as they all did, as if he thought I was mad. 'What's she wantin' wi' me?' he said; and then, 'I did nae harm, even if I did throw a bit stane at it—and it's nae sin to throw a stane.'

'You rascal!' said Mr Pitmilly, giving him a shake; 'have you been throwing stones? You'll kill somebody some of these days with your stones.' The old gentleman was confused and troubled, for he did not understand what I wanted, nor anything that had happened. And then Aunt Mary, holding my hands and drawing me close to her, spoke. 'Laddie,' she said, 'answer the young lady, like a good lad. There's no intention of finding fault with you. Answer her, my man, and then Janet will give ye your supper before you go.'

'Oh speak, speak!' I cried; 'answer them and tell them! you saw that window opened, and the gentleman look out and wave his hand?'

'I saw nae gentleman,' he said, with his head down, 'except this wee gentleman here.'

'Listen, laddie,' said Aunt Mary. 'I saw ye standing in the middle of the street staring. What were ye looking at?'

'It was naething to make a wark about. It was just yon windy yonder in the library that is nae windy. And it was open—as sure's death. You may laugh if you like. Is that a' she's wantin' wi' me?'

'You are telling a pack of lies, laddie,' Mr Pitmilly said.

'I'm tellin' nae lees—it was standin' open just like ony ither windy. It's as sure's death. I couldna believe it mysel'; but it's true.'

'And there it is,' I cried, turning round and pointing it out to them with great triumph in my heart. But the light was all grey, it had faded, it had changed. The window was just as it had always been, a sombre break upon the wall.

I was treated like an invalid all that evening, and taken up-stairs to bed, and Aunt Mary sat up in my room the whole night through. Whenever I opened my eyes she was always sitting there close to me, watching. And there never was in all my life so strange a night. When I would talk in my excitement, she kissed me and hushed me like a child. 'Oh, honey, you are not the only one!' she said. 'Oh whisht, whisht, bairn! I should never have let you be there!'

'Aunt Mary, Aunt Mary, you have seen him too?'

'Oh whisht, whisht, honey!' Aunt Mary said: her eyes were shining—there were tears in them. 'Oh whisht, whisht! Put it out of your mind, and try to sleep. I will not speak another word,' she cried.

But I had my arms round her, and my mouth at her ear. 'Who is he there?—tell me that and I will ask no more—'

'Oh honey, rest, and try to sleep! It is just—how can I tell you?—a dream! Did you not hear what Lady Carnbee said?—the women of our blood—'

'What? what? Aunt Mary, oh Aunt Mary—'

'I canna tell you,' she cried in her agitation, 'I canna tell you! How can I tell you, when I know just what you know and no more? It is a longing all your life after—it is a looking—for what never comes.'

'He will come,' I cried. 'I shall see him to-morrow—that I know, I know!'

She kissed me and cried over me, her cheek hot and wet like mine. 'My honey, try if you can sleep—try if you can sleep: and we'll wait to see what to-morrow brings.'

'I have no fear,' said I; and then I suppose, though it is strange to think of, I must have fallen asleep—I was so worn-out, and young, and not used to lying in my bed awake. From time to time I opened my eyes, and sometimes jumped up remembering everything: but Aunt Mary was always there to soothe me, and I lay down again in her shelter like a bird in its nest.

But I would not let them keep me in bed next day. I was in a kind of fever, not knowing what I did. The window was quite opaque, without the least glimmer in it, flat and blank like a piece of wood. Never from the first day had I seen it so little like a window. 'It cannot be wondered at,' I said to myself, 'that seeing it like that, and with eyes that are old, not so clear as mine, they should think what they do.' And then I smiled to myself to think of the evening and the long light, and whether he would look out again, or only give me a signal with his hand. I decided I would like that best: not that he should take the trouble to come forward and open it again, but just a turn of his head and a wave of his hand. It would be more friendly and show more confidence,—not as if I wanted that kind of demonstration every night.

I did not come down in the afternoon, but kept at my own window up-stairs alone, till the tea-party should be over. I could hear them making a great talk; and I was sure they were all in the recess staring at the window, and laughing at the silly lassie. Let them laugh! I felt above all that now. At dinner I was very restless, hurrying to get it over; and I think Aunt Mary was restless too. I doubt whether she read her 'Times' when it came; she opened it up so as to shield her, and watched from a corner. And I settled myself in the recess, with my heart full of expectation. I wanted nothing more than to see him writing at his table, and to turn his head and give me a little wave of his hand, just to show that he knew I was there. I sat from half-past seven o'clock to ten o'clock: and the daylight grew softer and softer, till at last it was as if it was shining through a pearl, and not a shadow to be seen. But the window all the time was as black as night, and there was nothing, nothing there.

Well: but other nights it had been like that; he would not be there every night only to please me. There are other things in a man's life, a great learned man like that. I said to myself I was not disappointed. Why should I be disappointed? There had been other nights when he was not there. Aunt Mary watched me, every movement I made, her eyes shining, often wet, with a pity in them that almost made me cry: but I felt as if I were more sorry for her than for myself. And then I flung myself upon her, and asked her, again and again, what it was, and who it was, imploring her to tell me if she knew? and when she had seen him, and what had happened? and what it meant about the women of our blood? She told me that how it was she could not tell, nor when: it was just at the time it had to be; and that we all saw him in our time—'that is,' she said, 'the ones that are like you and me.' What was it that made her and me different from the rest? but she only shook her head and would not tell me. 'They say,' she said, and then stopped short. 'Oh, honey, try and forget all about it—if I had but known you were of that kind! They say—that once there was one that was a Scholar, and liked his books more than any lady's love. Honey, do not look at me like that. To think I should have brought all this on you!'

'He was a Scholar?' I cried.

'And one of us, that must have been a light woman, not like you and me—But maybe it was just in innocence; for who can tell? She waved to him and waved to him to come over: and yon ring was the token: but he would not come. But still she sat at her window and waved and waved—till at last her brothers heard of it, that were stirring men; and then—oh, my honey, let us speak of it no more!'

'They killed him! I cried, carried away. And then I grasped her with my hands, and gave her a shake, and flung away from her. 'You tell me that to throw dust in my eyes—when I saw him only last night: and he as living as I am, and as young!'

'My honey, my honey!' Aunt Mary said.

After that I would not speak to her for a long time; but she kept close to me, never leaving me when she could help it, and always with that pity in her eyes. For the next night it was the same; and the third night. That third night I thought I could not bear it any longer. I would have to do something—if only I knew what to do! If it would ever get dark, quite dark, there might be something to be done. I had wild dreams of stealing out of the house and getting a ladder, and mounting up to try if I could not open that window, in the middle of the night—if perhaps I could get the baker's boy to help me; and then my mind got into a whril, and it was as if I had done it; and I could almost see the boy put the ladder to the window, and hear him cry out that there was nothing there. Oh, how slow it was, the night! and how light it was, and everything so clear—no darkness to cover you, no shadow, whether on one side of the street or on the other side! I could not sleep, though I was forced to go to bed. And in the deep midnight, when it is dark dark in every other place, I slipped very softly down-stairs, though there was one board on the landing-place that creaked—and opened the door and stepped out. There was not a soul to be seen, up or down, from the Abbey to the West Port: and the trees stood like ghosts, and the silence was terrible, and everything as clear as day. You don't know what silence is till you find it in the light like that, not morning but night, no sunrising, no shadow, but everything as clear as the day.

It did not make any difference as the slow minutes went on: one o'clock, two o'clock. How strange it was to hear the clocks striking in that dead light when there was nobody to hear them! But it made no difference. The window was quite blank; even the marking of the panes seemed to have melted away. I stole up again after a long time, through the silent house, in the clear light, cold and trembling, with despair in my heart.

I am sure Aunt Mary must have watched and seen me coming back, for after a while I heard faint sounds in the house; and very early, when there had come a little sunshine into the air, she came to my bedside with a cup of tea in her hand; and she, too, was looking like a ghost. 'Are you warm, honey—are you comfortable?' she said. 'It doesn't matter,' said I. I did not feel as if anything mattered; unless if one could get into the dark somewhere—the soft, deep dark that would cover you over and hide you—but I could not tell from what. The dreadful thing was that there was nothing, nothing to look for, nothing to hide from—only the silence and the light.

That day my mother came and took me home. I had not heard she was coming; she arrived quite unexpectedly, and said she had no time to stay, but must start the same evening so as to be in London next day, papa having settled to go abroad. At first I had a wild thought I would not go. But how can a girl say I will not, when her mother has come for her, and there is no reason, no reason in the world, to resist, and not right! I had to go, whatever I might wish or any one might say. Aunt Mary's dear eyes were wet; she went about the house drying them quietly with her handkerchief, but she always said, 'It is the best thing for you, honey—the best thing for you!' Oh, how I hated to hear it said that it was the best thing, as if anything mattered, one more than another! The old ladies were all there in the afternoon, Lady Carnbee looking at me from under her black lace, and the diamond lurking, sending out darts from under her finger. She patted me on the shoulder, and told me to be a good bairn. 'And never lippen to what you see from the window,' she said. 'The eye is deceitful as well as the heart.' She kept patting me on the shoulder, and felt again as if that sharp wicked stone stung me. Was that what Aunt Mary meant when she said yon ring was the token? I thought afterwards I saw the mark on my shoulder. You will say why? How can I tell why? If I had known, I should have been contented, and it would not have mattered any more.

I never went back to St Rule's, and for years of my life I never again looked out of a window when any other window was in sight. You ask me did I ever see him again? I cannot tell: the imagination is a great deceiver, as Lady Carnbee said: and if he stayed there so long, only to punish the race that had wronged him, why should I ever have seen him again? for I had received my share. But who can tell what happens in a heart that often, often, and so long as that, comes back to do its errand? If it was he whom I have seen again, the anger is gone from him, and he means good and no longer harm to the house of the woman that loved him. I have seen his face looking at me from a crowd. There was one time when I came home a widow from India, very sad, with my little children: I am certain I saw him there among all the people coming to welcome their friends. There was nobody to welcome me,—for I was not expected: and very sad was I, without a face I knew: when all at once I saw him, and he waved his hand to me. My heart leaped up again: I had forgotten who he was, but only that it was a face I knew, and I landed almost cheerfully, thinking here was some one who would help me. But he had disappeared, as he did from the window, with that one wave of his hand.

And again I was reminded of it all when old Lady Carnbee died—an old, old woman—and it was found in her will that she had left me that diamond ring. I am afraid of it still. It is locked up in an old sandal-wood box in the lumber-room in the little old country-house which belongs to me, but where I never live. If any one would steal it, it would be a relief to my mind. Yet I never knew what Aunt Mary meant when she said, 'Yon ring was the token,' nor what it could have to do with that strange window in the old College Library of St Rule's.

Eric Linklater

A seam of Scottish myth, history and culture runs through much of Eric Linklater's work. He had strong roots in Orkney and the North where he was brought up, and yet he was born in Penarth, South Wales, in 1899.

As Robert Bruce's biographer, and a friend of James Bridie and Compton Mackenzie, it is not surprising that Linklater should have been swept up in the rise of Scottish nationalism in the 1930s. By then a professional writer, he stood as the Scottish National Party's Parliamentary candidate for East Fife in 1933. His failure in this campaign and a general disillusionment with the party caused him to leave it in the same year, drawing on the experience to write *Magnus Merriman*.

Despite his prolific output and popular success at large with novels such as *Juan in America* (1931), and *Private Angelo* (1946), Linklater has received little critical attention in Scotland. A writer with a down-to-earth style and a delight in linguistic curiosities, he has a heightened sense of place and a lively satirical eye. He knew exactly how to tell a story and 'Kind Kitty', based on a poem by William Dunbar, draws its readers along unlikely paths which are sometimes dark, sometimes cheerful. Eric Linklater died in Aberdeen in 1974.

Kind Kitty

Thay threpit that scho diet of thrist, and maid a gud end.
Efter hir dede, scho dredit nought in hevin for to duell,
And sa to hevin the hieway dreidles scho wend.
DUNBAR

NINE OUT of ten people in Edinburgh never look at anything but the pavements and the shallow shop-windows and the figuration of neighbours as belittled as themselves. This is for safety, and to keep their wits from wondering, because whoever will raise his head suddenly to the Castle may see Asgard looming in the mist, and the hills above Holyroodhouse, that one day are no more than slopes for children to play on, the next are mountains that thrust huge shoulders through the clouds and bare their monstrous brows in the heights of the sky. So also if you look down at the houses that press numerously against the outer walls of Holyrood you may see nothing but a multitude of mean roofs. But you may as easily surprise a coven of witches dancing in the smoke, and warlocks leaping on the chimney pots.

This was a sight that Kind Kitty saw whenever she came up out of the Canongate to sit on a seat in the gardens under the Calton Hill, with a little flat bottle of whisky in her pocket, and a bonnet with a broken feather precariously pinned to her dirty grey hair.

Kind Kitty was never afraid to look at the hills and the air-drawn heights of the town, for though they might steal her wits away she had no wealth or position that needed her wits' attention and nothing to lose, though her thoughts took holiday for days on end, but a dozen hens and the wire-netting that confined them. It was the odour of hens that strangers first noticed, and most urgently disliked, when Kitty sat down beside them in the Gardens. It overcame the other smells that accompanied her, of smoke, of clothes incredibly old, of a body long unwashed, of yesterday's beer and the morning's dram. It was a violent unexpected smell, and Kitty's casual neighbours would soon rise and leave her. Then she would grumble through her old blue lips, and peer after them malevolently with her red and rheumy eyes, and unwrapping a piece of newspaper from the little bottle she would take a quick mouthful of whisky. 'Tae hell with you, then, for a high-minded upstart,' she would mutter, and wipe her mouth, and a water-drop from the end of her nose, with the back of her bony hand. But in a minute or two she would forget the insult, when her bleary eyes were captured by witches and warlocks dancing in the smoke, or by a flank of the Pamirs that pushed its stony ribs against the firmament. Then she would think of life and death, of the burnside in Appin where she had been born, of the great soldier, Sir Hector McOstrich, and the lovely wicked Lady Lavinia. The weave of life, like gunmetal silk shot with bright yellow, shone for her, at such an angle, with the remote and golden-lovely frailty of sunset after a rainy day. Misery in the morning was forgotten, and squalor after noon, beneath the aureate sky, returned like rain to the deeps of the earth.

But sooner or later the sunset would fade from her thoughts, the hills diminish, the warlocks dissolve into bitter vapour, and her belly protest its emptiness with loud exclamatory repetition. Then, with a twitch of her bonnet, a hitch to her dusty skirt, and a pull at her broken stays, she would rise in a sudden temper, and muttering furious complaints against the littleness of small whisky bottles, she would hobble back to the Canongate and stop to stare balefully at The Hole in the Wall, whose doors were not yet open. 'The mealy-mouthed thowless thieves,' she would mutter. 'The bletherin' kirk-gaun puggies!' And she would spit on the pavement to show her contempt for the law, and those who made it, that public-houses should be closed while thirst still grew unchecked.

It was drink, not food, that her empty stomach clamoured for. She ate little, and took no pleasure in such tasteless stuff as bread and potatoes and tinned beef. But for beer and black stout and whisky she had so great a love that her desire for them was unceasing, and her relish for their several flavours more constant than any carnal love. Except for a shilling or two that she was sometimes compelled to pay for rent, and a few coppers that went on corn for her hens, she spent all her money on drink and still was dry-mouthed for three or four days out of seven. She had the Old Age pension, and ten shillings a week was paid her, though unwillingly, by Sir Hector's grandson, who was not a soldier but a stockbroker, and bitterly resented such a burden on his estate. This income might have been sufficient to preserve her from the most painful and extreme varieties of thirst had she been content to drink draught ale, and that in solitude. But Kitty was both extravagant and generous, she liked whisky and good company, friendship and bottled beer, and twenty shillings a week was sadly insufficient for such rich amusement. Many of her friends were poorer than herself, and none was more wealthy, so their return for Kitty's entertainment was always inadequate. They would sometimes treat her to half a pint of beer, more rarely to a nip of whisky, but usually they repaid her with cups of tea, or half a herring, which gave her no pleasure whatever. She never calculated the profit and loss of good-fellowship, however, and so long as her neighbours had lively conversation and a cheerful spirit she would share her last shilling with them.

But a friend of hers, an old cast whore called Mima Bird, found a ten-shilling note one Christmas, and buying a dozen bottles of Bass, invited Kitty to come and drink six of them. The nobility of this entertainment inspired Kitty with a great desire to emulate it, not in vulgar competition, not for the ostentation of surpassing it, but simply to give again, and enjoy again, the delights of strong liquor and warm fellowship, so after much thought, and with high excitement, she formed a plan and made arrangements for a Hogmanay party that would put the Old Year to bed with joy and splendour.

New Year's Eve fell on a Saturday, and on Friday Kitty drew her Old Age pension and cashed the ten-shilling order that came from young Mr McOstrich. But a pound was not nearly enough to furnish such a party as she intended. She went to see James Campbell, the landlord of The Hole in the Wall, and after long discussion came to an agreement with him, and pledged her whole income for the first two weeks in January in return for thirty-three shillings in ready money and the loan of five tumblers. These were the best terms she could get, for Campbell was a hard man.

But Kitty did not waste much time in bemoaning so heavy a rate of interest. She had no reverence for money, as respectable people have, nor concern for the future; and her mind was occupied with entrancing preparations for the party. She bought two bottles of whisky, two dozen bottles of beer, and a dozen of stout. Nothing like so huge and extravagant an array had ever been seen in her dirty little kitchen in Baxter's Close, and the spectacle filled her with excitement that yielded presently to a kind of devotion, and then became pure childlike joy. She set the beer, orderly in rank, on the table, with the two whisky bottles on the mantelpiece, and the porter like a round fender before the empty fire. Then she stood here and there to admire the picture, and presently rearranged the bottles and marshalled the beer, like a fence, in front of the wire-netting that closed her dozen hens in a small extension of the kitchen that might, with a more orthodox tenant, have been the scullery. The hens clapped their wings, and encouraged her with their clucking. Then she made patterns and plans on the floor, now a cross, before which she signed herself with the Cross, and now a rough plan of Tearlach's Hall, in Appin, where Sir Hector and Lady Lavinia had lived in pride and many varieties of sin. Her old hands took delicately the smooth necks of the bottles, she patted into place a label that was half-unstuck, she made a shape like a rose, the bottles standing shoulder to shoulder in the middle, and the tears ran down her cheek to see the loveliness of that pattern. Weary at last, replete with happiness, she fell asleep with a bottle of whisky in her arms.

When morning came she woke in pride to be confronted with such riches, and her demeanour, that only her hens observed, was uncommonly dignified. Setting the bottles on the table, according to their kind and now without fantasy, she carefully considered her arrangements and debated their sufficiency for the imminent party. Was her house properly furnished for entertainment? There were five tumblers that she had borrowed, one that she possessed, a bed where four might sit, a chair, a stool, and more drink than had ever been seen in one room in all her memory of Baxter's Close. What else could be needed for the pleasure of her guests?

A thought entered her mind that she first repelled and then suffered to return. Some of her visitors might like something to eat. If that were so, it would be a great nuisance, and for a little while Kitty thought impatiently about the frailties of humankind and the monstrous demands that people made for their contentment. But presently she counted her money and found she had still four shillings left. So she put on her bonnet and went out shopping.

The wind blew coldly down the Canongate, with a flourish of rain on its ragged edge, but Kitty, with money in her purse and in her heart the intention of spending it, was too important to notice such small discomfort, and going first to a baker's she bought for two shillings a Scotch bun. With that fierily sweet and bitter-black dainty under her arm she turned and walked slowly, over greasy pavements, to a corn chandler's in the High Street, where for ninepence she obtained a large bag of Indian corn for her hens. Then she returned to the Canongate, and having purchased three-pennyworth of cheese she entered The Hole in the Wall at the very moment when its doors opened, and made a satisfying meal off a shilling's worth of draught beer and the bright wedge of American cheddar.

The afternoon was slow in passing, but Kitty amused herself with ingenious new arrangements of the bottles, and with feeding her hens, and soon after six o'clock her first guest arrived, who was Mima Bird, the old whore. Then came Mrs. Smiley, who made a small living by selling bootlaces; Mrs. Hogg, who should have been well-off, her husband having had both his legs shot off while serving in the Black Watch, but he spent all his pension on threepenny bets and twopenny trebles; old Rebecca Macafee, who had been a tinker till she married a trawler's cook, who deserted her, and varicose veins kept her from the country roads; and Mrs. Crumb, who had a good job as a lavatory attendant, but had to support a half-witted husband and three useless sons. These were Kind Kitty's oldest and favourite friends, and when she saw them all sitting in her kitchen, each with a dram inside her to warm her stomach and loosen her tongue and flush her cheeks, each with a glass of beer or stout in her hand and another bottle beside her, then she was so happy that all of a sudden she cackled with laughter, and rocked to and fro on her stool, and began to sing an old song in a loud hoarse voice:

> O Sandy, dinna ye mind, quo' she,
> When ye gart me drink the brandy,
> When ye yerkit me owre among the broom,
> And played me houghmagandy!

'It's better among the broom than in the Meadows on a cauld winter night, or up against the wall of Greyfriars Kirk with a drunken Aussie seven foot high,' cried Mima Bird.

'Ay, but they'd money to spend, had the Aussies,' said old Rebecca, 'and faith, they spent it.'

'It was a fine war while it lasted,' sighed Mrs. Hogg, whose husband, for three good years, had been more use to the Black Watch than he had ever been to her.

'The boys did well enough,' said Kitty, 'but the generals and the high heid yins were a pack of jordan-heidit losingers.' And she thought, sadly and lovingly, of Sir Hector McOstrich, who would have shown them how to win battles had not shame, not war, untimely killed him. But far-off thoughts could not long endure the loud immediacy of her cummers, whose laughter grew more frequent, whose tales and jolly memory became with every passing minute more rich and lively and delectable. Now and again their laughter would wake even the corn-fed hens to responsive clucking and scratching; and in the smoky light of a dingy lamp the coarse and weather-beaten cheeks of the six old women, their wrinked eyes and creasy necks, were lovely with a life invincible. The air was full of the rich odours of beer and stout, and ever and anon its heavy layers would lift and waver before the genial shock of a great crackling belch. Kitty gave them another dram, and thick slices of black bun.

> If whisky was a river, and I was a duck,
> O whisky! Johnny!
> I'd dive to the bottom and I never would come up,
> O whisky for my Johnny!

sang old Rebecca. 'When that man I was married on, and a hog-eyed lurdan he was,' she said, 'would come home from sea, he was so thick with salt it would fill you with thirst to smell him half-way up the stairs.'

'You must have robbed a bank to give us a party like this,' said Mrs. Crumb. 'It beats the High Commissioner's garden-party at Holyrood just hollow. Why, we've drink to every hand, and the very best of drink at that, but there, so they tell me, the ministers' wives are fair tumbling over each other, and tearing each other's eyes out, to get to the eatables and the drinkables, and them nothing but lemonade and ha'penny cakes.'

'It's the very best party I ever was at,' said Mrs Hogg.

'It's the only one I've ever been to,' said Mrs Smiley, and that was a lie, but she thought it was true and began to cry, and got another dram to stop her.

So the evening wore on, and by half-past eleven there was nothing left in the glasses but dry feathers of froth, nothing in the bottles but a remembering air. By then, however, it was time to go out and join the multitude, coming from all directions, that was crowding the pavement before St Giles and filling the night with a valedictory noise. These were the common people of Scotland, come to tread underfoot, as bitter ashes, their lost hopes of the Old Year, its miseries they had survived, and to welcome the New Year with hope inexpugnable and confidence that none could warrant and none defeat. The procession of the months would give them neither riches nor wisdom, beauty nor holiness, but under every moon were many days of life, and life was their first love and their last. So the bells rang loudly as they might, the little black bottles were offered to friend and stranger—for all were brothers out of the same unwearying and shameless womb, and many were drunk enough to admit the relationship—hands were held in a circle by unknown hands, songs were sung, and a boisterous dance was trodden. The New Year was made welcome like a stranger in the old days of hospitality, though none knew whether he was whole or sick or loyal or lying.

Now when the old women, who had spent such a fine evening with Kitty, came out into the night, the cold air beat on their foreheads and made worse confusion of their befuddled minds, so that four of them lost control of their legs and nearly all cognizance of the world about them. Mrs Smiley lay in the gutter and slept, and Mrs Hogg, lying curiously across a barrel, slept also. Mrs Crumb, walking in a dwaum, clung to the arm of a kind policeman, and old Rebecca, having bitten the hand of an officer of the Salvation Army, vanished in the darkness of a near-by close. But Kitty and Mima Bird staggered valiantly along and came near enough to St Giles to be caught in the crowd and to join their cracked voices in song, to lurch bravely in the dancing, and to crow their welcome to the infant year.

It was late the next morning when Kitty woke on her dirty and disordered bed. Her boots had made it muddy, her broken bonnet lay on the pillow beside her. How she had reached home she could not remember, nor did she worry her aching head to try. Her mouth was parched and sour, her eyes smarting, her stomach queasy. She lay for a long time before she had the strength or courage to move, and then agonizingly sat up, her head splitting beneath a great jolt of pain, and wretchedly set her feet to the floor. She groped among the debris of the feast, holding bottle after bottle with shaking hands to the dim grey square of window to see if any sup remained. But they were all as empty as though a hot wind of the desert had dried them, till at last, hidden by the greasy valance of the bed, she found one that held—O bliss beyond words!—a gill of flat beer. This she drank slowly and with infinite gratitude, and then, taking off her boots and putting her bonnet in a place of safety, she returned to bed. 'What a nicht with Burns!' she murmured, and fell asleep.

In the middle of the night she woke with a raging thirst. Headache and nausea had gone, but her whole body, like a rusty hinge, cried for moisture. Yet water was no good to her. She filled her rumbling belly with it, and it lay cold and heavy in her stomach and never penetrated the thirsty tissues. Her tongue was like the bark of a dead tree, her mouth was a chalk-pit, her vitals were like old dry sacks. Never before had she known such thirst. It seemed as though drought had emptied her veins, as rivulets go dry in the high noon of summer, and her bowels resembled the bleached and arid canvas of a boat that has drifted many days beneath the parching pitiless sun of Capricorn. In this agony, in this inward and ever-increasing Sahara, she lay till morning, while her very thoughts changed their direction with a creak and a groan.

But when the time came for it to open, she went to The Hole in the Wall and pleaded with James Campbell for a little credit, that she might save her life with a quart or two of beer. He, however, refused to let her have a single drop, not a sparrow's beakful, till she had paid into his hands, on the following Friday, her Old Age pension and her ten shillings from young Mr McOstrich. Then, he said, out of pure Christian kindliness he would let her drink a pint or so on consideration of her pledging to him another week's income. Nor could he be moved from this cruel and tyrannous decision.

It seemed to Kitty, as she walked home, that her body at any moment might crumble into dust and be blown away. She opened her mouth to suck in the wind and the rain, but the wind changed in her throat to a hot simoom, and choked her with a sandstorm of desire for the slaking gold and cool foam of bitter beer. She sat in her dark room gasping for assuagement, and tormented by the vision and the gurgling noise of ale cascading into glass. The marrow dried in her bones.

But despite the unceasing torture she would not yield to the temptation to beg sixpence or a dram, supposing they had it, from her friends. To sorn like a tinker on those whom she had so lately entertained like a queen was utterly impossible. Her spirit was too proud to stoop so low for comfort. Her torment must continue. She had nothing to sell, nothing that anyone would conceivably buy, not even her hens, for they were long past laying and too thin to be worth the plucking. She was shipwrecked, and she must endure till time should rescue her.

But she had not so long to wait for relief as she feared, for about six o'clock in the evening, when The Hole in the Wall was open again for those who had money, her hens began clacking and chacking as though they were mad, and anyone who had been there might have seen Kitty's head fall to one side, and one hand slide stiffly from the arm of her chair. She was dead, and it was thirst that had killed her. Thirst had sucked out the vital essence of her life, and left nothing but dry tubes and a parched frame behind. Her body was dead and as dry as a powdery sponge in a chemist's shop.

Some time later her soul felt better, though not yet at ease, when she found herself walking along Death's Road in the worlds beyond this world. She was still thirsty, but not agonized with thirst. She was worried by the flies and the midges on the lower part of the road, and she was angry to find herself dead; for she had enjoyed being alive. But she kept bravely on her way, knowing the proper thing to do, and she felt exceedingly scornful of the innumerable travellers who grumbled at stones in the way—for it was not a motor road—and complained about the lack of signposts, and sulkily lay down in the shadow of a hedge to wait for a bus that would never come.

The road climbed slowly round the side of a hill whose top was lost in a luminous mist. After a few hours Kitty became reconciled to death, and trudged on with growing curiosity. The farther she went the lonelier the road became, till for a mile or two she saw no one at all. Then, at a fork in the road, she found a group of some twenty people, very well dressed for the most part, who were discussing which way they should go. For on the left hand the road led downhill to a valley shining in the sun, but on the right it climbed steeply and narrowed in a few hundred yards to a mountain track. The majority of the disputing travellers favoured clearly the low road, but a dubious minority furrowed their brows and looked without relish at the upward path. The debate came to an end as Kitty drew near to them. A well-bred female voice, like a ship's bell in the night, exclaimed: 'The idea is absurd. As though such a wretched little path could lead to anything or anywhere!' 'Unless to a precipice,' added a tired young man. And the party, with scarcely a glance at Kitty, turned downhill with resolute steps or a shrug of the shoulders.

'Tyach!' said Kitty, and went the other way.

The path she took was not unlike the little road that leads to Arthur's Seat. The resemblance comforted her, and so did the mist, which was like a Scots haar with the sun coming through it. The track bent and twisted and crossed a depression between three hills. It rose into the mist. She walked for a long time in a sunny vapour, and lost her breath, and grew thirsty again.

Then the view cleared, and on the forefront of a great plateau she came to a high wall, with a tall white gate in it, and beside the gate a house with an open door, two bow-fronted lower windows, and three upper ones, from the centre of which jutted a green holly bush. So Kitty knew it was a tavern, and taking no notice of the ivory gate in the wall she walked gladly in and rapped on the bar. But when she saw who came to answer the summons, she was so astounded and so abashed that she could not speak, though a moment before she had known very well what she meant to say.

It was a lady with high-piled golden hair who came to serve her—but the gold was dim, the colours of her dress were faded (it had been fashionable when King Edward VII was crowned), her mouth had forgotten laughter—and Kitty, seeing not only all that had changed but that which was unchanged, knew her at once.

'Well,' said the lady, 'and what can I give you?'

'Oh, your ladyship!' stammered Kitty, and twisted her dirty old hands in joy and embarrassment.

Then, before either could speak again, a tall thin man came in through the outer door with a basket on his arm. He had a nose like a hawk's beak, a pair of fine moustaches like the wings of a hawk, he wore a deer-stalker's cap and an old Norfolk jacket, and the basket on his arm held a loaf of bread, a beef-bone, and some vegetables. He put the basket on a table and murmured to the lady with the dimmed golden hair, 'A customer, my dear? Things are looking up, aren't they?'

'Sir Hector!' said Kitty in a trembling voice.

But though she recognized them, they did not remember her, for she had lived longer than they had, and life had used her inconsiderately. It was only after long explanation, after much exclamation, that they knew her, and saw faintly in her dissipated features the sweet young lines of Kitty of the Burnside. Sir Hector was visibly distressed. But Kitty, giving him no time to speak his pity, indignantly asked, 'And what are you doing here, in a pub at Heaven's gate, who never soiled your hands with work of any kind on earth below? Is there no respect in Heaven? Or has someone been telling lies about you, and dirty slander, as they did in Appin, and London, and Edinburgh too?'

'We have been treated with understanding and forgiveness,' said Lady Lavinia; and Sir Hector loudly cleared his throat and added, 'It was a situation of great difficulty, a very delicate situation indeed, and we have no complaints to make. None whatever,' he said, and took his message basket into the kitchen.

But Kitty was sorely displeased by the indignity of their condition, for in her youth they had been great and splendid figures—though shameless in their many sins, dissolute in all ways, and faithful only to their mutual love—and in her loyalty she vilified the judgment of Heaven that kept them beyond its gate. She swore that if they were not good enough for God's company, then He could do without hers also. She wouldn't go to Heaven. Not she, she said. Not though God and all His holy angels came out to plead with her. 'Be damned if I'll consort with you,' she would say, and that would teach them what other people thought of their treatment of a great gentleman like Sir Hector and a lady like Lady Lavinia.

So for a few days Kitty stayed in the inn by Heaven's gate, and the beer there was as good as she had ever tasted, and her heart was glad to be in such grand company. But she could not restrain her curiosity to see what Heaven was like, and one morning she knocked on the ivory door, and when St Peter opened it she did her best to slip inside. But St Peter pushed her back and asked her who she was. Nor did he seem much impressed when she told him.

'And how did you get here?' he asked.

'Well,' said Kitty, 'it all began with a Hogmanay party in Baxter's Close in the Canongate.'

'That's enough,' said St Peter. 'We want none of your kind here. And he shut the door in her face.

Now having been refused admission, Kitty's curiosity became overwhelming, and she made up her mind to enter Heaven by hook or crook. So she walked up and down muttering angrily, till she thought of a trick that might beat St Peter's vigilance, and the following morning she knocked again on the ivory door.

St Peter frowned angrily when he saw who it was, but before he could speak, Kitty exclaimed, 'There's an auld friend of yours in the pub ootbye that's speiring for you, and would like you to go and have a crack with him.'

'What's his name?' asked St Peter.

'I just canna mind on,' Kitty answered, 'but he's a weel-put-on man with whiskers like your own.'

'It's not like any friend of mine to be spending his time in a public-house,' said Peter.

'You wouldna deny an auld friend because he likes his glass, would you?'

Now at that moment Kitty had a stroke of luck, for beyond the wall a cock crew loud and piercingly, and Kitty said quickly, 'You'll remember that once before you cried out you didna ken a man you kent full well. You'll not be wanting to make the same mistake again, I'm thinking?'

At that St Peter's face grew dark red with rage and shame. But he tucked up his gown and went swiftly out and over to the inn, leaving the gate of Heaven open. And Kitty, as soon as his back was turned, scuttled inside.

It seemed to her that Heaven had a rather deserted look. She had expected to see well-dressed crowds and a fine air of prosperity and well-being. She had hoped to associate with lords and ladies, or at least with wealthy people of the kind that lived in Heriot Row and did their expensive shopping in Princes Street. But the only people she saw were almost as shabbily dressed as she was, and even they were few in number.

She stopped and spoke to a mild little man who sat on a green chair beneath a white-flowering tree. 'The others will have gone for a picnic?' she said. 'Or they'll be busy with their choir practice?'

'There are no others,' he answered. 'At least, not here. Some of the farther regions, that people of an older birth have chosen, are well enough populated, but here we are very few in number. So many on earth to-day have lost their faith. . . .'

'The glaikit sumphs!' said Kitty, and continued her walk, but without much enjoyment. She was saved from boredom, indeed, only by discovering, in the shelter of a little wood, a henhouse with a run attached, in which a score of finely feathered Rhode Island Reds were gravely scratching, their ruddy plumage a very pretty contrast to the green leaves and white sand. While Kitty stood watching them with interest and admiration, she was surprised, and somewhat perturbed, by the approach of Our Lady and a young woman in a khaki shirt and cotton breeches.

Kitty most reverently curtsied, Our Lady as graciously smiled, and the young woman in the breeches went into the hen run. Presently she reappeared with a dejected look on her face and two small eggs in her hand.

'Now really,' said Our Lady, 'that's *most* disappointing. Two eggs to-day, three yesterday, and four the day before. They're getting worse and worse. I do think you might persuade them to do better than that, Miss Ramsbottom.'

'I'm giving them the very same feeds that were recommended by the Government College of Dairying and Poultry Management,' said Miss Ramsbottom unhappily.

'Well, if that doesn't suit them, why not try something else?'

'But I don't know anything else. We weren't taught anything else in the Government College. It took us so long to learn. . . .'

'You let me look after them, Your Ladyship,' said Kitty. 'I kept a dozen hens in a back kitchen in Baxter's Close, in the Canongate in Edinburgh, and fed them on anything I could find, or on nothing at all, and they laid like herring-roe for eight or nine years, some of them, till the poor creatures were fairly toom, and nothing could be done with them at all. But with bonny birds like these we'll have eggs dropping all day, like pennies in the plate at a revival meeting.'

'All right,' said Our Lady, 'I'll give you a trial and see how you get on. And if there's a choice—though there hasn't been for a long time past—it's the brown eggs that I prefer, especially for breakfast, though the white ones are good enough for omelettes, of course. Now come along, Miss Ramsbottom, and I'll find something else for you to do.'

So Kitty was given work in Heaven, and for several weeks she was happy enough to be looking after such handsome and well-disposed fowls, for under her care they became not merely prolific but regular in their habits. Two circumstances, however, kept her from setting down in whole contentment, one being the lack of congenial company, the other the fact that in Heaven there was nothing to drink but light wines and beer, and the beer was poor in quality.

She took to wandering far afield, and found that regions more remote from the gate were fairly thickly populated. But many of the inhabitants, to her disgust, were foreigners, and even among those of Scottish or English origin she found few with whom she had much in common. Yet she continued to explore the upper reaches of Heaven, for having met Our Lady she was seized with ambition to encounter God the Father and the Son of Man.

It was after a very long walk that by chance she saw God. He was sitting in a pleached arbour drinking wine with a bald man in doublet and hose, his head the shape of an egg, and another in sombre garments, with a broad bony forehead, untidy thick hair, and a wild mouth. Their voices were loud and magnificent, and a pleasant lightning played about the forehead of God the Father.

'I wrote your true morality,' said the bald man, 'when I made Parolles say "Simply the thing I am shall make me live."'

'And I,' said the man with the bony forehead, 'I wrote your pure wisdom in the third movement of my Emperor concerto, when I put the Hero—the Conqueror, the Fool—in the middle of a ring, and fenced him round with dancing countryfolk and laughter that would not stop.'

'So you're my Moralist, and you're my Philosopher?' said God the Father. 'And what was I when I said "Let there be light"? Simply the Artist for art's sake?'

'A pity you hadn't also said "Let there be understanding,"' said the man with the bony forehead.

'Then would you have robbed poor dramatists of their trade,' said the bald man.

Now this kind of conversation, though it appeared to please its participants, had no interest for Kitty, and without waiting to hear more she went on past the pleached arbour, and came presently to a little rocky foreland in the cliff of Heaven, and looking over the edge she saw something of the world below.

She had never known till then what evil there was upon the earth. But looking down, through the clear light of Heaven, she saw lies and tyranny and greed, misery like a dying donkey in the sand and greed like a vulture tearing its vitals. She saw hunger and heard weeping. She saw a fool in black uniform who had made his people drunk with lying words and threatened all Europe with war. She saw bestial stupidity consume the horde of humanity like vermin on a beggar's skin. And then she found that she was not alone on the little foreland, for in a cleft of the rock was the Son of Man, weeping.

So Kitty, in a great hurry to escape unseen, came quickly away from there, and without waiting to look at anything else, returned to her henhouse and the comforting plumpness of her Rhode Island Reds. She was hot and leg-weary after her long walk, and very depressed by what she had seen of the farther parts of Heaven. She wanted to sit down in a comfortable chair, and take off her boots, and drink a quart or two of good strong ale. She needed ale, and plenty of it, to soothe and reassure her. But as luck would have it, the beer that night was thin as a postcard, sour as vinegar, and there was very little of it. Kitty lost her temper completely, and let anyone who cared to listen know just what she thought of Heaven and the only brewer—since men brewed their own—who had ever succeeded in swindling his way into it. At dinner-time the next day she repeated the whole story, for again the beer was small in quantity and less in quality, a cupful, no more, and little better than swipes.

She rose from the table in fury, and went straight to the gate, which was unattended. She threw it open, and without any feeling of regret heard it slam behind her.

But in the tavern below the wall, with a tankard of their own brewing before her, she soon found good temper again, and told Sir Hector and Lady Lavinia a fine story of the hardships she had had to endure.

'Not that I wasn't real pleased to be working for Our Lady,' she said, 'and a fine time *she* had while I was there, with two good brown eggs to her breakfast every morning, but apart from her the company was poor—no gentry at all—and there were sights there that I wouldna care to see again, and talk that made no sense, and the beer was just a disgrace. It's maybe all right for them that like it, and God knows I wouldna say a word against the place, but I think I'll be better suited here, if you'll keep me. I can peel the tatties and scrub the floor and clean your boots, and if you won't grudge me a nip and a pint when my work's done, I'll be far happier here than in ahint that wall of theirs. And I wouldna find it easy to get by yon birkie with the keys again,' she added.

There, then, in the inn at Heaven's gate, Kind Kitty found her proper place. There she is still, doing a little work and drinking a good deal, and whomsoever Death takes from this world, whose legs and faith are strong enough for the hillward path, will do well to stop there and drink a pint or two for the good of the house and his own comfort. For Kitty's presence is sure proof that the ale is still good. Had its quality failed she would have gone elsewhere long before now.

Jessie Kesson

Jessie Grant Macdonald was born in Inverness in 1916 and spent her early years living with her mother in Elgin. Their poverty meant she was sent to an orphanage at Skene, Aberdeenshire, and from there took the almost inevitable step into service until 1934, when, aged nineteen, she married John Kesson and became a farmer's wife. She has since had many occupations including twenty years as a social worker in Glasgow and London and a spell producing Woman's Hour. It was a chance meeting with the Aberdeen novelist Nan Shepherd on an Elgin train in 1941 that encouraged Jessie Kesson into writing. Since then she has produced many radio plays and three novels, two of which she has adapted for cinema. She has published one collection of short stories, *The Apple Ripens*, and her short fiction shares themes and melodies with her novels.

Jessie Kesson combines an immediacy and intimacy normally found in autobiography with a control and imaginative flair from the best of fiction. It seems likely that her own early life has given much to her caring, down to earth portrayal of young girls who are often alone, if not lonely. In 'Until Such Times' the narrator seems to be speaking to a secret friend or an older self, which creates the impression of an unspoken history shared with her reader.

Until Such Times

THEY'RE COMING the day.' Grandmother bustled into the kitchen, waving a letter aloft. 'Postie's just brought a line. Now! If,' she said, pausing to consider the matter, '*If* they were to catch the through train, they should manage to win here in time for a bite of dinner.'

'I'd be the better of a clean shawl, then,' the Invalid Aunt suggested, 'if they're coming the day.'

—A suggestion that stripped Grandmother clean of the good humour that had been over her. 'My hands are never out of the wash tub!' she snapped. 'The shawl that's on you is clean enough! It's barely been on your back a week! And, as for you! . . .' Grandmother's face bent down till it was level with your own. '*You* can just sup up your porridge! There's a lot of work to be got through. If they're coming the day. Your Aunt Millie and Cousin Alice.'

'A lot of help she'll be to you. That one!' the Invalid Aunt said. 'Her Cousin Alice is a different kettle of fish. Another bairn altogether. Well brought up. And biddable.'

'Alice is neither better nor worse than any other bairn!' Grandmother snorted, before turning in attack on you again. 'And there's no call for you to start banging the teapot on the table!'

'The din that one makes,' the Invalid Aunt grumbled, 'is enough to bring on one of my heads!'

'For pity's sake, Edith! She's only a bairn.'

Times like these, you loved Grandmother. Knowing she was on your side. Times like these, you hated the Invalid Aunt. Sat huddled in her shawl on the bed-chair by the window. The smell of disinfectant always around her. And that other smell of commode. The medicine bottles along the window-sill for when 'the head came on her' or 'the heart took her'. Even the Invalid Aunt's medicine bottles had taken on malevolence, getting you off to a bad start with Grandmother, at the very beginning of your stay.

'You *understand*! You understand, bairn. I'm telling you NOW! And I don't want to have to tell you again! You must never touch your Aunt Edith's medicine bottles. Never! Ever!'

'But she said the heart took her!'

'Not even when the heart takes her,' Grandmother had insisted. 'Mind you on that! you must never touch Aunt Edith's medicine bottles. Not as long as you are here!'

But you weren't here to stay forever! Your Aunt Ailsa had promised you that. You was only here to stay . . . 'Until Such Times', Aunt Ailsa had said on the day she took you to Grandmother's house . . . 'Until Such Times as I can find a proper place for you and me to bide. For you should be at school. But the authorities would just go clean mad if they found out they had a scholar who lived in a Corporation lodging house. And spent most of her time in the Corporation stables. Sat between the two dust cart horses! so You are going to school. And biding with Grandmother . . . Until Such Times . . .' You could never tell when Until Such Times had passed. But you began to recognise its passing. With Grandmother bringing each week to an end, always on the scold, on Sunday mornings.

'Learning your catechism on the *Sabbath*! Five minutes before you set off for the Sunday School! I told you to learn it last night!'

But you had learned it 'last night'. You knew it 'last night'. 'It's just . . .' you tried to explain to Grandmother, 'it's just the words. They might all change in the night. I'm looking up to make *sure*!'

'It's just . . .' Grandmother always maintained, 'it's just that you didn't put your mind to it, last night! So! Let's hear it now, then! What is the Chief End of Man?'

'Man's Chief End is to glorify God and enjoy Him forever—'

It was the coming of the dark night that told you summer was at an end. 'A *candle!!!* A candle up to her *bed*!' The Invalid Aunt had protested, prophesying that 'They would all be burned alive in their sleep!' And so paving the way for Grandmother's instant rejection of your request for a candle. 'It was only,' Grandmother had pointed out, 'the shadows of the fir trees that you've seen, moving against your window, and you should be used to that by this time! There was nothing,' she tried to assure, 'nothing to be feared of in the wood. It's a blithe place for a bairn. Wait you!' she had exhorted. 'Just wait you till summer comes round again!' —an exhortation that had dismayed you, that had extended time beyond all comprehension of its passing self.

'I'm *saying*!' Grandmother grabbed the teapot from your hands. 'I'm saying there's a lot of work to be got through. With your Aunt Millie and Cousin Alice already on their road!'

'If it had been *Ailsa* that was coming,' the Invalid Aunt said, 'she would have jumped to it! My word! She would that!'

But it *wasn't* your Aunt Ailsa that was coming. She never 'dropped a line'. She just arrived. Unexpected. Unannounced.

How you wished that she could have arrived unseen. That the wood, which hid everything else, could have hidden Aunt Ailsa, too. But the kitchen window looked out on the road, and on all who passed along it, and the Invalid Aunt's voice was always the first to rise up in forewarning. 'God help us! *She's* on her way! Ailsa! Her ladyship! Taking up the whole of the road. Looks like she went into the Broadstraik Inn. And didn't come out till closing time!'

How you wanted to leap up off your stool, and hurtle yourself down the road to warn Aunt Ailsa. 'Walk straight, my Aunt Ailsa. Walk as straight as you can! They've seen you coming. They're all watching behind the curtains.'

'Thank God it's not Ailsa that's coming,' the Invalid Aunt concluded. 'We can do fine without her company!'

For once, you found yourself in agreement with the Invalid Aunt. Albeit with a sense of betrayal, and a pain for which you had not found the source, hidden somewhere, within the memory of your Aunt Ailsa's last—and first—'official' visit.

You had recognised the man and his pony and trap, waiting at the small wayside railway station, but had not realised that he, too, was awaiting the arrival of your Aunt Ailsa. Not until he came towards you, in greeting . . . 'You mind on me? Surely you mind on me!' he had insisted, flummoxed by your silence. 'You'll mind on the pony then! I'll warrant you've forgotten the pony's name.'

'He's Donaldie,' you said, willing enough to claim acquaintance with the pony. 'He's Donaldie. His name's Donaldie.'

The cat, Aunt Ailsa grumbled, as the man elbowed her towards the trap, must have got her tongue, for this was a poor welcome, considering Aunt Ailsa had come all this way.

It was the man! you protested HIM. Donaldie's dad. 'He belongs to his pony! Not to US. Not to you and me!'

It was only when they reached the wood that the old intimacy warmed up between them. Whoaing Donaldie to a halt, Aunt Ailsa spoke in the tone of time remembered, when the world was small enough to hold what she used to describe as . . . you and me. Ourselves two. And the both of us . . .

'You know,' Aunt Ailsa had confided, 'how Grandmother hates me smoking my pipe. So we're just going to take a turn up the wood for a smoke. I want you to do a small thing for me. To bide here, and keep an eye on Donaldie. We'll not be long. About five minutes just,' she emphasised, presenting you with another aspect of time.

'Five minutes *must* be up now, Donaldie,' you confided to the pony, munching away on the grass verge. His calm acceptance of passing time beginning to distress you, since animals differed from yourself in appearance only, never in understanding. 'It must be up, Donaldie. I've counted up to hundreds.'

'I know something about you, Donaldie,' you boasted, beginning to be irritated by the pony's indifference. 'Something about all horses. Something Aunt Ailsa once told me. All horsemen have a secret word of command. ''The horseman's *knacking* word,' she called it. 'But no horseman will ever tell the secret word. He would lose his power, that way of it. I don't know the secret word,' she admitted to the pony. 'But you might know it, Donaldie. If I could just find it.'

Time poised upon, and passing within, all the words you could remember. Tried out and tested, with no reaction from the pony.

'Maybe,' you suggested at last, 'maybe the secret word's in Gaelic . . . Ay Roy. Ay Roh

El Alooran
El Alooran

Ay Roh Ay Roh
Ay Roh.

'Stop wheebering away to yourself, there!' Aunt Ailsa commanded, as they turned up the track to Grandmother's house. 'And pay attention to what I am telling you! Not a word out of your head to Grandmother. Not one word about Donaldie's dad! We never saw him the day. We never set *eyes* on him. Just you mind on that.'

'Mind now,' Grandmother was saying. 'When your Cousin Alice comes the day, just you play quiet in the clearing. You know how her mother hates Alice getting her clothes all sossed up in the wood.'

'That one wouldn't worry,' the Invalid Aunt assured Grandmother. 'She would rive in the bushes till she hadn't a stitch to her back. It's high time she took herself through to the scullery and made a start on the dishes!'

'You cannot expect her to be stood out in the cold scullery all morning-!' Grandmother snapped.

'But I'm needing the commode!' the Invalid Aunt protested. 'I'm needing to pay a big visit. And I can't do a thing! Not with that one. Stood there. All eyes!'

'She's taking no notice, Edith! She's got better things to look at, than you sat stuck there on the commode. Come on, bairn!' Grandmother said, elbowing you out of the kitchen.' It's time you and me took a turn up the wood for a burthen of kindlers. And a breath of fresh air!'

'I'm needing the commode.' The Invalid Aunt's whine followed them to the porch door. 'I'm leaking! You know fine I can't contain!'

I can contain
I've never wet myself
Nor ever will again

'That!' Grandmother said, when she caught up with you at the clearing, 'is a bad thing to say. And a worse thing to *think*!'

'I beg pardon.' Your apology was instant. And genuine. Moments shared alone with Grandmother were too rare, too precious, to be wasted in acrimony.

'I grant you grace,' Grandmother acknowledged, spreading herself down and across the log. 'But, if that's what they're learning you at the school . . .'

School, like Grandmother herself, was a separate thing, and shared only at times like these, beyond influence of the house and the Invalid Aunt.

'If,' you said, squeezing yourself down on the log beside her, 'if we were sitting out in the porch, on a fine summer evening, and a weary, thirsty traveller came by and begged us for a drink of milk. And he had wings instead of ears. And wings instead of feet. Do you know what that man's name would be?'

'Wings instead of ears, did you say!'

'And wings instead of feet!' you reminded Grandmother.

'No,' she admitted. 'You've gotten me fair beat there! I've never heard tell of that man before!'

'His name would be Mercury. He's in my school reader. He can fly all round the world in a minute!'

'I can well believe that!' she conceded. 'With all that wings he's gotten.'

In moments like that, with the mood of acceptance over Grandmother, a positive admission of time, and its passing, seemed feasible.

'I wouldn't need a candle at night, now,' you boasted. 'I'm not feared of the wood, now.'

'Of course you're not feared,' Grandmother agreed. 'The nights are stretching out, now.'

'I still wouldn't need a candle!' you insisted. 'But that's *one* thing! I won't be here when the dark nights come again. That's *one* thing!' you claimed, jumping down off the log. 'I won't be here when the dark nights come again. Do *you* think I'll still be here when the dark nights come again?'

'That's ahrd to say,' Grandmother pulled herself up off the log, and stood, considering, 'Hard to tell. But *no*! she decided at last. 'No. I should hardly think you'd still be here, when the dark nights come again.'

Until Such Times
As we go home
A Hundred Hundred miles
And all the People
They bow down
And everybody smiles . . .

'I know,' Cousin Alice claimed, when they reached the clearing, 'I know why Grandfather says we mustn't go down through the woods where the men are working.'

'So do I though,' you assured her. 'It's because they *swear*! Something cruel! Grandmother says it's because they come from the south. And I know the swear the men say! It's a terrible swear. It begins with F! But mind!' you urged Cousin Alice. 'Don't you say it. *Ever*! They would just murder *me*! For telling!'

She hadn't heard that word before, Cousin Alice admitted. But you had heard it. Hundreds of times. In the Corporation lodging house. It didn't sound terrible then. Just like all the other words. It didn't sound terrible, until one day in the wood, when one of the wood men shouted it out.

'You should have seen the look on Grandfather's face!' you said to Cousin Alice. 'I wanted to cry out to him . . . it wasn't me that swore, Grandfather! It wasn't *me*! Just to make Grandfather speak to me. For once. And to let him know that I don't swear. And I wanted to stand as quiet as anything, so that the twigs wouldn't crackle, and Grandfather wouldn't see me at all. Sometimes,' you confessed to Cousin Alice, 'sometimes I'm never sure what to do . . .'

'Ankle strap shoes, like what Alice has got! Whatever would you be wanting next!' the Invalid Aunt wondered. 'Alice's Mother and Father worked hard for Alice's shoes!' she informed you. 'And Alice took good care of them when she got them!'

'Sorrow be on shoes!' Grandmother snapped. 'The lark needs no shoes to climb to heaven. Forbye!' she assured you. 'Thin shoes like yon wouldn't last you a week in this wood!'

'They wouldn't last you a day!' the Invalid Aunt said. 'But then, there's just no comparison!'

She would like you to be jealous of Alice, the Invalid Aunt. And that was the strange thing, although you envied Alice's shoes, you was never jealous of Alice herself. But glad for her. Proud of her. Willing to claim acquaintanceship. The glory that was Alice, somehow reflecting on yourself . . . Look everybody! Just look! This is Alice. She's *my* cousin! My cousin Alice. Did you ever see anybody so beautiful. So dainty. In all your life! With long golden hair. And blue ribbons. She's my cousin! My cousin . . . Alice. *Look*! Everybody just LOOK! That's *my* grandfather's horses coming up the road. They're his horses . . . my grandfather.'

'My conscience, bairn!' Grandmother edged you out of her road, and away from the window. 'You should know every tree from this scullery window by heart! For I never did see anybody who could stand so long. Just looking!'

That was about all you was good for, the Invalid Aunt confided to Grandmother. It was high time, she insisted, that Ailsa found a place for herself and that bairn! But, being man-mad, a bairn on her hands would fair clip Ailsa's wings.

'Be quiet Edith!' Grandmother admonished. 'It's your sister you're speaking about.'

'Sister or no sister,' the Invalid Aunt said, 'Ailsa died to me a long time ago.'

My Aunt Ailsa died to me
—Words of lament forming themselves in your mind—
A long long time ago
A dirge for a death, beyond your comprehension, singing in your head.

'The *world*!' Grandmother announced, 'must surely be coming to an end!' For, she informed you, this was only the second time your Aunt Ailsa had bothered to write!

'If she's bothered to write,' the Invalid Aunt said, 'she must be on the cadge for something or other. Either that, or she's lost her job again. It's my opinion . . .'

'There's a time and a place for opinions,' Grandmother declared, taking you by the hand into the scullery . . . 'Your Aunt Ailsa is coming to see you the day,' she confided. 'She might have some good news for you. So! Would it not be a good idea for you to take a turn up the wood for some dry kindlers for the fire.'

Until Such Times had maybe arrived at last. The very thought of it fixed your feet to the cement of the scullery floor. With the voices from the kitchen rising and falling to the rise and fall of your own heart beats . . .

It was to be hoped, the Invalid Aunt was saying, that this chield would marry Ailsa this time. Though any man that did that had all the Invalid Aunt's sympathy! Either that or he must be a poor, simple creature that was of him!

Neither poor nor simple, Grandmother pointed out. A decent enough chield. A disabled war soldier.

That would fit the bill! the Invalid Aunt maintained. Knowing *Ailsa*, she would have her eye on his bit pension! And lucky to get that! Better women than Ailsa had never even got the *chance* of a man! It was the Invalid Aunt's opinion that Ailsa had never 'let on' about the bairn.

O but she did! Grandmother confirmed. She said in her letter that she was bringing him to see the bairn.

And that, the Invalid Aunt concluded, would be enough to put any man clean off! Unless of course, it was somebody they didn't know.

'We know of him,' Grandmother admitted. 'Summers. Dod Summers. His father's got that croft down by the railway.'

'I'm with you now!' the Invalid Aunt's voice shrilled out in triumph. 'Peg Leg Summers.' So that's who's she's gotten. Old Peg Leg Summers. And he's got no pension. He shouldn't have been in the war in the first place. Well, well! Even I can mind on him! He used to go clop, clop, cloppin round the mart on a Friday!

'Listen now,' Grandmother urged you. 'When your Aunt Ailsa comes the day, she'll maybe be bringing somebody with her . . .'

'She wouldn't!' you protested. 'I know she wouldn't. My Aunt Ailsa never *would*!'

'Good grief, bairn! What ails you?'

'What on earth are you on about?' Grandmother insisted, puzzled by your distress.

'My Aunt Ailsa. She wouldn't. She'd *never* marry a man with a wooden leg!'

'*Listening* again!' The Invalid Aunt snorted. 'Lugs cocking at the key hole!'

'Look a here. Just you look a here now,' Grandmother said, easing you down on your stool by the door. 'A wooden leg's nothing. Nothing at all just. Many a brave man has a wooden leg. You like biding with your Aunt Alice,' she reminded you. 'Who has been making sore lament to get back to her Aunt Ailsa? Well then! You'll be happier with your Aunt Ailsa than you've been here. And fine you know that . . .'

'I wish to God she'd stop blubbering,' the Invalid Aunt complained. 'She should be thankful that somebody's willing to give her a home!'

'Now, listen, bairn, just you go and wash your face,' Grandmother suggested. 'And put on a clean pinny. You want to look your best to meet your Aunt Ailsa. But, first things first. I'll away to the well for some fresh water. You can follow on with the little pail.'

'Are you still blubbering there.' The Invalid Aunt's voice, battening itself against your hearing, was powerless to reach the horror of your imagination. 'You heard your Grandmother! You could at least obey her. But no faith you! Obedience would be some much to expect! *My*! But you're stubborn! Just like Ailsa. The living spit of the mother of you . . .'

'She's my Aunt Ailsa,' you said, protective of a relationship that was acceptable. 'She's my Aunt Ailsa. . . . She's not my *mother*!' The implication of the Invalid Aunt's words had penetrated at last, sending you hurtling towards her bed chair. 'She's my Aunt Ailsa!' Grasping the aunt by the shoulders, you tried to shake her into understanding. *My mother* is ladies I cut out from pictures in books. Ladies I pick out passing in the street! You know fine she's not my mother! You're just saying that because . . . because you're ugly! And you smell terrible! You're just a *fucker*!

. . . It wasn't *me* that swore, Grandfather. It wasn't me . . .

'My Aunt Ailsa's coming!' you shouted to Grandmother, bent over the well at the edge of the wood. 'She's all by herself. She wouldn't. I knew she wouldn't. Marry a man with a wooden leg!'

'I doubt you're right,' Grandmother agreed, as you stood together watching Aunt Ailsa coming up the track. 'Ah well!' she sighed, 'maybe it's all for the best. Who knows! Who can tell! You'd better run on and meet her, then. You haven't even washed your face!' Grandmother admonished. 'Nor changed your pinny! Whatever keepit you so long?'

'It was Edith,' you told Grandmother. 'I think the heart took her. She was making that funny noise.'

'Heaven above! O good grief.' The water from the pail that Grandmother dropped swirling round your feet.

'I didn't touch her medicine bottles!' you reassured her retreating figure. 'I didn't *touch* them!'

James Allan Ford

'Pitmedden Folk' takes us back to an East of Scotland boyhood, choosing as its subject a pleasure central to many childhood memories—the visit to a loved and elderly relative. Such scenes are often softened by nostalgia and the special bond between the very young and the very old has become something of a threadbare cliché.

James Allan Ford, however, has chosen his moment well and looks at the one trip a boy makes to his grandfather's farm which will be different from all the others. The strong comforting presence of Grandad Reedie is suddenly absent, confined to a sick bed and failing fast.

The boy begins to appreciate the fallible humanity of his parents and the social gulf they have all crossed, leaving Pitmedden behind. Willie Webster, the friend of so many summer holidays, will be trapped within the confines of a rural community, while our central figure moves on to better things. The boys' futures have already been decided. Ford makes us reconsider the standards by which we measure success and the apparently arbitrary forces which shape even children's lives.

Born in Auchtermuchty and brought up in Edinburgh, Ford has a genuine feel for the language of the East of Scotland. Serving with distinction in the Far East during the Second World War, Ford was also a prisoner of war under the Japanese.

His experiences during this period formed the basis for several of his five novels, while *A Judge of Men* has drawn on his later career in the legal profession. Before his retirement in 1979, Ford was both Registrar General and Principal Establishment Officer of Scotland.

In the clear, economical prose of 'Pitmedden Folk', he shows that he is equally at home with the more concentrated discipline of the short story.

Pitmedden Folk

THE JOURNEY to Pitmedden had always been longer than the journey back. But this time it seemed even longer, as if Pitmedden had become further from Edinburgh than ever before.

It was only on my mother's insistence, and with an ill grace, that my father had allowed me to go with them this time, and he started making up for it as soon as we were on the road. He was in a touchy mood, of course, after being taken down a peg by my mother, and his voice was sharper than usual as he laid down the law on what I could do and what I should not do when we reached my grandfather's smallholding. 'This is a sick visit, not a holiday. You'll not get up to any mischief with Willie Webster and his like. You've your new school uniform on, remember, and you'll keep it clean and do nothing to disgrace it. Are you listening?'

'Ye-es,' I drawled with a hint of defiance.

My mother turned round and gave me one of her looks—the look that pleaded with me not to provoke him. Although she had spoken against him when he had argued that I should stay in Edinburgh with my aunt, she sided with him in most things. She was always trying to persuade me that he was strict with me only because he wanted me to follow his example and get on in the world. 'He's come a long way since he ran barefoot in Pitmedden,' she often said. 'We have to keep up with him. We're Pitmedden folk, and Pitmedden folk hang together.' Hunched in the back seat of the new car, our first car, I stared sullenly at his balding head. It was the only bare part of him now.

Rain fell in torrents from the low clouds darkening the sky. We were travelling in midwinter, only a few days before Christmas, and the countryside I knew so well in the green and gold of summer was now hardly recognisable, stripped to its dark skin, wet bone. Rain and resentment made a misery out of what had always before been the happiest of journeys for me—a journey that had seemed long only because of my impatience to reach Pitmedden and a freedom I could never find in Edinburgh. Nothing raised my spirits until my father lost his way.

'We must have taken the wrong turning at the last junction,' he said coolly, as if we were all to blame.

My mother's impatience got the better of her. 'We should have gone by the train as usual.'

I knew better than to say anything, but I watched him with spiteful pleasure as he turned the car and headed back towards the junction. It was not often that I had the chance to see him taken down two pegs in one day.

He answered her as he sometimes spoke to me, separating his words to make each one painfully clear. 'What was the point of all that saving to buy a car, if we're not going to use it?'

'The point at the minute,' she said recklessly, 'is that we're wasting time.'

She had been impatient to reach Pitmedden ever since we had heard, the day before, in a letter from his neighbour Ag Lister, that Grandad Reedie was ill. I shared her love of her father, who was the greatest man in all the world of my boyhood—as wise as Solomon, as strong as Samson, and as tolerant as my father was strict—but on this occasion I did not fully share her impatience, for I was too intent on watching my father and waiting for him to make lame excuses for losing his way or maybe even to come off his high horse and apologise.

I was cheated. He said nothing until he was able to announce: 'We're back on course now. We'll not be more than a few minutes later than we expected to be.'

In the ordinary way, she would have let it rest at that, but she was not herself. She turned on him and said, 'We're four months late already.'

She was harking back to the argument over our summer holidays. But her reminder had more effect on me than on my father. He drove on without a word or sign of irritation, while my own spirits sank again. That year, in spite of all her arguments and all my pleas, he had taken us to North Berwick instead of to Pitmedden for our holidays. It was the first time in my life that we had not gone to Pitmedden in the summer. Easier at North Berwick for him to keep in touch with the office, and a better golf course into the bargain, were the reasons he had given me for the change. But my mother had told me the true reason. Now that he could afford to send me to a good school, she had explained, he wanted me to set my sights higher than Pitmedden, where—to his way of thinking—I learned nothing but coarse language and rough ways of living.

As we drove northwards through the rain, I stared at his head in resentful silence. He had turned his back on Pitmedden, my mother had told me, after his own parents had died and he had buried himself in his work. I felt like turning my back on him, for I did not want to follow his example. What was the point of getting on in the world, if it took me away from Pitmedden and the only real liberty I knew?

We reached Pitmedden about midday, with only fair weather and a blink of sunshine to welcome us. That was a new thing. Ever since my other grandparents had died and we had started staying with Grandad Reedie for our holidays, he had met us at the station with his governess-cart and driven us at the pony's walking-pace up through the village, and folk had come to their doors to welcome us, for we were well-known in Pitmedden. This time, as we drove through in our new car, nobody seemed to recognise us.

When we drew up outside the gate to Grandad's holding at the top end of the village, Ag Lister came out of her cottage across the road to speak to my mother. They stood in the middle of the road, and I could hear only snatches of Ag's story: 'Didna want tae worry ye . . . no that bad till three-fower days syne . . . keepit the hoose as clean as I could . . . Wullie's been seein tae the beasts . . .' When my mother came back to us, she had tears in her eyes. But she smiled at me and said: 'Ag's been nursing him, God bless her. Pitmedden folk are the kindest in the world.' Then, after blowing her nose, she gave my father a worried look and said: 'We'll have to go round the back. The front door's locked, she says.' That was another new thing. Doors were locked in Edinburgh, but not in Pitmedden.

The yard was a sea of mire after the rain. 'What a taft!' my father said, and told me to stay by the car until he could unlock the front door. He and my mother went through the gate and round the gable-end of the house, walking like hens as they picked their muddy way.

My father's word had never carried much weight with me in Pitmedden. He had spent most of his holidays on the nine-hole golf course and on outings with my mother to visit old acquaintances, while I—even in the days when we were staying with my other grandparents at the lower end of the village—had spent all the time I could on or around the holding, helping Grandad Reedie with his work or, with his encouragement, guddling trout in the burn or running wild along the slopes on the other side of the burn, where the goats were tethered and geese and turkeys were fattened for the Christmas market. With little hesitation I left the car and followed my parents' trail round the gable-end to get a full view of the heart of the holding.

The steading was not like Farmer Lumsden's steading further up the road. It was really just two old cottages and a stable standing in one block opposite the back of the house and connected to it by a lean-to cart-shed. And the cottages in particular were in a pretty bad state. Year by year I had seen the stonework crumble, the plaster break away from the laths, and the timber rot. And yet both buts and bens were used to the full. The ducks were kept penned in one room overnight, safe from foxes; hens had their nesting-boxes in the other room; one kitchen was used for storing bags of feeding-stuffs and tubs of the brock that was boiled up in a great black cauldron for the pigs; and the other was an Aladdin's cave filled with the oldest, most fascinating and most mysterious things I had ever come across—tools and ironmongery, broken harness and rope-ends, furniture, ornaments, books, paintings, postcards, empty tin boxes . . . There were rats and mice under the floors, and bats hanging from the rafters, and exposed lintels to swing from, and logs to be axed into kindling for the fire under the cauldron . . . It was adult territory open to boys, a place for testing strength and courage, a place of perfect liberty where I could, like Willie Webster, pee from a window into the burn, a place for old clothes and dirt from head to foot. Standing at the opposite side of the yard in my school uniform, doing nothing but look around, was yet another new thing for me. It was like being in a museum.

The air was still. I could hear the companionable chatter of the burn, the crooning and crackling of hens in the kitchen where the treasure lay, the inviting nicker of the pony in the stable, and then, like the sound of the serpent in the Garden of Eden, the shrill whistling of Willie Webster. He was coming up from the pig styes and was screened from me at first by the jungle that had once been Tibbie Webster's flower garden. Tibbie had been my grandfather's second wife and had never been called anything but Tibbie Webster except by vanmen and shopkeepers, who had called her Mrs Reedie, and by Willie and myself, who had called her Gran. Willie had been brought up by her after his mother's death, and had stayed on with Grandad Reedie after Tibbie's death. I never knew what to make of Willie Webster. Although he was only a few months older than me, we had very little in common. For one thing, he was not only an orphan but also a bastard and, apart from the times when he boasted that his father had been a full corporal in the Black Watch, he was touchy on the subject; for another, he hardly ever attended school, preferring leatherings to book-learning, and read and wrote like someone still in Primary; and—most important of all, for it was the difference that attracted me to him—he was a regular tearaway who smoked and swore, farted in any company, stole money from his Gran's purse and bottles of beer from the lorries delivering to the pub and the licensed grocer, and took girls up to the wood behind Ag Lister's cottage. He was part of the excitement of holidays in Pitmedden. When we were not fighting, as we often were, he led me into all sorts of devilment I could never experience in Edinburgh.

He came into view with a pail in his hand and, catching sight of me, shouted: 'Christ, whut brings you here? An whut the hell are ye supposed tae be in that rig-oot?'

It was hardly a welcome, but I was not put out, for Willie and I had always taken time to come to terms.

When he reached the yard and noticed our car outside the gate, his eyes widened. 'Jesus, dinna tell me ye've a motor an aa?'

I smiled. There was always a terrible rivalry between us. 'We're just up for the day—to see if we can help Grandad.'

'Help Grandad,' he repeated in sneering mimicry. 'Toonies are nae help here. Ye can get the hell oot o ma yaird as quick as ye like.'

'It's not your yard. We've more right than you to be here. We're his only real kin.'

'Kin, ma erse! Ye're no Pitmedden folk.'

That stung me. In my mother's world there were only two kinds of people—Pitmedden folk and Others—and she had never left me in any doubt about which were the better. 'We are so,' I shouted.

'Ye're a toonie, an a bairn forby. It taks a Pitmedden body like masel tae help the auld yin. Christ, I'm lookin efter the hail jing-bang here!' He held his arms out, boasting control of the entire holding.

There was as much envy as anger in me. 'I've helped Grandad here before, and if I had old clothes with me I could do it again.'

He sneered. 'The auld yin aye let on ye were helpin, but he was playin a bairn-game wi ye, juist. An it's no him that's rinnin things noo. I'm the gaffer noo. He'll dae nae mair roond here. He's ready tae snuff it.'

I was shocked, although I knew that he was just trying to make me cry. 'You're a dirty liar,' I shouted, bunching my fists. I had bled his nose and blackened his eyes often enough in the past to make him wary of my fists. Although he was a head taller than me, he was thin and round-shouldered and, for all his swaggering, a coward at heart.

Keeping a narrow eye on me, he said soberly: 'Ask Ag Lister or Eck Tamson. He's ready tae kick the bucket.'

It was unthinkable that my grandfather, as strong as Samson the last time I saw him, was now dying. My other grandparents had died, and Tibbie Webster had died, but Grandad Reedie was different . . . yet, Willie's manner shook my conviction.

He stuck out his jaw and, jerking his head aside, spat between tight lips. It was a trick I had never been able to imitate without slavering on my chin, and it gave him another advantage over me.

'It was Eck Tamson let it oot first. Askit whut I'd dae when the auld yin's deid.' Seeing that he had the edge on me, he started sneering again. 'Ye'll no ken Eck? He's a place o his ain up the road, but he whiles helps the auld yin tae—cuttin pigs' balls an siclike. Ye'll never hae seen a pig cut, hae ye? The auld yin wouldna let a bairn see that.'

All my anger and envy and shock came together, and I took an awkward swing at him, which he dodged. 'Shut yer face, Webster. I'm no a bairn—an I'm no a bastard like you.' I had found my Pitmedden tongue and felt surer of myself. I threw another punch at him, but the mire made me heavy-footed and he managed to wrap his long arms around me, slinging his pail across the yard. Then he tried to topple me, jeering, 'We'll see whut ye look like wi a slaister of Pitmedden glaur ower yer bonnie claes.'

My father came out the back door, stumped over to us and tore us apart. 'You should be black ashamed of yourselves, bawling and bickering like tinks when the old man is—' He gave me a push towards the door. 'Away and sit with him while I go for the doctor.'

Willie was first to move.

'I wasn't talking to you,' my father said.

Willie turned on him defiantly. 'It's no your hoose. I bide here, an I'll no be shut oot by ony fat-ersed toonie.'

By rights, he should have had his ears warmed, but my father simply glowered at him.

'Sit quiet with him,' my mother said in a quavery voice. 'I'm going to make him something to drink.'

'There's a hauf of whusky Eck Tamson brocht him,' Willie told her.

She laid her hand gently on his shoulder, and he drew away. 'You're a good lad, Willie,' she said, and left us.

He went across to the bed, hooked his thumbs in his belt, and raised his voice to ask, 'Hoo's the auld yin noo?'

'A wee thing tired, Wull.'

I was startled by the weakness of the voice and shy of the strange face on the pillow. It was too thin and waxy-looking to be my grandfather's face.

'It's no Jamie, is it?' The words were Grandad Reedie's although neither the face nor the voice was. Every year he had pretended he could hardly recognise me because I had grown so much.

'Yes—ay, it's me.'

'He'll no hear ye.' Willie was almost shouting.

'Hae ye seen the new pownie, Jamie?'

'Fourteen hauns,' boasted Willie. 'I'll let ye see her efter.'

I could find nothing to say myself. I was uneasy in the presence of the strange-looking old man.

'Ye'll hae tae see tae things the-nicht again, Wull. I'll no be . . .' The old man's lips kept moving silently for a while, then closed. His eyes closed too, and he lay so still that I thought he had died.

Willie bent over him and touched his nose. 'He's no deid yet. When folk dee, ye can squeeze their noses intae ony shape, like cannle grease.'

I was half-shocked, half-fascinated. I was also humbled. What was all my book-learning in face of Willie's knowledge of death, the cutting of pigs and suchlike dark things? How would I ever again think of myself as one of the Pitmedden folk?

Willie pulled a thorn stick from under the bed. 'This is for skelpin the bogles.'

'There's nae sic thing.'

'Mebbe no, but the auld yin's been seein them, an I had tae lock the door an bring him this stick.'

I looked at the shiny face on the pillow and looked quickly away again. Grandad Reedie had never been frightened of bogles or anything else.

'No that he could dae ony skelpin. He's weak as a bairn. Afore he gaed aff his legs, Eck Tamson aince helpit him up the road for an airin, an comin back by himsel doon the brae he couldna stop at the hoose. I had tae rin oot an get a grip on him an turn him in at the yett, or he'd hae keepit teeterin doon till he came tae the first dyke.'

He giggled, and I almost giggled too at the thought of a runaway old man. Then, recalling that the runaway had once been my Grandad Reedie, I felt confused and ashamed and turned to go. There was nothing of my real grandfather left in that room.

'You can stay with him,' I said to Willie.

'Christ, it's time I was feedin the pownie.'

While I hesitated, my father returned with the doctor.

Willie went to feed the pony. He seemed willing enough to let me help, but I was content to watch him from the back door—not because I was afraid of dirtying my uniform but because I had lost interest. The magic had gone from the place. Without my grandfather to help me see it through his eyes, I could see nothing but ruins and mire. I was looking at it through my father's eyes now, and what a taft it was!

When Willie came back to join me, he lit a cigarette and said in a casual but important voice, 'I'll hae tae muck oot that stable the-morn.'

He could no longer rouse my envy. The thought of his life there, labouring day in, day out, wet or shine, winter and summer alike, made me shrink. He was more of a prisoner than I was in Edinburgh.

We stood in companionable silence at the back door until we heard a stirring behind us, at the other end of the long stone-flagged lobby. My mother was going into the kitchen, sobbing. My father and the doctor were coming slowly along the lobby, talking in low voices. I heard my father say something about Willie and Perth. And Willie heard it too, for he swung round and shouted: 'If ye think I'll bide wi ma forty-second cousin in Perth, ye've another think comin. I'm bidin here.'

My father came out and told us, 'Grandad Reedie passed away a few minutes ago.' He looked me in the face, then turned to Willie. 'I know how you feel but you can't stay here on your own.'

'I've been ma lane for a lang time.'

'But it's leased property, and you're not old enough to take over the tenancy.'

'Christ, I'm auld enough tae dae the wark, am I no?'

The doctor tried to pat him on the back, but Willie stepped away. 'You're the speak of Pitmedden, lad. You've worked right well. But in the eyes of the law you should still be attending school.'

Willie scowled at the yard and spat. 'I'm no gaun tae Perth.'

My father glanced at the doctor, and they started to make for the gate.

'Perth's quite a nice place,' I said.

Willie ignored me. Pitmedden folk could be terrible thrawn. He shouted after the two men: 'I'll bide wi Eck Tamson. He's got the room, and he could dae wi anither pair o haunds.'

My father and the doctor did not turn back.

Willie started swearing, one foul word after another. To my amazement, he started crying too. That was yet another new thing of this strange day. All I could do for him was turn away and spare him the shame of being watched.

I had never felt more wretched in all my life, and I was beginning to guess why my father had not wanted to bring me to Pitmedden. I waited impatiently for him to return.

When at last he came back, he looked from my clean face to Willie's dirty, tear-smudged face and said to him, 'I'll hae a word wi Eck the-nicht.' He had not, after all, lost his Pitmedden tongue. But I could not find my own again.

'When are we going home?' I asked.

He gave me a longer look this time, and shook his head as if he had found me wanting. 'We'll have to get things sorted out here, and it can't be done in one day.' He turned from me and clapped his hands together. 'Come on, the pair of you, and we'll see if there's something for us to eat.'

Willie hung back.

'He was an auld man, Wull,' said my father, speaking more gently than he had spoken to me. 'He was gled tae be unyokit.'

'Auld bugger,' said Willie shakily. 'Never even askit tae see me.'

Brian McCabe

FEATHERED CHORISTERS

Brian McCabe (b.1951), has written radio drama, short stories and articles, along with two published collections of poetry. He shares many Scots authors' fascination with the young mind, using the child's viewpoint to open unexpected doors on conflicts and tensions the adult world would prefer to hide away. Along with R.D. Laing he seems to view mental imbalance or breakdown more as the product of a warped society than the result of a biological or personal defect. McCabe introduces his readers to the profoundly shocking concept that children, far more than adults, are sensitive and prone to mental collapse.

This was Brian McCabe's first published short story. It appeared in *Scottish Short Stories* in 1979. Through his conversation with an imaginary companion from Mars, we build a grim picture of a young boy's home, the constraints of his education and his far from rosy future. McCabe spatters the piece with the commands and reprimands of a world which is rapidly closing around the boy, and makes characteristic use of poetic and fantastic images to deal with topics which the reader would find difficult to reach by rational thought alone.

Feathered Choristers

Hello. I'm outside the door again, I can talk to you. You're not like anybody else in the class. You're from Mars, you're a Martian. That's why I can talk to you, because I'm not like anybody else in the class either. Sometimes you sit beside me don't you, when you want to ask me a question. Like what is one take away one on Earth. And I tell you the answer, nothing. Or when you want to tell me an answer, you materialise like in *Star Trek*. Just for a thousandth billionth of a second, then vanish back to Mars. Nobody sees you except me, nobody wants to. Nobody knows how to see you except me. See the dust in the air up there, where the sun's coming through the window? You're like the dust in the air—nobody notices you except me. And your voice is like interference on the radio—nobody wants to hear it except me. *You* can see everything. You can see through people, and you can see through walls. You've got X-ray eyes, that's why. I wish I had X-ray eyes. Cheerio.

Hello, come in, are you receiving me? My situation is an emergency, I have lost all contact with the *Enterprise*. I've been put outside the door again, because of my abominable behaviour. I am on the brink of disaster, and the teacher says my behaviour is detrior-hating. It means getting worse. This is an SOS. I will continue until I am rescued or until my Oxygen runs out. I'll tell you what's been happening to me down here on the planet Earth. Last week she made me sit next to the Brains. The Brains is an Earthling, species girl. With red hair, freckles and specs. I had to sit next to the Brains. She was always too hot, always wheezing and sweating, and her legs were always sticking to the seat. It was the noise I hated, the noise her legs made when she unstuck them from the seat. And she wouldn't let me use her red pencil, to colour in the sea. I know the sea's supposed to be blue on *Earth*, but on Mars it's red isn't it? And when I took that red pencil of hers out of her hand and broke it, the Brains started crying. It wasn't real crying, it was a special Earthling kind of crying. Sometimes they cry outside but not inside, it's more like watering eyes. And in the middle of the crying she said something about my clothes, because I've got a patch on the back of my trousers. I can't see it, but everybody else in the class can. So I got her back in the playground. I went into the Earthling boys' toilets and I drew up some of the water, the pisswater in the pan, into my new fountain pen. Then I squirted it into her face, and it went all over her specs. And that's how I got into trouble last week, all because I got a new fountain pen. I don't like using these

Earthling fountain pens much, they make too much of a fucking mess. Yesterday the teacher held my writing up for everybody in the class to look at, so they wouldn't write like me. See I don't write like anybody else, see I write in a kind of Martian. Nobody can read it except me and you, it's in code that's why. See all the mistakes are secret for something, every blot is a secret wee message. But I got into the worst trouble for squirting piss into the Brains's face. The Mad Ringmaster got me, watch out for the Mad Ringmaster. Over and out, cheerio.

Hello, come in Mars, do you read me? My position is getting more abominable by the minute. So now she makes me sit on my own, so you can sit in the seat next to me. But you shouldn't materialise like that in the class, when everybody's listening to the radio. Everybody was listening to Rhyme Time, a programme of verse for Earthling children. Everybody thought it was interference, but I knew it was your voice talking to me. And I got put outside the door again because of you. Don't try and deny it, I did. It was that poem called Spring, all about the cuckoo and whatnot. And you were asking me what that poem was all about, because there aren't any birds on Mars, are there? And I saw you out of the corner of my eye, except you kept disappearing and coming back. Materialising. When I throw a stone in a puddle, everything disappears and comes back. That's what you're like, a reflection. So I had to tell you what Spring is and what a cuckoo is, so I started making the noise a cuckoo makes. *Kookoo, kookoo*—it sounds like its name. She thought I was taking the piss out of the programme, but I wasn't. I was talking to you in the secret wee voice, the one I'm talking in now. Billy Hope, she said, this is a classroom not a home for mental defectors. Go and stand outside the door, come back when the poetry programme's finished. But it isn't finished, because when I put my ear on the door I can hear it going on. She said it was bad enough having to put up with interference on the radio, without having to toler-hate interference from me.

I can't stand poetry anyway, it's worse than long division.

Maybe the next time you materialise, I'll use some sign-language to talk to you. I could scratch my nose for Hello. Everybody would think I was just scratching my nose. But then, if I had an itchy nose and I scratched it, maybe you'd think I was saying Hello. And if I stuck my tongue out for Cheerio, I'd get put outside the door every time I said Cheerio to you because of my abominable behaviour. I just put my ear to the door again and I heard the interference. It was you asking me another question, asking me what behaviour means. The answer is, I don't know.

I'll tell you something though: my mother's got a screw loose, has yours?

Over and out cheerio.

Hello come in are you receiving me? Listen: You were born on the same day as I was, at exactly the same time, except *you* were born on

Mars. You go to a primary school on Mars, and you're in 4B like me. You're last in the class on Mars, except it's great to be last on Mars. It's like being top of the class on Earth. And 4B is better than 4A there isn't it, because everything's a reflection the other way round. You're like me the other way round. If I looked at you too much, I'd go cross-eyed like the Brains. See when you materialise in the seat that's empty, the seat next to mine—that's you doing your homework, isn't it? It's like Nature Study, except you're doing it on us the Earthlings. I bet you're glad you're not at a school on Earth. With a voice that sounds like interference, you'd get put outside the door every day. I wish you'd take me to your Martian school with you. Then I'd be top of the class—I mean last—and then *I'd* be called the Brains. We'd be first—I mean last—equal. In the Martian primary school we'd get put outside the door for coming top of the class, because that's what the prize is on Mars. On Earth it isn't a prize, nobody likes it down here. And when you're put outside the door on Mars, you can travel through space and time. You can visit other planets. Down here there's nothing to do outside the door, there's nothing to look at. Nothing except the door. And the corridor, and the clock. Earthling clocks tell the time, every tick means a second. A second, a second, a second. No it doesn't *say* it, it tells the time with its hands. No it doesn't really have *hands*, it's a machine. No it doesn't have a mind, Earthling machines don't have minds. But cuckoo clocks say the time, they say *koo-koo, koo-koo*. But birds are different from clocks. See the birds on the windowsill up there, I think they're pecking for crumbs. You should do some Nature Study on them, because there aren't any birds on Mars, are there?

Or maybe there are some birds on Mars, but they look more like cuckoo clocks. But the clocks on Mars fly round and chirp the time.

Anyway I'll tell you what to say about Earthling birds. Put down that they've got wings, beaks, claws, feathers, tails and they fly. They eat worms and crumbs, and sometimes they migrate. It means go to Africa. See when they peck for crumbs they look like they're bowing, like actors at the end of a pantomime. Maybe they're all going to migrate to Mars, so they're bowing to say cheerio. I don't know if birds've got minds, but they must have minds to tell each other it's time to migrate. But they don't look like they've got minds, because they move about in wee jerks like clockwork. Clocks don't have minds. But birds fly, clocks don't. But aeroplanes and spaceships fly and they don't have any minds. Tell you what, put down that you don't know if birds've got minds or not, but put down that the Earthling people *do* have minds in their heads. Now I bet you're wondering what all this has to do with Nature Study. I bet you're saying to yourself, this sounds more like Martian poetry to me. But have you ever thought that the two subjects might be quite the very same? Especially when there's interference on the radio, the two subjects sort of blur with each other, don't they?

I'll tell you something else: my mother put her head in the gas oven and she lost her mind.

Cheerio.

Listen if you don't pay attention, you'll never learn anything. Materialise *this instant*. That's better. If I catch you disappearing again or tuning out, I'm just going to have to make an example of you. Is that clear? Or else I will put you outside the door of your capsule and you will die. You're not stupid, you're lazy. You're a lazy, little *Martian*. You have opened my eyes more than once today and your behaviour is getting deterior-hating. Right, we're going to do some more Martian Nature Study. Any more interference out of you and I will give you long division or even poetry. Put this down:

Nature Study On The Planet Earth.

Under that, put this:

On the Planet Earth, everything is the other way round. Most Earthling birds don't have names and their mothers forget what to call them when they go to visit the nest. The only ones with names are crows, thrushes, blackbirds, sparrows, eagles, vultures and cuckoos. The rest are just called birds. Cuckoos are off their heads, they lay their eggs in the gas oven. My mother can be heard on the first day of Spring, and the noise she makes sounds like her name. She is cuckoo so she lives in a home, her home in another bird's nest. Behaviour means going to Africa, or else abominable long division. A bird is a flying machine, with a screw loose. Cuckoo clocks have minds, as well as hands, faces and speckled breasts. At dawn you can hear them tick, and every tick means deterior-hating. Spring is the time of the year when you scratch your nose for Hello and stick out your tongue for Cheerio. Poetry is people pecking for crumbs without minds in their heads. After a pantomime, the actors migrate. I am dust in the air, I am a reflection. I am the only Earthling with a mind, and the mind is interference from another programme. Koo-koo, koo-koo.

Cheerio.

Come in again, do you read me, hello. See that door along there, behind that there's a wee room where you go to get smallpox jags. On the wall there's this chart with letters on it. On the top line the letters are huge, you'd have to be blind not to read them. But they get tinier and tinier as they go down, till you can hardly even see them. See this chart is for testing Earthling eyes. If you don't get far enough down, you get specs. I got specs, but I smashed them on the way to school because everybody was calling me four-eyes.

Nobody's going to call me four-eyes.

The Brains wears specs, but nobody calls her four-eyes. Probably because she's always had specs, so nobody notices them. If you ask me, the Brains was probably *born* with specs on. And I had to get specs because of you. Don't try and deny it. It's with looking at you when you materialise, now my eyes are the wrong way round. I wish I had X-ray eyes, then I could see into all the classrooms, I could see what's happening inside them. The last time I was in that room, that room with the chart on the wall, I got drops in my eyes that made me see a bit like a Martian. People didn't have edges, they sort of merged with each other. Blurred. But once when I was taken into that room this nurse in a white coat gave me a book to look at. It was a Martian book. Every page was covered all over with hundreds of coloured dots. They looked like they were moving, sort of swarming like wasps. It was like what you see when you look at the sun too long, hundreds of coloured dots moving round. Then this nurse asked me if I could make out the shape or the number. Everybody in the class had to do it, it was a test. I'll tell you this, I was great at it. I was better than anybody else in 4B. If we got tests in making out the shape or the number instead of tests in long division, I'd be getting fucking gold stars every time.

The trouble is we didn't get marks for it. It was to find out if we were colourblind. I'm not colourblind, I *know* the sea's supposed to be blue. It isn't though is it, when you look at it up close? When my mother used to take me to the seaside, the sea always looked more sort of like the colour of piss. And what about the Black Sea, what colour's that? I should ask the teacher: please Miss, is the Black Sea black? Miss, is the Red Sea red? What colour's the Dead Sea, Miss? Is that the one he walked on, or is that the one he parted? Miss how could he part a *sea*? Keep the noise down, it was a miracle. A miracle is something that doesn't happen every day on Earth. On Mars, everything that happens is called a miracle.

She put her head in the Dead Sea. Her mind got walked on, and parted. Keep the noise down, it was a miracle, miracle, miracle.

Over and out.

Hello. See it might be okay getting put outside the door, except everybody sees the patch. That's the deterior thing about it. See everybody knows I've got a patch in the back of my trousers, but when I'm walking out to the door everybody sees it at once. And I can feel this evil thing behind me, like an actor in a pantomime. Maybe people are like birds and don't have minds in their heads, maybe I'm the only Earthling with a mind. Everything else is a pantomime: everything everybody says, everything everybody does. Maybe even the Mad Ringmaster hasn't got a mind. I don't know if he has got a mind, because I can't be him. I've got to be me. But I know I've got a mind, but everything else could be a sort of colourblind pantomime. Like the Brains crying outside but not inside when I broke her fucking coloured pencil and squirted the piss on her specs. And the way my mother used to cry when she was losing her mind. She still does when I go to see her, but it's just like watering eyes. The tears drip out of her eyes like when a tap needs a new washer. She lost her mind, that's why. When you lose your mind on Earth, you go into a home for mental defectors. I've still got a mind, so I'm not going to be going into a home.

Hello mind, take me to Mars.

On Mars, everybody has a mind and you can *see it*. It looks like a page in that colourblind book. You look at all the swarming dots, you don't know what it is, then you make out the shape or the number. And that's what they're thinking, that's the thought. On Earth, people have to use words. They have to talk to each other, or write letters to each other, or phone each other up. If you want to talk to a lot of people at once, you have to be a teacher. Either that or you have to be on the radio or the t.v. Then you can talk to hundreds of people at once. Like the weatherman who was on before the Rhyme Time programme, except there was a lot of interference. Well, he was probably talking to about a million people at once. That's what I'm going to be when I grow up, I'm going to be the weatherman.

Cheerio.

Hello come in are you receiving me. In a few minutes there will be Clock Talk, a programme of verse for cuckoos. Before that we have a weather report from Mars:

> *This is the Martian weather forecast. Tonight it is going to rain smallpox. The air will be full of interference, and the sea will be going on fire later on. Don't part it or walk on it, and don't go out without getting your jags. Tomorrow morning, the sun is going to be a shape or a number. If you can't make it out, you're colourblind. The clouds are going to start off huge and get tinier and tinier as they go down. If you can't read them, you'll get specs. There will be a lot of abominable behaviour later on, so don't get put outside the door. There will be no gold stars for anybody this week, or the next. Instead the sky is going to be covered in mistakes and blots. In the North, and South, and East, and West, there will be some scattered showers. You're bound to get drops in your eyes. The planet is changing shape. Watch out for meteors. Cheerio.*

But if other people don't have minds, there isn't much point in talking to them, is there? Not even to one of them. Maybe you should score out the bit about Earthling people having minds, and put down that some do and some don't. And she doesn't talk to anybody else except herself. See she lost her mind, then went into a home, and now she's got *two minds*. And one mind talks to the other mind, I think. But I wonder if the other mind can hear it. Maybe it's more like interference. But what I can't understand is how one mind take away one mind equal two minds.

Over and out.

Hello this is an SOS. My Oxygen supply is running low and I have made no contact with the *Enterprise*. Beam me up before it's too late.

See down there over that balcony, that's the Assembly Hall. It means prayers. You put your hands together and you say: *Our Father Which Art in Heaven, Hallo'ed Be Thy Name.* Then the Mad Ringmaster stands up and everybody else sits down and listens. He makes a speech about the school. If you've squirted piss on somebody's specs, he reads out your name and you have to report to his study along the corridor there. Or if something's happened in the school, the Mad Ringmaster announces it. Like when one boy died, he announced it so that everybody would know. He said: *Today there is a shadow among us.* He's like you that boy, dematerialised. Nobody can see him. See he fell from a tree, and the blood ran over his brain. His soul went to Heaven, and his mind is a shadow among us. On Mars you probably have a different kind of assembly. You probably just sit in a big circle holding hands, passing messages to each other through your fingertips. Because hundreds of Martians can get together and think *one* thought, because you can sort of merge, can't you? Blur with each other.

I wish I was an alien being. Maybe the next time you materialise, if you touch me we'll maybe merge.

So I had to report to his study. I told everybody about it in the playground, I was the centre of attention. Attention is what you pay for somebody talking to you. It's like buying something with money, you have to pay it to hear what they say. I told them all your name for him, the Mad Ringmaster, but everybody just said his name's Williams. You call him that because that's sort of what he looks like, with his big black gown and curly mustache. And his belt instead of a whip. And I told everybody what he said to me in his study, when he was giving me the belt. You'd better start crying. See, he wanted me to cry on the outside, the way the Brains did, the way my mother does. Like an actor in a pantomime. Then he could make an example of me. He could take me back into the class crying and then I'd be an example.

I am an example. But what am I an example of? I'm an example of *you*, the other way round. I should tell the teacher:
Please Miss, I'm the wrong way round. Billy Hope, this is a classroom not a home for mental defectors. Go and stand outside the door. You can come back in when you're the right way round.

But if the Mad Ringmaster ever gets me again, I'm definitely going to go to Mars. He'll have to announce it at assembly: *There is a shadow* . . . no not a shadow . . . *there is a reflection among us. He got put outside the door, and the blood ran over his brain.* I wish you would exterminate the Mad Ringmaster, make *him* a shadow among us. Put him in a box and bury him, bury him in the Dead Sea. It's wrong to hope somebody dies, except on Mars. What's wrong here on Earth is right on Mars, or at least it's not wrong. Because not wrong isn't the same as right always is it?

Like when you get a test, and you don't know some of the answers. So you don't put anything down, you just leave them blank. Well, you're not wrong, are you? But you're not right either, or they'd give you marks. They'd give you a couple of marks for leaving it blank, but they don't, except on Mars.

You know something, if they gave her a test she wouldn't be able to answer any of the questions. She'd got nothing out of a hundred. *Here comes the Mad Ringmaster.*

I'm inside the class again, I can't talk to you. He got me again, for getting put outside the door. He wanted me to cry on the outside again, to make me an example. But I didn't, I cried inside. My hands are on fire, they're Martian hands. Touch my fingertips, touch. Send messages through my fire. Don't ask me any more questions, blur with me. My hands are full of a thousand stings, so are yours. It feels like a swarm of wasps, a thousand stings. You can feel the message, so can I. It's sore, that's the message. The teacher's reading that poem called Spring from a book. Pay attention, pay attention. Cheerio.

'Billy Hope, stop blowing on your hands. I'm going to read the first verse again, the one you missed because of interference. Perhaps you can tell us what it means, Billy. Listen to the words very carefully:

Pretty creatures which people the sky
Are thousandfold this day,
Feathered choristers, they that sing
The livelong day away.

Now, Billy, I want you . . .'

I am an alien being and I people the thousandfold sky.

'I want *you* to tell the class . . . what the feathered choristers are.'

My Mother put her head in the sky and her mind flew away.

'Birds.'

Ian Hamilton Finlay

Ian Hamilton Finlay has enjoyed several different, equally creative careers. Born in Nassau in the Bahamas, Finlay was brought up in Scotland. He came to the fore during the 1960s as a major concrete poet. His first collection of short stories, *The Seabed and Other Stories*, appeared in 1958. He has published numerous volumes of poetry and other works, including a manual on translating.

As Finlay continued his work he became increasingly involved with its visual and physical presentation. In 1969 he moved with his wife to live in Dunsyre, where he set up the Wild Hawthorn Press, producing prints, booklets and cards, which combine words, ideas and images with a beautiful simplicity. These have brought Ian Hamilton Finlay an international reputation, enhanced by the pieces he has designed in stone, wood and glass. He has also been involved in creative landscaping, a discipline he has applied to his own garden to great effect.

Finlay's prose shows a clarity and apparent simplicity which it shares with much of his other work. In 'The Old Man and the Trout' a strong visual sense is also evident. The story brings us a sub-text as rich as the minutely described surroundings through which his characters move. The style adopted for the piece is childlike but never childish, and it makes full use of an observer for whom the adult world is still a curiosity, though its complications are fast approaching.

The Old Man and the Trout

HE WAS tenant of a red-roofed cottage where we spent a summer holiday once. I suppose I must have been about eleven or twelve years old at the time. It was late on in the summer evenings the old man used to spin me his sleepy yarns. While he yarned we sat together on his wooden garden-bench, in view of his green and yellow honey-suckle bushes full of late-shift bees. Behind us was a big field of ripening corn, with a lot of poppies like blood-spatters in it, bright crimson in the rusty gold. The old man sat well forward, his vein-knotted arms laid flat along his trousers which were pulled up tight, showing his carefully polished boots.

I can't remember much of what the old man said. Mostly he talked about his mole-trapping days, or about his own boyhood, when he'd lived down South. He still had a trace of the Southern way of talking and it was perhaps that that gave his voice such a tickly, sleepy sound. But somehow the mole-trapping was not true to the old man's character as I saw it. A lot of things I said or did would bring a momentary clot of sadness into his hazel eyes.

Once I talked the old man into taking me out fishing. I made him give a solemn promise to catch me a trout. I couldn't catch a trout myself, hard as I tried, every day. Still, the fish there were lovely to look at—fat and sleek, though a bit on the fly side, I thought.

When the old man had said he would take me fishing, we went round to the back of the cottage to gather worms from the hen-coop. The coop was round in the long, narrow garden the old man looked after, with the help of his sister, who was tying string round the currant bushes just then, as we began to dig the worms. The old man suffered from rheumatism, so he held the worm-tin while I dug at the dunged soil with a fork.

It must have been a very hot day, for I remember the old man had first unbuttoned his waistcoat, then taken it off and hung it on a bush. His woolly vest showed white through the slits in his thick, grey shirt. Once I broke a worm in half as I was pulling it from its escape-hole, and he stepped forward and ground the bits to nothing with his polished boot. 'They have feelings the same as we do,' he said, looking at me gently. As he spoke, the apple in his throat wobbled up and down, and I was suddenly saddened to see the brown crinkles in his neck, where his shirt-collar was missing. Then his sister called over to him from among the currant-bushes, and while he was gone to help her knot the string, I gathered up the worms and we were ready to start.

I took my rod from the shed where I always left it, never taking the pieces down, or untying the hook. It was an old shed. In the dusty corners of it stood cobwebbed washing-mangles, and the kind of big, brass basins in which black-currant jam is made in season. There was a steady drip of sunlight through the tiles down to the floor of brown earth. I liked just to stand in there, sniffing the dusty-damp smell which reminded me of something—something I could almost, but never quite remember.

The blue tar on the road had melted in the heat, and I left the marks of my rubber-heeled shoes on it as I walked along. At first, the old man carried the fishing rod while I was left to carry the tin of worms. It was an old treacle tin with a tight-fitting lid in which I had made a few holes with a hammer and nail. 'They have to breathe the same as we do,' I thought of the old man saying. I carried the tin inside my shirt to keep the worms cool and wet. I was scared they might close up like accordions and become no good for the trout.

It was almost no distance from the cottage down to the stream. On the way, though, we had to go by the Big House. Just as we drew level with the lawn, with its neat rhododendron bushes, the old man put the fishing rod into my free hand, and looked away into the fields on the other side of the road, as if he had caught sight of something. I could not see anything there myself. He took back the rod as soon as we were by the Big House and in sight of the stream.

Now that I could see the water running out from the bridge, I thought it might be better after all if it was me who fished. But I waited behind the old man while he slowly climbed the fence. Then we began to make our way down the bank of the stream which was grown all over with a strange kind of weed, like garden rhubarb that had jumped a wall and gone wild. This weed, said the old man, would hide us from the trout.

Instead of starting to fish right away, as I knew we ought to, we walked on down to the deep corner pool. There, the old man stopped, and soon we sat down among the false rhubarb. Flies buzzed round us noisily. A motor-bicycle whizzed up the road, leaving its sound spread out behind it like a long, black snake.

The pool was dappled on the far side with the shadows of trees. The clear water, as it swirled among their roots, was soiled by a drain that poured out rusty stuff, the colour of spate. It certainly was a fine place to fish the worm. I knew that several big trout lived under the trees, for I had often seen them feeding there, from the other bank. They always ignored the worms I threw down to them, except when I threw just the worms without the hook.

At length, the old man screwed himself up to spear on a worm. He told me to sit still where I was, and not to stand up, or shout, or I would scare the fish. Then he began to crawl towards the pool carrying the rod in one hand, and, with the other, clearing away the stems of the weed. The big green leaves kept closing back like the sea. I had to stand up just a little to see him cast. He threw the worm out in a way I thought terribly clumsy. It fell just by luck, though, in the mouth of the drain and began to float down slowly into the shadow of the trees.

To my surprise, the old man laid down the rod with its tip balanced on the edge of a rhubarb leaf. He crawled back towards me, and I could feel him creak. Seeing that I had half-stood up, he waved his hand at me, and I dropped down so as not to spoil his crazy fishing. At the same time I kept my eye on the tip of the rod. Almost at once, it was jerked down from the leaf. A trout had taken the worm. I shouted, and the old man stood up and made a grab for the butt.

Except once in a fishmonger's shop, I had never been so near to a big trout. While the old man wound hurriedly at the handle of the reel, the trout followed upstream in a slow, aloof sort of way. At first, I thought he was going to snag the gut on the barbed-wire cattle-fence which ran across the shallow water at the top of the pool. But he suddenly turned and swam back down towards the roots of the trees. He could not quite reach them because of the dragging line. He leaped out from the water with a big splash then surprised us both by swimming almost to our feet. I could see the red spots on his sides, and his baleful eyes. Then he swam away again, taking the slack of the line.

While the trout splashed in the water, in the shadow of the trees, the old man looked around for a place to land him but there was simply nowhere. The banks were steep, and we had no landing-net. It was a rotten situation.

At length the fish began to turn sideways on the top of the water, and the old man reeled him across the pool till he lay right below us. He lay almost on his back, with his mouth opening slowly and regularly as a clock ticks at night. All at once I felt sorry for him and I wished we had him on the bank.

The old man handed me the rod, and began to push up his jacket sleeve to above his elbow. Then he kneeled down over the trout, and closed his fingers on it, below the gills. He was raising it from the water when suddenly it slipped, and he was left holding only the gut, broken off a good way above the hook. I dropped the rod and looked after the fish as it swam away, with my hook in it.

The old man stood quite still for several minutes, looking after the trout. Then I picked up the rod and the worm-tin, and we walked up the road to the house, saying not a word to each other. I was worried about losing the hook but, as it happened, I had another one hidden away among the hankies in my drawer. I stopped worrying. I went in for my tea, and while I was eating I saw the old man's stooped figure cross the window, and I heard his chair scrape back as—it must have been—he took off his boots.

When I had finished my tea, I went out and sat on the bench sort of waiting for the old man. He didn't come, so in the end I went along and knocked on his door. It was his sister who answered my knock. She was wiping her red hands on a white dish-cloth, while behind her I could see the wallpaper with its pattern of faded roses, and a wooden coat-stand with a pair of the old man's galoshes down below. She took me through to the kitchen where the old man was sitting in a chair drawn in by the fire.

When he saw me come in he sat up. A grey shawl was thrown about his shoulders. He had taken his stocking-soles to ease his feet, and his boots were laid by in the hearth, the firelight dancing in the polished leather. His sister told me he got the rheumatism from being down at the stream fishing, but the old man said it was a sure sign of rain. That cheered me up.

I did not wait long in the old man's private kitchen. He was going to bathe his feet in a papier-mâché basin which his sister carried through from the scullery, and put down for him on the woolly rug. I waited only till she had filled the basin. I heard him groan as he bent forward to drag off his socks; and afterwards, when I was in the garden, I heard the water gurgling away mysteriously down the hidden drain.

Sure enough, there was rain as the old man's rheumatism prophesied. The big drops splashed on the honeysuckle bushes, outside the window, all night. I woke up early. After breakfast, though, it was still raining and I wasn't allowed to go out. Then in the afternoon it faired up, and I was let take my rod from the shed, with its new, puddled floor. The smell in there was a whole lot different that day—sad and exciting somehow. I didn't have to waste time digging for worms. They had come up to the top of the ground, and one or two of the pink ones had wriggled across the road and were squashed thinly on the blue tar. All I had to do was to lift them up.

The sunlit water looked like lentil soup. Twigs and other things were bobbing round in black-ripples, and I let my worm drop in beside them and I caught a good trout. I ran back across the fields and gave it in to the old man. His sister was pleased. She put the fish on a white platter, with little bits of green grass still sticking to its red-spotted sides. I went in to stare at it several times before it was gutted and fried.

The next day the water was almost clear again and I couldn't get any bites. I went down, after a while, to the corner pool, to see if I could spot the big trout. I saw one big fish, but I didn't think it was him, so I went on down to the next pool, and the next one again. This pool was like a big deep hole, with a lot of rotten branches half-buried in the mud down at the bottom of it. It was a pool where you could easily lose all your hooks.

I was just going to walk right by the pool, as I usually did, when my eye caught on something that was glinting down on the mud. I clambered down the bank and I picked up a dead branch which snapped. I threw it away. When I had found a branch strong enough, I thrust it down through the water, and poked at the big fish to get him where I could lift him out. Little pieces of mud flaked off the bottom and whirled round him like smoke. He sank up and down like a balloon each time I thrust. When at last I was able to get hold of him, I dropped him on the bank and he was quite stiff. A blue-bottle came and crawled on his eye but I shooed it away.

After I had looked at him for a long time, I took out my pen-knife and got back my hook. It was a little rusted, of course, but there was enough of the bloodied gut left to tie back on my line. I wondered what I ought to do with the trout and, eventually, I pushed him into a hole in the bank and pulled the long grass down on top.

When I had done fishing and got back to the house, the old man was sitting out on the garden bench waiting for me. His rheumatism was a bit better, and he yarned for a while about moles, and said it was an awful pity we'd lost the big trout. It was on the tip of my tongue to tell him what had happened, but I never did for I guessed that if I had it would have broken his heart.

Allan Massie

There has always been a strong connection between Scotland's authors and its wider cultural and political life.

It was not so long ago that MacDiarmid, Gunn and many others were actively involved in Scottish Nationalism and the hopes it aroused. With his piece, 'In the Bare Lands', Allan Massie examines the curious relationship between a country and those who seek to shape its culture.

Born in Singapore in 1938, Allan Massie was brought up in Aberdeenshire. Returning to Scotland after a period spent teaching in England and several years in Rome, he devoted all his energies to writing. His first novel *Change And Decay in All Around I See* appeared in 1978. He has also produced a study of Muriel Spark, with several more novels, including the very successful *Augustus*, and he writes regularly on books and Scottish affairs.

'In The Bare Lands' shows a bleak picture of a Scottish literary idol with feet of clay. Through the figure of Urquhart, who is exiled in Italy and hiding behind a manufactured Scottishness, and his disaffected interviewer, young, cold and bored, Massie offers a grim account of the health of Scotland, a nation which has lost much of its original culture and invented or romanticised more.

In the Bare Lands

No, you most certainly can't see him.'

Giles was accustomed to flat refusals. They didn't faze him.

'I don't want to intrude,' he said. 'I did write, you know, and I've come a long way.'

It was cold on the steps of the seedy-looking house which had certainly seen better days.

The woman—you could imagine from her cheek-bones she had once been beautiful—didn't seem impressed.

'You didn't get a reply, did you?'

Giles nodded.

'I know he's very old,' he said. 'I would have telephoned but you're not in the book.'

'Are you surprised?' she said.

'I'm a perfectly respectable person. I'm not a journalist if that's what you're afraid of.'

'I don't care who you are. Can't you see that?'

'I'm afraid it's beginning to rain.'

The wind which had been blowing for the last two days was now swirling heavy gouts of rain with it. The house—why had it been built facing north—lay or, rather, crouched directly in its path. Further up the mountain it might be snowing.

'Couldn't you just let me in to explain myself. It reminds me of trying to sell encyclopaedias, standing here.'

He turned up the collar of his Donegal tweed coat.

'That couldn't do any harm, could it, Miss Urquhart? You are Miss Urquhart, aren't you, his daughter, I mean?'

When she didn't reply, he turned for a moment and looked back down the valley. There were meadows a couple of hundred feet below and a sort of byre or bothy standing alone. It was a limestone country.

'I've got very respectable credentials,' he said, 'even a letter of introduction. Mr Alkins said he would write too.'

'Henry Alkins?'

'Yes, of course.'

It was the first sign that she might relent and he followed it up, though he knew well that what would really count was his docile dejection—his air of a spaniel that isn't being taken for a promised walk.

'I know there's been a postal strike,' he said, 'perhaps both our letters got lost that way.'

'I don't know what you want,' she said. 'You can't have sold encyclopaedias.'

'Not very successfully, I'm afraid.'

There was no point in telling her that he'd never come near to needing to do anything like that; friends' accounts had only established it in his mind as the most pathetic of imaginable holiday jobs.

'Well,' she said, 'he's out just now.'

'In this weather?'

'It's the lambing season.'

She pointed to the byre below.

'You can come in and talk to me if you like. I'll give you some tea. It's English.'

They entered a narrow hall. There was a heavy oak chest and the walls were painted white. The paint had been done a long time ago.

Miss Urquhart said,

'We'll go in here. There are no comfortable rooms in this house. I sometimes think that's why my father chose it.'

'The bare lands the surgeon's scalpel,' said Giles.

'Oh,' she looked at him with surprise, 'you do know a little then. I promised you tea. Or would you rather have kirsch? It's local.'

'I'd love both. I'm afraid that's very greedy.'

Giles gave her his little boy smile—he had been brought up by a maiden aunt while his parents were on a tea-plantation in Assam.

'There is whisky,' she said, 'but that's his.'

She went out through a door at the back of the small room to make the tea. Giles stood by the fire and looked around. It was like a Victorian art photograph—'Cottage in the Hebrides', perhaps. There should be an old woman with a shawl round her head sitting at her spinning-wheel by the fire. The only thing that spoiled the effect was the book-case which ran along the wall beside the door they had come in by. Giles examined it. There were two shelves of Urquhart's books—poetry, history (damned tendentious history he could imagine), political philosophy, social studies, six volumes of autobiography—Christ, he hadn't realised he'd written so much, and most of it crap. He pulled one out, not bothering to choose.

'The warder had knowledge of which my fellow-prisoners were ignorant. He knew he was a prisoner more closely confined than they.'

What bloody arrogant nonsense. He put the book back.

He had a feeling, rare to him, of being out of place. If Judkins thought up any more of these bright assignments he could bloody well follow them up himself.

He sat down—the chair had a straight back and the seat was too short—and pulled out Simon Lumsden's letter. It was brief and badly typed, the signature barely legible. He supposed it might do, though he, remembering Lumsden's animosity, could read reluctance between the lines.

'Simon Lumsden's the man to go to,' Judkins had said.

'Isn't he dead?'—his memory of Lumsden was very vague—his name surely hadn't appeared in the papers for at least a decade.

'No, he lives in Gravesend, but he isn't dead.'

It was the nearest approach to a joke Judkins could assemble from his card-index mind.

'And what if he won't see me?'

The whole project was unattractive—he would far rather stay in Venice instead of having to drive into the mountains above Bolzano. It was typical of Judkins to come up with something like this—'we've got the unit there, kill two birds with one stone,' he could just hear him say it, even though Judkins was more the type of sentimental moron who would put out a bird table in his suburban garden.

'Lumsden'll see you,' he had snickered. 'All you need do is go along with a bottle of brandy in one hand and a bottle of Scotch in the other.'

'But I thought they quarrelled. Will Lumsden's letter do any good?'

'You can get off your arse and try.'

Miss Urquhart came back into the room and set a tray down. She poured two cups of very dark tea.

'Milk and sugar?'

'Both, please.'

She handed him the cup and a small glass of kirsch and passed a plate with caraway-seed cake on it.

'It's a little stale, I'm afraid. He's finished with politics. You know that? That's why we live out here. He doesn't even like to talk about them. I don't know when he last wrote to the newspapers.'

'Well, he's eighty-five, isn't he?'

'The last visitor we had, sometime back in the autumn, didn't realise that. He was still looking for lead from him. He was a boy from Glasgow University. I'm Edinburgh myself.'

'I'd better explain why I've come.'

'There's no point in that. I only asked you in because it's pleasant to talk English now and then.'

She must have seen surprise on Giles's face.

'He'll only talk Gaelic to me. That shows what he feels.'

'I didn't realise . . .'

'He only learned it in prison, you know. In the second war, not the first.'

'I thought,' Giles had done his homework, 'he belonged to the Lallans school at one time.'

'That was before the working-man let him down.'

'You sound bitter.'

'Bitter? You're quite a wit, aren't you?'

Giles began to feel his resentment deepen.

'I've a letter from Simon Lumsden,' he said, handing it over.

'Poor Simon,' she replied. She only just glanced at the letter and laid it aside. 'How is he?'

It wasn't really a question to be answered.

'We haven't seen him for years. Simon had no ideas, you know. He just wanted a cause to attach himself to. Don't look at me like that, please. What do you imagine I think about when I'm sitting here? What have I to think about? The Workers' Republic of Scotland or the Union of Celtic Commonwealths?'

'I haven't said anything. I thought you said he was finished with politics'—if you call that sort of nonsense politics, he nearly added.

'Precisely.'

'Look,' said Giles, 'I didn't want to come here.'

'I used to think I was in love with Simon,' she said. 'I wanted to be. He did too. Oh well, do you know my fate? I chose the wrong man to save.'

She started to try to laugh and then to light a cigarette and then to cry—she stopped frozen between the attitudes.

Giles said,

'It's a television programme. My boss thought of calling it "A Leader in Search of a Party". It's his notion of Pirandello, half-baked, you know, but that's his style, it needn't be as awful as it sounds . . .'—he was speaking too fast, almost unaware of what he was saying and at any moment the ice would break and she would cry.

But instead the door opened and a very tall old man came in. He walked very erect, no suggestion of a stoop. He was wearing a plaid and looked . . . Giles had once spent a wet afternoon in Aberdeen and between closing and opening time gone into the Municipal Art Gallery (it was a choice between that and 'Sex—Swedish-Style', and though he detested great Galleries and would run a mile rather than visit the Uffizi or the Prado, he had in certain moods a weakness for provincial ones) and there seen a Landseer of truly impressive ineptitude entitled 'Flood in the Highlands', depicting what he took to be a Laird surrounded by family and retainers with assorted livestock perched on cliffs or struggling in the flood-waters . . . yes, Urquhart looked exactly like Landseer's conception of a Highland chief. He might even have modelled for the painting, or, more probably, based his conception of himself on it.

He didn't look at Giles but said something in what was presumably Gaelic to his daughter. She replied in the same language. Giles couldn't avoid the impression that hers sounded more fluent, even more natural.

Urquhart's hand disappeared somewhere under his plaid and emerged with a key. He unlocked a heavy deal cabinet, took out a bottle of whisky (Talisker, Giles enviously observed) and poured himself a half-tumbler which he swallowed at one gulp. He made another brief remark to his daughter, filled his glass, replaced the bottle, locked the cabinet and marched out of the room.

'Well?'

'I told you it was pointless.'

'What in fact did he say?'

'He told me to tell you to get the hell out of here. That's a paraphrase. It's more vivid in the Gaelic.'

'I see.'

They could hear footsteps overhead.

'Well, I never really thought anything would . . .' He tried to think of just what he'd like to do to Judkins. 'Do you think I could have another drop of kirsch before I go. It's really rather good.'

The footsteps marched up and down like a man pacing his cell.

'He'll live to be a hundred, I know he will,' she said, but she filled his glass. 'You can buy it in the village below.'

Giles drank it quickly and shrugged himself into his overcoat. Or something in a cage.

'Thanks, I will, I certainly will.'

He might as well get something out of the trip. Mind you, for the first time he conceded that Judkins had a point. Visually it would be damned good, but, still, if the old loony would only speak Gaelic—well, there were bloody few Gaelic speakers and most of them probably had no TV reception. He'd tell Judkins he'd sent him on a two hundred mile round trip to interview a monoglot Gael—that'd puzzle him.

'And give my love to Simon. For what it's worth.'

'He won't live to be a hundred, that's for sure. I'm not likely to see him again. He didn't like me much.'

'No,' she said.

It was sleet that was being blown on a diagonal by the wind now. He got into the hired Fiat, and turned, surprising himself, to say something, he didn't quite know what, something to bring life to her, even perhaps just thank you, but the door was already shut, and he drove down into the valley, the sleet changing to a thin rain as he descended.

Muriel Spark

With *The Prime of Miss Jean Brodie* (1961), Muriel Spark has surely earned a place in posterity. Spark was born in Edinburgh in 1918, and she began her writing career in London as a critical journalist and editor of *Poetry Review.* In 1951 she was converted to Catholicism and began to write fiction when her entry for *The Observer's* short story competition won first prize. Her first novel, *The Comforters* was published in 1957 and she has gone on to produce almost twenty more, along with books of criticism, poetry, short stories and drama.

Muriel Spark is able to detach herself from her characters, and yet this approach, with its sharp crafted prose, still serves to keep the reader alert and to create its own very convincing reality. We are shown a blend of human strengths and failings, of grubbiness and profound spirituality, and behind it all, a wicked sense of humour.

In 'The Black Madonna' a fastidiously liberal couple are given increasingly serious challenges to all they believe themselves to be. Their good will, their good works and the infinite pains they take to appear unaware of 'different social grades' are captured with ruthless accuracy. Then, in a brilliant leap of invention, Muriel Spark turns this world upside down, bringing bourgeois religous observance face to face with the truly miraculous.

The Black Madonna

When the Black Madonna was installed in the Church of the Sacred Heart the Bishop himself came to consecrate it. His long purple train was upheld by the two curliest of the choir. The day was favoured suddenly with thin October sunlight as he crossed the courtyard from the presbytery to the church, as the procession followed him chanting the Litany of the Saints: five priests in vestments of white heavy silk interwoven with glinting threads, four lay officials with straight red robes, then the confraternities and the tangled columns of the Mothers' Union.

The new town of Whitney Clay had a large proportion of Roman Catholics, especially among the nurses at the new hospital; and at the paper mills, too, there were many Catholics, drawn inland from Liverpool by the new housing estate; likewise, with the canning factories.

The Black Madonna had been given to the church by a recent convert. It was carved out of bog oak.

'They found the wood in the bog. Had been there hundreds of years. They sent for the sculptor right away by phone. He went over to Ireland and carved it there and then. You see, he had to do it while it was still wet.'

'Looks a bit like contemporary art.'

'Nah, that's not contemporary art, it's old-fashioned. If you'd ever seen contemporary work you'd *know* it was old-fashioned.'

'Looks like contemp—'

'It's old-*fashioned*. Else how'd it get sanctioned to be put up?'

'It's not so nice as the Immaculate Conception at Lourdes. That lifts you up.'

Everyone got used, eventually, to the Black Madonna with her square hands and straight carved draperies. There was a movement to dress it up in vestments, or at least a lace veil.

'She looks a bit gloomy, Father, don't you think?'

'No,' said the priest, 'I think it looks fine. If you start dressing it up in cloth you'll spoil the line.'

Sometimes people came from London especially to see the Black Madonna, and these were not Catholics; they were, said the priest, probably no religion at all, poor souls, though gifted with faculties. They came, as if to a museum, to see the line of the Black Madonna which must not be spoiled by vestments.

The new town of Whitney Clay had swallowed up the old village. One or two cottages with double dormer windows, an inn called 'The Tyger', a Methodist chapel and three small shops represented the village; the three shops were already threatened by the Council; the Methodists were fighting to keep their chapel. Only the double dormer cottages and the inn were protected by the Nation and so had to be suffered by the Town Planning Committee.

The town was laid out like geometry in squares, arcs (to allow for the by-pass) and isosceles triangles, breaking off, at one point, to skirt the old village which, from the aerial view, looked like a merry doodle on the page.

Manders Road was one side of a parallelogram of green-bordered streets. It was named after one of the founders of the canning concern, Manders' Figs in Syrup, and it comprised a row of shops and a long high block of flats named Cripps House after the late Sir Stafford Cripps who had laid the foundation stone. In flat twenty-two on the fifth floor of Cripps House lived Raymond and Lou Parker. Raymond Parker was a foreman at the motor works, and was on the management committee. He had been married for fifteen years to Lou, who was thirty-seven at the time that the miraculous powers of the Black Madonna came to be talked of.

Of the twenty-five couples who live in Cripps House five were Catholics. All, except Raymond and Lou Parker, had children. A sixth family had recently been moved by the Council into one of the six-roomed houses because of the seven children besides the grandfather.

Raymond and Lou were counted lucky to have obtained their three-roomed flat although they had no children. People with children had priority; but their name had been on the waiting list for years, and some said Raymond had a pull with one of the Councillors who was a director of the motor works.

The Parkers were among the few tenants of Cripps House who owned a motor car. They did not, like most of their neighbours, have a television receiver, for being childless they had been able to afford to expand themselves in the way of taste, so that their habits differed slightly and their amusements considerably, from those of their neighbours. The Parkers went to the pictures only when *The Observer* had praised the film; they considered television not their sort of thing; they adhered to their religion; they voted Labour; they believed that the twentieth century was the best so far; they assented to the doctrine of original sin; they frequently applied the word 'Victorian' to ideas and people they did not like—for instance, when a local Town Councillor resigned his office Raymond said, 'He had to go. He's Victorian. And far too young for the job'; and Lou said Jane Austen's books were too Victorian; and anyone who opposed the abolition of capital punishment was Victorian. Raymond took the *Reader's Digest*, a magazine called *Motoring* and *The*

Catholic Herald. Lou took *The Queen, Woman's Own* and *Life*. Their daily paper was *The News Chronicle*. They read two books apiece each week. Raymond preferred travel books; Lou liked novels.

For the first five years of their married life they had been worried about not having children. Both had submitted themselves to medical tests as a result of which Lou had a course of injections. These were unsuccessful. It had been a special disappointment since both came from large sprawling Catholic families. None of their married brothers and sisters had less than three children. One of Lou's sisters, now widowed, had eight; they sent her a pound a week.

Their flat in Cripps House had three rooms and a kitchen. All round them their neighbours were saving up to buy houses. A council flat, once obtained, was a mere platform in space to further the progress of the rocket. This ambition was not shared by Raymond and Lou; they were not only content, they were delighted, with these civic chambers, and indeed took something of an aristocratic view of them, not without a self-conscious feeling of being free, in this particular, from the prejudices of that middle class to which they as good as belonged. 'One day,' said Lou, 'it will be the thing to live in a council flat.'

They were eclectic as to their friends. Here, it is true, they differed slightly from each other. Raymond was for inviting the Ackleys to meet the Farrells. Mr Ackley was an accountant at the Electricity Board. Mr and Mrs Farrell were respectively a sorter at Manders' Figs in Syrup and an usherette at the Odeon.

'After all,' argued Raymond, 'they're all Catholics.'

'Ah well,' said Lou, 'but now, their interests are different. The Farrells wouldn't know what the Ackleys were talking about. The Ackleys like politics. The Farrells like to tell jokes. I'm not a snob, only sensible.'

'Oh, please yourself.' For no one could call Lou a snob, and everyone knew she was sensible.

Their choice of acquaintance was wide by reason of their active church membership: that is to say, they were members of various guilds and confraternities. Raymond was a sidesman, and he also organised the weekly football lottery in aid of the Church Decoration Fund. Lou felt rather out of things when the Mothers' Union met and had special Masses, for the Mothers' Union was the only group she did not qualify for. Having been a nurse before her marriage she was, however, a member of the Nurses' Guild.

Thus, most of their Catholic friends came from different departments of life. Others, concerned with the motor works where Raymond was a foreman, were of different social grades to which Lou was more alive than Raymond. He let her have her way, as a rule, when it came to a question of which would mix with which.

A dozen Jamaicans were taken on at the motor works. Two came into Raymond's department. He invited them to the flat one evening to have coffee. They were unmarried, very polite and black. The quiet one was called Henry Pierce and the talkative one, Oxford St John. Lou, to Raymond's surprise and pleasure, decided that all their acquaintance, from top to bottom, must meet Henry and Oxford. All along he had known she was not a snob, only sensible, but he had rather feared she would consider the mixing of their new black and their old white friends not sensible.

'I'm glad you like Henry and Oxford,' he said. 'I'm glad we're able to introduce them to so many people.' For the dark pair had, within a month, spent nine evenings at Cripps House; they had met accountants, teachers, packers and sorters. Only Tina Farrell, the usherette, had not seemed to understand the quality of these occasions: 'Quite nice chaps, them darkies, when you get to know them.'

'You mean Jamaicans,' said Lou. 'Why shouldn't they be nice? They're no different from anyone else.'

'Yes, yes, that's what I mean,' said Tina.

'We're all equal,' stated Lou. 'Don't forget there are black Bishops.'

'Jesus, I never said we were the equal of a Bishop,' Tina said, very bewildered.

'Well, don't call them darkies.'

Sometimes, on summer Sunday afternoons Raymond and Lou took their friends for a run in their car, ending up at a riverside road-house. The first time they turned up with Oxford and Henry they felt defiant; but there were no objections, there was no trouble at all. Soon the dark pair ceased to be a novelty. Oxford St John took up with a pretty red-haired bookkeeper, and Henry Pierce, missing his companion, spent more of his time at the Parkers' flat. Lou and Raymond had planned to spend their two weeks' summer holiday in London. 'Poor Henry,' said Lou. 'He'll miss us.'

Once you brought him out he was not so quiet as you thought at first. Henry was twenty-four, desirous of knowledge in all fields, shining very much in eyes, skin, teeth, which made him seem all the more eager. He called out the maternal in Lou, and to some extent the avuncular in Raymond. Lou used to love him when he read out lines from his favourite poems which he had copied into an exercise book.

Haste thee, nymph, and bring with thee
Jest and youthful jollity,
Sport that . . .

Lou would interrupt: 'You should say jest, jollity—not yest, yollity.'

'Jest,' he said carefully. 'And laughter holding both his sides,' he continued. '*Laughter*—hear that, Lou?—*laughter*. That's what the human race was made for. Those folks that go round gloomy, Lou, they . . .'

Lou loved this talk. Raymond puffed his pipe benignly. After Henry had gone Raymond would say what a pity it was that such an intelligent young fellow had lapsed. For Henry had been brought up in a Roman Catholic mission. He had, however, abandoned religion. He was fond of saying, 'The superstition of today is the science of yesterday.'

'I can't allow,' Raymond would say, 'that the Catholic Faith is superstition. I can't allow that.'

'He'll return to the Church one day'—this was Lou's contribution, whether Henry was present or not. If she said it in front of Henry he would give her an angry look. These were the only occasions when Henry lost his cheerfulness and grew quiet again.

Raymond and Lou prayed for Henry, that he might regain his faith. Lou said her rosary three times a week before the Black Madonna.

'He'll miss us when we go on our holidays.'

Raymond telephoned to the hotel in London. 'Have you a single room for a young gentleman accompanying Mr and Mrs Parker?' He added, 'a coloured gentleman.' To his pleasure a room was available, and to his relief there was no objection to Henry's colour.

They enjoyed their London holiday, but it was somewhat marred by a visit to that widowed sister of Lou's to whom she allowed a pound a week towards the rearing of her eight children. Lou had not seen her sister Elizabeth for nine years.

They went to her one day towards the end of their holiday. Henry sat at the back of the car beside a large suitcase stuffed with old clothes for Elizabeth. Raymond at the wheel kept saying, 'Poor Elizabeth—eight kids,' which irritated Lou, though she kept her peace.

Outside the underground station at Victoria Park, where they stopped to ask the way, Lou felt a strange sense of panic. Elizabeth lived in a very downward quarter of Bethnal Green, and in the past nine years since she had seen her Lou's memory of the shabby ground-floor rooms with their peeling walls and bare boards, had made a kinder nest for itself. Sending off the postal order to her sister each week she had gradually come to picture the habitation at Bethnal Green in an almost monastic light; it would be bare but well-scrubbed, spotless, and shining with Brasso and holy poverty. The floorboards gleamed. Elizabeth was grey-haired, lined, but neat. The children well behaved, sitting down betimes to their broth in two rows along an almost refectory table. It was not till they had reached Victoria Park that Lou felt the full force of the fact that everything would be different from what she had imagined. 'It may have gone down since I was last there,' she said to Raymond who had never visited Elizabeth before.

'What's gone down?'

'Poor Elizabeth's place.'

Lou had not taken much notice of Elizbeth's dull little monthly letters, almost illiterate, for Elizabeth, as she herself always said, was not much of a scholar. 'James is at another job I hope that's the finish of the bother

I had my blood pressure there was a Health visitor very nice. Also the assistance they sent my Dinner all the time and for the kids at home they call it meals on Wheels. I pray to the Almighty that James is well out of his bother he never lets on at sixteen their all the same never open his mouth but Gods eyes are not shut. Thanks for P.O. you will be rewarded your affect sister Elizabeth.'

Lou tried to piece together in her mind the gist of nine years' such letters. James was the eldest; she supposed he had been in trouble.

'I ought to have asked Elizabeth about young James,' said Lou. 'She wrote to me last year that he was in a bother, there was talk of him being sent away, but I didn't take it in at the time, I was busy.'

'You can't take everything on your shoulders,' said Raymond. 'You do very well by Elizabeth.' They had pulled up outside the house where Elizabeth lived on the ground floor. Lou looked at the chipped paint, the dirty windows and torn grey-white curtains and was reminded with startling clarity of her hopeless childhood in Liverpool from which, miraculously, hope had lifted her, and had come true, for the nuns had got her that job; and she had trained as a nurse among white-painted beds, and white shining walls, and tiles, hot water everywhere and Dettol without stint. When she had first married she had wanted all white-painted furniture that you could wash and liberate from germs; but Raymond had been for oak, he did not understand the pleasure of hygiene and new enamel paint, for his upbringing had been orderly, he had been accustomed to a lounge suite and autumn tints in the front room all his life. And now Lou stood and looked at the outside of Elizabeth's place and felt she had gone right back. On the way back to the hotel Lou chattered with relief that it was over. 'Poor Elizabeth, she hasn't had much of a chance. I like little Francis, what did you think of little Francis, Ray?'

Raymond did not like being called Ray, but he made no objection for he knew that Lou had been under a strain. Elizabeth had not been very pleasant. She had expressed admiration for Lou's hat, bag, gloves and shoes which were all navy blue, but she had used an accusing tone. The house had been smelly and dirty. 'I'll show you round,' Elizabeth had said in a tone of mock refinement, and they were forced to push through a dark narrow passage behind her skinny form till they came to the big room where the children slept. A row of old iron beds each with a tumble of dark blanket rugs, no sheets. Raymond was indignant at the sight and hoped that Lou was not feeling upset. He knew very well Elizabeth had a decent living income from a number of public sources, and was simply a slut, one of those who would not help themselves.

'Ever thought of taking a job, Elizabeth?' he had said, and immediately realised his stupidity. But Elizabeth took her advantage. 'What d'you mean? *I'm* not going to leave my kids in no nursery. *I'm* not going to send them to no home. What kids needs these days is a good home life and that's what they get.' And she added, 'God's eyes are not shut,' in a tone which was meant for him, Raymond, to get at him for doing well in life.

Raymond distributed half-crowns to the younger children and deposited on the table half-crowns for those who were out playing in the street.

'Goin' already?' said Elizabeth in her tone of reproach. But she kept eyeing Henry with interest, and the reproachful tone was more or less a routine affair.

'You from the States?' Elizabeth said to Henry.

Henry sat on the edge of his sticky chair and answered, no, from Jamaica, while Raymond winked at him to cheer him.

'During the war there was a lot of boys like you from the States,' Elizabeth said, giving him a sideways look.

Henry held out his hand to the second youngest child, a girl of seven, and said, 'Come talk to me.'

The child said nothing, only dipped into the box of sweets which Lou had brought.

'Come talk,' said Henry.

Elizabeth laughed. 'If she does talk you'll be sorry you ever asked. She's got a tongue in her head, that one. You should hear her cheeking up to the teachers.' Elizabeth's bones jerked with laughter among her loose clothes. There was a lopsided double bed in the corner, and beside it a table cluttered with mugs, tins, a comb and brush, a number of hair curlers, a framed photograph of the Sacred Heart, and also Raymond noticed what he thought erroneously to be a box of contraceptives. He decided to say nothing to Lou about this; he was quite sure she must have observed other things which he had not; possibly things of a more distressing nature.

Lou's chatter on the way back to the hotel had a touch of hysteria. 'Raymond, dear,' she said in her most chirpy west-end voice, 'I simply *had* to give the poor dear *all* my next week's housekeeping money. We shall have to starve, darling, when we get home. That's *simply* what we shall have to do.'

'O.K.,' said Raymond.

'I ask you,' Lou shrieked, 'what else could I do, what *could* I do?'

'Nothing at all,' said Raymond, 'but what you've done.'

'My own *sister*, my dear,' said Lou; 'and did you see the way she had her hair bleached?—All streaky, and she used to have a lovely head of hair.'

'I wonder if she tries to raise herself?' said Raymond. 'With all those children she could surely get better accommodation if only she—'

'That sort,' said Henry, leaning forward from the back of the car, 'never moves. It's the slum mentality, man. Take some folks I've seen back home—'

'There's no comparison,' Lou snapped suddenly, 'this is quite a different case.'

Raymond glanced at her in surprise; Henry sat back, offended. Lou was thinking wildly, what a cheek *him* talking like a snob. At least Elizabeth's white.

Their prayers for the return of faith to Henry Pierce were so far answered in that he took a tubercular turn which was followed by a religious one. He was sent off to a sanatorium in Wales with a promise from Lou and Raymond to visit him before Christmas. Meantime, they applied themselves to Our Lady for the restoration of Henry's health.

Oxford St John, whose love affair with the red-haired girl had come to grief, now frequented their flat, but he could never quite replace Henry in their affections. Oxford was older and less refined than Henry. He would stand in front of the glass in their kitchen and tell himself, 'Man, you just a big black bugger.' He kept referring to himself as black, which of course he was, Lou thought, but it was not the thing to say. He stood in the doorway with his arms and smile thrown wide: 'I am black but comely, O ye daughters of Jerusalem.' And once, when Raymond was out, Oxford brought the conversation round to that question of being black *all over*, which made Lou very uncomfortable and she kept looking at the clock and dropped stitches in her knitting.

Three times a week when she went to the black Our Lady with her rosary to ask for the health of Henry Pierce, she asked also that Oxford St John would get another job in another town, for she did not like to make objections, telling her feelings to Raymond; there were no objections to make that you could put your finger on. She could not very well complain that Oxford was common; Raymond despised snobbery, and so did she, it was a very delicate question. She was amazed when, within three weeks, Oxford announced that he was thinking of looking for a job in Manchester.

Lou said to Raymond, 'Do you know, there's something *in* what they say about the bog oak statue in the church.'

'There may be,' said Raymond. 'People say so.'

Lou could not tell him how she had petitioned the removal of Oxford St John. But when she got a letter from Henry Pierce to say he was improving, she told Raymond, 'You see, we asked for Henry to get back the Faith, and so he did. Now we ask for his recovery and he's improving.'

'He's having good treatment at the sanatorium,' Raymond said. But he added, 'Of course we'll have to keep up the prayers.' He himself, though not a rosary man, knelt before the Black Madonna every Saturday evening after Benediction to pray for Henry Pierce.

Whenever they saw Oxford he was talking of leaving Whitney Clay. Raymond said, 'He's making a big mistake going to Manchester. A big place can be very lonely. I hope he'll change his mind.'

'He won't,' said Lou, so impressed was she now by the powers of the Black Madonna. She was good and tired of Oxford St John with his feet on her cushions, and calling himself a nigger.

'We'll miss him,' said Raymond, 'he's such a cheery big soul.'

'We will,' said Lou. She was reading the parish magazine, which she seldom did, although she was one of the voluntary workers who sent them out, addressing hundreds of wrappers every month. She had vaguely noticed, in previous numbers, various references to the Black Madonna, how she had granted this or that favour. Lou had heard that people sometimes came from neighbouring parishes to pray at the Church of the Sacred Heart because of the statue. Some said they came from all over England, but whether this was to admire the art-work or to pray, Lou was not sure. She gave her attention to the article in the parish magazine:

> While not wishing to make excessive claims . . . many prayers answered and requests granted to the Faithful in an exceptional way . . . two remarkable cures effected, but medical evidence is, of course, still in reserve, a certain lapse of time being necessary to ascertain permanency of cure. The first of these cases was a child of twelve suffering from leukaemia. . . . The second . . . While not desiring to create a *cultus* where none is due, we must remember it is always our duty to honour Our Blessed Lady, the dispenser of all graces, to whom we owe . . .
>
> Another aspect of the information received by the Father Rector concerning our 'Black Madonna' is one pertaining to childless couples of which three cases have come to his notice. In each case the couple claim to have offered constant devotion to the 'Black Madonna,' and in two of the cases specific requests were made for the favour of a child. In *all* cases the prayers were answered. The proud parents. . . . It should be the loving duty of every parishioner to make a special thanksgiving. . . . The Father Rector will be grateful for any further information. . . .

'Look, Raymond,' said Lou. 'Read this.'

They decided to put in for a baby to the Black Madonna.

The following Saturday, when they drove to the church for Benediction Lou jangled her rosary. Raymond pulled up outside the church. 'Look here, Lou,' he said, 'do you want a baby in any case?' – for he partly thought she was only putting the Black Madonna to the test – 'Do you want a child, after all these years?'

This was a new thought to Lou. She considered her neat flat and tidy routine, the entertaining with her good coffee cups, the weekly papers and the library books, the tastes which they would not have been able to cultivate had they had a family of children. She thought of her nice young looks which everyone envied, and her freedom of movement.

'Perhaps we should try,' she said. 'God won't give us a child if we aren't meant to have one.'

'We have to make some decisions for ourselves,' he said. 'And to tell you the truth if *you* don't want a child, *I* don't.'

'There's no harm in praying for one,' she said.

'You have to be careful what you pray for,' he said. 'You mustn't tempt Providence.'

She thought of her relatives, and Raymond's, all married with children. She thought of her sister Elizabeth with her eight, and remembered that one who cheeked up to the teachers, so pretty and sulky and shabby, and she remembered the fat baby Francis sucking his dummy and clutching Elizabeth's bony neck.

'I don't see why I shouldn't have a baby,' said Lou.

Oxford St John departed at the end of the month. He promised to write, but they were not surprised when weeks passed and they had no word. 'I don't suppose we shall ever hear from him again,' said Lou. Raymond thought he detected satisfaction in her voice, and would have thought she was getting snobbish as women do as they get older, losing sight of their ideals, had she not gone on to speak of Henry Pierce. Henry had written to say he was nearly cured, but had been advised to return to the West Indies.

'We must go and see him,' said Lou. 'We promised. What about the Sunday after next?'

'O.K.,' said Raymond.

It was the Saturday before that Sunday when Lou had her first sick turn. She struggled out of bed to attend Benediction, but had to leave suddenly during the service and was sick behind the church in the presbytery yard. Raymond took her home, though she protested against cutting out her rosary to the Black Madonna.

'After only six weeks!' she said, and she could hardly tell whether her sickness was due to excitement or nature. 'Only six weeks ago,' she said – and her voice had a touch of its old Liverpool—'did we go to that Black Madonna and the prayer's answered, see.'

Raymond looked at her in awe as he held the bowl for her sickness. 'Are you sure?' he said.

She was well enough next day to go to visit Henry in the sanatorium. He was fatter and, she thought, a little coarser: and tough in his manner, as if once having been nearly disembodied he was not going to let it happen again. He was leaving the country very soon. He promised to come and see them before he left. Lou barely skimmed through his next letter before handing it over to Raymond.

Their visitors, now, were ordinary white ones. 'No so colourful,' Raymond said, 'as Henry and Oxford were.' Then he looked embarrassed lest he should seem to be making a joke about the word coloured.

'Do you miss the niggers?' said Tina Farrell, and Lou forgot to correct her.

Lou gave up most of her church work in order to sew and knit for the baby. Raymond gave up the *Reader's Digest*. He applied for promotion and got it; he became a departmental manager. The flat was now a waiting-room for next summer, after the baby was born, when they would put down the money for a house. They hoped for one of the new houses on a building site on the outskirts of the town.

'We shall need a garden,' Lou explained to her friends. 'I'll join the Mothers' Union,' she thought. Meantime the spare bedroom was turned into a nursery. Raymond made a cot, regardless that some of the neighbours complained of the hammering. Lou prepared a cradle, trimmed it with frills. She wrote to her relatives; she wrote to Elizabeth, sent her five pounds, and gave notice that there would be no further weekly payments, seeing that they would now need every penny.

'She doesn't require it, anyway,' said Raymond. 'The Welfare State looks after people like Elizabeth.' And he told Lou about the contraceptives he thought he had seen on the table by the double bed. Lou became very excited about this. 'How did you know they were contraceptives? What did they look like? Why didn't you tell me before? What a cheek, calling herself a Catholic, do you think she has a man, then?'

Raymond was sorry he had mentioned the subject.

'Don't worry, dear, don't upset yourself, dear.'

'And she told me she goes to Mass every Sunday, and all the kids go excepting James. No wonder he's got into trouble with an example like that. I might have known, with her peroxide hair. A pound a week I've been sending up to now, that's fifty-two pounds a year. I would never have done it, calling herself a Catholic with birth control by her bedside.'

'Don't upset yourself, dear.'

Lou prayed to the Black Madonna three times a week for a safe delivery and a healthy child. She gave her story to the Father Rector who announced it in the next parish magazine. 'Another case has come to light of the kindly favour of our "Black Madonna" towards a childless couple . . .' Lou recited her rosary before the statue until it was difficult for her to kneel, and, when she stood, could not see her feet. The Mother of God with her black bog-oaken drapery, her high black cheekbones and square hands looked more virginal than ever to Lou as she stood counting her beads in front of her stomach.

She said to Raymond, 'If it's a girl we must have Mary as one of the names. But not the first name, it's too ordinary.'

'Please yourself, dear,' said Raymond. The doctor had told him it might be a difficult birth.

'Thomas, if it's a boy,' she said, 'after my uncle. But if it's a girl I'd like something fancy for a first name.'

He thought, Lou's slipping, she didn't used to say that word, fancy.

'What about Dawn?' she said. 'I like the sound of Dawn. Then Mary for a second name. Dawn Mary Parker, it sounds sweet.'

'Dawn! That's not a Christian name,' he said. Then he told her, 'Just as you please, dear.'

'Or Thomas Parker,' she said.

She had decided to go into the maternity wing of the hospital like everyone else. But near the time she let Raymond change her mind, since he kept saying, 'At your age dear, it might be more difficult than for the younger women. Better book a private ward, we'll manage the expense.'

In fact, it was a very easy birth, a girl. Raymond was allowed in to see Lou in the late afternoon. She was half asleep. 'The nurse will take you to see the baby in the nursery ward,' she told him. 'She's lovely, but terribly red.'

'They're always red at birth,' said Raymond.

He met the nurse in the corridor. 'Any chance of seeing the baby? My wife said . . .'

She looked flustered. 'I'll get the Sister,' she said.

'Oh, I don't want to give any trouble, only my wife said—'

'That's all right. Wait here, Mr Parker.'

The Sister appeared, a tall grave woman. Raymond thought her to be short-sighted for she seemed to look at him fairly closely before she bade him follow her.

The baby was round and very red, with dark curly hair.

'Fancy her having hair. I thought they were born bald,' said Raymond.

'They sometimes have hair at birth,' said the Sister.

'She's very red in colour.' Raymond began comparing his child with those in the other cots. 'Far more so than the others.'

'Oh, that will wear off.'

Next day he found Lou in a half-stupor. She had been given a strong sedative following an attack of screaming hysteria. He sat by her bed, bewildered. Presently a nurse beckoned him from the door. 'Will you have a word with Matron?'

'Your wife is upset about her baby,' said the matron. 'You see, the colour. She's a beautiful baby, perfect. It's a question of the colour.'

'I noticed the baby was red,' said Raymond, 'but the nurse said—'

'Oh, the red will go. It changes, you know. But the baby will certainly be brown, if not indeed black, as indeed we think she will be. A beautiful healthy child.'

'Black?' said Raymond.

'Yes, indeed we think so, indeed I must say, certainly so,' said the matron. 'We did not expect your wife to take it so badly when we told her. We've had plenty of dark babies here, but most of the mothers expect it.'

'There must be a mix-up. You must have mixed up the babies,' said Raymond.

'There's no question of mix-up,' said the matron sharply. 'We'll soon settle that. We've had some of *that* before.'

'But neither of us are dark,' said Raymond. 'You've seen my wife. You see me—'

'That's something you must work out for yourselves. I'd have a word with the doctor if I were you. But whatever conclusion you come to, please don't upset your wife at this stage. She has already refused to feed the child, says it isn't hers, which is ridiculous.'

'Was it Oxford St John?' said Raymond.

'Raymond, the doctor told you not to come here upsetting me. I'm feeling terrible.'

'Was it Oxford St John?'

'Clear out of here, you swine, saying things like that.'

He demanded to be taken to see the baby, as he had done every day for a week. The nurses were gathered round it, neglecting the squalling whites in the other cots for the sight of their darling black. She was indeed quite black, with a woolly crop and tiny negroid nostrils. She had been baptised that morning, though not in her parents' presence. One of the nurses had stood as godmother.

The nurses dispersed in a flurry as Raymond approached. He looked hard at the baby. It looked back with its black button eyes. He saw the name-tab round its neck, 'Dawn Mary Parker.'

He got hold of a nurse in the corridor. 'Look here, you just take that name Parker off that child's neck. The name's not Parker, it isn't my child.'

The nurse said, 'Get away, we're busy.'

'There's just a *chance*,' said the doctor to Raymond, 'that if there's ever been black blood in your family or your wife's, it's coming out now. It's a very long chance. I've never known it happen in my experience, but I've heard of cases, I could read them up.'

'There's nothing like that in my family,' said Raymond. He thought of Lou, the obscure Liverpool antecedents. The parents had died before he had met Lou.

'It could be several generations back,' said the doctor.

Raymond went home, avoiding the neighbours who would stop him to enquire after Lou. He rather regretted smashing up the cot in his first fury. That was something low coming out in him. But again, when he thought of the tiny black hands of the baby with their pink fingernails he did not regret smashing the cot.

He was successful in tracing the whereabouts of Oxford St John. Even before he heard the result of Oxford's blood test he said to Lou, 'Write and ask your relations if there's been any black blood in the family.'

'Write and ask *yours*,' she said.

She refused to look at the black baby. The nurses fussed round it all day, and came to report its progress to Lou.

'Pull yourself together, Mrs Parker, she's a lovely child.'

'You must care for your infant,' said the priest.

'You don't know what I'm suffering,' Lou said.

'In the name of God,' said the priest, 'if you're a Catholic Christian you've got to expect to suffer.'

'I can't go against my nature,' said Lou. 'I can't be expected to—'

Raymond said to her one day in the following week, 'The blood tests are all right, the doctor says.'

'What do you mean, all right?'

'Oxford's blood and the baby's don't tally, and—'

'Oh, shut up,' she said. 'The baby's black and your blood tests can't make it white.'

'No,' he said. He had fallen out with his mother, through his enquiries whether there had been coloured blood in his family. 'The doctor says,' he said, 'that these black mixtures sometimes occur in seaport towns. It might have been generations back.'

'One thing,' said Lou. 'I'm not going to take that child back to the flat.'

'You'll have to,' he said.

Elizabeth wrote her a letter which Raymond intercepted:

'Dear Lou Raymond is asking if we have any blacks in the family well thats funny you have a coloured God is not asleep. There was that Flinn cousin Tommy at Liverpool he was very dark they put it down to the past a nigro off a ship that would be before our late Mothers Time God rest her soul she would turn in her grave you should have kept up your bit to me whats a pound a Week to you. It was on our fathers side the colour and Mary Flinn you remember at the dairy was dark remember her hare was like nigro hare it must be back in the olden days the nigro some ancester but it is only nature. I thank the almighty it has missed my kids and your hubby must think it was that nigro you was showing off when you came to my place. I wish you all the best as a widow with kids you shoud send my money as per usual your affec sister Elizabeth.'

'I gather from Elizabeth,' said Raymond to Lou, 'that there *was* some element of colour in your family. Of course, you couldn't be expected to know about it. I do think, though, that some kind of record should be kept.'

'Oh, shut *up*,' said Lou. 'The baby's black and nothing can make it white.'

Two days before Lou left the hospital she had a visitor, although she had given instructions that no one except Raymond should be let in to see her. This lapse she attributed to the nasty curiosity of the nurses, for it was Henry Pierce come to say goodbye before embarkation. He stayed less than five minutes.

'Why, Mrs Parker, your visitor didn't stay long,' said the nurse.

'No, I soon got rid of him. I thought I made it clear to you that I didn't want to see anyone. You shouldn't have let him in.'

'Oh, sorry, Mrs Parker, but the young gentleman looked so upset when we told him so. He said he was going abroad and it was his last chance, he might never see you again. He said, "How's the baby?" and we said, "Tip-top".'

'I know what's in your mind,' said Lou. 'But it isn't true. I've got the blood tests.'

'Oh, Mrs Parker, I wouldn't suggest for a minute . . .'

'She must have went with one of they niggers that used to come.'

Lou could never be sure if that was what she heard from the doorways and landings as she climbed the stairs of Cripps House, the neighbours hushing their conversation as she approached.

'I can't take to the child. Try as I do, I simply can't even like it.'

'Nor me,' said Raymond. 'Mind you, if it was anyone else's child I would think it was all right. It's just the thought of it being mine, and people thinking it isn't.'

'That's just it,' she said.

One of Raymond's colleagues had asked him that day how his friends Oxford and Henry were getting on. Raymond had to look twice before he decided that the question was innocent. But one never knew. . . . Already Lou and Raymond had approached the adoption society. It was now only a matter of waiting for word.

'If that child was mine,' said Tina Farrell, 'I'd never part with her. I wish we could afford to adopt another. She's the loveliest little darkie in the world.'

'You wouldn't think so,' said Lou, 'if she really was yours. Imagine it for yourself, waking up to find you've had a black baby that everyone thinks has a nigger for its father.'

'It *would* be a shock,' Tina said, and tittered.

'We've got the blood tests,' said Lou quickly.

Raymond got a transfer to London. They got word about the adoption very soon.

'We've done the right thing,' said Lou. 'Even the priest had to agree with that, considering how strongly we felt against keeping the child.'

'Oh, he said it was a good thing?'

'No, not a *good* thing. In fact he said it would have been a good thing if we could have kept the baby. But failing that, we did the *right* thing. Apparently there's a difference.'

George Friel

The pernicious influence of poverty is a recurring theme in George Friel's work. It crushes out life and traps whole communities in a debilitating cycle of failures and retreats.

George Friel (1910–75), never forgot his origins. He had grown up as one of seven children in a tenement on the Maryhill Road in Glasgow. His short stories and novels are rooted in the darker side of that reality and a very personal lack of hope for the future. 'Onlookers' is no glowing stairheid fantasy. It captures minutely the small-minded, self-obsessed life in a neighbourhood where the demarcation lines are strictly drawn between opposite sides of the street, or even between one close and the next.

Friel, the English teacher, cared deeply about the use and usefulness of language and became increasingly bitter as he saw how society contrived to take the means of communication from those who seem to need it most. Thus the action and atmosphere of 'Onlookers' rests on a use of language which is both chillingly incisive and evocative, while the tenement dwellers are left to communicate in clichés and gestures borrowed from the cinema.

Onlookers

BEFORE THE newlyweds moved in, the single apartment looking on to the main road was occupied by a man and his wife who fought every night. Regularly, just after midnight, the woman's screeching harangue was heard rising above the deep growling of her husband, and their only child squalled in unheeded terror. The whole block lay wakened in darkness, waiting the climax. After the rumble of overturned furniture came the sharp report of hurtled crockery breaking against the wall, and then the woman's loud wails. The neighbours lived in expectation of murder, and with heterosexual sympathy the gossiping wives blamed the woman for provoking the poor man and not knowing when to hold her tongue. Unfriended and unregretted, the quarrelsome couple moved after four months, and the tenement looked forward to peace at midnight again and sleep unbroken by the noise of battle going on till two and three o'clock in the morning.

The newcomers were different. The neighbours were sure they would never quarrel outrageously, for Mrs Gannaway and her husband were clearly suited to each other, agreeably placid in temperament. And Mr Gannaway had a small tobacconist and newsagent's shop, on the same side of the street as his house. Because of his attentiveness, it was always busy, steadily gaining trade from the muddled stores kept by slovenly old women in the district. So his wife would never need to quarrel with him about money, as her predecessor in the single apartment had done with her husband, a man who had never worked.

The tenement returned to tranquillity then, and although Mrs Gannaway did not gossip with the neighbours and had no confidant among them, they had nothing against her. They saw her as a slow-moving, dreamy young woman, who smiled readily with a vague friendliness. And from the cut and cloth and number of her husband's suits, as well as from the changes in costume she had herself, they considered the newlyweds were quietly prosperous, free from the worry over money which obsessed everyone else in the tenement.

But slowly the matrons began to see something more than a leisurely content in Mrs Gannaway's slow walk and more than the happiness of an unworried bride in her bright colour. Mrs Higney declared that the young wife was consumptive, and before long all the wives in the block were taking her guess as a statement of fact, a statement made years ago by somebody, long forgotten, who had known it as a certainty. Within the year, Mrs Higney was proved correct. After a doctor had visited her for a month, Mrs Gannaway went to Ruchill Hospital, across on the north bank of the canal, to the sanatorium there for consumptives.

Mr Gannaway stayed on in the single apartment alone, attended more industriously than ever to his shop, and greeted his neighbours with brief politeness. His small business went on improving, and he increased its stock, throwing into contempt the paltry holdings of the old wives who had kept similar shops in the district long before him. Walking the few hundred yards from his shop to his home, he had the air of a man who knows he is doing well because he deserves to. His greetings to the neighbours he passed had in them something of tolerance for the shiftless and condescension to the unsuccessful, and he never mentioned his wife. As a result, the women on his own side of the street were not quite sure if they liked him or not; they were not quite sure if he were callous and secretive, or just naturally a man of few words.

But before she had been much longer than a month away, Mrs Gannaway came back from the sanatorium and slept alone every night on a long couch placed against the window, which was opened wide at top and bottom. And she rested. She rested all day. Peeping discreetly behind their curtains, the housewives on the other side of the street watched her and her husband at the window of the single apartment, and discussed with each other all they saw, alluding to it casually as if they had seen it just by accident.

Then at night, the tenement was again kept awake by a disturbance in the single apartment, less violent than it had suffered from the quarrelling of the couple who had previously lived there, and with none of its screaming terror. But it had a horror all its own, and aroused the neighbours more intermittently. It was the sound of the young wife coughing, and the way it seemed to choke and rack her made them shudder and turn round with the blankets pulled over their ears. Sometimes, when she was at her worst, she had barely time to recover her breath from one attack before she was in the grip of another, coughing harshly all through the night. And once they were sure she was as good as dead. A fit of coughing at three o'clock in the morning faded away in an exhausted rattling in her throat, and in the little brick boxes around and across from her the tenement-dwellers stared unsleepingly into darkness, waiting and wondering. But then they heard another spasm seize her, showing by its vigour that she was still very much alive. Some nights they heard an especially lengthy paroxysm end in a long low moaning, as if she were weeping.

'That's terrible!' muttered Mrs Higney. 'You'd think it was tearing her inside right out, the way it comes. She'll kill herself some night, coughing like that.'

And the woman in the little dairy down the street, which opened at six o'clock in the morning and served the early-rising matrons with rolls and milk, began to ask regularly, as a ritual greeting to her customers, 'Did you hear her last night? I think she's getting worse.'

'There was once I thought she had burst something,' the customer would answer. 'It seemed to be sort of wrenching her apart.'

'That cough alone,' said the dairywoman, 'would be enough to kill anybody. It's something awful.'

But as if to confute their pessimism and reject their robust sympathy, Mrs Gannaway began to get better. She coughed less often at night, and she began to get up oftener and go out for a walk. For nearly three months she seemed to improve, and the neighbours were almost forgetting she had ever been ill. Then, as if just idling for a few days, she returned to her couch alongside the window and lay there unmoving. She began to cough again at night, with fiercely concentrated attacks that left her gasping. But the neighbours had heard worse from her before, and insensitive to it by custom, they heard it drowsily only as a minor spasm and fell unworriedly asleep. And while they slept, Mrs Gannaway coughed despairingly on, coughed as if she were fighting to suppress it, with something apologetic in it all, until the attack won out in its full deathful insistence and left her helplessly panting in exhaustion, her head lolling over the edge of the couch.

Three weeks after she took to her bed again, early in a morning of April when the clear spring sunlight slanted over the tall tenements of the main road and made its tram-railed broadness seem clean and joyous, she died at the window while her husband, risen from his bed in the other corner of the room, sat on a chair beside her, chafing her hands in a panic.

'She's dead,' said the dairywoman to her first customer at six o'clock, so impatient to tell the news that she could not wait to hear the customer's order.

The stout, slippered matron who had come in for a dozen rolls and a pint of milk gaped in disbelief as she had seen film actresses do, and slowly said, 'But I thought she was getting better.'

'You should have heard her last night, just before she died,' said the dairywoman, nodding her head wisely to hint at all her customer had missed. And to every customer who came in that morning she said at once, 'Did you hear Mrs Gannaway was dead?' And every customer gaped a while and then slowly said, 'But I thought she was getting better.'

The funeral took place the following afternoon, and three deep against the kerb on both sides of the street the neighbours stood impatiently waiting for the coffin to be brought down to the hearse.

'There's nearly as big a crowd here as there was the time they buried the man Reid,' said Mrs Higney, looking round approvingly. 'You remember he cut his throat.'

With increasing boldness the matrons on the Gannaways' side of the street discussed Mr Gannaway with whispering hostility, their heads nodding in agreement as they listened to each other.

'If he had only cared to spend some money on her,' said Mrs Higney in low-voiced righteousness. 'God knows he could afford to. It's a wee Klondyke, that shop of his. But damn the ha'penny he ever spent to try and help the poor girl.'

'Imagine keeping her there in a single apartment,' whispered Mrs Farquhar. 'How did he ever expect any woman to get better in that place? Why, she hadn't even room to move!'

'He could easy have got her a better house than that,' said Mrs Stevenson, supportingly. 'A single apartment, on the money he's making in that shop! Just shows you how some folks'll put up with anything to save a shilling or two.'

'Aye, as long as they're all right,' said Mrs Higney. 'And damn the rest! And she came back from the sanatorium, where she might have stayed in comfort, just to do her duty as a wife. Fine way he showed his appreciation, letting her stick in that pokey wee place!'

'Even the other side of the street would have been better,' said Mrs Martin. 'We just get the sun for a couple of hours in the morning. They get it all the rest of the time over there.'

'The other side of the street!' cried Mrs Higney contemptuously. 'He could have got her a place in the country. But he never had a thought for that poor girl. All he could think of was his shop, his shop, all the time.'

'He was always running back there,' said Mrs Farquhar. 'He couldn't stay at home in peace with his wife. Afraid he'd miss a penny or two, maybe. Some husband he was, leaving her alone like that.'

'What kind of a life had she?' demanded Mrs Stevenson. 'Cooped up there in a single-end all day, with nobody to keep her company or give her a helping hand.'

'And he was never up nor down about it,' said Mrs Martin. 'Always the same smug smile when he passed you. Too sweet to be wholesome. And her there, hardly fit to raise a hand. She'd have been better staying in the sanatorium away from him, for all the attention she got when she was trying to do her best for him.'

'You'd never have thought his wife lay dying, to look at him,' said Mrs Farquhar. 'But that poor girl knew it. You could see she knew it.'

Over on the other side of the street, the matrons who, peeping behind their curtains, had watched the Gannaways at the window of the single apartment across from them, stood silently waiting. Then slowly, like the ripples in water caused by a thrown stone, talk moved among them in whispers.

'I'm sorry for that poor man,' said Mrs Houston. 'He must have had a terrible life with her. I've seen him at that window washing dishes.'

'Washing dishes!' cried Mrs Lennie. 'He did all the cooking and cleaning in that house. He even sewed on his own buttons.'

'She sat there all day doing nothing,' said Mrs Buchanan. 'Surely she could have done some wee thing for the man. But not a hand's turn did she ever do. She'd have been better staying in the sanatorium, instead of coming back to be a hindrance.'

'Oh, it wasn't good enough for her,' said Mrs Plottel. 'She was so sure she could do it all at home. Rest, says she. Rest and fresh air, that's all the treatment they give you. So she came back and slept there with those windows wide open. Quite content to let that poor fellow look after her, when there were proper nurses for her in Ruchill. What kind of a life had he?'

'Maybe he's better without her,' said Mrs Lennie. 'She had to go, sooner or later. And she was no wife to him. A wife only in name. He did all the housework. He even served her with her meals, and she slept alone on that couch every night.'

'And all day too,' said Mrs Houston. 'He had to get his brother to look after the shop for him. He was always running up from it to attend to her. And you never saw him complain. Always put a pleasant face on it. He took it well, that man. There's not many men would have even bothered with a sick wife the way he was.'

'Well, they can't say he wasn't good to her,' said Mrs Buchanan. 'He gave her every attention. He wanted her to leave that single apartment and take a house outside the city. But not she! She said she'd miss the view on to the main road.'

'I know he was never done giving her money,' said Mrs Houston. 'Do you know, a week before she died he gave her five pounds he won on a horse. And what do you think she did? She bought herself a fine new dress. It'll do me in the summer, says she!'

'It just shows you,' said Mrs Buchanan. 'They never believe they're bad, these consumptives . . . Look, there he is now!'

Bearing the front right-hand corner of the pall, Mr Gannaway came through the close. When the coffin was placed in the hearse, he turned with his brother and opened the door of the first carriage. Letting his brother enter first, he pulled out a handkerchief and blew his nose, fumbling as he did so to brush a corner of the linen over his eyes. Then, round-shouldered and head down, he went in beside his brother.

'That poor man!' whispered Mrs Houston. 'It's really better for him as it is, a young man like him, with all his life before him. And yet he feels it just the same. Did you see him wipe his eyes?'

'Did you see that?' whispered Mrs Higney. 'Wiping his eyes so as everybody can see him! Aye, it's easy to cry when it's too late. If he had only thought more about her when she was living, maybe she wouldn't be dead the day. A young woman like her, with all her life before her.'

Ronald Frame

Though he was born and brought up in Glasgow, Ronald Frame (b.1953) has moved his fictions beyond the city. His short stories and novels can boast an international selection of backdrops.

His prose is crisp, precise and well suited to his territory—the thoughts and dreams beneath a social façade and the constant tension between outward appearance and internal reality of each individual. Frame's characters are lonely and seem to move through a world of unspoken rules which are ready to be enforced at any moment. Beyond them all is a harsher and inescapable natural law.

In 'Paris', the two Glasgow spinsters are relics of a city and a way of living which has almost entirely disappeared. Through them we see the effects of the social and moral controls which still have a silent but powerful influence on polite Scottish society.

Their self-deception and in many ways destructive gentility allows us to consider the opportunities missed in every life and the very real courage it can take to face each day.

Paris

MISS CALDWELL was the smarter of the pair. At one time customers would tell her she looked like Rosalind Russell. Even in retirement she had kept her figure (with difficulty) and always wore a turban (in the French style) and good accessories and shoes. 'Shoes are a person's give-away,' she liked to say, speaking from her experience as a fashion buyer in one of the last of the great Glasgow stores in Sauchiehall Street, which had closed its doors at the tail-end of the 'sixties.

Miss McLeod wasn't so meticulous in her appearance, she chose to think she was more 'discreet'. She used to be a teacher in the prep department of a private boys' school in town and for years she'd worn a sexless black gown over her outfits, so variety hadn't mattered. She hadn't dared to change her ways since then and she dressed now as she'd always done, mutely and respectably, because she never knew when she might spot one of her old pupils in the West End, or be spotted by one of them unbeknown. Somehow she felt she owed it to them, not to seem any different from how they must remember her.

Miss Caldwell and Miss McLeod had met in the late 'sixties, as recently retired ladies and as habituées of Miss Barclay's tea-room in Byres Road. Before their introduction they'd each had a partner to have their coffee with, until at about the same time of one never-to-be-forgotten year they'd been abandoned—Miss Caldwell's fellow-buyer (from Wylie and Lochhead) had inexplicably been wooed by an elderly manufacturer of ball-bearings and married him and gone to live in a nice trim seaside bungalow in Largs; Miss McLeod's friend, who'd been a teacher like her (at the Academy), had returned at sixty-four years old to her calf-country in the windy Mearns—leaving the two Misses, Caldwell and McLeod, seated high-and-dry at adjoining tables and with no one in that roomful of spinsters to speak to.

It was an excellent accident which brought them together, the waitress in starched white linen muddling one's sponge eiffel tower with the other's french fancy. With a gracious wave of her hand and in a throaty voice Miss Caldwell had invited the quietly spoken, bespectacled, beanpole Miss McLeod to join her at her (superior) table in the narrow window wedge of the noisy, high-ceiling'd triangular room. That morning and all the Tuesday and Friday mornings that followed they got on pleasantly enough, just chatting about this and that. It turned out that they hadn't a vast amount in common—Miss Caldwell watched television, Miss McLeod listened to the radio; Miss Caldwell read the *Glasgow Herald*, Miss McLeod the London *Telegraph*. Something else happened to bind them, though. About the third month of the arrangement (they'd learned meanwhile to avoid the topics of television and radio, and referred hardly at all to their different reading) they simultaneously began—consciously, but neither admitting it—to slightly elaborate on what they'd both found they liked to discuss best, themselves.

Miss McLeod 'borrowed' the grandfather of a long-lost friend she'd done her teacher-training with to talk about, a colossal bushy-bearded man who'd been an artist in Paris: that way she felt she could expound with impunity on one of her great interests, Fine Art. Miss Caldwell, who sometimes suspected Miss McLeod dwelled too much on cerebral matters, invented a life which had her working in London in the 1930s, in an up-market store in Regent Street. She hadn't been so lucky, of course, but her stories about 'customers'—Nancy Cunard, Margot Asquith, Lady Mountbatten—sounded quite authentic when she recounted them from gossip she'd picked up from old-hands in the Glasgow store's staff rooms.

'Once Marlene Dietrich came in. Did you know she always travelled with thirty-two pieces of luggage? There was a film on television, on "Saturday Matinee", what was it called? "Shanghai Something"—'

When her memory faltered on a person or a place in her 'past' she was describing, then Miss McLeod (ever on the look-out through the steamy windows of Miss Barclay's for her boys of years ago) took her cue and struck up again about 'her' grandfather's years of exile from Scotland in fin-de-siècle Paris. Every time the city was mentioned Miss Caldwell, resembling one of the mannequins she talked about in her toning fawns and beiges and velvet turbans, would echo the word, 'Ah, *Paris*!', with her own interpretation of what it meant. When it was her turn to speak again she told Miss McLeod, who found it so hard to concentrate on such things and remember them, about the hundreds and thousands of French couturiers' wonders smothered in tissue paper she'd unwrapped from bandboxes in the shops that had been her life. To save the situation, Miss McLeod, awkward in her heather tweeds and oversized cameo brooches and her stout shoes that had a way of pinching her feet however sensible they looked, recited some more odds and ends of information she'd read about Parisian intellectual life in the 1890s.

'I'd love to go!' exclaimed Miss Caldwell in her pan-loaf front-of-shop vowels, 'wouldn't you?' Miss McLeod nodded and replied in her more sedate Kelvinside teaching voice, 'Paris in the springtime! It must be a sight worth seeing!' (Both felt rather sorry for having admitted so candidly in the early days of their friendship that, for all the places they claimed they had visited, they'd never been to lovely, immortal Paris on the Seine.)

Paris was often discussed, the word 'holiday' would crop up, yet they resisted being drawn into any of the half-dozen travel agents they passed leaving Miss Barclay's after coffee on their two social mornings a week.

They each thought they had their reasons. Miss Caldwell considered that her pension from the store was a little less generous than she might have expected after thirty years of service, and it was hard going keeping herself presentably dressed and stocked up with cosmetics, never mind indulging in foreign adventures. For her part Miss McLeod felt that being seen to be 'careful' with her funds gave her a sort of moral advantage as well as a modicum of mystery, qualities she believed she needed since she so patently lacked her companion's somewhat jaded elegance and style.

By tacit consent Paris remained for them how it had been all along—conveniently in the abstract—and they continued with their stories, retelling them with even more vigour as the months and seasons slipped by. Miss Caldwell talked with glee and much waving of her paste rings about the two elderly sisters who lived on the other side of Atholl Gardens from her, one of whom in middle age had decided on impulse to marry; and after the happy day and the wedding night, had returned the next morning to her sister's flat, suitcases in the taxi, and had never spoken to nor as much as set eyes on her husband in the eighteen years since. Miss McLeod's favourite story sounded more forced and even less likely: she said there was a man of ninety-five living near her in Huntly Gardens, who stayed in his flat alone but set eight places at his dining-table for dinner and ate his solitary evening meal with the members of his long-dead family for company; his windows were lit into the night as he played his wind-up gramophone and walked endless circles round the table and eight empty chairs.

In one sense the two ladies knew they weren't so very different themselves, although they pretended to be with their talk of London and fashion designers who were once well known and that coterie of accomplished painters the critics called the 'Glasgow Boys'. They were both unhappily—if hazily—aware of what was happening to them: that they were becoming afraid of real life and becoming more and more apart from it with the years. They never spoke of their shared fate: it was a truth too awful to encompass properly, encountered so late in the day as this, and neither of them dared to come too close to it, to hazard to that edge. So they held back and didn't speak of it and tried to appear content with the ritual as it had developed: continuing from week to week to week to steer the same wary circle around each other, forfeiting direct questions, working on instincts and imagined knowledge for the sake of harmony, each to preserve her own secrets, the little white lies.

Bizarrely it had taken them both a year and a half just to discover what the other's first name was. At last they'd found out an address too—extracted from countless hints and clues—and several times they'd individually tracked their way under cover of darkness and stood on mushy leaves under dripping trees in a sooty square to spy, but neither had invited the other to her home or could have contemplated it. There was a vague suggestion that Miss Caldwell's flat was filled with Hartnell and Balenciaga creations bought at cost price, and drawers of exotic turbans and gloves, and racks of shoes too good to soil on Glasgow's pot-holed streets; it was never established that on Miss McLeod's walls did *not* hang a gallery of inherited canvases by expensive artists which museums and salerooms would have fought with their claws to get hold of.

Miss Barclay's tea-room closed when the tenement building was scheduled to come down, and they tried other places: a Scandinavian smorgasbord room with dwarf log stools that gave them cramp, the Curler's Arms (nice, with wood fires—but sometimes there'd be a beery smell from the night before), then some of the little healthfood shops that opened up, which served thoughtful food but vile decaffeinated coffee with no taste. Miss McLeod suggested the Grosvenor Hotel on Great Western Road, and Miss Caldwell—anxious about the possible expense with the summer sales coming up—confected a tale she often repeated that season, to do with a man who'd once betrayed her by not showing up for a rendezvous. By way of reply Miss McLeod embellished a story about 'Alistair', who'd actually been her deceased sister's young man years ago, but it was left to Miss Caldwell to presume that *she* had been the object of his affections. 'Yes, I've had my chances all right,' they each told the other wistfully. And talked of Paris again—home of artistic genius and of Chanel's little black suit and that young whizz-kid Saint Laurent—and they agreed how wonderful it must be to live in such a place where romance was the very air you breathed.

Eventually, by mutual agreement, their two shared mornings a week were spent in the upstairs tea-room in the Art Galleries, that awesome edifice with a silhouette like giant red sandstone sugar sifters. Getting there involved a hike across Kelvingrove Park, but the subsidised cost of the coffee meant more to Miss Caldwell than the price of Rayne's shoe leather and although Miss McLeod knew that little parties from her old school regularly paraded the galleries of sculpture and Impressionist masterpieces under the supervision of those pert young wives in polo-necks and sling-backs who made teachers nowadays and who'd taken her place, she felt the walk down past the Gothic university with its turrets and steeples and the atmosphere of learning and 'mind' inside the Art Galleries somehow gave her a spiritual authority to compensate for her rather dowdy appearance, which no amount of effort seemed able to rectify.

They would amble round the exhibition rooms after their two coffees and one empire biscuit apiece. Miss Caldwell walked with majestic slowness and the semblance of keen attention—but didn't like to miss a chance to study herself in the glass panels in the frames. Miss McLeod screwed up her eyes behind her spectacles and memorised the artists' names on the plaques for later reference. In the French Room they stopped by the pretty Parisian views—Miss Caldwell (seeing through herself) claimed she liked the 'smudgy' Impressionist ones best, but wasn't able to remember a word of Miss McLeod's painstaking lectures from the times before, about the difference between Manet and Monet for instance. The two of them peered at Paris (Miss Caldwell carefully noting her reflection afloat over the images), they sat down on the benches to reflect, they grew almost tearfully nostalgic for the city neither had visited. (Now they each wished they hadn't confessed as much at the beginning but had left the matter open, as if it might seem they'd happened never to have mentioned the fact . . .)

One fateful day they stayed on for lunch in the Art Galleries and in the afternoon took the bus into town and went to the Glasgow Cinematheque (they preferred to call it by its former name, the 'Cally' cinema) and there (with OAP tickets) they settled down to watch *The Umbrellas of Cherbourg*, announced at the doors as part of something called a 'Jacques Demy Retrospective'. Cherbourg wasn't Paris, of course, but they'd come prepared to accept it as a substitute. Not that the closeness or not of the resemblance greatly concerned them when the lights dimmed in the over-heated auditorium. For they discovered with a most unpleasant shock that they weren't educated to suffer the conditions of modern film-watching. They didn't care for this seedy, heavy-breathing mid-afternoon clientele, not one bit. Glasgow wasn't what it was, they agreed in loud whispers. A woman with cropped hair and wearing a black plastic jacket kept watching them and a young couple in the darkness behind groaned grossly like animals. Miss Caldwell was too doubtful to venture into the 'Ladies' even and came out at the end feeling her finery was contaminated with the lives they'd been sitting so close to and also aware of a damp sensation at the tops of her legs; Miss McLeod emerged behind her into the cruel daylight of Sauchiehall Street, trembling like an aspen leaf, her legs scarcely able to support her, sick to the pit of her stomach, quite positive she'd recognised an old pupil at last, sitting in one of the rows in front with his arm wrapped caressingly around another man's shoulders.

1981's was a savage winter. Snow lay eighteen inches deep in Kelvingrove Park. Miss Caldwell in layers of outdated woollens huddled over a one-bar electric fire in her cavernous first-floor sitting-room. Listening to the radio in her gaunt damp flat, Miss McLeod was almost sure she heard the announcer say the name of her teacher-friend who'd returned to Aberdeenshire when he read out a news item about a woman having been snowed in and dying in a black-out. With this terrible new sadness to bear and no way of confirming it (the newsagent's was at the world's end), she lost much of her own will to live this winter out. Through the icy windows Huntley Gardens was like an arctic wilderness, beyond saving. A pipe had burst in the kitchen, now another split in the bathroom; the gas went funny and wouldn't light, she ran out of matches to try; the radio battery faded to nothing, and she retired without hope to bed, her head humming with memories. She'd exhausted the supplies of food in her larder, was too proud to use her phone to summon help and died of pneumonia and starvation in the course of three long days and nights when the snows blown from Greenland blizzarded across Glasgow's genteel West End and transformed it into a frozenly beautiful winter composition by Sisley or Pissarro.

To Miss Caldwell's surprise, weeks after the funeral and when the last of the snow had melted away, an envelope embossed with the address of a lawyer's office dropped through her letter-box. She picked it up, turned it over. She braved the cold in the kitchen and made herself a cup of instant coffee—she didn't go out now, she'd forgotten the taste of the real thing—and she postponed opening the envelope till she'd extricated all the excitement she thought she could stand. When she slit the gummed flap with a knife and unfolded the letter inside to read it, she wasn't disappointed by its news. Coming quickly to the point, her correspondent informed her that, after numerous gifts to family cousins, Miss Montague McLeod had stipulated in her will a bequest to be made to her, for a sum of £500.

Two or three days later, when she'd recovered from the shock, Miss Caldwell found her thoughts were turning again and again to an imagined version of Paris, which they'd spoken of so often and so fondly together. She even dreamed of the paintings in the galleries, sleeping slumped over her *Glasgow Herald*. She wondered once or twice if it could be a message from 'beyond'. Quite by chance she saw Perry Como on television singing 'April in Paris'; and the same week a holiday programme did a feature on bargain spring holidays in the city.

One chilly morning with a blue sky she donned a turban (black, out of respect) and a heavy tweed coat (belted and edged with white fur on the cuffs, so very different from the one her late friend used to wear) and walked down busy Byres Road—taking constant note of the state of frost on the slippery pavements—to one of the travel agents. (I do it as my own tribute to a remembered friendship, she persuaded herself.) In the brochures the assistant gave her which she took back home to read, she thought everyone in the illustrations of Paris looked so young. There were hardly any elderly people at all to be seen. It concerned her a little bit that no one in the photographs wore the same sort of clothes as hers or appeared to take the pains about dressing that she did.

Another blue morning with another blue sky overhead she took a brisk walk to a smart little complex of mews shops behind Byres Road, with a purpose already fixed in her mind. It was spring sale time, in one of the boutiques she knew what she would find: a rail of half-price couturier dresses. Inside, positioned at the rail, she only looked at the ones with Paris labels. She found those that were her own size and selected one in festive red jersey wool, with a pleated skirt and a gilt belt and a cowl neck to conceal her least flattering feature. In the mirror, walking like the restaurant mannequins of her working years, she thought they did each other justice, she and the dress. She was conscious of other shoppers interrupting their foraging just to look at her.

She paid for the dress and left the shop carrying it in a splendid silver-coloured plastic bag. On her way home she went into a building society office and opened an account for the £400 left from the lawyer's cheque. It would be a nice little nest egg, she told herself: something put away—plus interest. For a rainy day. For when the bills became even harder to pay. She reflected that sometimes—very occasionally—a little madness was permissible, like the dress: but prudence was safer, in the long run. Nest eggs and rainy days, for when the bills became headaches you went to bed with and woke up with. Such is life, being canny, sensible. If I doubt it, she explained to herself for consolation's sake, think of my friend Monty McLeod, obviously so careful with her money.

Finishing her business in the building society, she noticed the cashier looking at her swanky bag. 'I'm going to a wedding,' she told him, unable to help herself.

She walked back outside through the revolving smoked glass doors, into what was left of the blue frosty morning, disturbed at her untruth. (Her radar set her on the right track home, and she walked automatically.) Even the sun shining now wasn't able to lift her spirits. Her good sense—the red dress and the lie about the wedding excepted—made her feel despondent. When on earth *would* she wear the dress?

Safely past the Grosvenor Hotel and temptation, her legs slowed. Suddenly she felt a panicky fear at the cargo in her bag; she *feared* it, the dress, wrapped like treasure in green tissue paper. (She wanted to smile and shrug her shoulders, she couldn't.) But what she feared even more she realised was still to come, and it was worse than dying in the street could be or hearing a ghost at her shoulder. She envied Monty McLeod her escape, envied her it bitterly. Oblivion couldn't be worse than that ice-box bedroom at the back of the flat and the bleak lightbulb in the fringed shade.

Or maybe—could it have been—she'd intended to help her, her Tuesday and Friday friend whose appalling end had been reported on the front page of the *Herald*, the money gifted to her was supposed to be buying her some comfort?

She continued to walk but slowing her steps still more, to allow the thought to register. It was coming to her, as all important things had a way of doing, out of the blue. She took advantage of the pause to draw her breath and looked down at her silver carrier-bag.

She was remembering something: waking in her armchair one night and hearing the man on the God-slot saying 'It's the mysteries that save us.'

Half-way along Grosvenor Terrace, in the middle of the pot-holed pavement, she stood considering the words. *It's the mysteries that save us.*

Would her friend have known and been able to tell her what the 'mysteries' were? Or could you only discover for yourself?

Did a 'mystery' need to be religious? What about—even— pirouetting for the tarnished oval of mirror in the wardrobe: could that possibly count? Or having a catnap dream in her big comfy armchair? Looking at pretty, 'smudgy' pictures on a gallery wall? Joining in the silly words of a song and hearing Perry Como with a voice like maple syrup say it was called 'the cork-popping Champagne City'?

James Kelman

NOT NOT WHILE THE GIRO

Kelman's landscapes will be familiar to anyone who knows the inner cities, their housing schemes, wastelands and tenement buildings. He was born in Glasgow, in 1946, and has mostly lived there, so he writes with a Glasgow accent, in much the same way as William Faulkner wrote with an accent. But Kelman's world is far from mystical. It is often all too real, not to mention realistic.

Other Scots have portrayed working class life, but no one has done it so faithfully. Kelman is writing from within, and so strong is this first sympathy that you feel he must have experienced what he writes about, even if the character in question is twice his age. In this way he has given a voice to the inarticulate, making art out of their everyday life and work, and, most especially, out of a faithful representation of their speech. If his subject matter is more or less the same, his approach is varied. He uses irony, satire, humour and a strong even a surreal sense of the absurd, and at best, Kelman's stories mirror Chekhov's dictum that a short story should be a glance; we glimpse something while passing, and from that glance we are able to tell what came before and what will come after. He has devised a way of conveying the consciousness of his characters, even though their emotional states may be a secret from themselves.

Not not while the giro

of tea so I can really enjoy this 2nd last smoke which will be very very strong which is of course why I drink tea with it in a sense to counteract the harm it must do my inners. Not that tea cures cancer poisoning or even guards against nicotine—helps unclog my mouth a little. Maybe it doesnt. My mouth tastes bad. Hot and kind of squelchy. I am smoking too much old tobacco. 2nd hand tobacco is stiff, is burnt ochre in colour and you really shudder before spluttering on the 1st drag. But this is supposed to relieve the craving for longer periods. Maybe it does. It makes no difference anyway, you still smoke them 1 after the other because what happens if you suddenly come into a few quid or fresh tobacco—you cant smoke 2nd hand stuff with the cashinhand and there isnt much chance of donating it to fucking charity. So you smoke rapidly. I do—even with fresh tobacco.

But though the tea is gone I can still enjoy the long smoke. A simple enjoyment, and without guilt. I am wasting time. I am to perambulate to a distant broo. I shall go. I always go. No excuse now it has gone. And it may be my day for the spotcheck at the counter. Rain pours heavily. My coat is in the fashion of yesteryear but I am wearing it. How comes this coat to be with me yet. Not a question although it bears reflecting upon at some later date. Women may have something to do with it. Probably not, that cannot be correct. Anyway, it has nothing to do with anything.

I set myself small tasks, ordeals; for instance: Come on ya bastard ye and smoke your last, then see how your so-called will fucking power stands up. Eh! Naw, you wont do that. Of course I wont, but such thoughts often occur. I may or may not smoke it. And if it does come down to will power how the hell can I honestly say I have any—when circumstances are as they are. Could begin smacking of self pity shortly if this last continues. No, yesteryear's coat is not my style. Imitation Crombies are unbecoming these days, particularly the kind with narrow lapels. This shrewd man I occasionally have dealings with refused said coat on the grounds of said lapels rendering the coat an undesired object by those who frequent said man's premises. Yet I would have reckoned most purchasers of 2nd hand clothing to be wholly unaware of fashions current or olden. But I have faith in him. He does fine. Pawnshops could be nationalized. What a shock for the small-trader. What next that's what we'd like to know, the corner bloody shop I suppose. Here that's not my line of thought at all. Honest to god, right hand up that the relative strength of the freethinkers is neither here nor there. All we ask is to play up and play the game. Come on you lot, shake hands etcetera. Jesus what is this at all. Fuck all to do with perambulations to the broo.

Last smoke between my lips, right then. Fire flicked off, the last colour gone from the bar. Bastarn rain. The Imitation Crombie. And when I look at myself in the mirror I can at least blow smoke in my face. Also desperately needing a pish. Been holding it in for ages by the feel of things. Urinary infections too, they are caused by failing to empty the bladder completely ie. cutting a long pish short and not what's the word—flicking the chopper up and down to get rid of the drips. Particularly if one chances to be uncircumcised. Not at all.

In fact I live in a single bedsitter with sole use of confined kitchenette whose shelves are presently idle. My complexion could be termed grey. As though he hadnt washed for a month your worship. Teeth not so good. Beard a 6 dayer and of all unwashed colours. Shoes suede and stained by dripping. Dripping! The jeans could be fashionable without the Imitation Crombie. Last smoke finished already by christ. Smile. Yes. Hullo. Walk to door. Back to collect the sign-on card from its safe place. I shall be striding through a downpour.

Back from the broo and debating whether I am a headcase after all and this has nothing to do with my ambling in the rain. A neighbour has left a child by my side and gone off to the launderette. An 18 month old child and frankly an imposition. I am not overly fond of children. And this one is totally indifferent to me. The yes I delivered to the neighbour was typically false. She knew fine well but paid no attention. Perhaps she dislikes me intensely. Her husband and I detest each other. In my opinion his thoughts are irrelevant yet he persists in attempting to gain my heed. He fails. My eyes glaze but he seems unaware. Yet his wife appreciates my position and this is important since I can perhaps sleep with her if she sides with me and has any thoughts on the subject of him in relation to me or vice versa. Hell of a boring. I am not particularly attracted to her. A massive woman. I dont care. My vanities lie in other fields. Though at 30 years of age one's hand is insufficient and to be honest again my hand is more or less unused in regard to sexual relief. I rely on the odd wet dream, the odd chance acquaintance, male or female it makes no difference yet either has advantages.

Today the streets were crowded as was the broo. Many elderly women were out shopping and why they viewed me with suspicion is beyond me. I am the kind of fellow who gets belted by umbrellas for the barging of so-called 'infirm' pensioners while boarding omnibuses. Nonsense. I am polite. It is possible the Imitation Crombie brushes their shoulders or something in passing but the coat is far too wide for me and if it bumps against anything is liable to cave in rather than knock a body flying. Then again, I rarely wear the garment on buses. Perhaps they think I'm trying to lift their purses or provisions. You never know. If an orange for example dropped from a bag and rolled in my direction I would be reluctant to hand it back to its rightful owner. I steal. In supermarkets I lift flat items such as cheese and other articles. Last week, having allowed the father of the screaming infant to buy me beer in return for my ear, I got a large ashtray and two pint glasses and would have got more but that I lacked the Imitation Crombie. I do not get captured. I got shoved into jail a long time ago but not for stealing cheese. Much worse. Although I am an obviously suspicious character I never get searched. No more.

My shoes lie by the fire, my socks lie on its top. Steam rises. Stomach rumbles. I shall dine with the parents. No scruples on this kind of poncing. This angers the father as does my inability to acquire paid employment. He believes I am not trying, maintains there must be something. And while the mother accepts the prevailing situation she is apt to point out my previous job experience. I have worked at many things. I seldom stay for any length of time in a job because I cannot. Possibly I am a hopeless case.

I talk not at all, am confined to quarters, have no friends. I often refer to persons as friends in order to beg more easily from said persons in order that I may be the less guilty. Not that guilt affects me. It affects my landlord. He climbs the stairs whenever he is unwelcome elsewhere. He is a nyaff, yet often threatens to remove me from the premises under the misapprehension I would not resort to violence. He mentions the mother of this infant in lewd terms but I shall have none of it. Maybe he is a secret child molester. I might spread rumours to pass the time. But no, the infant is too wee. Perhaps I am a latent molester for even considering that. Below me dwells the Mrs Soinson, she has no children and appears unaware of my existence. I have thought of bumping into her and saying, Can I watch your television.

Aye, of course I'll keep the kid for another bastarn half hour. Good christ this is pathetic. The damn parent has to go further messages. Too wet to trail one's offspring. I could hardly reply for rage and noises from the belly and sweet odours from the room of a certain new tenant whom I have yet to clap eyes upon though I hear she is a young lady, a student no doubt, with middle class admirers or fervent working class ones or even upper class yacht drivers. I cannot be expected to compete with that sort of opposition. I shall probably flash her a weary kind of ironic grin that will strike her to the very marrow and gain all her pity/sympathy/respect for a brave but misguided soul. What sort of pish is this at all. Fuck sake I refuse to contemplate further on it although I only got lost in some train of thought and never for one moment contemplated a bastarn thing. I day dream frequently.

This infant sleeps on the floor in an awkward position and could conceivably suffocate but I wont rouse her. The worst could not happen with me here. Scream the fucking place down if I woke her up.

I am fed up with this business. Always my own fault with the terrible false yesses I toss around at random. Why can I not give an honest no like other people. The same last time. I watched the infant all Friday night while the parents were off for a few jars to some pub uptown where this country & western songster performs to astonishing acclaim. Now why songster and not singer. Anyway, they returned home with a 1/2 bottle of whisky and a couple of cans of lager so it wasnt too bad. This country & western stuff isnt as awful as people say yet there are too many tales of lost loves and horses for my liking although I admit to enjoying a good weepy now and then unless recovering from a hangover in which case—in which case . . . Christ, I may imagine things more than most but surely the mother—whom for the sake of identity I'll hereon refer to as Greta. And I might as well call him Percy since it is the worst I can think of at present—displayed her thigh on purpose. This is a genuine question. If I decide on some sort of action I must be absolutely sure of my ground, not be misled into thinking one thing to be true when in fact the other thing is the case. What. O jesus I have too many problems to concentrate on last week and the rest of it. Who the hell cares. I do. I do, I wish to screw her, be with her in bed for a lengthy period.

Oxtail soup and insufficient bread which lay on a cracked plate. Brought on a tray. Maybe she cant trust herself alone with me. Hard to believe she returned to lunch off similar fare below. I cant help feeling nobody would offer someone soup under the title of 'lunch' without prior explanation. Tea did of course follow but no further bread. I did not borrow from her. I wanted to. I should have. It was necessary. I somehow expected her to perceive my plight and suggest I accept a minor sum to tide me over, but no. I once tried old Percy for a fiver on his wages day. He looked at me as if I was daft. Five quid. A miserable five. Lend money and lose friends was his comment. Friends by christ.

Sucked my thumb to taste the nicotine. A salty sandish flavour. Perhaps not. In the good old days I could have raked the coal embers for cigarette ends. Wet pavements. I am in a bad way—even saying I am in a bad way. 3.30 in the afternoon this approximate Thursday. I have until Saturday morning to starve to death though I wont. I shall make it no bother. The postman comes at 8.20—7.50 on Saturdays but the bastarn postoffice opens not until 9.00 and often 9.05 though they deny it.

I refuse to remain here this evening. I will go beg in some pub where folk know me. In the past I have starved till the day before payday then tapped a handful on the strength of it and . . . christ in the early days I got a tenner once or twice and blew the lot and by the time I had repayed this and reached the Saturday late night I was left with thirty bob to get me through the rest of the week ie. the following 7 days. Bad bad. Waking in the morning and trying to slip back into slumber blotting out the harsh truth but it never works and there you are wide awake and aware and jesus it is bad. Suicide can be contemplated. Alright. I might have contemplated it. Or maybe I only imagined it, I mean seriously considered it. Or even simply and without the seriously. In other words I didnt contemplate suicide at all. I probably regarded the circumstances as being ideal. Yet in my opinion

No more of this shite. But borrowing large sums knowing they have to be repaid and the effects etc must have something to do with the deathwish. I refuse to discuss it. A naive position. And how could I starve to death in two days, particularly having recently lunched upon oxtail soup. People last for weeks so long as water is available.

Why am I against action. I was late to sign-on this morning though prepared for hours beforehand. Waken early these days or sometimes late. If I had ten pence I would enter supermarkets and steal flat items. And talking about water I can make tea, one cup of which gives the idea if not the sustenance of soup because of the tea bag's encrustation viz crumbs of old food, oose, hair, dandruff and dust. Maybe the new girl shall come borrow sugar from me. And then what will transpire. If

Had to go for a slash there and action: the thing being held between middle finger and thumb with the index slightly bent at the first joint so that the outside, including the nail, lay along it; a pleasant, natural grip. If I had held the index a fraction more bent I would have soaked the linoleum to the side of the pot. And the crux is of course that the act is natural. I have never set out to pish in that manner. It simply happens. Everyman the same I suppose with minute adjustments here and there according to differing chopper measurements. Yet surely the length of finger will vary in relation. Logical thought at last. Coherence is attainable as far as the learned Hamish Smith of Esher Suffolk would have us believe. I am no Englishman. I am for nationalization on a national scale and if you are a smalltrader well

No point journeying forth before opening time.

It is possible I might eat with the neighbours as a last resort and perhaps watch televison although in view of the oxtail soup a deal to hope for. But I would far rather be abroad in a tavern in earnest conversation with keen people over the state of nations, and I vow to listen. No day dreaming or vacant gazing right hand up and honest to god. Nor shall I inadvertently yawn hugely. But my condition is such company is imperative. I can no longer remain with myself. And that includes Percy, Greta and the infant, let us say Gloria—all three of whom I shall term the Nulties. The Nulties are a brave little unit gallantly making their way through a harsh uncaring world. They married in late life and having endeavoured for a little one were overwhelmed by their success. The infant Gloria is considered not a bad looking child though personally her looks dont appeal. She has a very tiny nose, pointed ears, receding hair. Also she shits over everything. Mainly diarrhoea that has an amazingly syrupy smell. Like many mothers Greta doesnt always realise the smell exists while on the other hand is absolutely aware so that she begins apologising left right and centre. Yet if everybody resembles me no wonder she forgets the bastarn smell because I for the sake of decency am liable to reply: What smell?

Greta is a busy mum with scarce the time for outside interests. There is nothing or perhaps a lot to say about Percy but it is hell of a boring. The point is that one of these days he shall awaken to an empty house. The woman will have upped and gone and with any sense will have neglected to uplift the infant. Trouble with many mothers is their falling for the propaganda dished out concerning them ie. and their offspring—Woman's Own magazines and that kind of shite. Most men fall for it too. But I am being sidetracked by gibberish. No, I fail to fit into their cosy scene for various reasons the most obvious of which is 3's a crowd and that's that for the time being.

But dear god I cannot eat with them tonight. They skimp on grub. One Saturday (and the straits must have been beyond desperation if Saturday it truly was) they sat me down and we set to on a plate of toast and tinned spaghetti. For the evening repast! My christ. But what I said was, Toast and spaghetti, great stuff. Now how can I tell such untruths and is it any wonder that I'm fucking languishing. No, definitely not. I deserve all of it. Imitation tomato sauce on my chin. And after the meal we turn to the telly over a digestive smoke and pitcher of coffee essence & recently boiled water; and gape our way to the Late Weather. I could make the poor old Nulties even worse by saying they stand for God Save The Queen Of The Great English Speakers but they dont to my knowledge—it is possible they wait till I have departed upstairs.

I have no wish to continue a life of the Nulties.

Something must be done. A decisive course of action. Tramping around pubs in the offchance of bumping into wealthy acquaintances is a depressing affair. And as far as I remember none of mine are wealthy and even then it is never a doddle to beg from acquaintances—hard enough with friends. Of which I no longer have. No fucking wonder. But old friends I no longer see can no longer be termed friends and since they are obliged to be something I describe them as acquaintances. In fact every last individual I recollect at a given moment is logically entitled to be termed acquaintance. And yet

Why the lies, concerning the tapping of a few bob; I find it easy. Never in the least embarrassed though occasionally I have recourse to the expression of such in order to be adduced ethical or something. I am a natural born beggar. Yes. Honest. A natural born beggar. I should take permanently to the road. The pubs I tramp are those used by former colleagues, fellow employees of the many firms which have in the past employed me for mutual profit. My christ. Only when skint and totally out of the game do I consider the tramp. Yet apparently my company is not anathema. Eccentric but not unlikeable. A healthy respect is perhaps accorded one. Untrue. I am treated in the manner of a sick younger brother. It is my absolute lack of interest in any subject that may arise in their conversation that appeals to them. I dislike debates, confessions and New Year resolutions. I answer only in monosyllables, even when women are present: Still Waters Run Deep is the adage I expect them to use of me. But there are no grounds for complaint. Neither from them nor from me. All I ask is the free bevy, the smoke, the heat. It could embarrass somebody less sensitive than myself. What was that. No, there are weightier problems. The bathwater has been running. Is the new girl about to dip a daintily naked toe. Maybe it is Mrs Soinson. Or Greta. And the infant Gloria. And Percy by christ. But no, Percy showers in the work to save the ten pence meter money. Petty petty petty. I dont bathe at all. I have what might be described as an allover-bodywash here in the kitchenette sink. I do every part of my surface bar certain sections of my lower to middle back which are impossible to reach without one of those long stemmed brushes I often saw years ago in amazing American Movies.

Incredible. Someone decides to bathe in a bath and so the rest of us are forced to run the risk of bladder infection. Nobody chapped my door. How do they know I didnt need to go. So inconsiderate for fuck sake that's really bad. Too much tea right enough, that's the problem.

No, Greta probably entertains no thoughts at all of being in bed with me. I once contemplated the possibility of Percy entertaining such notions. But I must immediately confess to this strong dislike as mutual. And he is most unattractive. And whereas almost any woman is attractive and desirable only a slender few men are. I dont of course mean slenderly proportioned men in fact—what is this at all. I dont want to sleep with men right hand up and honest to god I dont. Why such strenuous denials my good fellow. No reason. Oho. Honest. Okay then. It's a meal I need, a few pints, a smoke, open air and outlook, the secure abode. Concerted energy, decisive course of action. Satisfying gainful employment. Money. A decidable and complete system of life. Ungibberishness. So many needs and the nonexistent funds. I must leave these square quarters of mine this very night. I must worm my way into company, any company, and the more ingratiatingly the better.

Having dug out a pair of uncracked socks I have often made the normal ablutions and left these quarters with or without the Imitation Crombie. Beginning in a pub near the city centre I find nobody. Now to start a quest such as this in a fashion such as this is fucking awful. Not uncommon nevertheless yet this same pub is always the first pub and must always be the first pub in this the quest.

Utter rubbish. How in the name of christ can one possibly consider suicide when one's giro arrives in two days' time. Two days. But it is still Thursday. Thursday. Surely midnight has passed and so technically it is tomorrow morning the next day—Friday. Friday morning. O jesus and tomorrow the world. Amen. Giro tomorrow. In a bad way, no. Certainly not. Who are you kidding. I have to sleep. Tomorow ie. tonight is Friday's sleep. But two sleeps equal two days. What am I facing here. And so what. I wish

To hell with that for a game.

But I did move recently. I sought out my fellows. Did I really though. As a crux this could be imperative, analogous to the deathwish. Even considering the possibility sheds doubt. Not necessarily. In fact I dont believe it for a single solitary minute. I did want to get in with a crowd though, surely to christ. Maybe I wasnt trying hard enough. But I honestly required company. Perhaps they had altered their drinking habits. Because of me. In the name of fuck all they had to do was humiliate me—not that I would have been bothered by it but at least it could have allayed their feelings—as if some sort of showdown had taken place. But to actually change their pub. Well well well. Perhaps they sense I was setting out on a tramp and remained indoors with shutters drawn, lights extinguised. My christ I'm predictable. Three pubs I went to and I gave up. Always been the same: I lack follow through. Ach.

Can I really say I enjoy life with money. When I have it I throw it away. Only relax when skint. When skint I am a hulk—husk. No sidesteps from the issue. I do not want money ergo I do not want to be happy. The current me is my heart's desire. Surely not. Yet it appears the case. I am always needing money and I am always getting rid of it. This must be hammered home to me. Not even a question of wrecking my life, just that I am content to wallow. Nay, enjoy. I should commit suicide. Unconsecretated ground shall be my eternal resting spot. But why commit suicide if enjoying oneself. Come out of hiding Hamish Smith. Esher Suffolk cannot hold you.

Next time the landlord shows up I shall drygulch him; stab him to death and steal his lot. Stab him to death. Sick to the teeth of day dreams. As if I could stab the nyaff. Maybe I could pick a fight with him and smash in his skull with a broken wine bottle and crash, blood and brains and wine over my wrist and clenched fist. The deathwish after all. Albeit murder. Sounds more rational that: ie. why destroy one's own life if enjoyable. No reason at all. Is there a question. None whatsoever, in fact I might be onto something deep here but too late to pursue it, too late. Yet it could be a revelation of an extraordinary nature. But previously of course been exhausted by the learned Smith of Esher decades since and nowadays taken for granted—not even a topic on an inferior year's O-level examination paper. He isnt even a landlord. I refer to him as such but in reality he is only the bastarn agent. I dont know who the actual landlord really is. It might be Winsom Properties. Winsom Properties is a trust. That means you never know who you are dealing with. I dont like this kind of carry on. I prefer to know names.

Hell with them and their fucking shutters and lights out.

It isnt as bad as all that; here I am and it is now the short a.m.'s. The short a.m.'s. I await the water boiling for a final cup of tea. Probably only drink the stuff in order to pish. Does offer a sort of relief. And simply strolling to the kitchenette and preparing this tea: the gushing tap, the kettle, gathering the tea-bag from the crumb strewn shelf—all of this is motion.

My head gets thick.

One of the chief characteristics of my early, mid and late adolescence was the catastrophic form of the erotic content. Catastrophic in the sense that that which I did have was totally, well, not quite, fantasy. And is the lack by implication of an unnatural variety. Whether it is something to do with me or not—I mean whether or not it is catastrophic is nothing to do with me I mean, not at all. No.

Mr Smith, where are you. No, I cannot be bothered considering the early years. Who cares. Me of course it was fucking lousy. I masturbated frequently. My imagination was/is such I always had fresh stores of fantasies. And I dont wish to give the impression I still masturbate; nowadays, for example, I encounter difficulties in sustaining an erection unless another person happens to be in the immediate vicinity. Even first thing in the morning. This is all bastarn lies. Why in the name of fuck do I continue. What is it with me at all. Something must have upset me recently. Erotic content by christ. Why am I wiped out. Utterly skint. Eh. Why is this always as usual. Why do I even

Certain clerks behind the counter.

I mend fuses for people, oddjobs and that kind of bla for associates of the nyaff, tenants in other words. I am expected to do it. I allow my—I fall behind with the fucking rent. Terrible situation. I have to keep on his right side. Anyway, I dont mind the oddjobs. It gets you out and about.

I used to give him openings for a life of Mrs Soinson but all he could ever manage was, Fussy Old Biddy. And neither he nor she is married. I cant figure the woman out myself. Apart from her I might be the longest tenant on the premises. And when the nyaff knows so little about her you can be sure nobody else knows a thing. She must mend her own fuses. I havent even seen inside her room or rooms. It is highly possible that she actually fails to see me when we pass on the staircase. The nyaff regards her in awe. Is she a blacksheep outcast of an influential family closely connected to Winsom Properties. When he first became agent around here I think he looked upon her as easy meat whatever the hell that might mean as far as a nyaff is concerned. And she cant be more than fifty years of age, carries herself well and would seem an obvious widow. But I dispute that. A man probably wronged her many years ago. Jilted. With her beautiful 16 year old younger sister by her as bridesmaid, an engagement ring on her finger just decorously biding her time till this marriage of her big sister is out of the way so she can step in and get married to her own youthful admirer, and on the other side of poor old Mrs Soinson stood her widowed father or should I say sat since he would have been an invalid and in his carriage, only waiting his eldest daughter's marriage so he can join his dearly departed who died in childbirth (that of the beautiful 16 year old) up there in heaven. And ever since that day Mrs Soinson has remained a spinster, virginal, the dutiful but pathetic aunt—a role she hates but accepts for her parents' memory. Or she could have looked after the aged father till it was too late and for some reason, on the day he died, vowed to stay a single lassie since nobody could take the place of the departed dad and took on the title of Mistress to ward off would-be suitors although of course you do find men more willing to entertain a single Mrs as opposed to a single Miss which is why I agree with Womans Lib. Ms should be the title of both married and single women.

In the name of god.

Taking everything into consideration the time may be approaching when I shall begin regularly paid, full-time employment. My lot is severely trying. For an approximate age I have been receiving money from the state. I am obliged to cease this malingering and earn an honest penny. Having lived in this fashion for so long I am well nigh unemployable and if I were an Industrial Magnate or Captain of Industry I would certainly entertain doubts as to my capacity for toil. I am an idle goodfornothing. A neerdowell. The workhouse is too good for the likes of me. I own up. I am incompatible with this Great British Society. My production rate is less than atrocious. An honest labouring job is outwith my grasp. Wielding a shabby brush is not to be my lot. Never more shall I be setting forth on bitter mornings just at the break of dawn through slimy backstreet alleys, the treacherous urban undergrowth, trudging the meanest cobbled streets and hideously misshapen pathways of this grey with a heart of gold city. Where is that godforsaken factory. Let me at it. A trier. I would say so Your Magnateship. And was Never Say Die the type of adage one could apply to the wretch. I believe so Your Industrialness.

Fuck off.

Often I sit by the window in order to sort myself out—a group therapy within, and I am content with a behaviourist approach, none of that pie-in-the-sky metaphysics here if you dont mind. I quick-fire trip questions at myself which demand immediate answers and sometimes elongated thought out ones. So far I have been unsuccessful, and the most honest comment on this is that it is done unintentionally on purpose, a very deeply structured item. Choosing this window for instance only reinforces the point. I am way way on top, high above the street. And though the outlook is unopen considerable activity takes place directly below. In future I may dabble in psychiatry—get a book out the library on the subject and stick in, go to nightschool and obtain the necessary qualifications for minor university acceptance whose exams I shall scrape through, industrious but lacking the spark of genius, and eventually make it into a general sanatorium leading a life of devotion to the mental health of mankind. I would really enjoy the work. I would like to organise beneficial group therapies and the rest of it. Daily discussions. Saving young men and women from all kinds of breakdowns. And you would definitely have to be alert working beside the average headbanger or disturbed soul who are in reality the sane and we the insane according to the learned H.S. of Esher S. But though I appear to jest I give plenty thought to the subject. At least once during their days everybody has considered themselves mad or at least well on the road but fortunately from listening to the BBC they realise that if they really were mad they would never for one moment consider it was a possible description of their condition although sometimes they almost have to when reading a book by an enlightened foreigner or watching a heavy play or documentary or something—I mean later, when lying in bed with the lights out for example with the wife fast asleep and 8½ months pregnant maybe then suddenly he advances and not too accidently bumps her on the shoulder all ready with some shite about, O sorry if I disturbed you, tossing and turning etc, but I was just wondering eh . . .And then it dawns on him, this the awful truth, he is off his head or at best has an astonishingly bad memory—and this memory, under the circumstances may actually be at worst. And that enlightened foreigner is no comfort once she will have returned to slumber and you are on your own, alone, in the middle of the night, the dark recesses and so on dan d ran dan. But it must happen sometimes. What must fucking happen.

The postoffice may be seeking reliable men. Perhaps I shall fail their medical. And that goes for the fireservice. But the armed forces. Security. And each branch is willing and eager to take on such as myself. I shall apply. The Military Life would suit me. Uplift the responsility, the decision making, temptations, choices. And a sound bank account at the wind up—not a vast sum of course but enough to set me up as a tobacconist cum newsagent in a small way, nothing fancy, just to eke out the pension.

But there should be direction at 30 years of age. A knowing where I am going. Alright Sir Hamish we cant all be Charles Clore and Florence Nightingale but at least we damn well have a go and dont give in. Okay we may realise what it is all about and to hell with their christianity, ethics, the whole shebang and advertising but do we give in, do we Give Up The Ghost. No sirree by god we dont. Do you for one moment think we believe someone should starve to death while another feeds his dog on the finest fillet of steak and chips. Of course not. We none of us have outmoded beliefs but do we

I cannot place a finger somewhere. The bastarn rain is the cause. It pours, steadily for a time then heavier. Of course the fucking gutter has rotted and the constant torrent drops just above the fucking window. That bastard of a landlord gets nothing done, too busy peeping through keyholes at poor old Mrs Soinson. I am fed up with it. Weather been terrible for years. No wonder people look the way they do. Who can blame them. Christ it is bad, the weather, so fucking consistent.

Depresses everything. Recently I went for a short jaunt in the disagreeable countryside. Fortunately I got soaked through. The cattle ignored the rain. The few motor cars around splished past squirting oily mud onto the Imitation Crombie. I kept slipping into marshy bogs from whence I shrieked at various objects while seated. It wasnt boring. Of yore, on country rambles, I would doze in some deserted field with the sun beating etc the hum of grasshoppers chirp. I never sleep in a field where cattle graze lest I get nibbled. The countryside and I are incompatible. Everybody maintains they like the countryside but I refuse to accept such nonsense. It is absurd. Just scared, to admit the truth—that they hate even the idea of journeying through pastureland or craggyland. Jesus christ. I dont mind small streams burning through arable-land. Hardy fishermen with waders knee-deep in lonely inshore waters earn my total indifference. Not exactly. Not sympathy either, nor pity, nor respect, envy, hate. Contempt. No, not at all. But I heroworship lighthousekeepers. No. Envy is closer. Or maybe jealousy. And anyway, nowadays all men are created equal. But whenever I have had money in the past I always enjoyed the downpour. If on the road to somewhere the rain is fine. A set purpose. Even the cinema. Coat collar upturned, street lights reflecting on puddles, arriving with wind flushed complexion and rubbing your damp hands, parking your arse on a convenient convector heater. But without the money. Still not too bad perhaps.

According to the mirror I have been going about with a thoughtful expression on one's countenance. I appear to have become aware of myself in relation to the field by which I mean the external world. In relation to this field I am in full knowledge of my position. And this has nothing to do with steak & chips

Comfortable degrees of security are not to be scoffed at. I doff the cap to those who attain it the bastards. Seriously, I am fed up with being fed up. What I do wish

I shall not entertain day dreams
I shall not fantasise
I shall endeavour to make things work

I shall tramp the mean streets in search of menial posts or skilled ones. Everywhere I shall go, from Shetland Oilrigs to Bearsden Gardening Jobs. To Gloucestershire even. I would go to Gloucestershire. Would I fuck. To hell with them and their cricket & cheese. I refuse to go there. I may emigrate to The Great Englishes—o jesus christ Australia & New Zealand. Or America and Canada.

All I'm fucking asking is regular giros and punctual counter clerks.

Ach well son cheer up. So quiet in this dump. Some kind of tune was droning around a while back. I was sitting clapping hands to the rhythm and considering moving about on the floor. I used to dream of playing the banjo. Or even the guitar, just being able to strum but with a passable voice I could be dropping into parties and playing a song, couple of women at the feet keeping time and slowly sipping from a tall glass, 4 in the a.m.'s with whisky on the shelf and plenty of smokes. This is it now. Definitely.

black and white consumer and producer parasite thief come on shake hands you lot

Well throw yourself out the fucking window then. Throw myself out fuck all window—do what you like but here I am, no suicide and no malnutrition, no fucking nothing in fact because I am leaving, I am getting to fuck out of it. A temporary highly paid job, save a right few quid and then off on one's travels. Things will be done. Action immediate. Of the Pioneering Stock would you say. Of that ilk most certainly Your Worship. And were the audience Clambering to their feet. I should think so Your Grace.

The fact is I am a late starter. I am

I shouldnt be bothering about money anyway. The creditors have probably forgotten all about my existence. No point worrying about other than current arrears. The old me wouldnt require funds. A red & white polkadot handkerchief, a stout sapling rod, the hearty whistle and hi yo silver for the short ride to the outskirts of town, Carlisle and points south.

It is all a load of shite. I often plan things out then before the last minute do something ridiculous to ensure the plan's failure. If I did decide to clear the arrears and get a few quid together, follow up with a symbolic burning of the Imitation Crombie and in short make preparations to mend my ways I could conceivably enlist in the Majestic Navy to spite myself—or even fork out a couple of month's rent in advance for this dump simply to sit back and enjoy my next step from a safe distance and all the time guffawing in the background good christ I am schizophrenic, I never thought I acted in that manner yet I must admit it sounds like me, worse than I imagined, bad, bad. Maybe I could use the cash to pay for an extended stay in a private nursing home geared to the needs of the Unabletocope. But can it be schizophrenia if I can identify it myself. Doubtful. However, I regard

I was of the opinion certain items in regard to my future had been resolved. Cynical of self, this is the problem. Each time I make a firm resolution I end up scoffing. Yes. I sneer. Well well well, what a shite. That really does take the biscuit. And look at the time look at the time.

Captains of Industry should create situations for my ilk. The Works Philosopher I could be. With my own wee room to the left of the Personnel Section. During teabreaks Dissidents would be sent to me. Militancy could be cut by half, maybe as much as 90%. Yet Works Philosophers could not be classed as staff, instead they would be stamping in & out like the rest of the troops just in case they get aspirations, and seek reclassification within Personnel maybe. Gibberish. And yet fine, that would be fine, so what if they got onto the staff because that would leave space for others and the Dissident next in line could become the new Works Philosopher and so on and so forth. And they would stick it, the job, they would not be obliged to seek out square squarters whose shelves are crumb strewn.

I shall have it to grips soon. Tomorrow or who knows. After all, I am but 30, hardly matured. But fuck me I'm getting hell of a hairy these days. Maybe visit the barber in the near future, Saturday morning for instance, who knows what is in store. Only waiting for my passion to find an object and let itself go. Yes, who can tell what's in store, that's the great thing about life, always one more fish in the sea, iron in the fire; this is the great thing about life, the uncertainty and the bla

Jesus what will I do, save up for a new life, the mending of the ways, pay off arrears, knock the door of accredited creditors, yes, I can still decide what to do about things concerning myself and even others if only in regard to me at least it is still indirectly to do with them and yet it isnt indirect at all because it is logically bound to be direct if it is anything and obviously it is something and must therefore be directly since I am involved and if they are well

well well, who can tell what the fuck this is about. I am chucking it in. My brain cannot cope on its own. Gets carried away for the sake of thought no matter whether it be sense or not, no, that is the last fucking thing considered. Which presents problems. I really do have a hard time knowing where I am going. For if going, where. Nowhere or somewhere. Children and hot meals. Homes and security and the neighbours in for a quiet drink at the weekend. Tumbling on carpets with the weans and television sets and golf and even heated discussions in jocular mood while the wives gossip ben in the kitchen and

Now then: here I am in curiously meagre surroundings, living the life of a hapless pauper, my pieces of miserable silver supplied gratis by the Browbeaten Taxpayer. The past ramblings concerning outer change were pure invention. And comments made about one's total inadequacy were done so in earnest albeit with a touch of pride. Even the brave Nulties are abused by me, at least in respect to grub & smokes. And all for what. Ah, an ugly sight. But this must be admitted: with a rumbling stomach I have often refused food, preferring a lonely smoke and the possible mystery of, Has he eaten elsewhere . . . and if so with whom. Yet for all people know I have several trunks packed full of articles, clothes and whatnot. Apart from a couple of clerks nobody knows a thing about me. I could be a Man About Town. They probably nudge each other and refer to me as a bit of a lad. I might start humping large suitcases plastered with illegible labels. Save up and buy a suit in modern mode. Get my coat dyed, even stick with its symbolic burning. Or else I could sell it. A shrewd man I occasionally have dealings with rejected this coat. But I did ask a Big price. Shoes too I need. Presently I have what are described as Bumpers. Whereas with real leather efforts and a new rig out I could travel anywhere and get a new start in life. I could be a Computer Programmer. But they're supposed to reach their peak at 21 years of age. Still and all the sex potency fucking peak is 16. 16 years of age by christ you could not credit that. Ach. I dare say sex plays more of a role in my life than grub. If both were in abundance my problems could only increase. Yet one's mental capacities would be bound to make more use of their potential without problems at the fundamental level.

But

the plan. From now on I do not cash giros. I sleep in on Saturday mornings and so too late for the postoffice until Monday mornings by which time everything will be alright, it will be fine, I shall have it worked out and fine and if I can stretch it out and grab at next Saturday then the pathway shall have been erected, I shall have won through.

Recently I lived in seclusion. For a considerable period I existed on a tiny islet not far from Toay. Sheep and swooping gulls for companions. The land and the sea. After dark the inner recesses. Self knowledge and acceptance of the awareness. No trees of course. None. Sheer drops from mountainous regions, bird shit and that of sheep and goats as well perhaps, in that kind of terrain. No sign of man or woman. The sun always far in the sky but no clouds. Not tanned either. Weatherbeaten. Hair matted by the salt spray. Food requires no mention. Swirling eddies within the standing rocks and nicotine wool stuck to the jaggy edges, the droppings of the gulls.

Since I shall have nothing to look forwards to on Saturday mornings I must reach a state of neither up nor down. Always the same. That will be miserable I presume but considering my heart's desire is to be miserable then with uncashed giros reaching for the ceiling I can be indefinitely miserable. Total misery. However, to retain misery I may be obliged to get out and about in order not to be always miserable since—or should I say pleasure is imperative if perfect misery is the goal; and, therefore, a basic condition of my perpetual misery is the occasional jaunt abroad in quest of joy. Now we're getting somewhere Sir Smith, arise and get your purple sash. And since ambling round pubs only depresses me I must seek out other means of entertainment or henceforth desist this description of myself as wretch. And setbacks and kicksintheteeth are out of the question. Masochism then. Is this what

Obviously I am just in the middle of a nervous breakdown, even saying it I mean that alone

But for christ sake saving a year's uncashed giros is impossible because the bastards render them uncashable after a 6 month interval.

Walking from Land's End to John O'Groats would be ideal in fact because for one thing it would tax my resistance to the utmost. Slogging on day in day out. Have to be during the summer. I dislike the cold water and I would be stopping off for a swim. Yet this not knowing how long it takes the average walker . . . well, why worry, time is of no concern. Or perhaps it should be. I could try for the record. After the second attempt possibly. Once I had my bearings. Not at all. I would amble. And with pendants and flags attached to the suitcase I could beg my grub & tobacco. The minimum money required. Neither broo nor social security. The self sufficiency of the sweetly self employed. I could be for the rest of my life. The Land's End to John O'Groats man. That would be my title. My name a byword, although anonymity would be the thing to aim for. Jesus it could be good. And far from impossible. I have often hitched about the place. Many times. But hitching must be banned otherwise I shall be saving time which is of course an absurdity—pointless to hitch. And yet what difference will it make if I do save time because it can make no difference anyway. None whatsoever. Not at all. And if it takes 6 weeks a trip and the same back up I could average 4 return trips a year. If I am halfway through life just now ie. a hundred and twenty return trips then in another hundred and twenty trips I would be dead. I can mark off each trip on milestones north & south. And when the media get a grip of me I can simply say I'll be calling a halt in 80 trips time. And I speak of returns. That would be twenty years hence by which time I would have become accustomed to fame. Although I could have fallen down dead by then through fatigue or something. Hail rain shine. The dead of winter would be a challenge and could force me into shelter unless I acquire a passport and head out to sunnier climes, Australia for example to stave off the language barriers yet speech need be no problem since communication will be the major lack as intention perhaps. No, impossible. I cannot leave The Great British Shores. Comes to that I cannot leave the Scottish ones either. Yes, aye, Scotland is ideal. Straight round the Scottish Coast from the foot of Galloway right round to Berwick although Ayrshire is a worry its being a very boring coastline. But boredom is out of the question. Ayrshire will not be denied. So each return trip might involve say a four month slog if keeping rigidly to the coast on all minor roads particularly when you consider Kintyre—or Morven by fuck and even I suppose Galloway itself to some extent. But that kind of thing is easily resolved. I dont have to restrict myself to mapped out routes from which the slightest deviation is frowned upon. On the contrary, that last minute decision at the country crossroads can only enhance the affair. And certain items of clothing are already marked out as essential items. The stout boots and gnarled staff to ward off country animals after dusk. A hat & coat for wet weather. The Imitation Crombie may suffice. Though an anorak to cover the knees would probably reap dividends. And after a few return trips—and being a circular route no such thing as a return would exist ie. I would be travelling on an arc—the farmfolk and country dwellers would know me well, the goodwives leaving thick winter woollies by the side of the road, flasks of oxtail soup under hedges. Shepherds offering shelter in remote bothies by the blazing log fires sipping hot toddies for the wildest nights and plenty of tobacco always the one essential luxury, and the children up and down the land crying, Mummy here comes the Scottish Coastroad Walker while I would dispense the homespun philosophies of the daisy growing and the planet as it revolves etc. A stray dog joining me having tagged along for a trip at a safe distance behind me I at last turn and at my first grunt of encouragement it comes bounding joyfully forwards to shower me in wet noses and barked assurances to stick by me through thick & thin and to eternally guard my last lowly grave when I have at length fallen in midstride plumb tuckered out after many years viz 12 round trips at two years a trip. Yet it might be shorter than that. While the hot days in central summer are the busloads of tourists arriving to see me, pointed out by their driver, the Legend of the North, the solitary trudging humpbacked figure with dog & gnarled staff just vanishing out of sight into the mist, Dont give him money Your Lordship you'll just hurt his feelings. Just a bite of your cheese piece and a saucer of milk for the whelp. Group photographs with me peering suspiciously at the camera from behind shoulders at the back or in the immediate foreground perhaps, It is rumoured the man was a Captain of Industry Your Grace, been right round the Scottish Coastroad 28 times and known from Galloway to Berwick as a friend to Everyone. Yes, just a pinch of your snuff and a packet of cigarette-papers for chewing purposes only. No sextants or compasses or any of that kind of shite but

J. M. Barrie

During the last decades of the nineteenth century the Kailyard nourished all that was mawkishly escapist and unremittingly sentimental in Scottish writing. It gave rise to a glut of short fiction which amply displayed what J. H. Miller in *The New Review* of 1895 descrbed as a 'diseased craving for the pathetic,' and in which the huge populations concentrated in Scotland's cities could enjoy a version of country life which was familiar enough to be funny and foreign enough to be patronised.

Kailyard fiction was commercially successful, but with few exceptions, the writers attracted to the genre were second rate. One of these exceptions was James Matthew Barrie (1860–1937). The third of ten children, he was born to a weaver in Kirriemuir and educated in Forfar, Kirriemuir, Glasgow and Dumfries. He left Edinburgh University in 1884 with an MA degree and moved into journalism.

Tiny in stature and enormously ambitious, Barrie was destined for popular success, especially as a playwright for the London stage. He began his literary career with stories based on the tales his mother Margaret Ogilvy had told him about the Kirriemuir of her youth. So it was that memories of a small Angus town of forty years earlier were eventually published as *Auld Licht Idylls* (1888), the first of Barrie's Kailyard pieces. There were to be five other collections, ending with a disturbingly self-revealing biography of his mother.

'Cree Queery and Mysy Drolly' comes from *Auld Licht Idylls.* Barrie's stance is that of a sympathetic but slightly patronising observer, and his story is aimed squarely at our moral and sentimental sympathies. Yet it is a disconcertingly exact picture of human suffering in the harshest poverty, and it leaves a number of unanswered questions in the reader's mind.

Cree Queery and Mysy Drolly

THE CHILDREN used to fling stones at Grinder Queery because he loved his mother. I never heard the Grinder's real name. He and his mother were Queery and Drolly, contemptuously so called, and they answered to these names. I remember Cree best as a battered old weaver, who bent forward as he walked, with his arms hanging limp as if ready to grasp the shafts of the barrow behind which it was his life to totter uphill and downhill, a rope of yarn suspended round his shaking neck, and fastened to the shafts, assisting him to bear the yoke and slowly strangling him. By and by there came a time when the barrow and the weaver seemed both palsy-stricken, and Cree, gasping for breath, would stop in the middle of a brae, unable to push his load over a stone. Then he laid himself down behind it to prevent the barrow's slipping back. On these occasions only the barefooted boys who jeered at the panting weaver could put new strength into his shrivelled arms. They did it by telling him that he and Mysy would have to go to the 'poor-house' after all, at which the grey old man would wince, as if 'joukin' from a blow, and, shuddering, rise and, with a desperate effort, gain the top of the incline. Small blame perhaps attached to Cree if, as he neared his grave, he grew a little dottle. His loads of yarn frequently took him past the workhouse, and his eyelids quivered as he drew near. Boys used to gather round the gate in anticipation of his coming, and make a feint of driving him inside. Cree, when he observed them, sat down on his barrow-shafts terrified to approach, and I see them now pointing to the workhouse till he left his barrow on the road and hobbled away, his legs cracking as he ran.

It is strange to know that there was once a time when Cree was young and straight, a callant who wore a flower in his buttonhole, and tried to be a hero for a maiden's sake.

Before Cree settled down as a weaver, he was knife and scissor-grinder for three counties, and Mysy, his mother, accompanied him wherever he went. Mysy trudged alongside him till her eyes grew dim and her limbs failed her, and then Cree was told that she must be sent to the pauper's home. After that a pitiable and beautiful sight was to be seen. Grinder Queery, already a feeble man, would wheel his grindstone along the long high road, leaving Mysy behind. He took the stone on a few hundred yards, and then, hiding it by the roadside in a ditch or behind a paling, returned for his mother. Her he led—sometimes he almost carried her—to the place where the grindstone lay, and thus by double journeys kept her with him. Every one said that Mysy's death would be a merciful release—every one but Cree.

Cree had been a grinder from his youth, having learned the trade from his father, but he gave it up when Mysy became almost blind. For a time he had to leave her in Thrums with Dan'l Wilkie's wife, and find employment himself in Tilliedrum. Mysy got me to write several letters for her to Cree, and she cried while telling me what to say. I never heard either of them use a term of endearment to the other, but all Mysy could tell me to put in writing was—'Oh, my son Cree; oh, my beloved son; oh, I have no one but you; oh, thou God watch over my Cree!' On one of these occasions Mysy put into my hands a paper, which, she said, would perhaps help me to write the letter. It had been drawn up by Cree many years before, when he and his mother had been compelled to part for a time, and I saw from it that he had been trying to teach Mysy to write. The paper consisted of phrases such as 'Dear son Cree,' 'Loving mother,' 'I am takin' my food weel,' 'Yesterday,' 'Blankets,' 'The peats is near done,' 'Mr Dishart,' 'Come home, Cree.' The Grinder had left this paper with his mother, and she had written letters to him from it.

When Dan'l Wilkie objected to keeping a cranky old body like Mysy in his house Cree came back to Thrums and took a single room with a hand-loom in it. The flooring was only lumpy earth, with sacks spread over it to protect Mysy's feet. The room contained two dilapidated old coffin-beds, a dresser, a high-backed arm-chair, several three-legged stools, and two tables, of which one could be packed away beneath the other. In one corner stood the wheel at which Cree had to fill his own pirns. There was a plate-rack on one wall, and near the chimney-piece hung the wag-at-the-wall clock, the timepiece that was commonest in Thrums at that time, and that got this name because its exposed pendulum swung along the wall. The two windows in the room faced each other on opposite walls, and were so small that even a child might have stuck in trying to crawl through them. They opened on hinges, like a door. In the wall of the dark passage leading from the outer door into the room was a recess where a pan and pitcher of water always stood wedded, as it were, and a little hole, known as the 'bole', in the wall opposite the fireplace contained Cree's library. It consisted of Baxter's 'Saints' Rest', Harvey's 'Meditations', the 'Pilgrim's Progress', a work on folk-lore, and several Bibles. The saut-backet, or salt-bucket, stood at the end of the fender, which was half of an old cart-wheel. Here Cree worked, whistling 'Ower the watter for Chairlie' to make Mysy think that he was as gay as a mavis. Mysy grew querulous in her old age, and up to the end she thought of poor, done Cree as a handsome gallant. Only by weaving far on into the night could Cree earn as much as six shillings a week. He began at six o'clock in the morning, and worked until midnight by the light of his cruizey. The cruizey was all the lamp Thrums had in those days, though it is only to be seen in use now in a few old-world houses in the glens. It is an ungainly thing in iron, the size of a man's palm, and shaped not unlike the palm when contracted, and deepened to hold a liquid. Whale-oil, lying open in the mould, was used, and the wick was a rash with the green skin peeled off. These rashes were sold by herd-boys at a halfpenny the bundle, but Cree gathered his own wicks. The rashes skin readily when you know how to do it. The iron mould was placed inside another of the same shape, but slightly larger, for in time the oil dripped through the iron, and the whole was then hung by a cleek or hook close to the person using it. Even with three wicks it gave but a stime of light, and never allowed the weaver to see more than the half of his loom at a time. Sometimes Cree used threads for wicks. He was too dull a man to have many visitors, but Mr Dishart called occasionally and reproved him for telling his mother lies. The lies Cree told Mysy were that he was sharing the meals he won for her, and that he wore the overcoat which he had exchanged years before for a blanket to keep her warm.

There was a terrible want of spirit about Grinder Queery. Boys used to climb on to his stone roof with clods of damp earth in their hands, which they dropped down the chimney. Mysy was bed-ridden by this time, and the smoke threatened to choke her; so Cree, instead of chasing his persecutors, bargained with them. He gave them fly-hooks which he had busked himself, and when he had nothing left to give he tried to flatter them into dealing gently with Mysy by talking to them as men. One night it went through the town that Mysy now lay in bed all day listening for her summons to depart. According to her ideas this would come in the form of a tapping at the window, and their intention was to forestall the spirit. Dite Gow's boy, who is now a grown man, was hoisted up to one of the little windows, and he has always thought of Mysy since as he saw her then for the last time. She lay sleeping, so far as he could see, and Cree sat by the fireside looking at her.

Every one knew that there was seldom a fire in that house unless Mysy was cold. Cree seemed to think that the fire was getting low. In the little closet, which, with the kitchen, made up his house, was a corner shut off from the rest of the room by a few boards, and behind this he kept his peats. There was a similar receptacle for potatoes in the kitchen. Cree wanted to get another peat for the fire without disturbing Mysy. First he took off his boots, and made for the peats on tiptoe. His shadow was cast on the bed, however, so he next got down on his knees and crawled softly into the closet. With the peat in his hands, he returned in the same way, glancing every moment at the bed where Mysy lay. Though Tammy Gow's face was pressed against a broken window he did not hear Cree putting that peat on the fire. Some say that Mysy heard, but pretended not to do so for her son's sake, that she realized the deception he played on her, and had not the heart to undeceive him. But it would be too sad to believe that. The boys left Cree alone that night.

The old weaver lived on alone in that solitary house after Mysy left him, and by and by the story went abroad that he was saving money. At first no one believed this except the man who told it, but there seemed after all to be something in it. You had only to hit Cree's trouser pocket to hear the money chinking, for he was afraid to let it out of his clutch. Those who sat on dykes with him when his day's labour was over said that the weaver kept his hand all the time in his pocket, and that they saw his lips move as he counted his hoard by letting it slip through his fingers. So there were boys who called 'Miser Queery' after him instead of Grinder, and asked him whether he was saving up to keep himself from the workhouse.

But we had all done Cree wrong. It came out on his deathbed what he had been storing up his money for. Grinder, according to the doctor, died of getting a good meal from a friend of his earlier days after being accustomed to starve on potatoes and a very little oatmeal indeed. The day before he died this friend sent him half a sovereign, and when Grinder saw it he sat up excitedly in his bed and pulled his corduroys from beneath his pillow. The woman who, out of kindness, attended him in his last illness, looked on curiously, while Cree added the sixpences and coppers in his pocket to the half-sovereign. After all they only made some two pounds, but a look of peace came into Cree's eyes as he told the woman to take it all to a shop in the town. Nearly twelve years previously Jamie Lownie had lent him two pounds, and though the money was never asked for, it preyed on Cree's mind that he was in debt. He paid off all he owed, and so Cree's life was not, I think, a failure.

Lewis Grassic Gibbon

CLAY

Lewis Grassic Gibbon, (James Leslie Mitchell 1901–35), was born on his father's farm at Auchterless in Aberdeenshire. He was educated in the area and worked as a journalist in Glasgow before enlisting as a soldier, and then as a clerk in the RAF. The army gave him opportunities to travel which formed the inspiration, settings or background for a number of books he wrote under his own name. He became a full-time writer in 1929 and settled in England, in Welwyn Garden City, with his young wife Rebecca Middleton, who came from the croft next to his family home. Mitchell is best known for his magnificent novels of North East life, *Sunset Song*, *Cloud Howe* and *Grey Granite*, which make up the trilogy called *A Scots Quair* written by 'Lewis Grassic Gibbon', a name he borrowed from his mother's family. Mitchell died of a perforated ulcer at the tragically early age of thirty-four.

Many of Mitchell's recurring concerns can be found in his stories, especially his fierce sense of place, and a poetic involvement with the beauty and harshness of life on the land. This is matched by his narrative style, by way of a talking voice, seemingly effortless, which is colloquial and lyrical at the same time, as if to assume a world of shared experience with the reader.

'Clay' is such a work, carrying dourness and determination at the heart of the story, yet it is clearly symbolic and explores the author's own ambivalence, his love and hatred for the 'red clay of the Mearns' and its people.

Clay

THE GALTS were so thick on the land around Segget folk said if you went for a walk at night and you trod on some thing and it gave a squiggle, it was ten to one you would find it a Galt. And if you were a newcomer up in the Howe and you stopped a man and asked him the way the chances were he'd be one of the brood. Like as not, before he had finished with you, he'd have sold you a horse or else stolen your watch, found out everything that you ever had done, recognized your mother and had doubts of your father. Syne off home he'd go and spread the news round from Galt of Catcraig that lay high in the hills to Galt of Drumbogs that lay low by Mondynes, all your doings were known and what you had said, what you wore next your skin, what you had to your breakfast, what you whispered to your wife in the dead of night. And the Galts would snigger *Ay, gentry, no doubt,* and spit in the vulgar way that they had: the average Galt knew less of politeness than a broody hen knows of Bible exegesis.

They farmed here and they farmed there, brothers and cousins and half-brothers and uncles, your head would reel as you tried to make out if Sarah were daughter to Ake of Catcraig or only a relation through marrying a nephew of Sim of High Rigs that was cousin to Will. But the Galts knew all their relationships fine, more especially if anything had gone a bit wrong, they'd tell you how twenty-five years or so back when the daughter of Redleaf had married her cousin, old Alec that now was the farmer of Kirn, the first bit bairn that came of that marriage—ay, faith, that bairn had come unco soon! And they'd lick at their chops as they minded of that and sneer at each other and fair have a time. But if you were strange and would chance to agree, they'd close up quick, with a look on their faces as much as to say *And who are you would say ill of the Galts?*

They made silver like dirt wherever they sat, there was hardly a toun that they sat in for long. So soon's they moved in to some fresh bit farm they'd rive up the earth, manure it with fish, work the land to death in the space of their lease, syne flit to the other side of the Howe with the land left dry as a rat-sucked swede. And often enough as he neared his lease-end a Galt would break and be rouped from his place, he'd say that farming was just infernal and his wife would weep as she watched her bit things sold here and there to cover their debts. And if you didn't know much of the Galts you would be right sorry and would bid fell high. Syne you'd hear in less than a six month's time that the childe that went broke had bought a new farm and had stocked it up to the hilt with the silver he'd laid cannily by before he went broke.

Well, the best of the bunch was Rob Galt of Drumbogs, lightsome and hearty, not mean like the rest, he'd worked for nearly a twenty-five years as his father's foreman up at Drumbogs. Old Galt, the father, seemed nearly immortal, the older he grew the coarser he was, Rob stuck the brute as a good son should though aye he had wanted land of his own. When they fell out at last Rob Galt gave a laugh *You can keep Drumbogs and all things that are on it, I'll soon get a place of my own, old man.* His father sneered *You?* and Rob Galt said *Ay, a place of my own and parks that are* MINE.

He was lanky and long like all of the Galts, his mouser twisted up at the ends, with a chinny Galt face and a long, thin nose, and eyes pale-blue in a red-weathered face, a fine, frank childe that was kindness itself, though his notion of taking a rest from the plough was to loosen his horses and start in to harrow. He didn't look long for a toun of his own, Pittaulds by Segget he leased in a wink, it stood high up on the edge of the Mounth, you could see the clutter of Segget below, wet, with the glint of its roofs at dawn. The rent was low, for the land was coarse, red clay that sucked with a hungry mouth at your feet as you passed through the evening fields.

Well, he moved to Pittaulds in the autumn term, folk watched his flitting come down by Mondynes and turn at the corner and trudge up the brae to the big house poised on the edge of the hill. He brought his wife, she was long as himself, with a dark-like face, quiet, as though gentry–faith, that was funny, a Gald wedded decent! But he fair was fond of the creature, folk said, queer in a man with a wife that had managed to bring but one bairn into the world. That bairn was now near a twelve years old, dark, like her mother, solemn and slim, Rob spoiled them both, the wife and the quean, you'd have thought them sugar he was feared would melt.

But they'd hardly sat down a week, in Pittaulds when Rachel that would trot at the rear of Rob, like a collie dog, saw a queer-like change. Now and then her father would give her a pat and she'd think that he was to play as of old. But instead he would cry *Losh, run to the house, and see if your mother will let you come out, we've two loads of turnips to pull afore dinner.* Rachel, the quean, would chirp *Ay, father,* and go blithe to the shed for her tailer and his, and out they would wade through the cling of the clay and pull side by side down the long, swede rows, the rain in a drifting seep from the hills, below them the Howe in its garment of mist. And the little, dark quean would work by his side, say never a word though she fair was soaked; and at last go home; and her mother would stare, whatever in the world had happened to Rob? She would ask him that as he came into dinner—*the quean'll fair have her death of cold.* He would blink with his pale-blue eyes, impatient, *Hoots, lassie, she'll take no harm from the rain. And we fair must clear the swedes from the land, I'm a good three weeks behind with the work.*

The best of the Galts? Then God keep off the rest! For, as that year wore on to its winter, while he'd rise at five, as most other folk did, he wouldn't be into his bed till near morning, it was chave, chave, chave till at last you would think he'd turn himself into an earthworm, near. In the blink of the light from the lanterns of dawn he would snap short-tempered at his dark-faced wife, she would stare and wonder and give a bit laugh, and eat up his porridge as though he was feared he would lose his appetite halfway through, and muck out the byre and the stable as fast as though he were paid for the job by the hour, with a scowl of ill-nature behind his long nose. And then, while the dark still lay on the land, and through the low mist that slept on the fields not a bird was cheeping and not a thing showing but the waving lanterns in the Segget wynds, he'd harness his horses and lead out the first, its hooves striking fire from the stones of the close, and cry to the second, and it would come after, and the two of them drink at the trough while Rob would button up his collar against the sharp drive of the frozen dew as the north wind woke. Then he'd jump on the back of the meilke roan, Jim, and go swaying and jangling down by the hedge, in the dark, the world on the morning's edge, wet, the smell of the parks in his face, the squelch of the horses soft in the clay.

Syne, as the light came grey in a tide, wan and slow from the Bervie Braes, and a hare would scuttle away through the grass and the peesies waken and cry and wheep, Rob Galt would jump from the back of Jim and back the pair up against the plough and unloose the chains from the horses' britchens and hook them up to the swiveltrees. Then he'd spit on his hands and cry *Wissh, Jim!* no longer ill-natured, but high-out and pleased, and swink the plough into the red, soaked land; and the horses would strain and snort and move canny and the clay wheel back in the coulter's trace, Rob swaying slow in the rear of the plough, one foot in the drill and one on the rig. The bothy billies on Arbuthnott's bents riding their pairs to start on some park would cry one to the other *Ay, Rob's on the go,* seeing him then as the light grew strong, wheeling, him and his horses and plough, a ranging of dots on the park that sloped its long clay rigs to the edge of the moor.

By eight, as Rachel set out for school, a slim, dark thing with her well-tacked boots, she would hear the whistle of her father, Rob, deep, a wheeber, upon the hill; and she'd see him coming swinging to the end of a rig and mind how he once would stop and would joke and tease her for lads that she had at the school. And she'd cry *Hello father!* but Rob would say nothing till he'd drawn his horse out and looked back at the rig and given his mouser a twist and a wipe. Syne he'd peck at his daughter as though he'd new woke *Ay, then, so you're off,* and cry *Wissh!* to his horses and turn them about and set to again, while Rachel went on, quiet, with the wonder clouding her face that had altered so since she came to Pittaulds.

He'd the place all ploughed ere December was out, folk said that he'd follow the usual Galt course, he'd showed up mean as the rest of them did, he'd be off to the marts and a dealing in horses, or a buying of this or a stealing of that, if there were silver in the selling of frogs the Galts would puddock-hunt in their parks. But instead he began on the daftest-like ploy, between the hill of Pittaulds and the house a stretch of the moor thrust in a thin tongue, three or four acre, deep-pitted with holes and as rank with whins as a haddock with scales, not a tenant yet who had farmed Pittaulds but had had the sense to leave it a-be. But Rob Galt set in to break up the land, he said it fair cried to have a man at it, he carted great stones to fill up the holes and would lever out the roots when he could with a pick, when he couldn't he'd bring out his horses and yoke them and tear them out from the ground that way. Working that Spring to break in the moor by April's end he was all behind, folk took a laugh, it served the fool fine.

Once in a blue moon or so he'd come round, he fair was a deave as he sat by your fire, he and your man would start in on the crops and the lie of the land and how you should drain it, the best kind of turnips to plant in the clay, the manure that would bring the best yield a dry year. Your man would be keen enough on all that, but not like Rob Galt, he would kittle up daft and start in to tell you tales of the land that were just plain stite, of this park and that as though they were women you'd to prig and to pat afore they'd come on. And your man would go ganting wide as a gate and the clock would be hirpling the hours on to morn and still Rob Galt would sit here and habber. *Man, she's fairly a bitch, is that park, sly and sleekèd, you can feel it as soon as you start in on her, she'll take corn with the meikle husk, not with the little. But I'll kittle her up with some phosphate, I think.* Your man would say *Ay, well, well, is that so? What do you think of this business of Tariffs?* and Rob would say *Well, man, I just couldn't say. What worries me's the park where I've put in the tares. It's fair on the sulk about something or other.*

And what could you think of a fool like that? Though he'd fallen behind with his chave on the moor he soon made it up with his working at night, he fair had a fine bit crop the next year, the wife and the quean both out at the cutting, binding and stooking as he reapered the fields. Rachel had shot up all of a sudden, you looked at her in a kind of surprise as you saw the creature go by to the school. It was said that she fair was a scholar, the quean—no better than your own bit Johnnie, you knew, the teachers were coarse to your Johnnie, the tinks. Well, Rachel brought home to Pittaulds some news the night that Rob came back from the mart, he'd sold his corn at a fair bit price. For once he had finished pleitering outside, he sat in the kitchen, his feet to the fire, puffing at his pipe, his eye on the window watching the ley rise up outside and peer in the house as though looking for him. It was Rachel thought that as she sat at her supper, dark, quiet, a bit queer, over thin to be bonny, you like a lass with a good bit of beef. Well, she finished her meat and syne started to tell the message that Dominie had sent her home with; and maybe if she was sent to the college she'd win a bursary or something to help.

Her mother said *Well, Rob, what say you to that?* and Rob asked *What?* and they told him again and Rob skeughed his face round *What, money for school? And where do you think that I'll manage to get that?*

Mrs Galt said *Out of the corn you've just sold,* and Rob gave a laugh as though speaking to a daftie—*I've my seed to get and my drains to dig and what about the ley for the next year's corn? Damn't, it's just crying aloud for manure, it'll hardly leave me a penny-piece over.*

Rachel sat still and looked out at the ley, sitting so still, with her face in the dark. Then they heard her sniff and Rob swung round fair astonished at the sound she made. *What ails you?* he asked, and her mother said *Ails her? You would greet yourself if you saw your life ruined.* Rob got to his feet and gave Rachel a pat. *Well, well, I'm right sorry that you're taking't like that. But losh, it's a small bit thing to greet over. Come out and we'll go for a walk round the parks.*

So Rachel went with him half-hoping he thought to change his mind on this business of college. But all that he did on the walk was to stand now and then and stare at the flow of the stubble or laugh queer-like as they came to a patch where the grass was bare and the crop had failed. *Ay, see that, Rachel, the wretch wouldn't take. She'll want a deep drill, this park, the next season.* And he bent down and picked up a handful of earth and trickled the stuff through his fingers, slow, then dusted it back on the park, not the path, careful, as though it were gold-dust not dirt. So they came at last to the moor he had broken, he smoked his pipe and he stood and looked at it *Ay, quean, I've got you in fettle at last.* He was speaking to the park not his daughter but Rachel hated Pittaulds from that moment, she thought, quiet, watching her father and thinking how much he'd changed since he first set foot on its clay.

He worked from dawn until dark, and still later, he hove great harvests out of the land, he was mean as dirt with the silver he made; but in five years' time of his farming there he'd but hardly a penny he could call his own. Every meck that he got from the crops of one year seemed to cry to go back to the crops of the next. The coarse bit moor that lay north of the biggings he coddled as though 'twas his own blood and bone, he fed it manure and cross-ploughed it twice-thrice, and would harrow it, tend it, and roll the damn thing till the Segget joke seemed more than a joke, that he'd take it to bed with him if he could. For all that his wife saw of him in hers he might well have done that, Mrs Galt that was tall and dark and so quiet came to look at him queer as he came in by, you could hardly believe it still was the Rob that once wouldn't blush to call you his jewel, that had many a time said all he wanted on earth was a wife like he had and land of his own. But that was afore he had gotten the land.

One night she said as they sat at their meat *Rob, I've still that queer pain in my breast. I've had it for long and I doubt that it's worse. We'll need to send for the doctor, I think.* Rob said *Eh?* and gleyed at her dull *Well, well, that's fine. I'll need to be stepping, I must put in a two-three hours the night on the weeds that are coming so thick in the swedes, it's fair pestered with the dirt, that poor bit of park.* Mrs Galt said *Rob, will you leave your parks, just for a minute, and consider me? I'm ill and I want a doctor at last.*

Late the next afternoon he set off for Stonehive and the light came low and the hours went by, Mrs Galt saw nothing of her man or the doctor and near went daft with the worry and pain. But at last as it grew fell black on the fields she heard the step of Rob on the close and she ran out and cried *What's kept you so long?* and he said *What's that? Why, what but my work?* He'd come back and he'd seen his swedes waiting the hoe, so he'd got off his bike and held into the hoeing, what sense would there have been in wasting his time going up to the house to tell the news that the doctor wouldn't be till the morn?

Well, the doctor came in his long brown car, he cried to Rob as he hoed the swedes *I'll need you up at the house with me.* And Rob cried *Why? I've no time to waste.* But he got at last into the doctor's car and drove to the house and waited impatient; and the doctor came ben, and was stroking his lips; and he said *Well, Galt, I'm feared I've bad news. Your wife has a cancer of the breast, I think.*

She'd to take to her bed and was there a good month while Rob Galt worked the Pittaulds on his own Syne she wrote a letter to her daughter Rachel that was fee'd in Segget, and Rachel came home. And she said, quiet, *Mother, has he never looked near you? I'll get the police on the beast for this,* she meant her own father that was out with the hay, through the windows she could see him scything a bout, hear the skirl of the stone as he'd whet the wet blade, the sun a still lowe on the drowsing Howe, the dying woman in the littered bed. But Mrs Galt whispered *He just doesn't think, it's not that he's cruel, he's just mad on Pittaulds.*

But Rachel was nearly a woman by then, dark, with a temper that all the lads knew, and she hardly waited for her father to come home to tell him how much he might well be ashamed, he had nearly killed her mother with neglect, was he just a beast with no heart at all? But Rob hardly looked at the quean in his hurry *Hoots, lassie, your stomach's gone sour with the heat. Could I leave my parks to get covered with weeds?* And he gave her a pat, as to quieten a bairn, and ate up his dinner, all in a fash to be coling the hay. Rachel cried *Aren't you going to look in on mother?* and he said *Oh, ay,* and went ben in a hurry. *Well, lass, you'll be pleased that the hay's done fine—Damn't, there's a cloud coming up from the sea!* And the next that they saw he was out of the house staring at the cloud as at Judgment Day.

Mrs Galt was dead ere September's end, on the day of the funeral as folk came up they met Rob Galt in his old cord breeks, with a hoe in his hand, and he said he'd been out loosening up the potato drills a wee bit. He changed to his black and he helped with his brothers to carry the coffin out to the hearse. There were three bit carriages, he got in the first, and the horses went jangling slow to the road. The folk in the carriage kept solemn and long-faced, they thought Rob the same because of his wife. But he suddenly woke *Damn't, man, but I've got it! It's* LIME *that I should have given the yavil. It's been greeting for the stuff, that park on the brae!*

Rachel took on the housekeeping at Pittaulds, sombre and slim, aye reading in books, she would stand of a winter night and listen to the suck and slob of the rain on the clay, and hate the sound as she tried to hate Rob. And sometimes he'd say as they sat at their meat *What's wrong with you, lass, that you're glowering like that?* and the quean would look down, and remember her mother, while Rob rose cheery and went to his work.

And yet, as she told to one of the lads that came cycling up from Segget to see her, she just couldn't hate him, hard though she tried. There was something in him that tugged at herself daft-like, a feeling with him that the fields mattered and mattered, nothing else at all. And the lad said *What, not even me, Rachel?* and she laughed and gave him that which he sought, but half-absent like, she thought little of lads.

Well, that winter Rob Galt made up his mind that he'd break in another bit stretch of the moor beyond the bit he already had broke, there the land rose steep in a birn of wee braes, folk told him he fair would be daft to break that, it was land had lain wild and unfed since the Flood. Rob Galt said *Maybe, but they're queer-like, those braes, as though some childe had once shored them tight up.* And he set to the trauchle as he'd done before, he'd come sweating in like a bull at night and Rachel would ask him *Why don't you rest?* and he'd stare at her dumbfounded a moment: *What, rest, and me with my new bit park? What would I do but get on with my work?*

And then, as the next day wore to its close, she heard him crying her name outbye, and went through the close, and he waved from the moor. So she closed the door and went up by the track through the schlorich of the wet November moor, a windy day in the winter's nieve, the hills a-cower from the bite of the wind, the whins in that wind had a moan as they moved, not a day for a dog to be out you would say. But she found her father near tirred to the skin, he'd been heaving a great root up from its hold, *Come in by and look on this fairely, lass, I knew that some childe had once farmed up here.*

And Rachel looked at the hole in the clay and the chamber behind it, dim in the light, where there gleamed a rickle of stone-grey sticks, the bones of a man of antique time. Amid the bones was a litter of flints and a crumbling stick in the shape of a heuch.

She knew it as an eirde of olden time, an earth-house built by the early folk, Rob nodded. *Ay, he was more than that. Look at that heuch, it once scythed Pittaulds. Losh, lass, I'd have liked to have kenned that childe, what a crack together we'd have had on the crops!*

Well, that night Rob started to splutter and hoast, next morning was over stiff to move, fair clean amazed at his own condition. Rachel got a neighbour to go for the doctor, Rob had taken a cold while he stood and looked at the hole and the bones in the old-time grave. There was nothing in that and it fair was a shock when folk heard the news in a two-three days Rob Galt was dead of the cold he had ta'en. He'd worked all his go in the ground nought left to fight the black hoast that took hold of his lungs.

He'd said hardly a word, once whispered *The Ley!* the last hour as he lay and looked out at that park, red-white, with a tremor of its earthen face as the evening glow came over the Howe. Then he said to Rachel *You'll take on the land, you and some childe, I've a notion for that?* But she couldn't lie even to please him just then, she'd no fancy for either the land or a lad, she shook her head and Rob's gley grew dim.

When the doctor came in he found Rob dead, with his face to the wall and the blinds down-drawn. He asked the quean if she'd stay there alone, all the night with her father's corpse? She nodded *Oh, yes,* and watched him go, standing at the door as he drove off to Segget. Then she turned her about and went up through the parks, quiet, in the wet, quiet gloaming's coming, up through the hill to the old earth-house.

There the wind came sudden in a gust in her hair as she looked at the place and the way she had come and thought of the things the minister would say when she told him she planned her father be buried up here by the bones of the man of old time. And she shivered sudden as she looked round about at the bare clay slopes that slept in the dusk, the whistle of the whins seemed to rise in a voice, the parks below to whisper and listen as the wind came up them out of the east.

All life—just clay that awoke and strove to return again to its mother's breast. And she thought of the men who had made these rigs and the windy days of their toil and years, the daftness of toil had been Rob Galt's, that had been that of many men long on the land, though seldom seen now, was it good, was it bad? What power had that been that woke once on this brae and was gone at last from the parks of Pittaulds?

For she knew in that moment that no other would come to tend the ill rigs in the north wind's blow. This was finished and ended, a thing put by, and the whins and the broom creep down once again, and only the peesies wheep and be still when she'd gone to the life that was hers, that was different, and the earth turn sleeping, unquieted no longer, her hungry bairns in her hungry breast where sleep and death and the earth were one.

S. R. Crockett

Like his contemporary Ian Maclaren (pseudonym of the Reverend John Watson) S.R.Crockett (1860–1914) was both a Free Church minister and a Kailyard novelist.

His Galloway sketches were gathered together in *The Stickit Minister* (1893), having first appeared in the Christian Leader. He can write well, with strong dialogue and natural description, but his endings are often contrived towards a rather too comfortable or sentimental conclusion. Crockett nudges his readers, making sure we get the point.

'The Tutor of Curlywee' obviously fosters one of Scottish culture's favourite notions about the love of learning to be found in its self-reliant rural communities. Yet this was the system which educated Robert Burns and Thomas Carlyle. There is a fine irony in Crockett's narrative tone when he describes the grand importance of a Minister of Education, so pleased with his hard-won Bill which will bring enlightenment to the common people.

Though the charm is beguiling, this attitude effectively wrote the rural poor out of existence using them as set dressing for moralising romps disguised as country life viewed from the manse window.

The Tutor of Curlywee

THE MINISTER of education started to walk across the great moors of the Kells Range so early in the morning that for the first time for twenty years he saw the sun rise. Strong, stalwart, unkemp, John Bradfield, Right Honourable and Minister of the Queen, strode over the Galloway heather in his rough homespun. 'Ursa Major' they called him in the House. His colleagues, festive like schoolboys before the Old Man with the portfolios came in, subscribed to purchase him a brush and comb for his hair, for the jest of the Cabinet Minister is even as the jest of the schoolboy. John Bradfield was sturdy in whatever way you might take him. Only last session he had engineered a great measure of popular education through the House of Commons in the face of the antagonism, bitter and unscrupulous, of Her Majesty's Opposition, and the Gallio lukewarmness of his own party. So now there was a ripple of great contentment in the way he shook back locks which at forty-five were as raven black as they had been at twenty-five, and the wind that blew gently over the great billowy expanse of rock and heather smoothed out some of the crafty crow's feet deepening about his eyes.

When he started on a thirty-mile walk over the moors, along the dark purple precipitous slopes above Loch Trool, the glory of summer was melting into the more Scottish splendours of a fast coming autumn, for the frost had held off long, and then in one night had bitten snell and keen. The birches wept sunshine, and the rowan trees burned red fire.

The Minister of Education loved the great spaces of the Southern uplands, at once wider and eerier than those of the Highlands. There they lie waiting for their laureate. No one has sung of them nor written in authentic rhyme the strange weird names which the mountain tops bandy about among each other, appellations hardly pronounceable to the southron. John Bradfield, however, had enough experience of the dialect of the 'Tykes' of Yorkshire to master the intricacies of the nomenclature of the Galloway uplands. He even understood and could pronounce the famous quatrain—

> The Slock, Milquharker, and Craignine, / The Breeshie and Craignaw; / The five best hills for corklit, / The e'er the Star wife saw.*

* In old times the rocks and cliffs of the Dungeon of Buchan were famous for a kind of moss known as 'corklit,' used for dyeing, the gathering of which formed part of the livelihood of the peasantry. At one time it was much used for dyeing soldiers' red coats. *Harper's Rambles in Galloway.*

The Minister of Education hummed this rhyme, which he had learned the night before from his host in the hall tower which stands by the gate of the Ferrytown of Cree. As he made his way with long swinging gait over the heather, travelling by compass and the shrewd head which the Creator had given him, he was aware about midday of a shepherd's hut which lay in his track. He went briskly up to the door, passing the little pocket-handkerchief of kail-yard which the shepherd had carved out of the ambient heather. The purple bells grew right up to the wall of grey stone dyke which had been built to keep out the deer, or mayhap occasionally to keep them in, when the land was locked with snow, and venison was toothsome.

'Good day to you, mistress,' said the Minister of Education, who prided himself on speaking to every woman in her own tongue.

'And good day to you, sir,' heartily returned the sonsy, rosy-cheeked goodwife, who came to the door, 'an' blithe I am to see ye. It's no that aften that I see a body at the Back Hoose o' Curlywee.'

John Bradfield soon found himself well entertained—farles of cake, crisp and toothsome, milk from the cow, with golden butter in a lordly dish, cheese from a little round kebbuck, which the mistress of the Back House of Curlywee kept covered up with a napkin to keep it moist.

The goodwife looked her guest all over.

'Ye'll not be an Ayrshire man nae, I'm thinkin'. Ye kind o' favour them in the features, but ye hae the tongue o' the English.'

'My name is John Bradfield, and I come from Yorkshire,' was the reply.

'An' my name's Mistress Glencairn, an' my man Tammas is herd on Curlywee. But he's awa' ower by the Wolf's Slock the day lookin' for some forwandered yowes.'

The Minister of Education, satisfied with the good cheer, bethought himself of the curly heads that he had seen about the door. There was a merry face, brown with the sun, brimful of mischief, looking round the corner of the lintel at that moment. Suddenly the head fell forward and the body tumultuously followed, evidently by some sudden push from behind. The small youth recovered himself and vanished through the door, before his mother had time to do more than say, 'My certes, gin I catch you loons—,' as she made a dart with the handle of the besom at the culprit.

For a little John Bradfield was left alone. There were sounds of a brisk castigation outside, as though some one were taking vigorous exercise on tightly stretched corduroy. 'And on the mere the wailing died away!'

'They're good lads eneuch,' said the mistress, entering a little breathless, and with the flush of honest endeavour in her eye, 'but when their faither's oot on the hill they get a wee wild. But as ye see, I try to bring them up in the way that they should go,' she added, setting the broomstick in the corner.

'What a pity,' said the Minister of Education, 'that such bright little fellows should grow up in this lonely spot without an education.'

He was thinking aloud more than speaking to his hostess. The herd's wife of Curlywee looked him over with a kind of pity mingled with contempt.

'Edicated! Did ye say? My certes, but my bairns are as weel edicated as onybody's bairns. Juist e'en try them, gin it be your wull, sir, an' ye'll fin' them no that far ahint yer ain!'

Going to the door she raised her voice to the telephonic pitch of the Swiss *jodel* and the Australian *'coo-ee.'*

'Jee-mie, Aä-leck, Aä-nie, come ye a' here this meenit!'

The long Galloway vowels lingered on the still air, even after Mistress Glencairn came her ways into the house. There was a minute of a great silence outside. Then a scuffle of naked feet, the sough of subdued whispering, a chuckle of interior laughter, and a prolonged scuffling just outside the window.

'Gin ye dinna come ben the hoose an' be douce, you Jeemie, an' Rob, an' Alick, I'll come till ye wi' a stick! Mind ye, your faither 'ill no be lang frae hame the day.'

A file of youngsters entered, hanging their heads, and treading on each other's bare toes to escape being seated next to the formidable visitor.

'Wull it please ye, sir, to try the bairns' learning for yoursel'?'

A Bible was produced, and the three boys and their sister read round in a clear and definite manner, lengthening the vowels it is true, but giving them their proper sound, and clanging their consonants like hammers ringing on anvils.

'Very good!' said John Bradfield, who knew good reading when he heard it.

From reading they went on to spelling, and the great Bible names were tried in vain. The Minister of Education was glad that he was examiner, and not a member of the class. Hebrew polysyllables and Greek proper names fell thick and fast to the accurate aim of the boys, to whom this was child's play. History followed, geography, even grammar, maps were exhibited, and the rising astonishment of the Minister of Education kept pace with the quiet complacent pride of the Herd's Wife of Curlywee. The examination found its climax in the recitation of the 'Shorter Catechism'. Here John Bradfield was out of his depth, a fact instantly detected by the row of sharp examinees. He stumbled over the reading of the questions; he followed the breathless enunciation of that expert in the 'Caratches', Jamie, with a gasp of astonishment. Jamie was able to say the whole of *Effectual Calling* in six ticks of the clock, the result sounding to the uninitiated like the prolonged birr of intricate clockwork rapidly running down.

'What is the chief end of man?' slowly queried the Minister of Education, with his eye on the book.

'Mans-chiefend-glorfyGod-joyim-f'rever!' returned Jamie nonchalantly, all in one word, as though someone had asked him what was his name.

The Minister of Education threw down his Catechism.

'That is enough. They have all done well, and better than well. Allow me,' he said, doubtfully turning to his hostess, 'to give them each a trifle—'

'Na, na,' said Mistress Glencairn, 'let them e'en do their work withoot needin' carrots hadden afore their nose like a cuddy. What wad they do wi' siller?'

'Well, you will at least permit me to send them each a book by post—I suppose that you get letters up here occasionally?'

'Deed, there's no that muckle correspondence amang us, but when we're ower at the kirk, there yin o' the herds on Lamachan that gangs doon by to see a lass that leeves juist three miles frae the post office, an' she whiles fetches ocht that there may be for us, an' he gi'es it us at the kirk.'

John Bradfield remembered his letters and telegrams even now entering in a steady stream into his London office and overflowing his ministerial tables, waiting his return—a solemnizing thought. He resolved to build a house on the Back Hill of Curlywee, and have his letters brought by way of the kirk and the Lamachan herd's lass that lived three miles from the post office.

'Oot wi'ye!' said the mistress briefly, addressing her offspring, and the school scaled with a tumultuous rush, which left a sense of vacancy and silence and empty space about the kitchen.

'And now will you tell me how your children are so well taught?' said John Bradfield. 'How far are you from a school?'

'Weel, we're sixteen mile frae Newton Stewart, where there's a schule but no road, an' eleven frae the Clatterin'Shaws, where there's a road but no schule.'

'How do you manage then?' The Minister was anxious to have the mystery solved.

'WE KEEP A TUTOR!' said the herd's wife of Curlywee, as calmly as though she had been a duchess.

The clock ticked in its shiny mahogany case, like a hammer on an anvil, so still it was. The cat yawned and erected its back. John Bradfield's astonishment kept him silent.

'Keep a tutor,' he muttered; 'this beats all I have ever heard about the anxiety of the Scotch peasantry to have their children educated. We have nothing like this even in Yorkshire.'

Then to his hostess he turned and put another question.

'And, if I am not too bold, how much might your husband get in the year?'

'Tammas Glencairn is a guid man, though he's my man, an' he gets a good wage. He's weel worthy o't. He gets three an' twenty pound in the year, half score o' yowes, a coo's grass, a bow o' meal, a bow o' pitatas, an' as mony peats as he likes to cast, an' win', an' cairt.'

'But how,' said John Bradfield, forgetting his manners in his astonishment, 'in the name of fortune does he manage to get a tutor?'

'He disna keep him. *I* keep him!' said Mistress Glencairn with great dignity.

The Minister of Education looked his genuine astonishment this time. Had he come upon an heiress in her own right?

His hostess was mollified by his humbled look.

'Ye see, sir, it's this way,' she said, seating herself opposite to him on a clean-scoured, white wooden chair, 'there's mair hooses in this neighboorhood than ye wad think. There's the farm hoose o' the Black Craig o' Dee, there's the herd's hoose o' Garrary, the onstead o' Neldricken, the Dungeon o' Buchan—an' a wheen mair that, gin I telled ye the names o', ye wadna be a bit the wiser. Weel, in the simmer time, whan the colleges gang doon, we get yin o' the college lads to come to this quarter. There's some o' them fell fond to come. An' they pit up for three or fower weeks here, an' for three or four weeks at the Garrary ower by, an' the bairns travels ower to whaur the student lad is bidin', an' gets their learnin'. Then when it's time for the laddie to be gaun his way back to college, we send him awa' weel buskit wi' muirland claith, an' weel providit wi' butter an' eggs, oatmeal an' cheese for the comfort o' the wame o' him. Forbye we gather up among oorsels an' bid him guid speed wi' a maitter o' maybe ten or twal' poun' in his pooch. *An' that's the way we keep a tutor!*'

George MacDonald Fraser

During a varied literary career, George MacDonald Fraser (b. 1925), has brought his readers two enduringly popular anti-heroes, first with the caddish Flashman in the *Flashman* novels, and then in more recent stories featuring Private McAuslan, the Dirtiest Soldier In The World.

Fraser served his time as a lieutenant in the Gordon Highlanders and as a journalist in Scotland, England and Canada, finally becoming Deputy Editor of the *Glasgow Herald*. He has also produced several notable screenplays. In his prose we can see the journalist at work, gathering significant details to reinforce a lively and engaging story line. The McAuslan tales are also filled with a genuine love of their subject—that strange, corporate identity which is a Highland regiment. Fraser portrays this miniature society with a light touch which allows the laughable to become poignant and the absurd to appear entirely human.

'The General Danced at Dawn', the title story of Fraser's first McAuslan anthology, hardly features the infamous private. Instead it brings to life the everyday detail of battalion existence with some beautifully compact writing. The camaraderie underlined by a communal history does much to explain the long, if sometimes bloody, love affair between Scots and their military past.

The General Danced at Dawn

FRIDAY NIGHT was always dancing night. On the six other evenings of the week the officers' mess was informal, and we had supper in various states of uniform, mufti and undress, throwing bits of bread across the table and invading the kitchen for second helpings of caramel pudding. The veranda was always open, and the soft, dark night of North Africa hung around pleasantly beyond the screens.

Afterwards in the anteroom we played cards, or ludo, or occasional games of touch rugby, or just talked the kind of nonsense that subalterns talk, and whichever of these things we did our seniors either joined in or ignored completely; I have seen a game of touch rugby in progress, with the chairs and tables pushed back against the wall, and a heaving mass of Young Scotland wrestling for a 'ball' made of sock stuffed with rags, while less than a yard away the adjutant, two company commanders, and the MO were sitting round a card table holding an inquest on five spades doubled. There was great toleration.

Friday night was different. On that evening we dressed in our best tartans and walked over to the mess in twos and threes as soon as the solitary piper, who had been playing outside the mess for about twenty minutes, broke into the slow, plaintive *Battle of the Somme*—or, as it is known colloquially, 'See's the key, or I'll roar up yer lobby.'

In the mess we would have a drink in the anteroom, the captains and the majors sniffing at their Talisker and Glen Grant, and the rest of us having beer or orange juice—I have known messes where subalterns felt they had to drink hard stuff for fear of being thought cissies, but in a Highland mess nobody presses anybody. For one thing, no senior officer with a whisky throat wants to see his single malt being wasted on some pink and eager one-pipper.

Presently the Colonel would knock his pipe out and limp into the dining-room, and we would follow in to sit round the huge white table. I never saw a table like it, and never expect to; Lord Mayors banquets, college dinners, and American conventions at a hundred dollars a plate may surpass it in spectacular grandeur, but when you sat down at this table you were conscious of sitting at a dinner that had lasted for centuries.

The table was a mass of silver: the horse's-hoof snuff-box that was a relic of the few minutes at Waterloo when the regiment broke Napoleon's cavalry, and Wellington himself took off his hat and said, 'Thank you, gentlemen'; the set of spoons from some forgotten Indian palace with strange gods carved on the handles; the great bowl, magnificently engraved, presented by an American infantry regiment in Normandy, and the little quaich that had been found in the dust at Magersfontein; loot that had come from Vienna, Moscow, Berlin, Rome, the Taku Forts, and God knows where, some direct and some via French, Prussian, Polish, Spanish, and other regiments from half the countries on earth—stolen, presented, captured, bought, won, given, taken, and acquired by accident. It was priceless, and as you sat and contemplated it you could almost feel the shades elbowing you round the table.

At any rate, it enabled us to get through the tinned tomato soup, rissoles and jam tart, which seemed barely adequate to such a splendid setting, or to the sonorous grace which the padre had said beforehand ('I say, padre, can you say it in Gaelic?' 'Away, a' he talks is Glesca.' 'Wheesht for the minister'). And when it was done and the youth who was vice-president had said, 'The King,' passed the port in the wrong direction, giggled, upset his glass, and been sorrowfully rebuked from the table head, we lit up and waited for the piper. The voices, English of Sandhurst and Scottish of Kelvinside, Perthshire, and Peterhead, died away, and the pipe-major strode in and let us have it.

A twenty-minute pibroch is no small thing at a range of four feet. Some liked it, some affected to like it, and some buried their heads in their hands and endured it. But in everyone the harsh, keening siren-sound at least provoked thought. I can see them still, the faces round the table; the sad padre, tapping slowly to *The Battle of the Spoiled Dyke*; the junior subaltern, with his mouth slightly open, watching the tobacco smoke wreathing in low clouds over the white cloth; the signals officer, tapping his thumb-nail against his teeth and shifting restlessly as he wondered if he would get away in time to meet that Ensa singer at the club; the Colonel, chin on fist like a great bald eagle with his pipe clamped between his teeth and his eyes two generations away; the men, the boys, the dreamer's eyes and the boozer's melancholy, all silent while the music enveloped them.

When it was over, and we had thumped the table, and the pipe-major had downed his whisky with a Gaelic toast, we would troop out again, and the Colonel would grin and rub tobacco between his palms, and say:

'Right, gentlemen, shall we dance?'

This was part of the weekly ritual. We would take off our tunics, and the pipers would make preparatory whines, and the Colonel would perch on a table, swinging his game leg which the Japanese had broken for him on the railway, and would say:

'Now, gentlemen, as you know there is Highland dancing as performed when ladies are present, and there is Highland dancing. We will have Highland dancing. In Valetta in '21 I saw a Strip the Willow performed in eighty-nine seconds, and an Eightsome reel in two minutes twenty-two seconds. These are our targets. All right, pipey.'

We lined up and went at it. You probably know both the dances referred to, but until you have seen Highland subalterns and captains giving them the treatment you just don't appreciate them. Strip the Willow at speed is lethal; there is much swinging round, and when fifteen stone of heughing humanity is whirled at you at close range you have to be wide awake to sidestep, scoop him in, and hurl him back again. I have gone up the line many times, and it is like being bounced from wall to wall of a long corridor with heavy weights attached to your arms. You just have to relax and concentrate on keeping upright.

Occasionally there would be an accident, as when the padre, his Hebridean paganism surging up through his Calvinistic crust, swung into the MO, and the latter, his constitution undermined by drink and peering through microscopes, mistimed him and received him heavily amidships. The padre simply cried: 'The sword of the Lord and of Gideon!' and danced on, but the MO had to be carried to the rear and his place taken by the second-in-command, who was six feet four and a danger in traffic.

The Eightsome was even faster, but not so hazardous, and when it was over we would have a breather while the adjutant, a lanky Englishman who was transformed by pipe music into a kind of Fred Astaire, danced a 'ragged trousers' and the cooks and mess waiters came through to watch and join in the gradually mounting rumble of stamping and applause. He was the clumsiest creature in everyday walking and moving, but out there, with his fair hair falling over his face and his shirt hanging open, he was like thistledown on the air; he could have left Nijinsky frozen against the cushion.

The pipe-sergeant loved him, and the pipe-sergeant had skipped nimbly off with prizes uncounted at gatherings and games all over Scotland. He was a tiny, indiarubber man, one of your technically perfect dancers who had performed before crowned heads, viceroys, ambassadors, 'and all sorts of wog presidents and the like of that'. It was to mollify him that the Colonel would encourage the adjutant to perform, for the pipe-sergeant disliked 'wild' dancing of the Strip the Willow variety, and while we were on the floor he would stand with his mouth primly pursed and his glengarry pulled down, glancing occasionally at the Colonel and sniffing.

'What's up, pipe-sarnt,' the Colonel would say, 'too slow for you?'

'Slow?' the pipe-sergeant would say. 'Fine you know, sir, it's not too slow for me. It's a godless stramash is what it is, and shouldn't be allowed. Look at the unfortunate Mr Cameron, the condition of him; he doesn't know whether it's Tuesday or breakfast.'

'They love it; anyway, you don't want them dancing like a bunch of old women.'

'No, not like old women, but chust like proper Highlandmen. There is a form, and a time, and a one-two-three, and a one-two-three, and, thank God, it's done and here's the lovely adjutant.'

'Well, don't worry,' said the Colonel, clapping him on the shoulder. 'You get 'em twice a week in the mornings to show them how it ought to be done.'

This was so. On Tuesdays and Thursdays batmen would rouse officers with malicious satisfaction at 5.30, and we would stumble down, bleary and unshaven, to the MT sheds, where the pipe-sergeant would be waiting, skipping in the cold to put us through our session of practice dancing. He was in his element, bounding about in his laced pumps, squeaking at us while the piper played and we galumphed through our eightsomes and foursomes. Unlovely we were, but the pipe-sergeant was lost in the music and the mists of time, emerging from time to time to rebuke, encourage and commend.

'Ah, the fine sound,' he would cry, pirouetting among us. 'And a one, two, three, and a one, two, three. And there we are, Captain MacAlpine, going grand, going capital! One, two, three and oh, observe the fine feet of Captain MacAlpine! He springs like a startled ewe, he does! And a one, two, three, Mr Elphinstone-Hamilton, and a pas-de-bas, and, yes, Mr Cameron, once again. But now a one, two, three, four, Mr Cameron, and a one, two, three, four, and the rocking-step. Come to me, Mr Cameron, like a full-rigged ship. But, oh, dear God, the horns of the deer! Boldly, proudly, that's the style of the masterful Mr Cameron; his caber feidh is wonderful, it is fit to frighten Napoleon.'

He and Ninette de Valois would have got on a fair treat. The Colonel would sometimes loaf down, with his greatcoat over his pyjamas, and lean on his cromach, smoking and smiling quietly. And the pipe-sergeant, carried away, would skip all the harder and direct his running commentary at his audience of one.

'And a one, two, three, good morning to you, sir, see the fine dancing, and especially of Captain MacAlpine! One, two, three, and a wee bit more, Mr Cameron, see the fine horns of the deer, Colonel sir, how he knacks his thoos, God bless him. Ah, yes, that is it, Mr Elphinstone-Hamilton, a most proper appearance, is it not, Colonel?'

'I used to think,' the Colonel would say later, 'that the pipe-sergeant must drink steadily from three AM to get into that elevated condition. Now I know better. The man's bewitched.'

So we danced, and it was just part of garrison life, until the word came of one of our periodic inspections, which meant that a general would descend from Cairo and storm through us, and report to GHQ on our condition, and the Colonel, Adjutant, Regimental Sergeant Major and so on would either receive respective rockets or pats on the back. Especially the Colonel. And this inspection was rather more than ordinarily important to the old boy, because in two months he and the battalion would be going home, and soon after that he would be retiring. He should by rights have retired long before, but the war had kept him on, and he had stayed to the last possible minute. After all it was his life: he had gone with this battalion to France in '14 and hardly left it since; now he was going for good, and the word went round that his last inspection on active service must be something for him to remember in his old age, when he could look back on a battalion so perfect that the inspecting general had not been able to find so much as a speck of whitewash out of place. So we hoped.

Now, it chanced that, possibly in deference to the Colonel, the very senior officer who made this inspection was also very Highland. The pipe-sergeant rubbed his hands at the news. 'There will be dancing,' he said, with the air of the Creator establishing land and sea. 'General MacCrimmon will be enchanted; he was in the Argylls, where they dance a wee bit. Of course, being an Argyll he is chust a kind of Campbell, but it will have to be right dancing for him, I can assure you, one, two, three, and no lascivious jiving.'

Bursting with zeal, he worked our junior officers' dancing class harder than ever, leaping and exhorting until he had us exhausted; meanwhile, the whole barracks was humming with increased activity as we prepared for inspection. Arab sweepers brushed the parade ground with hand brushes to free it of dust, whitewash squads were everywhere with their buckets and stained overalls; every weapon in the place, from dirks and revolvers to the three-inch mortars, was stripped and oiled and cleaned three times over; the cookhouses, transport sheds, and even the little church, were meticulously gone over; Private McAuslan, the dirtiest soldier in the world, was sent on leave, squads roamed the barrack grounds continually, picking up paper, twigs, leaves, stones, and anything that might offend the military symmetry; the Colonel snapped and twisted his handkerchief and broke his favourite pipe; sergeants became hoarse and fretful, corporals fearful, and the quartermasters and company clerks moved uneasily in the dark places of their stores, sweating in the knowledge of duty ill-done and judgement at hand. But, finally, we were ready; in other words we were clean. We were so tired that we couldn't have withstood an attack by the Tiller Girls, but we were clean.

The day came, and disaster struck immediately. The sentry at the main gate turned out the guard at the approach of the General's car, and dropped his rifle in presenting arms. That was fairly trivial, but the General commented on it as he stepped out to be welcomed by the Colonel, and that put everyone's nerves on edge; matters were not improved by the obvious fact that he was pleased to have found a fault so early, and was intent on finding more.

He didn't have far to look. He was a big, beefy man, turned out in a yellowing balmoral and an ancient, but beautifully cut kilt, and his aide was seven feet of sideways invisibility in one of the Guards regiments. The General announced that he would begin with the men's canteen ('men's welfare comes first with me; should come first with every officer'), and in the panic that ensued on this unexpected move the canteen staff upset a swill-tub in the middle of the floor five seconds before he arrived; it had been a fine swill-tub, specially prepared to show that we had such things, and he shouldn't have seen it until it had been placed at a proper distance from the premises.

The General looked at the mess, said 'Mmh,' and asked to see the medical room ('always assuming it isn't rife with bubonic plague'); it wasn't, as it happened, but the MO's terrier had chosen that morning to give birth to puppies, beating the adjutant to it by a short head. Thereafter a fire broke out in the cookhouse, a bren-gun carrier broke down, an empty cigarette packet was found in 'B' Company's garden, and Private McAuslan came back off leave. He was tastefully dressed in shirt and boots, but no kilt, and entered the main gate in the company of three military policemen who had foolishly rescued him from a canal into which he had fallen. The General noted his progress to the guardroom with interest; McAuslan was alternately singing the Twenty-third Psalm and threatening to write to his Member of Parliament.

So it went on; anything that could go wrong, seemed to go wrong, and by dinner-time that night the General was wearing a sour and satisfied expression, his aide was silently contemptuous, the battalion was boiling with frustration and resentment, and the Colonel was looking old and ill. Only once did he show a flash of spirit, and that was when the junior subaltern passed the port the wrong way again, and the General sighed, and the Colonel caught the subaltern's eye and said loudly and clearly: 'Don't worry, Ian; it doesn't matter a damn.'

That finally froze the evening over, so to speak, and when we were all back in the anteroom and the senior major remarked that the pipe-sergeant was all set for the dancing to begin, the Colonel barely nodded, and the General lit a cigar and sat back with the air of one who was only mildly interested to see how big a hash we could make of this too.

Oddly enough, we didn't. We danced very well, with the pipe-sergeant fidgeting on the outskirts, hoarsely whispering, 'One, two, three,' and afterwards he and the adjutant and two of the best subalterns danced a foursome that would have swept the decks at Braemar. It was good stuff, really good, and the General must have known it, but he seemed rather irritated than pleased. He kept moving in his seat, frowning, and when we had danced an eightsome he finally turned to the Colonel.

'Yes, it's all right,' he said. 'But, you know, I never cared much for the set stuff. Did you never dance a sixteensome?'

The Colonel said he had heard of such a thing, but had not, personally, danced it.

'Quite simple,' said the General, rising. 'Now, then. Eight more officers on the floor. I think I remember it, although it's years now . . .'

He did remember; a sixteensome is complicated, but its execution gives you the satisfaction that you get from any complex manoeuvre; we danced it twice, the General calling the changes and clapping (his aide was studying the ceiling with the air of an archbishop at a cannibal feast), and when it was over the General actually smiled and called for a large whisky. He then summoned the pipe-sergeant, who was looking disapproving.

'Pipe-sergeant, tell you what,' said the General. 'I have been told that back in the Nineties the First Black Watch sergeants danced a thirty-twosome. Always doubted it, but suppose it's possible. What do you think? Yes, another whisky, please.'

The pipe-sergeant, flattered but slightly outraged, gave his opinion. All things were possible; right, said the General, wiping his mouth, we would try it.

The convolutions of an eightsome are fairly simple; those of a sixteensome are difficult, but a thirty-twosome is just murder. When you have thirty-two people weaving and circling it is necessary that each one should move precisely right, and that takes organization. The General was an organizer; his tunic came off after half an hour, and his voice hoarsely thundered the time and the changes. The mess shook to the crash of feet and the skirling of the pipes, and at last the thirty-twosome rumbled, successfully, to its ponderous close.

'Dam' good! Dam' good!' exclaimed the General, flushed and applauding. 'Well danced, gen'men. Good show, pipe-sarn't! Thanks, Tom, don't mind if I do. Dam' fine dancing. Thirty-twosome, eh? That'll show the Black Watch!'

He seemed to sway a little as he put down his glass. It was midnight, but he was plainly waking up.

'Thirty-twosome, by Jove! Wouldn't have thought it possible.' A thought seemed to strike him. 'I say, pipe-sarn't, I wonder . . . d'you suppose that's as far as we can go? I mean is there any reason? . . .'

He talked, and the pipe-sergeant's eyes bulged. He shook his head, the General persisted, and five minutes later we were all outside on the lawn and trucks were being sent for so that their headlights could provide illumination, and sixty-four of us were being thrust into our positions, and the General was shouting orders through cupped hands from the veranda.

'Taking the time from me! Right, pipers? It's p'fickly simple. S'easy. One, two, an' off we go!'

It was a nightmare, it really was. I had avoided being in the sixty-four; from where I was standing it looked like a crowd scene from *The Ten Commandments*, with the General playing Cecil B. de Mille. Officers, mess waiters, batmen, swung into the dance as the pipes shrilled, setting to partners, circling forwards and back, forming an enormous ring, and heughing like things demented. The General bounded about the veranda, shouting; the pipe-sergeant hurtled through the sets, pulling, directing, exhorting; those of us watching clapped and stamped as the mammoth dance surged on, filling the night with its sound and fury.

It took, I am told, one hour and thirteen minutes by the adjutant's watch, and by the time it was over the Fusiliers from the adjoining barracks were roused and lined along the wall, assorted Arabs had come to gaze on the wonders of civilization, and the military police mobile patrol was also on hand. But the General was tireless; I have a vague memory of him standing on the tailboard of a truck, addressing the assembled mob; I actually got close enough to hear him exhorting the pipe-sergeant in tones of enthusiasm and entreaty:

'Pipe-sarn't! Pipey! May I call you Pipey? . . . never been done . . . three figures . . . think of it . . . hunner'n-twenty-eightsome . . . never another chance . . . try it . . . rope in the Fusiliers . . . massed pipers . . . regimental history . . . please, Pipey, for me . . .'

Some say that it actually happened, that a one hundred and twenty-eightsome reel was danced on the parade ground that night, General Sir Roderick MacCrimmon, KCB, DSO, and bar, presiding; that it was danced by Highlanders, Fusiliers, Arabs, military police, and three German prisoners of war; that it was danced to a conclusion, all figures. It may well have been; all I remember is a heaving, rushing crowd, like a mixture of Latin Carnival and Scarlett's uphill charge at Balaclava, surging ponderously to the sound of the pipes; but I distinctly recall one set in which the General, the pipe-sergeant, and what looked like a genuine Senussi in a burnous, swept by roaring, 'One, two, three,' and I know, too, that at one point I personally was part of a swinging human chain in which my immediate partners were the Fusiliers' cook-sergeant and an Italian café proprietor from down the road. My memory tells me that it rose to a tremendous crescendo just as the first light of dawn stole over Africa, and then all faded away, silently, in the tartan-strewn morning.

No one remembers the General leaving later in the day, although the Colonel said he believed he was there, and that the General cried with emotion. It may have been so, for the inspection report later congratulated the battalion, and highly commended the pipe-sergeant on the standard of the officers' dancing. Which was a mixed pleasure to the pipe-sergeant, since the night's proceedings had been an offence to his orthodox soul.

'Mind you,' he would say, 'General MacCrimmon had a fine agility at the pas-de-bas, and a decent sense of the time. Och, aye, he wass not bad, not bad . . . for a Campbell.'

William Boyd

NOT YET, JAYETTE

With his short stories, novelist William Boyd coaxes his readers into uncomfortable and even disturbing territories.

His settings, ranging from Los Angeles to Africa and Vietnam, are more than exotic backdrops. Like his characters, they introduce us to alternative values and ways of life, showing how fine the line is between the socially acceptable and the shocking.

Boyd, like his work, is widely travelled. Born in Ghana, in 1952, he was a student at Nice, Glasgow and Oxford Universities. For three years he lectured in English at St Hilda's College, Oxford, before turning to full-time writing. He has published one collection of short stories, *On the Yankee Station*. Taken from this book, 'Not Yet, Jayette' is narrated by a typically fallible central figure, through whom a whole society is laid bare.

Not Yet, Jayette

THIS HAPPENED to me in L.A. once. Honestly. I was standing at a hamburger kiosk on Echo Park eating a chilé-dog. This guy in a dark green Lincoln pulls up at the kerb in front of me and leans out of the window. 'Hey,' he asks me, 'do you know the way to San José?' Well, that threw me, I had to admit it. In fact I almost told him. Then I got wise. 'Don't tell me,' I says. 'Let me guess. You're going back to find some peace of mind.' I only tell you this to give you some idea of what the city is like. It's full of jokers. And that guy, even though I'd figured him, still bad-mouthed me before he drove away. That's the kind of place it is. I'm just telling you so's you know my day is for real.

Most mornings, early, I go down to the beach at Santa Monica to try and meet Christopher Isherwood. A guy I know told me he likes to walk his dog down there before the beach freaks and the surfers show up. I haven't seen him yet but I've grown to like my mornings on the beach. The sea has that oily sheen to it, like an empty swimming pool. The funny thing is, though, the Pacific Ocean nearly always looks cold. One morning someone was swinging on the bars, up and down, flinging himself about as if he was made of rubber. It was beautiful, and boy, was he built. It's wonderful to me what the human body can achieve if you treat it right. I like to keep in shape. I work out. So most days I hang around waiting to see if Christopher's going to show then I go jogging. I head south; down from the pier to Pacific Ocean Park. I've got to know some of the bums that live around the beach, the junkies and derelicts. 'Hi Charlie,' they shout when they see me jogging by.

There's a café in Venice where I eat breakfast. A girl works there most mornings, thin, bottle-blond, kind of tired looking. I'm pretty sure she's on something heavy. So that doesn't make her anything special but she can't be more than eighteen. She knows my name, I don't know how, I never told her. Anyway each morning when she brings me my coffee and doughnut she says 'Hi there, Charlie. Lucked-out yet?' I just smile and say 'Not yet, Jayette.' Jayette's the name she's got sewn across her left tit. I'm not sure I like the way she speaks to me—I don't exactly know what she's referring to. But seeing how she knows my name I think it must be my career she's talking about. Because I used to be a star, well, a TV star anyway. Between the ages of nine and eleven I earned twelve thousand dollars a week. Perhaps you remember the show, a TV soap opera called 'The Scrantons'. I was the little brother, Chuck. For two years I was a star. I got the whole treatment: my own trailer, chauffeured limousines, private tutors. Trouble was my puberty came too early. Suddenly I was like a teenage gatecrasher at a kids' party. My voice went, I got zitz all over my chin, fluff on my lip. It spoilt everything. Within a month the scenario for my contractual death was drawn up. I think it was pneumonia, or maybe an accident with the thresher. I can't really remember, I don't like to look back on those final days.

Though I must confess it was fun meeting all the stars. The big ones: Jeanne Lamont, Eddy Cornelle, Mary and Marvin Keen—you remember them. One of the most bizarre features of my life since I left the studio is that nowadays I never see stars any more. Isn't that ridiculous? Someone like me who worked with them, who practically lives in Hollywood? Somehow I never get to see the stars anymore. I just miss them. 'Oh he left five minutes ago, bub,' or 'Oh no, I think she's on location in Europe, she hasn't been here for weeks.' The same old story.

I think that's what Jayette's referring to when she asks if I've lucked-out. She knows I'm still hanging in there, waiting. I mean, I've kept on my agent. The way I see it is that once you've been in front of the cameras something's going to keep driving you on until you get back. I know it'll happen to me again one day, I just have this feeling inside.

After breakfast I jog back up the beach to where I left the car. One morning I got to thinking about Jayette. What does she think when she sees me now and remembers me from the days of 'The Scrantons'? It seems to me that everybody in their life is at least two people. Once when you're a child and once when you're an adult. It's the saddest thing. I don't just mean that you see things differently when you're a child—that's something else again—what's sad is that you can't seem to keep the personality. I know I'm not the same person anymore as young Chuck Scranton was, and I find that depressing. I could meet little Charlie on the beach today and say 'Look, there goes a sharp kid.' And never recognise him, if you see what I mean. It's a shame.

I don't like the jog back so much, as all the people are coming out. Lying around, surfing, cruising, scoring, shooting up, tricking. Hell, the things I've seen on that sand, I could tell you a few stories. Sometimes I like to go down to El Segundo or Redondo beach just to feel normal.

I usually park the car on Santa Monica Pallisades. I tidy up, change into my clothes and shave. I have a small battery powered electric razor that I use. Then I have a beer, wander around, buy a newspaper. Mostly I then drive north to Malibu. There's a place I know where you can get a fair view of a longish stretch of the beach. It's almost impossible to get down there in summer; they don't like strangers. So I pull off the highway and climb this small dune-hill. I have a pair of opera glasses of my aunt's that I use to see better—my eyesight's not too hot. I spotted Rod Steiger one day, and Jane Fonda I think but I can't be sure, the glasses tend to fuzz everything a bit over four hundred yards. Anyway I like the quiet on that dune, it's restful.

I have been down on to Malibu beach, but only in the winter season. The houses are all shut up but you can still get the feel of it. Some people were having a bar-b-q one day. It looked good. They had a fire going on a big porch that jutted out high over the sand. They waved and shouted when I went past.

Lunch is bad. The worst part of the day for me because I have to go home. I live with my aunt. I call her my aunt though I'm not related to her at all. She was my mother's companion—I believe that's the right word—until my mother stuffed her face with a gross of Seconal one afternoon in a motel at Corona del Mar. I was fifteen then and Vanessa—my 'aunt'—became some kind of legal guardian to me and had control of all the money I'd made from 'The Scrantons'. Well, she bought an apartment in Beverly Glen because she liked the address. Man, was she swallowed by the realtor. They built these tiny apartment blocks on cliff-faces up the asshole of the big-name canyons just so you can say you live off Mulholland Drive or in Bel Air. It's a load. I'd rather live in Watts or on Imperial highway. I practically have to rope-up and wear crampons to get to my front door. And it is mine. I paid for it.

Maybe that's why Vanessa never leaves her bed. It's just too much effort getting in and out of the house. She just stays in bed all day and eats, watches TV and feeds her two dogs. I only go in there for lunch; it's my only 'family' ritual. I take a glass of milk and a salad sandwich but she phones out for pizza and enchiladas and burgers—any kind of crap she can smear over her face and down her front. She's really grown fat in the ten years since my mother bombed out. But she still sits up in bed with those hairy yipping dogs under her armpits, and she's got her top and bottom false eyelashes, her hairpiece and purple lipstick on. I say nothing usually. For someone who never gets out she sure can talk a lot. She wears these tacky satin and lace peignoirs, shows half her chest. Her breasts look like a couple of Indian clubs rolling around under the shimmer. It's unfair I suppose, but when I drive back into the foothills I like to think I'm going to have a luncheon date with . . . with someone like Grace Kelly—as was—or maybe Alexis Smith. I don't know. I wouldn't mind a meal and a civilised conversation with some nice people like that. But lunch with Vanessa? Thanks for nothing, pal. God, you can keep it. She's a real klutz. I'm sure Grace and Alexis would never let themselves get that way—you know, like Vanessa's always dropping tacos down her cleavage or smearing mustard on her chins.

I always get depressed after lunch. It figures, I hear you say. I go to my room and sometimes I have a drink (I don't smoke, so dope's out). Other days I play my guitar or else work on my screenplay. It's called 'Walk. Don't Walk.' I get a lot of good ideas after lunch for some reason. That's when I got the idea for my screenplay. It just came to me. I remembered how I'd been stuck one day at the corner of Arteria boulevard and Normandie avenue. There was a pile of traffic and the pedestrian signs were going berserk. 'Walk' would come on so I'd start across. Two seconds later 'Don't Walk' so I go back. Then on comes 'Walk' again. This went on for ten minutes: 'Walk. Don't Walk. Walk. Don't Walk.' I was practically out of my box. But what really stunned me was the way I just stayed there and obeyed the goddam machine for so long—I never even thought about going it alone. Then one afternoon after lunch it came to me that it was a neat image for life; just the right kind of metaphor for the whole can of worms. The final scene of this movie is going to be a slow crane shot away from this malfunctioning traffic sign going 'Walk. Don't Walk.' Then the camera pulls further up and away in a helicopter and you see that in fact the whole city is fouled up because of this one sign flashing. They don't know what to do; the programming's gone wrong. It's a great final scene. Only problem is I'm having some difficulty writing my way towards it. Still, it'll come, I guess.

In the late afternoon I go to work. I work at the Beverly Hills Hotel. Vanessa's brother-in-law got me the job. I park cars. I keep hoping I'm going to park the car of someone really important. Frank—that's Vanessa's brother-in-law—will say to me 'Give this one a shine-up, Charlie, it belongs to so and so, he produced this film,' or 'That guy's the money behind X's new movie,' or 'Look out, he's Senior Vice-President of Something incorporated.' I say big deal. These guys hand me the keys—they all look like bank clerks. If that's the movies nowadays I'm not so sure I want back in.

Afternoons are quiet at the hotel so I catch up on my reading. I'm reading Camus at the moment but I think I've learnt all I can from him so I'm going on to Jung. I don't know too much about Jung but I'm told he was really into astrology which has always been a pet interest of mine. One thing I will say for quitting the movies when I did means that I didn't miss out on my education. I hear that some of these stars today are really dumb; you know, they've got their brains in their neck and points south.

After work I drive back down to the Santa Monica pier and think about what I'm going to do all night. The Santa Monica pier is a kind of special place for me: it's the last place I saw my wife and son. I got married at seventeen and was divorced by twenty-two, though we were apart for a couple of years before that. Her name was Harriet. It was okay for a while but I don't think she liked Vanessa. Anyway, get this. She left me for a guy who was the assistant manager in the credit collection department of a large mail order firm. I couldn't believe it when she told me. I said to her when she moved out that it had to be the world's most boring job and did she know what she was getting into? I mean, what sort of person do you have to be to take on that kind of work? The bad thing was she took my son Skiff with her. It's a dumb name I know, but at the time he was born all the kids were being called things like Sky and Saffron and Powie, and I was really sold on sailing. I hope he doesn't hold it against me.

The divorce was messy and she got custody, though I'll never understand why. She had left some clothes at the house and wanted them back so she suggested we meet at the end of the Santa Monica pier for some reason. I didn't mind, it was the impetuous side to her nature that first attracted me. I handed the clothes over. She was a bit tense. Skiff was running about; he didn't seem to know who I was. She was smoking a lot; those long thin menthol cigarettes. I really didn't say anything much at all, asked her how she was, what school Skiff was going to. Then she just burst out 'Take a good look, Charlie, then don't come near us ever again!' Her exact words. Then they went away.

So I go down to the end of the pier most nights and look out at the ocean and count the planes going in to land at L.A. International and try to work things out. Just the other evening I wandered up the beach a way and this thin-faced man with short grey hair came up to me and said 'Jordan, is that you?' And when he saw he'd made a mistake he smiled a nice smile, apologised and walked off. It was only this morning that I thought it might have been Christopher Isherwood himself. The more I think about it the more convinced I become. What a perfect opportunity and I had to go and miss it. As I say: 'Walk. Don't Walk.' That's the bottom line.

I suppose I must have been preoccupied. The pier brings back all these memories like some private video-loop, and my head gets to feel like it's full of birds all flapping around trying to get out. And also things haven't been so good lately. On Friday Frank told me not to bother showing up at the hotel next week, I can't seem to make any headway with the screenplay and for the last three nights Vanessa's tried to climb into my bed.

Well, tonight I think I'll drive to this small bar I know on Sunset. Nothing too great, a little dark. They do a nice white wine with peach slices in it, and there's some topless, some go-go, and I hear tell that Bobby de Niro sometimes shows up for a drink.

Neil Munro

HURRICANE JACK

Neil Munro (1864–1930), came to Glasgow from Inverary on Scotland's West Coast. For a while he worked in a lawyer's office. Then he turned to journalism and became editor of the *Glasgow Evening News*, writing articles, sketches and the Para Handy stories under the pseudonym of Hugh Foulis. Eventually he admitted their author's true identity. He did this reluctantly wanting to disclaim the popularity of the Foulis work in favour of more serious ambitions as poet and novelist.

In his first collection of stories, *The Lost Pibroch*, which appeared in 1896, Munro views the romantic pull of Highland culture with a gently ironic tone. This pattern recurs throughout his serious work, and in his best novels, *John Splendid* and *The New Road*, he sees romanticism as destructive and dangerous. On the other hand there is something engagingly romantic about Para Handy and his disparate crew on a steam cargo boat for hire. Theirs is a timeless world as they sail up and down the west coast of Scotland, untouched by events outwith their locality, untouched by anything other than themselves and what they encounter. It is like an industrial version of the Celtic twilight, yet the stories are saved from sentimentality by their comic inventiveness and the eccentricity of the characters.

The Para Handy tales were enormously popular. Much later they became associated with a highly successful television series, which at times concentrated more on visual humour than on the texts. This is a pity, for Munro's prose is crammed with sly asides and an enduring delight in its West Coast setting. 'Hurricane Jack' introduces a character who crops up from time to time as an occasional member of the crew.

Hurricane Jack

I VERY OFTEN hear my friend the Captain speak of Hurricane Jack in terms of admiration and devotion, which would suggest that Jack is a sort of demigod. The Captain always refers to Hurricane Jack as the most experienced seaman of modern times, as the most fearless soul that ever wore oilskins, the handsomest man in Britain, so free with his money he would fling it at the birds, so generally accomplished that it would be a treat to be left a month on a desert island alone with him.

'Why is he called Hurricane Jack?' I asked the Captain once.

'What the duvvle else would you caal him?' asked Para Handy. 'Nobody ever caals him anything else than Hurricane Jack.'

'Quite so, but why?' I persisted.

Para Handy scratched the back of his neck, made the usual gesture as if he were going to scratch his ear, and then checked himself in the usual way to survey his hand as if it were a beautiful example of Greek sculpture. His hand, I may say, is almost as large as a Belfast ham.

'What way wass he called Hurricane Jeck?' said he. 'Well, I'll soon tell you that. He wass not always known by that name; that wass a name he got for the time he stole the sheep.'

'Stole the sheep!' I said, a little bewildered, for I failed to see how an incident of that kind would give rise to such a name.

'Yes; what you might call stole,' said Para Handy hastily; 'but, och! it wass only wan smaal wee sheep he lifted on a man that never went to the church, and chust let him take it! Hurricane Jeck would not steal a fly—no, nor two flies, from a Chrustian; he's the perfect chentleman in that.'

'Tell me all about it,' I said.

'I'll soon do that,' said he, putting out his hand to admire it again, and in doing so upsetting his glass. 'Tut, tut!' he said. 'Look what I have done—knocked doon my gless; it wass a good thing there wass nothing in it.'

'Hurricane Jeck,' said the Captain, when I had taken the hint and put something in it , 'iss a man that can sail anything and go anywhere, and aalways be the perfect chentleman. A millionaire's yat or a washing-boyne—it's aal the same to Jeck; he would sail the wan chust as smert as the other, and land on the quay as spruce ass if he wass newly come from a baal. Oh, man! the cut of his jeckets! And never anything else but 'lastic-sided boots, even in the coorsest weather! If you would see him, you would see a man that's chust sublime, and that careful about his 'lastic-sided boots he would never stand at the wheel unless there wass a bass below his feet. He'll aye be oiling at his hair, and buying hard hats for going ashore with: I never saw a man wi' a finer heid for the hat, and in some of the vessels he wass in he would have the full of a bunker of hats. Hurricane Jeck wass brought up in the China clupper tred, only he wassna called Hurricane Jeck then, for he hadna stole the sheep till efter that. He wass captain of the *Dora Young*, wan of them cluppers; he's a hand on a gaabert the now, but aalways the perfect chentleman.'

'It seems a sad downcome for a man to be a gabbert hand after having commanded a China clipper,' I ventured to remark. 'What was the reason of his change?'

'Bad luck,' said Para Handy. 'Chust bad luck. The fellow never got fair-play. He would aye be somewhere takin' a gless of something wi' somebody, for he's a fine cheery chap. I mind splendid when he wass captain on the clupper, he had a fine hoose of three rooms and a big decanter, wi' hot and cold watter, oot at Pollokshaws. When you went oot to the hoose to see Hurricane Jeck in them days, time slupped bye. But he wassna known as Hurricane Jeck then, for it wass before he stole the sheep.

'You were just going to tell me something about that,' I said.

'Jeck iss wan man in a hundred, and ass good ass two if there wass anything in the way of trouble, for, man! he's strong, strong! He has a back on him like a shipping-box, and when he will come down Tarbert quay on a Friday night after a good fishing, and the trawlers are arguing, it's two yerds to the step with him and a bash in the side of his hat for fair defiance. But he never hit a man twice, for he's aye the perfect chentleman iss Hurricane Jeck. Of course, you must understand, he wass not known as Hurricane Jeck till the time I'm going to tell you of, when he stole the sheep.

'I have not trevelled far mysel' yet, except Ullapool and the time I wass at Ireland; but Hurricane Jeck in his time has been at every place on the map, and some that's no'. Chust wan of Brutain's hard sons—that's what he iss. As weel kent in Calcutta as if he wass in the Coocaddens, and he could taalk a dozen of their foreign kinds of languages if he cared to take the bother. When he would be leaving a port, there wassna a leddy in the place but what would be doon on the quay wi' her Sunday clothes on and a bunch o' floo'ers for his cabin. And when he would be sayin' goodbye to them from the brudge, he would chust take off his hat and give it a shogle, and put it on again; his manners wass complete. The first thing he would do when he reached many place wass to go ashore and get his boots brushed, and then sing "Rule Britannia" roond aboot the docks. It wass a sure way to get freend or foe aboot you, he said, and he wass aye as ready for the wan as for the other. Brutain's hardy son!

'He made the fastest passages in his time that wass ever made in the tea trade, and still and on he would meet you like a common working-man. There wass no pride or nonsense of that sort aboot Hurricane Jeck; but, mind you, though I'm callin' him Hurricane Jeck, he wasna Hurricane Jeck till the time he stole the sheep.'

'I don't like to press you, Captain, but I'm anxious to hear about that sheep,' I said patiently.

'I'm comin' to't,' said Para Handy. 'Jeck had the duvvle's own bad luck; he couldna take a gless by-ordinar' but the ship went wrong on him, and he lost wan job efter the other, but he wass never anything else but the perfect chentleman. When he had not a penny in his pocket, he would borrow a shilling from you, and buy you a stick pipe for yourself chust for good nature—'

'A stick pipe?' I repeated interrogatively.

'Chust a stick pipe—or a wudden pipe, or whatever you like to call it. He had three medals and a clock that wouldna go for saving life at sea, but that wass before he wass Hurricane Jeck, mind you; for at that time he hadna stole the sheep.'

'I'm dying to hear about that sheep,' I said.

'I'll soon tell you about the sheep,' said Para Handy. 'It wass a thing that happened when him and me wass sailing on the *Elizabeth Ann*, a boat that belonged to Girvan, and a smert wan too, if she wass in any kind of trum at aal. We would be going here and there aboot the West Coast with wan thing and another, and not costing the owners mich for coals if coals wass our cargo. It wass wan Sunday we were passing Caticol in Arran, and in a place yonder where there wass not a hoose in sight we saw a herd of sheep eating grass near the shore. As luck would have it, there wass not a bit of butchermeat on board the *Elizabeth Ann* for the Sunday dinner, and Jeck cocked his eye at the sheep and says to me, "Yonder's some sheep lost, poor things; what do you say to taking the punt and going ashore to see if there's anybody's address on them?"

'"Whatever you say yoursel'," I said to Jeck, and we stopped the vessel and went ashore, the two of us, and looked the sheep high and low, but there wass no address on them. "They're lost, sure enough," said Jeck, pulling some heather and putting it in his pocket—he wassna Hurricane Jeck then—"they're lost, sure enough, Peter. Here's a nice wee wan nobody would ever miss, that chust the very thing for a coal vessel," and before you could say "knife" he had it killed and carried to the punt. Oh, he iss a smert, smert fellow with his hands; he could do anything.

'We rowed ass caalm ass we could oot to the vessel, and we had chust got the deid sheep on board when we heard a roarin' and whustling.

'"Taalk about Arran being releegious!' said Jeck. "Who's that whustling on the Lord's day?"

'The man that wass whustling wass away up on the hill, and we could see him coming running doon the hill the same ass if he would break every leg he had on him.

'"I'll bate you he'll say it's his sheep,' said Jeck. "Weel, we'll chust anchor the vessel here till we hear what he hass to say, for if we go away and never mind the cratur he'll find oot somewhere else it's the *Elizabeth Ann.*"

'When the fermer and two shepherds came oot to the *Elizabeth Ann* in a boat, she wass lying at anchor, and we were all on deck, every man wi' a piece o' heather in his jecket.

'"I saw you stealing my sheep," said the fermer, coming on deck, furious. 'I'll have every man of you jiled for this."

'"Iss the man oot of his wuts?" said Jeck. "Drink—chust drink! Nothing else but drink! If you were a sober Christian man, you would be in the church at this 'oor in Arran, and not oot on the hill recovering from last night's carry-on in Loch Ranza, and imagining you are seeing things that's not there at aal, at aal."

'"I saw you with my own eyes steal the sheep and take it on board," said the fermer, nearly choking with rage.

'"What you saw was my freend and me gathering a puckle heather for oor jeckets," said Jeck, "and if ye don't believe me you can search the ship from stem to stern."

'"I'll soon do that," said the fermer, and him and his shepherds went over every bit of the *Elizabeth Ann*. They never missed a corner you could hide a moose in, but there wass no sheep nor sign of sheep anywhere.

'"Look at that, Macalpine," said Jeck. "I have a good mind to have you up for inflammation of character. But what could you expect from a man that would be whustling on the hill like a peesweep on a Sabbath when he should be in the church. It iss a good thing for you, Macalpine, it iss a Sabbath, and I can keep my temper."

'"I could swear I saw you lift the sheep," said the fermer, quite vexed.

'"Saw your auntie! Drink; nothing but the cursed drink!" said Jeck, and the fermer and his shepherds went away with their tails behind their legs.

'We lay at anchor till it was getting dark, and then we lifted the anchor and took off the sheep that wass tied to it when we put it oot. "It's a good thing salt mutton," said Hurricane Jeck as we sailed away from Caticol, and efter that the name he always got wass Hurricane Jeck.'

'But why "Hurricane Jack"?' I asked, more bewildered than ever.

'Holy smoke! am I no' tellin' ye?' said Para Handy. 'It wass because he stole the sheep.'

But I don't understand it yet.

Douglas Dunn

Douglas Dunn was born in Renfrewshire in 1942, but is associated with Hull where he went to University, worked as a librarian, later became a fellow in Creative Writing and encouraged a new generation of writers. Dunn has published a number of highly acclaimed books of poetry, being awarded the Whitbread Prize for *Elegies* in 1986. He now lives in Tayport in Fife and has published a collection of short stories, *Secret Villages*.

His prose has the melancholy edge and attention to detail found in his verse, with a surprising sense of humour which delights in bringing the accepted clichés of Scottish life under the microscope and finding new truths behind the pretence.

Here he looks closely at our image of the wily Highlander and his dependence on unsuspecting tourists. The beautifully judged, formal and ironic tone of 'The Canoes' shows us the minds and spirits which live beyond the picture postcards, and while it retains the beauty of the scene, it also conveys the grey lives of a people left stranded by their past. As Dunn reminds us, there is a long and historical answer to the Englishman's question, 'How much do I owe you?'

The Canoes

PETER AND Rosalind Barker began their holiday on Loch Arn on an evening in the first week of August. We were standing by the rail of what is known in our village of Locharnhead as the Promenade—a name that does no more than repeat the intent of the old Duke, who paid for its construction many years ago as a means of employing our fathers. It is just a widening of the pavement by the side of the road that runs along the head of Loch Arn and then peters out in an unpaved track a mile farther on. We have ten yards of Promenade, and that is not much of a walk. Our fathers used to lean on a low stone wall there. Now, as the old Duke considered this wall a symbol of our fathers' idleness, the job of knocking it down for good wages was meant to be significant. As a boy, I remember the old Duke's rage when, within a day of the work's completion, as he found our fathers loafing on the splendid new barrier they had just built, he craned from the window of his big car and cursed them to lean perpetually on a hot rail by the hearths of damnation. On summer evenings, therefore, we stand where our fathers stood, and one or two very old men sometimes stand beside their sons. For the most part we keep our mouths shut and enjoy the mild breeze that whispers across the water.

The Barkers looked a prosperous young couple. Mr Barker could have been no more than thirty years of age; his wife might have been a year or two younger. Their skins were already tanned, which I thought strange for two people at the start of their holiday. Mrs Barker wore a broad red ribbon in her fair hair, and I was pleased to see that her husband was not the sort of young man whose hair hides his ears and touches his shoulders. They both wore those modern clothes that, in my opinion, look so good on young, slender, healthy men and women. And I noticed that they wore those useful shoes that have no laces but can just be kicked off without your stooping to struggle with ill-tied knots as the blood rushes to your head.

Mr Barker parked his car in the place provided by the County Council, adjacent to the jetty. The jetty was paid for by the old Duke. It is announced as Strictly Private Property on a wooden notice board, though few people here can be bothered to read notices. The paint has long since peeled from it, and its message is rewritten in the badly formed letters of the new Duke's son's factor. Perhaps more would be done for the attractions of Locharnhead, which stands in need of a coat of paint throughout, if it was not the sort of place you can only get back from by returning along the arduous way you came.

Our eyes swung genially to the left to inspect the new arrivals—all, that is, except those of Martin MacEacharn, who is so dull of wit he proclaims himself bored with the examination of tourists. They are a kind of sport with the rest of us. Much amusement has been given to us by campers and hikers and cyclists in their strange garbs and various lengths of shorts and sizes of boots. We tell them they cannot light fires and pitch their tents where they are permitted to do so; and we tell them they may light fires and pitch tents to their hearts' desire where gamekeepers and bailiffs are guaranteed to descend on them once it is dark and there will be no end of inconvenience in finding a legal spot for the night.

Young Gregor remarked enviously on the couple's motorcar. It was low to the ground, green, sleek, and new, and obviously capable of a fair rate of knots. Magee, whose father was an Irishman, ambled over toward Mr and Mrs Barker, pretending he was too shy to speak to them. They were admiring the fine view of the long loch from the jetty. Mr Barker had his arm around his wife's shoulders and was pointing to various phenomena of loveliness in the scenery. They are a familiar sight to us, these couples, who look and behave as if they feel themselves to have arrived in a timeless paradise of water and landscape and courteous strangers in old-fashioned clothes. On fine summer evenings the stillness of the water may be impressed on all your senses to the abandonment of everything else. Our dusks are noted far and wide and remembered by all who have witnessed them. On Loch Arn at dusk the islands become a mist of suggestions. There are old songs that say if only you could go back to them once more, all would be well with you for ever.

Mr Barker noticed Magee beside him and said, 'Good evening,' which Magee acknowledged with his shy smile and slow, soft voice. 'You'll be looking for me, perhaps,' Magee said. All of us leaning on the rail of the Promenade—Muir, Munro, Young Gregor, MacMurdo, MacEacharn, and myself—nodded to each other. When the couple saw us, we all nodded a polite and silent good evening to them, which we believe is necessary, for they have heard of our courtesy, our soft-spoken and excellent good manners and clear speech. All except Martin MacEacharn extended them the thousand welcomes; he was undoubtedly thinking too hard in his miserable way about the Hotel bar behind us and for which he had no money to quench his thirst.

'If you're the boatman, then, yes, you're the man we're waiting for,' said Mr Barker to Magee. My, but he had a bright way of saying it, too, though we all thought that a couple who possessed two long kayak canoes on the trailer behind their motor car had no need of a boatman. He towered over Magee, who is short, wizened, bowlegged, and thin, though his shoulders are broad. Mrs Barker, too, was a good half foot taller than him.

'Well, I think I can just about more or less manage it,' said Magee, with a quick look at his watch, which has not worked in years. 'Yes,' he said, for he must always be repeating himself, 'just about. Just about, if we're handy-dandy.'

'Handy-dandy?' said MacMurdo with contempt. 'Where does he pick them up, for goodness' sake?'

Magee, as we all knew, was desperate for a bit of money, but a lethargic disregard of time is obligatory in these parts. Or that, at least, is the legend. What I will say is that if Magee is late for his dinner by so much as half a minute, his wife will scatter it, and probably Magee as well, before her chickens. Social Security keeps him and the rest of us alive, and I have yet to see a man late for his money. If it ever came to the attention of the clerk that Donal Magee turns a bob or two with his boat, then he would be in deeper water than the depths of Loch Arn, some of which, they say, are very deep.

It soon became clear why the Barkers couldn't paddle themselves out to Incharn. Gear and suitcases are awkward to transport by canoe. Magee, a lazy man, turned round to us with a silent beckoning. He was asking us to lend him a hand but was frightened to say so aloud for fear that our refusals might ruin the atmosphere of traditional, selfless welcoming he had created with such skill and patience. We turned away with the precision of a chorus line it was once my good fortune to see in one of these American musical films—all, that is, except Martin MacEacharn, who wasn't looking.

Once Magee had loaded his boat and tied the canoes to its stern, the flotilla set off in the dusk like a mother duck followed by two chicks. I treated them to one of my lugubrious waves, which I am so good at that no one else is allowed to make one while I am there. How many times, after all, have the holiday types said to us, 'We will remember you forever'? It is a fine thing, to be remembered.

Incharn is a small and beautiful island. That, at any rate, is how I remember it, for I have not stepped ashore there since I was a boy. A school friend of mine, Murray Mackenzie, lived on Incharn with his mother and father. Only one house stands there among the trees, with a clearing front and back, between the low knolls at each side of the small island. When the Mackenzies left for Glasgow, or whatever town in the south it was, Murray was given a good send-off at school. We had ginger ale, sandwiches, and paper streamers. The minister of the time presented him with a Holy Bible, in which we all inscribed our names in their Gaelic forms.

For a good few years the house lay empty. None of the Duke's men were inclined to live there and put up with rowing back and forth on the loch to get to work and come home from it. A childless couple took its tenancy. The man was a forester, and every day he rowed his boat to a little landing stage by the loch side and then followed the steep track over the hill. But his wife was visited by another boat, at whose oars sat Muir's elder brother, a self-confident and boastful lad who had spent four years at sea with the P & O Steam Navigation Company. Still, the poor woman must have been lonely on Incharn, all by herself most of the day, and she would have grown sick of it, especially in winter, waiting for her man to row back in the early dark; and it would have been worse if there had been a wind blowing or a bad snow. Muir's elder brother went back to sea without so much as a farewell to his fancy woman, and he has never been heard of since. She was found by her husband, standing up to her middle in the waters by the pebble beach, shivering and weeping but unable to take that last step—and one more step would have been enough, for it shelves quickly to the depths. They, too, left, soon after that, and the island and its house lay empty. To row past it used to give me the shudders. I was a young man then, and had been away, and would go away again.

For a number of years the house has been rented in the summer months. The Duke's factor will accept only those who are highly recommended by the solicitor in London who handles the Duke's English business.

Magee and his hirers were soon no longer visible to the naked eye. We lounged by the rail, which has been rubbed by our hands and elbows to a dull shine. Muir, I think, remembers his lost brother when he looks toward Incharn, though he is too sullen to say so.

'Another couple to Incharn, then,' said Munro. 'Now, there's been more folk through the door of that house in a couple of years than there have been kin of mine through the door of my mother's house.' He always calls his house his mother's. She has been dead for twenty years; but we are born in houses, as well as of mothers.

'It's a sad thing that no one will lend a man the price of a pint of beer,' said MacEacharn.

'If we wait for Magee returning,' said the cool, calculating, and thirsty MacMurdo, 'then we'll have the price of several apiece. A twenty-minute drag over the loch is worth a pound or two.'

'Aye,' said Young Gregor, 'and don't forget the twenty minutes back.'

Eyes tried to focus on Incharn as its form vanished into the dusk. Lips were wetted by tongues as we imagined the pints of beer to which Magee might treat us on his return if we behaved nicely toward him or threatened him with violence. But Magee was in one of his funny moods. He is not the man to stand up to a woman like his wife. Munro has said, 'I'm glad I am married to the woman who accepted my proposal, but I'm doubly thankful I'm not married as much as all *that*.'

Magee did not come back but illustrated once again how he has inherited from his father an aptitude for the evasion of responsibilities. He beached his boat a few hundred yards to the right of us, where there is a spit of sand, and then went home in the dark with his money, hoping perhaps to buy a few hours of peace and quiet through giving his wife a cut of his boatman's fee.

That Magee had been well paid is a matter of which I am certain. A couple of nights after the arrival of Mr and Mrs Barker, I had nothing to do, and Magee agreed that I go with himself and another English couple to Inverela, where there is another house on the new Duke's son's estates. It stands by the loch side and cannot be reached by road unless you park a mile from it and then walk along a narrow track. To go by boat is only sensible.

'Well, well, then,' Magee began as we were taking our leave of the Englishman on Inverela's tiny landing stage. His wife, by the way, was running around cooing about how wonderful it was, but we took no notice of that. 'I hope the weather stays fine and the loch remains as calm as a looking glass all the while you are here.' Highly impressed by this eloquent desire for their comforts, the Englishman gestured for his wife to come over and hear this, because it was obvious that Magee was far from finished. 'And may there be no drop of rain, except perhaps once or twice in the night, to make your mornings fresh and to keep the leaves as green as you wish to see them.' They settled back before this recitation. 'And may your sleep be undisturbed and tranquil and you have no reminder whatsoever of the cares of the world, which I am told are the very devil outwith of Loch Arn. And, to translate from our Gaelic'—of which Magee knows one curse, two toasts, and a farewell—'may your bannocks never freeze over or your hair fall out, and may you never forget to salt your potatoes.'

I imagined how that couple would say to each other, as soon as our backs were turned, that it was true after all: the people here speak better English than the English. In that matter, the explanation is to be found in the care with which our kinsmen of long ago, in their clachans by the shores of Loch Arn, set about forgetting their original tongue so that their children, and their children's children, and all their posterity would converse in translation.

As Magee stepped into his boat, it was in the way of a man who expects to be paid nothing at all for his troubles. His grateful employer was shuffling in his jacket for money—a sight studiously avoided by Magee's little blue eyes, which are too close together. The Englishman had a look of prosperity about him and a willingness to be forthcoming. 'Ah . . . ah . . .' The Englishman was a bit embarrassed. 'How much do I owe you?'

Now, there can be a long and historical answer to that one, but Magee thought for a moment with one hand on his chin while the other removed his hat and began scratching his head. 'How . . . how much would you say it was worth?'

'Would a fiver do?' asked the Englishman. His wife nudged him. Magee, like myself, was quick to notice that this woman, in a hat of unduly wide brim—dressed, it seemed to me, for a safari—was a touch on the overpaying side of humanity.

I was all for putting an end to Magee's playacting and stretching my own hand out to receive the note. But Magee began ponderously calculating: 'Now, then . . . It is thirty minutes out, after the ten minutes it took to get you aboard, and unloading you took another ten minutes, while it will take us another thirty to get back home. . . .'

That was a fine stroke of obscurity, for the man was nudged once more by his grinning wife, and he produced another fiver. Two fivers together was more than the government gave you for having no job. Magee looked at the notes as if insulted. 'Now, that seems a lot to a man like myself . . . sir,' he said. 'How does the seven pounds strike you . . . sir? You see, it's the fair price.'

'A bit of a problem there,' said the gent. 'I haven't a single note on me.'

'Then, in that case,' said Magee, a bit too quickly, 'I'll take the ten pounds and I'll see you when you come to Locharnhead.'

'How will we get there?' asked the woman, who was already blinking in a soft hail of midges.

'By that boat there,' said Magee, who pointed to a beached rowing boat that belonged to the house. 'Or you may walk by the track, on your right.'

'Ah. I see. Yes, indeed. On the right, you say?'

'On the right, sir. But you will be quicker by the loch.'

I remember it took the Englishman four hours to row to Locharnhead the following day, for that canny son of an Irishman had been to Inverela that morning to hide one of the oars. Magee did well with a sort of contract for their subsequent transportation.

'Ten pounds for a night's work, Magee,' I said on our return voyage. 'Is it not a liberty to take so large a sum, even from an Englishman who looks as though he can well afford it?'

'Do you want a drink?' he asked. 'Or do you want a *good* drink?'

'You know me,' I said.

'Then hold your hush and don't whine at me for a hypocrite. Because daylight robbery is exactly what it is, and you and the rest of them will sup on the benefit of it. Though I'll tell you true enough that if he didn't look such a pig of a rich man in his pink shirt and white breeks, I'd have let him off with the three pounds the factor says is the fixed charge to Inverela.'

We passed Incharn on the return trip in the late dusk. I waved to its holiday tenants, who had lit a fire on the beach. That couple we'd just left at Inverela could not be imagined lighting a bonfire. I had a feeling the Barkers would have been glad of our company if we had called on them for a few moments, but the thirsty lads, we knew, would be waiting for us on the Promenade, and with me in the boat Magee would have no chance of getting up to his tricks. In the light of their bonfire Mr and Mrs Barker looked like people of the far long ago, when, we are told, there was great happiness and heroism in the world. Or it may just have been the way they carried their youthfulness that led me to think so.

'Now, I hope you didn't fleece that nice couple of the Barkers there.'

'What kind of a thief do you take me to be? I asked for the factor's fixed charge, and they were kind enough to pass me a fiver.'

'Aye, well, there will be no more work for you out of that pair. These two are water babies.'

A day or two later I was walking on the hill. My old pal Red Alistair was, I knew, reluctantly laying down a drain on the Duke's lower pastures—the one he was meant to do the year before but didn't get around to finishing. He is called Red on account of the political pamphlets he inherited from his father. He is annoyed by the nickname, being twice the Tory even than the new Duke's son, and he keeps his legacy of pamphlets in deference to his father's memory. As I was looking for Red Alistair, I found the minister scrutinizing the loch through his spyglass.

'Now, there's a sight I've never seen on the loch before,' he said. 'There are two canoes on it today.'

He gave me his glass and I had a clear view of Mr and Mrs Barker in single line ahead. They wore yellow waterproof jackets and sensible life jackets as well, which was a relief to me.

'Is there any chance of that becoming popular?' I asked the minister, after I had told him who the two canoeists were and what nice people they had turned out to be.

'You should ask that of Young Gregor. He's the boy who's daft on boats round here, though if he ever opens that marina he does nothing but talk about, we will become a laughing-stock for our broken craft, and make no mistake.'

He was as disappointed in Young Gregor as we all were. 'Go, for God's sake, to a southern city,' we urged the boy. 'There's nothing here but old men and the bed-and-breakfast trade.' Lack of capital was what he complained of—that and the poor show of enthusiasm he received from the manager of the Bank, which comes twice a week to Locharnhead in a caravan.

'These canoes can fairly shift some,' said the minister. 'My, if I was young, I'd be inclined to try my hand at that. What an emblem of youth is there before our eyes.'

'We should encourage Young Gregor in it,' I suggested. 'These craft appear to have no engines at all.'

'That boy will break my heart. Is there nothing that can be found for him to do?'

'Can you imagine any woman from round here sporting about on the water like that?'

'Our women are not so much bad-natured as unpredictable,' he decided. 'By and large, though, it might be the bad nature you cannot predict. But we have known great joys in our time. There is no sweeter thing in this life than an harmonious domesticity. You know, I even miss the bad nature of my late wife.' He paused as he peered through his telescope. 'They are a tall couple, these English Barkers.'

'They tell me she is called Rosalind.'

'Now, that is a name from Shakespeare, I believe.'

'Then it's a fair English name,' I remember saying, 'for a young woman as handsome as Mrs Barker and with a true demeanour to go with it.'

'It makes a change from Morag, or Fiona, I'll say that much,' said the minister.

For many more minutes we stood there on the hill, exchanging the spyglass as we watched the two canoes.

'What day is it?' asked the minister.

'I think it must be Thursday, for I saw the women waiting on the fishmonger's van.'

Mr and Mrs Barker visited the Hotel bar in the early part of some evenings for a drink and a bite to eat. While they were inside, we took the opportunity of examining their Eskimo craft—not, of course, that there is much to look at in a kayak canoe. I studied them longer than the others had the patience for. A jaunt in one of them would have been very satisfying. To have asked Mr Barker might have been thought a bit eccentric of me, though I doubt if he would have taken it as an impertinence. Their canoes had a very modern look to them, as, indeed, had that bright and lively couple with their air of freedom.

'Aye,' said MacMurdo, who joined me on the jetty, 'that must be a fine and healthy outdoor sport for them—the sort of thing that could set you up for the winter and keep you well.' MacMurdo, fresh-faced as he is for his years, is housebound for three months of the calendar with the sniffles. When the Barkers came back, we stood to one side and said our soft 'Good evening' together, which they returned. Then we watched them slip into their canoes and paddle away into the early dusk.

'It's the best time of all to be on the water,' said MacMurdo. 'Just look at the beauty of it over there. The whole world is getting itself ready to settle down for the night.'

'Do you think he'd mind if I asked him—I mean, if he'd let me take his canoe out for a few minutes?'

'What's so special about one of these canoes?'

'They strike me for one thing as an exciting little sort of a craft, that's what. Now, look there, and see how close you would be to the water.'

'A man of your age . . . A boat like that is for young things.'

'It would be interesting to *me*.'

A man like myself might be expected to resent these folks who come up from the south like swallows to take their ease on a country that has brought me no prosperity. All the same, no one can tell me better than I tell myself that I am as lazy as any man born. Part of my trouble is that I have become content enough on plain victuals in modest quantities and two packets of Players a week. What jobs I've done in other parts than this one did not contribute much to my happiness. But there are things I've seen, and people I've met, I would not do without if I had my chance again. When the mobile library, which is a wonderful thing, calls at Locharnhead, I am the first man aboard and the last man out. That is not hard, as the only other reader in our community, apart from the youngest MacMurdo when he's at home, is Mrs Carmichael, wife of our stingy publican and the Hotel's cook. By the way, I once ate a large dinner there. It was not worth the money, and Magee and the rest of them watched me through the window for all five courses, screwing up their faces and licking their chops in an ironic manner. MacEacharn, I noticed, was there, too, but that obstinate man wasn't even looking.

But for all the large contrast between myself and the likes of Mr and Mrs Barker, it made me mellow and marvellously sad to watch them paddle in the still waters of Loch Arn at dusk, going toward Incharn, where the Mackenzies once lived, and that unhappy couple who followed them.

Incharn, as I have said, is a beautiful island. A good number of trees grow there, and on the side you cannot see from the head of the loch there is low ground and a growth of reeds of which nesting swans and water-fowl are appreciative. This is the most beautiful side of all, though you can only see it properly from the water, which means that it has been observed by few people. Facing Locharnhead, the beach is of fine pebbles, and it slopes quickly into the water. Crab apples grew there when my friend Mackenzie lived on it, and that bitter fruit made grand jelly in his mother's big copper pan. They had a black leaded stove of great size, which Mrs Mackenzie kept as spotlessly black as a Seaforth's boots, and we were famous for the spit and polish. Mrs Mackenzie would do her washing in a wooden tub on the beach, and her suds floated and spread as Murray and I threw stones at the scattering patches of foam. People on holiday do no washing at all, I'm told. Sometimes I felt like telling Mr and Mrs Barker about Incharn, but I never got round to it. They might have been interested. Magee has been known to tell those he ferries to the island of the tragedy that befell there. In his story, the woman drowned herself, and her demented husband first slew her lover with his bare hands and then committed his own life to the chill waters, but it was not that way. For all I know, the Barkers heard that story from Magee; but if they did, they were too happy to pay it any heed.

At night you can see the small lights of the cottage if its blinds or curtains are not drawn. In our famous dusks and sunsettings, the lights seem to spread in the open and watery mist, and they float above the island like benedictions. A man can look toward Incharn and feel drawn toward it. Muir's brother may have felt that, too, for whether the beauty of a place discriminates among those who are to be compelled by it is not a subtlety I am prepared to go into. Incharn draws a charitable thought from me, at any rate. But then I was always a bachelor, though not because I wanted to be one; and so I am always glad of something that holds disgruntlements at bay. All winter long I look forward to the holiday couples. It would please me more if Mr and Mrs Barker were to come back, with their frail canoes, and the way they splashed each other with water off their paddles, and capsized and rolled over under the water and came back up again as my heart beat with admiration for them—and, above all, the way they just followed each other about on the still water.